SAMSON'S LION

A NOVEL FOR THE MILLENNIUM

By Alex Wolf

FIRST PRINTING:
January 2000

Published by
TMS Publishing Co.
P.O.B. 21578
Baltimore, MD 21282
(410) 764-8810
www.samsonslion.com
E-mail: inquire@samsonslion.com

ISBN: 0-9677044-0-5
Library of Congress Catalogue Number: 99-076403

Typography by TMS Publishing Co.

Cover Design by Bill Hackney at **Staiman Design**, Baltimore MD
(410) 580-0100

Printed and bound in the United States of America by
Gem Printing, Baltimore MD
(410) 764-1617

Foreword

Although the reader may become so involved in *Samson's Lion* that he comes close to mistaking it for reality, it must be borne in mind that this is a work of fiction. The author disavows knowledge of any factual inside information that may have found its way into the story. The reader will certainly find authentic, researched historical episodes within the book, but they don't involve classified or mystical information. With the exception of ideas, events and characters which are well-known and readily found in the public record, all other names have been randomly selected and the story is purely the product of the author's imagination.

Due to the plethora of characters, foreign names, and aliases, we have provided, at the end of the book, an alphabetic index of all significant characters' names. We hope this will assist the reader in avoiding confusion and keeping track of the story. Foreign and other uncommon terms can be found in an alphabetical glossary after the Index of Character Names.

Acknowledgments

I would like to thank the friends and family members who reviewed the work and offered valuable suggestions: B. Fleischman and Dr. B. Miller for their thoughtful copy editing and meticulous proofreading, Y. Fleischman for his knowledge of martial arts, Y. B. M. for his technical suggestions on submarines, C. Harris for his geological information, Dr. S. Langermann for his epidemiological advice, B. Simon for his expertise on Iran, Y. A. and D. Richards for their expertise on weapon systems, E. Feldman, Y. Marsh and Y. Golani for their valuable suggestions, S. Apisdorf for his publishing assistance, my father, for his philosophical criticisms, my wife who edited the entire work, creating a pleasurable read from a great story, and most notably, renowned author and editor Libby Lazewnik, who took the book from a pleasurable read to a polished gem.

Be inspired and enjoy,

Alex Wolf
January, 2000

TABLE OF CONTENTS

May 29, 1999, International Press Release:

The Israeli Navy announced today that the wreckage of a submarine it lost in January of 1968 has been found at the bottom of the Mediterranean Sea. The same sonar imaging equipment that discovered the remains of the Titanic fourteen years ago was used to locate the ill-fated sub.

As in the case of the Titanic, the hull of the submarine was found broken into two sections on the ocean floor at a depth of twenty-eight-hundred meters.

No trace of the crew's remains was evident.

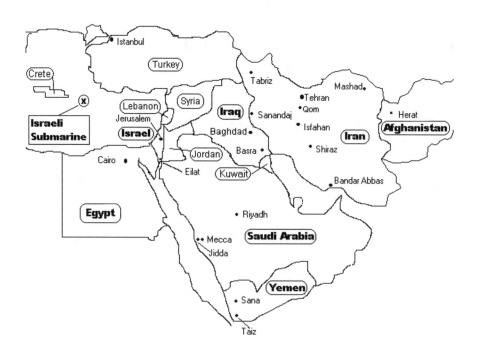

The Middle East

PRELUDE:

ATTACK AND RETRIBUTION

"His hand against everyone, and everyone's hand against him"

Genesis 16:12

Chapter 1

July 1, 2002, 1:13 a.m. (GMT+2), Zahal Surveillance Command HQ, Tel Aviv, Israel:

"Shlomo!" the console operator shrieked at his superior, "Six Shahab-5s launched from Sanandaj, bearing 255, Mach 6.62!"

The cavernous room was instantly plunged into a state of frenzy. Nine minutes later, the first missile splashed harmlessly into the sea. Three more instantaneously disintegrated over Jordan, after direct hits by Arrow IIIs. The fifth missile's guidance system was damaged by the percussion of an exploding Arrow that missed, but caused the Shahab to veer off course and crash in the heart of the Negev Desert. The last missile exploded in an orange grove in the center of Israel.

It took twenty minutes for the Israeli population to awake to the wails of emergency sirens and prepare their gas-resistant sealed shelters — four minutes too late for several apartment blocks in the southeast corner of Ramle. The deadly nerve gas diffused into the atmosphere and sank down to snuff out the lives of those hapless residents. Emergency vehicles, bearing heavily suited personnel who scoured the area for damage, came across the two lone buildings that had suffered casualties.

July 2, 2002, 9:06 a.m. (GMT+2), Dam Control Room, Aswan Egypt:

"Abdallah, come quickly." Faruk, the control room operator, called anxiously to his boss. "The seismograph needle has gone haywire. It's been showing minor tremors since yesterday. Now there's a 2.1 shock centered right on the dam! It's strange — the needle is moving up, but I don't feel anything."

Just as he spoke these last words, a coffee mug on the hardwood table began to rattle. Abdallah set his hand on the mug, and could feel the glass vibrating at what he thought might be about fifty cycles. Then the amplitude started to increase, although the frequency remained constant or slightly diminished. The needle on the seismograph had edged up to 2.3 when the phone rang.

"What's going on? Is everything under control?" The excited voice at the other end belonged to the Egyptian Minister of the Interior.

"We're experiencing a tremor. No problem... yet. The dam can easily withstand a major quake of up to 7.5 without serious effect. But it's odd that this tremor has sustained for so long and is growing in amplitude."

"Where's it centered?" the minister asked.

"Just a moment, sir, while I check our instruments."

In the silence that followed, the minister babbled nervously, "Our news media have not yet reported any Israeli retaliation for the Iranian attack yesterday morning. The whole world knows that we have joined the Pan-Moslem coalition, which has been threatening the Zionist state. We will force them to make more accommodations to the Palestinians.... Well? Answer me! Where is the quake centered?"

Faruk's eyes were glued to the scope, which now was registering 2.5 and climbing. The operations room, although built into the superstructure along the top of the dam, was now vibrating audibly. The window glass and other materials whose natural harmonics were excited by the low frequency rumbling formed a nerve-racking cacophony. As the needle on the seismograph and the amplitude on the oscilloscope kept creeping up, the noise increased proportionally.

"Minister Al Hambra," Abdallah said gravely into the phone, "the epicenter is below my feet."

"Oh, no!" The Cairo minister's wail was deafening in the dam manager's ear. It was suddenly amplified by another, much louder, electronic wail rising up from the Aswan Dam itself.

"What's that?" Al Hambra screeched.

"Sir," Abdallah exclaimed, "that alarm is from the lake level indicator. The water is draining out too quickly. I have noticed a slight abnormal reduction in level since yesterday, but put it down to the heat."

"The dam, the dam, has it cracked?"

"No sir, the dam is solid as iron. I can't explain why or where so much water... that's 30,000 liters per second... is leaking from. Let's see, from the time this emergency began fifteen minutes ago, the lake has lost another twenty-seven million liters...." He shook his head in wonder.

Seconds later, the needle shot up to 7.7. The room was now rocking in a wave motion, and the phone went dead. The lights went out for a second until a secondary generator kicked in. The power outage was not due to any damage. It was caused by an automatic sensor shutting down the entire generating station. All power to Cairo ceased.

"Faruk, let's get out of here. This place is going to blow. This is no earthquake. It's an Israeli bomb or something. The dam is going to burst!"

The two men ran out of the control room and along the top of the dam to the east gate, which led to the main Aswan road. They were four hundred meters from the end of the gargantuan structure, when Abdallah turned around. He witnessed the control room being cast down like a matchbox by a torrent of water from Lake Nasser into the lower Nile. The fissure in the concrete started to spread in both directions, east and west. Five hundred ton chunks of concrete, steel and earth were swept away like pebbles. Abdallah put every gram of strength he possessed into the effort to outrun the crumbling wall coming at him like a mad pursuer. Although Faruk was also running as fast as his squat one hundred twenty-kilogram body could carry him, Abdallah quickly left him behind. He reached virgin bedrock and raced another hundred meters up the trail. There, gasping and sweating, he turned again — just in time to see Faruk go over the falls and disappear into the maelstrom of turbid water one hundred ten meters below. Niagara Falls would only describe one small corner of the mass of water that would reach Cairo seven hours later.

Abdallah, beginning to breathe more normally now, glanced around him. No other person was in view. As his eyes went back at the awesome cascade of water, thirty-seven years of memories began swimming in his head. All at once another thought dawned on him, a dreadful thought: millions of human beings downriver were doomed. His eyes filled. Slowly, with bowed shoulders, he turned and walked away.

July 1, 2002, 7:30 a.m. (GMT+3.5), Isfahan, Iran

The morning paper was delivered. Anxiously, Farshid Levihayim read the lead article.

> **Only two hours ago, our military fulfilled our Prophet's highest commandment. After suffering the presence of the devil for fifty-four years, he has now ceased to exist. A battery of two-hundred Shahab missiles loaded with VX gas have miraculously all hit their marks in occupied Palestine. They have decimated the infidels who have defiled holy ground. Within five hours, the gas will have become totally inert. Occupying forces from our nation and eleven brother Moslem countries will enter the territory and gather the millions of Jewish carcasses into a huge pyre.**
>
> **We welcome our brother Palestinians to expand their recently-declared independent state to all of their ancestral grounds.**

He skimmed the piece a second time, then ran for the telephone. Almost of their own accord, his fingers dialed the number of the man who served as president of the three hundred remaining members of the Isfahan Jewish congregation.

"Yosef," Farshid said urgently, "did you hear the news?"

"I certainly did," the other answered in a grave voice. "Terrible, just terrible."

"Israel is sure to retaliate at many Arab and Moslem targets in response to last night's poison gas attack. I doubt it will be a mere tactical strike. In fact, it will probably be massive! We must call for a day of prayer immediately. Perhaps, that way, we can stave off the Angel of Death from our community."

"But Farshid," the president protested, "the Israelis know about us. They'd never attack our city, jeopardizing Jewish lives."

"You are wrong, my friend. This is serious war. It may even be World War III in the making, God forbid. In war there are sacrifices; there always are. We have no control over our destiny. You know as well as I that the government will never let the Jews leave the city at this time. The streets are crawling with police." He shook his head, though the other man could not see him. "No, my friend, our destiny is in the hands of God now. Call up the other six trustees. I will also continue the chain call, and even knock on doors if necessary. Every man, woman and child must be in the synagogue by 9:00 a.m. for a day of fasting and prayer."

"Of course, of course." The president capitulated at once. "Farshid, ever since the last rabbi left for America, you have been our de facto rabbi. Your counsel has always been wise. I will make the calls immediately."

As word of attacks on Qom, Mashad and numerous Arab cities began to inundate the Iranian news media that morning, large crowds gathered to angrily denounce Israel and the Jews. The Iranian president sent a large contingent of police to protect Jewish homes and the synagogue.

By 8:45, Jews were flowing into the synagogue — all the city's Jews, young and old. Even the physically impaired were wheeled into the large, ornate, stone building.

"Mr. Levihayim!" Captain Nemat Hawaga addressed Farshid as the latter directed the traffic entering the building, "What's going on here? It is not Sabbath or a holiday."

"No, it's not. But we feel that the volatile situation calls for a special prayer service."

The policeman shrugged. "You have nothing to worry about. The police will protect your community. It is an order from the President."

"Captain Hawaga, we have the utmost trust in our President and in the power of the police to protect our community. All the same, our wise men have advised us that the situation in the world is so tenuous that we all must pray for peace... for Iran, and for the world."

"I understand." The officer nodded sagely. "I commiserate with you Jews for having brethren who are Zionist murderers. My own cousin was executed in the holy city of Qom last year for stealing cars. He had been a miserable blight on the family — but I don't blame my aunt, uncle and other relatives for the black sheep, as I don't blame you for those Zionist infidels. A day of prayer? A good idea, yes. I will order barricades to be placed around the synagogue. The Moslem populace will be kept one hundred meters away."

The barricades went up just as the last members of the community slipped into the synagogue — and just as a huge crowd of protesters gathered around the restricted area. On the southern side of the synagogue, a fight broke out between police and a band of three hundred militant Hizbullah members. Heads were cracked, and forty people were arrested before Captain Hawaga retrieved control of the situation. He sent the violent troublemakers to an adjacent park to conduct a verbal assault instead.

At 9:25 a.m., Farshid Levihayim shut and locked the huge metal doors of the synagogue building. He would have closed all of the outside window shutters as well, but they had been bricked up ever since the massive riots during the revolution, twenty-four years before. Just a few years prior to that time, Levihayim had been appointed by the other trustees to oversee a general renovation of the building. Under those circumstances, sealing the windows had seemed the prudent move, even if not aesthetically pleasing.

Once everyone was gathered safely inside, the cantor began reciting Psalms of David, which the congregation repeated after him, line by line. The prayers came to an abrupt halt at 10:06, when a large shock rocked the building. Pandemonium erupted. Farshid Levihayim ran up to the podium.

"Friends, now is not the time to stop our prayers to God! Now is the time to increase our fervor, for God shall surely listen to our supplication and save us from the violence out in the streets."

Raggedly, the prayers resumed. Levihayim stayed up on the podium beside the cantor. Within a minute of the blast, the three hundred people in the sturdy building could hear the screams of a frenzied mob approaching from the outside. The congregants were first disconcerted and then frightened as streams of water began leaking from all the walls. Someone shouted, "The Fundamentalists have broken through! The police have given up. We're all going to die!"

Just seconds later, a seven thousand strong roar rose up outside, immediately followed by a frantic banging at the door. The congregation was horrified and very close to panic. Levihayim called out, "Silence, silence! We must pray harder. Put greater feeling into your prayer. Don't think about what is going on outside. That is in God's hands!" He turned. "Cantor, the time has come for you to blow the Shofar."

The cantor took out the Shofar from a cloth satchel, put it to his lips, and began blowing the spine-tingling series of notes that the congregants were accustomed to hearing on the High Holy Day of Rosh Hashanah. He had completed the first thirty notes and was bringing the ram's horn to his lips in preparations for the next series, when the banging on the door ceased. A murmur from the congregation was audible again. The cantor raised the Shofar to his mouth, and blew the next thirty notes. By the time he finished, the noise of the crowd outside had substantially subsided.

Another member of the congregation cried, "It is a miracle of God! We are spared. Let us go outside to see our enemies retreat." There was a stir as others began to act on this idea.

"*Stop!*" roared Farshid Levihayim. "No one is to leave the building until after the sun sets. We have dedicated an entire day to prayer and fasting. By our Holy Law, we must finish the day without interruption, even if the Almighty may have already sent His angels to help us."

Three men disregarded Levihayim's admonition, and made for the door. Levihayim raced off the podium to block the door, although he knew that none of the three possessed a key to the deadbolt. Other men came to his aid, and the violators were sent muttering back to their seats.

The prayers continued until sundown. At 7:45 p.m., the evening service finished. Farshid Levihayim turned the key of the deadbolt lock, which opened the outer heavy metal doors. To the frustration of the worshipers, who were in a hurry to return home to eat, the doors would not open.

"They've blockaded the doors from the outside!" one woman screamed.

"Just keep pushing," Farshid Levihayim ordered. "We haven't heard anyone out there since the morning. We'll get the doors opened." The four strongest young men got into position, and heaved forward against the door. It budged, opening a crack. All at once, the mass of people waiting near the door backed away as a foul stench from outside effused into the building. It took five more heaves before the door was sufficiently ajar for a man to step through. Shmuel Moinzada was the first one out.

There was an instant of stunned silence. Then he screamed, "There are dead people all around! Hundreds, maybe thousands — at least fifteen piled against the door." He flung out his arms. "God has saved us and destroyed our enemies. It's a miracle!"

The crowd broke into cries of awed jubilation. "God is the Almighty. God is the Almighty!"

As they chanted this refrain over and over, Joseph Saadatmand, the community president, pulled Farshid Levihayim aside. "Farshid, I know you are a God-fearing man — but this is just too uncanny."

He stared at his friend of thirty years, trying to elicit a response. But none came, except for an extended hand and a subdued wish. "Yes, Joseph, uncanny. Let us pray this dose of medicine will, once and for all, heal the illness that has afflicted the hearts of our oppressors."

July 1, 2002, 4:45 a.m. (GMT+4.5), Mujahedin terrorist camp near Herat, Afghanistan:

"So, Mahmud, which do you prefer, the AK-74 or the M-16?"

"Some choice; Russian slime or American infidels! Though I must admit that they make damn good weapons." Mahmud creased his brow thoughtfully. "Let's see. The .556 American round is cheap, available, accurate, and very effective in the way the bullet tumbles upon impact — sort of a flying buzzsaw blade. The Russian .554 round is an obvious copy, the bullet almost identical in size and shape. But the casing is nothing but an — ouch!" He slapped a hand to the back of his neck. "Damn it, something just stung me!"

When he removed his hand, it was splattered with a bit more blood than the typical mosquito bite should elicit.

Sirhan said helpfully, "Mahmud, your neck is bleeding."

"Thanks for the tip." Sourly, Mahmud wiped his hands on his pants.

"What happened? Did you pick at a scab?"

"No, Sirhan. I was bitten by something. Strange that it should bleed so much."

Sirhan shrugged. "Strange that you should have been bitten at all. The mosquitoes have been gone for over a month now, and the bees and wasps don't come out until much later in the day. Let me have a look."

Sirhan took out a handkerchief and wiped away the blood. The entire area surrounding the bite, some twenty millimeters in diameter, was visibly swollen.

"This needs attention. I'm going to call a camp doctor."

He dialed the number of the infirmary on his cell phone. Alerted by his companion's concerned expression, Mahmud asked sharply, "What's the matter? What's going on?"

Sirhan spoke briefly into the phone, then switched it off and set it down with a distinctly worried air. "It seems you weren't the first one to be bitten. The infirmary has received over four hundred calls, and men have been streaming in since the sun rose."

A tiny, black, humped-backed fly landed on the back of Sirhan's left hand. It looked like nothing he had ever seen before. He could hardly feel its weight on his skin. It would have been a simple matter to slap it away, but Sirhan was curious.

Two seconds later, he felt a sharp pain on his hand. A drop of blood oozed from the site. With his right hand he swooped down, hoping to trap the tiny creature. He quickly placed a plastic cup over the palm of his hand. The fly bumped frantically against the cup's sides.

"Mahmud, hurry! Slip a sheet of paper under the mouth of the cup," Sirhan Kalami barked at his underling, who immediately complied.

Making sure the lip of the cup remained flat against the paper, Sirhan carefully set it down on the table. Although the cup was not crystal clear, he could make out something minuscule fluttering inside. He grabbed his cell phone.

"This is Major Sirhan Kalami. I want to speak to the master. It's urgent."

"Master Rastafani is very busy now. There seems to be some kind of infestation in the camp. Many men have been bitten. It's all highly unusual," the secretary replied in an agitated voice.

"That's why I'm calling. I've discovered something about this problem. Put the master on the phone." Sirhan's tone was almost frantic. The secretary told him to hold.

A moment later, a new voice came on the line. It was crisp and authoritative. "This is Omar Rastafani. What have you learned about this unusual insect — a menace that afflicted me not ten minutes ago?"

"Did the master see the insect?" Sirhan asked excitedly.

"No. I could find no trace of it, nor did I feel anything touch me. The infirmary reports the same thing. No one has seen the little pest."

"I have, master! I have it right in a cup — alive. It's a little black fly, the likes of which I have never seen before. Nor would I have believed any man who would have told me that such a small bite could draw so much blood." Sirhan drew a deep breath. "It must be an American or Israeli conspiracy. Those infidels couldn't scratch our surface with all of their cruise missiles, so they've sent flies instead."

Rastafani bawled, "Stop talking rubbish, Major! There is a time and a place for nonsensical propaganda, but this is not one of them. I just want to find out what's going on. Remain at your barracks. I'll be there immediately. Don't do anything with that fly."

"Yes, master."

Sirhan hung up the phone and stared, mesmerized, by the shadowy fluttering of the unfamiliar insect. The skin on the back of his left hand turned a brighter red, and began to throb.

Rastafani's helicopter landed on the campus of Herat University at 5:37 a.m.

Professor Ibrahim Hilwani, head of entomology, had been awakened from his slumber and directed to meet the millionaire rebel leader at the professor's office. Carefully, Rastafani handed him the cup containing the imprisoned fly. He led them next door to his lab, where he placed the cup — still sealed with a sheet of paper — into a finely meshed cage. The professor sat down to study the creature, jotting notes from time to time. Rastafani and his two companions, Major Sirhan Kalami and Captain Mahmud Jebli, watched with ill-concealed impatience.

The professor turned at last to face his visitors. "Please sit down gentlemen." He waited until they were seated in a rough semicircle around the cage. "I will be frank with you. I've never seen this species before, except in textbooks. It will take me a few minutes to identify it. I have to connect to some sources on the Internet to find a little more information."

The professor left the room for about thirty minutes, leaving the others to cool their heels near the insect's cage. On his return, he announced calmly, "I have found it. It is a black fly."

Rastafani half-rose from his seat. "Thank you very much," the rebel leader retorted angrily. "It's quite obvious that it's a fly, and it's black, but what *about* it?"

"Yes, and what can we do about it?" Major Sirhan added, scratching furiously at the back of his hand.

"In a moment, my good sirs, in a moment. This subspecies of *Simulium venustum* is native to five counties in the American state of Maine. Its bite is considered quite vicious for such a small insect. It slits open the skin with its razor-sharp mandibles, and injects an anticoagulant. This causes the bite to bleed at least twenty times the amount of blood that the fly can actually lap up. A nasty little thing.

"The literature I've found states that the sore can last up to two weeks. In about ten percent of the victims, the bite will become locally infected, treatable by calamine and topical antiseptics. But the good news is that it does not carry any known diseases. So I suggest you wash the area with soap, apply some calamine for the itching and some Neosporin to prevent infection, and forget about it."

Rastafani looked around at his officers, then back at the Professor. "How the hell did these things get here? Hundreds...." He broke off as his cell phone rang. "Yes? Yes... Yes.... What are you saying?" He listened a moment longer while a series of expressions — none of them happy — crossed his face. With a "Goodbye, I'll be in touch," he replaced the phone in his pocket.

"Professor Hilwani, since daybreak the reported incidents of insect bites have increased greatly. So far, three thousand two hundred men have suffered bites from this damned fly. Would you tell me this: how the hell did they get from Maine, in the cursed United States, to Afghanistan — thirteen thousand kilometers away?"

The professor was silent for a moment. Then he lifted his hands, palms upward. "I have no idea. I can only tell you about its physical characteristics. I can't tell you who transported them. I am an entomologist, not an insect smuggler."

Rastafani said suspiciously, "You mean they couldn't have arrived here by natural means? Perhaps in the cargo of a ship, or in the wheel-well of a plane?"

"Impossible. They are environmentally bound to their local region, which must be cool and have fast-flowing streams for breeding. Why, I would assume...." The professor looked at his watch, which was flashing 7:14 a.m., "that in four hours, as the coolness of early morning is replaced by a forty-degree sun, none of these flies will be left alive. They will die, shrivel up, and disappear into the dust of the earth. A minor incident, quickly over and quickly forgotten." As he spoke these last words, the professor laughed.

Major Sirhan showed the back of his hand to the professor, who exhibited surprise at the size of the weal left by the bite. He examined it narrowly, then said, "Let me go back to the literature. Perhaps I missed something. I thought I read that the bite leaves a bump only a tad larger than that of a mosquito."

An hour later, during which time Rastafani had been furiously making and receiving calls, the professor returned. "Major, the weal you displayed is unusually large." Mahmud, showing him an even larger bump on the back of his neck, spoke up for the first time. "The Master has also reported having been bitten."

All eyes turned expectantly on Rastafani. The rebel leader's dark-complected face flushed in embarrassment. It was obvious that the master's bite was on a compromising site of his body. Rastafani declined to reveal himself, but confirmed that he too, suffered a similarly exaggerated swelling.

Slowly, the professor said, "This is really out of my area. I will call my friend Professor Alwazi in epidemiology." In silence, he led the way back to his office. Behind him, he overheard Rastafani, on his cell phone, passing on some of the information he had gleaned from the professor. He laid particular emphasis on the fact that the bites were purportedly harmless. Meanwhile, reports of bites by the thousands were continuing to pour in.

At 10:00 a.m., the phone rang. It was Professor Alwazi, with the results of the blood tests he had taken.

"Ibrahim," Alwazi said in a furious voice, "they are infected with the very trypanosome I developed in my lab together with you! How on earth did your flies get released in the rebel camp? The blood sample contained ninety percent Alpha Modula — the most virulent strain. You know as well as I that all those bitten will die within forty-eight hours. I can't understand it. We developed this pathogen to punish the Zionists and their American lackeys. You better have a good explanation or I'm going to the authorities."

Rastafani and his officers were listening closely. Hilwani smiled, the phone pressed to his ear. "So you say the tests are negative? Good!"

"Have you gone mad?" Alwazi shouted. "I just told you, thousands will die!"

"Okay, very good. Come over to my office right away. There are some people here who would like to meet you."

Ten minutes later, Alwazi pressed a buzzer in the hall to announce his presence. "Gentlemen," Professor Hilwani told his guests, "Please excuse me. I must go out for a few minutes. I must look up one additional source and consult with my colleague. Then I think I may have the correct explanation of these unusual events. Please wait for me here."

The two professors met in the hall, and proceeded to the lab. They entered the lab and took a look at the black fly. Alwazi was shocked to see it lying dead at the bottom of the cage. Its wings had shriveled and the tiny body had already dried up to a significant degree. Professor Hilwani clapped his hands together. "Aha, you see? That last gene splice I tried worked perfectly. The survival period of the fly was reduced to ten hours after being vectored. There are doubtless no more to be found outside, in the camp."

Alwazi stared at him, saying slowly, "Ibrahim, something very sinister is happening. I think you know more than you've shared with me. Wasn't Rastafani the one who funded the development of our little parasite? That's what you've been telling me for the past seven years." He waited for a response. When none was immediately forthcoming, he demanded, "Tell me now! Exactly how did the flies get into the rebel camp?"

Hilwani's manner was soothing. "Alwazi, my friend, you are the foremost epidemiologist from Tehran to Karachi. I almost match your ability in the field of entomology."

"What are you saying?"

"What I'm saying is that you are mixed up in this disastrous experiment as much as I am. If it's my head, it's yours, too. Don't ask me any more questions, and I won't have to explain any further. I like you. You're a fine fellow — a bit of a sucker, but still fine. No one but you and I know about the experiment gone awry. The evidence from my department — that is, the flies — has all but self-destructed, as you witnessed in that cage. I suggest that you destroy all remaining vials of the trypanosomes, what you've called your *Trypanosome alwazei*. Then both of us will be safe from suspicion."

"But four or five thousand of our people will die! We have the medicine, if administered within the next few hours, to save them."

"In order to save them, we would have to reveal what happened. Then we are in trouble, you understand. Very serious trouble."

"No, I don't understand. I'm going to report this immediately," Alwazi retorted. Defiantly, he started out of the lab.

Alwazi most certainly didn't understand, for as he turned to depart, he felt a hypodermic needle pierce his rear. Thirty seconds later his unconscious frame was stuffed into a laboratory locker.

Hilwani strode back into his office, where he was pounced upon by the three anxious officers. "What does it all mean?" Rastafani asked.

"Take it easy. There is no problem. But just to cover a minuscule eventuality, allow me to examine you for a moment, Master Rastafani," the professor instructed calmly.

Rastafani hesitated, then gave his grudging consent. The professor lifted up the rebel leader's long black beard and began feeling about his pharynx. "I am just checking your glands. I feel a little swelling. Do you sense anything?"

"No. Well, perhaps a little," answered the millionaire-turned-rebel, beginning to shake.

The other two officers who had been bitten began to palpate their own necks. Sirhan reported that his glands were beginning to feel sore. Rastafani demanded that they be taken to the University hospital at once.

Professor Hilwani dialed his phone and ordered a medical doctor sent out to them at once.

As the trio of victims waited, Sirhan spoke up. "I thought you said this fly doesn't carry disease. Why, then, are we feeling sick?"

"I can't answer that. I told you — this fly is a foreigner. I only repeated to you what I found in the literature."

Fifteen minutes went by and no doctor arrived. It was noon. By now, the Master and Sirhan began complaining that they felt feverish and were experiencing pain in the pharyngeal and lymph glands, which had begun to swell. "Where the hell is the doctor?" yelled Rastafani. He got up and walked to the door, shaking and sweating. He turned the knob to exit, but the professor's door was locked.

"Open this door," Rastafani commanded in an angry but weakened tone. As he turned around, he jumped in fright. The oversized cylinder of a noise suppressor connected to an H&K USP 9mm was pointed directly at his chest.

"Go sit down, Mr. Rastafani," Hilwani said softly. "That's it, next to your friends." As Rastafani complied, he passed in front of Major Kalami. Hilwani just caught a glimpse of Kalami's right hand making its way to his side. As Rastafani cleared the major, a dull thud and a flash emanated from the professor's pistol. A hundredth of a second later, two extra cavities were added to the major's heart, one anterior, one posterior.

"Now sit down!" barked the professor. Shakily, the rebel leader complied.

"Rastafani, I know that you two are not feeling too well. But I have excellent news for you. Assuming you keep your hands in front of you, unlike your moribund friend, you will be joining him in eternal paradise within twelve hours. However, if you wish to enjoy the extra time in eternal bliss instead of here on my couch, I will be happy to oblige you." Hilwani waited for the full import of his words to sink in. "Now, my friend, please take out your cell phone and detach the battery. There is no need for you to be interrupted while contemplating the erotic bliss you may anticipate soon... in the next world." Rastafani obeyed. Though he was able to speak only with increasing difficulty, he croaked, "Who are you? What are you doing?"

Hilwani gave him a seraphic smile. "'Who am I?' you ask. I am a memory. I am a leaf blown in the wind. I don't really exist. 'What am I doing?' you want to know. I am an entomologist. I work with insects. I study them. I see what makes them live and what makes them die. I learn how they naturally evolved, and — yes, how they can artificially evolve. In other words, how they can be genetically engineered. I study the diseases they carry and how they are vectored.

"I apologize for not having been perfectly honest with you, when you first sought my advice. But I will be now — perfectly. The actual species of black fly that bit you is classified as *Simulium hilwanei*. Do you understand? I developed it from the venustum subspecies. How does it vary from its progenitor? It was developed to become the host of the *Trypanosome alwazei*. That title should also be revealing. This protozoan is a variant of the *Trypanosome gambiense*, of African Sleeping Sickness fame. It was genetically isolated from its prototype as being five hundred times more resistant to the body's autoimmune system. Thus, it reproduces and infects the body, as you are experiencing, by taxing the inflammatory cells within a few hours instead of months.

"Now you know what I know. Who am I? I am entitled to ask you the same question. But I won't, because I already know. You are Omar Rastafani, a great philanthropist. Why, it was through your own magnanimity that the parasite which now afflicts your own blood was developed.

"You are also a man of God. You pray with fervent devotion, five times each day, for Allah to destroy the Jews. As you must know, your Moslem colleagues recently made a futile attempt to accomplish just that."

Hilwani leaned back against his desk, the H&K trained relentlessly on his captives.

"But most notably," he finished, "you are a murderer. Very soon now to be retired."

Chapter 2

July 2, 2002, 4:25 a.m. (EDT), The Oval Office of the White House:

Five-and-a-half thousand miles away, the receiver was lifted from its hook.

"Benari, this is President Lewis. Are you insane?"

"Excuse me, Mr. President?" The voice at the other end was calm and urbane.

"*No more.* Do you hear me?"

"Mr. President, what are you talking about?"

"You know what I'm talking about. Cut the bull!"

There was a pause. Then the Israeli Prime Minister said thoughtfully, "I suppose you're referring to the problems some of our Middle East friends have been suffering of late."

"Damn it! You know what I'm talking about. I said stop the bull."

"When are you going to let our spy, Rabinowitz, out of jail?"

"Don't bother me about that traitor, Rabinowitz. I'm warning you, Benari: if there's one more strike, I'll take action."

"Action, Mr. President?" Benari's voice hardened. "We've had enough action. We took two missile hits. Now someone — some group, or maybe the Almighty Himself — seems to feel the time has come for the Arabs to taste a little of their own medicine. We've been on the taking end for fifty-four years, you know."

"Listen to me, Danny. The Arrow IIIs have them under control. You only lost twenty-six people...."

"It's twenty-eight now."

"I'm sorry, twenty-eight. But they've lost 320,000, and the toll rises every hour."

"Abe, they used gas! You hear me? Gas, Mr. President — VX-4!" Benari shouted.

"But your people were prepared. You'll weather this until we can get the situation under control. There has to be some semblance of balance, Danny. The genie is out of the bottle now. There's still a chance we can put it back — but not if you pull the pin on one more neutron device or whatever the hell you're doing over there! Damn it. Damn it!" The President of the United States broke down in an uncontrollable sob. It was all of twenty seconds before he was able to compose himself.

"All right," he said, breathing deeply to steady himself. "You hit Isfahan, Qom and Mashad. The Iranians, maybe, deserved a little punishment. The latest tolls indicate 100,000 dead in those holy cities. In Egypt you flooded out some 185,000. What did they do to deserve this?" President Lewis's composure was dangerously close to cracking again.

"*We* hit? Our aircraft and ballistic missiles never left the ground. Shame on you, Abe. Where's your gratitude? I thought you'd be thrilled to have that Afghan terrorist camp wiped out. You spent three hundred twenty million dollars in cruise missiles — according to our best estimate, that's about 8.2 million per confirmed kill. In the meantime, over twelve hundred innocents have died, and more than 54,000 have been wounded from fourteen embassy bombings perpetrated by that scum. Rumor has it, the original box of flies cost $129.95 from a lab supply house in Bangor. Of course the R&D to vector the disease must have cost a little more than that. But why are you blaming Israel? From what I understand, it was our mutual terrorist enemy that picked up the tab."

"You Jews are smart."

"What do you mean, you Jews? *We* Jews!"

"Look here, the Egyptians were the first to make peace. Couldn't you have cut them some slack? You had to smash the Aswan High dam? The most vital and vulnerable resource in the whole damn country!"

"Was that meant to be a pun?" asked the Prime Minister.

"Very funny," the President sneered. "Answer me, Danny."

Benari's tone was the audial equivalent of a shrug. "Our seismologists reported a major earthquake in the region. I guess, Mr. President, they will have to rename it the Aswan Low Dam, if they want to be impeccably honest. Besides, the Egyptians should also be thankful. Lake Nasser was a terrible breeding ground for schistosomiasis...."

The bantering mood departed as swiftly as it had come. Benari spoke clearly and distinctly into the phone, as though on a lecturer's podium.

"But since when have Arabs been honest? Since Oslo? No, Mr. President, Egypt has — or should I say, *had* — the strongest military in the Arab world, and they're on our flank. Perhaps your reconnaissance didn't pick up that they had twenty divisions sneaking toward the border. Ours did. As I showed you in the past, Mr. President, our fathers have sinned. Those sins must be paid for.

"In '48 we had no arms, yet against all odds we survived. We even got a contiguous country instead of the patchwork mess the UN offered. Then, in '56, we capitulated, along with the Brits and the French, to your snake Dulles, and gave back the 'peace' we fought for. In '67 we stopped at the Jordan River, Mount Hermon and the Suez Canal. We could have, and should have, taken the cakewalk into Amman, Damascus and Cairo. We should have created a Palestinian state right then, somewhere in the million square miles of Arab lands. Instead we left them to prosper in the West Bank and Gaza, three thousand square miles of land which we so desperately needed to ensure our security.

"In '73 we were almost lost. Why? Because of forbearance to the Americans, who swore Sadat would never attack. We survived by the skin of our teeth, when Nixon realized that he had been *had* by the Arabs. He managed to dump enough supplies for us to make it — barely. Then, in '82, we went into Lebanon to wipe out the PLO scum, whom King Hussein had chucked out of Jordan on their butts. We made it to Beirut, and installed a democratic government in the war-ravaged hell-hole that had once been the Switzerland of the Middle East. Then your gung-ho president, Reagan, told us to get out — that he would manage things fine on

his own, right there in Dodge City. That, after we had made all the sacrifices....
Well, he wasn't in there very long before he received his lesson in Arab etiquette: I
refer to the occasion when two hundred forty-one of his marines, caught napping,
found themselves blown to pieces. Then he got the hell out of there, and let the
damn Syrians fill the vacuum. Has any peace come to that region in the past twenty years?

"After that came the intifada, which we treated with kid gloves. In '93 we
signed Oslo. This was our greatest blunder. It was like handing our enemy the gun
to shoot us with. Peace, all in the name of peace. 'Look,' you said, 'it worked with
Sadat. It can work with the Palestinians.' We went along. The Palestinians broke
every obligation they had agreed to in the accord. Still, we gave in. The
Palestinians promised to change the charter calling for our destruction — later. We
said okay. Okay, you can supply your police with automatic combat arms. Okay,
you can have three times as many police as agreed to. Okay, you can let terrorists
operate with impunity from your domain. Okay, we'll sign another giveaway package in Wye, Maryland, and yet another in Sharm el Sheikh, to strengthen and confirm the Oslo suicide compact. Okay, okay, okay — anything you want! You'd
think we were talking about a scene from the Three Stooges, if not for the lives
being threatened and lost. Yes, our fathers have sinned, and we must pay the price.

"That price is this: our foresworn enemies must be kicked swiftly and kicked
hard, so that they won't forget. When they yell 'uncle' for the tenth time, *perhaps*
then they will begin to mean it. Mr. President, whoever is causing them their present troubles is waiting for the real 'uncle' to be called."

There was a silence at the other end that stretched for perhaps half a minute.
Then Lewis continued as if he hadn't heard a thing Benari had said.

"But why Riyadh, Kunetra, Aleppo, Basra? What did you hit them for? I suppose you're readying a massive hit for Baghdad. I'm surprised it's still on the map."

Dryly, Benari rejoined, "I can only guess that those behind the attacks are saving the best for last. Indeed, the Iraqis deserve a few days to soil their pants before
they get their just desserts. You're crying, but I'm sure Bush and Schwartzkopf are
not. Most good-intentioned people resent being duped."

President Lewis made a manful effort to change the tone of the conversation.
"Look here, Danny, even I have only so much power. I have little control, at this
point, over the Russians and the Red Chinese. I'm losing control over my own people. The vermin are crawling out of the woodwork. Not since the oil crisis of '73,
when we heard, 'Burn Jews, not oil,' has there been such an anti-Semitic clamor.
Right now, it looks like the first Jewish president may very well be the last. The
Arabs once trusted me. My platform was, 'Elect Lewis, avoid Middle East war.' I've
failed. I have no reason to exist in the eyes of half the people. What can I do?"

"You can go home," the Israeli PM said stoically.

"I *am* home, you fool," Lewis yelled.

"No, Abe, you're not. You're a Jew. Your home is Israel." The phone clicked
hard in Benari's ear, and went dead.

Chapter 3

A new Israeli submarine was scheduled to arrive from England for a gala welcoming ceremony in Haifa on January 26, 1968.

It never showed up.

After two weeks of searching, no signal was heard, nor did any trace of the vessel turn up. The sub was declared lost.

The Israeli Minister of Defense released a statement to the effect that it was futile to spend any more resources looking for the sub. The area of the Mediterranean Sea in which it was assumed to be lost — somewhere between Greece and Egypt — was so vast that locating a single sunken vessel was considered virtually impossible. Someday, perhaps, the technology would be developed which would enable detection of the metal hull lying somewhere on the bottom of the sea. In the meantime, there was no hope of finding any survivors. The nation was in mourning.

February 15, 1968, The Prime Minister's Cabinet room:

Sitting on one side of the table was the Israeli government's entire cabinet. On the other side sat the top brass of the Israeli Navy.

"Admiral Arel, what happened to the sub?" the Prime Minister asked.

The admiral replied with cool professionalism. "We think it is lost."

"How does a sub get lost? Let's cut to the chase. We all know the sub is lost. I want to hear every plausible explanation that you have considered over the past two weeks."

The admiral sighed. "We really have no leading theory. Our last radio transmission was forty-one hours before the sub was to arrive in Haifa. The captain asked for permission to use the extra time until the welcoming ceremony in Haifa, to test some new tracking equipment off the coast of Egypt. Permission was denied. But maybe they didn't listen. Maybe they were detected by the Egyptians, and sunk."

"Didn't listen?" howled the PM. "What kind of Navy is this? Anyone does what he wants? Orders, no orders, it's a free-for-all! We seem to have reverted to the days of the Judges: 'There was no king, every man did that which was right in his eyes'."

The admiral said soothingly, "It's just an idea. It's probably not true. Mr. Prime Minister, we select and train outstanding people. Sometimes it goes to their head. Neither our schools nor our military nor our Special Forces training teaches that there is a Power above Who must be obeyed. Instead, we teach that the Zionist

State is the supreme entity that we must strive to defend and maintain. A State is the creation of man, and it is led by men. Here we have a man or a group of men into whom it has been drilled that they're the elite of the nation. Of course, Mr. Prime Minister, it is feasible that orders were not followed. Some men are above orders. Some men don't believe that there exists any Power higher than themselves."

The PM looked stonily into the face of Admiral Arel. With enforced calm, he said, "Let's hear the other theories."

"Our last radio transmission was from the vicinity of the Greek islands, about five hundred fifty kilometers from Haifa. Perhaps the sub had an accident — just a plain, bad luck accident. It might have been bearing down on a rock jutting up from the ocean floor, and couldn't evade it in time. It's almost impossible to speculate until we find the remains."

"That's plausible," the PM admitted. "What else has been proposed?"

"Well," the admiral began slowly, "there are a lot of Russian advisors and their ships in the area, especially near Egypt. Perhaps the sub was captured and the crew exiled to Siberia."

"That sounds far-fetched," the PM said at once. "Don't you think we would have heard something about this through various diplomatic channels?"

"You know the Russians — notoriously unpredictable. The world has been looking for Wallenberg for twenty-three years. You'd think they'd have released something about him by now."

The Prime Minister leaned forward and said with quiet emphasis, "Let me ask you this, Admiral. Is it possible that the submarine had inherent defects that could have led to its loss?"

The Admiral stared silently at the PM. The PM turned to look around the room, first at the other naval officers present and then at his own cabinet. His eyes stopped at his Minister of Defense. "What do you know about this submarine, Moshe? Maybe it wasn't the right design for our needs? Maybe the British failed to give proper training? Nu, what do you think?"

"Levi, I am aware that the sub underwent some major renovations before we took possession. I assumed the ministry approved the designs. I didn't personally study the plans, nor would I know if they were flawed. But it was the British who executed the work. I suppose we could start by investigating the job they did. Let's send a contingent over to England to investigate the shipyard where the work was done."

Admiral Arel spoke up. "We have Admiral Benun here. He was in charge of purchasing and overseeing the modifications. Admiral Benun, do you have anything to note about the renovations or the quality of the British work?"

Benun became very still. The naval commander repeated. "Ozer, wake up. I asked you to take the floor."

All eyes were on Benun. He knew the truth, but couldn't get it out of his mouth. Everyone in the room had the eerie feeling, the pit-in-the-stomach sensation, that something terrible was about to be said — something that could shed light on the tragedy that had befallen the nation.

At length, Benun mustered his courage and spoke. "There was one minor modification that was questionable from an engineer's point of view."

"What does that mean, Admiral Benun?" asked the PM anxiously. "Come to the point."

"The Mossad needed a modification, and submitted a design. It was for a large escape chamber that would make possible an underwater exit for thirty men."

"So?" the PM prompted. "Who made the design, Admiral — the British, or our guys? Somebody must have approved it."

"Actually, it was the Mossad who submitted the design."

"Did it have Navy approval?"

"The Navy doesn't have the authority to disapprove it. State Security always pulls rank."

"Were you aware of problems with the design?"

"I'm not a submarine engineer."

"Answer the question!" bellowed the Prime Minister. "Whether your head rolls or not is unimportant. We must get to the bottom of this, *now*."

Benun clenched his fists, then thrust them out of sight behind his back. Lifting his head, he confessed, "My British counterpart, a submarine engineer who was in charge of the project, warned me there were problems with the design."

"Problems, Admiral? That is a nebulous term." The Prime Minister's patience was wearing visibly thin. "To what extent did he indicate the problem could manifest itself at sea?"

Benun rose slowly from his seat, looked around the room, closed his eyes, and spoke in a hollow voice.

"He said it would sink. He predicted it wouldn't last two hundred hours."

Into the shocked silence, the Prime Minister said, very quietly, "Can you explain to me why you allowed the design to be implemented?"

"I didn't want to. I worked with the British to modify the design, to remove the problem. The Mossad overruled me. They insisted on the original design. The modified design allowed only ten men at a time to exit or enter. They said it wasn't good enough. The weight from the huge water-filled section at the top of the hull, the escape chamber, caused an unmanageable imbalance in the boat."

The PM's voice was filled with wonder. "And the British agreed to build such a flawed design?"

"Yes," Benun sighed. "After I signed the liability waiver they demanded."

February 15, 1968, British Admiralty, London, England:

"Captain Weatherby, how nice to see you. I'm glad you called this meeting. I assume it's about the Israeli sub that was lost a few weeks ago."

"Yes, Admiral. That's exactly what it was about. Here you are, sir." Weatherby handed the Naval Commandant a document, which contained several attachments.

The Admiral read the document first.

Dec 27, 1965

I, the undersigned, Admiral Ozer Benun of the Israeli Navy, hereby authorize the work, as outlined in the attached blueprint supplied by the Israeli Government, to be executed as specified. I acknowledge that British Naval Engineering, Submarine Design, considers the design to be seriously flawed to an extent that, if implemented, could cause instability in the craft.

(Signed) Ozer Benun

The Commandant glanced up. "So they tried to live dangerously. Ever since they trounced the stupid Arabs last summer, those Israeli fat-heads think they're gods. Maybe this will take them down a peg. A little humility would do them a world of good. You did the right thing, Weatherby."

"What do you mean, sir? By agreeing to do the bloody job? Or by making Benun sign the waiver?"

"Both, both, my man. We are off the hook. But I question whether we should make these facts public. It is still embarrassing that British shipwrights, under the supervision of our Navy, built a boat so flawed that it didn't even make it to home port. It could be difficult to sell the international community on the fact that the arrogant Israelis are totally to blame." He tapped the document thoughtfully against his open palm. "We'll wait and see. In the meantime, how many copies of the design and this waiver are extant?"

"This is the original and only copy of the waiver, sir. I didn't even make a copy for the Israelis. There are a few copies of the sub design down at the shipyard. Benun obviously also has copies in Israel."

"Gather all the copies you can find. This material will remain with me. Now, by authority and subject to the Official Secrets Act, you will never say a word to anyone about this without my express permission."

Weatherby straightened up and nodded. He understood the consequences of failing to remain tight-lipped. With a deferential salute, he left his commanding officer's office.

By the next day, all hard copy in Britain concerning the ill-fated Israeli submarine, *Davar*, was in the hands of the Commandant of Her Majesty's Royal Navy.

February 17, 1968, Jerusalem, Israel:

"Nobody knows the truth about the sub," the Prime Minister told the head of GSS.

"How could they?" came the terse response.

"The rumor is beginning to circulate that our design was flawed. As long as it remains just a rumor — one theory among various others — it will serve us well. But I am concerned that there might be too much talk about this. It may even make the press." The Prime Minister's eyes reflected his distaste at that possibility.

"I wouldn't worry, Mr. Prime Minister. Colonel Schwartz collected all copies of the design before the sub went down. I suggest we see if there is any way we can work with the British to keep the facts quiet."

"Very good. I want you to fly to England today, and see what you can do. I'll give you a letter. We have a delegation of naval men heading there next week. Try to make a deal before they arrive."

The security chief stood up, holding out a confident hand. "I think we'll be okay," he said with a smile. The two shook hands and parted company.

Later that same evening, the head of Israeli Intelligence met with the Commandant of the British Navy in London. After a forty minute meeting, it was agreed, for the mutual interests of both countries, that the issue of the design modifications would remain permanently sealed.

The following week, three cabinet ministers and four top brass naval officers arrived in Portsmouth to lead an investigation. Benun introduced the entourage to Captain Weatherby. But when Weatherby brought out the blueprints of the sub, there was no trace of any major frame modifications. Benun was astounded and greatly discomfited.

"What's going on here? Where is the actual design, Captain?"

"This is it, Admiral Benun. Does your memory fail you?" Weatherby asked innocently.

"But what about the design modifications I brought? What about the waiver? I must show these documents to our group."

Weatherby allowed a moment to elapse before answering. When he did, his voice was gentle.

"Admiral Benun, it has been several years. I think you must have confused this project with some other one you were involved with." He waved a hand at the blueprints. "This is all that there is."

Benun was highly embarrassed. He had been made to look a fool in front of the top brass. At the same time, he became aware of another, even stronger feeling — of relief. He smelled a coverup, one that, perhaps inadvertently, covered up his own part in the debacle as well. He shrugged his shoulders at the others in the group and said curtly, "There's nothing for us here. Let's go home."

The matter was buried.

Chapter 4

June 1968, Heichal Shlomo, The Chief Rabbinate, Jerusalem:

Slowly, the rabbi shook his head. "Reb Shlomo, you say we can permit the wives of the men lost on the sub *Davar* to remarry? I wish I could agree — but the Law is clear. Men lost in a great body of water, where a witness standing upon the shore cannot see to the other side, cannot be presumed dead. They may have found some plank or flotation device and made their way to safety, out of the view of the witness."

"Yes, Reb Isaac, you are correct. But the public will never accept such a harsh pronouncement upon those poor women. We must find a way to free them to remarry."

"Of course we must explore every possible avenue, but we can't violate the Law of the Torah. Our sages have worked tirelessly to free *agunot* through the ages. I have gone through all the literature and the precedents, but I cannot find anything like this."

Reb Shlomo spoke with urgent persuasiveness. "You are right Isaac; this case is unique. But we can find greater leniency. I have ascertained that when a submerged sub sinks, it is less likely to survive than when a regular ship sinks. The chances, in fact, are close to impossible. Usually, when a conventional ship sinks, the passengers are cast into the sea. In this case, men on board the sub cannot get out to even attempt to swim to the surface."

"Why not, Shlomo?" Reb Isaac argued. "When they realized the sub was sinking, all they had to do was open the door and swim up to the surface."

Smiling, the other rabbi said, "Isaac, my friend, you spent fifteen years studying in *kollel*, but maybe you should have gone to college for a while. You might have learned that under the water there is a huge amount of pressure against the hatch, and it can't be opened. Besides, there would be no way a man's lungs could survive the pressure until he reached the surface." His manner grew brisk. "I think we have an acceptable presumption that such an accident is impossible to survive. We have a precedent from the case of a man who fell into a pit of snakes and scorpions. In modern times, our Sages have permitted women to remarry whose husbands were on airplanes that crashed into the sea and the bodies never recovered. Such a thing, too, is impossible to survive."

"But Shlomo, how do you know the submarine was under the water when it vanished? Maybe it was on the surface? Maybe some enemy captured the men alive? Even the government claims it hasn't the foggiest idea where it was when it was lost."

"Yes, Isaac, you are right. We *don't* know. But for that we also have a precedent from our Sages. In the case of a well-known personality, we presume that if he doesn't show up after awhile, he must be dead. With communications available today, anyone is considered like a well-known personality. Certainly an entire submarine, with all its crew, must be compared to the well-known personality. Surely, if the boat were captured, the enemy couldn't or wouldn't have kept it quiet. Besides, we have the opinion of one great Sage who explains that even in the case of a man lost in a large body of water, if he fails to return after many years, he is presumed dead."

Reb Isaac stood up and began pacing the room as he formulated his counter-argument. "Yes, Shlomo, indeed, all that you have said is perfectly true. But let me portray this hypothetical scenario. Maybe there never *was* any accident. So far, there hasn't been a shred of evidence to indicate the fate of the sub. No bodies swept up on any shore, no floating debris found anywhere, no oil slick, nothing at all."

"What are you saying? There is no word from the sub. Doesn't that prove its crew must be dead?"

"Who says they are dead? Maybe the military or the Mossad sent them on a secret mission and doesn't want foreign governments to be aware of it. Perhaps the entire disappearance is a ruse!"

Reb Shlomo threw him a look of mingled pity and exasperation. "Oh Isaac, what's gotten into you? You have time to read spy novels? What you're saying is ludicrous — even scandalous. You think our government would do such a thing to these poor wives? To knowingly send away their husbands, allowing the wives and the whole world to presume them dead? That's the most ridiculous thing I've ever heard from a great Torah scholar like yourself!" He slapped a hand down on the table and said decisively, "I am signing the permission document for the wives to remarry. And you will sign it along with me."

Defeated, Reb Isaac slumped back into his chair. He remained lost in thought for several moments before rousing himself to say, "All right, I was only speculating on the most extreme possibility. But if you say that it is too far-fetched, and that according to Halacha we don't even have to take the possibility into consideration, I'll sign along with you." He hesitated. "Please, when discussing the case, don't mention that I raised this possibility. It would be embarrassing for the Torah if it became known that I entertained such an idea."

"Of course Isaac." Reb Shlomo smiled graciously, then handed his partner a pen. "Just sign here below my name. And don't worry — I won't mention your silly theory to a soul."

PART ONE:

ABDALLAH IBN GAƧH

"But also the nation that they will serve, I shall judge"

Genesis 15:14

Chapter 5

On November 4, 1942, Nazi Field Marshal Erwin Rommel met defeat in El Alamein, Egypt. On that same day, Alon Barnash was born in Alexandria, one hundred kilometers to the east. His father was a wealthy corporate magnate, owning the controlling interest in an industrial machine plant providing employment for some twelve hundred people.

All of that changed dramatically when Nasser overthrew King Farouk and nationalized the company.

At first, Rahamim Barnash continued to manage the plant. Three months later he was replaced by an Arab, second cousin to Nasser's wife. And six months after *that*, all his assets were seized — including his accounts in Beirut. The family was reduced to penury.

The Barnashes managed to flee to France, along with thousands of others who understood that Jews were no longer welcome in Egypt. Within a year, the family found a new home in Kiryat Gat, Israel. Young Alon had little recollection of his birthplace, nor — aside from the fact that he spoke the language like a native — did he take much interest in it.

Now, for the first time since he'd left at the age of eleven, Alon was about to set foot on his native soil.

April 1968, the Red Sea off the coast of Egypt:

Toward the end of the month, when the moon was new, Alon Barnash surfaced in the warm waters of the Red Sea. He estimated that he was some four hundred meters off the coast. Burdened only with a waterproof knapsack, the swim ashore took no more than eighteen minutes. As he hauled himself out of the water in the darkness, he fought an almost irresistible urge to hurl his knapsack into the night and return the way he'd come.

The struggle lasted all of five seconds. Alon stood upright, slung the knapsack more firmly over his shoulder, and began walking. The knapsack contained Arab clothing, an Arab identity card issued in the name of Abdallah Ibn Gash, a Helwan 9mm pistol and — most notably — fifty thousand Egyptian pounds in cash.

Alon hitched a ride into the city of Aswan, where he rented the most frugal apartment he could find in the middle-class section of town. Over the next three months, he frequented the cafes and men's clubs where he could be sure of meeting people — the right people. On Fridays, he was a regular at the mosque for prayer. On Saturday nights, he was a regular in the Europskaya, the local Russian saloon which had been set up to accommodate the plethora of dam workers common to the region for the past ten years. While his Russian friends swilled their vodka, Abdallah Ibn Gash, faithful Moslem, sipped his hot tea.

In the summer of 1968, he found a job teaching science in the local high school. By that time he was on his way to becoming very popular in the right circles. Neither his persona nor his behavior aroused the slightest suspicion in Aswan.

Abdallah poked his head into the teacher's lounge at the Saladin High School, where he had just begun to teach. As he'd hoped, it was empty save for one person. He stepped inside and cleared his throat. The young woman looked up, a question in her eyes.

"Hello, Miss Baktari. I hope I'm not interrupting you at anything urgent."

The other teacher shook her head, blushing faintly. "No, that's all right."

Abdallah sat down in the armchair opposite hers, his manner becoming subtly less formal. "I'm new here, Miss Baktari — and frankly, I'm anxious to hold onto the students' attention. One sure way of losing it would be to teach them things they've already learned. We're about to do the chapter on geology. Could you clue me in as to how much of this material was covered in your general science class last year?"

"Mr. Ibn Gash —"

"You can call me Abdallah."

She smiled shyly. "Well, in that case, it would only be fair to call me Fatima."

"It's my pleasure to call you Fatima," Abdallah said, his deep blue eyes looking directly into hers. She blushed and looked away.

"Mr. Ibn Gash —"

"Abdallah!"

"I mean Abdallah. I'll show you my worksheets from last year...." She gathered her courage. "Why are you looking at me like that?"

"Like what... Fatima?"

"There's a twinkle in your eye. I'd heard that you were a devout Moslem!"

"What makes you think I'm not devout?" He leaned forward earnestly. "Listen here — I'm a single man. I came here from Alexandria not long ago; I have no family left. So I guess you can say I'm on my own." Ibn Gash took his eyes off the young woman and cast them sadly on the ground.

"I'm sorry."

"But that doesn't answer your question. I have a very special relationship with God, but I suppose you can consider me modern in many ways." He looked at her with open curiosity. "You yourself don't seem to be the most religious Moslem in the world. You are, after all, university educated."

"We are not Arabs; my family moved from Iran seven years ago," Fatima explained. She seemed unaccountably uneasy.

"I see. The Shah has made a great many changes in Iran — brought it into the twentieth century. Why did your family leave? I'd have thought that the present political climate would suit you."

"Actually, my father was appointed to the Iranian diplomatic mission in Cairo."

"Well, now. That explains everything!" Abdallah beamed. "Except for the fact that you are not yet married."

Fatima Baktari flushed crimson. "Now you're getting personal, Mr. Ibn Gash. You will find the worksheets in the office tomorrow." She beat a hasty retreat.

Three days later, Ibn Gash approached Miss Baktari in the schoolyard after class.

"Miss Baktari, thanks for the work sheets — they saved me about a week's hard labor. Now, please listen to me." With his penetrating eyes upon her — eyes which, though she would never have admitted as much, had intruded on her dreams for three nights running — Fatima felt mesmerized, almost under a spell. "I'm sorry about my remark to you the other day. You were absolutely in the right. I should never have become so personal. But it's lonely here in Aswan.... Very few educated people, except for the engineers at the dam — when they're sober. Like you, I am single, though I don't want to remain that way. I've been teaching here for nearly three weeks, and I must admit, I've been watching you." He smiled engagingly. "In fact, I'll be perfectly honest: I like you."

Fatima Baktari turned away. "Don't think I haven't noticed. But I don't think we are for each other."

Ibn Gash seized her hand and turned her toward him. "Why do you say that? You know nothing about me."

"True — but I know about myself. It won't work."

"Try me. What's the problem?"

"I am a modern liberal Iranian. My father is just like the Shah. Publicly he's a good Moslem, but privately... privately...."

"He's not very devout?"

"Exactly."

Shrewdly, he guessed, "And you, also, are not the most devoted follower of the Prophet? And you think that would bother me?"

"Well.... Yes. But there are other problems. Please, Mr. Ibn Gash...."

"Abdallah."

"Abdallah. We are from completely different backgrounds. I don't even like to talk about it. You are Arab, I am Iranian. We are simply — different."

Abdallah was dimly aware of the schoolyard noises all around him. The strong September sun beat down on his head, but he was too intent to feel the heat. "Fatima, I don't care about family stock. Didn't your own Shah marry an Egyptian? I don't even care about the fact that your family is not so religious; anybody can change. Both of us are, at least nominally, Moslem. I really think this could work for us. A single man like me, with no family. A single girl like you, a foreigner in a strange land. Why are you so closed to the idea?" He stopped. "Is there someone else?"

"Look, Abdallah, I told you there are other problems. I'm probably older than you — I'm twenty-nine." With that, Fatima climbed into her Volkswagen and drove off.

The next few months were busy ones for Abdallah. After school hours he became very friendly with the assistant manager of the Aswan High Dam Power station, and even arranged to bring his class for a tour. At his friend's invitation he began spending a great deal of time at and around the dam. By November of 1968, he gave notice to the school that he would not be returning the following year; he had accepted a job with the dam authority.

The job actually began, on a part-time basis, immediately. As he juggled his teaching schedule and his hours at the dam, Ibn Gash continued to woo Fatima Baktari. He took her to the dam often, winning her company on the pretense of educational experience. One evening, as he stopped his car to let her off at her home, he faced her abruptly.

"Fatima, the time has come. I want to marry you."

Her smile was still a little shy, still a little sad. "Abdallah, I would very much like that... but I think we will remain just good friends."

"Why, why? You have been like this ever since we began to speak with each other. I swear to Allah, you can trust me! You have a problem, Fatima. Or maybe more than just a problem: a secret. What is it? Do you have some sort of genetic illness? I don't care. I don't even care that you are three years older. I love you. No matter what the trouble is, I will love you."

Fatima began to cry. "You — you've been very insightful. A genetic illness...." Through her tears, her lips twisted in a wry smile. "You swore by the Prophet that I could trust you. I have never told anyone about my 'problem'. Now it is out of sight and out of mind — but if it became known, it would most certainly become a major problem. I would probably have to leave Egypt."

"Never mind, my dear. Tell me what it is. You deserve peace of mind."

"Abdallah, I ask only one thing. Swear to me that you won't reveal my secret. I am assuming that you will never want to speak to me again, but I'll take my chance. Just swear that you won't tell or — or take revenge."

"I swear it. But you talk as if this is some terrible thing. Look here, I love you. I want to marry you, even if you once worked as a harlot. That's it, isn't it? Well, you see — I don't care."

Fatima slapped Ibn Gash gingerly across the face. "The only contact I've allowed between us is holding hands, and you accuse me of harlotry! I swear to you, I am a virgin."

"I'm sorry, I'm sorry. I wasn't serious." Ruefully, he rubbed his stinging cheek. "It's just that you've been hinting at your awful secret for two months now. Put me out of my suspense, Fatima! What is it?"

Fatima looked up at him with a half-smile. "All right, I forgive you. And I apologize for the slap." As her thoughts returned to her present quandary, her voice sharpened again with anxiety. "I'm terribly nervous. I will tell you — but then, please, let's just part company. No recriminations, all right? Remember, you swore to me." She sat trembling in the passenger seat, waiting for his answer. Abdallah merely nodded, peering intently into Fatima's eyes.

She drew a long breath and confessed, "My mother is a Jew."

Covering her eyes, Fatima broke into deep, shuddering sobs.

Ibn Gash was taken by surprise. Whatever he had expected, it had not been this. He was not prepared for this development... though the tentative, joyous relief that seeped through him told its own story. Fatima looked up at him through her fingers. "Abdallah, you look shocked. I guess you ought to be. I'll — I'll say good-bye now. Please remember your promise."

She yanked open the passenger door. As she started to climb out of the car, Abdallah grabbed her hand and pulled her back in. For an instant, she almost believed she felt the cold steel of a honed blade at her throat....

"Fatima, call your father in Cairo. We must be married before the next new moon."

Disbelievingly, she looked up into his face, his deep blue eyes. "You still want me?"

"I still want you. Your father married your mother; I will marry you, even if you insist on a Jewish ceremony."

Two weeks later Abdallah married Fatima Baktari. The Mullah of Cairo himself performed the ceremony, which was followed by a modern reception at the Iranian embassy. The following week, the couple moved into Fatima's apartment, which was far more comfortable than Abdallah's.

On November 26, exactly seven months from the day Alon Barnash became Abdallah Ibn Gash, he drove a passenger truck — rented to take his class on a field trip to Lake Nasser — back to the shore of the Red Sea.

To his new bride, he explained that he was taking his class on a two-day camping trip to the lake. At the lake, Ibn Gash told the class that he had to drive into town for supplies and would be back in a few hours. When the glowing dial of his wristwatch showed exactly 9:00 p.m., he signaled nine times with a flashlight toward the open water — and waited. Half an hour later, he could just make out the forms of eight men coming up the deserted rocky beach, dragging a large crate. He signaled three more times. They were upon him within minutes.

"Alon," Gutzi Karmel called softly.

"Abdallah," he answered at once. "Always Abdallah Ibn Gash."

"Abdallah, then — how've you been?" Gutzi shined a light in his face. "You old Arab, what have you been up to in the past half-year?"

"Everything has gone as planned. I think God is with us."

"You mean Allah." Gutzi chuckled.

"I mean God. I've landed a job working at the dam. Everybody knows and trusts me there; I don't even have to show my ID to enter the control area anymore. I know the place like the back of my hand." He peered at the shadowy figures waiting behind Gutzi. "Say, how come I didn't get a ninth man? I have a work schedule all figured out."

Gutzi shrugged. "This is it, pal. We've made all the rounds. You were dropped off after the North American contingent. Then we worked our way back toward the Persian Gulf, letting off passengers. Rafi himself was last to go...."

"Where?" Alon asked, excited.

"Hey, you know the rules. I can't tell you that."

"Okay, okay, I was just testing you." Alon was disappointed.

"We have four more guys back on the sub. They're going to complete the operation. I guess we'll have to stay an extra day or two."

"I guess so.... By the way, I get a Mazel Tov."

"What are you talking about?" Gutzi asked in surprise.

"I got married last week."

Gutzi's face fell, but he said only, "You follow orders well. How do you find being husband to a *shiktza* — and an Arab at that?"

"I wouldn't know. She's Jewish."

Gutzi became agitated. "I hope you've maintained your secrecy! You know the rules."

"Absolutely. I don't think you get the picture, Gutzi. I still bow down on the mat five times a day and spend my Fridays at the mosque. You can be sure that nobody hears me whispering *Shema Yisroel,* the only prayer I know by heart." Alon smiled thinly. "She nearly died when she revealed to me that her mother is Jewish. She thought I would kill her, denounce her, or at the very least never want to see her again. She's astonished at my reaction — and very grateful. To Fatima, I'm a devout but modern-minded Moslem. That's the way life will remain for me. I accept it." His manner became brisk. "Now, we have plenty of work to do. Let me show you a cave I found, about seven hundred meters from the entrance to the control area. It's perfect for our work."

The ride through the mountains from the coast to the dam went uneventfully. Abdallah drove the tender up to the cave and got out. He carefully scouted the surroundings, then motioned for the others to follow. After climbing down a small shaft, they found themselves in a cavern twenty meters wide and four meters high. The cavern was piled high with equipment — good equipment. Diesel compressors, pneumatic hammers and drills, plenty of flexible extension rods and several wheelbarrows.

"Where did you get this stuff?" one of the Israelis asked.

"This dam is a big, big project. It's operational but not quite finished — maybe another eight or ten months. There's a lot of equipment around. Probably too much. That's typical of Russian largess. Believe me, these aren't the first things to disappear. One thing you learn about communism is that nobody really cares." He turned to face his men. "If we all work hard for about nine days, I figure we can penetrate the upper layer of bedrock granite. According to this geological survey," Abdallah pulled out a large map of the area and directed his flashlight on the small area around the cave, "the granite substrate continues about sixty meters down. Below that is a layer of non-consolidated material...."

Shimon Boker broke in. "I didn't major in geology; I'll be specializing in bridges and buildings. Explain the term 'non-consolidated material', please."

"Sand, my friend," Abdallah said. "Plain old silicon dioxide. Now let me continue. This layer extends about four hundred fifty meters down. Below that — folded, mildly disturbed sandstone/limestone. The sandstone/limestone forms alternating plates that reach below the scope of this survey. Now, the Nile itself carries a huge amount of silt out of the mountains of Central Africa; the riverbed contains so much mud and clay that there is very little seepage to the strata below. In constructing the dam, engineers inserted an inner core of clay to further minimize seepage into the dam's foundation.

"Actually, the valley is quite fertile on the east bank. The west bank is another story. It's as though the river were a great boundary between the living and the dead.... In any case, what we have to do is get through that first substrate of granite. I need a shaft, just large enough for a man. After that, I'll take it from there. I've got an unlimited amount of time to finish the job.... We hope."

"Sounds pretty grandiose," Gutzi remarked.

"The dam is also grandiose. We'll just be evening the score.... Though who knows? By the time this work is near completion, ten or twelve years from now, we may be at peace with Egypt and all of this will have been for nothing."

"Peace? You're crazy. These guys will never make peace. After three wars, they're still talking like they want to start another."

Abdallah shrugged. "Look, we're not politicians, we're technicians. Let's get to work."

Over the next nine days, the nine men worked ten hours a night, drilling and removing chips of stone. They lived in the cave, no very arduous feat for men with their training. They had brought along scuba breathing regulators. Abdallah had "requisitioned" a three hundred meter roll of high-pressure air hose, which was adapted to connect the regulators to the air-compressors. An air intake shunt was directed outside the cave for each of the three active compressors. Although diesel smoke billowed out of the cave entrance, it was virtually invisible at night. Connecting exhaust hoses to the outside would have generated too much noise — something that the darkness couldn't have concealed. Abdallah came on a tour of inspection every three or four days, laden with food and other supplies.

Finally, fifty meters below the surface, the solid granite turned to large boulders sitting in sand. Another ten meters, and the boulders became mere pebbles. The men's work was complete. At 2:00 a.m., Abdallah drove up with a tender he had rented earlier in the day, and made the three-hour trip to the coast. He waved goodbye to his mates, the closest friends a man could hope for. Under cover of the night he let a tear fall. It was very possible that he might never see these men again. They were just another part of the awesome package of people and things he'd been forced to renounce in the service of his mission....

When his friends had disappeared, Abdallah restarted the truck's engine. The return trip was quiet and very lonely. He thought fleetingly of Fatima, and of the secrets he could never share with her. The loneliness intensified.

He reached Aswan in the early hours of the morning. His friends had vanished without a trace — but they had left behind a serious souvenir for Abdallah to remember them by: a three hundred kilo wooden crate equivalent to approximately fifty kilotons of explosives.

One morning, two months after saying his last farewell to his friends, Abdallah Ibn Gash opened the Al Ahram newspaper to an article that had caught his eye.

Exactly one year ago, the Zionist State revealed that it had lost a submarine somewhere in the Mediterranean. An extensive search found no trace of the vessel.

Yesterday, February 9, 1969, a fisherman off the coast of Khan Yunis in Zionist-occupied Egypt, hauled in an Emergency Buoy Marker from the sunken vessel. Captain Bishara Abu Dib of the Egyptian Navy has now disclosed that his destroyer fired depth charges at an alien submarine off the coast of the Nile Delta last year, at about the time the submarine was reported lost.

Apparently, he hit his mark.

Chapter 6

Many facets of the Arabic culture meshed perfectly with Alon Barnash's long-term project — and none more so than the fact that men and women did not socialize together. The woman was viewed as a beast of labor, a sow to nurse her young and a receptacle to satisfy her husband when he wasn't out with his buddies. The highly educated Ibn Gash household was unusual in that husband and wife conducted an atypical intellectual intercourse. Still, Abdallah spent a great deal of time outside the house as compared to his Western counterpart.

Fatima accepted this as a fact of life, and even considered herself lucky to have a man who spent so much time with her outside the bedroom setting. So when Abdallah told her that he was headed out to the Shesh-Besh (backgammon) club for the evening, or the Russian saloon, or just to chew the fat over at the dam control, it was inconceivable that she should challenge him, check on his whereabouts, or even try to contact him there.

This unquestioning acceptance worked to his advantage. Two or three times a week, he would ride his motorbike seven kilometers to the dam, conceal the bike behind the rocks, move two small flat stones that covered the entrance to the cave, and continue his monotonous work.

The routine never varied. Placing a compressed-air regulator over his face, he started up the diesel compressor and continued the job of loosening and pulverizing compacted sand. He would fill a large bucket with approximately one hundred kilos of the debris, step up on it, and pull on another rope. This engaged a reduction-geared windlass attached to the drive shaft of the diesel engine. The windlass raised the loaded bucket — along with Abdallah — to a position from which he could dump the contents into a wheelbarrow. He would then walk the wheelbarrow to the extremity of the cavern and empty it. The shaft was dug at a twenty-five-degree slope, so that climbing up posed no real problem even if the windlass should fail.

After six months and a penetration of one hundred fifty meters, he spent the next two weeks — six sessions lasting five hours each — digging a chamber about two and a half meters in diameter and one hundred thirty-five centimeters high. The next full session was spent lowering the smallest compressor down to the new chamber. He was now in the position to efficiently continue his excavation of the tunnel. Of course, the deeper he dug, the more his average daily rate of progress began to drop off: it took him longer and longer to get up and down the shaft to dump his load. Every few months, Abdallah would rent a decent-sized truck for the day. Under cover of the night, he would siphon the filled fuel tank into five individual forty-liter tanks he kept in the cave.

After seventeen months of digging, his windlass unwound three hundred meters of cable. The time had come to dig out a second large chamber and move the power plant down to the next level. In addition, he had to start looking around for more air hose. The year was late 1970, and the dam was complete. All the construction equipment — that is, all that remained — had been sent back to Russia, and extra supplies were hard to come by. After some thought, Abdallah suggested to his wife that they visit her family in Cairo for a week. While there, he found one hardware store that sold painting equipment. He purchased a medium-sized electric compressor, five spray-paint canisters and nozzles, twenty liters of various colored paints, and a two hundred meter roll of air hose. To the curious salesman he explained that the numerous compressors for his auto painting business required that large quantity of hose. To his wife, he explained that the apartment needed a good painting, which she couldn't deny. When they got home, he threw all the equipment into storage — except for the hose, which found its sly way into the cave.

Meanwhile, above ground, Abdallah Ibn Gash prospered. He lived a life devoid of controversy and therefore devoid of suspicion. In February of 1971, Fatima gave birth to a fine-looking son weighing 3.8 kilos. They named him Mustafa. When the baby was one week old, the couple took up Fatima's mother's offer to stay with her for a month. Abdallah seized the opportunity to stock up on more air hose and other equipment that was hard to come by in any other part of Egypt.

Two days after their arrival at the Baktaris' luxurious Cairo residence, he walked into the bedroom that had been allotted to them, and found Fatima standing by the bedroom wastebasket. She started at his entrance, blushing fiercely. It was clear that he had taken her by surprise. Curious, he crossed the room to where she stood.

Fatima had been discarding a bloody length of gauze in the wastebasket.

"What's that?" Abdallah asked.

"Oh, that — that...." She drew a deep breath. "That's from the baby's circumcision."

"The baby is not even two weeks old, and you had him circumcised already? I remember my grandfather telling me about his circumcision when he was thirteen years old," Abdallah lied glibly to his unsuspecting wife of two years. "That practice is a thing of the past. In my family, we would be circumcised at two, three, or even up to six months. But what was your hurry to have our little baby cut so young?" He paused, then added suspiciously, "I've heard that the Jews cut at eight days."

Fatima's response was hurried and nervous. "Darling, mother explained that it is the custom of Iranian Moslems to circumcise baby boys at eight or ten days. I was just following my family's tradition."

"Tradition, my eye!" Abdallah said with an impressive show of anger. "Your mother is a Jew. I'll bet she was Jewing my son. A curse upon her head!"

"Please, Abdallah," Fatima cried. "Jew, Arab, what's the difference? Aren't we all children of Abraham? You swore to me that my mother's Jewish background didn't matter to you. Now, of all times, are you going to let that fact come between us?"

Abdallah softened. It would never do to let his wife suspect that he had grasped the entire scenario from his first glimpse of the bloodied bandage. At the same time, he had no desire to distress Fatima more than he must to keep up pretenses. "No, my dear. I made a promise to you, and I mean to keep it. Only," he frowned, "I never thought it would come to this — imposing a Jewish practice on my own son!"

Fatima began to bawl louder than the baby. Abdallah found himself only with great difficulty holding back a torrent of laughter.

When Fatima's mother returned home, Abdallah confronted her.

"I understand you had my son circumcised yesterday," he said in a stern but controlled voice.

The fifty-two-year-old matron, caught off guard, thought rapidly. "Yes, that's true. So what? Don't all good Moslems carry on that tradition?"

"Don't you think the father should have been informed? And tell me, who was the circumciser? A doctor or a mullah?"

Mrs. Baktari was silent.

"Mother-in-law, please answer me. Mustafa is your grandson, but he's my son," Abdallah stated with emphasis. "Did you hire a Jew rabbi? Tell me the truth. Your highly-educated daughter married a man of similar intellect, you know. You won't get anything past me."

Mrs. Baktari was trapped. She had no choice but to be candid.

"Yes, I hired the old rabbi. He's performed thirty thousand circumcisions over the past forty-five years. Why shouldn't I have hired him? If you were sick, would you hesitate to be treated by a Jewish or a Christian doctor? If you were in legal trouble, would the lawyer's religion make any difference to you?" She shrugged. "When you want a professional to do a job, you hire the best you can find. Back in Iran, all the Moslems used the Jewish ritual circumciser. He simply did the best job."

"I'll bet. It was probably just the 'Westernized' Moslems like you and your Shah who did that. A real Moslem would never hear of using a Jew. Besides," he snapped, "it seems you were in quite a hurry to get the cutting done."

"I didn't know how long you and Fatima would stay in town. I just wanted to make sure the expert could schedule Mustafa before you leave. Well, he had an open appointment — and I took it."

Abdallah decided it was time to pull out the stops. "Mother-in-law, you can't pull the wool over the eyes of Abdallah Ibn Gash!" He whirled around to shout at his wife, in the next room. "Fatima! Pack up. We're leaving!"

"Please, Abdallah," Fatima moaned from her bed. "I'm so weak; I can't go. I need my mother. My first baby, my first baby, and all this has to happen to me." She resumed her wailing.

Abdallah felt that his ruse had succeeded sufficiently. It was time to show some measure of compassion.

"Oh, all right," he said grudgingly. "You can stay, if you wish. But I'm leaving tomorrow. I shouldn't be away from work for so long in any case. You can wire me when you want to come home."

Abdallah left the next day, still stern in manner but refraining from overt complaints about his mother-in-law's behavior. Fatima was relieved. As soon as her husband had left, she turned tearfully on her mother.

"Mother, I told you not to do it. Don't you see what damage it's caused? I love Abdallah, and I'm sure he feels the same toward me. Was it worth jeopardizing our marriage?"

With dignity, Mrs. Baktari drew herself up and said, "My daughter, I am a Jew. That makes you Jewish, and my grandson, too."

"That's what you say. According to Islamic law, which Abdallah believes in, Mustafa is a Moslem just like his father. I don't understand you, Mother. Why this sudden insistence on pushing the Jewish issue? It doesn't concern me in the least. Although your background was never a secret to me, you never raised me as a Jew, nor practiced anything Jewish yourself." Pettishly, Fatima added, "If all this is really so important to you, why did you marry my father in the first place?"

Mrs. Baktari looked down, somber, as she answered her only child in all honesty.

"My daughter — my beloved daughter. I was young and foolish. My parents were very traditional. They bought meat only from the Jewish butcher. They fasted on the Day of Atonement. But they were very westernized. I was taught tolerance in the home and, in the late thirties, sent to university. My father was friendly with Jew and non-Jew alike. That is how I was raised.

"But when I came home one day in the middle of my second year at school with a non-Jewish boyfriend, my parents were aghast. I couldn't comprehend it; their attitude seemed to turn back the clock by five hundred years. I was nineteen when I married your father. He was from a prominent family, very close with Reza Shah, and he insisted I quit school when I became his wife — which I did. I had no need for a career in any case. It took years for my parents to get over the fact that I had married a non-Jew, and even then, I could tell that the hurt in their hearts would never completely heal.

"That was thirty-four years ago." She gazed earnestly at her daughter. "Fatima, sometimes it takes time to wake up. It takes an event to pull a person out of a deep slumber. I saw your son — my first and only grandson — and memories of my parents and grandparents suddenly awoke in me. The night you arrived, I cried till morning. By the time the sun had risen, I'd decided that thirty-five years of defying my parents, my family, and my own people was long enough. Perhaps it was the maternal instinct of survival that made the decision for me. I knew I had to see my Jewish grandson brought into the covenant of Abraham, our forefather."

She drew a deep breath, then continued, "You walked out of the room when the rabbi performed the circumcision. But I was there. I told the rabbi to name the child Moshe, for he was pulled from the waters of Egypt just like our great leader of long ago. That was the least I could do for the legacy of my people."

Fatima regarded her mother steadily, eyes damp. She said nothing. Presently, her mother added softly, "I won't interfere again in the life of your family. It would be arrogant of me to insist that you change your ways to those that I'd abandoned for most of my own life. That decision will be up to you."

Fatima cleared her throat and asked hesitantly, "And father...?"

"I love your father, and I'll stay with him until I die. That was a decision I must live with. But I wished to give my grandson — your precious son — a beginning in life that I know is right. What happens later is out of my hands. Do you understand, Fatima?"

Fatima's answer was to burst into tears, face buried in her mother's shoulder.

The two women sat for a long while on the edge of the bed, weeping. Then the baby woke up and joined the chorus. His mother took him out of his bassinet to be nursed. Her tears turned to joy as she watched her little Mustafa, or Moshe — she wasn't quite sure who he really was — fall peacefully asleep in her arms. There was no need for Abdallah to know all the details, she decided as she crooned over her infant. The truth was buried in the mists of time. The baby was hers, hers and Abdallah's — that was all that mattered.

It was good to be back. During the six weeks his wife stayed in Cairo, Abdallah was able to double his average excavation efforts. On the last day, he broke past the three hundred fifty meter mark. When he returned to Cairo for his wife and child, he said nothing about the circumcision or the acrimonious clash with his mother-in-law.

Grateful for his silence, Fatima went happily home.

Chapter 7

Another year passed. On the second of March 1972, Abdallah hit rock. The tightly packed, non-consolidated material became, unquestionably, consolidated. The angle of the shaft — so straight that one could see a bright Primus lamp in the cavern from four hundred fifty meters down — was directed at bringing the shaft's bottom even with the northern edge of the dam's outer wall. As yet, the shaft was not beneath the dam itself. The origin of the shaft, at ground level, was seven hundred meters from the edge of the river.

Now Abdallah was able to continue extending the shaft horizontally, another four hundred meters along the sandstone strata, to arrive under the dam. From that point, another fifteen hundred meters remained to reach the spot directly beneath the center of the dam — the spot which was destined to become final resting place for a fifty kiloton bomb.

Abdallah found that digging along the sandstone floor was easier, and his progress improved slightly. By the outbreak of the Yom Kippur War in October of 1973, he, one lone man, had completed over half the distance to the goal he had set since hitting the substrate.

The October war came as a great surprise. Although Abdallah was keen on the news, especially when it touched Israel, he was not in a good position to spy on the military-strategic complex of the Egyptian government. The buildup around the Suez Canal certainly had been rumored for several weeks, but nobody in his right mind had actually thought that Egypt was prepared to attack Israel.

Abdallah had been "sick" in bed for the two days prior to the outbreak of the war. He always seemed to fall ill at around that time of the year, totally losing his appetite. But in 1973, just as the radio was blaring, "Our troops have retaken our stolen land from the cursed Israelis. Long live President Sadat; he has succeeded where Nasser failed! Our troops are now on the outskirts of Tel Aviv. Soon the enemy will be driven into the sea," Abdallah jumped out of his sickbed. He kissed his wife and two-year-old son, saying as he left that he must join the national forces for victory. He promised to return when the enemy was vanquished. Fatima begged him not to go. She wept copiously as he gathered his clothes, plenty of food, and other gear from around the house.

"What's the matter with you?" he demanded. "You almost sound as if you're unhappy about the fact that, after twenty-five years of being a curse, Israel's existence is about to end!"

She wrung her hands. "No, Abdallah, that's not it at all. I'm just so scared. Maybe they have a trick up their sleeve. They are such a powerful nation, and they have the U.S. backing them. I think, somehow, they will survive.... I don't want you to go. I'm afraid."

"You sound like you want the Israelis to survive," said Abdallah, with fire in his eyes.

"Of course not! But — they're human beings too, aren't they?"

"Thieves, who have stolen Arab lands."

Fatima was in no mood for politics. She clutched at his sleeve. "Please, Abdallah, I'm a woman alone with a small toddler. I have nobody here but you. Please don't go."

He embraced her warmly, saying, "Don't be afraid, dearest. Allah will have mercy on us." With that, he was out the door.

It was evening. Desolate, Fatima watched from the window as her husband sped off on his motorbike, apparently afire to offer himself to the Egyptian army with no time lost.

But he did not head for the recruiting office. Instead, Abdallah drove with headlong speed to his cavern. Anxiously, he rode down his windlass cable. Although the last large chamber was only eighty meters back from the end of the shaft, he began working feverishly to dig another here, at the closest point to the center of the dam. He would have to make do with a subterranean shock less than a quarter of the way to the center, the weakest portion of the dam. He worked all that night and the two next to excavate a chamber two meters long, two meters wide and one-and-a-half meters high. He finished just after dawn on the third day, praying fervently that his diesel exhaust had gone unnoticed.

Satisfied that this new chamber was minimally sufficient for its purpose, he rode the dirt bucket back up to the top. By now, the ride took more than half an hour to complete. The wooden crate that had sat peacefully dormant for four-and-a-half years was about to go into action.

Abdallah pried the crate open. Inside was a cylinder, sixty centimeters in diameter and one hundred eighty centimeters long. He was well-trained in what he must do to make it work. Attached to both ends were thick rings. He removed the bucket from the end of the cable, attached the cylinder to the snap-lock, and rolled it toward the mouth of the shaft. Then he slowly rode down on top of the bomb, descending through the granite by the force of gravity, down past the tightly compacted sand, until he and the bomb reached rock-bottom below.

He rolled the cylinder into the first large chamber whose floor rested upon the sandstone layer. Pulling a long, windlass cable after him, he crawled to the recently formed chamber at the end of the tunnel. There he drilled a pilot hole into the sandstone below and began to twist a one-meter-long corkscrew anchor into it. After three turns, he attached a clamp head to the pneumatic drill, locked it onto the eye of the anchor and pulled the trigger. In six seconds, only the eye of the anchor was exposed — an anchor that was meant to withstand one thousand kilos of force. He attached a seven-centimeter swivel pulley to the eye and wrapped the windlass cable through the pulley. A tug on the windlass control cord, and more cable began feeding out: another seven hundred meters up the shaft back to the cylinder.

Abdallah was perspiring profusely in the eighty-degree heat of the underground passageway as he attached the snap-lock to the handle of the cylinder. Another pull on the windlass control cord, and the direction of the reduction gear was reversed. In this way, Abdallah Ibn Gash dragged the three hundred kilo load to what might well be its final destination.

Much sweat — four-and-a-half years worth — had evaporated since Abdallah had begun his ambitious project, and the infrastructure of destruction was not as ready as he had hoped. There was a great deal more work needed, years more, to complete the project according to plan. But as fate would have it, Abdallah had run out of time. The outbreak of hostilities with Israel had precipitated a crisis that he was forced to meet with shortcut measures. He would just have to pray for a small miracle.

Now the real work began: that of arming a dormant but gargantuan tool of destruction.

Abdallah removed four screws, lifted up a panel and exposed the guts of the device. He labored to throw all the proper switches and plug all the loose wires into their proper jumper pins. He watched as the diodes lit up in sequence, closely following the schematic. His every move was deliberate and utterly cautious, or as cautious as his trembling hand could manage. Had he made the same moves to put together a Heathkit, it would have taken him perhaps forty minutes; now he needed five hours.

At last he finished. Now all that was left to do was unspool eleven hundred meters of electrical wire as he made his way back to the top. This wire he connected to a throw switch. The switch did not set off the device: the Mossad had never billed this as a suicide mission. It activated a timer. In eighteen hours, the equivalent of 50,000 tons of TNT would rock the bottom of one of the biggest tubs in the world. Abdallah only hoped that it would be enough to pop the cork.

Four days after he'd bid his wife farewell, Abdallah showed up at home. "My dear, pack up, we're leaving the country." He pulled out two Air France tickets from Cairo to Paris.

Fatima was completely bewildered. "I don't understand. When you ran out a few days ago, you couldn't wait to join the campaign against the enemy. Now you want to flee the country. What's gotten into you?"

"They wouldn't accept me. They said my job at the dam was too important. But having listened to the news and having thought about what you said, I think you might be right. The Israelis are the sneakiest people on earth. Maybe this whole war was a ruse. Somehow those devils figured out how to draw the Egyptians and Syrians into a war, only to hit back with a devastating blow."

"But Abdallah, all the news reports are saying that the Arab forces are succeeding. The Israelis have been pushed out of Sinai. That's not just propaganda, I heard as much on BBC International. The Syrians have recaptured Mt. Hermon and Kunetra; soon, the entire Golan will be back in their hands. The situation looks very bleak for Israel. What leads you to believe that things will turn around against us?"

Abdallah said excitedly, "That's just it, dearest. The Israelis have set us up. Precisely because things look so bleak for them, they will feel justified in pulling the trigger on a nuclear bomb. Allah knows they have the bomb, and are itching to use it on us...." He seized her hands. "I have a hunch they may try to hit the dam first. That's why I want to get you and Mustafa out. I don't care what the military says — I don't want to be anywhere near that dam when it blows! Now hurry up and pack, Fatima. We have to be in Cairo by 12:00 p.m. tomorrow for the flight."

By evening the situation was dire for Israel. They had just about run out of munitions, and no European country would permit the use of their airbases for American transports.

Abdallah was glued to the radio all afternoon. He kept switching channels, trying to catch the news from various international short-wave broadcasts. By this time, Fatima had become resigned to their plan.

"Abdallah, I think it will be good for us to get out of the country. I just heard from my parents. They're leaving for Iran this evening. My mother was frantic on the phone, until I told her we're flying to Paris tomorrow. She was overjoyed to hear it." She frowned at her husband, twiddling radio dials with intense concentration. "Please, can't you stop switching the channels like a madman? You're making me nervous!"

Abdallah continued as if he hadn't heard a word she'd said. Every few minutes, he would lock onto a frequency for one or two minutes, listening to what seemed to be nothing but noise. Fatima had never seen her husband this disturbed before. She attributed his reaction to the precarious situation and Abdallah's extreme interpretation of it.

Only little Mustafa was able to sleep that night. At two a.m., Abdallah abruptly switched off the radio and climbed out of bed. He told his wife that he had to go out to dam control to set the systems and brief the staff on emergency procedures. Fatima was sleepy, frightened, and at a total loss to understand her husband's erratic behavior. All this agitation was completely out of character for Abdallah. She was anxious to get to the airport and out of the country, where she and her family might have a chance at normalcy again.

Abdallah's heart was pounding like a sledgehammer gone mad. The signal had been given. Israel was standing on the brink.

The signal to red alert, which affected his phase of the project, was transmitted in code over a predetermined order of frequencies. All day long, he had been listening for that code. At two hours after midnight, with a suddenness that had taken his breath away, it had come.

The drive to the dam took him no more than twenty minutes. He went first to dam control, where he sat for three hours, discussing the war with his friends. He gave no hint of nervousness, nor any sign that he thought there was a possibility that Egypt might lose. There was an air of celebration in the control room, as though Egypt had already emerged victorious. The night shift laughed and joked throughout the night.

At 5:00 a.m., just before dawn, Abdallah stopped his car about one hundred meters from the cave entrance and opened the hood. Glancing around to make certain he was unobserved, he sprinted behind the rocks to his clandestine cavern. Within thirty seconds he was headed back to his car. The ground beneath his feet was ticking. He had engaged the switch. He checked his watch: exactly 5:09 a.m. GMT+2.

He had climbed into his car and was on the point of closing the door when a voice from behind startled him.

"Abdallah, what are you doing here?" It was Kalim, the turbine engineer.

In the dim interior of the car, Abdallah put his hand on the Helwan 9mm he kept under the seat.

"Kalim! You really shouldn't sneak up on people like that. You scared me to death!"

"Sorry about that. But what's the matter — car trouble?"

Abdallah grinned. "Not really. I just felt the strong urge to take a leak."

"No problem, friend," Kalim said, grinning back. "Have a good day. Hope to see you at the club tomorrow; there's a real bash planned. Israel will certainly be in hell by then."

"Sure, sure. See you then." With an airy wave, Abdallah drove off.

At 6:30 a.m., Ibn Gash drove his family to Aswan's miserable excuse for an airport. By 7:15, the DC-3 was high above the desert skies, following a path along the Nile due north toward Cairo International Airport. At 12:30 p.m. GMT, the Air France 747 set down at Orly. Grabbing a cab, the Middle Eastern couple, fluent in French, checked into a medium-quality hotel on the outskirts of downtown Paris.

Immediately, Abdallah switched on the large Grundig short-wave and sat intensely beside it, to Fatima's intense frustration.

"I thought we came here to forget the war. Yet the first thing you do is turn on the radio?"

Worn out by his travels, Mustafa was fast asleep in his cot. Fatima sat down next to her husband on the bed and put her arms around him. Ignoring her advances, he cocked his ear at the radio, as he had done before they left, flipping stations as nervously as an antelope in a lion's den. Then he caught hold of a French language broadcast of Kol Israel. He listened intently.

"The military news liaison has just released a report that can be interpreted as the first good news since the outbreak of the war. The Egyptian line of two thousand tanks has stopped at the border with Israel. No one can explain why. The meager lines of Israeli armor, which had been shattered over the past four days, have not been significantly reinforced. We have also just received word that Spain has granted permission for limited stopovers of American Military equipment transports. The first shipments should arrive in Tel Aviv by tomorrow morning."

"Abdallah, Abdallah," called his wife, still trying to pull him away from the radio. "Why are you listening to that? Isn't it nothing but idle enemy propaganda?"

Abdallah turned to her with a strange smile. "No, my dear, it is not. Remember, that was an internal Israeli broadcast. Israel doesn't believe in duping its own people. They are too threatened, and must remain alert to the actual situation. I'm afraid you were right. It looks like they may survive after all.... But it's also obvious now that my assessment was wrong. The Americans probably convinced them not to use nukes, and, in return, they're resupplying Israel with conventional weaponry."

Abdallah scanned the channels one more time. Finally he locked onto a frequency which seemed to issue squeaks and squawks of meaningless noise. He listened closely for a minute, then turned off the radio.

"Dear," Fatima suggested in all sincerity, "maybe you should see a good specialist here in Paris. Something is wrong with you."

Abdallah turned to her, elated. "What's wrong with me? We are safe. I think the war will end in more or less a draw. It would have been nice if we could have rid the world of the Israeli menace, but that day may have to wait."

"Why were you listening to all that noise? You did the same thing last night, back home."

"That's not noise, dear. Those are legitimate frequencies — emergency frequencies. We listen quite often to them at the dam. Those noises are prepared by the radio stations before they go on the air. If they don't start broadcasting within a minute or two, it means they've canceled the broadcast for that time-slot." He smiled. "My dear, you have a lot to learn."

Fatima shrugged and said, "You're right, as usual. But, please, can't we begin to relax? I'm exhausted."

"My dearest, of course you can relax. But I can't; I'm still too jumpy." He stood up and stretched his arms above his head. "You know, I think you struck upon a good idea. I'm heading out to see a specialist."

"What? So suddenly? Abdallah, can't you even get a little sleep first?"

Abdallah pulled two thousand francs from his wallet and handed the wad to his wife. "Here, this should take care of you and Mustafa until I get back."

Bewildered, Fatima asked, "When will that be?"

"Tomorrow.... Hopefully." With that, he was out the door.

Fatima lay down on the bed and cried herself to sleep.

Abdallah made his way back to the airport and went up to the counter. "I'd like a ticket for the next flight to Cairo."

The agent took her time looking through the computer screen. "We have a flight going tonight at 11:21 p.m. That is the first opening."

"That won't do." Abdallah looked up at the CRT in the main corridor. The time was 2:15 p.m. GMT. "I see you have a flight leaving in nine minutes from Gate fourteen. I'll take that one."

"It's full," the ticket agent said sternly.

Abdallah looked up at the screen again and spoke quickly. "Then I'll take the flight to Casablanca leaving at 2:45."

The ticket agent looked at Abdallah as if he were a certified lunatic. Abdallah counted out the money in large bills, told the agent he had no luggage, and ran off to the gate. He quickly showed his ticket to security, passed through the metal detector, butted his way into the line at passport control, and made it to Gate fourteen just as the passengers for the last fifteen rows of the plane were called.

Toward the back of the line, he spotted an older man who walked with a cane, boarding pass clutched in his hand. The man had a simple air about him. Coming up from behind, Abdallah said softly, "Excuse me, sir. I'm from Air France. If you will come with me a minute, we'd like to change your seat for a more comfortable one."

Innocently, the passenger followed him back toward the terminal. The old man was astute enough to ask, "Isn't the plane boarding now?"

"Don't worry, it will wait for you. We just have to go back to the desk for a minute. Your boarding pass, please." The man handed over the pass.

Abdallah sat the man down in a lounge chair and told him he'd be back in a few minutes.

The plane landed in Cairo at 7:45 p.m. GMT+2. Abdallah ran directly to the domestic flight desk, where he discovered, to his dismay, that there was no direct flight to Aswan until six the following morning. Again, he looked up at the trusty flight info CRT, and found a flight leaving for Khartoum forty minutes later. He raced back to International flights, bought his ticket and boarded.

Abdallah kept his eyes glued to his watch from the moment the flight took off. At 9:59 p.m., one hour and twenty minutes into the flight, ten thousand meters above the ground, Abdallah Ibn Gash fell off his seat into the isle of the Ilyushin 96M-jetliner. He clutched at his chest, and began breathing with great distress. Two Sudanese stewards ran over to the stricken man and called for any doctor who might be on the plane. None came forward. One of the stewards ran to the cockpit; a moment later, the copilot came running out.

Abdallah held his breath. The light complexion of his face took on a distinctly bluish tinge, and the plane started descending very quickly. Announcements were made in Arabic, French and English to fasten seat belts, as the plane would be making an emergency landing in Aswan to discharge an ill passenger.

During the ride to the hospital from the airport, Abdallah suddenly stopped his pathetic gyrations, pulled the oxygen mask off his face, and said to the paramedic, "I think I'm okay now. It was just an asthma attack. I get those occasionally when flying, when the cabin pressure is low. I suppose the Russian airliners don't maintain the same level of cabin pressure as American jets."

The surprised medic said, "Mister, you sure caused a lot of trouble, making them land the whole plane and all."

Abdallah shrugged. "They couldn't throw me out. Where am I, anyway?"

"Aswan, Egypt. Say, you speak Arabic just like an Egyptian. You're not Sudanese?"

"Who told you I was? Can't you see the color of my face? What a coincidence — I live in Aswan! I'm feeling much better. Could you take me home?"

The medic stared at him. Serenely, Abdallah stared back. Slowly, the medic turned to shout at the driver, "Hey, Hassan, this guy's okay now. He lives right here in Aswan and wants a ride home."

The driver frowned, indicated that something was fishy about the whole incident, and said, "I think we'd better get the patient to the hospital, just to make sure he's all right."

Abdallah pulled out one hundred Egyptian pounds from his wallet and handed it to the paramedic, who immediately said to the driver, "Hassan, I just checked him, he's all right. He couldn't be better, in fact. Just drive him home."

Abdallah got out of the ambulance a block away from his home, took out his motorbike, and sped back to his cavern. It was 10:51 p.m. when he arrived. It was at this point that he ran into a problem that seemed to overshadow those he'd conquered in returning home from Paris. A large troop of soldiers had been stationed around the dam that day, and were scrupulously patrolling the entire area. The Egyptian government had become belatedly wary about that fact that the dam stuck out as an ideal target....

"What's going on?" Abdallah asked one of the soldiers, less than seventy-five meters from the concealed entrance to his cave.

"Who are you?" the soldier countered.

Abdallah took out his ID and handed it to the guard, who carefully perused it by flashlight before handing it back. Astonished, he said, "You work here, and you didn't hear the President declare this region on high alert today? They're suspicious that the Israelis may have designs on the dam."

"No, I was out of town. I just got back," answered Abdallah. "Why are you patrolling this area? There's nothing doing over here."

"I could ask you the same question. There's no access from here to the dam. I was told this is just an old shunt road that hasn't been used since the dam was excavated ten years ago." The soldier's eyes narrowed. "So, mister, what are you doing here?"

Abdallah gave him a sheepish half-smile. "Look, I suppose you're going to figure it out anyway in a few minutes, so I'll tell you now. I'm supposed to meet someone here."

The soldier's flashlight was aimed at Abdallah's face. He caught the smile and the wink very clearly.

"You have a wife?" asked the soldier, ten years Abdallah's junior.

"Yeah, I guess you could say that. A real horse, she weighs close to one hundred forty kilos."

Abdallah could see by the penumbra of his flashlight that the soldier was beginning to sympathize with him. He fought to keep his mounting impatience from his face. It was one minute past eleven when the soldier said, "Have fun. I'll see what I can do."

The soldier told the other member of the patrol to cover an area down the road. To Abdallah's chagrin, he received an argument in return.

"The country is at war, and you're worried about helping some philanderer get his kicks? We're assigned to this road. We're staying right here, Mister." The soldier directed his attention at Abdallah. "I don't think you should be around here. Now, take your motorbike and get out or I'll call the MPs."

"Look, I've got to take a leak," Abdallah said, falling back on this trusty ruse. He headed for the cave; time was running out. The soldier who had foiled his amorous plans followed close behind.

"Hey man, can't I have some privacy?" Abdallah yelled.

"Look, I don't know who you are or what you're really doing here. Just do your business and leave."

By this time, the two had walked around some large rocks and were just above the cavern entrance. Abdallah tripped on a rock in the dark, grasped his ankle and began to writhe in pain. The soldier knelt to examine his foot. Abdallah quickly grabbed his neck in a chokehold and applied strong thumb pressure to the man's carotids. "That's what you get when you prevent a man from having his fun, you dog."

Thirty seconds later, the conscientious soldier was unconscious. Abdallah quickly moved the rocks aside, went down the three meters to the cavern, and threw the switch. It was 11:05 on his watch. Just as quickly, he made his way back up, covered the entrance, walked past the still figure of the soldier, and made his way back to his motorbike. As he was starting it, the soldier who a few minutes earlier had lent him a sympathetic ear came closer to ask, "Where's Muamar?"

"He had to take more than just a leak. He'll be along," said Abdallah, and rode off in a cloud of dust.

Chapter 8

Abdallah went directly to the Aswan central post office and phoned Fatima in Paris.

"I was called back to Aswan — an emergency. Look, you stay put until the war is over."

Fatima wondered unhappily if her husband had really lost his mind. However, stuck in Paris with a small child, she was in no position to do anything about it. She had plenty of money but was lonely and miserable, and just barely survived until Abdallah picked her up at the Aswan airport four weeks later.

Three weeks after it had begun, the war was over. It ended in a stalemate. The Egyptians and Syrians were embarrassed; although they'd had the huge advantage of a sneak attack on the Jews' holiest day of the year, they were unable to capitalize on it. The Israelis were satisfied with the fact that they were still in existence. Abdallah was greatly relieved, Fatima frustrated and distraught.

But it was at this juncture that Abdallah's behavior miraculously reverted to normal. All Fatima's prodding never induced him to reveal a thing. A month later, the matter had been buried in the recesses of familial history and forgotten.

It did, however, take six months longer until the military patrols were withdrawn from around the dam. The interval proved a godsend for Abdallah: with extra time on his hands, he spent more of it with his wife and child, the final step in mollifying Fatima's melancholia over his bizarre wartime activities.

By the summer of 1976, Abdallah's tunnel had progressed to a point directly below the center of the dam. Over the years he had acquired much better drilling equipment and the operation proceeded at a faster clip than during the seven years past. He calculated, mathematically, that even were he to stop work now, there remained a seventy-five percent probability that the device would work. But Alon Barnash, like the others, had been chosen for the project because — apart from his other talents — he had the determination and dedication to complete his task. And so, after transferring the device to the last large chamber, where it would remain, Abdallah began drilling and digging again.

This time, he drilled straight down, through the first layer of sandstone. It took him only two weeks to penetrate this softly consolidated substrate, and he was surprised when his ten-centimeter drill head penetrated to a hollow area. Within an hour of this penetration, he lowered himself about four meters to a solid limestone floor. The cavern between the layers extended about ten meters. Thereafter, the gap between the layers narrowed to a point that he could not traverse even by crawling on his stomach. However, after drilling about thirty-five meters horizontally, he hit another hollowed cavern. Now his progress became swift; much of the terrain was naturally hollow, and he was able to dump his diggings on the spot, without the long journey back to the entrance cavern.

North View

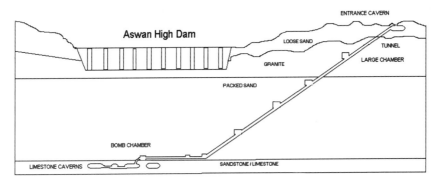

Top View

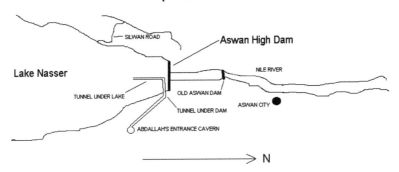

It took him only six months to complete a five hundred meter pathway south under the dam, so that he was now directly below the deepest area of Lake Nasser. He actually dug one hundred meters further than necessary, to position himself under the beginning of the lake beyond the wide reaches of the rock-filled dam. He was seeking a cavern larger than the smallish ones he came upon every ten meters or so. At the end of one hundred meters, he hit one that was three meters high, twenty meters long and fifteen meters wide. Now he began to dig his way up.

This work, too, was a great relief compared to the past years of toil: it was hardly necessary to remove the rock and sand, for, as he dug, gravity carried them down to cavern below. Every once in a while he would have to sweep the debris from under the tunnel, which he was digging at a twenty-five-degree angle. Still, his progress was very swift. In only three months, he hit granite, and he knew that soon he would reach water. He couldn't be sure exactly how thick the granite layer was at the spot he was drilling. After grinding his way fifty meters through solid rock, he began making sixty centimeter test bores with a twelve-millimeter bit, prior to drilling out the full meter width of the tunnel. Naturally, this slowed his progress, but by this point he was so close to the end that it didn't really matter. Besides, he didn't want to get killed by a torrent of water rushing in at him at one hundred eighty pounds of pressure per square inch....

After seven weeks and fifty-five meters of granite, his careful test probes paid off. When he drilled his thin probe bit a distance of forty centimeters, a trickle of water began to dribble down on him. He replaced the probe bit with his ten-centimeter carbide hammer-drill tool, and removed a chunk of rock thirty centimeters wide and twenty centimeters deep. Replacing the twelve-millimeter probe bit, he pushed it another ten centimeters — and was through. The stream of muddy water hit the bottom wall of the angled tunnel like a fire-hose jet, flowing all the way down, five hundred fifty meters, to the cavern below.

Abdallah was well prepared for this eventuality, which had been built into his original plan. He removed a ninety-centimeter rod that was attached to his belt, a mushroom shaped pliable rubber stopper attached to its top end. It was actually a large truck tire plug. He pushed hard through the narrow hole against the pressurized water streaming down, twisting and turning the handle of the rod until it broke through to the top. The mushroom-shaped rubber stopper fanned out and plugged the hole. Only a slight trickle continued to flow, but Abdallah was not concerned.

Thus, after eight years, in about the same amount of time it had taken to build the dam itself, the infrastructure to "unbuild" it was in place. Over the next three weeks, Abdallah completed the project by planting a one-kilo stick of C-4 plastic explosive every eight meters, in a line, along the five hundred meter sand layer, and four sticks every eight meters in the granite layer up to the top of the Lake Nasser shaft. They were wired to explode in sequence, one second apart, from the bottom up. At the very top, just under the lakebed, he planted fifty sticks. Abdallah calculated that these excavating explosions would double — at least — the rate of water flowing down to the hollow rock layers, besides opening up the top. His design was simple: the underground shock would move the rock plates, causing the ground to collapse under the dam. By filling the rock layers with water, they would become twenty times less stable because of the lubricating effect of the fluid. Abdallah determined that if and when it became necessary to implement his life's project, he would begin to flood the substrata at the same time as he set off the timer for the nuclear device. In eighteen hours, his shaft could direct over 1.6 billion liters of water to lubricate and soften the earth below the dam. If left for a few years, the water alone would probably undermine the subterranean stability and collapse the entire structure.

"Abdallah," Fatima said one day to her transformed husband, "I can't understand you. Since we've been married, you've never spent so much time at home. Not that I have any complaints, you understand.... But I can't help being curious. You seem suddenly to have stopped going to the clubs and hanging out with your buddies."

"My dear, I've always given you more attention than the average man of my people."

"Yes, of course, Abdallah. I've really appreciated that."

"But now Mustafa is already six, almost seven. As a baby, there was only so much that I, a man, could take of smiling and playing with the little one. It is for the mother to raise and care for the small children. Now our little Mustafa is beginning to develop his learning ability and his intellect. The time has come to spend more time with my son, to impart to him the traditions of his people."

"I see." Fatima was noncommittal. Her manner said, more clearly than words, "We'll see...."

Despite his wife's skepticism, Abdallah was true to his word. He continued to spend a relatively greater amount of time with her, but also, she observed, spent far more time with his son than any of her students' father's did. Abdallah bought a small motor boat, which he kept at the Lake Nasser marina, thirty kilometers south of Aswan. He would take the boy water-skiing several times a week even during the school year. He made sure Mustafa finished all of his schoolwork properly and insisted that he excel in all of his studies.

By the time Mustafa was eight and a half, he was skilled enough in water-skiing to ride and jump waves, even on one ski, and to execute turnarounds and other spectacular tricks. At this time, Abdallah began to teach him the fundamentals of maintaining an outboard engine. Mustafa could soon drive the boat, even towing a skier, and attend to most of the regular maintenance. His father was proud. Next, Abdallah taught his son to work with hand tools, both power and manual. By the time Mustafa was nine, he was designing and building dog and bird houses for the neighbors. Through their shared interests, Abdallah and Mustafa became almost inseparable.

But along another vein, Fatima was greatly alarmed at the friction between them. Inevitably, whenever Abdallah scolded Mustafa to buckle down in his study of Islam, an altercation would ensue. Even when Mustafa was a small boy of six, his father had insisted that he accompany him to Mosque on Fridays. Fatima tried arguing with her husband, but he refused to listen. The strictness his father imposed upon him with respect to worship formed a part of Mustafa's earliest recollections — a singularly painful part. When prostrated on the carpet, facing Mecca to praise Allah, the little boy would pick up his head to scout around, often laughing with other boys performing similar antics. His father would smack him soundly and direct the boy sternly back to his prayers. "Allah is great and Mohammed is his Prophet." Once, when Mustafa was almost eight, Abdallah slapped the boy's face so hard that the sound ripped like a gunshot through the acoustically vibrant domed building. Startled, many of the eight hundred men, prostrated on the ground, glanced up to locate the source of the sudden clap. Mustafa was mortified. His anger stung more than his burning cheek.

Abdallah made Mustafa learn verses of Koran by heart, sometimes for hours at a time without respite. This upset Fatima the most, but she was powerless to do anything about it. If she attempted to remonstrate, Abdallah would remind her that she was too liberal and order her sharply to stay out of religious matters. When Abdallah was away at work, Mustafa would openly complain to his mother about his father's stringent and uncompromising religious demands. During Ramadan, a month of fasting, Mustafa would actually become ill. At the tender age of ten he lost two or three kilos and felt tired and lethargic for most of the day. If his father noticed him swallowing his spittle, or even thought he was trying to do so, the boy would receive an impetuous whack across the cheek. Fatima found herself in a quandary in which she felt utterly helpless to act. How to modify her husband's draconian spiritual impositions upon her son? She had no recourse but to bear them stoically and urge her son to do the same. Ironically, despite Abdallah's unbending religious domination over his son, in every other area father and son were as close as they could be.

During the Ramadan of Mustafa's twelfth year, Fatima became so alarmed over her son's health that she acted in desperation: she made an appointment to see the Imam of Aswan.

She and her son stood before the elderly, robed Imam. He addressed her first. "So, Mrs. Ibn Gash, this is your Mustafa. Yes, I have seen him many times. His father has been conscientious about bringing him to mosque since he was very small." The Imam motioned Mustafa closer. He placed a hand beneath the boy's chin and lifted it up a little, studying the sullen expression on the boy's face.

"Imam Achmed, I hate to say this, but my husband is too strict with the boy. He is a deeply devout man, and perhaps he can't grasp that his son is still a child, too young to understand the imperatives of the Sharia."

The Imam nodded thoughtfully. "Yes, Mrs. Ibn Gash, I have noticed over the years how determined your husband is to impart the tradition to your son. Perhaps it is because the boy is his only child that Abdallah is so concerned to make sure he will carry on the message of the Prophet."

"Perhaps so, Imam, but I can't take it any more! Strangely, they have a wonderful relationship in secular matters. My husband has taught Mustafa all sorts of things, and despite Abdallah's strict treatment in religious matters the boy bears no constant hate for his father. I am only afraid that the day will come when Abdallah goes too far —" She lowered her voice to a near whisper — "if he hasn't already. I'm afraid he may really hurt the boy, and alienate him altogether."

The Imam gazed into Mustafa's eyes as if reading the riddle of his future there. Fatima caught her breath and firmly blinked back the incipient tears. In a tone that was almost brisk, she asked, "A practical question, Imam. As you can see, the boy is not well. Can I give him food during the day, even though Ramadan will not be over for another ten days?"

"Perhaps you could give him more to eat at night."

She shook her head vigorously. "It doesn't work that way with Mustafa. He doesn't have a big appetite to begin with. Once he grows accustomed to a reduced diet, he can't digest too much at one time."

"In that case, I will grant him a dispensation. He does seem troubled." The Imam smiled at Mustafa, who returned the smile uncertainly.

"Sir," Fatima begged, "could you write a letter for me to that effect? I wouldn't want to hide anything from my husband."

"Madam, I cannot do that. I suggest, instead, that we accord your husband a hearing on his behavior toward your son. Perhaps we will find that he has been generally too strict with your son. On the other hand, perhaps not...."

Two days later, Fatima and Abdallah appeared together before the Imam. Fatima was pleasantly surprised that Abdallah had agreed to go; she had anticipated some recrimination for summoning her husband to the equivalent of a religious court hearing. But her heart soon dropped again. In the course of the interview, it was Abdallah who prevailed. He convinced the Imam that he was carrying on a longstanding family tradition, a method of upbringing that had for generations ensured that the devout lifestyle be handed down from father to son. He described the beatings he had received from his father and grandfather as a young boy, for the sin of insolence toward Islam. It was only after the message had been pounded into him for the umpteenth time, he said, that he had finally come to understand the beauty and wisdom of the faith and its teachings.

This, he claimed, had occurred at the age of fourteen. Abdallah promised his wife, in front of the Imam, that after the age of fourteen he would no longer impose religion on his son. By that age, he was certain, the boy would from his own volition adhere to the religious principles he'd been taught. Fatima rode home dissatisfied but resigned to the decision. She was now totally powerless to even raise the subject again.

One day in 1979 found the Ibn Gash family glued to their radio as President Anwar Sadat delivered an impassioned speech in the Israeli parliament. He spoke brilliantly, in his classic Arabic style, stating that hostilities between Egypt and Israel were ended and that a peace accord would soon be invoked.

Fatima turned a hopeful face to her husband. "Dear, what do you say about President Sadat? Can you believe it?"

"Yes, dear, I think the man is for real. We have lost four wars to the Israelis. The Russians got fed up with us after the disastrous 1967 war and we had to seek better relations with the U.S. Now, we all know that the Jews control the U.S...."

"Please Abdallah," she frowned. "You are such an intelligent man. Why do you speak like the pea-brained fanatics about the Jews?"

"Aha — that's the Jewish blood that flows through your veins!" Abdallah smiled to rob his words of offense. "Look my dear, I'm just stating facts. I'm not saying the Jews control the whole country, just that they wield enough power and have enough financial resources to sway the American government in the direction of staunch support of the Zionist State. Let us say it's a bone thrown to the Jews — a price that gentile America sees as reasonable in return for Jewish money and support on other issues. It's all politics."

He stood up and began pacing the living room, his analysis flowing fluently. Fatima and Mustafa, the former on the sofa and the latter sprawled comfortably on the rug, listened with interest.

"Now, Sadat, is just as smart as any politician alive. He's come to the realization that, militarily, the Arab world is just no match for the Israelis. Likewise, he now realizes that he can no longer play the Russians and Americans against each other. He has a chance now to retrieve the Sinai Peninsula for our country, along with the Abu Rodis oil fields whose revenue has been so sorely lacking for the past twelve years. And mark my words: for making peace with Israel, he will get a phenomenal financial aid package out of the Americans, maybe even one that rivals the handout given to the bloodsucking Israelis. He can only gain and has very little to lose. Of course, he will be condemned by the rest of the Arab world.... But just wait. When they see how we're prospering, they'll follow suit. Just give them time."

"You don't seem to object to this spectacular shift in policy," Fatima remarked dryly. "I would have imagined you'd be outraged."

"Fatima, we've been married ten years and I see you still don't understand me. Perhaps you were right when we were first going out — when you felt our difference in background might make us incompatible." He grinned. "But I still love you."

Fatima shook her head. After a decade, her Abdallah remained an enigma.

*   *   *

After the Camp David Accords were signed, Abdallah made one of his infrequent visits to his cavern. He would go once every eight weeks to inspect the tunnels, making sure they remained intact and hadn't suffered from any ground shifts. He also checked that the circuits in the fusing mechanisms of his detonation systems were in working order, and that the batteries were well charged. He had set up sensors to help him be sure that the moisture level in the tunnels was low. This did not, however, obviate the need to crawl into the entire system for periodic inspections.

This time, he climbed down to where the nuclear device was lying dormant, and disconnected all of the arming circuits. It was unlikely that anything could trigger the device accidentally, but under the present political climate he thought it better to return it to non-alert status.

*   *   *

In 1985, on Mustafa's fourteenth birthday, Abdallah proved true to his word: he stopped pestering the boy about Islam. That Friday, Mustafa failed to show up at the mosque for the first time in almost nine years. Fatima found him soundly asleep in bed. She tried to wake him so that he could make a later prayer service than the 6:30 a.m. one his father regularly attended.

He turned away, his bedclothes in a tangle. "Ma, leave me alone. Can't I taste my freedom just for one week? I'll be back next week. I just need some extra rest. I'm tired."

"Mustafa, is this how you act at the first opportunity to praise Allah from your heart, without your father forcing the matter upon you?" his mother asked, true enthusiasm markedly missing from her manner.

Mustafa's answer was to pull the sheet over his head. Fatima watched him for a moment, then quietly left the room.

At 9:00 a.m., Abdallah walked into the house and made straight for the kitchen.

"Fatima," he called, "did Mustafa go to mosque today?"

Fatima, stirring something busily, with her back to her husband, did not answer immediately. Coming closer, Abdallah asked, "Fatima, didn't you hear me?"

"I don't want to get involved. Ask him yourself."

"That's how a good Moslem mother answers her husband?! Don't you feel a responsibility to wake him up and help him fulfill his religious obligations?"

Fatima felt the old frustration at her husband overcoming her again.

"Abdallah, ever since the boy was born you took full charge of his religious education and upbringing." She began to raise her voice. "And now you want me to start pushing where you've stopped! Well, I have news for you. Maybe in your family ramming religion down the throat has carried on the tradition from father to son through the generations. We happen to be living in a new and modern world that conflicts with the old. Had we been nomadic Bedouins living in goatskin tents, maybe your harsh methods would still have worked. But both of us are scientists and engineers. We live between two worlds, one arcane and confining, the other new and progressive. I'm not going to say anything more to my son on the subject of Islam. You pounded it into him for all these years. If it is really ingrained in his heart, you don't need me — and if it's not, nothing I can say will help him now."

They locked eyes for a long moment. Slowly, Abdallah lifted his shoulders, then let them fall. "You are very wise, my Fatima," he said softly. "I won't talk to you again about this subject. Our son's fate in his own hands now — and the hands of Allah."

"Amen!" Fatima beamed, and clapped her hands in joy.

Abdallah entered his son's bedroom and gazed upon his slumbering son. Mustafa had thrown off the sheet and lay facing upward. A certain peace seemed to lie on his features. Almost as if he sensed his father's presence hovering over him, he blinked, stirred, and opened his eyes.

"F-father," he stammered, with a wild look at his bedside clock, "I didn't realize what time it was!"

Abdallah smiled. "My son, as I promised years back, when you turn fourteen you are on your own. I won't, I can't, force you any longer to do that which is right in the eyes of Allah. But I must warn you — the fires of hell burn hot. You will curse yourself for the vain pleasures you enjoyed when your flesh is singed in a fire hotter than the sun for half an eternity. You will curse yourself for not living a virtuous life for the short sixty or seventy years we are given, in return for eons of pleasure in the next world."

"But father, all I did was sleep a little late this one time. I didn't do anything really bad."

"That is not for you to determine, my son. You passed up an opportunity to praise Allah."

"So I'll do it right here on my bedroom floor. Just as soon as I get dressed."

"But you missed going to the Mosque on this, our holy day of the week."

"I am sorry father. I'll try harder next week."

The following week, Fatima stepped into her son's room at 6:00 a.m. and attempted to wake him. She didn't feel obligated to do so, but felt she should try.

"Mustafa, it's time to get ready for mosque."

He groaned, eyes still tightly sealed. "Yeah, Ma, I'm getting up." He clutched his middle. "Ooh, I have a stomach ache. I must have had too much felafel last night. Oh, my stomach!" Mustafa got up and made his way to the bathroom. He didn't come out until his father had left for mosque.

The third week, Mustafa pleaded a headache. On the fourth week, his mother didn't bother going to his room.

Each Friday, after his father would returned from prayers, he would gently but emphatically warn his son of the hellish tortures in store for him. In flowery terms, he described all the missed pleasures, the sweet fruits, the delicious meats and the harems of beautiful wives that Mustafa would never enjoy in paradise because of his indolent behavior. After a month, Mustafa — knowing himself safe from corporal punishment — stopped listening. He presented no counter arguments: he simply insisted that he hadn't done anything wrong.

Apart from these Friday skirmishes, their relationship flourished. Mustafa had grasped most of the technical skills imparted to him by his father, and became proficient in many of them. Even at the age of twelve, he had entered and won major junior competitions. Now at fourteen, he was winning open-age form and skill competitions. He was the top student in the class, even though he had skipped two years, and completed the eleventh grade just after his fifteenth birthday. At sixteen, he divulged to his mother that he wanted nothing to do with religion.

Fatima stopped short of preparing food for Mustafa during Ramadan, but she made no effort to keep him from helping himself to meat sandwiches and pints of leben from the refrigerator. He had the courtesy and the good sense not to eat in his father's presence. Along with being a great student, he really was a very good boy. He was respectful, even of those whom he didn't personally like, and helpful to his parents and grandmother. This last became a source of concern for Abdallah. The devout Moslem voiced his displeasure at his son's close and time-consuming relationship with his Jewish grandmother. But this was another area where Mustafa simply, and politely, refused to listen to his father.

Chapter 9

In 1980, after the Iranian Islamic Revolution, the deposed Shah went to live in Egypt. Dr. Baktari, Fatima's father, who had served the Shah's government, asked for asylum also. He remained in Cairo to personally service the Shah. As per protocol, the Shah was surrounded by massive security, and despite the presence of Islamic zealots in Egypt, he was quite safe. Dr. Baktari, in his new capacity, benefitted from that security and maintained his standard of living by working for the Shah instead of the Iranian government.

This situation was short-lived. The Shah took ill, and moved to the U.S. for treatment. He never recovered. As soon as he left the country, the veil of security around his retinue was lifted. In 1981, two days after President Anwar Sadat's assassination, Dr. Batkari was found dead in a Cairo alley, a victim of foul play. Mrs. Baktari was handed an apology and a pension by the Egyptian government. She moved to Aswan to be near her daughter and grandson.

Over the years, she had kept her word to Fatima and Abdallah and had not spoken to Mustafa about her background. While genuinely mourning her husband, she felt at the same time a tremendous relief, as though a great load had been lifted from her shoulders. She found her mind churning with thoughts and regrets about her lost heritage and the follies of her youth. It was extremely difficult to maintain her promised silence.

She was unaware, at first, that Mustafa had stopped following the Islamic faith after winning his "freedom" at fourteen. When she found out — some six months after she moved to town — she was overjoyed. More than ever, she longed to share her true self with her grandson. Despite her inner turmoil, she maintained her silence in this area while firmly encouraging her relationship with her grandson. Their two spirits grew close.

It was April of 1987, and Mustafa was about to graduate high school, as valedictorian. In addition to being a member of the Egyptian national water-ski team, he had won a full college scholarship for placing in the top ten in a national computer programming competition. Fatima Ibn Gash and her mother went about glowing with happiness. Abdallah was proud and gratified over his son's accomplishments, and was not hesitant in letting Mustafa know it. Still, he never ceased to exhibit a modicum of resentment over his son's abandonment of Islam. It was the single thorn in the otherwise pleasant garden of their lives.

"Mother, look at this." Mustafa showed his mother a flyer he'd received from a friend at school.

Fatima read the pamphlet with consternation.

STUDENT EXCHANGE PROGRAM

The Education Ministry is sponsoring a program in conjunction with the Israeli education ministry. The six-week program will include a two-week tour of Israel and Palestine, two weeks in an Ulpan (intensive Hebrew language course), and two weeks with a family (Israeli or Palestinian). The program will cost five-hundred Egyptian pounds per student, all expenses covered. Financial assistance is available for eligible students. Only fifty places are available.

"I really don't think your father will go for this."

"But Mom, Khalid Abdan is going; he's one of my best friends. His parents are pretty religious."

"Maybe publicly," she sniffed. "I've heard that Kamal Abdan drinks. Mustafa, if it were up to me, I'd let you go. I'm just afraid to anger your father. You know how sensitive he becomes on issues like this. Isn't it enough that he tolerates your attitude toward Islam?"

"I only want to apply for the program. Who says I'll be accepted? I'll need your signature."

Fatima thought long and hard. She loved her son and trusted him. She cared nothing about his religious indifference, and thought the exchange-student experience would be a beneficial one for the mature and intelligent teen. On the other hand, she loved and was dependent on her husband, and didn't want to step on his toes. Mustafa's education and intellectual development could be advanced just as easily by staying in Egypt, or perhaps a trip to Europe or America. Why, of all places, should he go to Israel? She shuddered to think of her Abdallah's probable reaction.

For the time being, she held her tongue. Nothing was mentioned to Abdallah about his son's controversial plans. But, as Fatima might have predicted, the following day her mother informed her in no uncertain terms that she must sign the application.

"All right," Fatima surrendered, reluctantly affixing her signature to the form her son held out. "But I warn you — this doesn't mean you have our permission to go."

"Thanks, Mother!" Mustafa was jubilant.

Three weeks later, Mustafa received a letter from the education ministry. The news was staggering. Not only had he been accepted into the exchange program, but due to his outstanding scholastic performance, all his expenses would be paid! Eyes sparkling, Mustafa showed the letter to his mother.

"Speak to your father," she said shortly. "I'm staying out of this."

Abdallah listened quietly to his son's careful presentation, then ran his eyes over the printed information Mustafa offered. When he was through reading, he looked up and met his son's anxious eyes.

"Mustafa," he said, "I think this is a good idea." He signed all the parental consent forms, and the deal was done.

Fatima was flabbergasted. That night, they had scarcely entered the bedroom when she whirled on her husband. "I still don't understand you! After eighteen years of marriage, you're still a mystery to me. You're always berating the Zionist State, even though you seem to feel that peace between Egypt and Israel is advantageous. Naturally, I assumed that letting your son spend six weeks there would be out of the question. What in the world induced you to agree?"

Stretched out on his bed, Abdallah smiled. "Simple. Do you really think the true intention of our education ministry was to foster closer relations with the Zionists? The government wants to grasp every opportunity for our intelligent and talented youth to familiarize themselves with Israel from the inside." He began to tick off on his fingers. "First, the Israelis have been very successful in many technical and social areas where we could use improvement. Second, while I'm not saying that our government is sending this contingent as spies, there's no doubt that they'll pick up useful information — information that will be beneficial for our security. I am certain that the government expects some of these kids to eventually choose a career in government, and knowledge of the land and language of our potentially hostile neighbor will come in handy.

"Mustafa is an ideal candidate to participate in this program. The government was very insightful to offer him a full scholarship to go. Now, my dear, do you understand?"

"Yes, of course." She sat at the edge of the bed. "I guess I just don't think along the same lines as you do."

"That's for sure. I think you still have the Jew mentality infiltrating your subconscious mind."

"Abdallah! You always say that." She pouted. "Sometimes I wonder whether you really love me."

"My dear, why not simply resign yourself to the fact that you will never fully understand me? Of course I love you. One thing has nothing to do with the other."

Fatima fell asleep that night as bewildered as ever.

Chapter 10

On a Friday in late June of 1987— Mustafa, together with forty-nine other teens, three adults, and one tour guide — was walking from the tour bus, which had parked outside the Dung Gate of the Old City of Jerusalem, toward the Al Aqsa Mosque.

"We are now about to enter one of the holiest sites of our Islamic tradition," said Tarik, the Palestinian tour guide. "We will not enter the mosque just now, in order not to disturb the worshipers. First, we will proceed to the Dome of the Rock, the very site from which our Prophet ascended to heaven over thirteen hundred years ago."

Mustafa hurried unobtrusively to where Dr. Muhamma, the Egyptian Education Ministry representative, was standing. Drawing him aside, he said in an undertone, "Dr. Muhamma, I really have no interest in seeing the Dome of the Rock, or any of the other holy sites up on that hill. I would really prefer to wait down here until the group returns to the bus."

"Mustafa, I'm surprised at you."

Mustafa shrugged. "I guess you could say I'm a bit more secularly oriented than some of the others. Besides, that's an awful lot of steps. I'm a little tired from the crammed tour of the past week."

"Well... I suppose it's all right." Muhamma looked at his watch. "Just be back on the bus in forty-five minutes. That's at 2:30."

After the rest of the group began the ascent to the mosque, Mustafa remained in place on the plaza, fascinated by the flow of humanity to and from the nearby Western Wall, the last remnant of Solomon's Temple and Judaism's holiest site. Some wore black robes and round wide-brimmed hats, long sidelocks dangling in front of their ears. Some wore shorts and short-sleeved shirts, their only concession to religious tradition a brightly-colored skullcap. Mustafa followed the flow until he was facing the wall itself.

It stood about twenty meters high and ninety long. Toward bottom, the wall was made of huge stone blocks; nearer the top, the stones were much smaller and more neatly cemented together. From the cracks between the stones sprouted weeds; Mustafa couldn't understand why they hadn't been removed. As he stared at the people praying against the wall, an old man approached to hand him a makeshift paper skullcap. In Hebrew, the man said, "Here, put this on and go say a little prayer."

Mustafa, not understanding, responded in French, "I don't understand Hebrew, do you speak French?"

The old man, Nissim Abulafia, was the caretaker of the Western Wall. He had held the position for twenty years, ever since Israel had taken over the site after the Six-Day War. He understood a little French from his native Morocco, but his practiced ear immediately picked up the boy's Egyptian accent. He spoke up in Arabic.

"You're from Egypt, aren't you?"

"Yes. From your accent, I gather you're from Tunis or Algeria."

"Morocco. I came here to our homeland thirty-four years ago. Now put on the Kippa and go pray by the Wall."

"You don't understand," Mustafa protested. "I'm an Arab — a Moslem. Well, maybe the Moslems consider me an infidel.... I don't practice the religion, but my father is very devout."

The old man looked intently at Mustafa, who began to feel uncomfortably self-conscious during the scrutiny. In his Moroccan-accented Arabic, Abulafia stated, "You're a Jew."

Mustafa was taken aback. It wasn't possible to be offended by the ranting of some old-world peasant, but he felt the need to set the record straight. "No, sir," he said politely. "I just told you I'm Arab. More accurately, half Arab. My mother is Iranian. But she, too, is Moslem."

"You're a Jew," repeated the old man.

Mustafa found himself at a loss. Here was an old-fashioned character — some kind of nut case by the looks of him — trying to convince a modern, intelligent, computer-age young man of something that he knew was ridiculous.

"How do you know I am a Jew?" Mustafa challenged. "You never saw me in your life until three minutes ago!"

"You're a Jew." These seemed to Mustafa to be the only words the old man knew.

"Mister, I just came from Cairo with a group of students, who are now praying up there." Mustafa pointed toward the Al Aqsa Mosque.

"You're a Jew," came the worn refrain.

Laughing, Mustafa shrugged and began to walk away. The man followed him. "Here." He handing Mustafa the makeshift skullcap, which resembled a black coffee filter, to wear on his head. "Put this on and go pray at the Wall."

Mustafa took it, stared at the dome-shaped paper bell in his fingers, and looked up at the elderly lunatic, who said again, "You're a Jew."

As if in a dream, Mustafa put the cap on his head and walked slowly to the Wall. He noticed that thousands of folded scraps of paper were stuffed in the cracks between the giant stones. He picked one out and carefully unfolded it. The note was written in Hebrew. He folded it and put it back in the place he had taken it from. The third one he unfolded was in English, which he was able to understand. It read, "Dear God, my son Arnold has abandoned our people. He has a non-Jewish girlfriend and lives like a bum. Please God, help him to return to his people."

For the second time that morning, Mustafa was taken aback. He understood that all the notes were probably prayers and requests for heavenly assistance. As he was stuffing the note back into the Wall, a tapping on his shoulder startled him.

He jumped in fright, caught red-handed in the severe offense of removing notes from the Wall.... But the bearded man behind him, when Mustafa turned, merely smiled and said, in English, "Do you have a place to eat for Sabbath?"

The American wore a tieless white shirt under a slightly shabby black suit and sported a featherless black fedora hat on his head. Slowly, Mustafa said, "I don't speak good English. Maybe you speak French?"

"Oh, great, my wife is fluent in French! We'll see you tonight — 7:30." The man handed Mustafa a card, which had his address on it, and quickly vanished into the milling crowd on the plaza.

Mustafa stared down at the card in his hand. The invitation had caught him by such surprise that he hadn't had the presence of mind to say a word as the fellow had departed. Who was he, and what was this all about?

The card read,

Rabbi Meir Schuman
34 Arzei Habira
Jerusalem Israel
tel. 565783

Mustafa slipped the card into his pocket and walked back to the table at which old Nissim Abulafia was sitting. He dropped the Kippa back in the bin and, for the first time looked directly at the old man, who was smiling. Mustafa wheeled away. He had taken four steps in the direction of the Dung Gate before he heard the familiar voice call softly, in Arabic, "*You're a Jew.*"

The group was staying at the Ambassador Hotel in East Jerusalem, not far from the American Consulate, which in turn was quite close to the old Mandelbaum Gate border crossing. At about 7:30 that evening, a small group of students decided to go for a walking tour of the area with Tarik, the Palestinian guide.

"And over here, where you see some remnants of barbed wire by the sides of the road, stood the Mandelbaum Gate. For nineteen years this gate was manned by UN guards who escorted Israeli convoys up to Mt. Scopus, which Israel held onto during the armistice of 1949. Foreigners, who had permission to enter Jordan from Israel, also crossed the frontier at this point. During the 1967 war, bitter fighting took place right at this point, until the Israelis broke through the lines. The Jordanian soldiers fought gallantly, but could not prevail to defend against the heavily American-supplied Israeli army....

"We have arrived at Nabi Samwil Street. If you look out to the right, at the lights on the mountain several kilometers in the distance, you will see the tomb of Samuel the Prophet. This street used to lead to the tomb before the division of the city in 1948. Now, as we walk up toward the ultra-religious Jewish quarter known as Meah Shearim, we are passing some of the newer Jewish neighborhoods built in the past fifteen years. Compare the buildings on the left to those on the right, which were built nearly one hundred years previously.... Here, on the left, we have Arzei Habirah — luxury dwellings built by the Israelis for modern ultra-religious Jews — fanatic Jews, we might call them — while in East Jerusalem, many of our Arab brethren wallow in squalor."

One of the students began to challenge the tour guide on his political commentary. Mustafa Ibn Gash pulled the card he had received earlier that afternoon from his pocket and checked the address. Silently, he reasoned, "Since I'm so close, I'll knock on his door. Curiosity, that's all."

He raised his voice. "Tarik, I'm going to see someone in this neighborhood. I'll get back to the hotel on my own later."

"But I can't let you do that. You must stay with the group!" The tour guide was nervous. "Who would you know here, anyway?"

"Tarik, I appreciate your excellent knowledge of Jerusalem, but perhaps you don't quite grasp the mission of this program. We're supposed to meet and get to know the Israelis. That is exactly what I am going to do. I'll see you back at the hotel." Ignoring Tarik's continued protests, Mustafa walked off toward the entrance of the housing complex known as Arzei Habira.

It took him only five minutes to find number thirty-four. He identified Mr. Schuman's apartment from the oval olivewood name plaque, written in both English and Hebrew characters, affixed to the door. He hesitated, then shrugged and pressed the doorbell.

The door swung open almost at once. The man he'd met at the Western Wall stood there, smiling.

"Welcome!" He gestured for Mustafa to precede him through the door. As the teenager stepped inside, Schuman jokingly scolded, "It's 8:30 — you're an hour late. But you're very welcome anyway." He led Mustafa to the dining area.

The entire family was seated around the long table, which was set with a white cloth and elegant china. A festive meal was obviously in progress. Schuman offered Mustafa a skullcap and pulled out a chair for him.

Schuman's seven-year-old daughter, dressed in a pretty skirt and blouse with dark hair gleaming on her shoulders, spoke up anxiously. "Abba aren't you going to tell him he mustn't ring the bell on the Sabbath?"

"Shhh, Batya, he doesn't know anything... yet." Turning to Mustafa, he signalled to his wife to translate for their French-speaking guest. "I am Meir Schuman. What's your name?"

Mustafa looked around. Every eye was fixed expectantly on him. Surely these were the fanatic Jews of which Tarik, the tour guide, had spoken. The boys had long sidelocks curled behind their ears. The girls' dresses had sleeves to the wrist and hemlines well below the knee. It reminded him of the way the more orthodox Moslems dressed their girls.

He turned back to Schuman. "My name is Mustafa."

Schuman thought this an odd name for a Jewish boy; then again, twenty years ago the only name he'd been known by was Myron.

"Mustafa, I am going to assume you haven't heard Kiddush (the Sabbath blessing over wine) yet, so I will say it for you."

Schuman poured wine into a silver chalice, then chanted the one-minute prayer in Hebrew. When he finished, Mrs. Schuman instructed Mustafa to say Amen, which he did. Schuman poured off a few CCs into another glass, which he handed to his young guest. Mustafa took a cautious sip. It was the first time in his life that the youth had tasted wine. Adhering to strict Moslem code, his parents never brought alcohol into the house.

Unprepared for the burning sensation as the wine went down his throat, Mustafa began coughing. He had also drunk it too fast. Schuman came over and patted his back vigorously until the coughing stopped.

"Th-thank you," Mustafa gasped.

"Don't mention it. Here, this is our next stop." His host led him into the kitchen, filled a wide-mouthed cylindrical cup with water, and demonstrated to Mustafa how to pour it on his hands. Mrs. Schuman explained in French that Jews wash in this manner before eating bread. Watching closely, Mustafa managed to imitate Schuman's every move. Back at the table, the Schumans pointed to Hebrew words in English transliteration on the pages of a small booklet, telling Mustafa that he would now say the blessing prior to eating bread. Mustafa did as he was asked.

"Mustafa, would you like to try a piece of my homemade Gefilte fish?" asked Mrs. Schuman.

"What's that?"

The Schumans exchanged a baffled glance. How could any Jew, even the most spiritually estranged, be ignorant of this celebrated Jewish gastronomic staple?

The patty of sweetly spiced, cooked ground fish was brought to Mustafa. After one bite, it was obvious he really didn't want any more. Mrs. Schuman told him in French that Sabbath was for enjoyment, and he didn't have to eat anything at the table he didn't like. Next, he was brought a bowl of chicken soup. This he ate with relish, especially the thin noodles floating in the fatty liquid. His host waited until Mustafa's first hunger was satisfied.

"So, Mustafa, you must be a student. What do you study?"

"Mostly computers. What else?" Mustafa smiled, and the family laughed. Encouraged, he added, "Do you have a computer? I'll show you a neat simple BASIC program I wrote."

The children, though clearly eager to show him their somewhat antiquated XT, returned a few words which Mrs. Schuman automatically translated as, "It's Sabbath, we don't use the computer."

"Why not? What's wrong with using a computer on what you call Sabbath?"

"Don't you know that we don't work on Sabbath?" they asked in surprise. Schuman leaned back, content to let this conversation between the children and Mustafa continue.

"I don't know much at all about it. I'm really not so interested in religion. Would you like to hear about water-skiing? At that, I am a champion in my country!"

"Sure! The children listened in fascination as Mustafa described the fancy maneuvers that had won him the junior championship when he was twelve. They drank in Mustafa's adventures: moving at high speed through the water, the near collisions, the engine failure in the middle of an important run. Their interest impelled him to continue with other stories: about the time he had fixed a competitor's engine at the age of fourteen, and the way he'd once figured out how to remove a broken propeller without the proper tool. After about half an hour of this conversation, Mr. Schuman broke in gently, in English. "Children, children, can't we talk more about Sabbath matters? Mustafa does not have a very strong background in Judaism. Let's try to impart some of the serene beauty of Torah to him." He directed his attention at Mustafa. "Does your family attend a reform synagogue in... I didn't get where you're from."

"I'm from Egypt."

"Egypt!" Schuman exclaimed, surprise stamped on his features. "I thought you were from France. I've heard there are some fifty or a hundred Jewish families still living there. Egypt, eh? Alexandria or Cairo?"

"Neither," Mustafa said. "I'm from Aswan."

"Aswan? How interesting! Have you ever seen the dam?"

"Everybody asks me that. Of course I've seen it. My father is one of the top control engineers at the dam. We also have a speedboat on Lake Nasser. That's where I do most of my skiing."

"That's fantastic. I didn't realize there are Jews in Aswan. You probably don't even have a synagogue over there."

"Mr. Schuman, I don't know of any Jews in Aswan, and there's definitely no synagogue."

Schuman and his wife looked at each other in astonishment.

"Mustafa, I saw you praying at the Western Wall this afternoon. You *are* a Jew, aren't you?"

"No. I'm not Jewish. Is there something wrong?"

Meir Schuman fumbled for words. Mrs. Schuman recovered first, and it was she who answered.

"No, there's nothing wrong. It's just that.... We thought.... Well, since you were wearing a Kippa and praying by the Wall, we assumed you were a Jew."

"An old guy, I guess he worked there, handed me a skullcap and told me to say a prayer. I didn't feel like offending him. Besides, he was pretty insistent. As for my religion, I was raised Moslem, but I'll tell you the truth, I think it's mostly old-fashioned nonsense. But my father — oh, my father, is he strict? He prays five times a day. Goes to Mosque on Fridays, fasts Ramadan. He keeps everything. I think he's still upset I didn't turn out the way he wanted."

"What about your mother?" asked Mrs. Schuman.

"Yeah, she was born Moslem, but she's more like me. She wouldn't admit it, but I think she shares my attitude straight down the line. The same goes for my grandmother. My mom and her mother are from Iran. They settled in Egypt thirty years ago. My grandfather was very close with Shah Mohammed Pahlavi and worked in the diplomatic mission in Cairo. Those fanatic Moslems murdered him, just after Sadat was killed."

The Schumans were upset, but not devastated. It had happened three times before that they had taken in a young man visiting the Western Wall who turned out not to be Jewish. But this was the first time they had invited an Arab in error.

Mustafa saw the disappointment on their faces. "Look, I have no resentment with Jews at all. I've even had arguments with my father about the politics. He's like Mubarak — he believes the peace with Israel is beneficial for the time being, but he doesn't think we should get too close. I can't see why not. We're not living in the dark ages, although most Arabs behave like we do. We live in the computer generation and the era of science. Don't get me wrong; there's nobody who knows engineering, geology, and hydrodynamics better than my dad. But when it comes to religion, he's still from the old school." He shook his head. "It's almost as if he had two personalities... I've never understood that about him. When I was a kid, he used to beat the heck out of me when I wasn't a good enough Moslem. My mom also knows science — she teaches it in high school. She has a modern attitude. Out of my father's presence, she doesn't give a hoot about religion."

"They let a woman teach high school science?" Schuman asked, surprised.

"Look, Egypt has a lot of fanatics, but the government, from Nasser's time, really started modernizing the country. It's sort of like Iran during the Shah's time, but not quite so avant garde. Now look at Iran — clear back to the twelfth century, those fools. Yeah, in Egypt they're trying to keep some kind of balance in their modernization. They don't want to tick off the really devout too much. My mom still wears a scarf on her head when she teaches. And long sleeves and a long dress." Mustafa looked at Mrs. Schuman, "Something like the way you dress, except that you don't wear a head covering."

The Schumans laughed. Mrs. Schuman responded, "Mustafa, all Orthodox married Jewish women cover their heads. We're just allowed to wear a wig."

"Hey, that's neat. I'll have to tell my mom about that. She hates that drab black scarf. I'll bet she'd love to wear a wig instead." He made a face. "But I don't know how the Mullah would feel about it!"

They all laughed. The tension that had arisen when Mustafa revealed his non-Jewish identity had all but disappeared. The main course of chicken and rice was served. Then dessert. The conversation afterwards lasted until 1:30 a.m. The chemistry between Mustafa Ibn Gash and the Schuman family, children as well as adults, was tangible. Finally Mustafa noticed the clock and commented, "The others back at the hotel are probably thinking the worst has happened to me. They probably figured I've been killed by a fanatic West-Bank Jewish settler."

He thanked his hosts warmly and bid them good bye. They, in turn, bid him "Good Shabbos."

Chapter 11

Dr. Muhamma had given Mustafa a form for his host family to fill out. The following Monday, during the afternoon siesta which both Jews and Arabs observed in the Holy Land, he strolled over to the Schumans' and knocked on the door. He waited a few minutes, and knocked again. Still no answer. He knocked a third time, very loudly, and Mrs. Schuman appeared at the door. "Why didn't you ring the bell? I couldn't hear a thing over the washing machine."

He gave her a sheepish grin. "Well, I saw that the children were upset the last time I came and rang the bell. I thought it might disturb you."

"No, Mustafa, that's not it."

"Then what...?"

"Never mind, it's not important. What brings you by?"

"Here." He handed her the forms, which were in Hebrew and Arabic. She read about the student exchange program and its goals. Mrs. Schuman found herself unable to answer Mustafa on the spot. Although she and her husband would never have considered asking the youth to leave their home the other night simply because he turned out not to be Jewish, hosting a non-Jew for two weeks was a different matter entirely. In any case, taking in an Arab student seemed to her more appropriate for a secular Israeli family. Still, she didn't have the heart to tell him so.

"I'll have to discuss this with my husband." She gave Mustafa the phone number and told him to call back in a few days.

At about the same time that Mustafa was knocking at the Schumans' door, Meir Schuman was back on the beat at the Western Wall, searching for lost Jewish souls to pick up. He came upon Nissim Abulafia with his pile of paper skullcaps.

"Nissim," said the veteran soul-snatcher to the old custodian, "do you remember giving a Kippa to a French-speaking teenager last Friday?"

"The Egyptian boy?" Abulafia asked immediately.

"Yes, that's the one. How did you know he was Egyptian?"

"What do you think? I spoke to him. As soon as he opened his mouth, I caught the accent."

"Well, I have news for you, Reb Nissim," Schuman sighed, "He's a *goy* — an Arab. He was just on tour and came over to see the Wall."

"He's a Jew," said Nissim Abulafia.

"What are you talking about? Did he tell you so? I also assumed he was a Jew. I invited him over last Friday night, and he showed up. Would you believe it? We didn't find out he's a *goy* until an hour into the meal."

"He's a Jew," the elderly caretaker repeated doggedly.

Meir Schuman shook his head, exasperated. "Reb Nissim, he must have bamboozled you. I'll bet he just wanted to get a closer look at the Wall. He must have thought we don't let Arabs approach Judaism's holiest site."

"He's a Jew."

Schuman stared at the old man. Then, abruptly, he switched tactics. "All right, he's a Jew. How do you know?"

"I looked at his face. He's a Jew."

"You mean, he was born to Jews and somehow adopted by Arabs?"

"What do you think I am, a prophet or something? How would I know how he came to think he was an Arab? All I know is that he's Jewish."

"But you claim to know, beyond a shadow of a doubt, that he's a Jew?"

"Can you see when it is night? Can you see when it is day? I can see when a person is a Jew or not a Jew, just the same way." The old man smiled.

Perplexed, Schuman thanked him and walked away. Business was slow that day; he didn't pick up anyone at the Wall. When he arrived home that evening, he said to his wife, "Leah, I'm sorry I didn't ask Mustafa where he was staying. According to old Nissim Abulafia, the boy's a secret Jew."

"You're kidding! Well, here's something that will comfort you. Take a look at this." Mrs. Schuman handed her husband the host-form that Mustafa had dropped off.

Schuman looked over the papers, took out a pen, and signed them immediately. "This is amazing. You know, as I left the Wall today, I started to think about Reb Nissim's insistence that Mustafa is a Jew. I concluded that Nissim was losing it.... Now, I'm convinced it must be true. This is providential!" He thought for a moment, then added, "Now I understand why we clicked so well last Friday night. Mustafa didn't seem any different from an alienated Jewish youth from Los Angeles or Kansas City."

"He seemed to fit right in," his wife agreed. "We were all so comfortable together."

"How remarkable are the ways of the Almighty! Completely on his own, apparently without even knowing he was Jewish, Mustafa turned his back on the religion in which he was raised." He shook his head in wonder. "Providence...."

Upon the completion of the Hebrew-language Ulpan course three weeks later, Mustafa was dropped off at the Schuman home. He had barely set his bags down in his room — that is, the room he was to share with the four Schuman boys — before Meir Schuman all but dragged him out of the house.

"Where are we going, Meir?" Mustafa asked as they walked briskly to the "fanatic" Jewish neighborhood of Meah Shearim.

"I want to introduce you to a great rabbi."

"Is that something like a Jewish Mullah?" The question was posed in broken, but surprisingly passable Hebrew.

"That's right. Hey, you speak a pretty good Hebrew for only a couple of weeks of Ulpan."

"In the evenings, after class, I spent some time comparing Hebrew to Arabic. Structurally, they are very close to each other, and a lot of the words are similar. But why are we in such a hurry to see your rabbi? You're trying to convert me?"

"No, Mustafa," Schuman laughed. "No more questions, now. You'll find out in due time."

Schuman entered the office of Rabbi Meshizahav, the famous mystic and palm reader, alone, while a mystified Mustafa cooled his heels in a small waiting room.

"Rabbi, I am going to bring in a sixteen-year-old boy who was raised in Egypt by Arabs. I have reason to believe that he may be Jewish. Can you tell just by looking at him, or by reading his palm?"

"Bring him in. We'll see," the rabbi answered.

The boy was called in to stand before the rabbi. He found himself at the receiving end of a scrutiny similar to the one he'd undergone by Nissim Abulafia at the Western Wall. Without a word, the rabbi seized Mustafa's right hand and began tracing the lines on it with his finger. After three minutes of examination, Rabbi Meshizahav looked up at Meir Schuman, and said in Yiddish, "There's no doubt about it. But I am the one who is amazed. How did *you* find out?"

"You know old Nissim Abulafia, who hands out Kippot at the Wall?"

"Aha, so you have discovered his secret?"

"What secret?" Schuman demanded.

"Never mind that for now. Let's concentrate on the youth."

Mustafa knew himself to be the subject of their conversation, but he didn't understand a word of Yiddish. In his two-week-old Hebrew, he asked. "What's going on? What's this about?"

Schuman asked the rabbi whether he should tell him the truth. The rabbi carried on a long conversation with Schuman, asking how he'd met the boy and what he was doing in Israel. In the end, the rabbi advised Schuman not to say anything until Mustafa's program was about to end — just a day or two before the boy would was slated to return home.

Mustafa fit into the Schuman family like a glove on a hand. They didn't pressure him about religion at all. But often Mustafa himself would ask about the unusual practices he witnessed every day, every hour, in the Schuman home. Mustafa made the first few inquiries just to be cordial. Soon enough, he found himself growing curious about the new world he had entered. After three days in the Schuman home, Mustafa's insightful questions about the Jewish religion were drawn from a profound interest.

True to his word, he showed the children the computer games he had programmed. He also showed the family his photo albums, which he had brought from Aswan. Mrs. Schuman noted that no pictures of his father were to be found in the album. Surprised, Mustafa mused that it was always his father who took the pictures.

"I've been here only a week, but I feel like part of the family," Mustafa told Mrs. Schuman one afternoon, while she was doing the laundry (she forever seemed to be doing laundry). "Aswan, Egypt is old, dirty, and provincial compared to Jerusalem — the Jewish part of Jerusalem, that is. The Arab section reminds me of Aswan. The more I walk the streets, the more I see of your and Meir's friends and neighbors, the more I feel like staying here. I told you before that I can't stand Islam?"

"Yes, you did."

"But I can't seem to get it out of my head. For sixteen years I grew up among my Arab people — and now, in just a few weeks, I feel like I only want to be with Jews. My father will take me to a shrink, if he ever finds out my feelings." He made a motion with his finger suggesting a slitted throat.

"I don't know about that, Mustafa," Leah Schuman said, as she shoved an armful of whites into the dryer. "From what you've told us, your father sounds like a very intelligent and sensitive man. Just be honest and open with him — I'll bet he'll respect you for it more than you can imagine. And it certainly sounds like your mother and grandmother would be likely to support you."

"Maybe." Mustafa sounded dubious — and continued to look worried. Leah's heart went out to the youngster. What new twists lay in Mustafa's future, she wondered as she sorted through a pile of colored clothes, and what role did she and Meir have in all of it?

That day, Meir Schuman stopped off at the home of Rabbi Auerbach, one of Israel's most prominent Halachic authorities, to ask his opinion of Mustafa's case. After explaining the entire situation, Schuman asked the Rabbi, "I am aware that the rabbi may be leery of basing a decision of Jewish law on the evidence of Kabbalistic intuition. But the whole scenario seems to be divinely inspired."

"Yes, Meir, it certainly does. Yet I would tell you — and this is only my personal opinion, you can go ask others if you wish — that according to Halacha, despite the positive indications, we cannot be sure the boy is Jewish. Perhaps you could contact his parents in Egypt to find out if he was adopted, or if they have any insight as to where he came from. For all we know, perhaps the Kabbalists discerned some Jewish ancestry in his mother. Perhaps she herself doesn't even know her true background!

"There are many possibilities. If you can find out, good; if not, and the boy would like to be considered a Jew, he will have to undergo a conversion process."

The last two weeks of the program flew by like a dream for Mustafa. Although they never imposed any religious observance upon him, the Schumans were astonished to see the youth, reared in Islam, move toward the Judaism he witnessed daily with as much depth of understanding and enthusiasm as the typical American *Ba'al Tshuvah*.

Two days before the group was scheduled to return to Egypt, all the students — along with one host family member each — were invited to a closing convention to discuss their experiences. Tzvi Schuman, who was also sixteen, and the only Israeli wearing a Kippa on his head, attended with Mustafa.

The discussion went as might be expected. The theme of almost every speech was, "I thank our hosts for offering us this enlightening experience, and hope that this program, and similar ones, will foster peace between our peoples."

One aspect of the convention did deeply affect Mustafa in a personal way. The host family member who accompanied Meluk Ashrawi, a young man of perhaps eighteen or nineteen, kept staring at Mustafa. Mustafa had a mischievous urge to stare back. For over an hour the two played cat and mouse: as soon as Mustafa would raise his eyes to see if the young man was staring, the Israeli would look away. But each time Mustafa looked away and then glanced back again, the young fellow would be gazing at him. It was unsettling.

"Tzvi," whispered Mustafa, who was sitting next to him, "Do you see that guy sitting over there, about eight seats from the end of the row?"

"Yeah. What about him?"

"Do you know him, by any chance? He came with a student from Luxor by the name of Meluk. They're sitting together."

Tzvi located Meluk by the prominent name badge worn by all those present.

"Mustafa, I don't know any secular Israelis. We Orthodox have our own insulated society here in Israel." He squinted at the Israeli's badge. "I see his name is Ariel Mizrachi. If you have an interest in meeting him, let's go over during the next break." He glanced at Mustafa curiously. "Why do you ask?"

"I don't know. I think he's been staring in this direction."

At that moment, Mizrachi turned his head to direct his look at Mustafa yet again. Mustafa kept his eyes riveted to a spot directly ahead of him. Mizrachi kept staring.

"I think you're right, Mustafa," Tzvi whispered into his ear.

Mustafa turned to face Mizrachi, who immediately switched his gaze to the speaker at the podium.

Tzvi Schuman looked at Mizrachi, then at Mustafa. There was something strange going on....

Then, like the proverbial ton of bricks, the answer hit him.

"Mustafa, that fellow — look at him again! Something about him reminds me of you. That's it! He must have noticed that you look like him, and is trying to pinpoint exactly how."

Mustafa now began to stare at Ariel Mizrachi with purpose. Mizrachi turned toward him, met his gaze, and glanced away — then looked back to find Mustafa's gaze unwavering. A minute later, the two were studying each other intently, all pretense dismissed. During the first break, Tzvi dragged Mustafa along to meet Ariel Mizrachi face to face.

"Hi, I'm Tzvi Schuman from Jerusalem. My family hosted Mustafa Ibn Gash. He's from Aswan."

Mizrachi looked uncomfortable. "I'm Ariel Mizrachi from Ramat Gan. I never would have thought a Charedi would host an Arab student. That's pretty good." He kept his gaze studiously averted from Mustafa, clearly trying to avoid taking note of the resemblance between himself and the Arab youth standing opposite him — a resemblance even more striking from up close. To Tzvi, he said challengingly, "You probably sit in a yeshiva all day. Why can't you at least go to Nachal, where you'd serve a little in the army?"

"A minute ago, you seemed to realize that you may have some misconceptions about us," Tzvi said quietly. "If you like, I'll explain to you how our learning in yeshiva benefits the nation as much as your military service." He paused. "Hey, you look over eighteen. Why aren't *you* in the army?"

"I am!" Mizrachi answered indignantly. "The navy, actually. Right now, they're paying for my medical school education. I'll start active service in five years, when I get my MD. My father served in the navy; I'm following in his footsteps."

This exchange went on in a Hebrew that was too fast for Mustafa to follow. Brazenly, Tzvi said to Mizrachi, "My friend Mustafa here thought you might have been looking his way a little too often during the speeches."

"Well, *he* was looking at *me*," came the defensive reply.

"You two look alike, did you notice that?" Mizrachi blushed at Tzvi's remark, but before he could frame an answer Meluk Ashrawi rose from his seat to join them. He said something to Mustafa in Arabic that neither of the two Jews understood. Then Meluk spoke again, in a decent English this time, directing his remarks to Ibn Gash and Mizrachi. "You two could pass for brothers. Hey, Khalid, Hassan, Mohammed — come over here a minute!" Some of the other Egyptian students and their host family members were drawn to the scene. "Look at these two. Notice anything funny?"

The group looked the pair over, as though they were specimens under a microscope. One of the students thought they didn't look the least bit similar, but all the others noticed the definite, if subtle, resemblance. A few even agreed with Meluk: they could almost have passed for brothers.

The program resumed again a few minutes later, and the other students sloughed off the weird coincidence. But not Mustafa and Ariel.

At 8:00 p.m., the convention closed with a banquet. Mustafa found a moment to seek out Ariel Mizrachi alone. "Care to take a walk?"

Mizrachi hesitated, then shrugged. "Why not?"

Ben Yehuda Street was quiet, its shops shuttered for the night. "If it was only our appearance that was similar, I wouldn't be so curious," Mustafa said as they strolled along. "But I've also noticed an inflection in your voice that is similar to mine."

"I have to admit you're right. But you're an Egyptian Arab, and I'm a Sephardic Jew." Mizrachi glanced sidelong at Mustafa. "My father was from Egypt, you know. My mother told me he was born in Alexandria."

"What a coincidence!" Mustafa exclaimed. "My father is also from Alexandria."

"Really? That *is* strange."

Enthusiastically, Mustafa said, "Hey, why don't we go over to your house right now? I'd like to meet your father." His time in Israel had all but done away with any shyness he might once have felt at meeting strangers.

To his dismay, Mizrachi's expression tightened. "I never knew my father. He was accidentally killed while serving in the navy. I was just a baby then. I don't even remember him."

"I'm sorry." Mustafa tried to lighten the atmosphere. "Well, I guess I won't be meeting Mr. Mizrachi...."

"Oh, you could meet him — my stepfather, that is. He adopted me when I was a kid and I took his name. My real father's name was Alon Barnash. My mother never speaks about him. I suppose the memory is too painful."

The rest of the walk was accomplished in a silence that was tinged with sadness. With a feeling that was almost regret, Mustafa bid Ariel Mizrachi farewell and returned to the Schuman residence.

The next day, Meir Schuman took Mustafa aside. "We've very much enjoyed having you, and hope you will come back to visit us. Our house is open to you."

Mustafa smiled gratefully. "Thank you. I do hope to come back someday soon."

"Good...." Schuman took a breath, then plunged into speech again. "Mustafa, there's something I must tell you. Please don't get upset. Do you remember the Rabbi I took you to, the day you came here to stay?"

"Of course — who could forget him? He gave me the willies." Mustafa glanced keenly at Schuman. "What did he tell you? You said, at the time, that it would have to wait. I guess the time has come."

"Yes, the time has come. Now, please don't take offense."

"Please," Mustafa said urgently. "Just tell me."

"All right. The rabbi told me that he'd looked into your soul — and seen that you are really a Jew." Quickly, he held up a hand. "Now I know that sounds like a lot of hocus-pocus, but for many reasons I suspect there's something to it. Mustafa, do you know if you were adopted?"

Mustafa sat with a blank stare for a minute. Then he turned to Meir Schuman and said, with the calm assurance of a man many years older, "Mr. Schuman, this is going to sound crazy — but I have no doubt that I am a Jew. Something inside me clicked immediately with your family, with your community. On the day you met me, at the Western Wall, the old Moroccan guy who gives out the Kippot told me that I was Jewish. At first I thought he was senile, but I guess maybe he was on to something. I don't know how he knew; maybe he's one of those people you call a *Tzadik*." He faced his friend with solemn directness, tinged with quiet despair. "Meir, I want to be a Jew like you, but I don't know what to do. I have to go home."

"We'll deal with that when the time comes. First, what about the question I asked you?"

Mustafa shook his head firmly. "I am naturally born to my parents. Couldn't you tell that from the photographs I showed you?"

"I remember remarking that there were no pictures of your dad."

"That's true. But you saw my mom. Anyway, I have no doubt about it: I was not adopted."

"In that case, do you know anything about your mother's ancestors? In Jewish Law, if your mother is Jewish, you are Jewish, regardless of the father's background."

Mustafa frowned. "I'm quite certain she's Iranian for many generations back. Her maiden name is Baktari. I think that could be either Jewish or non-Jewish.... But I know that the family was — nominally, at any rate — Moslem." He thought for a moment, then said, "Look, my mother's mother is still alive. I'm very close to her. I suppose I could ask her if she has any Jewish ancestry."

"Good! You do that. But for now, without any solid evidence, in order to observe Judaism you would have to go through a conversion — simply to eliminate any doubts. Would you consider that?"

"Let's go now," Mustafa said at once. He got up and started for the door.

"Not so fast," Schuman laughed. "Let me explain how it works. First you will have to be circumcised."

"But that's been done already. I can't be circumcised twice, can I?"

"No, but the custom is to spill a drop of blood as a sign of the covenant. Just a little pinprick."

"I think I could manage that, Meir. Anything else I should know about?"

"After the symbolic circumcision you immerse in a ritual bath and, in front of three judges, accept the responsibility of observing Jewish Law. That's all. It could take just twenty minutes. In general, we don't accept converts until they have shown themselves to be genuinely committed and have spent several years studying Judaism. But in cases where the person's status is merely in doubt, the rabbis will perform the conversion process right away."

Meir Schuman removed a Hebrew letter from an envelope, explaining to Mustafa that it contained a recommendation from a great rabbi to the rabbinical court to carry out the conversion process without delay.

As they went downstairs and out of the building, Mustafa's heart was pounding so loudly he was sure his friend could hear it. His emotions were in too much turmoil to allow for easy conversation, and Schuman seemed to respect his need for private thought. In silence, the pair walked twenty minutes to another housing development on the opposite side of Meah Shearim, to the apartment of Yossel the *Mohel*.

Yossel scanned the letter, called in a neighbor (three Jewish men had to witness the event), took out an alcohol swab and a small sterile scalpel blade, and instructed Mustafa to lower his pants and sit down.

Mustafa complied. Yossel looked carefully at the site which he proposed to nick with his blade. His scrutiny seemed exaggerated for such a simple procedure. Suddenly, he tossed the unused alcohol swab into a trash bin, and spoke to Schuman in rapid Hebrew. "This boy is already circumcised. You can go."

"We know that, Reb Yossel. But you read Rabbi Auerbach's letter. The boy needs to spill a drop of blood and go through the whole conversion process."

"Do you know who you're talking to?" asked Yossel, only half in jest.

"Of course. The greatest Mohel in the world!"

"That's right," Yossel smiled. "And I am telling you that this boy was circumcised at the age of eight days, and by a real *Mohel*. Here, look at that scar." Yossel pointed to the relevant site on the boy's anatomy. "You see how fine a ring was formed?"

"Yes, but the boy was raised Moslem. They circumcise, too."

"Of course they do — but never at eight days. These days, they wait a few months, or even years. In the old days, they did it at the age of thirteen. Now look over here." Yossel pointed to a small ventral scar. "You see this? You won't find that mark on a Moslem job. I tell you, this boy had a real *Mohel*, and he was eight days old. He's good to go."

With finality, Yossel threw the unused scalpel blade in the garbage and told Mustafa to pull up his pants.

"Mustafa," Schuman said slowly to the bewildered youth, "do you understand what happened? Yossel the *Mohel* is certain you had a proper Jewish circumcision at eight days. Something in your family seems to have been kept a secret from you. If I were you, I'd do some serious investigation when you get home."

Mustafa thought for a moment. "I don't get it. I'm certain my mother and father are my real parents. Are you trying to tell me that they were Jewish, and then, after I was born, suddenly converted to Islam? That's ridiculous!"

"I'm not telling you anything. I'm just suggesting that you do some digging into your past. There's a mystery here, Mustafa."

Mustafa's face grew set. "Look, Meir, I don't really care. I just want to be a Jew. Let's go do the rest of it."

From Yossel's house they proceeded to the rabbinical court. The rabbis read the letter and demanded a certificate of circumcision. Schuman explained that Yossel was certain the boy had been circumcised already in accordance with Jewish Law. That was sufficient for the rabbis. Mustafa was taken to the Zupnick Mikva nearby. Three rabbis waited there. They asked if he was prepared to observe Torah Law.

"I am," Mustafa answered solemnly.

"How are you going to keep kosher in Aswan, Egypt?" asked the elder rabbi.

"I'll become a vegetarian. But I don't think I'll stay there. I'll go to a school right here in Israel and only return to Egypt for visits."

The rabbis, understanding that the boy was probably already Jewish, refrained from putting him through the wringer that a conventional convert must go through. As they watched, Mustafa immersed in the ritual pool. When he came out, he was pronounced a bonafide Jew.

On their walk back to Arzei Habirah, they stopped in a bookstore and purchased the articles that Mustafa — now Mordechai — would need in his Jewish observance. Since there was no time for him to attend classes, Meir also recommended several books which would educate Mordechai in the practices he needed to know. The next day — the last before the group's departure for Egypt — Meir Schuman gave Mordechai a crash course in practical Judaism. He promised to enroll the boy in a Jewish college on his return to Israel. Mordechai was ecstatic over his new status, and kept pinching himself to make sure he wasn't dreaming. It was certainly real — though the way it had come about had a dreamlike quality that filled him with wonder. There was no question in his mind that this trip, and its consequences, had been ordained and orchestrated by God.

As he prepared to board the bus for the airport, Mordechai said, "Meir, I don't even have the words to thank you and your family. I owe you so much...."

"Nonsense," Meir said briskly, to cover the emotion he felt at Mustafa's departure. "You did it all yourself."

"No, that's not true. I had help." Mustafa gave Meir a radiant smile. "After two-and-a-half years of abandoning religion, I now see why God allowed it to happen — so that I could come here and find myself."

Chapter 12

Mordechai Ibn Gash arrived home early Friday morning, anxious to tell his family about his adventures — and to hear the truth about his religious status. His initial remarks to his mother and grandmother were noncommital. When they pressed him for specifics about the trip, he smiled and said, "Let's wait until father comes home from the mosque." Nothing in his manner betrayed the enormous changes he had undergone, or the nervousness he felt at the impending meeting with his father. While he felt no compunction about the revelation he was about to make — his parents had, after all, hidden some deep, dark secrets from him for all the years of his life — he couldn't help regretting the pain his story would cause his fiercely religious father.

Abdallah walked through the door at eight. He hurried over to hug and kiss his son. When all four were gathered around the kitchen table, Mordechai came right to the point.

"The trip was great. I saw a lot and learned even more. Most of all, I was lucky enough to stumble onto the truth."

His grandmother paled. Bewildered, Fatima asked, "What are you talking about, Mustafa?" Abdallah looked steadily at his son, but said nothing.

"The most notable event of the past six weeks was that I found out that I was born a Jew." Mordechai gazed in turn at each member of his family. "Please, Mom, Dad, Grandma — tell me the whole truth."

The ladies were struck dumb. Abdallah's face was grim, but not overly surprised. Mordechai pressed, "Go ahead and tell me. Mom, Grandma — you know, don't you?"

"Mustafa," Fatima said, "your mind has cracked! You spend six weeks in Israel, and you come home *majnun*. We're taking you to see a doctor, a psychiatrist, immediately." She emitted a brief bark of near-hysterical laughter. "A Jew? Are you crazy, Mustafa? Your father would kill you if you were a Jew!"

Instinctively, all eyes turned to Abdallah. His face was as impassive as if it had been carved from marble.

Slowly, Mordechai nodded. "I understand, Mom. You have to say something like that. Look, I'm being perfectly honest with you. Please tell me the truth — because I'm about to drop the second bomb of the morning." The two ladies visibly tensed. "I've committed myself to being an observant Jew. My name is now Mordechai."

For the first time, Mrs. Baktari spoke. "Mustafa — my Mustafa!" she cried, as the tears began to run unchecked down her lined cheeks. She threw her arms around the boy and hugged him tightly. "Your name is not Mordechai."

He pulled back slightly. "Why do you say that, Grandma? I chose the name myself."

"Because your name is Moshe." The words emerged with difficulty through the outpouring of tears. It was some minutes before she was sufficiently composed to speak clearly. Letting go of the boy, she said, "I am a Jew. My parents were traditional, but modern. I married your grandfather — may he rest in peace — who was not Jewish. But I am, your mother is — and you truly are. When you were born, your parents came to Cairo, and on the eighth day of your life I had the last Jewish *Mohel* in all of Egypt come from Alexandria to bring you into the covenant of Abraham, our forefather." She gazed at him lovingly, pure joy shining from her tired eyes. "But how could you have found out?"

"They have holy men in Israel, many of them," Moshe answered. "They saw me and told me; after two weeks, I knew it must be true. Dad...." Moshe directed his attention at his father. "Did you know about all this?"

"Yes," came the simple, but astonishing, answer. "I knew your mother was a Jewess when I married her, and I found out that your grandmother had you circumcised."

Moshe drew a deep breath. "Dad?"

"Yes, my son."

"What are you going to do now?"

"Nothing," Abdallah shrugged, palms upward in the classical gesture of futility. "What can I do? You want to be a Jew? You're a big boy, I'm not going to stop you. Just use your good sense. We're living in an Arab nation. Keep it discreet."

Abdallah knew without looking that his wife and her mother were flabbergasted at his cavalier attitude about the shocking news. He turned to address them directly. "Look, when my son lived as a total infidel, he kept no religion at all. At least now he will pray to God — and I can be sure he won't be eating pork!" He smiled wryly. Fatima, in response, gave the same, hysterical bark of laughter.

"Dad," Moshe said sympathetically, "this is big of you. Thank you. And don't worry — I don't intend to tell anyone around here." He paused, then continued in a rush, "The truth is that I want to go back to Israel to study. I have to catch up on sixteen lost years."

Abdallah looked intently at his son. "Go, if you must, but keep this very quiet. When you go back there, don't tell people about your background. It could come back here and get me in trouble."

"I would never do anything to hurt you. I'll even take on a different last name."

The hours flew by as Moshe told his family about the trip. Finally, he came to the last day, and the convention.

"As I've been telling you, amazing things happened to me throughout the entire trip. But one of the strangest of all was when I met an Israeli named Ariel

Mizrachi." Intent on his story, Moshe didn't notice the way Abdallah's ears pricked up. "The students stood us next to each other, and some of them claimed that we could pass for brothers. It was true — we shared an uncanny likeness. He's about two or three years older than I am. Now don't fall off your seats, but he told me his father, a Sephardic Jew, was born in Alexandria. Just like Dad."

Fatima looked at her husband, who had placed a hand over his face. "Did you know a Jewish family in Alexandria by the name of Mizrachi?"

It was a physical effort for Abdallah to remove his hand and answer her. The words emerged casually, betraying none of the strain that lay behind. "Actually, it was a common name for Jews here in Egypt — maybe the most common. I must have known a few Jews by that name when I was growing up."

Moshe opened his mouth, but his father had continued speaking. "I was always puzzled about why the Jews of Egypt looked like the Moslems. When the dam was being built, there were a few Russians who told me they came from Jewish ancestry — although they hardly knew what that meant — and they looked exactly like the other Russians. It's curious." Abdallah shrugged, and made a gesture that seemed to dismiss the subject. To Moshe, he said, "So tell me more about your plans, my son...."

That evening, Moshe invited his parents and grandmother to hear him break his teeth in Hebrew over the Sabbath blessings. He had no wine, but Meir Schuman had told him he could use the readily available pita bread instead. Fatima and Mrs. Baktari remained in the kitchen to listen. Abdallah declined.

Later that evening, Moshe found his father reading by himself on the porch. "Dad, I want to tell you more about this Ariel Mizrachi. Besides the fact that his father was born in Egypt, his name wasn't originally Mizrachi. His biological father is dead. Mizrachi adopted him when his mother remarried. His original last name was... was... I don't recall clearly. Barnat, I think, or Banash, something like that."

Abdallah turned his face toward the street to conceal an irrepressible tear. He said nothing.

"Dad.... What's the matter?" Moshe peered at his father in the dim porch light. "Did you know somebody like that when you were young?"

Still gazing sightlessly at the traffic below, Abdallah told his son, "It's been a long time. I'm not sure. Sometimes weird coincidences happen.... Let's drop the subject, all right?"

"Okay, Dad. I don't want to upset you." Moshe stepped back into the house.

Abdallah rained tears onto the street below for a few minutes longer, then wiped his face vigorously and followed his son inside.

Chapter 13

One month after Moshe Ibn Gash returned home to Aswan, he was back in Jerusalem, where he became known as Moshe Mitzri. Meir Schuman enrolled the youth in a beginner's Yeshiva (Jewish studies college). Ironically, he was able to pay full tuition from the grants and scholarships he was awarded by the Egyptian government. By the end of 1988, Moshe Mitzri was indistinguishable from the typical *Charedi* (ultra-religious) Israeli Jew. He picked up Hebrew like a native, and made significant progress in his studies. His mentors recommended that he visit his family in Egypt only sparingly. When he did return for a visit, he removed his black hat and suit and donned the typical clothing of the middle-class, modern, Arab teen of Aswan.

After his first year in Israel, his parents and grandmother became convinced that he was completely serious about Jewish observance. This was not merely some passing fad. The youth had poured all of his intellect and talent into his newly-discovered lifestyle. Fatima was completely at a loss to understand why Abdallah, that devout Moslem, seemed so complacent when his *"Yeshiva Bachur"* son came home to visit.

"Mustafa."

"Please, Dad — it's Moshe now."

"Okay, Moshe. But to the outside you must remain Mustafa."

"Of course, Dad, of course." The youth had displayed an ever-growing maturity, and a corresponding discretion, about his religious preference.

"I know you are bent on spending all of your time learning about your religion. But is it possible for you to combine those studies with useful pursuits, perhaps by studying some scientific subject?"

Moshe stiffened. "Dad, there is nothing more useful in life than study and living by Torah."

"I never thought I'd see the day that my son would become a fanatic," Abdallah lamented. "If only you had put those energies into the study of the Koran!"

"Dad, I'm not a fanatic — but you'll never understand, and I don't expect you to. I'll tell you what. I was actually thinking about this before you brought it up. I've heard of an excellent program, where I'd spend several hours in the morning in Torah studies, and the afternoon learning physics."

"Physics? Just physics? No liberal arts electives, no literature, no biology, no history?"

"Just physics. Their program in optics, computers and electronics is considered the best in Israel."

"You amaze me, Moshe. I certainly like that idea better than what you're doing now."

Moshe Mitzri applied, and was accepted, to the Jerusalem Technological Institute for the '88-'89 school year. His scholarship was so outstanding that he earned his diploma in only three years, completely at the expense of the Egyptian government. In June of 1992 he returned to Egypt — but this time, he was detained at the border crossing at Ismailia. Granted a telephone call, he told his father that the government wished to interrogate him. Abdallah set out at once on the nine-hour drive to Ismailia.

Upon his arrival, he learned that Moshe had been released two hours previously. "Thanks for coming, Dad," Moshe grinned. "It got me a ride home, anyway."

It was the first opportunity the two had found in a long time for a real talk, man to man. Abdallah wanted to know what Moshe had reported to the government questioners.

"No, Dad, they have no idea that I live as a Jew. I did show them my degree and explained that my intention is to use my knowledge for the sake of our homeland — to seek a job in computer engineering. I assured them that I have no allegiance to Israel. Of course, I took the posture that Egypt is at peace with Israel, and that I intended to remain coolly associated with my colleagues to the east. I thought I did a really good job of toeing the standard party line."

With a quick, intent glance, Abdallah asked quietly, "What do you really feel, my son?"

Moshe hesitated. "Look, Dad, you're very smart. I'm a Jew. I feel like I've been one all my life. And that's true, isn't it?"

Abdallah didn't answer right away. A kilometer or two of highway unrolled beneath them before he spoke.

"I suppose so," he said at last. "According to the Jews, you're a Jew."

"Look, Dad, I haven't figured out exactly how serious Sadat was when he signed the peace accord. I also don't know what's in Mubarak's mind. Does anybody? We see so many mixed signals. In some ways, there seems to be a high degree of cooperation between Israel and Egypt. On the other hand, occasionally the Party newspapers here back the Palestinian terrorists, the mortal enemies of Israel."

"Answer me this, Moshe. If it turned out that the peace, although it's lasted for thirteen years now, was only a facade — or perhaps that it is sincere for now, but some event in the future will cause it to break down — whose side would you be on? Who would you fight for?"

Moshe noticed that his father's knuckles, wrapped around the steering wheel, were white. "Dad, why are you putting me on the spot like this? You were raised as a devout Moslem, and I know that you're a patriotic Egyptian. I consider you an honest and serious man. I respect you for what you are. But I am just as sincere in carrying on my heritage. I am a Jew.

"I am also an Egyptian national, and I do feel an allegiance to the land of my birth. But I will be perfectly frank with you: the Land of Israel is the homeland of my ancestors, and I now consider it my homeland. I have a lot of American friends — American Jews, that is — and they all feel the same way. Even though they're always gloating about how great American life is for the Jews, they still have that special, spiritual connection with Israel. The whole world, especially the Arab world, considers America practically married to the Jewish State. But if that situation should somehow change, I have no doubt where the American-born Jews living in Israel would put their allegiance." He stopped, then finished in a low voice, not looking at his father. "In so many words, that's my answer. I hope you can respect it."

Without a word, Abdallah pulled the car over to the side of the deserted road. He turned to stare at his son, wearing the most serious face Moshe had ever seen on his father. After a minute, Abdallah began to smile. Relieved, Moshe followed suit. Abdallah's smile soon turned to laughter. As the absurdity of his twenty-four years of deception filled his consciousness, the laughter grew more uncontrolled. Tears of hilarity squeezed from the corners of his eyes, to fall unnoticed onto his chin, his shirt, his lap.

Moshe's smile disappeared.

"Dad, what's the matter? Are you okay?"

The laughter continued. Moshe became first concerned, then frightened. At twenty-two years of age, he had never seen such a display from his father. Had the strain of having a Jewish son affected Abdallah's mind?

He was debating the wisdom of leaving the car and seeking help, when Abdallah stopped laughing. He gave Moshe a radiant smile, then said in perfect Hebrew, "I am the luckiest man alive to have a son like you."

The words struck Moshe like a shock wave. Stunned into immobility, he stared at his father in complete incomprehension. Then he began to shake. His hands trembled uncontrollably and his mouth worked as he attempted to frame a question. In the same language, he stammered, "F-father, how do know how to speak Hebrew so well? Were you trained by the secret service to spy on Israel?"

Smiling, Abdallah shook his head. "My poor Moshe, you don't know what to think. A spy?" He chuckled. "I suppose you could say I'm a spy — actually, a special covert agent. But Moshe...."

"Yes, Dad?" Moshe found he could breathe again.

"I am no Egyptian spy. I am an agent for Israel: the Mossad Aleph-Shin. And... I confess my sin, I've been fooling you all along. I am a Jew, just like you."

Moshe Mitzri Ibn Gash felt dazed, as though he were deep in some dream — or just waking from one. It was some seconds before his mind began working again. Slowly, he asked, "I suppose Mom knows about this?"

"She knows nothing. She was raised in Islam — a very liberal Moslem. All her life, she has known that your grandmother is Jewish. You should have seen the look on her face when she revealed her awful secret to me, after I proposed to her."

"You mean you didn't know she was Jewish when you were about to marry her?"

"That's right. It was as great a shock to me as the one you just received a few minutes ago...." Abdallah turned sober. "Moshe, I had a specific purpose in telling you this now. That purpose does not exist for your mother. If you love your country and your people, you will maintain the same silence that I have to your mother for the past twenty-four years."

Suddenly, a terrible fear washed over Moshe. In blind panic he wrenched open the car door, jumped out, and began to run. Abdallah threw open his own door and left it that way as he pursued his son.

"Moshe, stop! What happened?" the distraught father shouted from one hundred meters behind.

Turning, Moshe saw that Abdallah had stopped running. He stopped, too, and caught his breath. Some of the fear drained away. He began to think.

When his father had approached close enough to hear, Moshe held up a hand. "That's far enough. Now tell me the truth. You're really an Egyptian agent, right? The police contacted you from the border when I was being interrogated. You're merely testing me to see if I would betray the land of my birth."

"No, no, no! That's crazy! I told you the truth, Moshe. Now come back to the car. I don't like broadcasting these matters, even though there's not a soul around for ten kilometers." When his son did not budge, Abdallah's tone turned pleading. "Please, I swear I told you the truth. What lunacy entered your mind just now?"

Still maintaining his distance, Moshe spoke in a very serious tone. "Then tell me this: why, for the first fourteen years of my life, did you do everything in your power to ensure that I would grow up a devout Moslem? I still shudder sometimes when I think of the beatings you gave me."

Abdallah was dumbstruck for a moment. Moshe anxiously looked on, bracing himself for his father's response. It came in an explosion of convulsive laughter. The fit of unbridled mirth eclipsed even Abdallah's earlier display, just before he had shocked his son by revealing his true identity. Moshe worked up the courage to move closer. Abdallah's raging hilarity seemed harmless enough. Moshe could not know it, but the strain of so many years of deception — and the necessary distance it had placed between Abdallah and his loved ones — was telling now in this fit of laughter, a very close cousin to tears....

Moshe began to be seriously concerned when his father started gasping for breath.

"Dad, Dad, what happened? What did I say?" Grasping his father's arm, he walked beside him back to the car. Slowly, Abdallah's fit ran its course. When he was able to talk again, he drank in a lungful of air and said, "My son, on everything you hold holy I promise you this: my devotion to Islam is, and always has been, one hundred percent bogus. It was just an aspect of my cover. Don't you understand? By shoving Islam down your throat for fourteen years, I succeeded in indoctrinating you beyond my wildest dreams. It was like shooting a dead-center bull's-eye. For you see, Moshe, it was my intention to drive you *away* from the religion, not toward it."

Moshe sat in astonished silence, digesting what he had just heard. As the reality sunk in, his own inner wellspring of laughter let loose. It caught Abdallah up again, and the sounds of the joyous peals rang out in the heat of the day.

Moshe abruptly stopped laughing. Turning urgently to his father, he said, "I just thought of something! I don't believe it!"

"What's that?" asked Abdallah.

"Dad, were you ever married before? Before you came here to spy?"

Abdallah looked straight ahead at the road. His face had grown still and sad. "Yes, my son. I was." A tear welled up in his eye.

"Dad, the Israeli whom I met four years ago, when I first went to Israel. Ariel was his name. Ariel Mizrachi. I never saw him again...." As Moshe spoke, the tear in Abdallah's eye began to flow freely down his cheek. "Dad, is he...?"

"Yes, Moshe — I've no doubt of it. He must be Ariel, the son of Alon Barnash. *I* was Alon Barnash. It's incredible, but there it is: by sheer chance, you met your half-brother."

Moshe began to cry along with his father.

After some time, Abdallah placed a hand on his son's shoulder. "Moshe, you must not seek him out. You must never reveal a thing we have spoken about today. This is a matter of extreme importance. Ariel believes his father is dead. That's the way it must remain."

"What about your first wife? What does she know?"

"I can't read her mind, but as far as I know, she also thinks I'm dead."

Outraged, Moshe demanded, "But Father, how could you have done a thing like that? You left a woman thinking you were dead. She remarried and probably has children from Mizrachi. Dad, they're *Mamzerim* (illegitimate, and prohibited from marrying other Jews) and they don't even realize it. Do you understand what you've done?"

Abdallah switched on the engine. "Moshe, we have another six hours until we get home. I'm going to explain to you exactly who I am, what my mission is, and how critical and calculated every move I have made has been. But just to allay your present concern — I don't understand why I did it, but I gave my wife a *get* (Jewish divorce) before I disappeared."

Moshe was flabbergasted. "Then maybe she knows you're alive?"

"She knows nothing. Now listen to the story. I suppose I should start with the episode at GSS headquarters in December of 1965...."

Over the next four hours, Alon Barnash outlined the entire plan to his son, along with much of the significant history that formed its background.

Chapter 14

November 1965, MOSSAD Headquarters:

"Admiral Benun, we're going to need a sub," Colonel Rafael Schwartz — number-one man, project designer, and commander of Mossad Aleph-Shin (Samson's Lion) — briefed a naval honcho at a special meeting.

"That should be no problem," the Admiral answered enthusiastically. "We have two on order from the Brits. WWII leftovers. We're getting a great deal on them, even with the upgrades we ordered."

"Could you add one to that order?"

The Admiral frowned. "A great deal, I said — but those subs are still costing us a pretty penny. Right now our plans don't call for more than two."

"I understand, Admiral Benun. That's why I suggested that you order another. That way, you'll still have your two for the navy."

"Listen, Schwartz, *I'm* no spook. Talk straight, man."

"It's simple," Rafi Schwartz said. "We need the sub on a permanent basis. Part of an ongoing project."

The admiral was flustered and angry. "Look here, I understand the necessity of covert operations — but maintaining and operating a submarine is a job for the Navy. We'll coordinate use of our equipment for your projects, but you can't have your own sub. We are not a rich country. It's an outrage to throw out $50,000,000 in equipment for some wild project that probably won't ever get off the ground."

Schwartz saw that arguing would prove counterproductive at this point, and a waste of precious time. Respectfully, but in a tone that would brook no contradiction, he said, "Admiral Benun, I can't tell you any more. The GSS will reimburse the $50,000,000. Please put in the order for three subs." He paused a beat, then added, "I understand you'll be in Portsmouth next month to work with the British on design modifications. Before you leave, I'll have our blueprint ready for the boat we need. Maybe you'll have a more sympathetic understanding after you see it."

"Yes sir," the Admiral said.

The following month, a small contingent of Israeli military personnel, led by Admiral Ozer Benun, was standing on the southern coast of Great Britain, in a closely guarded shipyard containing four T-class submarines. Captain Hillman Weatherby of British Naval Intelligence headed up a team of his nation's marine engineers designated to work on the Israeli order.

"You did a smart move by ordering another sub, Admiral Benun. We've had very serious inquiries into the Tornado — Egypt and Morocco, primarily. That sub

would have sold soon, and to someone you might not have been happy about."
He began walking, headed for the nearest structure. "Let's go into engineering and
take a look at the plans you have in mind for this boat."

Admiral Benun carefully removed an E-sized blueprint from a long cardboard
tube and unfurled it on an open drafting table. The British officer/engineer studied
it in silence. He started from the stern and scanned the plans up and down to the
bow, pausing now and then to take a puff from the stogy hanging from his bottom
lip. The scrutiny took him a full half-hour, during which time he made no com-
ments and asked no questions.

At last, he turned away from the blueprint, pulled the cigar from his mouth,
and stated flatly, "Mr. Benun, it won't work."

Benun grew crimson with anger, liberally tinged with embarrassment. There
had been a certainty in the British officer's assertion that made him very uneasy.
"What are you talking about? We had our best engineers working on this design.
Of course it will work.... What won't work?"

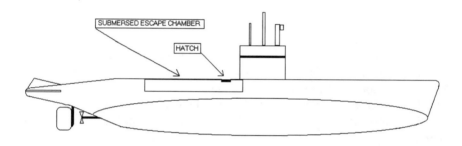

"This section over here." Weatherby pointed to a large, sealed, empty area
located at the top of the hull, just behind the sail of the sub. "This is marked *sub-
mersed escape chamber*. You obviously want to be able to chuck out a group of
divers or frogmen without surfacing. But this design will cause the entire water
frame to become unbalanced. We just shoot out our men through a dual hatched
tube. That is how everyone does it."

"I'm aware of that, Weatherby," Admiral Benun said, his manner cold as ice
now. "But our operations call for a group of twenty or thirty divers to exit at once.
Filling and emptying a single tube would mean two hours to put out twenty men
— and two hours for them to return. Maybe you Brits take tea while getting your
men out. We require efficiency."

Weatherby didn't betray the slightest sign that he'd taken the remark personally. He puffed thoughtfully for a moment, then plucked the cigar from his mouth,
tipped a bit of ash on the blueprint, and faced his Israeli counterpart. "This design
is garbage. The sub won't last two hundred hours before it joins the junk-pile of
maritime debris on the ocean floor." He shrugged a cool shoulder. "But it's your
money, and your men."

Ozer Benun was a good military man. His planning of battle strategy in the
1956 Sinai campaign had catapulted him in just ten years up the ranks to the posi-

tion he currently held. As a rule, his mind easily grasped the general, as well as the specific, advantages and drawbacks of the equipment that fell within his purview. He lacked formal technical training, however, and neither knew nor understood the subtle nuances of dynamic equilibrium assessment. When briefed on the design modifications by Rafi Schwartz, he had no way of knowing that the escape chamber with its specialized gear would impact on the balance of the entire vessel. He now stood before a foreigner whom he knew was telling the truth. But that truth rent a gash in the invincibility of the Israeli Security Service, and was a source of profound embarrassment for its go-between — himself.

He stood nonplused for a few moments, then dropped his brazen stance and asked seriously, "What, exactly, is wrong with our design?"

The British officer appreciated being consulted, rather than dictated to, by the Israeli. Weatherby began to analyze the design more carefully, stopping to jot down some calculations. As he worked, he engaged his Israeli counterpart. "Let me explain the problem to you, Admiral. The hull of any surface ship displaces a specific volume of water. We have Archimedes to thank for quantifying that physical phenomenon for us. That volume, when applied to the size of the ship, is measured in tons of water. But what is actually more critical is the volume of air that is displaced. Air means buoyancy. The ship is constructed of steel and other materials that are heavier than water. The buoyancy is what keeps the thing afloat.

"Of course, the ship is designed to carry a load. That load — whether freight or passengers — adds weight and displaces air space in the hull, thereby reducing buoyancy. Thus, a loaded ship will draw deeper in the water. Theoretically, a ship can be loaded until the side of the hull remains just above the waterline, but overloading beyond the point of minimum certified freeboard would be a harbinger of disaster. The upshot is this: a ship can run empty, or carry a load triple or more of the ship's own weight. Is this clear?"

Benun did not relish being spoken to like a schoolboy, but he was reluctant to offend Weatherby, who had shifted into a very useful instructional mode. "Yes, perfectly clear. Carry on."

"Now, in addition to the weight versus buoyancy issue, we have an issue of stability. For several thousand years, mankind has known that the modified flat-bottom or V-hull model is hydrodynamically stable. That is, it requires a force to cause a ship to list sideways, to port or starboard. Remove the lateral force, and the boat will tend to right itself. This remains true as long as the Center of Gravity (CG) remains low. If the CG is too high in the vessel, and the vessel lists to the extent that the force vector of the CG is laterally shifted beyond a point of no return, the boat will obviously capsize. In a cargo ship, the CG is relatively easy to position: by placing the heaviest loads at the bottom of the holds, and by making sure that the cargo is not loaded in such a way that the CG force vector would not be dangerously shifted under severe weather conditions.

"We see, then, that these two factors are independent of each other. In theory, we can have a perfectly stable boat that will immediately sink. If we fill the bottom of the hold with lead until the sides of the hull draw below the water line, that's the same as saying that the buoyancy of air displacement falls below the weight of the ship.

"We can also have a ship that has an overwhelming proportion of buoyancy in relationship to its material weight, yet it, too, will surely sink. This would be in a case where nothing at all is placed in the holds: all the weight is piled high on the upper deck, raising the CG to a point that challenges the hydrodynamic stability of the hull. One slight lateral shift, and the boat goes over.

"However, even in this scenario there is one redeeming factor. That is, although the extra-high weight will have a tendency to raise the CG due to its physical location on the ship, the additional weight will also displace buoyancy and cause the ship to draw deeper in the water.

"Our sub, when on the surface, has the dynamics of any surface vessel. At the same time, it must be designed to abide by the rules of submarine dynamics, which has some characteristics that closely resemble those of a spacecraft. Unlike a surface ship, when a submarine is submerged there is very little latitude in total material weight. The buoyancy must closely match this weight, so that the sub will neither rise to the surface nor sink to the bottom. Descension and ascension are controlled by 'flying' the submarine by its fore and aft diving planes. So the first principle is that the ballast tanks are filled to exactly balance the weight of the boat against its buoyancy when the ballast contains only air.

"The second principle is that there must be dynamic stability by weight distribution of the entire vessel. Whereas, on a surface vessel, the CG is much less critical as long as the hull has sufficient buoyancy, in a sub the CG plays a much more critical role, despite the fact that the buoyancy is perfectly balanced. A surface ship, as I pointed out, has a redeeming feature in its stability, even if loaded high. That is, the added weight will sink the hull lower into the water, to some extent mitigating the impact of the elevated CG.

"But in a submarine, these circumstances don't exist. As in a spaceship, there is no force from below that counters even the slightest lateral force from tipping the vessel. Weights cannot be added to strategic locations to balance the CG, for, as mentioned, the total weight is very specific. Therefore, when we design a sub, we take into consideration every weight variable — the engine, the batteries, the torpedoes, the compressed air tanks, the fuel tanks, the fresh water tanks, the movement of crew throughout the vessel — and then we plot a polygonal graph which represents a lateral view of the sub. The CG force vector must remain inside the polygon or dynamic stability is lost, and the sub will go down. We design the sub with fore and aft ballast tanks to keep the CG within the polygon."

Weatherby paused to take a puff. Shoving the cigar to a corner of his mouth, he added, "As a matter of fact, the CG must be plotted two dimensionally. Many a sub has gone down because it became too nose-heavy or tail-heavy.

"The specific problem with the design in your blueprints is this." Weatherby pointed to a line, which split the top third of the sub's hull and denoted a compartment, anterior to the sail.

"This escape chamber is about two meters high and about sixteen meters long. I have calculated that the added weight, when flooded for underwater exit — although seemingly minimal — and the position of that weight, puts the CG force vector outside of the theoretic polygon. Even the most drastic weight redistribution by adjusting ballast will not safely relocate the CG within the polygon." He fixed his eyes on the Admiral. "I suppose you do intend to use the thing to send out men?"

"Of course," Benun said. "Why else would we need it?"

Weatherby's gaze grew stern. "Remove the buoyancy of air filling that compartment and the resulting top-heaviness, and your sub will just roll over and sink. A sub is not a jet fighter with the pilot tightly strapped in, nor a spacecraft devoid of gravity, where there is no upside-down or right-side-up. An upside-down sub is a sub that is totally out of control — and one that will go straight to the bottom."

Benun was convinced. He couldn't fathom how Israel's finest had come up with such a reckless design. Nonetheless, he had a great desire to see the project to fruition. Swallowing his pride, he asked Captain Weatherby, "How would you suggest a way that we might accomplish our requirements and still ensure the stability that you say is lacking in this design?"

Weatherby brushed away the remnant of cigar ash on Benun's blueprint and, pencil in hand, began marking the blueprint. Occasionally he would take out a thick reference book, then step over to the adding machine and quickly punch in some numbers. Returning to the drafting table, he leaned over to alter a line segment only slightly larger than a speck on the large sheet in front of him. The two men pored over that table for six hours.

"Here we have it," Weatherby said at last, triumph in his tone. This design allows for your escape port, albeit less than half the size, and the perfect balance of the boat." He went on to describe the technical changes that made all of this possible. "We can't do anything with the ballast tanks; may as well build a new sub. The hatch will have to be moved ten meters toward the bow. The hydraulic pumps will have to be moved to the lower deck and we'll need forty-four extra meters of piping, which we could run along the starboard tubing feed. The chamber must be reduced to five meters in length. You will only be able to exit ten men at a time, but that's the best I can do."

The explanation expanded to consume three quarters of an hour, before Benun interrupted.

"Captain, I believe you, but I don't think it's necessary to go into all the details with me. Let me send a copy of this design to headquarters in Israel, and I am quite certain it will be approved."

Benun stood with Weatherby by the huge blueprint machine as it noisily rattled off an exact duplicate of the British engineer's new design. Then Benun asked for a second copy. "I'll take the entire blueprint back with me. In the meantime, I'd like to send just the section showing the area of modification from our embassy, by diplomatic facsimile."

On the following day, having faxed the revised portion of the blueprint to Rafi Schwartz at GSS HQ, Admiral Ozer Benun was about to exit the Israeli embassy in London when he was paged to the front desk. Benun picked up a phone.

"This is Schwartz," came the familiar voice. "Call me back on a secure wire." The connection was broken before the Admiral could respond. Ten minutes later, Benun was in a special office next to the ambassador's residence, at one end of a diplomatic-encoded line to Israel. The ambassador himself had dialed a long series of numbers to establish the necessary connection. He passed the handset to the

Admiral and exited the room. Benun, in turn, entered his own long series of numbers on the keypad, and Rafi Schwartz came to life on the other end.

"Benun, we will go with the original design. You had no authority to listen to an alternative."

"But...."

"No buts, Admiral. That's an order."

"Are you saying that Weatherby is lying about the flaw in your design? Why? You'll have every chance to review both his design and the completed job. What motive could he possibly have?"

"I'm not saying he has any bad motive. From the perspective of his training and knowledge of sub design, he is probably completely sincere. But our engineers have spent months working out this design, and we need it executed exactly the way it appears on the blueprint. That," Colonel Schwartz repeated emphatically, "is an order."

The Admiral exploded. "You don't seem to care about your nation's men or resources! You won't even submit the newer design for review. Are you a submarine engineer? You're a spook, a man of stealth. What do you know about making a machine work? Less than I do, that's certain. Weatherby is serious about your flawed vessel. It's a death ship, which I cannot allow to be commissioned in my Navy."

Schwartz was silent for a long moment. There were things, many things, that even Benun was not permitted to know. Gently, he said, "Mr. Benun, we can't discuss this now. I'll speak to you when you return. Tell the British to await further instructions before beginning the work."

Within three days, Benun flew back and forth from Israel. He entered Weatherby's office and said, "Captain, I thank you for your concern and for all the effort you put in. But the design must be exactly as we specified originally."

"Will you sign a disclaimer? I won't authorize the job until you do so."

Benun took a pen from his pocket.

January 10, 1968, Portsmouth, England:

The newly-constructed Israeli submarine, renamed *Davar*, set sail with seventy men aboard. Three women stood on the dock as the ribbon was cut and the slender boat steamed past the Isle of Wright toward the English Channel. The previous evening, their husbands, Eli Kedem, Shefi Mordechai and Alon Barnash, had called the office of Rabbi Karlin in Bnei Braq to complete a procedure they had launched at the behest of another member of the outfit, Benny Harkesef. The rabbi could distinguish the sniffles of weeping men on the other end of the line: they had just authorized a proxy to divorce their wives.

Now those same three brave men, standing on the deck of the departing sub, again broke into uncontrollable sobs as they waved good bye to their smiling (soon to be ex-)wives, who were waving back from the shore.

Thirty hours later, the sub — having run five hundred kilometers into the Atlantic on its maiden voyage — submerged for the first time. Just below the surface, the nose of the sub surged down. Fore and aft diving planes were immediately adjusted to compensate for the slight bow-heaviness created by the added buoyancy of the vacant escape chamber. Once the sub was leveled, traveling at ten knots to maintain stability, the valve on the escape chamber was opened and the huge cylinder partially flooded with twenty tons of water, neutralizing its buoyant effect and allowing the sub to level off without having to pitch the diving planes. Now the sub could safely slow down or even stop underwater without rolling or flipping over.

"Battle stations! Everyone man your battle station," came the captain's voice over the PA system. "Load torpedoes into all tubes and charge tubes for launch."

The men aboard had been thoroughly trained for this *exercise*. "Fire, torpedo one. Fire two. Fire three." All eight fore and aft torpedoes were fired. Again came the command, "Load torpedoes into all tubes and charge for launch." Again all of the torpedoes were fired. After the third cycle, there were no more torpedoes left to launch. All twenty-four one-ton guided-bombs had hit the target perfectly, and detonated.

The target was the ocean floor two thousand meters below.

Twenty-four tons is a lot of weight to lose all at once, especially in a sub whose initial design balance has been thrown off by major retrofitting. For now, blowing out half the water sitting in the modified section seemed to be the most prudent move.

Three hours later, the lights of a cargo ship three hundred kilometers off the coast of Portugal became visible over the horizon. The prearranged meeting took place in a spot that was off the conventional shipping lanes, and lasted only forty-five minutes. Twenty-five crates, about eight meters long and seventy-four centimeters square — built to just fit through the main hatch of the sub — were lowered by crane from the surface ship down to the torpedo rooms. The crates were marked in English and Hebrew: DANGER LIVE TORPEDOES. The sub then returned to the stealth of the black waters below. Six hours later, the sub came to rest on a sand bar which rose up from the ocean floor to a depth of twenty meters below the surface.

In the meantime, the contents of the crates were carefully unloaded in the previously emptied interior of the sub. The crates marked with an Aleph were opened first. Inside were twenty six-millimeter-thick steel cylinders, each forty-six centimeters in diameter and ninety-four centimeters long. Each cylinder was rabbeted around the inside edge at one end, and on the outside by the exact same three mm by three mm groove. The cylinders were designed to be connected. Filling the entire cylinder, except for the exposed lip of the rabbeted ends, was solid lead. Indeed, each section weighed over seventeen hundred kilos.

Packed carefully inside each crate, was also a connecting-boss, a five-meter-long piece of steel which resembled a modified "I" beam. The modification had been made to the top horizontal flange, which now curved slightly concave to flush fit an 8.5-meter-diameter tube — the submarine's hull. The other horizontal flange was more steeply concave to fit a forty-six-centimeter-diameter tube — the lead-filled cylinders. The flanges were fifteen centimeters wide, connected by a channel sixty centimeters wide and 2.5 cm thick. One of the crates contained the structure's fore and aft caps. The fore cap resembled a torpedo head, the aft cap, a conical structure tapering down to a point.

Twenty men donned their diving suits and tanks, hauling along the parts of their apparatus that required assembly. These were six common engine lifts, found in any mechanic's shop. In addition, they carried with them underwater welding equipment and a number of twenty millimeter ratchet handles, each fitted with a five-centimeter socket. They climbed through the hatch leading to the escape chamber and sealed the hatch behind them. A minute later, after all regulators were in place, torrents of water began to rush in. Ten minutes later, the tank was full: one hundred fifty tons of water.

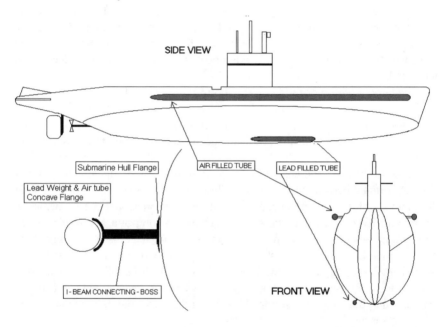

The frogman closest to the escape hatch spun the locking wheel, and the round door came open. The twenty men climbed out and banged twice on the hull near the forward torpedo tubes. Inside the sub, personnel were busy filling the torpedo tubes with items they were clearly never designed to hold. The equipment they inserted had, however, been designed to fit and maneuver through those tubes. Turbulent bubble streams emanated from the tubes, and the equipment was quickly spit out onto the soft ocean floor. The I-beam connecting-bosses came first. Behind them came the cylindrical lead-filled sections, whose exact fit through the tubes matched that of a real torpedo and served to push the connecting-bosses ahead.

Four well-trained frogmen carried a section of connecting-boss. Using tape measures, they found the exact predesignated location on the bottom/side of the hull, and fitted the slightly concave flange against the hull. Two other divers began spot-welding the boss against the hull. The next section of connecting-boss was lined up behind the first and welded in place. Next, a lead-filled cylinder section was rolled alongside of the hull, just below the connecting-boss. It was lifted into place with the engine hoist until it nestled securely in the concave flange of the I-beam, now firmly attached to the sub's hull. Four pre-drilled and tapped holes were lined up with corresponding holes on the flange. Another frogman, with a net full of galvanized stove bolts and a huge ratchet, quickly tightened the unwieldy piece in place.

The next section was lifted so that the interior and exterior rabbeted grooves were aligned, pressed against each other, and mated in place. All the sections were constructed in this way on both sides of the hull's bottom. Five hours after the operation had started, the last tail cone was seated and locked into place.

The craft now took on the weird appearance of a submarine with helicopter landing rails. But these ten-meter rails added close to 34 tons of weight to a point just even with the bottom of the hull. After finishing their work, the divers gathered up the engine lifts and bound them tightly to the deck. The rest of the equipment, which wasn't as bulky, was brought back into the escape chamber with the divers. Compressed air entered the chamber, forcing out the water through the opened valve until hardly a drop remained behind. The divers rejoined their colleagues below.

Ten hours later, the sun had set above. The captain pumped compressed air into the ballast tanks and the sub began very slowly to rise. Even with all the water blown out of its tanks, and the additional buoyancy of the air-filled escape chamber, the newly added weight extended the time it normally took for a sub to surface. Using the engine lifts, in conjunction with other hoisting equipment that all subs must carry, the work of fabricating the complementary buoyancy began, by dint of adding air tubing above. When the radar room confirmed that there were no vessels within view above the horizon, and no aircraft approaching, the crew on deck began welding the connecting-bosses in place. Along the port and starboard hull, one meter below the water line, they worked to set sixty-five meters of the sixty-centimeter supports in position. The engineers had calculated that it would take that length of buoyant, air-filled tubing, close to the top of the vessel, to counter the weight of the lead at the bottom. The net effect was to lower the CG by twenty-eight centimeters. Not much, considering the overall size of the vessel — but enough to restore it to within the critical polygon of dynamic stability when the escape chamber was flooded.

This job would take much longer since all connections were done by welding; there were no pre-tapped bolt threads. In addition, the joints between the sections had to be welded airtight. The work proceeded only at night, with the sub submerged out of sight during the day. It was impossible for arc welding to be concealed very well at night, but at least passing planes would not have the opportunity to take a critical look at what was going on below. During the three nights that most of the crew labored to finish the work, twice they received the signal from the radar operator to turn off the welding equipment. Each time, a plane approached overhead and flew safely by.

When the work was done, a pressure gauge was screwed into a tapped hole and air pumped in under pressure. The port-side air-ballast tube was filled with three hundred psi of air — over twenty atmospheres. The gauge needle was dead still: a perfect seal. The air pressure was reduced to one hundred fifty psi so that when the submarine submerged to normal cruising depth, the air ballast tubes would be under reduced ambient water pressure. Next, the starboard tube was filled. At two hundred twenty-four psi, a stream of bubbles could be seen rising to the surface. The hole, no larger than a pencil lead, was twenty-two meters from the tail-end of the tube. The Israelis were prepared for all eventualities. The smallest operator in the mission was a twenty-three-year old kibbutznik. As brilliant as were all aboard the mission, Amos Karmel was not nicknamed Gutzi for nothing. He was one hundred forty-five centimeters tall and, though in excellent physical condition, wore a size thirty-three Cadet suit. Gutzi entered the tube and crawled the twenty-two meters, acetylene torch in hand, until he heard the banging above him. He couldn't actually see the hole; it didn't take a straight path through the slightly incomplete weld. One man on the outside tried to blow some air inside by cupping a hand around the air nozzle on the site of the exterior puncture. Gutzi could see some bubbles coming through, but could not pinpoint the hole's precise location. He took out his brazing rod and slapped a five-centimeter square area of weld around the spot.

Twenty minutes later, the rear cap was resealed, and the pressure test began anew. This time, when the gauge reached two hundred eighty-five pounds, the needle started to fall. It came back to two hundred fifty — and stopped. No leakage could be detected from the outside. The crew spent two hours trying to find the source of the problem, but came up empty. Three hundred psi were pumped into the tube. The men carefully examined it, all sixty-five meters. Nothing.

"I have no time for this," Shefi Mordechai told Gutzi Karmel impatiently. "Push it up to four hundred psi!" he yelled from down the gangway.

"I hope it won't explode."

"Don't worry. It will surely blow out at a joint. Make sure you're not standing next to any joints."

As the air filled, a small stream of bubbles became apparent at a point along the flange weld. The spot was marked by crayon, the tube cap unsealed, and Gutzi Karmel crawled his way in — this time only eleven meters — to fix the hole.

The work was complete. The *Davar* was now perfectly balanced.

Chapter 15

For a few minutes after his father finished speaking, Moshe sat awestruck.

"An amazing story, isn't it?" Abdallah asked.

Moshe turned to his father and said, "I'm overwhelmed not just by the boldness, but even more by the brilliance of the plan. Answer me this, Dad, what happened to the sub in the end? Where is it now?"

"I can't say for sure. I was among the first to be let off. But Rafi — Colonel Schwartz, that is — had planned to scuttle the *Davar* in the Mediterranean along its original route, somewhere between Crete and Israel. Sinking it in twenty-eight hundred meters of water would make the sub break up upon hitting the ocean floor. Schwartz was quite certain that, by luck or advancing technology, the vessel would eventually be found. If that occurred before the completion of the operation, he wanted no suspicions aroused. Since it would be broken into pieces, the long-term effects of the sea water and ocean currents would ensure that no crew remains would be expected to be recovered."

"But, Dad, what if they had found the wreck shortly after it was scuttled?"

Abdallah shrugged. "Rafi did the best he could...." He frowned, struck by a thought. "Aha! Now I understand."

"What's that, Dad? What just dawned on you?"

"About a year after I returned to Egypt, I read in the papers that our sub's emergency buoy washed up on the coast of Gaza. The Egyptian Navy took credit for sinking it. This happened at about the time the last of the personnel on board should have been put ashore; I'm quite certain the last stop was Europe. I'll bet Rafi left instructions that the buoy be released off the coast of Egypt to mislead those searching for the sub." He turned to his son, eyes sparkling. "Moshe, it's been twenty-four years and they still haven't found it. The technology is there — look how they located the Titanic back in '85. I wouldn't be surprised if Rafi planted other physical evidence making the sinking of the sub appear like an accident." He shook his head in admiration. "That Rafi doesn't cease to amaze me. Maybe he isn't just a man!"

Moshe was a mature young man possessing all his father's acting ability, along with his intelligence. To his mother and grandmother, nothing had changed in the odd relationship between the Moslem father and Jewish son. He even got a job in his father's division at the dam, where his talents quickly became apparent. Before long, he was given charge of the computer control system. Fatima began to notice that her husband, and the son whom none of the Arab coworkers realized practiced Judaism (with his father's help, Mustafa had negotiated a four-day-a-week contract), stayed out together at least once a week.

"Abdallah, you haven't been out to the club with your buddies this much since Mustafa was a young boy," Fatima remarked to him one day.

"That's right, my dearest. But now that he's a big boy, I can take him along with me. So don't feel so bad."

Abdallah took Moshe to his cave and explained the entire setup. The first time they crawled down through the tunnel to the device, Moshe noted the ancient circuits controlling it.

"Dad, would you let me modernize this system? I could set this up so that the entire thing could be controlled via digital signal from something like a TV remote, in your pocket."

Abdallah beamed. "That's why I brought you here, son."

Over the next year, Moshe spent all his free time designing an A-D converter, which he hooked up to a PC. This not only replaced all the crude functions of the original timing and ignition circuits, but added many more modifiable options and remote monitoring capabilities. He was able to purchase most of the components he needed from a large electronics supply house in Cairo. A few he smuggled in when returning from his infrequent visits to Israel.

In March of 1994, while in the cave finishing up the digital transceiver needed to process the signals from the remote controller, Moshe announced, "Dad, as you know, I came back from Israel this time with the VLSI chip that I just soldered into the computer here. But I also accomplished something else before I left Jerusalem."

"What's that, son?"

"I'm engaged!"

Abdallah threw his arms around his son. "Mazal Tov!"

"Thanks. Cheryl's a nice girl. You'll like her."

"I'm certain of that, Moshe. Where are you going to live?"

"Well, that may be a problem. But maybe not. My work here is finished. All the tests show the system will work like a champ. I hope we'll never know. I might just have to say goodbye to you and Mom. I'm hoping that within the next few years I'll be able to advance this system so you can return to Israel. We'll be able to maintain full control from there. But the only way I see a possibility of that happening, is by telephony or satellite communication."

Abdallah shook his head. "I don't know, Moshe. Even the best electronic system can go awry. My life has already been dedicated to this work. I'm not going to take the slightest chance of jeopardizing the mission." He grinned, adding, "Besides, I really like your mother. I really believe she's a great lady, even though I've been scamming her for twenty-six years."

"Dad, don't you think you can tell her everything by now? She wouldn't turn you in."

"No, she wouldn't. But Moshe, one of the most important principles of the undercover trade, is never to reveal anything without a good reason. When I was prepared to marry her, I never dreamed I would have a son like you. I truly believe the Hand of God was in everything that happened. But I also believe that I must stick to my training and the mission, with cold exactitude."

"But Dad, I was not part of the plan," Moshe argued. "I was an accident."

"How dare you say that? You, a *Charedi Jew!*"

"I didn't mean it in that way. Of course, it was providential. I just meant that you never thought you would have a son, whom you could entrust with the secret, who would have the talents and knowledge to participate in the project."

His father cupped his chin reflectively in the palm of his hands. "You're right, and you're wrong. The Mossad — Rafi Schwartz, that is — thought of everything.... Well, almost everything. If I could show you my notes (but of course, I had to destroy them), you would have seen that a component of this mission, for those to whom it was applicable, was to pass it along to a worthy and qualified successor. I lucked out in having both a qualified and a worthy son."

"Not lucked out, Dad. You just got through saying it was the Will of God." The pair broke into laughter.

Suddenly, they heard the rocks at the cave's mouth being hurriedly shoved aside. Before they had time to react, two men jumped down, one wielding a gun. The unarmed man was well known to Ibn Gash senior and junior. He was Balbek, head turbine engineer of the dam's power plant.

Balbek looked around with avid curiosity. "Well, Abdallah, what do you have here? A hideout of sorts?" He pointed. "What's this, an old compressor? Tell me, what do you do here? Been digging for something?" The curiosity was quickly replaced by cold suspicion.

"Balbek, how did you find us here?" Abdallah feigned trepidation. "Tell that man to put down his gun — someone could get hurt!"

"I don't think that would be too wise... unless of course, you have a reasonable explanation for all this. I've been following you for the past month. Every time, you just seemed to disappear into the hills. Well, last week, I came very close to interrupting your party here, but I had a feeling that something sinister might be going on. I didn't want to take any chances." Balbek gloated. "It looks like I was right, hey?"

Mustafa interjected, "Look here, Balbek, that's ridiculous. If you had such thoughts, why didn't you just report them to the police?"

"I didn't report them because your father has been working here for so long that I would have been laughed away. No, I had to discover for myself what was going on. Now — talk!" Balbek aimed his flashlight at his partner's pistol, then swung it back to spotlight his captives. "What is going on?"

Abdallah's demeanor was calm as he said, "You know how dedicated I am to the dam. About twelve years ago, before you came to work here, I suggested that the dam authority build a monitoring station just outside the immediate vicinity of the dam. They didn't listen to me, didn't consider it worth the costs. So I built it on my own."

The turbine engineer exploded in a derisive snort. "Balbek is not so stupid! You expect me to believe that? I'll bet you've uncovered some antiquities, thought you could turn a handsome profit. That's it, hey? Well, Balbek wouldn't want the genius Abdallah to become too greedy."

"No, Balbek," Abdallah said quietly. "There are no antiquities under the ground here. But you're an electrician."

"An engineer also!" yelled Balbek.

"Yes, that's what I meant. I just meant that you don't know geology and seismology. Those are my specialties. I have reason to believe that there are geological conditions — conditions which the sixties technology couldn't pick up — which severely endanger the stability of the dam. For my own sake, just as a hobby, I put together this monitoring station so that I could warn all the skeptics if and when things ever deteriorate. Come on over here." Abdallah gestured at the PC on the other side of the cave, which actually was the central brain of the triggering system.

Balbek glanced at his colleague, still pointing his Glock-17 at the two secret Jews. Then, blustering, he moved closer to Abdallah and demanded that he switch on the computer. Abdallah seated himself on a chair directly in front of the console, and offered Balbek a crate beside him. Although each man had a flashlight, the surrounding cave was very dark. The man with the gun was approaching the computer when he suddenly shouted, "Balbek, there's a mine shaft here!" He aimed his flashlight down the shaft, but couldn't see to the bottom. "Balbek, I wouldn't trust these guys. This is too fishy. I think we're sitting on a gold mine."

Wheeling around, the gunman ordered Moshe to go over to where his father was sitting. But before Balbek could rise from his crate, Abdallah had him in a chokehold from behind. It was a move he knew well.

"Put down your gun, or I'll break Balbek's neck!" yelled Abdallah.

The armed interloper directed his beam toward the two men on the ground next to the computer. He could see Balbek's head jerk forward a few centimeters. Moshe instantly switched off his flashlight and scooted away. The gunman lost him in the darkness.

"Never! You let him go, or I'll kill your son."

It was a standoff. The gunman scanned the chamber for two seconds, then aimed his light at Balbek, still firmly ensconced in a chokehold, before scanning again. Abdallah's old Helwan 9mm was hidden in a cabinet near the entrance. Moshe knew where it was. Abdallah couldn't move from his position; he prayed that Moshe would be able to get to the weapon. Time passed; it felt like hours. Balbek was now only semiconscious, and incapable of trying to make a sudden move. The gunman took Abdallah at his word about being prepared to kill Balbek if he used his gun. None of the three knew Moshe's exact whereabouts in the cave. After what seemed an eternity, the gunman backed off toward the cave's entrance.

Abdallah's mind spun fruitlessly. There was a very real danger that the other might get out and notify the authorities, but there was little that Abdallah could do to stop him. He and the gunman had their flashlights trained on one another. The gunman was on the steep slope now, walking backwards.

Just as the gunman was about to pop his head up through the opening, there was a loud crack, a tremendous flash of light, and a scream from the cave entrance. Abdallah couldn't imagine what had happened, but his beam caught the violent fall of the gunman back to the cave floor, his Glock clattering from his hand. With ninety kilos of flesh still leaning against his chest, Abdallah watched as Moshe ran over and picked up the gun.

"Wow!" Moshe shouted. "It worked!"

"What worked?" asked the stunned father.

"My TASER." Moshe grinned sheepishly. "I forgot — you wouldn't know about that. I used to come here a lot without you. I have this cave completely wired up."

"What are you talking about, Moshe?"

Moshe spread his arms. "Buried just behind a thin layer of dirt, this room is a veritable capacitor. While I was building your remote controller to blow up the dam, I also built another, simpler one, which uses an infrared signal that can set off a 300,000-volt charge in any of six locations. I've got one by the entrance to the shaft, one by the computer station.... You get the picture." He nodded at the prone figure of the gunman. "That jerk was standing, at first, just where he was safe. But once I saw him backing toward the entrance, I knew I had him." The grin made another appearance. "I'll bet you were sweating bullets."

Abdallah shuddered. "You have that right."

"The TASER could have zapped him from up to one meter, but when I pushed the button on the remote I always keep in my pocket, his head was practically touching it."

Standing up and stretching his cramped limbs, Abdallah asked, "How come you never told me about this?"

"Hey, Dad, that's a funny question coming from you. You had me in the dark about yourself for twenty-one years. I'm entitled to pull one on you, no?"

Abdallah felt like laughing, but he couldn't afford the luxury just then. He had to decide what to do with the two intruders. Though he was pretty certain that no one else was privy to Balbek's suspicions — the engineer's greed would have seen to that — he was nonetheless in the grip of a quandary.

He peered at the gunman. "Moshe, how powerful was the shock? Is he dead?"

"You know, Dad, I'm really not sure. I know electronics, but little about physiology. The power on that zap was about nine milliamps. What are we going to do with these guys?"

"Well, I spent ten years of my life digging deep holes in the ground. I suppose I'll have to get out my shovel again." With that, Abdallah wound his right arm tightly around the engineer's neck and pressed as hard as he could with his left forearm against the back of Balbek's head. There was a resounding pop as Balbek's neck was broken. The carcass slumped to the floor. Abdallah ran over to the gunman, whom he had never seen before, and felt his pulse. He was alive.

"Moshe, I'll give you the honors."

Moshe still holding the gun, began to visibly tremble. "Look, Dad, I'm a *Yeshiva Bachur* (rabbinical student). You're the trained killer."

His father studied him for a long moment before saying, with a shrug, "Okay, you win. But I hope you won't be so soft if my life were endangered."

"Don't worry, Dad. If I had to, I could pull the trigger." Moshe spread his hands. "But you can have the honors this time."

Abdallah took the gun from his son, put the barrel to the gunman's head, and pulled the trigger. *Click.* The Glock decocked. Abdallah pressed the magazine release with his right thumb. A full magazine of seventeen nine-millimeter rounds dropped into his left hand.

"Moshe, if you ever carry a Glock, do me a favor. Don't keep it unchambered."

"But, Dad, the Israeli military always carry their Glocks unchambered. They're trained to cycle the slide as they pull the gun from the holster."

"I guess that's a good policy for dummies, so they shouldn't shoot off a foot. I think you're pretty smart. You carry chambered."

"Yes, sir."

Abdallah replaced the magazine and chambered a round. On the ground, the gunman groaned and began to come around. Moshe told his father to wait. The man sat up, completely disoriented.

"What's your name?" Abdallah demanded.

The man stared back into the flashlight shining on his face with a dull expression. He then started to mumble some incomprehensible words.

"Dad, it looks as though his brain is fried. I know that even the Israeli police stun guns don't exceed 200,000 volts. I wasn't too concerned about the consequences when I fashioned this one. I think he may not fully recover."

"On the other hand, maybe he will. Let's take him out of the cave."

With much prodding, they finally got the man out of the cave. They found a Volkswagen Jetta parked near the road two hundred meters away. Moshe returned to the cave and found the keys in Balbek's pocket.

"What took you so long?" asked the anxious father, when Moshe reappeared fifteen minutes later.

"I pulled Balbek's carcass out of the cave."

"What for? I thought we'd find him a nice final resting place somewhere under his beloved dam."

"Dad, I thought of an idea. I read a lot of Tom Clancy."

Abdallah cuffed his son playfully on the arm. "Hey, boy, what are you looking at fiction for? You have an old man to ask about these things."

Moshe refused to be distracted. Eagerly, he said, "Dad, what do you think would happen if our friend here, with the scrambled brain, drove the Volkswagen?"

"He couldn't drive a car straight for fifty meters."

"Exactly."

"Of course," Abdallah said thoughtfully. "Sounds good to me. Bring the body and let's go."

The next evening, as they were lingering over dessert, Fatima said, "Abdallah, you knew Anwar Balbek, didn't you?"

"Of course. He worked down by the turbines. This is good pudding, Fatima."

"Did you know his cousin, Fuwad Jawash?"

"No, can't say that I was ever introduced to him."

"I just heard on the news that they were both killed in an auto accident."

Abdallah paused with his spoon halfway to his mouth. "Gee, that's too bad. Was anyone hurt in the other car?"

"It wasn't a collision. Their car went out of control on a dirt road off of Silwan. It went over the edge of the road, and crashed into the lake seventy meters below."

"How tragic."

"You don't sound too sympathetic."

"Fatima, my dear, Balbek wasn't one of my friends, and I didn't even know his cousin."

"I understand." She pouted. "Still, you could be a bit more sympathetic; they both left families. The police couldn't find out what they were doing over there."

"Look, Fatima. I know the region well. There's nothing over there. Maybe they were up to no good." He sighed theatrically. "But I'm used to your cushy feelings. It must be the Jewish blood that flows in your veins."

"Abdallah!" screamed the frazzled wife. "You always say that!"

"I'm sorry, my dear. I still love you."

Chapter 16

Moshe finished up the last details before his marriage. He had computerized the system on which his father had been working for twenty-five years. Now he trained his father in its use and modification. The computer savvy son was surprised at the older man's adeptness at grasping the new concepts of the digital era. His fiancé was an American Syrian who had been studying in a girl's seminary in Israel. Moshe was married in Long Branch, New Jersey, and found a high-paying computer job in Minneapolis, where the young couple settled.

Though Moshe had hoped there was some way Abdallah and Fatima could attend the wedding, Abdallah could not allow it, and Moshe understood. But now he had family in the U.S. With the help of the Shah's son, his seventy-five-year-old grandmother emigrated to America. Mrs. Baktari also chose to settle in Minneapolis, where she openly returned to Judaism. Moshe would visit his parents twice a year, but always alone. Thus, life continued for another seven years.

Turning on the radio to the 8:30 news on June 30, 2002, Moshe heard that Iran had attacked Israel with poison gas. He stiffened, as though shell-shocked. Then, coming to life again, he leaped convulsively at the phone. It was 2:35 a.m. in Aswan when the ringing of the phone woke his father.

"Hello.... Oh, Mustafa it's you." Abdallah shook his head to clear it. "What's going on?"

"Dad, it may be war. Turn on your radio. I'll catch the next flight to Cairo if you think you could use my help."

Instantly, Abdallah was fully awake. Crisply, he ordered, "Make arrangements, go to the airport, and wait. I'll call you on your cell phone within the hour."

Abdallah went into the dining room to listen to his Grundig short-wave. Quiet as he was, Fatima awoke and padded after him. As she had in the past, she watched her husband listen intently to a bewildering assortment of squawks and squeals issuing from the radio. Abdallah would listen for about thirty seconds to one frequency before tuning in to another. He did this several times, and then switched off the radio.

"Expecting a station to go on the air?" asked Fatima, startling Abdallah. He hadn't noticed her observing him.

"Why, yes, of course," he said easily. "I see your memory has held up pretty well over the past thirty years." Soberly, he added, "Fatima, that was Moshe on the phone. Our Moslem countries have made a surprise attack on Israel."

"Oh, no, not again! I thought we were at peace."

Abdallah walked to the window and looked out at the sleeping street. "We must stand up for our Palestinian brothers. The Israelis have violated every provision from the Oslo accords to the Wye accords of '98. Iran has shot off numerous poison gas missiles. Our nation has four hundred thousand troops moving toward El Arish right now. It seems that the leaders of twelve Moslem nations have determined that now is the time. It is do or die." He turned abruptly to face his wife, his expression grim. "Fatima, I'm deathly afraid. This time the Israelis may pull out all the stops. We're getting out. Moshe is on his way here now."

"If what you say is true, why on earth should he come here now?" In Fatima's face, fear battled with astonishment.

"There may be difficulties in our escape from the country. We're not young anymore; we may need our son to help us."

Slowly, Fatima said, "Abdallah, every time there is a crisis, you seem to fall to pieces. I sure hope this one is over soon, so that you will come back to your senses."

He smiled. "I have no argument with you there, my dear." He walked over to the sofa, sat down and patted the place next to his. Fatima took his cue and settled in, he continued, "Let's just try to stay calm. In another day or two, we will leave. Maybe we can reach the U.S. and settle there."

Fatima had thought herself beyond being surprised at anything her husband might say or do, but this took her aback. "Abdallah, I thought you were a patriotic Egyptian!"

"I am, my dear. I'm just not so sure there will be an Egypt left in a few days.... The Israelis are wily; we can't anticipate how they will react. Besides, can't I be a patriotic Egyptian in exile?"

"But —"

"Why are you complaining? You've wanted to be near your mother ever since she had that stroke two years ago. Mustafa and Cheryl have taken wonderful care of her. Now here's a chance for us to be there ourselves."

"Abdallah, you've been a thirty-three year enigma to me." In profound resignation, Fatima shook her head. "Will I ever understand you?"

"Maybe one day, my dear. Maybe.... But for now, I want you to pack up. Just the valuables and your essentials."

Abdallah had received the same signal that had come twenty-nine years before: FULL RED ALERT, proceed to detonate. Moshe had everything set up so that his father no longer had to make the trip out to the cave to trigger his system, but he did so anyway. He left the house at 4:45 a.m., calling Moshe on his cell phone.

When the call came, Moshe was at British Airways gate twenty-two at St. Paul-Minneapolis International. He had purchased a ticket for a direct flight to London leaving at 11:05 p.m. CDT. As the minutes ticked away he kept glancing nervously at his watch. The call came. One word was spoken. "Come!"

At 6:10 a.m. on July 1, 2002, Abdallah, sitting in front of his computer console in a cave about one kilometer from the Aswan High dam, keyed in the last digit of a ten digit code, held his breath and pushed the ENTER key. He had one window of <u>Windows 2000</u> opened to the seismographic program that Moshe had written. This program received digital information from sensors that the father and son had planted years before hundreds of meters below the earth. He watched as the screen indicated the sequential detonations of explosives, which were expanding the shaft leading from the limestone substrate to the bottom of Lake Nasser. After seventy-two seconds, the final and greatest blast sent a minor rumble up the shaft, six meters from where Abdallah was sitting. His computer showed that the explosives had functioned exactly as planned. There were now approximately 25,000 liters of water flowing down that shaft every second, filling the limestone caverns that sandwiched the sandstone substrata. As time went on, the granite — hard as it was — was being eroded still further by the torrential flow of silty water. The flow rate was actually increasing with time.

The main device was no longer set on the eighteen-hour timer. It was triggered, after being armed by code from his console, by a remote hand controller, no bigger than a car alarm remote that Abdallah kept in his pocket. That device had four keys which had to be pressed in sequence to trigger the bomb, and it had a digital radio signal range of three kilometers from the dam. Abdallah had built a signal booster, a significantly larger device, which he had kept hidden near his office at dam control. But on this occasion, he decided not to use it. He would be present at the dam, to personally witness the fruits of over thirty years of his labor.

He arrived at the dam at 7:00 a.m.

Faruk, his assistant of fourteen years in dam control, was avid with the day's news. "Abdallah, what do you think is going to happen? You've heard the news of course?"

Abdallah shook his head and said, "Faruk, my friend, I've decided to retire. Perhaps I'll travel and spend more time with Mustafa and his children in America."

"At a time like this?" Faruk almost howled in surprised disapproval. "There could be a big war soon, if the Americans fail to restrain our... our neighbors to the east."

"I'm not worried," Abdallah shrugged. "The Americans know how to handle the Israelis. I just hope our Arab brothers will show some restraint."

"What do you mean? Don't you consider the mistreatment the Palestinians have suffered for the past fifty-three years worth fighting for?"

"Sure, it's worth fighting for. But Faruk, you are a young man. You have a lot...." Abdallah patted his rotund partner on the belly as he said these words, "to live for. I, on the other hand, am almost old. I will turn sixty in four months. I've done my service for Egypt and for Allah. I just want to live out my last few years in peace, safety and enjoyment." He sat down before his computer console, prepared to begin the day's work.

Farouk followed him curiously. "Hey, Abdallah, you always evade the guys when they bug you about the rumor that Mustafa married a Jew. Tell me, is it true?"

"Faruk, why do you and your buddies always pry into my private affairs?" Abdallah hesitated. "I'll tell you the truth if you promise to keep it discreet."

"Of course, of course! Faruk Ilsamik is a man of his word."

"In that case, I'll tell you — but you must never reveal this to anyone. I know I can trust you.... Mustafa is a spy for our country in America. He has a top-secret job in the computer department of an American government agency, and transmits all the secrets back to Cairo."

Faruk's eyes almost popped out of his head.

Persuasively, Abdallah went on, "But you know how much those rotten Americans hate the Arab and Moslem peoples, don't you, Faruk? They are controlled by the Jews, and, to a lesser extent, by Christians."

"Yes, yes, of course," Faruk said stoutly.

"Well, no Moslem could ever get security clearance. So do you know what my brilliant Mustafa did?"

"What, Abdallah? Tell me. I beg of you, tell me!"

Abdallah narrowed his eyes. "You swear never to tell a soul?"

"Never!"

"Mustafa became a Jew himself. He is under deep cover!"

His gullible assistant slapped his brow in amazement. "Unbelievable! But, privately, does he keep our holy faith?"

Abdallah sighed as he answered, "Faruk, I'm afraid I failed in that respect. By the time my boy was fourteen, he'd become an infidel. How it pains a father when his son breaks with the faith of his ancestors!" Faruk nodded sympathetically and patted the lamenting father on the shoulder. Abdallah straightened. "But in all other respects, Mustafa is a wonderful, patriotic son. I just have to accept my lot. Where he failed in Islam, he is making up in other ways."

Faruk nodded in commiseration, then let his eyes rove over the console. They widened.

"Abdallah, look here!" Faruk pointed to the lake level indicator. It was dipping ever so slightly. "How do you explain that?"

Abdallah made a good show of studying the reading. "Well, it *is* very hot today." They both looked at the thermometer, which showed forty-three centigrade. "Perhaps there is just more evaporation than usual. Or maybe they're fooling with the water flow at the Sudan cataract."

"They can't do that without informing us."

"Ah, what do you want from those Abeed? They do it all the time."

"I don't remember them doing that." Faruk was growing confused, both by the lake level reading and by Abdallah's explanations.

Abdallah stood up. "All right, I'll look into the situation. But for now, Faruk, you're the boss. I have to go home now for a few hours."

"But — but —"

"I'll be back." Abdallah left the room and headed for home.

He parked his motorcycle and transferred himself to his jeep. It was already noon, and Aswan was stirring with the prospect of war. So far there were rumors — only rumors, as the government had imposed a news blackout — that the Israelis had already retaliated for the early-morning missile attack. Abdallah retrieved the ten fifty-liter gasoline tanks that he had kept in storage for more than a score of years, and filled them at the local gas station.

As the pump meter registered two hundred liters, he heard the attendant shout over the intercom, "Hey, mister, that's a lot of gas you're buying! There are four cars in line at your pump."

Abdallah yelled back, "I'm stocking up for the backup emergency generator at the Nasser Medical clinic — in case of war!"

"Okay, then," the attendant reluctantly nodded. "Just hurry it up."

Ten minutes later, he capped the last jerry-can and returned home. By 3:00 that afternoon, Fatima was all packed and ready to go. Abdallah told her to make sure to call him on his cell phone between six and seven, to let him know when supper would be ready. She gave him an odd look, but agreed to do as he'd asked.

Moshe had caught an Air Kuwait flight from London, and at that moment was flying over the Alps. Abdallah calculated that Moshe would land just in time to catch the 7:30 p.m. shuttle to Aswan, which landed at 8:50.

At 3:45 p.m., Abdallah was back at the dam. Faruk was frantic about the lake level decline.

"Don't worry about it. I placed a call to the interior ministry in Cairo. They have my cell phone number and will get back to me as soon as they find out what this is about."

At 6:18, Abdallah's cell phone rang. As he took it out of his pocket, he glanced at Faruk, who turned around and pricked up his ears.

"Yes? Yes. Okay.... All right," Abdallah said into the phone.

"Abdallah, have you gone crazy again?" Fatima asked at the other end. "I know you like stuffed leaves and rice — why do keep repeating that it's all right? What are you talking about?... What? The Sudanese are shunting water from the Nile? Who cares what the Sudanese are doing upstream?"

"That explains it," Abdallah said. "And what measures have been taken, sir?"

"Abdallah," Fatima cried, "you've gone insane again! Will you see a doctor? Right now, before we leave?"

"I see," said Abdallah, nodding into the phone. "You've contacted the Sudanese minister of natural resources. Aha — so they've shunted off forty-percent of the Nile to fill their reservoirs in anticipation of a serious war. Have you told them of the damage they're doing to us? Hmm? They say we have more than enough water in the lake?... Yes, I see. All right, by tomorrow morning the situation should be resolved. Good, very good. Good-bye."

He hung up on his distraught wife. "Well, Faruk," Abdallah told his nervous assistant, "I suppose you overheard what the minister had to say. It's those Sudanese. But he assures me that the situation ought to be resolved by tomorrow." He glanced at his watch. "I must be off now. I'll be back tomorrow, about 7:00 a.m."

"But Abdallah, there could be an emergency!" Faruk protested.

"You have my phone number," Abdallah, halfway out the door, called over his shoulder. "Just call!" He was gone.

At 9:00 p.m., Abdallah arrived at Aswan's twenty-first century improved airport terminal — by now, just about fit for the Wright brothers' plane. Moshe met him outside the gate carrying only two pieces of hand luggage and, without a word, followed him outside to the jeep. As they were riding home, Moshe opened his mouth for the first time.

"Smells like gas."

Abdallah switched on the dome light. "Turn around."

"Gee, Dad, that's a lot of gas. Going on a safari?"

"I'm afraid we might have to. I just heard an hour ago that all international flights leaving the country have been suspended. Some of my old pals from the sub have pulled the trigger. There's fireworks in the air — thermal and political."

Moshe frowned. "What are we going to do?"

"I anticipated the closure of the airport. But we're getting out. Do you remember three years ago, when you came for the summer, the resort we went to for a week at Quseir?"

"Of course. After I showed off my trophies, the marina people agreed to rent out their Sea Ray. I was up on skis at seventy-five km per hour." Moshe smiled, remembering. "That was some thrill."

"You've been skiing lately?"

"I was just out at Mille Lacs last Sunday. I can still do a double turnaround off a three-meter ramp. Not bad for an old man of thirty-two, eh? What do you say, Dad?"

"You had a good teacher," his father smiled. "Moshe, how would you like to go skiing tomorrow back at Quseir? I called to reserve that Sea Ray."

Moshe studied Abdallah's face for a trace of a smile that would tell him his father was kidding. He found none. "Dad, the world's in a real mess now. I really don't think this is the time for fun in the sun."

"You misunderstand me, son. This has become part of the plan. I reserved the boat in your name. You're going to drive there tonight with Mom, and check into the resort. I scouted out the place last time. There's a cove three kilometers south of the marina. Tonight, after you take Mom to the room, drive back to that cove — it's a good thing we have a 4WD — and unload all the gas cans. Early tomorrow, while Mom is still sleeping, go down to the marina and make sure you take that boat out before 7:30 a.m. The timing is crucial; I want you to have that boat in hand before the dam goes. Ride it down to the cove and load the gas cans on board. I'll meet you at the cove between 12:00 and 2:00 p.m."

"What about Mom?"

"She'll be with me."

"Sounds like we're going some distance."

"Yeah. Home."

Moshe's breath caught in his throat. "Israel? Dad, don't you think there will be a lot of naval activity in the Red Sea? The Gulf of Aqaba is only twenty kilometers wide. It'll be crawling with people who would love to shoot lots of little holes in us!"

All his father would say was, "Don't worry." With that, Moshe was forced to be content. To himself, however, he could not hide the stark fact that he *was* worried. More than worried — panic-stricken.

Back at the house, Fatima let loose on her husband.

"Abdallah! Of all the crazy times to go on vacation. There's a war going on!"

"Not officially. You haven't heard that on our news."

"Not Egyptian news — but every other international news in the world. Why, just yesterday you, yourself, told me frantically that we must get out of the country. Now we're going deep-sea fishing and you want to see Moshe water ski. You're crazy! I'm not going. If you refuse to fly out tonight, then we won't. I, for one, am staying right here at home."

"My dear, the government has temporarily suspended international flights. Now, just relax. We'll take a little holiday at the coast and hopefully, in two or three days, we'll be able to get a flight out. Moshe here will take you to Quseir now."

"Now! At 10:00 at night — whatever for? You've lost your mind." Fatima wrung her hands. "You just can't take the fear of war. It's always been your problem, Abdallah. You've completely lost it." She began to cry uncontrollably.

Moshe stepped up to his mother and put a reassuring arm around her shoulders. "Mom, please, take it easy. I'm going to take you to the resort now. You can sleep in the car. We'll get there about 2:00 a.m. Dad reserved a room already. Everything will be all right."

Fatima stopped weeping for a minute. Lifting red-rimmed eyes to her son, she demanded, "Moshe, now you've gone crazy, too?"

"No, Mom. I've just come from America, where I heard the real news. Things are really not as bad as you've heard on BBC. The British have a habit of exaggerating."

"Your Dad always told me they're dead accurate."

Moshe shrugged. "Where's your stuff? I'll take it out to the car."

At 5:00 a.m., Abdallah was on his PC in his empty house, monitoring the soaking geological conditions under the dam that were as yet unknown to anyone else. The seismograph started showing activity, with a reading of 1.2. The terrain below the dam was beginning to shift. Still, the two hundred meter deep pilings under the concrete frame of the dam were not in jeopardy. When the seismograph showed a tremor of 1.4, the phone rang. It was Faruk.

"Abdallah, I think you ought to get over here. There's some tremor activity in the region."

"What's the reading? Two — two and a half?"

"Oh, no. Nothing like that. Just the low ones. But it seems to be getting worse."

Abdallah switched from alarmed mode to annoyed. "You're bothering me at seven o'clock for such nonsense? Maybe you are in line for some R&R?"

"Please, Abdallah. I'm worried."

With a long-suffering sigh, Abdallah said grudgingly, "Okay, I'll be right over."

*   *   *

By 10:00 a.m. on July 2, 2002, the only people left alive in the city of Aswan were those who happened to be sleeping in their boats parked in the driveway. There were not many of those. A torrent of water swept down over the city, as it had on Pharaoh's chariots some three thousand three hundred years before. A hundred kilometers to the north, near the Gulf of Suez, fifty-nine-year-old Abdallah Ibn Gash was driving as fast as he could on a Suzuki GSX-1300R Hayabusa, toward the Red Sea resort city of Quseir.

*   *   *

Just after 7:00 a.m., exactly two hours before the citizenry of Egypt would lose control of its collective bladder, Moshe Mitzri handed a VISA card to a clerk at the Quseir marina.

The clerk handed the card right back. "We don't rent out the Sea Ray. Our staff members are the only ones who drive it."

"Don't you remember me? I'm Mustafa Ibn Gash. I think you'll find the boat was reserved in my name."

The clerk behind the counter looked more carefully at the insistent customer.

"Oh, yeah! You're the water-ski champion of Egypt. Sure, no problem." Hero-worship lit his features as he hurried to complete the necessary paperwork. "I watched you the last time you were here. You were great! He pointed the place where Moshe was to sign. "But please, have it back before dark, between 6:00 and 7:00 p.m."

Moshe paid three hundred dollars, in advance, to rent the fastest water craft commercially available in the Middle East. Cranked out at full throttle, the eleven meter Sea Ray Sundancer could do one hundred km/h. Of course, at that speed, its twin 7.4 liter engines would guzzle three liters of gas to travel one kilometer. But at a nice cruising clip of sixty km/h, the boat could get one kilometer per liter.

Moshe had all the suitcases with him, and he placed them on the boat. He sped for the cove, loaded the gas cans and other materials stashed there into a corner of the deck, and covered them with a tarp. The work done, he sat down on board to wait anxiously for his passengers to arrive.

Abdallah walked into the resort at Quseir at 12:45 p.m., and found his wife looking wild-eyed in their room. He crossed over to give her a kiss, then stepped back to scrutinize her. "My dear, you don't look too good."

"My crazy husband, the whole world has gone crazy! Do you know where your precious dam is right now?"

"Of course. It's ten kilometers south of the beautiful city of Aswan. What's this all about, Fatima?"

"Were you at work at all this morning? What time did you leave?"

Abdallah looked at his watch. "I was at work for an hour. Everything is fine. I must have left at about 8:30 a.m.," he lied.

"At 9:10 this morning, the Israelis blew up the dam. Your beautiful city of Aswan lies under ten meters of water. Water that is heading in a tidal wave — straight for Cairo!" She buried her face in her hands as if, even now, the shock was too great for her to fully absorb.

Abdallah registered surprise, then regret. "What a shame! But it's a good thing we decided to take this vacation just now. Sounds like we could have gotten hurt had we been at home."

The sobbing Fatima was too distraught to remark on her husband's astonishingly mild reaction to her cataclysmic news. Taking her hand, Abdallah said gently, "Come my dear, I think you need some ocean air. I told Moshe to rent a boat. Let's go out for a ride."

Fatima was unresisting as a rag doll as her husband led her downstairs. Under her breath, he heard her muttering, "Why, God, did this have to happen to me? Why?"

Abdallah found the empty jeep and buckled Fatima into the front seat. As they drove leisurely down the coast road, Fatima regained control of her senses. She turned despairingly on her husband.

"I've never understood you, not since the day we were married. You are just so *weird*! Everything about your life is weird. They say you're an engineering genius. I think you're too fanatic in your Islam sometimes. On the other hand, your only son becomes an infidel, and it doesn't seem to bother you too much." She flung up her hands, then let them fall into her lap. "I give up, Abdallah. I just give up."

Abdallah made no comment. The road had unwound another kilometer when Fatima, sounding more like herself now, exclaimed, "Oh, Abdallah, I forgot some things back at the hotel. The sunscreen, a book I was reading — and lunch. We forgot lunch. Let's go back for a moment.... Abdallah, where are you going? I think we just passed the marina."

"Don't worry, my dear. Moshe took everything. He took food, he took drinks, he even took along all your luggage. It's all on the boat."

She stared. "Where are we going? I thought we were just going to be away for a few hours."

Abdallah didn't answer. He drove the jeep onto the rocky beach, and stopped right at the water's edge. The waves lapped the tires. Abdallah turned to his wife and said quietly, "Come, my dear. It's time to meet our son."

Abdallah waded through the water until it was up to his waist, dragging his wife behind. She was too drained, and much too confused, to argue about getting her dress soaked. As soon as they were aboard the boat, Moshe gunned the motor.

"Fun, isn't it Mom?" he yelled over the roar of the engine.

Fatima noticed the tarp-covered heap taking up half the deck. Curiously, she lifted the edge of the tarp. "Abdallah, Moshe — why is this boat full of gas cans?"

Neither answered her.

"My son, my husband, this boat isn't yours! You are pirates. My men are pirates!" She began to bawl again. But her weeping had no power to halt, or even slow, the seven hundred horses racing through the water. In ten minutes, the coast sank below the horizon. In an hour, the coastal Red Sea hills disappeared from view. Only the deep blue waters of the Red Sea surrounded the three seafarers in the stolen speedboat.

Abdallah spoke to his son, but in a language his wife couldn't understand. "Moshe, I'll take over driving. Fill up the boat's fuel tanks — they must be getting low by now."

Fatima asked, "Abdallah, what did you just say to Moshe? I didn't catch it."

"I told him to fill the tank, we're running out of gas. But we have plenty on board the boat. That's all I said."

"I don't care what you said. I didn't *understand* what you said! I didn't know you spoke any language other than Arabic, French and a broken English. Moshe, of course, speaks an educated English and fluent Hebrew."

Abdallah came to a decision. He turned to his wife, still holding the wheel, and grinned broadly.

"Abdallah, what's going on?" Fatima demanded. Their eyes held for a long moment, hers filled with questions, his with the answers he was finally ready to reveal.

Abdallah killed the engine. The boat came to a halt and bobbed idly in the waves. "Moshe," Abdallah said to his son in Hebrew, "I think the time has come to tell your mother. You may have the honors."

"What language are you speaking?" Fatima asked again.

"Now, Mom, take it easy. There's nothing to be nervous about. Dad was speaking to me in his native tongue. He said the time has come to tell you something."

"His native tongue is Arabic!" declared the troubled woman. "That wasn't Arabic. It sounded more like Hebrew... but that's crazy."

Fatima stared at Abdallah. He was smiling. "It's crazy," Fatima repeated slowly. "Abdallah, your native tongue is *Hebrew?* You're a Palestinian?"

Laughing, he said, "I suppose you could call me a Palestinian. Prior to 1948 the Land of Israel was called Palestine."

"What are you saying?"

Moshe interposed soothingly, "Mom, don't be too upset. I want you to think back. Do you remember when Dad proposed to you, and you told him you were a Jew?"

She shuddered. "I'll never forget that moment. I thought he'd walk out and I'd never see him again."

"But Dad wasn't as upset as you expected, was he?"

"N-no...."

"Mom."

Fatima tore her mind away from the past and met her son's eyes. "Yes?"

"I don't want *you* to get too upset about what I'm about to tell you. Promise?"

"Why shouldn't I promise?" She threw out her arms. "My family has gone totally crazy already. Do I have anything to lose?"

"Dad's a Jew."

Fatima fainted right into Alon's arms.

Chapter 17

They had been heading north-northeast, directly for the Straits of Tiran, traveling at a speed of fifty-five km/h for four hours. By Alon's estimate they were more than halfway there when he stopped the boat. It was still light at 5:45 p.m. in midsummer, and they took out the fishing gear.

"Dad, what are we going to do with all these fish?" Moshe asked as he hauled aboard another Moses Sole.

"They might come in handy. We can't go any farther until after dark. If a patrol boat spots us, I think we have a pretty authentic-looking ruse."

It wasn't long before his precautions justified themselves. The nine meter Egyptian Coast Guard boat made its appearance over the horizon at just after 7:00 p.m., half an hour before sunset.

"Moshe, go below deck. Here." Alon lifted the tarp, quickly located what he wanted, and unzipped a suitcase. Within seconds, his old Helwan pistol had changed hands.

The patrol boat, manned by three officers, pulled up alongside the speedboat. The Sea Ray had a small Egyptian flag waving from its pulpit and an Egyptian registration number painted on its hull.

"What are you doing out here so far from your port?" One of the officers, a swarthy individual of stern mien, barked out the question.

"We came to this spot to fish. I got a tip that right below us lie the Sinai shoals — the best fishing in the Red Sea. Look." Alon pulled up a stringer that had twelve fish attached.

"I've been patrolling these waters for four years and I've never seen anyone fishing here before," said the officer, suspicious.

"I told you, it was a tip. It's a secret that few anglers know about." Alon smiled deprecatingly. "If the whole world knew, the fishing wouldn't be much good, would it?"

The officer refused to soften. "You're almost a hundred kilometers from the coast. When did you leave port?"

"About 8:30 this morning."

"I see. Then you probably haven't heard the news."

"What news?"

"The Israelis have destroyed the Aswan dam. There are thousands of casualties — maybe tens of thousands. Don't you think you'd better be heading back? It will probably be all-out war soon."

"Soon!" Alon helped. "You just said they bombed the dam. It sounds like the war's already started! Fatima," he said urgently, with a wink out of the side of his face the Egyptian officer couldn't see, "did you hear that? The Israelis have bombed the dam! We'd better turn right around."

The officer corrected coldly, "I didn't say they bombed the dam, Mister. I said they destroyed it. From what I've heard, it just sort of gave way, and collapsed in on itself. But we know it must have been sabotage."

"Couldn't it have been an earthquake?"

"Well, some of the dovish pundits on the radio are claiming that that's what it was. But it came just a day after the Moslem coalition — which Egypt had joined — launched a missile attack on Israel."

Alon frowned. "I thought Iran was behind that."

"Yeah, it was pretty stupid of our government to join the coalition. Between you and me, I don't give two hoots about the Palestinians. They're not worth Egyptian lives. But I don't make the rules; I only enforce them."

One of the other Coast Guard officers noticed the blue tarp tied down, covering a large area near the rear of the deck. "What do you have there?" he asked, pointing.

"Oh, just some spare gas and some other gear that we didn't want to stow below."

The three officers conferred.

"Mohammed, let's board the boat," the first officer whispered. "Something's not right here."

"Oh, come now, Hassan. They're just an old couple out fishing," the second demurred. "You know, I think he's really on to something about this spot. Tomorrow, I'm going to bring along a fishing pole."

"Let's just see what's under the tarp. If it's nothing we'll leave."

The third officer objected, "You heard the old man. He wants to get back to port. We shouldn't hold them up."

"This will only take a few minutes."

The conference ended, and Hassan spoke up.

"We are going to board your boat for a minute. We want to make sure everything is in order on board. Then you will head back to port. You can follow us."

Hassan jumped down half a meter and was on the deck of the Sea Ray. He took a quick look around, then walked over to the tarp. It was firmly secured with bungee cords. He unhooked one and picked up the edge of the tarp. Fatima began to twist her hands nervously. Alon motioned for her to stay calm. It was crucial to allay these intruders' suspicions for as long as possible....

"You sure have a good supply of gas. Let's see, one, two, three — Hey! That's a lot of gas! The officer straightened up and went to undo the other side of the tarp to see exactly how many cans there were. He yelled back at his comrades, "Mohammed, come on over here for a minute. They have too many gas cans for a day's excursion."

Alon began to talk. "We knew this spot was pretty far out, we certainly didn't want to run out of gas in the middle of the sea."

The officer didn't answer him. The patrol boat circled around so that its starboard side was next to the Sea Ray's port side, adjacent to where the tarp was tied. Mohammed stood on the patrol boat's gunwale, poised to jump down onto the deck of the Sea Ray. Ibrahim stayed at the wheel of the patrol boat. Mohammed jumped. He was in midair when every ear caught the sound of a loud electrical zap. Mohammed fell into the sea.

Instantly, Hassan pulled his gun from his holster. Ibrahim, on the patrol boat, did the same.

"What happened?" he shouted at Alon, who was sitting next to his wife trying to calm her down.

"I don't know." Alon shook his head gravely. "Sounded like he shorted some wires and took a shock."

The unconscious officer was afloat in the water, buoyed by his life-vest.

"Jump in and pull him aboard," Hassan ordered Alon.

"Don't you see that you have my wife panic-stricken? Please, put away that gun. Besides, I can't swim."

Hassan looked at his partner, slowly drifting away in the subtle breeze. He hesitated, then threw his gun back on to the patrol boat. "Keep them covered, Ibrahim! I'm going in after Mohammed."

The head patrol officer, also wearing his life vest, dove into the water and swam the ten meters to his groggy mate. He turned around as he heard two shots ring out, and just managed to see Ibrahim fall out of sight to the deck of the patrol boat.

Moshe burst out of the cabin of the Sea Ray and jumped aboard the patrol boat. Alon gunned the Sea Ray's engine. Prudently, Hassan abandoned his unconscious crewman and swam frantically toward the patrol boat. He just managed to get a grip on the stern rail when Moshe jerked the throttle forward, following the Sea Ray, already one hundred fifty meters ahead. Hassan struggled to hold on, his feet pulled back in the wash of the speeding boat.

Moshe looked around. The officer's hands were still gripping the rail. He cranked the boat to full throttle, but the sixty km/h couldn't dislodge the tenacious hands of Lt. Hassan Morabi. As Moshe caught up to the Sea Ray, cruising alongside, Alon saw the problem. He cupped his hands to his mouth and yelled as loudly as he could, "Jerk it into reverse!"

Moshe nodded, and did as his father had said. The boat lurched back so forcefully that Moshe had to hold on to the wheel with all his might not to be pulled forward into the windshield. He heard the gears grind for a full ten seconds until the boat came to a complete stop and began to surge backward. Then he managed to look back — just in time to see Hassan, the lone pursuer, whose head had smashed against the rail — slip below the surface. Moshe stopped the boat after it had traveled backward only fifty meters. He leaned over and searched the water carefully, but saw no sign of Hassan. There was only a shredded strip of life vest and a deep red trail in the water. Moshe choked, and turned away.

The Sea Ray pulled up next to the patrol boat. "Dad, what do we do now?" Moshe asked, still paler than usual.

"I think we should scuttle the patrol boat." As they spoke, they could hear an operator's voice coming over the Patrol boat's marine radio: "Patrol boat twenty-six, what is your location? I repeat, your location?" Moshe switched off the radio.

Fatima looked on in incredulous silence as the two men worked quickly and surely, like professionals.

"Moshe, what did you have there, another TASER device?"

"Yes, Dad. Actually there are four planted along the gunwale compartments. I knew I would have a lot of time on my hands waiting for you and Mom to arrive. I figured it couldn't hurt to wire up the deck. Of course, I had a remote in my pocket. TASERs always come in handy."

"You sure have a fetish for electrocution."

"Everyone is entitled to one *mishigat*. Back at home in St. Louis Park, I have fourteen bug zappers strung around my yard like holiday lights. During the mosquito season, it sounds like a popcorn-feast."

Alon laughed. "From the day I took this job, I never expected to have an electronic wizard of a son to help me."

Moshe answered dryly, "Do you think *I* ever expected to have a secret agent for a Dad?"

It was well after dark before the two men were able, with the crude tools at their disposal, to rip a large hole in the sturdy fiberglass hull of the patrol boat. As the water started filling the ballast, the boat slowly receded deeper into the water. They had lashed the body on board to the deck with bungee cords. As the boat listed far enough to port, the water finally started gushing over the side, and the boat quickly slipped below the surface. The two sailors turned their attention next to another important piece of work. For the final leg of the journey, they thought it would be wise to sand off the Sea Ray's registration number — a job that took all of another half-hour — and to rip the Egyptian flag from the pulpit.

"Fatima," Alon said to his wife, "we've been working hard for our nation today, but you haven't lifted a finger. Here." He pulled a can of spray paint and a white sheet from his suitcase. "You've always been artistic — help out a little."

It was 8:40 p.m. and pitch dark when Alon took the G.P.S. from his pocket and instructed Moshe to take a heading of seventy-one degrees toward the Straits of Tiran, approximately five hours away. They cruised at a leisurely forty km/h — not to conserve fuel, but to minimize the roar of the engine, the only way they could be located at night. Moshe and Alon took turns; one drove while the other scouted the horizon for lights, which could indicate a ship. On two occasions, Alon took out his night vision binoculars after viewing lights just above the horizon. Both were large ships, probably cargo vessels, neither one closer than sixteen kilometers distant — too far to hear the Sea Ray.

At 3:30 a.m. on July 3, 2002, the trio on board the hijacked Egyptian speed-boat were able to distinguish the lights from land on two sides of a five-kilometer gap: the Straits of Tiran. Two large ships loomed ominously in the center of the gap, straddling the Straits less than two kilometers apart. It was too dark to identify their nationalities, but Alon had no doubt they were war ships, one a cruiser, the other a destroyer. It was likely that at least one of the ships was Israeli. The Israelis had learned their lesson thirty-four years before, when they had failed to patrol the Straits of Tiran. Nasser took immediate advantage by sealing it up, fomenting the Six Day War.

Alon and Moshe reasoned that it would be impossible to pass the ships without being seen, and probably fired at. There was plenty of activity on shore at the entrance to the Gulf of Aqaba, making it impossible for the Sea Ray to hug the shore and slip safely by the warships.

Alon decided to sit tight at a distance of twenty kilometers from the two ships. As soon as there was enough light to determine which one was Israeli — assuming that one *was* an Israeli ship — he would crank up the engine and make a dash for it.

No one on the Sea Ray slept; the adrenaline flowed too vigorously. At 5:30 a.m., the first hint of light began to radiate from the east. Moshe offered his father a *Talit* and *Tefilin*.

"It's been forty-five years since I've put these things on. I don't think I'm going to start now," the secular Jew told his rabbinic son.

"Abdallah, or whatever your name is," Fatima broke in.

"It's Alon. You know, I'll bet your mother gave you a Jewish name when you were born."

"That's true. I haven't thought about it for over fifty years. Let's see.... I can't remember."

"I know," Moshe interjected. "Grandma told me. It's 'Ahuva'. That's Hebrew for 'beloved'."

Alon Barnash was visibly shaken at the coincidence. Thirty-seven-year-old memories began swimming in his head. His wife noticed his agitation.

"What's the matter, Alon?" Fatima asked, concerned.

Alon took a long, steadying breath. "It's okay. Don't worry, I'm all right."

Fatima looked seriously at Alon, and said in a quiet but firm voice, "Please put those on, as Moshe requested, and pray. We are now a Jewish family."

Alon looked quizzically at his wife, then back at his son, who had taken the *Talit* out of its velvet bag and was extending it to his father. "Dad, you told me that for the past thirty years, you have been quietly saying *Shema Yisrael* while prostrated in the mosque. Can't you put these on, and just say the same prayer? It only takes a minute — and we may need all the help from God that we can get...."

Alon looked back at Fatima, who nodded. He took the *Talit* and put it on. Then his son helped him wrap the *Tefilin* on his left arm and head. Alon Barnash cried out the *Shema* prayer with all the faith he could muster. His son had exaggerated: it took no more than half a minute. Moshe removed the *Talit* from his father's shoulders and draped it over his own, then put on the *Tefilin*. He prayed for thirty minutes, until just before sunrise. Just as he was completing the last prayer, he heard his father exclaim in joy, "The ships — they're both Israeli!" Alon gunned the engine full throttle.

At that moment, a flare crashed into the water some two hundred meters in front of them. Fatima gasped, a hand to her mouth. Moshe looked behind, "A patrol-missile boat is on our tail — about eleven hundred meters behind us. Let's see." Moshe carefully focused his binoculars, "It's Saudi. Dad, crank it up."

"We're already moving as fast as we can. Is that thing gaining on us?"

"It's too close to call. I think maybe slightly. No, it's just about a dead heat."

The Saudi boat shot another flare, which hit down only fifty meters to port of the Sea Ray.

"Dad, they have a good fix on our distance. Why are they shooting flares at us?"

"I think they want us to stop."

"Should we?"

"I'm afraid that's not an option. We have no registration on the boat. We'll be assumed to be spies. Our Egyptian-accented Arabic probably won't get us out of this fix, and I already threw the fish overboard."

The minutes ticked by. It soon became apparent that the Saudi Patrol boat wasn't gaining — on the contrary, it was slipping back by a slight margin. The Israeli warships were now in full view, only eleven kilometers away.

"Moshe, Fatima, we have no choice — we're going to continue to run for the ships. Fatima, put the flag you made on the fish gaff, and wedge it into the hatch on top of the cabin. I want it as high up as you can extend it."

"But Dad," protested Moshe, "when the Saudis see that, they'll surely switch to live fire. We know that Riyadh and Mecca were hit yesterday."

"I know," Alon said soberly. "But I see no other choice. You just got through praying, my boy, and so did I. Fatima — Ahuva — I guess it's your turn now."

"I don't know how. At least, I don't know any Jewish prayers, just a few Islamic ones, and I wouldn't want to say those. I'm on your side now." She hesitated, then suddenly screamed at the top of her voice, "*Please God, save us now!*"

"That was great, Mom," Moshe yelled over the engine's thunder.

A minute later, Fatima was still holding the makeshift Israeli flag high, a small missile whizzed by, less than eight meters directly overhead. It crashed into the sea six kilometers ahead, and blew up between the Israeli ships. Moshe looked intently at the Saudi boat with his 10x50 binoculars. "They're readying another missile!"

As he shouted these terrified words, the missile was fired. It took only three seconds for the missile to traverse the twelve hundred meters that separated the Saudi gunboat from the Sea Ray. Alon swerved the boat so suddenly that Moshe was knocked off his feet. Fatima held on to the tightly wedged flagpole for dear life. The missile exploded in the water, forty meters to starboard. But fragments of molten metal hit the small craft, ripping a deadly gash in the hull that left a flap of fiberglass jutting out into the water. Though the engine was not affected, the boat began to zigzag uncontrollably as water rushed through the mauled fiberglass. The boat's velocity was seriously cut by the drag of the jagged hull. Even if it might still be possible for the Sea Ray to reach the Israeli ship before it sank, the reduced speed made it obvious that the Saudi boat could catch up to them first.

By this time, they were no more than four kilometers from the near Israeli vessel. The Saudi boat was only six hundred meters behind when Moshe bellowed, "Mom, Dad, get ready to jump in the water." As he was giving these instructions, another flash whooshed by, passing within sixty meters of the Sea Ray. But this time it was traveling in the opposite direction. The trio looked back, just in time to see the Gabriel missile detonate upon impact with the thirty meter patrol boat, creating a fireball so huge that the boat was instantly engulfed. Forty seconds later, when the flames diminished, there was nothing left on the surface of the water but smoldering debris.

The Sea Ray's hull was so full of water by now that Alon simply cut the engine. The three Jews had donned life vests immediately before starting their run for the Israeli cruiser. They saw the ship they were making for begin to steam in their direction. The rapidly approaching missile cruiser was eight hundred meters away when the bow of the Sea Ray slipped under the water. The three held hands in a circle, and waited in the warm waters of the Red Sea for the minute and a half it took for the ship to arrive.

Five minutes later they were on board. Home, at last.

"You were pretty lucky," the warrant officer in charge of the rescue said, in Hebrew, to the family. "What on earth was going on? Where did you come from? We couldn't make out any markings on your boat, except for your homemade Israeli flag. We thought it was some kind of enemy ruse at first. But when the captain saw the first missile fired at you, he ordered the crew to full alert. After the second missile, we knew those guys were serious about taking you out, and we fired. That's the first Gabriel I've shot — it's a pretty good missile. Slight overkill for a tiny patrol boat."

"As long as it was a kill. Thanks," Moshe said fervently. Fatima was too overcome to speak. Alon said nothing.

They were brought into the captain's stateroom and handed towels while a crew member went to find them some dry clothes. "Sorry, ma'am, we don't have a dress on board," a sailor told Fatima. She smiled and nodded, not understanding a word he had said.

The captain of the ship came in to confront his unexpected guests. "Okay, I believe you are Israeli. But who are you?"

Moshe pulled a soggy American passport from his pocket and handed it to the Captain.

"Mustafa Ibn Gash, born in Egypt, 1971, naturalized in 2000. What? Mustafa Ibn Gash? Are you sure you're a Jew? The captain noticed Moshe's sopping wool *Tzitzit.* "And you?" he asked Alon. "Another religious *yored* with an Arabic name?"

Alon said quietly, "Mossad Aleph-Shin 36."

The captain became deadly serious. He went at once to his secured radiophone and repeated the ID Alon had given him. As the captain waited for an answer, Alon took off his left shoe. The captain listened for a moment, then said into the phone, "Yes sir. Will do." He turned to Alon. "Let me see your left.... Ah! I see you were expecting this."

Alon held his big toe separated from the next digit, so that the Captain could clearly see the tiny brand mark that served to identify the claimant of that ID number. The Captain rose, and saluted Alon. Fatima watched, fascinated. She still did not know her husband's true last name.

"Colonel Alon Barnash. Welcome aboard, sir."

"Colonel?" Alon repeated in surprise. "The last time I was addressed as an officer, I was a captain."

"How long ago was that, sir?"

"Let's see... about thirty-four years ago."

"That's been quite a while. I suppose you were recently promoted, perhaps for some outstanding service to the nation. You would know about that, better than I.... In any case, that's what your ID came up with."

Fatima finally opened her mouth, to ask in plaintive Arabic, "Would somebody please tell me what's going on?"

Alon turned to smile at her. "We are just getting acquainted with Captain Shoval of the Israeli navy. Everything's just fine."

Shoval, startled, asked Alon, "Who's she, an Arab?"

"An Arab?! She's my wife, and as Jewish as the rest of us."

"Then why is she speaking in Arabic to you? Doesn't she speak Hebrew?"

"Not a word. But that's a long story."

"What's your relationship with Ibn Gash?" the captain asked.

Alon and Moshe looked at each other.

"He's my son. This woman is his mother."

"But his last name is different. What's going on?"

"That's also a long story."

"All you have are long stories? Don't you have any short stories?"

Alon thought for a moment about the captain's question. "No, only long ones."

"I suppose this is not the right time to interrogate you. A room is being readied for you three. I also called a doctor to check you out; you've had a pretty rough day. He's coming over in a tender from our flagship — the destroyer you noticed guarding the other side of the Straits."

At that moment, there was a knock on the door. The doctor came in, complete with little black bag. He pulled out a stethoscope, and looked at Fatima. Uncomfortable with all the men around, she said quickly in English that she felt fine, and that he should examine the men first. As he came face-to-face with Alon, the sixty-year-old Mossad agent noticed the name badge on the doctor's chest, and froze.

"Dad, what's the matter?" Moshe asked, watching the astonished play of emotions cross his father's face.

"Yes, what's the matter?" the doctor echoed playfully. "You scared of stethoscopes? It doesn't hurt at all. Just feels a little cold."

Moshe looked more closely at the doctor — and then, he, too, froze in bewilderment. It took a few seconds for him to regain his composure. But before he could say a word, both the doctor and the captain — not to mention the perpetually befuddled Fatima — were taken aback as Alon broke into an uncontrollable sob.

"Doctor," Moshe asked in a hushed voice. "Do you believe in miracles?"

The doctor glanced down at Moshe's torn and soaked fringed undergarment. "I know *you* do, you're *Charedi*. But me — no, I don't believe in miracles. There's an explanation to everything." The answer came with quick assurance.

"You don't understand," Moshe told him, "Not all miracles involve Manna falling down from heaven. Some are just an unimaginable juxtaposition of events."

"What are you getting at? I came to examine three people whom I was told had been pulled from the sea, and you're asking me about miracles?"

"Yes... Ariel."

"How did you know my name?!" demanded the stupefied doctor. His badge only indicated his first initial.

"We've met before. Fifteen years ago, before I had a beard. Before I even lived as a Jew."

Whirling around to address the captain, Dr. Mizrachi insisted, "I don't know these people. I'm afraid this one's becoming delusional." He pointed at Moshe. "We better get them ashore to a hospital as soon as possible. Order a helicopter to fly them to Eilat."

"Ariel," Moshe said with quiet emphasis, "I am your brother."

Mizrachi flushed crimson and grew tense as a coiled spring. Relentlessly, Moshe continued, "And the man crying near you is our father. Your real father."

Ariel was gripped by panic as he gaped at Alon. "That can't be. My father went down with the *Davar* thirty-four years ago. I still light a candle for his memory every Tevet 25. My father is dead."

"No, Ariel, he's right here. He did go down at sea thirty-four years ago, for the sake of our people. But now the sea has returned him."

With difficulty, Alon controlled his sobbing and gazed intently at Ariel, who trembled silently as he stared back.

The captain, not far from tears himself, opened his mouth to speak. "Major Mizrachi, I am as lost as you are — but I can swear to you that the man sitting opposite you is Colonel Alon Barnash, Mossad wing of the GSS."

Suddenly, as if a dam had burst, a torrent of tears gushed from the doctor's eyes. Alon and Ariel embraced.

PART TWO:

FARSHID LEVIHAYIM

"And this is the writing that was inscribed: Mene Mene Tekel Upharsin"

Daniel 5:25

Chapter 18

In the twentieth century, Shiraz was home to many of Iran's Jews. A larger community resided in the capital, Tehran, perhaps — but Shiraz was where the action was. So when Eli Kedem was deposited on a lonely shore on the coast of Iran, he did not make his permanent residence in Shiraz. He did spend his first year there, accepting humbling employment for the purpose of establishing Iranian residence — but for his long-term sojourn in the land, a smaller, less connected community suited him best.

In 1969, the start of his second year in Iran, Kedem — known now as Farshid Levihayim — purchased a residence in Isfahan, a dwindling Jewish community. At the time, the Jews were happy and safe, despite the fact that ninety-nine percent of the population was Moslem. There was one reason for this unusual relationship. His name was Shah Mohammed Reza Pahlavi. The Shah had a greater interest in reviving the glory of the ancient Persian Empire than in promoting Moslem/Arabic religious culture. As a result, devout clerics considered him an infidel. To the vast majority of the population, however, the Shah was a saint and a savior. His programs to modernize Iran — bringing it from the seventh century directly into the twentieth — coupled with the fabulous oil wealth, was a recipe for success. The progress and prosperity that increasingly made itself felt in Iran served to redirect the people's attention from religion to riches. This proved a godsend for the Jews.

In every other Moslem country where Jews had a presence, it was necessary for the government to expend vast resources to keep the populace from growling, or worse, at the Jews. On the one hand, when the Jewish State was founded it offered a refuge to all Jews under persecution. On the other, Israel's very existence was often the impetus for stepped-up persecution of Jews in many volatile regions of the Middle East. Iran's unique situation dictated that such sentiments found small foothold among the indigenous population. Anti-Semitism and anti-Israel feelings were left to a small fanatic fringe—themselves subject to harassment by the Shah's forces.

Tehran was too unbridled and avant-garde for the traditional Jews of Iran, whose ancestors had settled there twenty-four hundred years ago. Shiraz was more attractive to them, combining the cosmopolitan atmosphere with the old Middle-Eastern traditional flavor. The populace there had never indulged much in the Jew-baiting so popular in other Moslem countries. Indeed, Shiraz permitted the quintessential blend of spiritual and material well-being for the Jews.

Under those circumstances, how could an Israeli think about implementing "reverse infrastructure"? Why did the Mossad, in 1968, include Iran on its list of places to prepare for an offensive, defense policy?

The Shah himself offered the answer to that question. For a period of thirty years, he warned his friends, the Jews, to take their wealth and leave the country. Apart from being the only significant Moslem leader who was closely allied with the Jewish State, he was also far more adept at reading the *handwriting on the wall* than his great-great-granddad, Balshatzar.

Unlike those in Tehran and Shiraz, the Jews of Isfahan were never well-received by the populace. For that matter, the Shah himself was viewed with ominous eyes in that more-than-just-traditional city. The Jews living there were less sophisticated than those of Shiraz; it was inertia that kept them fixed in place. But even that inertia had finally reached its limits by the end of the Shah's days, and families began to move away.

This made Isfahan the perfect outpost for Farshid Levihayim. Soon after moving to town, he opened a business recycling automobile batteries. The business became very successful, and by 1975, eighty-five percent of the dead batteries from Tehran to Abadan found their way to his reprocessing plant in Isfahan. He was now the most prominent member of the Jewish community, though he always declined nomination as community president. Realizing it might be a long time (or never) before his purpose in Isfahan would be completed, Levihayim did not neglect to keep up the skills that would serve him in good stead. His mental agility was kept keen by running a successful business, while his bodily skills — he had a third Dan black belt in Shorin Ryu karate — were maintained by joining a local Kung Fu club. He found the three Japanese-style karate clubs in Isfahan to be below par. Within six months, he "earned" his brown belt, but refused to publicly demonstrate ability beyond that level.

"Farshid," said Joseph Saadatmand, a friend and prominent clothing merchant, "you have been living here for two years. Thank the Almighty, your business has grown. Why do you continue to spurn my efforts to help you find a wife? Everyone in the community considers you the most eligible bachelor. You are religious, rich, and good-looking. It's a shame! It isn't right — yes, it's a downright sin — for you to live in loneliness without a life partner."

Farshid gave his friend his trademark smile, charming and direct. "Joseph, I greatly appreciate your efforts on my behalf. But I've already met all appropriate girls in Isfahan: all three of them. None were my match, I'm afraid."

"But my cousin in Hamadan has a beautiful daughter. Didn't I suggest her to you once?"

"At least eight times, Joseph. I keep telling you she's too young."

"But it's been almost a year since I've mentioned the idea. She is older now!" Joseph was nothing if not persistent. "Perhaps you will reconsider?"

"Let me see, last year she was fourteen," Farshid said. "That would make her about fifteen now. I am a man of thirty — only twice her age.... No, Joseph, I don't think she will do for me."

"So when you are thirty-five and she, twenty — then she will be for you? Why waste five years of your life?" Joseph shook his head. "Farshid, you have been something of a puzzle ever since you moved to town. But you are still my good friend."

Farshid slapped the other man on the shoulder. "Of course, Joseph, and that's the way I would like it to remain. If it is the Will of God, I will find my mate. I'm just not in a hurry. I'd rather make the right decision than a hasty one."

Levihayim grew accustomed to the constant badgering by his best friend, Joseph, and the occasional harassment from others about his non-married status. Still, these torments forced him to defend himself, to invent excuses and concoct ruses — the most vital pastime of his existence.

*   *   *

"Daryoush," called Levihayim to his plant foreman, "I just got a call from our subcontractor in Mashad. He has a truck on its way here with two thousand batteries. I would like to process the entire carload into number-eight shot."

"Whew, that's a lot of tiny balls."

"True. But we just got in an order from a large ammunition company in South Africa. My contact in Pretoria indicates that the national police have decided to switch to fine bird shot for riot control." Levihayim smiled. "You see, Daryoush, other people's troubles can be our good fortune."

His foreman, like Levihayim's other employees, found himself irresistibly warming to that smile. "Yes, of course, sir. I'll grease the line myself."

Two hours later, a fifteen-meter tractor-trailer backed into the truck bay of Persian Gulf Lead, Ltd. A roller conveyor was extended directly into the rear of the truck. Two workers alternated placing the 15kg-20kg lead-filled rubberized cubes along its arm. Each battery flowed steadily until a sturdy metal flange knocked it on its side. At this point, a third worker would push the battery forward into the bite of a circular saw blade one meter in diameter. The top of the battery, terminals and all, was sliced off and directed to a garbage pit outside. A fourth worker dumped the lead plates and drained the remaining sulfuric acid from its casing into the main pit, lined with concrete, from which the noxious liquid was then pumped into an open-ground pit one hundred meters away. There it flowed down among the heap of casings, battery terminals and other refuse — an environmental nightmare.

Inside the main pit, a Bobcat shoveled the lead plates into a pile, where they would be left for a week to dry out in central Iran's arid air before processing. After drying, the lead was dumped into a blast furnace, which was constantly burning. The purified molten lead was shunted into a series of molds in a circle on a rail system, and cooled. The twenty-five kilo bars were moved to a warehouse, where they were stacked and stored.

Levihayim's company, Persian Gulf Lead, also had facilities — albeit limited — for fabrication. The vast majority of their orders for in-house fabrication was for ammunition: 9mm, one hundred fifteen-grain ball bullets, one hundred twenty-four-grain 7.62mm military rounds, and a drop-casting facility for making shot. PGL manufactured shot, from thirty-six grain #00 buck to #8 extra-fine bird shot.

"Boss, where are you going?" Daryoush called up to Levihayim one morning. His boss was seated behind the wheel of the tractor-trailer carrying twenty-five-kilo cubical cans of shot.

"I'm driving this load to Bandar Abbas myself. Colonel Botha of the South African police will be there to check the merchandise. I wanted to meet him in person; it's good for business."

Daryoush scratched his head in puzzlement at this departure from form, then shrugged and started back to the factory office.

The lead shot never traveled the nine hundred kilometers to the port. Colonel Botha wasn't waiting there in any case. In fact, it is questionable whether the man even existed. Levihayim drove the truck fifty kilometers out of town and waited at the side of the road. At 1:00 a.m., he turned the rig around and headed for the Great Synagogue of Isfahan. As an active trustee, he held the keys to the building, including those that fit the locks of a little-used storage cellar. The truck pulled up behind the building. Levihayim backed it up as close as possible to the steps of the cellar. The strong and agile thirty-year-old magnate unloaded eight hundred twenty-five kilo cans, stacking them quickly and neatly in one corner.

Over the next two years, the "Lead King of Iran" repeated this ceremony five times, always under the pretext of driving the truck to the Bandar Abbas port to meet the illusive Colonel Botha.

"Boss," Daryoush ventured, after the fifth time the lead was processed for the South African police, "How many times do you have to meet the colonel yourself? You really shouldn't be driving a truck."

Levihayim was seated behind his desk, with the foreman standing respectfully opposite him. He leaned back in his swivel chair, completely at his ease. "Daryoush, my good man. That is why I have made a small fortune, and you, even as plant manager, only earn a modest salary. It's all a question of business acumen. I know my customers and I know how to handle them. Besides, the South Africans want to keep this controversial import as discreet as possible. They have enough trouble maintaining their regime; the nations of the world are ready to isolate them to death. The last thing they need is for the media to hear that they're spraying unruly women and children with bird shot."

Daryoush was a loyal and efficient foreman, but incisive thinking was not his strong point. Levihayim's logic left him puzzled but acquiescent.

"Yes, boss, I'm sure you're right." A sudden grin split the olive face. "Besides, I'm sure the Shah does the same to his devout antagonists."

"Yes," his boss nodded. "But — fortunately for the Shah, and unfortunately for the devout — he happens to share their skin color."

Chapter 19

June 1972, Isfahan:

"Boss," the loyal plant manager said to Levihayim some weeks later, "Abdul is sick, Rajab lost his mother today and Kooreesh is stiff all over from his wrestling match last night. There is no one to make the Shiraz delivery this afternoon."

Levihayim looked up from the papers he had been reading. "Well, Daryoush, what about you?"

"You know how I feel about truck driving."

Slowly, Levihayim nodded. Daryoush became literally panic-stricken the moment he climbed into the cab of a truck. As a rule, this was a phobia that in no way detracted from his efficacy at his job. "So there is no one to go?" Levihayim frowned.

Daryoush hesitated, then blurted, "Boss, what about you?"

"Me?" Levihayim's brows lifted in surprise. "I run a multibillion rial business, Daryoush. Don't you think driving a truck would constitute a serious waste of my time?"

Now it was the foreman's job to register astonishment. "But boss, what about all the runs you insisted on making yourself to Bandar Abbas? You know — for that South African job."

"Oh yes, that." Levihayim had almost forgotten, and he was glad to forget. Hauling a total of eighty tons is a lot of work for one man. "Yes, Daryoush you are quite right. No man should be reluctant to soil his hands with honest labor. I'll do the driving myself." He set aside his pen and stood up. "By the way, how did Kooreesh do last night?"

"Oh, he lost again — but at least he's not in the hospital. He should be back at work by tomorrow."

All the way to Shiraz, a total of four hours' driving, Levihayim fretted over the waste of his valuable time. Upon his arrival, he thankfully dropped his load at Eurasia Paint works and turned the truck around for the long drive back to Isfahan.

Ten minutes later, while stopped at a light, Levihayim glanced to his right and noticed several men milling around outside a small building that was marked by Hebrew lettering over the door. During his stint in Shiraz, he'd attended a congregation two kilometers away. Now he was reminded of the existence of this other synagogue, recalling the one time he had stopped in to pray.

Instinctively — albeit with some reluctance — he called through the open passenger-side window, "What's the matter, gentlemen?"

"Are you a Jew?" they called back, practically in unison.

"Yes. What's the problem?"

"If you would be so kind as to park your truck, we won't have a problem at all. You see, we were one short for a minyan."

Levihayim was nothing short of desperate to get back to Isfahan. But he knew that the moment he'd shouted out his question through the window of his cab, he had obligated himself to descend from the driver's seat and accommodate these men, who were just as desperate to fill their quorum and begin the services. The weary lead-hauler moved closer to the curb and switched off his engine.

"Ah, here we have him — the tenth man for our afternoon prayer service!" the cantor announced triumphantly. The other congregants, impatient, threw the newcomer cursory nods of welcome and picked up their prayer books. Fighting off fatigue, Levihayim obligingly took his part in the service, then was cajoled into staying on for the evening service which would commence a half hour later.

The worshipers whiled away the thirty minutes in study or quiet conversation. One man, burly and genial, approached Levihayim.

"My name is Avraham Pinhasi. I don't think I know you." Glancing out the window, Pinhasi saw the large truck, with PGL, Ltd. Isfahan emblazoned along one side. "So you drive a truck and come from Isfahan?"

Levihayim grinned wryly. "Actually, I own the company. My driver was out sick today."

Pinhasi looked him up and down, marveling at how handsome and fit Levihayim appeared. He began to make mental calculations of the factory owner's earning ability, and came to the conclusion that it must certainly be adequate, at the very least. The only question was, "Is this young man married?" Pinhasi tackled the subject in roundabout fashion.

"You have family in Isfahan?"

"Actually, no. My father is no longer alive and my mother left Iran many years ago."

"Where is she, if I may ask?"

"She's in Israel."

"I'm surprised you didn't go with her."

"I've got a great business here. Israel is being run by a bunch of socialists — I could never do as well there. Why, we have thousands of Israelis here in Iran who have come to make big money. I think I'd just rather stay here."

Pinhasi nodded at this evidence of sound good sense. "You look about thirty," he remarked. "Isn't it time you married?"

With a good-humored grimace, Levihayim replied, "The men at my synagogue pester me about that too. I just haven't met the right one yet."

Pinhasi thought about his next move. His wife's second cousin would be a perfect match for this stranger. She was staying with them for the summer. Levihayim, he knew instinctively, would be a difficult catch. It would not do to scare him off.

He clapped Levihayim on the shoulder. "Listen, you look exhausted. Isfahan must be a good five hours' drive from here —"

"Four," Levihayim murmured.

"So I'm inviting you to my house. Please stay over. You can come with me to the synagogue in the morning and drive back in daylight."

Smiling, Levihayim shook his head. "Thanks, but I really must be heading back."

"Please. With so many people away, we have a hard time making the Minyan. At least come over for dinner tonight."

"I appreciate your offer, but I must refuse. Thanks all the same."

Pinhasi took a direct tack. "Mr. Levihayim," he said, "let me be honest with you. There is a young lady I would like you to meet. She lost her husband tragically a few years ago, but has no children. She is beautiful — though, I must admit, not overly orthodox."

"In that case, why suggest her to me? You can see for yourself that I'm an observant Jew. In fact, I serve as a synagogue trustee back in Isfahan."

Pinhasi dismissed this niggling concern with a wave of the hand. "I'm sure she would be as observant as you insist. But she's lived in Israel since she was ten years old. You know how it is over there. Israel is a more... liberal society. Please," he wheedled, "just come for dinner."

Levihayim thought about it for a moment. There might be possibilities here. Perhaps meeting an Israeli with only distant relatives in Iran was a good idea. He would never need to reveal his true identity; his accent was very good, and she would never know that he, himself, had immigrated to Israel from Tehran at the age of seven.

On the other hand, the freer he was of entanglements, the safer he would be. Besides, she might nag him to leave the country.

"I appreciate your intentions, Mr. Pinhasi, but she probably wants to go back to Israel."

"Well, why don't you ask her yourself?" Taking advantage of Levihayim's momentary hesitation, Pinhasi pressed his advantage. "Look, it will be nothing formal. I invited you, as an out-of-town guest, to drop in for a meal. She happens to be staying with us. If you don't like her, you just pick up and leave. No one is embarrassed, no real chance of hard feelings."

All around them, men had been picking up their prayer books in preparation for the evening service. At that moment, it began. The two men were forced to drop their talk until their prayers were completed.

The evening service over, Levihayim thanked his prospective host again but firmly declined his invitation to dinner. He mounted the driver's seat of his truck, threw the shifter into first and stepped on the gas. Pinhasi, following him, winced as the loudest grinding he had ever heard emanated from the rear axle of the truck. It lurched forward a few meters and came to a stop. Levihayim gave it some gas, but the old White Diesel only raced up. He switched off the engine and stepped down to join Pinhasi. "That's the third time the rear axle has gone on this truck in the past eighteen months."

"What are you hauling? Lead?" Pinhasi asked jokingly.

"Actually, that's exactly what I was hauling. I own Persian Gulf Lead, Ltd." Levihayim pointed at the side of the truck, dimly illuminated in the moonlight. His tone took on a resigned quality as he asked, "Is your invitation still open?"

"Please, please! Maybe it is the Will of God."

Levihayim walked the six blocks to Pinhasi's house. The elder man took out his key and, in the darkness, groped to find the keyhole. The door opened to a light-filled foyer. Levihayim stepped inside after his host, glancing over Pinhasi's shoulder into the living room beyond. He gasped, his face turning ash-white. Without a word, he turned and ran, as fast as his feet could carry him.

Two blocks away, at a main intersection, he hailed a passing taxi.

"Where to, Mister?" the driver asked, staring curiously at his breathless passenger.

"Isfahan."

Now it was the cab driver's turn to gasp. But before he could protest or even think, Levihayim waved a thick wad of bills in front of him and ordered him to drive. The man drove.

The next day, Levihayim sent a still-aching Kooreesh — the after-hours wrestler — down to Shiraz to see to the truck's repair and bring it back. Kooreesh found the truck where his boss had been forced to abandon it the night before, parked in front of the synagogue. A mechanic, hastily summoned, was inserting the axle into the housing when Avraham Pinhasi came by for his daily study session in the synagogue. Finding Kooreesh hovering impatiently by the huge lead transporter, Pinhasi asked, "You work for Levihayim?"

Kooreesh nodded a sour assent. "Truck broke down," he said, gesturing tersely. He winced as the motion brought a protest from sore muscles. "I'm bringing it back to Isfahan."

"I know the truck broke down. Levihayim came here yesterday, his truck broke down, and I invited him to my house. But the minute we stepped inside, he ran away as if he were on fire. What's the matter with him?"

"I don't know anything," groaned the driver, stooping to massage his aching right calf.

Pinhasi persisted, "Tell me. Is your boss a little nuts?"

"Farshid Levihayim? He's the smartest man I ever met. He treats all the workers like brothers — Jews and Moslems alike. I was taught to hate Jews. But after working for him for two years, I see that everything I was taught was a lie. Outright lies!" Kooreesh straightened painfully as he remembered something. "By the way, do you know Avraham Pinhasi? I have a letter for him from my boss."

Pinhasi started. "I am he." He grabbed the letter impatiently from the fat hand that extended it to him, and tore it open.

Dear Avraham,

I sincerely apologize for running off so wildly. I had just remembered a personal commitment, so imperative that I couldn't even spend the time to explain it to you. As for your cousin's daughter — although I would have preferred a woman who was never married, I have decided to take your advice and meet her. However, I will be too busy to journey to Shiraz in the near future. I will be happy to meet her here in Isfahan. Please call me at my office, tel. 355-785. I will send a car to bring her from the train station.

Sincerely,
Farshid Levihayim

The letter was handwritten, and dated one a.m. that morning, at which time Levihayim had presumably returned to his home in Isfahan.

Pinhasi ran home and showed the letter to his wife, who in turn showed it to their Israeli guest. She frowned.

"Are you sure he's not crazy? I don't know how I could bear another letdown in my life. Believe me, Auntie, you can't imagine how I've suffered."

Mrs. Pinhasi dismissed her relative's suffering with a wave of her hand. "Go meet him. Maybe he's a little eccentric, so what? He's rich, handsome, and very religious."

"But, Auntie, I'm not religious! Besides, Uncle says that this fellow has a well-established business in Isfahan. I don't know that I'd care to stay in Iran for the rest of my life."

"Just go for the day," Mrs. Pinhasi urged. "What do you have to lose? If you don't like him, or if you can't agree on these matters, nothing has been gained and nothing lost."

The following Monday, Daryoush picked up the young lady from the Isfahan Central Station and drove her the twelve kilometers to the lead factory at the edge of town. The plant manager led the woman — who had been instructed to don a Chador while in Isfahan — to his boss's office, ushered the woman inside, and closed the door behind her. Daryoush hadn't spoken a word to the lady after confirming her identity at the station, but vile thoughts entered his mind as he heard the door click into a locked position as he pulled it shut.

The young lady from Israel, stepping hesitantly into the office, was taken aback at the overt rudeness of the man she was meeting. Levihayim had his chair swivelled fully around, so that his back was to her as she entered.

The door slammed shut. Farshid Levihayim thrust out one hand and motioned for his visitor to come forward. No words were exchanged as the embarrassed woman slowly crossed the seven meters to his desk. The only thought that passed through her mind as she made her way was, "This man is really cracked! Why did I listen to Uncle and Auntie? What a waste of my time!"

As she came around the right side of the desk, Farshid swivelled his chair slightly to the left. When she was one meter away, he abruptly stood up, turned around — and caught the woman as she fainted dead away.

Levihayim sat down, holding the unconscious figure tightly in his arms. Gazing into her face, he began to cry.

"Ruchama, my dearest, wake up," he said softly in a choked voice. The drenching flow from his eyes soaked her cheek as he pressed his lips to it. Her eyes opened. Slowly, she sat up in his lap and looked deep into his eyes. As they embraced, her tears mingled with his. "This is a miracle from God. A true miracle!"

The euphoric dream lasted only a minute longer. Suddenly, Ruchama Kedem shot to her feet and traded her sobbing for screaming. "What have you done to me? What have you done? You filthy bum! You survived, but you didn't come back. Instead, you found wealth here in Iran — and abandoned me to a life of misery!"

Farshid stood up, too, wiping away his tears with a handkerchief. "Ruchama, my dear, I love you with all my heart, and I always have. Give me a chance to explain. But before I do, promise to stay with me. I promise I'll never leave you again. You can trust me now. Promise to trust me, and then I will explain."

The young woman looked intently at her husband through her tears — the husband who had disappeared and been declared dead, and who had hoodwinked her along with the rest of the world. What explanation could anyone offer for so evil and so thoughtless an act? She didn't understand. She felt shaken and angry. But the mere fact of his existence beside her, and the warmth and familiarity of his touch as he tenderly took her hand in his, convinced her. "I'm sorry. I trust you." The couple embraced again for a full minute. Then Farshid took her by the shoulders and held her away from him. "Sit down Ruchama. What I am about to tell you is so secret that it may shock you."

"A bigger shock than the one I received five minutes ago, doesn't exist." Shakily, she sat down in the swivel chair her husband had just abandoned.

He smiled. "Perhaps so. You must believe me when I say that I would have given my right arm to spare you what you suffered. When you hear what I have to say, I hope you will forgive me."

"Tell me, then." Ruchama was all impatience.

"All right. Bear with me, please. This will take a while...."

Three days later, the Pinhasis escorted their cousin Ruchama Kedem to the airport to catch a flight to Tehran — the first leg in her return trip to Israel.

"Ruchama," Mrs. Pinhasi said, distressed, "Please change your mind and stay. We expected you to stay another month. Just because it didn't work out between you and Mr. Levihayim, you didn't have to rush off like this."

"Thank you, Auntie, I wish I could. But I must accept my great-uncle's offer of a place in Los Angeles, in the United States. After being so rudely put off by Mr. Levihayim in that old-fashioned rat-hole, Isfahan, I just want to find a place where I will fit in."

Mr. Pinhasi spoke up. "Ruchama, Los Angeles is not a good place for you. We've heard so many stories about Iranian Jews who have completely abandoned their traditions in its permissive environment. I'm sorry they made you wear a Chador, but here in Shiraz and in Tehran the Shah has abolished the practice."

"Really, Iran is developing very rapidly. There is great opportunity here for a young modern woman," his wife added persuasively.

"Thank you, Auntie. My thanks to you, too, Uncle. But I think I'll pass." Ruchama stepped up onto the boarding ramp. With a final wave, she disappeared.

Ruchama Kedem never made the TWA flight in Tehran. Farshid picked her up from the airport and took her to a hotel twenty miles out of Tehran. It was late, and both were as excited as the day they were married. Farshid settled himself in bed as Ruchama went into the bathroom. Only seconds had passed before, without warning, he was startled out of his pleasurable mood by the sound of his wife's voice, screaming out his name. He jumped up and tried to turn the knob of the locked door.

"Eli!"

"Ruchama, you must not call me that anymore."

"I'm sorry — Farshid, my dearest. I just remembered something!"

"What's that?"

"I think we are divorced."

"*What?*"

"Just a moment while I unlock this door." Ruchama jiggled the knob and stepped out. Farshid reached for her hand, but she pulled it away, shaking her head. A moment later, seated in facing armchairs, she resumed the thread of her talk.

"Several months after you disappeared, a rabbi called and asked me to come see him in his office. He was very mysterious — and I was curious. When I got there, I found not one, but three rabbis waiting for me. One of them handed me a hand-printed document. I can still hear his words: 'Accept this divorce that your husband has delivered to you, and with it you shall be free to marry any man from this moment on'." She fixed her eyes on his. "Farshid, what do you know about this?"

Slowly, he brought a hand to his forehead. "I can't believe I forgot that. Yes, Ruchama, I did order a *Get* to be written for you. I didn't want you to be left with an ambiguous status, never able to remarry." The thought of Ruchama's belonging to anyone else was unbearable. He stretched out a hand. "My dear...."

Again, she shook her head. "I'm sorry, darling. You can't touch me until we are legally husband and wife again."

"But we're already here, and I love you so much. Dearest, we'll get remarried tomorrow. You can't imagine how much I've missed you."

"I've missed you, too, Farshid — but we must get married first." She gazed at him speculatively. "Uncle Avraham told me how religious you were. I see now that you had him fooled."

"Hey, since when did *you* become so religious? It didn't bother you much before we were married."

"That's true — but I was still in the Israeli army then. Anyway, you told me to always call you Farshid Levihayim. You are not Eli Kedem anymore. If I must call you Farshid, and I must keep kosher and observe Shabbat in your house, then we must be married before you touch me again."

Farshid stood up and said decisively, "Come on, then. Let's go see the rabbi in Tehran right now." He grabbed her hand, and she pulled it away. "Please, Farshid. We must wait. Just listen to me; I want to tell you what happened after you disappeared. It was back in April of 1968. I received the strangest call...."

"Mrs. Kedem, this is Rabbi Karlin in Bnei Braq. I want to express my grief and sorrow over your husband's disappearance."

"Thank you, rabbi. The outpouring of sympathy from everyone has been tremendous...." Ruchama hesitated. "But I don't think I know you. My husband never mentioned your name to me. Were you acquainted with him? I haven't had that many calls from rabbis. We are not religious people."

"Mrs. Kedem," said the rabbi, "I did have the privilege of meeting your husband. In the brief time I spoke to him, I received the distinct impression that he was a highly intelligent man, fully dedicated to his nation. I am calling you for a specific reason. Before your husband left, he asked me to take care of a certain matter, in case he didn't return. Unfortunately, he has not returned. Please be at my office tomorrow morning, so that the matter can be taken care of as he would have wished."

"Of course, rabbi. But it seems strange that he never mentioned anything about you, or this matter, to me."

"Mrs. Kedem, I promise you this — I will explain everything to you when I see you tomorrow."

AT 11:10 next morning, Ruchama Kedem walked into Rabbi Karlin's office. She took her seat beside two other women, who had arrived just before her. She recognized Naama Mordechai as the wife of one of her husband's colleagues, but was not familiar with Ahuva Barnash.

"Ladies," Rabbi Karlin began, sitting at his desk opposite them, "Thank you for coming here today. Again, I wish to express my sympathies to you and your families for the great tragedy that has befallen you and the nation. May the All-Merciful comfort you in your loss."

The ladies began to weep quietly, thanking the rabbi brokenly through their tears. He waited until they had regained a measure of control before continuing.

"There is a very important matter at hand. The government has declared the sub lost, and has given up hope that it will soon be found. There is no longer any hope of survivors. This leaves you in an untenable position. Although it may be premature to speak of this subject, you are all very young, and may wish to remarry sometime in the future. I understand that you, Mrs. Mordechai, gave birth to a daughter just two weeks before the tragedy." He swiveled in his chair. "And that you, Mrs. Barnash, have a six-month-old son. The children need a father and a breadwinner. Despite the tragedies that the Jewish people have suffered throughout history, there comes a point when we must go on with life."

"Rabbi," Ruchama Kedem said, lifting her head, "I wasn't married long, and I don't have any children. When Eli's sub was lost, I did contact the Chief rabbi's office. They informed me that I would have to spit at my husband's fourteen-year-old brother if I wanted to remarry. That is the sickest thing I ever heard of."

The rabbi smiled and held up a hand. "Mrs. Kedem, there are many misconceptions about the procedure you refer to. I'll be glad to discuss it at length with you later. Right now, we must conclude the business at hand.

"Before your husbands departed, they came to this office. Please, do not be shocked when I tell you that they prepared all the necessary paperwork to grant you a Jewish divorce, a *Get*."

The women gasped in surprise and confusion. Quickly, Rabbi Karlin said, "Let me explain. One of your husband's colleagues — I think he was with them on the sub, unfortunately — convinced them to grant each of you a Jewish divorce. Knowing the inherent dangers of submarine travel, as evidenced by mishaps in the past, your husbands were realistically concerned about the possibility of disappearing without a trace. Such an eventuality would leave you women in limbo — neither married nor legally widowed. Your husbands undertook the responsibility of ensuring that you, their beloved wives, would not suffer the problem of being forbidden to remarry.

"It is a little known fact that in the days of Kings Saul and David, it was a regular practice for all departing soldiers to prepare Jewish divorces for their wives, to go into effect in the event of the soldier's capture or disappearance in battle. The laws of declaring a man deceased without the usual proofs are very complicated. This procedure simplifies matters dramatically. For even if, by some miracle, the men on the sub really are alive but perhaps not in a position to return or even to contact you, you would still be able to remarry."

Ruchama Kedem began to weep copiously. "I don't want a *Get*! I'll remain married to my husband forever. I won't let him out of my heart."

In a soothing voice, Rabbi Karlin said, "Mrs. Kedem, please be calm. The fact that you accept the *Get* your husband prepared doesn't mean that you have to feel severed from him. Your husband is not from the priestly family of Aaron, a *Cohane*. If he were someday to return, you could remarry as if nothing had happened — unless you had married someone else in the interval. By our Law, once a woman marries another man, she may not return to her previous husband."

The rabbi addressed all three of the presumed widows. "Please, for your sakes and for your future, accept the *Get* today. Nobody is forcing you to remarry or to abandon your husband's memory. Trust me; I have vast experience in these matters. In the long run, it will be for your benefit."

The women cried, conversed, and commiserated with one another for about ten minutes. Ahuva Barnash, the most traditional of the three, then asked the rabbi a question that impressed him.

"Rabbi, I don't quite understand. If my husband is no longer living, how can the *Get* procedure have any validity?"

"Young woman, you ask an excellent question! The Talmud discusses this very issue at length. Indeed, if all those on board the submarine perished, then the procedure we are about to perform has no real significance. If, on the other hand, your husband is still alive and you are mistakenly permitted to remarry on the presumption that he is dead, there are dire consequences in Jewish Law. By going through with the *Get*, we are covering both possibilities, so that you may someday remarry without a shadow of doubt."

In a show of fortitude, the women straightened up and told the rabbi to proceed. The personnel of the rabbi's rabbinical court instituted the procedure of presenting to each wife the special handwritten document ordered by her husband. In the simple ritual, the husband's appointed proxy handed the *Get* to each woman while the rabbinical court looked on, and uttered the necessary declarations.

Rabbi Karlin informed each woman that she was now divorced, and was permitted to remarry after three months. Ahuva Barnash, whose sister had been divorced, then asked her second intelligent question of the morning.

"Rabbi, do we receive some kind of document certifying the *Get*? Perhaps we will be asked to present it at some time in the future."

"Mrs. Barnash, in a general sense you are right. But we have a special set of circumstances here. I presume that the Chief Rabbinate will be issuing you certificates allowing you to remarry, so you won't need one from our rabbinical court. As a matter of fact, it would probably be prudent of you, Mrs. Barnash and you, Mrs. Kedem and Mrs. Mordechai, not to mention to anyone that you went through with this procedure. It seemed to me that your husbands wanted it that way. I myself am not quite sure why they were so worried about keeping this matter confidential."

"Rabbi," Mrs. Barnash said, "I knew nothing of this entire matter until this morning; I certainly have no idea why it should be kept a secret. But if that was my husband's wish, I will fulfill it."

The others nodded in agreement. All three women thanked the rabbi and departed.

"That was quite an interesting story, Ruchama. It sounds almost as spooky as mine. I see now why you take this religious bit pretty seriously. By the way, did you ever go through *Halitza,* that other rabbinical ceremony, with my brother Nechemia?"

She nodded. "I had to. I wasn't going to mention anything about the *Get*, just as I had promised Rabbi Karlin. The Chief Rabbi's office insisted that I do it."

"Did you actually spit at him?" Farshid asked curiously.

"No, that's just a myth. But I was required to spit on the floor. Let's not talk about that anymore. Farshid, you have a mission. Now that I'm back in the picture, I have a responsibility to do everything I can to make sure it succeeds."

He looked at her face. The expression she wore was one of utmost seriousness. The fire of passion that had welled up in his body cooled down. He knew she was right.

At 10:15 p.m. they found Rabbi Ezra Sofer in his home study.

"It's very late. Is it something urgent?" the rabbi asked, looking from Farshid to Ruchama and back again.

"Very urgent," Farshid declared. "We want to be married right away."

"Very well. I'll try to schedule you for next week."

"No, rabbi," Farshid insisted. "We must be married now."

"That's impossible. You must wait at least one week, perhaps longer."

Farshid took out the ring he had purchased twenty minutes before at the gift shop of the Hilton. "Look here, rabbi — I'll give her the ring and you pronounce us married. Why a week?"

"When did you start planning this marriage?"

The couple looked at each other. "About three days ago," Ruchama told the rabbi honestly.

"Well, according to our Holy Torah, you..." directing his attention at the young lady, "must wait at least one week from that time and then immerse yourself in the ritual bath. That is, if the timing is correct. You know that much, don't you?"

Blank stares from both young people met the rabbi's eyes. He sighed.

"Nurit," he called to his wife, "come in here a minute, please." He directed an exasperated stare at the couple. "I think you need some training before you get married. That is, if you want *me* to marry you. I can't stand this waywardness some of our young people have fallen into. It's bad enough that you hardly know each other."

For the next eleven days, Ruchama became a guest in the rabbi's house. He assented to the couple's wish to make the wedding a very small affair. It would be held in the synagogue after the evening service, and the guest list would include only the fifteen or twenty elderly men who attended the services. Farshid gave the rabbi ten thousand rial. Then he returned to Isfahan to prepare his home for his bride.

By his wedding day, he was having second thoughts about the entire matter. Ruchama had informed him that she'd become convinced by Nurit Sofer to live the life of a religious Jewish woman.

"Are you crazy?" Farshid exclaimed incredulously.

Ruchama smiled. "I don't think you have much choice, Farshid. I know too much, and I don't think you would want to kill me." Her voice softened. "Besides, it's a miracle from God that we were reunited. You never intended it. By a series of circumstances, you had to drive to Shiraz yourself. Then you met my uncle, and your truck broke down. You yourself told me it was a miracle."

"That was just a manner of speaking."

"Are you saying it wasn't really a miracle, just a coincidence?"

"No, I never said that. Okay, so it was a miracle. But do we have to live so old-fashioned a lifestyle? I'm sure God understands that things have changed in the twentieth century."

Firmly, she said, "We will live a devout life together. I'm afraid your cover might be blown if we didn't."

"Is that why? I thought you said you really believe in this stuff."

"I do, Farshid. And I also believe that the work you are doing is being done for the sake of God and his people."

Farshid looked intently at his wife. He saw a strong woman, a good woman. He inclined his head, in respect and submission. "We'll have it your way."

Chapter 20

In 1976, on the recommendation of Farshid Levihayim, the seven trustees of the Isfahan Jewish community voted to renovate the synagogue building. More than one hundred twenty years had passed since the building was erected, and though it didn't exhibit too much wear, the motion was unanimously passed. Levihayim had hinted that PGL, Ltd. would pick up the entire tab.

Levihayim worked with the architect to design a new interior wall that would conceal the rough-hewn stone, the building blocks of the entire structure. The stone wall was studded with aluminum beams, which was paneled with Sheetrock toward the interior of the building. The studs left a fifteen-centimeter gap. Insulation would be blown in through special open plugs, where the wall joined the ceiling. Levihayim insisted on a sheath of Tyvek moisture barrier in the fifteen-centimeter gap, to seal both the inner stone surface and the backplane of the Sheetrock. Despite the added cost — which Levihayim bore in any case — the Tyvek was sealed watertight along all of its seams. The foam insulation would be sprayed into this waterproofed Tyvek sheath. When the work was done on the walls, Levihayim came before the board.

"Gentlemen, I must apologize. Over the past year and a half I've spent over 36,000,000 rials on the synagogue, but I am unfortunately not in a financial position at the moment to complete the insulation."

Joseph Saadatmand came to his friend's defense. "Farshid, your generosity over the past eight years has been without parallel. Besides, many of us on the board couldn't understand why you insisted on insulation in the first place. It is rare, even in the worst winter, for temperatures to fall below freezing. I am quite certain the new wall and the moisture barrier alone will make our congregants much more comfortable than in the past."

Farshid Levihayim was always the last man to leave the synagogue at night. He would remain to study. Then he would lock up, using the set of keys entrusted to him almost from his arrival in Isfahan. But, for several months after the first stage of the work was completed, Levihayim was not actually poring over the Talmud into the wee hours of the morning. He would descend to the cellar and bring up a ladder and a can of lead shot. This he would pour into the insulation plugs at the top of the wall. He could usually manage to dump ten cans per night, before retiring to his home. Ruchama accepted this routine. Little Shimon and baby Dalia often asked for their father; mother made up for him. It took Levihayim almost two years before he emptied the last can, which created a lead barrier around the entire structure. One other renovation, to which only Farshid and Ruchama were privy, was the extension of a few cold water pipes, now with valves hidden behind the insulation plugs in the wall.

Farshid Levihayim, although committed to his religion and growing increasingly devout in his personal life, recognized his obligation toward all the citizens of Isfahan. He used his wealth for numerous causes which endeared him to the people, and especially to the city's politicians. In the winter of 1977, he was invited to speak before the city council of Isfahan.

"Praise to Allah, I stand before you, the honorable fathers of Isfahan, to offer my participation in the development and well-being of our beautiful community. It is a community famous for its tolerance of the diverse groups that live within its borders. No man faces discrimination, be he Moslem, Jew, Christian, Zoroastrian or Bahai. We all live as brothers. The Almighty has been kind and blessed me with a moderate degree of wealth. I would like to use that blessing to further the outstanding blessing of brotherhood, which we all enjoy here in the city. Therefore, I propose and will fund the construction of prominent memorials in the parks and plazas of Isfahan."

Applause broke out. Levihayim raised his hands to quiet the assemblage. "What greater symbol of peace and brotherhood can there be than to publicly honor the great men of Iran by constructing memorial fountains where our people congregate to enjoy themselves? The fountains will hurl a glorious spray into the air. The children can wade in their shallows and collect rials that men of good will cast into its waters. The center structures, housing the pumps that circulate the water, will be built as memorial towers and inscribed with the names of our great leaders of the past, both kings and clerics. Our divine law forbids the graven image of a man; we will suffice without those idolatrous forms, and instead reserve our commemoration and dedications to a simple, tower-like structure. Let me show you some of the plans I've already worked out."

Levihayim unfurled blueprints bearing the designs of several fountains and memorials. The structures were up to ten meters in height; the fountains, fifteen meters in diameter. While passing around these sheets, the councilmen began numerous petty arguments, each vying to adorn his own neighborhood.

"Gentlemen, gentlemen, please. Insha Allah, no neighborhood will be left out. Neither park nor plaza will remain bare of these objects of beauty and contemplation. I will construct them at my lead works from the materials we process and from quality granite from the local quarries. This project will not be without its local economic benefits as well."

There was more applause and a round of hearty handshakes as Farshid Levihayim got up to leave. Within a week, all the necessary permits, variances, and waivers were lying on his desk at PGL, Ltd. The city council passed a resolution giving Levihayim full authority to choose the type of monument and the exact site of its construction, even granting him the authority to tear down an existing structure if necessary. He used this authority to its fullest, always yielding graciously to the wishes of the local politicians.

Building on this enthusiasm, Levihayim immediately expanded his company to process all nonprecious nonferrous metals. He began smelting copper, tin, nickel and aluminum. Most were processed into bars, but some he fabricated into beautiful fountain centers. He purchased pumps from England, which mechanized the fountains. Then, prior to installing his first pump in Reza Square, he put Daryoush in charge of the plant, and took his wife on a vacation to the beach.

"This is no vacation," Ruchama told her husband, while digging alongside him at a lonely beach, one hundred kilometers south of Abadan. "It's 2:00 a.m., chilly and damp. I hope this mission is as worthwhile as you claim."

"Just keep digging, my dear, and together we will pull up a treasure buried here many years ago."

After digging for over an hour, and to a depth of one hundred fifty centimeters, Farshid took out a sheet of paper containing the map he was working from. He studied it again while sitting on the sand as his wife kept digging. "Ruchama, I am certain we're digging over the right spot. Those guys from the Mossad are accurate to the millimeter."

But nothing was there. Farshid assumed that the hermetically sealed containers must be at least one-half by one meter, or close to it. The encoded map seemed to indicate that the cache was buried no more than 1.25 meters deep, but nothing was found except for some broken shards of glass and long buried driftwood branches.

Ruchama suddenly caught her husband's attention. "Farshid, take a look at this." A rusty length of metal, ribbed like a rebar rod, crossed the bottom of the narrow pit. Farshid dug toward the right to find its origin, but after scraping twenty centimeters along that side, the metal ribbing came to an abrupt end. Now he dug to the left. After about half a meter, the rod curved up toward the surface. Three meters from the pit, the rod leveled off at a depth of about fifty centimeters. Following the line to which the rod was pointing, Levihayim made a test bore two meters further along the route to which the bar was pointing. His shovel hit the rod. He made another test bore three meters further, and again the shovel hit the rod. After several more test bores, which took only four scoops of sand, he discovered the end of the rod, some thirty-one meters away from the site indicated on the map he had been given.

"Ruchama, let's start digging here. Those boys at the Mossad sure make things difficult."

"But secure," his wife added.

"I'll say." Farshid plied his shovel.

Twelve more scoops of earth, and the shovel hit something hard and metallic. The only two human hearts in twenty kilometers were pounding so hard, they could practically be heard for that distance. After another hour of digging, the couple lifted the handles of an anodized aluminum trunk, weighing at least forty-five kilos, and placed it in the trunk of their Chevy. Three more identical chests were pulled from the earth and placed in the car. They were not opened until safely stowed away in their bedroom at home, behind a locked door.

"Farshid, how are you going to open these?" asked Ruchama, as she observed her husband studying one of the seamless containers, in search of an opening.

"This thing is really machined well.... Aha, I found the seam! It's almost a perfect fit. I suppose they foresaw that it might be sitting out there for a long time. Now the trick is to open it."

"I don't understand," Ruchama frowned. "With all the training and technical sophistication, why didn't they teach you how these things are sealed, and how they are opened?"

"They did, my dear. But this is not what I was expecting. This was planted where we found it, perhaps six months or more after I was let off to establish myself. I can only guess that a newer and better technology was employed to seal the important contents than was available during my training. Look, there's no hurry. It will be several months before the fountains are ready to be installed. Let's sit on this for a few days. Hopefully, we'll figure it out."

Ruchama had an idea. "Why don't you get an acetylene torch from the factory?"

"Ruchama, sometimes you say the stupidest things!" Farshid laughed good-humoredly. "Do you know what's in here?"

"Not exactly."

"If you did, I don't think you would have made the suggestion. Obviously, the Mossad expected me to figure it out. It may take me a few days, that's all."

To his astonishment, Ruchama began to cry. "You don't have to call me stupid. I didn't have your training. You dragged me along to help you out. I was just trying to help."

Farshid looked away from his wife. "I'm sorry. I guess I'm just impatient to get these things opened. You have been helpful, my dear. We'll figure it out somehow."

The following day, as Ruchama was doing the laundry, her four-year-old daughter called, "Mommy, what's this?"

"What's what?" The busy mom was not paying much attention to the tot as she ironed shirts.

"This thing, Mommy. It looks like a rial bank, but it's very heavy."

Ruchama Levihayim glanced up from her ironing board. There, at the door, was little Dalia dragging a blanket behind her. On the blanket sat a rectangular metal box thirty centimeters long and twenty square. The mother, absorbed in her work, thought the child was playing a game.

"I give up. What is that? A toy daddy bought you?"

"No. I don't know what it is. I found it in your room, and there's a lot more in a big box."

It took all of three seconds for the facts to click together in Ruchama's mind. She dropped her iron and ran into the bedroom. There she saw one of the aluminum boxes that she had helped to dig out of its nine-year nest — its lid wide open. The cube that young Dalia had managed to pull out and drop onto her blanket on the floor was one of eight stacked in the trunk. She ran back, grabbed the object from her crying daughter, put it back in the crate and pushed shut the top. She heard several clicks, and the lid sealed itself tight again.

Ruchama ran to the phone. "Farshid, Farshid! Dalia opened the box!"

"What?"

"The box in our room. She opened it!"

"Which box? Calm down, Ruchama. Just take it easy, and tell me what you're talking about."

Ruchama was silent for a moment. Farshid only heard her breathing. Then, very calmly, she stated, "Dalia opened the aluminum case we dug up on the Gulf coast two days ago, and removed a square item that must weigh about six kilo. There are a total of thirty two in all of the cases together."

"What?" yelled Farshid. "Don't move. No, take the baby and get out of the house. No, wait till I get home. How on earth did she get it opened?"

The telephone clicked in Ruchama's ear. "Farshid, Farshid?" She hung up.

Farshid's actual drive home took him just nine minutes. The extra twelve were devoted to receiving a speeding ticket for going one hundred km/h in a fifty km/h zone. There was a sense of anti-climax when he finally entered the bedroom and saw his wife holding Dalia in her arms. She was sitting on her bed, opposite the top trunk on the floor, locked as before.

"What's going on?" he demanded. "You told me the box was opened."

"I put the cube back inside and shut the lid. It locked itself."

Farshid took the little girl from his wife's arms. "Dalia, honey. How did you open that box?"

"I didn't open it, Daddy."

"Now, now, you must always tell the truth. Mommy told me you opened it and took something out."

"I think it's a rial bank. Daddy, is it a rial bank? Can I keep it?"

"How did you take it out if you didn't open the box?"

"It opened by itself."

"When you came in the room, it was already open?"

"No," came the reply from the little girl.

"Well, suppose you tell me what you did right before it opened by itself?"

Dalia's thin shoulders rose and fell in a shrug. "I don't know. I was playing on it and it opened."

While Levihayim was giving his daughter the third degree, Ruchama was snooping around the case.

"Farshid, look over here," she called.

He put the child down and looked at the object of his wife's attention. It was a small scattering of black dust on the floor behind the trunk. Farshid picked up a pinch of the dust and rubbed it between his fingers. Then he smelled it, trying to figure out what it was.

"Daddy, what are you doing with that? That's from my MagnoMan."

The puzzled father bent down to the young child. "What's a MagnoMan?"

"It's a kind of game. But you don't really play it. You just play with it."

"How do you play with it?" asked Farshid. Ruchama was about to interrupt, but Farshid motioned for silence; he wanted to listen to the child.

"Well, you put that dust on a board that has faces on it, and then you make hair on the man. Or you can give him a beard." Dalia took out a little rod about the size of a pencil and a cardboard tablet with four faces in squares in each of the four corners. The title on the tablet was MagnoMan.

"Now daddy, dump that dust on the board and I'll show how I play."

The father complied. As the child flipped the cellophane sheet over the iron dust, dragged it with the magnetic wand, and formed a weird hair pattern on the female face, Farshid slapped his hand to his own face. "Ruchama, there's a magnetically activated lock mechanism inside the lid!"

He grabbed the wand from his daughter and started waving it around on the surface of the lid. Nothing happened. The little girl grabbed the wand back. "Daddy, you don't know how to do it. Watch me."

Farshid and Ruchama watched in awe as the little girl placed the thin cardboard sheet on the box lid, poured a little of the dust onto one of the squares, flipped the cellophane down and began to fashion a beard and hairdo. After about thirty seconds, they all heard a series of clicks, and the lid popped open one centimeter.

As it opened, the acrid smell of smoke wafted into the room.

In a panic, Farshid grabbed the child and ran toward the door. "Ruchama, get out, get out! It's about to blow!"

Farshid ran out into the street and down the block. He didn't pause for breath until he was two hundred meters from the house. He turned around, but his wife was nowhere in sight. "What have I done?" the distraught man asked himself. He set the child down and walked back to the house. When he came near, he glanced up at the window of his room.

Ruchama stood there, holding up one of his expensive shirts, perforated and blackened by her abandoned iron.

Levihayim entered the house and made his way straight to his bedroom, embarrassed. Dalia followed right behind him, trying to get his attention. "Daddy, why is your face red? Why did you run away? Why Daddy?"

He didn't answer her. He entered the room, to find his wife studying the weird cube in her hand.

"Mommy, is it really a rial bank?" the little girl asked eagerly.

"Dalia, go out now. I must talk with Mommy." The little girl opened her mouth to protest, but something in her father's face made her think the better of it. Farshid led her out of the room, handed her the MagnoMan, and shut the door.

"Farshid," Ruchama asked, "What is this thing?"

"Oh, that." He grinned. "It's a rial bank."

"Farshid!"

"It's a tactical thermal neutron bomb. When it is detonated, everything alive within five hundred meters will die. But structures aren't affected. Within a few seconds, after the radiation dissipates, the kill zone is safe to enter."

Ruchama started to shake. She tossed the six-kilo aluminum-cased object at her husband, who easily caught it.

"Now, now, that wouldn't have done you any good; you're standing only two meters from it."

Farshid put the bomb back in the case, sat down on the bed, and motioned to his wife to do the same. "Let me explain how it works. Actually, it's quite humane. These little metal cubes are individual tactical neutron bombs. Our politicians refer to them as 'Enhanced Radiation Weapons,' or ERWs. Although they're similar to fission devices, or atomic bombs, and fusion devices — hydrogen bombs — their destructive power doesn't lie in the production of heat and shock."

His voice took on a lecturing quality. Ruchama sat with furrowed brow, working hard to follow him. "In a fission thermonuclear weapon, different triggering or 'spark plug' devices are used to raise the energy needed to produce an uncontrolled chain reaction. This frees neutrons within the atom to bombard other atoms and split them. The actual splitting of the atom releases much more energy than the amount that's required to split it. If we stop there, we have an atomic bomb.

"A significant byproduct of this type of device, in addition to heat, is gamma ray radiation, which as everybody knows, effectively damages living organisms. Scientists can now utilize and channel the huge energy burst from a fission reaction to fuse two hydrogen atoms into one helium atom. When this reaction is accomplished, an incredibly greater magnitude of energy is released. This is the principle of the Hydrogen Bomb, whose energy is released largely in heat and proportionally produces lower levels of gamma radiation.

"But in our neutron bombs, the burst of neutrons generated by the initial fusion reaction is intentionally not absorbed inside the weapon to intensify heat levels, but allowed to escape instead. This intense burst of high-energy neutrons is the primary destructive mechanism, as opposed to the heat and gamma radiation. By using a deuterium-tritium gas mixture as the only fusion fuel, the neutron bomb thermonuclear reaction releases eighty percent of its energy as neutron kinetic energy — and it's also the easiest of all fusion reactions to ignite. Because neutrons are more penetrating than other types of radiation, many shielding materials that work well against gamma rays do not work nearly as well here. The term 'enhanced radiation' refers only to the burst of ionizing radiation released at the moment of detonation, not to any enhancement of residual radiation in fallout."

Ruchama looked like she had a number of questions and was trying to make up her mind which to ask first. Farshid, however, plowed right on.

"The fact is, these tactical neutron bombs that we dug up are primarily intended to kill people quickly within a limited range. By emitting large amounts of lethal neutron radiation — which is the most penetrating kind — ERWs maximize the lethal range of a given yield of nuclear device against people, even those behind metal or concrete barriers.

"A radiation dose of six hundred rads is normally considered lethal, but no effect is noticeable for several hours. Neutron bombs were intended to deliver a dose of eight thousand rads to produce immediate and permanent incapacitation. These miniature cubes, which weigh about six kilograms each, produce the equivalent of two hundred fifty tons of TNT. Everyone exposed and unprotected, within five hundred meters, will die quickly from the damage to the DNA in their body cells. Beyond this range, the effectiveness falls off rapidly. Still, without adequate protection there can be long-term damage. The best overall protection is not lead, although lead will protect against the small dosage of fission byproduct, the gamma rays. But the main barrier to an ERW detonation is water, which readily absorbs free neutrons." Farshid sat back, beaming. "There you have it, Ruchama, in a nutshell. Fantastic, isn't it?"

"I think it's horrible," Ruchama said, shuddering.

"All war is horrible. We won't be the ones to start it. We do, however, hope to end it — and the quicker, the better."

Chapter 21

Within the bronze shell of each monument fountain was a small power plant. At the base there was a four-horsepower pump, powered by a 240v, 25amp electric line drawn in under the fountain's pool. The pump could circulate two thousand liters per minute. Its blast sent water spraying thirty meters straight up in the air. On the inside wall next to the pump was an electric control panel. This controlled the pump and the lights, which would go on at dusk and turn off, together with the water, at 11:00 p.m. In addition, several wet cell batteries, under a constant trickle charge, were in place to maintain the fountain's timing circuit during the city's frequent electrical blackouts.

This much of the fountains' innards was known to the city fathers and their maintenance men. What they didn't know was that, behind the main circuit panel, the power leads continued on within the hollow shell of the monument, up to another small chamber at the top. The main jet pipe passed up through a false plate, sixty centimeters below the top of the tapering frame. Inside this area was a power-plant of an entirely different nature. Here, one of the small metal cubes which Farshid had dug up was firmly attached to a ledge. Beside it was a small circuit board that contained a radio receiver. The entire monument functioned as a perfect antenna.

The power leads from the batteries clandestinely emerged in this area and powered the circuit board and the contents of a small cubical aluminum case. Farshid kept two transmitters, one at home and one in the synagogue. Every system was tested for integrity. Ruchama would key in the frequency sequences necessary to trigger the devices, while Farshid himself was constructing them at his plant ten kilometers away. A buzzer in the top chamber would sound, indicating a successful connection. After all the systems were completed and well tested, Farshid made the final connections to the metal cubes. By the summer of 1978, twenty-seven of the most popular squares and parks in Isfahan were embellished with the fruit of Farshid Levihayim's generosity. They were also wired to invisibly poison the DNA of anything alive in their proximity. But only two people in all of Isfahan were aware of that fact.

MONUMENT FOUNTAIN

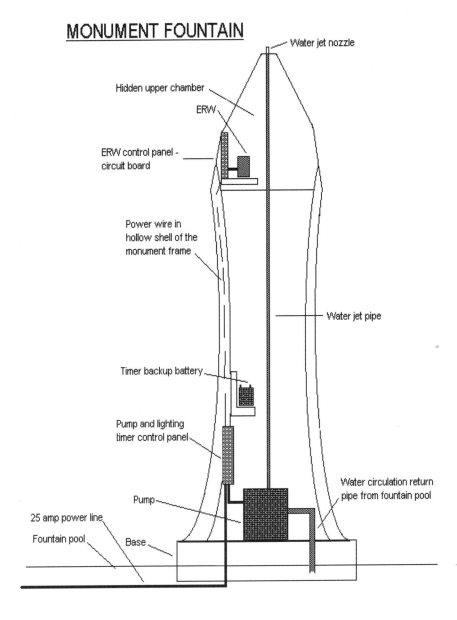

Water jet nozzle

Hidden upper chamber

ERW

ERW control panel - circuit board

Power wire in hollow shell of the monument frame

Water jet pipe

Timer backup battery

Pump and lighting timer control panel

Water circulation return pipe from fountain pool

Pump

25 amp power line

Fountain pool

Base

Over the years, Levihayim had noted the propitious occurrences that had graced his life since he set out on his mission. As he began to think earnestly about the possibility of a Providential Hand in his fate, it became more credible each day. His wife had come to that conclusion many years before, at the rabbi's house just before she remarried her husband. For Farshid, the hammer that drove in the final nail of his faith came along with the last monument he set in place in one of Isfahan's public parks.

Riots broke out across Iran. A week later, six hundred ardent Moslem revolutionaries would be killed by the failing Shah in the streets of Tehran. Isfahan, Qom
and Mashad were ready to convert to a fundamentalist government; those cities
had proclivities in that direction for years. In 1968, when Farshid Levihayim had
been let off on a lonely shore in Iran, the probability that his small cog in the overall operation would ever be implemented was remote — almost unthinkable. Now,
in 1979, within a few months, all of that changed dramatically. It dawned upon
Farshid that his, might actually turn out to be the most vital activity of all in saving
his people. Just perhaps, he thought, God had prepared the medicine before the
illness.

By December, the country was in chaos. The Bakhtiar regime set in place by
the Shah had completely failed to mollify the hardcore Moslems. Khomeini,
though still in exile, had been named the new king. Farshid requested a meeting
with the city council and preemptively requested that the fountain in Reza Pahlavi
Square, which was already plastered with posters of Khomeini, be officially reded-
icated to that cleric. Isfahan at that time was already firmly in the revolutionary
camp. The council wildly applauded Levihayim's suggestion. Three days later,
forty thousand people gathered in the square to watch the welding of the new two-
by-three meter plaque, covering the name of Pahlavi forever with that of Ayatollah
Ruhollah Khomeini.

As a tactical maneuver, the move was not just smart — it was brilliant. For in
addition to the unrestrained anti-Shah, anti-Western clamor of the masses, anti-
Jewish, anti-Zionist fervor had begun to emerge as well. After Levihayim's ploy,
police and revolutionary guards were sent into the Jewish neighborhoods to quell
any thoughts of revenge against the Jews. Farshid Levihayim also became known
as a supporter of the revolution.

"Don't you think you are going too far?" Joseph Saadatmand asked his friend
one day.

"No, Joseph. We must live with the reality. The House of Pahlavi is finished.
Khomeini and his kind will take over the country very shortly. I see the momentum
building toward a violent crescendo. We must be prepared to live with it, or to
leave."

Farshid rose to replenish the ice water in Joseph's glass. Outside, the broiling
Iranian sun had bleached the pavements a dazzling white, but Farshid's living
room was cool, its drapes closed against the glare. He resumed his seat, opposite
Joseph on the sofa, his own drink cradled in his hands. "But I also think that, anti-
Western as Khomeini may be, he truly believes in the law he reveres. He despises
corruption and will punish it wherever it rears its ugly head. Who knows? He may
even bring about a religious revival for our own people."

"Excuse me?" Joseph was startled.

"He will certainly outlaw disreputable hangouts; they will be torn apart by a
million pairs of bare hands. Women, even in Shiraz and Tehran, will have to cover
their bodies in public. Crime, corruption and irreverent behavior will be eradicated from public view. Don't our own Holy teachings preach those things?"

"Yes, that's true. But who says Khomeini will have control? Each fanatic will take the law into his own hands, in line with his own interpretation of Islam."

Levihayim rose and began to pace the room in time with his thoughts. "I agree with you there, my friend. That may be inevitable now, during the turmoil of the revolution. But as things settle down, it's my hope that they will go back to normal. A new standard of normalcy, to be sure, but still normal. The Iranians are more civilized than most Third-Worlders — and, for that matter, most Westerners."

"What, then, is your advice to the Jewish community?"

Levihayim thought a moment before replying, "Cooperation and adaptation. It is never wise to fight the inevitable."

Joseph rose, setting down his glass. "Farshid, the community has always benefitted from your counsel. I'll spread the word."

On the afternoon of January 7, 1979, the phone rang at the Levihayim residence. Ruchama answered. It was long distance from America.

"Hello, is Farshid home?" The far-off question reached Ruchama in a Shirazian Farsi.

"No, he's at his office. Who is this?"

"My name is Marad Barzadeh. Farshid Levihayim is my cousin and I'm calling to inquire if he's safe. I am an American citizen now, but I have a concern for my relatives in the present turmoil. If you need money or any other help, I will try to get it to you."

"I think you have the wrong party," Ruchama said, bewildered and suspicious. "My husband doesn't have any relatives by the name of Barzadeh, here, or in America."

"No, no, he is definitely my relative — all the Levihayims are related. I must apologize for never having contacted your family before. I came to America in '65 and haven't been back since. Please madam, do you need anything?"

Ruchama didn't know what to make of the caller. Her husband's original name, before it was changed to Kedem upon arrival in Israel, had been Golfeiz. On the other hand, if she argued too much with the mysterious caller, she might say something that would trigger an alarm. She injected a placating note into her voice.

"I'm really sorry, but I just don't know what to tell you. My husband and I have only been married seven years. I don't know all of his relatives. You could call back this evening, when he'll be home."

"Let me call him now. Where does he work?"

Ruchama wondered for a moment whether it was wise to divulge this information. In the end, however, she decided in favor of doing so. It was no secret that Farshid Levihayim owned a large lead factory in Isfahan; a refusal to supply the phone number would be highly unusual.

"He's president of Persian Gulf Lead," she said slowly. "The phone number is 355-785."

Marad chuckled. "Sounds like my cousin has made it big. Does he own the company?"

"Yes." Ruchama answered tensely.

"It's really hard to get through. The few lines available are jammed — but of course I'll try. In case I don't, tell him that I am now known as Raymond. I'm a university professor of mathematics. He may be surprised to know that I still keep kosher and go to synagogue every Sabbath. Farshid was very devout as a youth. Has he kept it up?"

Again, the nerves in Ruchama's mouth tensed up as she felt herself compelled to answer. As she spoke, she realized just how amateur a spook she was: she could only tell the truth. "Oh, Farshid is a top trustee of the community. Even the congregation's president consults him on all matters."

"That's really great. But answer me this, Mrs. Levihayim. Why would cousin Farshid move from Shiraz to Isfahan?"

Ruchama was about to fall apart. She was tempted to hang up the phone, but instead responded to the question as though a gun were pointed at her head. "It was before we were married. I suppose he had this business opportunity here that he couldn't pass up."

"I'd hate to live in Isfahan," Marad remarked. "The Moslems there have a reputation for being quite hostile to our people. Is that true?"

"Not completely. But my husband gets along quite well with the local politicians. He donates to non-Jewish causes as well as Jewish ones."

Ruchama felt comfortable divulging that particular piece of information. It always boded well to indicate a gregarious nature.

"That sounds very good. But are you sure you will be safe in Isfahan? The revolutionaries are unpredictable and may turn on the police and the city government."

"No, Mr. Barzadeh, we are safe. We must remain in Isfahan."

"Why?" he pressed. "Perhaps you should go to Shiraz for a few weeks until things settle down. Maybe you could even get out and stay in Israel with Farshid's parents."

"W-we couldn't do that. The business is still running, despite the revolution." Ruchama clutched the receiver so tightly that her knuckles turned white.

"Have you been in touch with the family in Israel?" the voice on the other end of the phone asked conversationally.

This was where Ruchama went to pieces. Belatedly, she realized that the whole conversation had been the fish chum. The last suggestion — that they go stay with Farshid's parents — had been the bait. She had not contradicted the caller. She had been duly hooked.

"No, no, we haven't been in touch with anybody. Excuse me, I — there's something I must see to. Thank you for calling. Good bye." She hung up the phone, trembling. What had she done?

When Farshid returned home, Ruchama said nothing — for the simple reason that she didn't know what to say. He noticed that something was amiss. "What's the matter, dear? You look very nervous."

"I guess the worry over the revolution is getting to me." She twisted her fingers together as she blurted, "Farshid, maybe we should leave Iran for a while."

"That's impossible, you know that. We have a mission here. Who knows what may happen? As soon as Khomeini gets in, he may lead the Holy War charge to dislodge the 'infidels' from Eretz Yisrael. No, this is the worst time to leave." He studied his wife with concern. "But maybe you should go, and take the children. You'd have to find someplace to live where you'd be a stranger. That's imperative."

"Farshid, I'm not leaving you now." She started to cry. He moved closer and took her in his arms. Ruchama was on the point of telling him about the call, when the doorbell rang.

Gently disengaging himself, Levihayim went to answer. He looked through the peephole and saw a short man with closely cropped hair and huge ears. The man had a foreign air, but that might have been attributable to the baggy overcoat that covered him from shoulder to ankle.

"What do you want?" Levihayim asked in Farsi.

"I need your help. Let me in," the man answered in English.

Now Levihayim asked in weak, but understandable English. "Who are you?"

"My name is Moss Farrell. I'm from Fort Worth, Texas, and I need your help."

This was incomprehensible to Levihayim. What kind of help could he extend to this American stranger? He had already committed himself publicly to the revolution and was reluctant to fraternize with Westerners. "If it's about business, call my office tomorrow."

"Mr. Levihayim, I need your help *right now*. I swear to God, I'm on the level. Just let me in."

Levihayim hesitated. "Is there anybody with you?"

"No, I'm alone. My driver's out waiting in the car."

"Wait there a few minutes."

Levihayim called Ruchama over to the door. He told her to wait until she saw him standing on their doorstep. He went out the back door and through the neighbor's courtyard to the street. He peered down the block in both directions. All he could see was the lone Peugeot-606 parked in front of his house, the driver listening to the radio. It appeared that this Farrell fellow was telling the truth about being alone. Farshid sneaked up behind the man waiting at his stoop and said quietly, "You may go in Mr. Farrell."

Farrell jumped as if he had been stuck with a needle, and whirled around. "Hey, you scared me!"

"I'm sorry. But, as you must be very aware, we live in troubled times."

"I may be more aware than you are. That's why I'm here."

Levihayim signalled to his wife through the peephole, and Ruchama instantly opened the door. Farrell was invited into the dining room. Within minutes, a tray of steaming tea was placed before the men. Farrell took off his coat.

"First, I want to ask if you know who I am?" he asked.

"No, I don't. Who are you?"

Farrell pulled several magazine articles from his pocket and handed them to Levihayim. "Better look at these. You'll find out who I am, and I won't have to sit here convincing you."

The articles were from Time and Newsweek. First Levihayim looked carefully at the pictures and ascertained that the man sitting at his table was the H. Moss Farrell described in the articles. He called Ruchama, who was fluent in English, to join them and quickly peruse the articles. She spoke aloud in Farsi as she read. "This man is very rich. He owns DIS, Digital Information Systems — the largest computer software company in the world."

"How rich?" asked Farshid. "About like us?"

Ruchama laughed and pointed at a line that showed the figure $500,000,000. Then she described his successful exploits in helping the American POWs and MIAs, some of whom were still languishing in Viet Nam. "Farshid, if these magazines are telling the truth, this man is an American super-patriot."

Farshid looked at Farrell, who was only trying to guess what the two Farsi speakers were saying.

"So you're a rich American patriot," Farshid said in his halting English. "What can I do for you? I have a small business reprocessing lead. If you need some lead bars, I think I can spare some from my inventory." He paused, studying his guest. "But you have hinted that you are not here about business."

Farrell crossed his arms. "Mr. Levihayim, I'll be real honest with y'all. Neither one of us has time to waste. Do you have a social security card?"

Levihayim felt for his wallet. "Of course. Everyone was issued one last year."

"We did the entire computerization of that system. We also computerized the National Bank, and were just getting set to do the income tax system when this country went to hell a few months ago. Your government hasn't paid our main contract since June. They owe us $7,000,000."

"I apologize for my government, but I'm afraid I have no connections or ability to help you. I would suggest you stop doing the work until you get paid."

"We did just that," Farrell said. "And that's the problem. Haven't y'all noticed that the whole social welfare system is at a standstill?"

"Mr. Farrell, the whole country is at a standstill."

"Yes, indeed." Farrell's manner grew brisk. "Well, to make a long story short, the government arrested our two top people in Tehran. I want to get them out of jail and out of the country. There's where I need your help."

Farshid began to laugh. "Mr. Farrell, I don't have any idea who told you I could help, but I can't. Maybe you don't realize it, but I am a Jew. Jews are a suspicious minority here in Iran. The Moslems hate us almost as much as you Westerners."

Farrell broke in, bristling. "I resent that. I don't hate Jews or anybody."

"I apologize for my poor English. I meant, as much as they, the Moslems, hate the West. In any case, as I told you before, I have a successful business, but I'm no billionaire, and I would like to keep a low profile. I must be truthful with you. The Shah was a brutal and corrupt leader. I have joined with those who would like to see the country become more... religiously traditional. Now, you'd better go — for your sake. Don't waste your time with me. You should spend it seeking help from a good source."

"Mr. Levihayim, or whoever you are. I know you can help me," Farrell declared emphatically.

Farshid and Ruchama looked at each other. "Ruchama, my dear, please leave us alone now." Both men were silent until the door had closed behind her. Levihayim turned to his visitor. "What did you mean, 'or whoever you are'?"

"Your name isn't Levihayim. You're an Israeli spy, aren't you?"

Slowly, and very emphatically, Farshid said, "Mr. Farrell, you have lost your mind. Leave my house at once, or I'll call the revolutionary guards. Maybe you'll wind up in jail with your friends. I see you already realize it is unlikely they will ever get out alive."

"Let's cut the bull. I know who you are, and you'd better help me." Farrell was deadly serious.

Without warning, Levihayim jumped on Farrell and easily grappled him to the floor. He got him in a chokehold from behind and said between clenched teeth, "Farrell, I don't know who you are or what you want. But I'll give you thirty seconds to confess, because you're going to die right here."

"Stop!" Farrell gasped. "You won't get away with this. My men in this country and the U.S. know who you are. If I don't come back they're instructed to leak your identity to the Khomeiniites. If I'm dead, you're dead."

Still holding onto the American, Levihayim paused to gather his wild thoughts. Farrell said persuasively, "Help me, and no one will know. I swear to God, I'm just trying to help my men. I've already spent $300,000. Money is no object to me. I'll pay you, too."

"Farrell! You're bluffing. What's my name?"

Farrell had indeed been bluffing. He wasn't sure of Levihayim's original name; he'd only had a hunch that he was a spy. It was now painfully, even dangerously, obvious that he had struck pay dirt.

Chapter 22

Bill Gordon and Paul Chislin, executives of DIS, had remained behind in Iran after a full employee evacuation. They hoped they could collect some of the debts owed to the company or, better yet, get the government contract back on track. Instead, on December 26, 1978, they were arrested.

No specific charges were brought against them. But the prosecutor, Hosain Dagat, told them that DIS was suspected of bribing the Minister of Social Welfare to get the contract. That minister was already in jail. As it turned out, the government really wanted to blackmail DIS into starting up the system, which was now shut down. Moss Farrell left his vacation resort, and began to work tirelessly to get his men released.

He found that all his clout in the American government was to no avail here. The Shah was still officially the ruler, but had just about lost his power base; within three weeks, he would leave his homeland forever. The Bakhtiar government was also rapidly losing its grip. But due to the DIS shutdown, no one in the ministry, including top officials, had been paid in months. The top brass wanted that system up and running. Since there was no money, their only recourse was to shake down DIS.

The novice government officials didn't know what they were up against in the person of H. Moss Farrell.

*   *   *

"Sam," the short magnate said to his right-hand man, Sam Kirby, "we're not getting anywhere through conventional means. I think the time has come to plan a way to bust our boys out. Call Tiger Crystal and tell him the situation. Crystal's the best man for the job."

Crystal flew into Fort Worth from Florida. So did eight other men who were familiar with Tehran. The group — which Crystal would lead — carefully studied all the information they could find about the prison and the surrounding terrain, formulated a plan, and started to train for it.

"I think we need an insider, someone who knows the country and has connections to get out," Farrell told his deputy. The two sat deep in thought in Farrell's luxuriant office. "Tell me, Moss," Sam said. "Why do you think you failed to get anyone's attention in the Carter White House?"

"I think their minds can only concentrate on one thing at a time. They're too busy with Sadat and Begin, and making the Camp David Accord work." Farrell shook his head impatiently. "Those Israelis, they're always dominating the news."

Kirby sat bolt upright. "Moss, that's it! You just found the ticket out for our men."

"What are you talking about?"

"The Israelis. Until a few months ago, there were as many Israeli technical people in Iran as Americans. I'll bet there are a few left who could help us."

"I'll bet not. Khomeini is virulently anti-Zionist. They'd be shot on sight."

"Of course, of course. But they must have spies sprinkled around — Mossad agents and the like. If we could find one of them, we have our ticket out. Any agent worth his salt would have his escape hatch all ready and waiting. We pay him, or do whatever we have to, so that he opens that window for us."

"Listen to yourself, Sam. You're basically saying the Israelis have the best undercover operation in the world. I'll grant you that. But that being the case, how on God's earth are we going to find one over there? Just like they know how to operate, they know how to cover up!"

Kirby sat lost in thought. Finally, he roused himself to say, "That's surely true, Moss. But our search can be narrowed down to the Jews of Iran. That's a whole sight less than the country's general population."

"Now you're talking nonsense. What are we going to do? Stand up in every Jewish temple and ask: will the real Mossad man please stand up?"

"Moss. What business are you in?" Kirby was smiling.

"Computer systems," Farrell snapped. "What are you getting at?"

"I think you have all the demographic data of Iran right here in this building. We have backup tapes of our work over there going back several years. Let's get our programmers down to work looking for our man."

Farrell was not yet convinced. "How are they going to do that? There are thirty million records to sift through. Are we going to profile every one of them?" He snorted. "Maybe we'll have our men back for the Millennium — if they're still alive."

Doggedly, Kirby asked, "Do you remember Dr. Raymond Barzadeh, professor of statistics at U. of T.?"

"Sure. We hired him as a consultant when we wrote the proposal to the Iranian government three years ago."

"Right. I'd invited him to lunch, but he wouldn't eat anything. That's when he told me he's a Jew. The man is a genius, and he's perfectly trustworthy."

A gleam sprang into Farrell's eye. "Get him on the phone right away. I'll call down to programming."

That same evening, Farrell caught a flight to Tehran. By the day after, Barzadeh was working with the programmers, giving linguistic and demographic hints on setting up their filter. They were to narrow the search to individuals with Persian-Jewish names whose information record indicated some kind of a discrepancy with earlier records. In creating the database, DIS had required the Iranian government to supply all the birth records that could be found, beginning in 1875. Most of this vital data was punched into the system. Some of the later data, however, was transferred from a crude system the Iranians had been working on without outside help in the late sixties. Included here was everyone born after 1940. The army had intended to computerize for the draft.

The programming team leader was Bart Hunslow. He was just the kind of guy that Farrell loved. A sharp mind, a leader among men and, most of all, he had served as a Navy Seal for three tours in Viet Nam. Hunslow was a Texan; 'yes sir' and 'no sir' were natural to his lexicon even before he became a military man.

"Mary," said Bart, to a morbidly thin, bespectacled young programmer under his wing, "let's think this through. Could anyone have added a record to the file without our knowledge? What would they have had to do?"

Mary pushed her glasses higher up on her nose, as though to help along her thought processes. "Well, in addition to adding the record, they'd have to change the trailer record — the one at the end of the file that has the counts."

"Yes. You're right," Bart nodded. "Otherwise, we would have gotten a failing error message saying that the number of records was incorrect. Okay, now let's assume they changed the count on the trailer record, too. How would we know they had plugged in a record?"

"If we know how many records we started out with, and how many were added and deleted, we could calculate how many should be on the final file."

"Good. See if we have that information," Hunslow ordered.

Mary was back in five minutes, rolling a cart full of tapes ahead of her. There was a tape containing the raw data from the Iranian army system, and several more with the birth information that had been manually keyed in from birth certificates. There were a lot of other tapes marked "Transactions", followed by a date. She had also located the first good tape containing the converted data in its final format, and the tapes with the most current data.

"We may have everything we need," she said, "but I'm not sure if we've got all the transactions. To check that, I'll print a dump of the header records. Each transaction run has a sequential number assigned to it. That number would appear on the header."

"Do that," Bart agreed. "But we don't know when a record might have been added. It might already be on that first file. Why don't you also write a program to see if the number of records on that tape equals the sum of the converted records?"

Mary returned a few hours later. "All the transactions were there. I'm glad I didn't scratch any of my old tapes. Charlie's been bugging me to do it, but I was too busy to get around to it. It doesn't look like any record's been inserted. All the counts matched perfectly, even the comparison of the first tape with the converted records."

Ron Bergel, another programmer on the project, threw in his two cents. "Maybe the record you're looking for wasn't inserted. If I were a spy or something and wanted to hack a system like this to gain a legitimate ID, I'd modify an existing record. The first red flag would be a difference in the count."

"You're right Ron — I already figured as much. But if they changed the count on the trailer as well, it wouldn't flag. For a short-term mission, that would be the easiest approach."

Hunslow decided that Ron was right. An undercover man would probably be spending many years on the job. If he had the capability and know-how — and certainly the Israelis did — he'd hack the system just as Ron had described.

"This was an easy first try," Hunslow said. "Now let's try the next most likely red flag. I think we have checksums on the trailer for last name, first name, and Social Security number. Let's see if those add up to the detail records."

"Wouldn't we have seen an error message if the checksums didn't balance?" Mary asked.

"I think we still have to give it a shot. There may have been some errors reported. But, since checksum errors aren't failing errors, they may have been ignored." Bart thought a moment. "If that's clean, I want you to rerun — starting from the first tape and applying each transaction tape to it. Let's see if we get any checksum errors. At the same time, I'll ask Bob Harris to work with Dr. Barzadeh to write a special filter program. But I don't know how much use it will be for us if we don't find any errors."

Seven more hours went by, and when the number crunching was done, still no red flag. The only checksum errors found were between the Iranian army tape and the first good file. These appeared in the Social Security number field. But Hunslow figured that one out quickly. He remembered that one of the problems during conversion had been nonnumeric Social Security numbers. The Iranians had typed in a lower-case l (EBCDIC hex value 93) instead of a numeric 1 (hex value F1), and the conversion program had changed these to numeric values. The difference in checksums could be calculated by choosing appropriate multiples of the hex 5E difference for each digit of the Social Security number.

Hunslow picked up the phone. "Harris, any progress with Barzadeh?"

"Yeah, the guy's a brain. After speaking with me for thirty minutes, he's telling me how to program the filter routines. We gave it a test run on one tape — L-O, about 3.8 million records. So far, we've sifted through two thousand. He says, they're eighty percent Jews for sure. Right now we're in middle of running the routine with three more filters based on the error patterns Barzadeh distinguished."

"When will that be done?"

"In about two hours."

An hour and forty-one minutes later, the phone rang in Hunslow's office. "This last run was close to ninety-five percent accurate according to Barzadeh. We came up with 16,654 records."

"Good! Run the job on all the tapes, A to Z. You've got four computers to work with."

Three hours later, 112,997 records were written to a file. With such a small database to work from, Hunslow grabbed the fastest 370 in the place and the team gathered to refine their search. A job was run to filter out all women, men between the ages of zero to twenty, and those sixty-five and up.

Mary spoke up. "Hey, what makes you think the person we're looking for isn't female?"

"Mary, trust me," said Hunslow.

This filter yielded a database of 39,121 records. Although the past eighteen hours of work made sense, they weren't sure what to do next. Barzadeh, along with Harris, who had graduated a crash course on Iranian Jewish names, started searching through the printouts. They were not quite sure what to look for, but hoped for some sort of digital sore thumb.

Hunslow had used the latest data he could find, which was dated July 10, 1978. He had Mary bring out all of the Iranian Social Security tapes. Now he wanted to run the same job on a set dated December 9, 1976. "What's this?" he asked, noticing the label on the tape. "It says DW checksum."

"Oh," said Mary, "That was a test I ran against the file. I made the checksum fields double words. Then I realized it wasn't necessary, it was just slowing down the run. So I changed it back to single word size. Thirty-two bits is plenty."

"Hey!" exclaimed Ron Begler. "That might be the answer. Maybe the data was hacked to match the thirty-two-bit checksum. They wouldn't bother to make sure that it would match up to sixty-four bits. They'd just assume the high order bits would drop off. Let's run a compare."

"Compare what?" asked Mary.

"Rerun your data, up to December 9, 1976, just the same way you did before, but use sixty-four-bit checksums," said Hunslow. "Let's see if they match the totals on your test tape."

Five hours later, Mary showed him the results. Hunslow scanned the printout. Suddenly, his eyes lit up. "Bingo! A mismatch. Now let's find that son of a gun."

"I don't see how," Mary protested, doing her ladylike best to stifle a huge yawn.

"We've got the filtering tools. We'll run them against both tapes. Then we just have to check all the differences between our filtered records on the two tapes. When we find the difference that equals the difference in the checksums, we've got him."

It didn't take long. Tapes spun, printouts were checked, and then a cheer went up from the group. They had a Social Security number, name and address. The disparate checksums pointed directly at the record whose keyname was Farshid Levihayim.

*   *   *

"Yes!" Farrell shouted in excitement from his roost in the Tehran Hyatt. "Isfahan, you say? I'm on my way."

Farrell told no one where he was going. He merely left a note with the front desk. If he didn't return within twenty-four hours, the number on the envelope was to be called, and the note picked up.

Chapter 23

Levihayim relaxed his grip on Farrell's neck.

"Please, Mr. Levihayim," Farrell urged. "I'm friend, not foe. I really don't know who you are or what you're up to, and I don't care. I just know that you can help."

Levihayim let the man go, apologized, and helped him to straighten out his jacket. Farrell sank back in his chair. Ruchama, hearing the commotion, had remained poised just outside the door. She entered the room now, and addressed Farrell directly. "Who is Barzadeh?"

Quizzically, Farshid turned to his wife and asked, "Who *is*... Barzadeh?"

Farrell lifted his hands. "Now listen to me, you two," he said in his heavy Texan drawl. "Dr. Raymond Barzadeh is an Iranian Jew from Austin, a professor there, who helped me track you down. You have a fine cousin in that man," Farrell said to Levihayim, who was completely befuddled.

Ruchama realized it was her turn. She spoke in Farsi. "Farshid, these people baited me this afternoon. I couldn't bring myself to tell you what a fool I had been. But I tell you now, with all my woman's intuition: Mr. Farrell is completely sincere."

Farrell didn't understand the words, but saw right through the expressions. "Thank you kindly, Ma'am."

"But Ruchama," Farshid responded in Farsi, "he knows too much. Even if he is one hundred percent trustworthy, we can't afford any red flags attached to us. We have our operation in place. I just want to sit tight and live the roles we've been playing for the past ten years. I hope to God that world peace will come, and the Messiah, if you will. But I must ensure that, if the time comes, what must be done will be done. I simply can't justify jeopardizing everything for his poor waifs."

"Do you know what he wants? Give him a chance. Hear him out."

"My dear, if I don't help him, he's threatened to reveal that we aren't kosher. From what he says, dispatching him would get us an automatic centerfold in the *Revolution Times*...." He stopped, then said slowly, "Wait. I have an idea."

Farshid directed his attention at Farrell and spoke in English. "Sir, tell me what you know about me, and how you found out."

"That's a reasonable request. You could have had that before you roughed me up. I have nothing to hide," Farrell replied with a touch of acerbity.

"Please accept my apologies. But, to be perfectly frank, you ought to consider yourself lucky. I was about to break your neck and dump your body into my blast furnace."

Farrell cringed. "I told you, we're in the computer software business. We did a bunch of contracts for your government, so we had all the vital data. We have the best programmers in the world and, luckily, the services of Dr. Barzadeh — your cousin." Farshid made a face. Farrell continued, "He actually helped us cull the Jewish names from all the demographic data. We ran all kinds of digital searches until we found that Farshid Levihayim didn't fit in quite right."

Farshid looked at Ruchama, "That's impossible. My tracks were supposed to be covered by our best computer people."

Again, Farrell guessed what he had said. "I'd say you Israelis are the *second* best computer people; we Texans are still the best. Look, honest, all we know is that y'all arrived here between 1966 and 1969, and that possibly your name was once Golfeiz."

Farshid's eyes belied his shock. These guys were good.

"That's it. Oh yes, your pretty little wife helped to confirm our suspicions in a lovely conversation with Dr. Barzadeh. You know — your long-lost cousin."

Farrell flipped a cassette tape on the table. Ruchama covered her face in shame. Farrell took a wad of C-notes out of his pocket and plunked them down on the table. There were two hundred of them. "Please, Farshid, I owe it to my men to give them the best shot I can. I've got the best breakout man that *ever* served the American Army, together with a team of great guys we put together. They're waiting in Tehran. But I need a native, and a smart one at that. One that I can trust sight unseen." He pointed a dramatic finger directly at Farshid's chest. "That's you!"

Ruchama looked up at her man. "Do it, Farshid. In the worst case scenario, I will carry out the project."

Farshid Levihayim picked up the five-centimeter thick stack of crisp bills. He looked at them for a few seconds and slipped them in his pocket. Farrell extended his hand and said, "Let's have a drink."

The next day, Farshid Levihayim rented a Range Rover. His company had three, but he wanted one without a readily traceable tag. He worked all day preparing his paperwork. He did this by getting real passes, vouchers, and references from the local Mullah, under his own name. Then he put some of his long unused Mossad talents back to work.

"How's this, Ruchama?" He showed her the copies he had made under the alias of Abbas Bolgazi. He donned the typical clothing of a common street revolutionary and even attached a false mustache to his clean-shaven face. His shoddy appearance, coupled with the shiny Range Rover, made him look the part of a rebel leader — a real takeover man.

He got through every road block in minutes, and every weapons search, even though he was carrying a Walther PPK. The man was a pro — a little rusty at this game, but a pro nonetheless.

When he arrived at the hotel, he was in the mood for a good joke. For one thing, he knew the Americans would enjoy a little show of bravado. For another, he wanted to establish his unquestioned authority in the eyes of his Western colleagues. He got the room number from the bellhop; it cost him only three hundred rials. Then he took the elevator to the twelfth floor and waited. Sure enough, within an hour he watched the elevator door open and a waiter from the restaurant carry a large tray toward room 1231.

"I'll take that, thank you," Farshid-Abbas told the hapless fellow, blocking his passage.

"That's for room...."

"Twelve thirty-one. I'm in their company. I'll take it." The immaculately dressed waiter looked distrustfully at the shabbily clad man. But he said nothing when Abbas stuffed ten thousand rials in the other's breast pocket and plucked the tray adroitly from his hands.

At the door, he adjusted the tray to leave one hand free, and knocked briskly. "Room service."

The door opened. Farshid held the tray at face level. Crystal's reaction showed deeper concern than the hotel's waiter had; he had much more at stake. "What's this?" he yelled. "They send in some grungy rebel from the streets?" The Tiger smelled a rat and lunged at Farshid. The able Mossad man, tray still balanced in his left hand, plunged his foot in the approaching man's instep. Crystal started falling forward. Farshid dropped into a quick squat and shoved his elbow hard in the sixty-year-old Tiger's ribs. The man went down on the floor, holding his side.

Farshid wheeled around and jumped on the bed, tray still in hand. He whipped out his PPK with his right hand and yelled, "Freeze!" He was now in total command of the room and all six of Farrell's cornered rescue squad. Tiger Crystal got up and looked at his attacker with a cold expression.

"In the name of Allah and the revolution, you're all under arrest. Stay where you are, or you'll be shot. You're spies. We know why you are here. You came to get your criminal accomplices out of prison."

Five of them were practically in tears. Only Tiger Crystal kept his stoic gaze on the man in the middle.

"You," pointing to Bud Caldwell, "pick up the phone and get Farrell over here right away." The men audibly gasped. This guy knew everything. Caldwell didn't move. Farshid pointed the gun straight at the Tiger's head, three meters away. "Call," he barked, "or this one won't stand trial." He shook the gun forward. "I just need dollars, you hear. I get dollars, then I leave." Caldwell called. Moss was only two floors above. "Moss, we have a problem. The rebels know everything. There's one of them in here. He's calling you down to the room. He says he'll shoot Crystal now, if you don't show up. He wants money, and then he says he'll leave.... Oh yeah, he's also got our food."

Farshid knew his man. Within three minutes there was a knock at the door. Farshid motioned to Caldwell to turn the knob and leave the door ajar, then return to his position. The door was pushed open all at once. Moss Farrell had a wad of bills, an unknown quantity, flapping in his hand. He looked up at Farshid and froze for a second. Then he doubled over in raucous laughter.

Still laughing uncontrollably, Farrell let go of the door and it slammed shut. Farshid was still holding the gun and the tray, his face impassive. The men were totally bewildered, so much so that their hands were still raised. After about half a minute, with Farrell still heaving with mirth, Tiger Crystal joined him — his laughter was so ferocious that the room began to shake. Farshid put the gun back in his pocket and set the tray down on the table.

"Gentlemen, enjoy your meal."

The mouths of five men still hung wide open.

Farrell was trying to talk, but he was hardly able to get two words out of his mouth, when the laughter overtook him again. "Meet... meet... Far—"

Farshid quickly corrected him. "Abbas Bolgazi."

Upon hearing the alias, Farrell's hysterics were back. Farshid took out the pistol and worked the slide. He dropped the empty clip, inserted the loaded one, and put the thing back in his waist holster.

Farrell finally gained control of himself and went over to hug Farshid. "This," he announced to the assemblage, "is our man in Iran. I hired him yesterday. He's the one we found...."

"Shhh!" Abbas hissed. From the men's changed expressions, it became obvious to Farshid that they had some prior knowledge about him. He wasn't happy about that, but was optimistic that if he succeeded in his mission and came out alive, they would owe him one. They could pay him by forgetting he had ever existed.

Chapter 24

For three hours, without uttering a word, Farshid listened to the men describe their plan and how they'd prepared for it. How they would pull a ladder out of a van, scale the prison wall as the prisoners were exercising in the prison yard. Jump over walls and barbed wire. Divert the guards' attention....

"So what do you say Mr. Bolgazi?" Caldwell asked, smiling proudly at the plan's ingenuity and daring.

"It's idiotic."

On every side, faces fell.

"And I am the idiot," Crystal said. "So let's hear what the pro would do."

"I'd sit back and relax," Bolgazi replied.

Farrell's long ears pricked up and his beady eyes lit with a fire. "My innocent men should just languish in jail? I'd rather send everyone home and pay the cursed $13,000,000 bail — ransom is what it really is."

"You won't have to pay the money. Your men won't languish very long — two months, at the most. Then they will be free."

"Oh yeah? Who's going to free them?" Farrell demanded.

"They'll just walk out," came the terse reply from the Jew in Moslem garb. He held up a hand. "Just listen to me. This is how I would handle this. You should definitely continue the legal efforts and talks with Dagat. Keep trying to bargain the bail down and keep complaining about how outrageous the arrests were. Keep insisting on the men's complete innocence. This will keep him off guard. If you were to cut off communications with him, you can be sure your men will be sent to some far-off prison, which will be the end of your visits to them and probably our chances of getting them out. Dagat will definitely suspect that you have foul play in mind.

"The best place for these men is right here in Tehran. When Khomeini returns — and my feeling is that will be within the month — full-blown revolution will erupt. The crowds will storm the Bastille, and all the prison doors will be opened. That's how your men will walk out."

Farrell began to rub his hand in open glee. "You could have something there, man!" he crowed. "A simple and bloodless solution!"

"Not a complete solution," Bolgazi warned. "Your real problem will be getting them out of the country. No doubt there is a stop order on them at all ports of exit. The powers that-be will definitely honor those orders, for they will have no idea who issued them. Of course, there's the possibility that Dagat will be deposed along with many of the bureaucrats of the Shah's regime, but I highly doubt it. I

understand that he's a prosecutor for the Ministry of Health and Social Services —
much too complex and benign an office for the Islamic Fundamentalists to dis-
mantle right away. They will be concentrating all their efforts on cleaning up the
military and the police. The way I see it, Dagat will survive the Revolution, especially since his job is, ostensibly, to root out corruption."

Bolgazi walked to the door. "Mr. Farrell, I have a business to run. Since it could
be several weeks before things start heating up, I'll return home. If you need me,
call my office and ask the agent answering the phone, 'Can you melt lead in
Tehran?' That will be my signal. In the meantime, forget about cracking through
the prison wall. You'll all be dead before you get three meters." He paused, then
asked, "Don't you have any trustworthy Iranians who worked for the company?"

"Why, yes, we do," answered Lamont Timmons, former director of personnel
in Tehran. "Javeed, a young entry level programmer, seemed the energetic type."

"Bring him here. But don't breathe a word about my origin. He'll know me
only as Abbas Bolgazi."

Javeed showed up two hours later. He entered the hotel room, shook hands
with all his friends from DIS, then turned around to look at Abbas Bolgazi. He
glanced at Caldwell and asked bluntly, "Who's the rebel clown?"

Without waiting for an answer, he stepped over to Abbas Bolgazi, who stood
motionless, watching him. Javeed poked at Bolgazi's mustache — and peeled it
off. Over his shoulder, Javeed tossed it back at the DIS men, "I hope you know
what you're doing. I could swear this guy looks like a Jew."

"This is your man, gentlemen," Bolgazi said. "Mr. Farrell, I don't know why
you wasted your money and efforts on me."

Javeed addressed him in rapid Farsi. "Don't be offended. Half my friends are
Jews. If Mr. Farrell picked you for his team, you must have something to offer. We'll
work together. I understand they want us to lead an overland passage to freedom
for Bill and Paul. I like the notion of there being two of us, instead of just me."

"Fine." Bolgazi studied the rambunctious twenty-three year-old. "Can you
take orders?"

"Sure. I can take all the orders I'm given." He grinned. "But I always do what
I want."

Bolgazi laughed and slapped Javeed hard on the back. "Ask our friends here
how I introduced myself to them. Ask Colonel Crystal."

After he heard the story, Javeed's humor subsided slightly. But being the
brazen daredevil that he was, Javeed decided to play a game of his own. It wasn't
enough to hear stories; he wanted to test Bolgazi himself. Javeed had a brown belt
in karate and was eager to test his own skills as well. Talking to Bolgazi in Farsi as
a distraction, he slowly approached. Suddenly, he sprang like a tiger with a punch
at Bolgazi's stomach.

The next thing Javeed knew, he was flying through the air. He had an odd
feeling that he'd been miraculously converted into a bird. He did a full somersault
and landed flat on his back on the queen-size bed two meters away.

When he'd caught his breath, he sat up and said, "I didn't know they took Jews into SAVAK."

Abbas smiled. "Javeed, my friend, I hope that the only talent we will need in this project will be in the use of our tongues. In that, I presume your skills are closer to mine. Perhaps not my peer, you understand, but not too far behind." Javeed laughed and nodded his head. Bolgazi continued in English, for the others' benefit. "Once Bill and Paul are out, someone must meet them and lead them to safety. That will be Javeed, myself, or both of us. As revolutionary leaders, we will have the power to safeguard them from the mob. Now we must formulate a plan to get them out of the country."

Lamont Timmons had been researching this. "I've checked out taking them by boat to Kuwait. We even have a man there, ready to get hold of the boat and other equipment."

Bolgazi thought for a moment. "Let's analyze this logically. We have two basic obstacles to overcome. The first, and I think most formidable, is getting through all the roadblocks and checkpoints that both the government and the rebels have set up. The second is getting the men across the border. From here to the Gulf coast is over fifteen hundred kilometers. Traveling the main roads, we can expect at least ten checkpoints, and as many as twenty. I passed through six, just driving from Isfahan.

"Once at the sea, there is a problem of Coast Guard patrols. You can be sure they have been intensified. On a moonless night, though, the chances are good. The overland leg is nearly impossible."

"I also considered that," Timmons said. "But anywhere we go, we're going to run into roadblocks."

"That's true," Bolgazi replied, "but the quality of the personnel at the roadblocks is a major factor. Our possible routes are to Azerbaijan, Afghanistan, or Turkey. The Russians rule Azerbaijan — a grim prospect. Afghanistan is a cinch to enter, but where would we go from there?" He spread his hands as his eyes swept the room. "Gentlemen, our best bet is Turkey. Three factors are in our favor. It is the closest border. Turkey is friendly with the west. But most of all, the bulk of the region we will be passing through is Kurdish."

"Why is that in our favor? The Kurds are wild men, primitive and dangerous," Timmons objected.

"Everything you've said is true. But with the right act, the Kurds can be more predictably manipulated. I am confident that Javeed and I will be able to handle them."

The decision was made: Turkey it would be. Equipment was purchased, including two Range Rovers. Papers were prepared, including professionally forged vouchers and passes by the expert, Abbas Bolgazi. Farrell returned to the States to arrange the logistics inside Turkey.

Chapter 25

On January 16, Bill and Paul were transferred to the Gasr Prison. Although practically impenetrable, this prison was much more comfortable than the Health Ministry's detention center. On February 1, 1979, Khomeini landed in Tehran. The response of the people was overwhelming. Millions poured into the streets to welcome him back. Even the most devout believer that the Shah would somehow prevail was forced now to bury his hopes. On February 2, the secretary of Persian Gulf Lead received a strange call. The caller wanted to know if the company would melt lead in Tehran.

"Just one minute. I'll connect you with Mr.... Let's see," she muttered under her breath. "Mr. Bolgazi."

Crystal was kept on hold for at least ten minutes. Finally the secretary came back on the line. "I'm still trying to find Mr. Bolgazi. Please continue to hold."

Crystal felt the sweat form on his ear, which remained plastered to the receiver. There was a knock at his door. Still holding the phone, Crystal walked over and opened it. He found himself standing face-to-face with Abbas Bolgazi.

The colonel hung up the phone. "That's what I call a quick response."

"I believe in doing the job right. With yesterday's news, I figured you would call," Bolgazi said. "Get Javeed over here. We're heading out as soon as he comes."

"Where are you going?"

"To the border. We have to 'grease the way'."

"We did that already, two weeks ago," Crystal told him.

"Good. I'd like to hear what you found out. But to be honest, it may as well have been two decades ago. The equation has completely changed."

Javeed arrived. Two hours later, they were on the road to Tabriz.

The situation had been altered dramatically. When Crystal and company had gone previously to visit the checkpoints, the government was still in control of them all. Now, twenty kilometers out of Tabriz, the government had completely abandoned the road until the Turkish frontier. Kurdish villagers came out to man the roads. They hated the government as much as the Khomeini rebels, but they had their own agenda.

"Abbas!" Javeed yelled, "there's a roadblock up the road." It was 9:00 p.m. and the pair was about one hundred seventy-five kilometers past Tabriz. "Looks like only one guy. From the looks of the shoulder, I think we could make it around him with this Range Rover."

"No, Javeed, we'll stop," Abbas decided. "You'll see what I mean."

The vehicle came slowly to a stop. Abbas rolled down the window. "What's the problem?"

"Where are you going?" demanded the young Kurdish guard.

"We're rebels. Can't you see? We're going up to the border to make sure the outpost guards have crossed over to the Islamic Revolution's camp." Abbas took out his vouchers from the Mullah of Isfahan. Javeed started digging for his. As the guard was reading the papers, rifle slung over his shoulder, twenty more armed Kurds came from nowhere and huddled around the car. Abbas looked at Javeed, who nodded his head. After a wait of twenty minutes, an old Jeep pulled up along side them. The driver motioned the Range Rover to follow.

Half an hour's drive up a bumpy dirt path brought them to the one shabby, solid structure in the tent village of Jabala Tarmuk. Inside, they were instructed to hand over their papers to the local chieftain, Nabi Fashwari. The guard at the road-block was illiterate, but he did recognize an official-looking seal. The chieftain, literate, carefully perused the documents. He had no phone; he relied on his own judgement of the travelers.

He had been plowing through the documents for a full five minutes when he abruptly handed them back and offered his hand. The two nervous men relaxed. They were invited to sit down, and hot tea was brought.

"So you've been appointed to relieve the Shah's, may he rot in Hell, border police?"

"Well, not exactly," said Javeed. Glibly, he continued, "We hope the crew that's there will change their loyalty. Our struggle is not with our people, but with the Shah, who oppressed the people. When the Islamic Republic gains full rule, the people will be truly free. All the people of the nation — Persian Moslems, Kurds, Zoroastrians, Communists, even Mujahedin — shall eat the fruits of the revolution... as long as they don't offend the true faith, of course."

Abbas nodded his head in agreement throughout this speech: Javeed was as adept with his tongue as he had hoped. Javeed concluded, "We are hoping the border guards will have already recognized the Revolution. But we must be sure. There are still some pockets of Shah loyalists around."

Now Abbas took the floor. "We should be returning to Tehran by tomorrow afternoon. Could you give us a pass, so that our journey can flow smoothly? We have much to do before the all-out Revolution begins."

The chieftain wrote out his typical pass and stamped it. Abbas thanked him.

"Oh yes, one more thing."

"What's that?" asked the chieftain.

"We have been able to help several foreigners, arrested by the corrupt regime of the Shah, to escape his clutches. They were arrested for transferring information to the Rebels. We will be bringing them to the frontier to get them out of the country. We need your help."

The rebel chieftain appeared to be dug in for a long session, and Abbas obligingly carried on the conversation. He praised the Kurds, cursed the Shah and Saddam Hussein, and then went on to other topics pleasing to the chieftain's ears.

Javeed, meanwhile, squirmed and fidgeted and consulted his wristwatch at frequent intervals. Finally, by 12:30 a.m., the chieftain asked his guests to stay overnight. Abbas, grateful for the hospitality, readily accepted.

"Abbas," Javeed whispered, lying near his buddy on a fur mat in the tent, "we could have been on the road. Why did you accept the chief's invitation?"

"It was getting late. It wasn't a good idea to continue on."

"It only got late because you kept rambling."

"What? You didn't enjoy the productive and edifying conversation?"

"I find my six-year-old nephew more enlightening than that cutthroat."

"Just go to sleep. We'll talk about it later."

At 3:30 a.m., Abbas stealthily departed the tent. Javeed lay still and waited a half-hour until Abbas returned. He didn't say anything.

The next day, after a light breakfast and profuse thanks, the pair got back into the Range Rover and continued their journey. Only six kilometers up the road, they were stopped at another roadblock. They were forced to go through the same routine here in Jabala Khandor.

"So, I imagine you were stopped down the road by Nabi Fashwari. May his name be blotted out!" the chieftain said.

"Yes, briefly. Why do you ask?"

"That thief has been a bone in my throat for twenty years. Every year, one third of our goats are missing from our flocks."

"Only twenty years?" asked Javeed.

"Well, before, under our grandfather, we were one tribe."

"Aha, so you and Nabi Fashwari are related?"

"Yes, unfortunately. He's my first cousin."

"Isn't it a shame that brothers can't live in peace?" Abbas asked rhetorically.

"Of course it's a shame. But if I got my hands on him, I'd kill him." Khalil Fashwari motioned with his finger across his neck.

Javeed boldly said, "From the way you talk, I'm surprised you haven't had fights among your tribes already."

The chieftain frowned. "In truth, we have had a few skirmishes between our villagers over the years. But my number-one wife always cajoles me into holding my sword back from her brother's neck."

Javeed and Abbas looked at each other, suppressed laughter dancing in their eyes.

Then Abbas got down to business. In less time than they might have believed possible, they received the necessary safe passage to continue toward the frontier. Three other checkpoints detained them for short stints, but their stay in these areas were not as involved as the ones they'd spent with the Fashwari rivals. The pair scouted around near the border and found a man who, in return for money, agreed to sneak them on horseback around the mountains and over the border. They did not take him up on his offer, but they now knew where to find him should they require his services.

The frontier outpost was still manned by loyalists to the government. Having been stationed there for the past two months, with another month to go in their tour of duty, the guards didn't seem to know exactly who was in charge in Tehran — nor did they seem to care. They did have a phone, but explained to Abbas and Javeed that it was usually impossible to get through.

On their way back late that afternoon, the car approached the Jabala Khandor village checkpoint once again. The guard recognized the vehicle immediately and waved them on. Two kilometers down the road, Abbas stopped.

"What's the matter?" Javeed asked.

"I've got to take care of something. I'll be back in about three hours."

"I'm going with you."

"No. You must stay with the car."

Abbas got out and opened the hood. Javeed jumped out of the passenger seat as a huge plume of steam billowed up from the engine.

"Looks like we blew a radiator hose." Abbas smiled at the concerned look on his friend's face as he folded his pocket knife and clipped it onto his belt. "Now just stay with the car. I'll take the jerry-can for water and get us some help."

The day soon grew dark. In the nearly two and a half hours that Abbas was away, two cars and a truck passed Javeed. At each offer of assistance, Javeed indicated that he would be all right, his partner had already gone for help. By the time Abbas returned, the engine had completely cooled down. He took a screwdriver from the toolbox, loosened the hose-clamp, cut off three-centimeters of the hose that he had punctured near the water inlet, and reattached it. Meanwhile, Javeed filled the empty radiator, and they were off.

"So what did you accomplish?" asked Crystal, as soon as they arrived back at the hotel.

"Oh, nothing much," Abbas mused as he chewed on a piece of bread. "Maybe we got a little experience in how to handle the natives up that way. I don't anticipate we'll have too much trouble. Some, maybe, but not too much.

"Still," he said thoughtfully as he reached for another slice of bread, "you never know...."

Chapter 26

True to Abbas' prediction, just one week to the day after he and Javeed returned from their excursion, the street skirmishes exploded into full-scale civil war. It was not long before the pockets of loyalist police and military dropped their guns and collapsed under the momentum of the Revolution.

Abbas and Javeed reached the Gasr prison early. Outside, men milled and shouted, their excitement rapidly approaching the point of violence, but still without focus. Abbas took quick advantage of the situation, directing Javeed to establish his leadership over a small group of street revolutionaries, then doing the same himself. As soon as Abbas had collected some forty or fifty followers, he called on them to overturn a nearby car. Then he ordered a twelve-year-old boy, armed with a coke bottle full of gasoline, to hurl it into the smashed windshield. Someone else, without need for direction, threw in a lit newspaper. Within seconds, the car was engulfed in dramatic flame. This show accomplished exactly what Abbas desired: there was soon a crowd of three hundred people clamoring around the bonfire.

At the right moment, the excitement having reached fever pitch, Abbas yelled, "The prison! Let's storm the prison! It holds our poor brothers — those whom the accursed Shah has tortured!"

A roar of agreement rose from the frenzied crowd. Abbas flung out an arm and pointed at a downed telephone pole. Some twenty young men ran to pick it up — but found that it weighed much more than anyone had imagined. Abbas commanded all the men to help. Another sixty men joined in and, with difficulty, lifted the pole off the ground. Walking as fast as they could, they rammed the pole against the heavy steel gate of the prison road entrance. The gate shook and rattled, but didn't budge, even after five or six strikes. Meanwhile, two or three of the ram-team fell dead in the street, shot by guards positioned at the prison's second-story windows.

Dozens of street rebels, armed with AK-47s, FLNs, M-16s, and an assorted mix of other non-fully-automatic weapons, began to return fire. In addition, Molotov cocktails by the dozens were heaved over the five-meter wall. Abbas discreetly removed himself from the path of the firefight. Around the corner, he found a small barred window on the main wall, near another entrance. Though their arms trembled with fatigue, the fearless rebels with the telephone pole followed Abbas's lead. The first ramming blow smashed out the two-centimeter bars like toothpicks. A slight, fourteen-year-old boy climbed through the window as others crowded around, shouting encouragement. He had reached a point about seven meters inside the courtyard when he was confronted by a prison guard, who drew his pistol and shot the boy dead. Within two seconds, the guard himself was lying dead, his body riddled with at least fifteen rounds from the spectators at the window.

Others began pouring through that window. Several more guards came out of the building, but at the sight of the torrent of people coming at them, they dropped their guns and ran back into the prison. The rebels shot off the huge padlock that secured the main gate. Two more rebels fell wounded from the ricochet of those bullets; nobody paid them much attention. The horde's energy was entirely focused on freeing the prisoners. Soon, there were thousands of people milling about the prison courtyard. Most were rebels, but hundreds were dressed in standard prison uniforms. Abbas and Javeed had set out to start a self-sustaining chain reaction — and their success was overwhelming.

Retired now from their leadership roles, the two went in search of Bill and Paul. They knew exactly where the American pair was being held — but by the time they arrived at that cell block, it was completely empty; every last prisoner had made good his escape.

Back on the street, they split up to find their men. By this time, there were tens of thousands of people in the street. The shooting had stopped. It was obvious that the soldiers had completely surrendered to the facts. Shouts of joy pierced the air, with impromptu celebrations taking place in the street. All this only added to the confusion and did nothing to help the DIS men, or their saviors.

Hours passed — maddening, frustrating hours — with no sign of the men.

"Javeed, go back to the hotel. Hitchhike if you have to. I'll never get my rental car out of here; there are too many people. I'll stick around and keep looking for our guys. Hopefully, I'll recognize them from the pictures. They may be hiding, afraid they'll be recognized as Americans."

"How do you hope to find them?" Javeed was discouraged. He waved a hand, adding, "This place is a madhouse."

"This particular place, yes. A few blocks away, though, the streets will be less crowded. I'll try to steal a car and patrol the area." Abbas clapped his young assistant encouragingly on the back, and ran off.

At 8:00 p.m., it was well after dark. Abbas assumed that the concealed Americans — for by now he was certain that they were deliberately hiding — might feel safe enough to emerge from their lair and make their way to the hotel. He decided to abandon the environs of the prison, around which he had been driving for hours, and make his way instead in the direction of the hotel, along the route they would be most likely to take. It was nearly an hour later, and some two kilometers from the prison, when he noticed two shadows dodging into a building to avoid his headlights. He pulled the car over to the curb and sprinted into the building after them. He heard nothing. Bill and Paul, if that's who it was, must be cowering in some nook in the pitch-dark ruin. Abbas didn't want to call out; he couldn't be sure these were his men.

Suddenly, he reflexively flung up his right arm to block an incoming blow. The man who had tried to administer that blow found himself unexpectedly airborne. Abbas switched on the flashlight in his hand — just as the second man was aiming a 1.3-meter metal bar at him. He squinted in the sudden light. Abbas took advantage of the split-second hesitation to shout, "Paul — stop. It's Abbas from the DIS group!"

Bill was aching, but was able to get up under his own steam. Half an hour later, in the hotel's parking lot, Abbas brought them clean business suits. They changed out of their grubby prison fatigues right there, in the stolen Paykan. Everyone in the hotel room was crying as the men, dirty-faced, but now well-dressed, stepped inside.

"I know you guys are entitled to a long rest. Especially after bumping into me," Abbas said. Everyone laughed. "But I'm afraid we must move. In two or three days, when a modicum of control returns to the prison, they may be after you. With a $13,000,000 bail on your heads, you guys are expensive pieces of meat."

Abbas could not prevail on Crystal and Caldwell to move out before the morning. Everyone was fatigued from the day's activities, their senses and reflexes at their lowest ebb. Impatient at the delay, his own nerves hyped up with adrenaline, Abbas passed a sleepless night.

No police came that night. But the next day, as the entire crew was on its way out through the main lobby, headed for the empty residence of an evacuated DIS employee, a troop of six plain-clothes men entered the hotel from the main entrance.

Fortunately, Abbas had instructed Caldwell not to go to the front desk to check out of the hotel. After inquiring at the desk, the police made straight for the elevators instead of backtracking out the front door. An hour later, all ten men made it to the safe house.

"Now you can relax for a few days," Abbas told his American friends. "It might even be to our advantage."

"Why is that?" Lamont Timmons asked. "The longer we wait, the more border ports could receive stop orders... and perhaps even pictures of our men."

Abbas waved this aside. "The pictures are nothing. To an Iranian, all Americans look the same. You've got the fake passports. That won't be our problem. Our main problem will be the avarice of the people we'll have to pass."

"We've got plenty of gelt," Crystal remarked.

Abbas looked up at him, shocked. He hadn't heard that word used since he'd left Israel, eleven years before. It was a common colloquialism used by Yiddish-speaking Jews.

"Gelt? What's that?" Abbas asked innocently.

"You know. Moolah, scratch, greenbacks."

"Oh, you mean money. Gelt? What language is that?"

"It's Yiddish," answered the Colonel.

"What's that?"

"You never heard of Yiddish? It's Jewish."

Abbas shrugged. "I thought the Jews speak Hebrew."

"Hey," Crystal said, "I thought Javeed said you're a Jew. Don't you know anything about your people?"

"Relax," Abbas advised. "Look, I never heard of Yiddish. The Jews here don't speak it."

"My grandmother, may she rest in peace, was from Russia. She lived in America for fifty years, but she didn't speak a word of English — only Yiddish."

"What are you saying, Colonel Crystal? *You*, a Jew? Javeed told me — with disgust, I may add — that you're a pig farmer."

"Well, I don't observe anything. My wife, may she rest in peace, wasn't Jewish. I don't really know anything about the religion, and I'm not interested."

Reading the Colonel's cue, Abbas changed the subject.

On the following day, Lamont Timmons was at DIS's main office to pay the remaining skeleton crew and close the place up for good. The phone rang; Timmons picked it up.

"This is Dagat," came the peremptory voice. "Where are your men?"

Abbas had briefed Lamont in preparation for this moment. "You mean they're not in Gasr?"

"Come on, Mr. Timmons, you know the revolutionaries stormed the prison and freed the prisoners. I expect you to turn the men back in to the authorities in accordance with the law!"

"Dagat," barked Timmons, "You are responsible for their safety. Three days ago, I demanded that you hand the men over to the American Embassy, and you refused to listen. You tried to shake down our company for $13,000,000, when our men were not even charged with a crime. You're damn straight we're concerned about our men! If they're hurt, we're going to make sure you will be in deep mud."

Dagat paused for a moment. When he answered, his manner was a shade less harsh. "Mr. Timmons, why don't we meet? I think I can be more flexible about the bail."

Timmons responded coldly, "Mr. Dagat, once you can give us information about our men and their condition, I'll be happy to speak to you. But you'd better find them safe and sound, you hear?" He ended on a shout.

Dagat apologized, and quickly ended the conversation. It was obvious that he had taken the bait.

Three days later, on February 14, the streets had calmed down enough to permit the three Range Rovers to find their way out of the city. They took the main highway toward Tabriz. The first leg of the journey went well, and by 4:00 p.m., the ten travelers stopped for the night at a hotel on the outskirts of the city.

It was the next day when things started to heat up.

The equation, Abbas saw, had already changed from the situation which had existed only twelve days before, when he and Javeed made the trip. Now only rebels manned the checkpoints. Many were unofficial, all were untrained. These checkpoints served a double-edged sword: the rebels were searching for weapons and loyalists, the former being easier to spot. Before they'd left, Crystal had insisted that weapons be left behind, and generally his dictate was wise. Although Abbas agreed with it, he made himself an exception to the rule. He was driving alone in his rented vehicle so that, even if he were caught, he would not necessarily indict the others.

At the first major roadblock, the cars were thoroughly searched. So were the men. By the third roadblock — all of them falling within a span of less than twenty kilometers — Javeed noticed that vehicles with certain grease pencil markings on the windshields were waved through. Abbas and Javeed went to work. After that, their progress became much swifter.

One hundred kilometers west of Tabriz, the road narrowed and deteriorated. The local populace deteriorated even more. The Kurds had always been a primitive and untamed people, but under the strong arm of the governments that ruled over them — Iran, Iraq and Turkey — there was a limit to what they could get away with. Now, with the Iranian government in turmoil, the mountain people brazenly took charge of their territory.

The first roadblock was in front of a bridge that spanned a narrow ravine. Neither Crystal in his excursion nor Abbas in his, had encountered any trouble traversing that spot. Now, ten machine-gun-toting men stood at the side of a makeshift gate.

"What's the problem?" Abbas asked from the lead car.

"Papers. Let's see your papers," demanded the group's spokesman.

"Can't you see, we have free passage granted from the Revolutionary Guard?" Abbas pointed to the markings in the corner of his windshield. The man studied the markings and then called over one of his cohorts. Altogether, five of the village vigilantes attempted to understand the scribbled glass.

"We don't recognize this. You're going to have to show us some ID," the spokesman decided at last.

Abbas wasn't keen on handing over his papers. These were not police or paramilitary of any type. They were common rogues out for intrigue and profit.

"I'm sorry, I didn't understand. You want a toll to cross the bridge — no problem. Just let the two cars behind me pass, and I will pay the toll for all three cars."

He handed the spokesman a crisp twenty dollar bill. The spokesman devoured the bill with his eyes, then waved the two DIS Range Rovers over the bridge. Abbas instructed them to stop one kilometer down the road, and to proceed one kilometer for every five minutes it took him to negotiate with the cutthroats.

Trying to calculate how much he could get away with, he handed two more twenty-dollar bills to the chief honcho. "That is the toll? Twenty per car?"

The man, smiling, nodded as he pocketed the money. But the others refused to move the log which made up the "toll gate." They began to argue with the spokesman in a language of which Abbas only caught a few words. Finally, after a half-hour, Abbas yelled from out of the window. "Who is in charge here? I am going to be late."

Seven of the ten men yelled, in virtual unison, "Me!"

Abbas got out of the car, went over to the first spokesman, who now seemed to have been demoted, and asked him for two of the twenties back. Abbas explained that since all these men were in charge, they were all entitled to an equal share of the toll. Just to be a nice guy, and so that he could get on, he would pay all ten "guardians of the bridge" one twenty dollar bill each. Cheers rose up from the group, even from the first spokesman, who was close to getting a bullet in the head, and the men rushed to roll the enormous log out of the way.

Abbas finally caught up with the others, ten kilometers down the road. Their progress was smooth until the caravan arrived at the edge of Jabala Tarmuk, fifty kilometers away. Although Abbas and Javeed had received assurances of safe passage from Chieftain Nabi Fashwari, the new political circumstances made Abbas doubtful. As it turned out, his fears were well founded.

"These papers are worthless," the guard said curtly, as the trio of cars waited at the side of the road. "How do we know they're not forged?"

"They are genuine documents!" Javeed said indignantly. But his protest was dismissed as summarily as the papers.

"You will follow us," came the reply. In short order, they were led into the presence of the chieftain himself.

"Your honor," Javeed told Nabi Fashwari urgently, "your word must be kept. Our friends here"— he pointed at the Americans — "have just escaped the injustice of the evil Shah."

Fashwari shrugged. "Then what is the problem? The Shah is out now. The Islamic Republic is in."

"That's true. But there are still elements of the Shah's regime that the new government has not yet been able to root out. These elements still wield power, and that power could harm all of us." He drew a breath. "Tell us what you want, but please hurry. We are scheduled to meet our friends at the Turkish border."

The Kurdish chieftain sat back at his leisure. "You and your friend are very smooth talkers — but you cannot fool Nabi Fashwari. I wish to know what you discussed with my dear cousin up the road, when I saw you last."

"Nothing much. We told him basically the same things we told you."

"You fool!" Fashwari shouted in a fit of anger. "I want to know what he said about me and my village. Did he threaten us?"

For the first time, Abbas joined the conversation. "He didn't threaten. He just said he would kill you when he had a chance." Javeed glanced quizzically at his partner. Behind them huddled the Americans, fearful and impatient and completely in the dark as to what the talk was all about. Twelve guards, pistols drawn but pointed toward the floor, surrounded them.

Nabi Fashwari grimaced as Abbas revealed his news. "No doubt you will be stopped at Jabala Khandor. I'm going to let you go now — but you must tell my cousin that if he does not wish to be wiped out, together with his seven wives and thirty-one children, he must continue to pay the tribute we have demanded, as in the past. He must not think for one moment that, just because the Shah's Kurdistan District Police have ceased to exist as a force, there will be any advantage in misbehaving."

"I imagine the tribute you're talking about involves goats."

Nabi Fashwari, who had been looking down while speaking, glanced up sharply. "Yes, goats. If he makes any trouble, we will raise the tribute to include one-third of his women."

In thankful silence, the men trooped back to their cars and were waved on by the pistol-toting guards. Three kilometers down the road, Abbas stopped the car for a conference.

"Gentlemen, we're in for some major trouble, caught up in a nearly impossible situation. I doubt if money can extract us from it. But Allah will be with us. We will proceed on our way. We may have to run this blockade, but don't worry. If all goes well, we won't be shot at.... At least, not much."

This did not prove very reassuring to the unarmed Americans, who had no choice but to follow the leader. To their surprise and dismay, Abbas then informed them that the leader was not going to lead. "I will remain behind again for a while. I have instructed Javeed what to do in case you run into major trouble."

"But how are you going to know? We don't have any radio communications," Caldwell demanded.

"I will know. Now get going," Abbas ordered.

The Americans hesitated. From the start, they had not liked Abbas Bolgazi's total domination. Still, they fully understood his militaristic attitude toward his mission. Besides, Farrell had strictly enjoined them to follow his orders.

True to the chieftain's prediction, the remaining two cars were stopped at Khalil Fashwari's roadblock, just down the hill from Jabala Khandor.

"What's the problem?" Javeed demanded. "We have safe passage from Khalil Fashwari." He took out one of the vouchers Abbas had forged in the name of the Imam of Isfahan. The guard looked it over carefully and was about to wave them on, when an older man came over and asked to see the paper.

"You idiot!" he yelled at the young patrolman. "You can't read past the first-grade level. This is not from the chief."

Javeed was able to pick up the gist of what had been said. He grabbed back the paper, looked at it again, and apologized.

"I'm sorry, this is the wrong paper. Myself, I didn't go to school past the second grade." Javeed offered a shamefaced smile. Then he handed the literate guard the real document, sealed with Khalil's Fashwari's ring. The guard read it carefully. Gruffly, he ordered, "Let's see all the passports in your party."

Javeed frowned, but he had no choice. He told the men to hand over their passports.

"Americans?"

"I told the chief I would be coming through with foreigners. He gave us his okay."

"But these are Americans." The guard looked up. "The chief is expecting you. I am instructed to bring you all up to the village. Where is your friend from your last journey to these parts?"

Losing patience, Colonel Crystal stepped up to Javeed's side. "What's all this about?" he barked. Javeed motioned to indicate the need for silence, then turned back to the guards.

"My friend didn't come along this time. Now, please let us through. Can't you see my men are getting nervous?"

"They might be worse than nervous when the chief has his way."

"Why, what have they done? We were assured by the chief when we passed through a few weeks ago that passage would be safe."

Without answering, the guard shoved Javeed with the barrel of his gun to indicate that he should walk. The others were herded together and walked from their vehicles toward the village. Javeed passed twenty dollars to the guard whose gun was nudging him, and whispered, "I'll give you another one of those after you tell me what's going on."

The man stepped up closer. In an undertone, he said, "Your papers are fake. Your story is fake. Chief Khalil went into Tabriz the day after you passed and called Isfahan. He thinks the capture of two of these Americans will earn him a reward of 10,000,000 rials." Javeed slipped out the twenty, and the hand behind him snatched it up.

When the group, urged on by six machine guns, was within five hundred meters of the village, a series of sudden explosions rocked the hilltop. The guards looked around in a panic. Someone yelled, "Nabi Fashwari has attacked!"

Less than a minute later, the guards — chattering among themselves in an attempt to decide what course to take — were joined by the remaining eight guards, running up the path from the highway. Now there were fifteen Kurds yelling all at once. Everyone turned around as a huge flash from Jabala Tarmuk lit the dusky sky. A gigantic fireball, reaching a height of two hundred meters, was clearly visible five kilometers down the mountain. Javeed seized his chance. He would put his talents as rebel leader to good use.

"Why are you men wasting your time with this nonsense?" he shouted. "Don't you see that full-scale war has broken out between the villages? You'd better join in the battle if you don't want your village exterminated. We just came from Jabala Tarmuk, and Nabi Fashwari swore he would destroy your chief and take away his wives."

In a frenzy of anger, the Kurds bellowed, "Let's go!" "Nabi Fashwari is a dead man!"

"Come on, guys," Javeed called urgently to his own men. "Back to the cars."

The DIS group broke into a ragged run. When they reached the bottom of the path, they saw the two guards who'd been left to man the roadblock. Abbas had already arrived and was being held at bay by one of the guards. Both turned as they heard the running footsteps coming toward them from around a row of trees. A shot rang out — it had the timbre of a .380 autopistol — and one of the guards stumbled and fell. The other, who couldn't have been a day over fifteen, dropped his gun and ran, howling for mercy. Tiger Crystal picked up the old Mosin Nagant rifle abandoned by the fleeing boy, and stashed it in the back of the Range Rover. The men scrambled back in to their cars and were off.

"Now, Javeed," Crystal demanded, "what the hell happened back there? I'm sure you and Abbas had something to do with it."

"We?" Javeed adopted the highly facetious manner for which Persians are renowned. "These two villages have had a rivalry going for decades. Very provincial people. If there were enough caves in these hills, they'd be living in them. But, yes, sometimes it takes a minor catalyst to encourage people to do what their hearts really desire." He grinned. "Jabala Tarmuk will have to go back to cooking over wood camp fires for the foreseeable future. I think their two thousand liter LP tank suffered an 'accident'."

The men in the car laughed. Bill asked, "But what about those explosions? How did you manage them?"

Javeed took a little black box with a small red button on it from his pocket. "Abbas gave me this toy as an Ashura present. It's some kind of radio transmitter."

The group laughed again — all except for Tiger Crystal. He was in awe of the professional who was leading this group out of the country. This Abbas Bolgazi was no common native, but a well-trained operative. Tiger had the savvy and the sensitivity not to ask too many questions.

*   *   *

The next roadblock was forty kilometers up the mountainous road, near the village of Raziya. Here Abbas shrieked frantically to the three scraggly sentries, "Do you know the village about forty kilometers back? We saw a roadblock there, but nobody was guarding it."

The sentries exchanged a glance. "Of course. You must mean Jabala Khandor. Chief Khalil is a second cousin of our chief."

"What about the next village down the road?"

"Of course, Jabala Tarmuk. The people of that village are also distantly related. Those two hate each other's guts," grinned the sixteen-year-old Kurd.

"Well, it's not just hate anymore," Abbas informed him grimly. "War has broken out between them. When we passed by an hour ago, the shooting and explosions were deafening. Do you have a phone in your village? I must call the district police."

"The closest phone is in the border town seventy kilometers up the road," said the boy, visibly concerned.

Abbas frowned impatiently. "We must hurry there, before the conflict spreads to all the villages in the region. Open that gate."

Before any of the three sentries could gather their wits, the boy was opening the gate. Abbas's car and Javeed's made it through and sped off. But the third car, which was driven by Tiger Crystal, was stopped and the gate closed. Tiger yammered in English, gesticulating wildly to let them know that he had to follow the other cars. The primitive road blockers could not understand a thing he said. They, in turn, were barking in Kurdish and broken Farsi for everyone to get out of the vehicle. No one understood. Three hundred meters up the road, Abbas stopped and threw a small plastic explosive out the car. Back at the checkpoint, the sound shocked the three mountain men into forgetting their argument with the foreigners. In single-file they ran toward the site of the explosion. Tiger got out of the car and opened the gate himself.

"We're going through. Get down low — we may have to take some fire," the colonel told his men.

He gunned the engine. One hundred fifty meters down the road, the three gun-toting vagabonds spun around as they saw the car coming at them at one hundred kilometers per hour. Two of them opened fire, one with an AK-47, the other with a Turkish Mauser. Tiger ducked as the windshield took eight hits. One section of glass, toward the upper center, caved in together with the rear view mirror. Thankfully, the road was straight for the seventy meters from the onset of the shooting; Crystal could afford not to raise his head as long as he held the wheel tight. In seconds, it was all over. The cowering men in the vehicle heard and felt the impact of something very solid bang onto the hood and smash through the already riddled window. Fifty meters down the road, Tiger sat up and jammed the breaks. Staring at him was a blood-soaked head, quite dead.

The other two sentries had jumped off the road onto the side. They quickly repositioned themselves and began shooting at the fleeing car. One bullet hit the rim of the spare tire, attached to the rear door of the vehicle. Bud Caldwell grabbed the Russian relic Tiger had procured at their previous stop, leaned out the window, and took a shot. The thug with the AK-47 fell back, blood spurting from his chest. A slight plume of steam began to emanate from under the hood as Tiger gunned the engine again. A bullet had just grazed the edge of the radiator. Once they were out of rifle range from the Kurds, Tiger stopped the car again, threw the Range Rover in reverse, and floored the gas. Everyone held on tight as the vehicle violently jerked back. The carcass stuck in the remains of the windshield was dislodged, sucking out along with it another mass of window glass from the top of the hood. Tiger was unconcerned about the wind that was now blowing in his face; at least his view was unobstructed now. He no longer had to twist his neck to peer from a small clear area where the orb of cracked glass didn't obscure his vision.

He jammed the stick into forward gear, joining the other two vehicles half a kilometer down the road. They re-formed into a three-car convoy, racing down the road as fast as they could drive. They had traversed no more than fifteen kilometers when the heat gauge indicated that the trailing Range Rover didn't have much life left. Five kilometers later, the engine seized. They all pulled over to the side of the road, and the men from the range Rover climbed into Abbas's car. Before they departed, Bud Caldwell and Lamont Timmons pushed the wreck toward the edge of the road and watched as the junked vehicle tumbled down to a valley four hundred meters below.

They reached the border at ten p.m. The police, not quite sure which government they were working for, nevertheless did their jobs as though nothing untoward was happening in their country. The passports underwent a routine check which, at first, aroused no suspicion, despite the fact that the ones Paul and Bill were carrying were not their own. Then the supervisor came out of his office and inspected the passports again. He did a double, then a triple-take, on Paul's. The picture didn't match the face. Tiger Crystal asked, "What's the problem officer?"

"This man here. He doesn't look like the picture on his passport."

Tiger snorted, "Can't you see he's sick? We've got to get him to a hospital. The closest one is no doubt in Turkey."

"Well, I'm going to have to check into this further." The supervisor disappeared into his office with the passport.

"At least," Paul whispered to Bud, "they don't know we're wanted."

Cautiously, Bud assented, "Yeah, it seems that way."

After fifteen minutes, Tiger Crystal, impatient — as were they all — knocked on the supervisor's door. There was no answer. He knocked again, louder this time. Finally, the man inside called angrily, "Come in!"

Tiger was in for precisely three minutes. He emerged with a smile on his face. Meanwhile, Abbas found a telephone and contacted the police emergency number.

"I want to report that the Jabala towns are fighting. We passed through that area a few hours ago, and the gunfire was horrific."

"Yes, we heard. Five hundred army troops are on their way to the scene from Tabriz. They should be there shortly." Smiling slightly, Abbas hung up.

"Let's go, we're cleared to pass," Tiger said as he walked briskly out of the frontier house. The men started back for the cars, but he stopped them. "No, fellows — we're walking across. The Range Rover has a new owner." The men looked at him strangely. "I signed Lamont Timmons' name and handed the keys and title to the supervisor."

His people began to smile, but Crystal motioned for them to move. They walked in a line around the locked chain. Two hundred meters down, they traded the freezing night for the Turkish border station.

Abbas had followed them half way.

"Good luck, gentlemen," he called. With hugs and a teary parting, they said their farewells.

"Oh, Colonel Crystal." Arthur Tiger Crystal turned around. "Here," Abbas handed him a wad of green bills.

"What's this?" Crystal asked, looking at the extended hand.

"This is the remainder of the twenty grand Farrell had given me. There's $16,500 here. Count it."

Crystal shook his head and emphatically demurred, "No sir, that's for you. You were worth ten times as much."

"I don't need it. The Mitzvah is my reward." The word slipped from Abbas's mouth.

Crystal frowned. "What's that? I've heard of a Bar Mitzvah, of course. My grandmother wanted me to have one when I was thirteen, but my parents didn't want to bother."

"Let's just say that Allah will provide me with the reward. Now give this money back to Mr. Farrell."

"I can't and I won't. I'm certain Farrell wants you to keep it. Besides, you're not done yet; you still have to get back home. It might come in handy."

In the face of the colonel's obstinacy, Abbas reluctantly tucked the wad back into his pocket. The two men shook hands, embraced once more, and went their separate ways.

Chapter 27

Farshid Levihayim got back into his rented Range Rover and changed into the business suit he had kept in his car. He shaved off the mustache and stubble from his face, which had grown in the past four days, and drove back very cautiously. Approaching the city of Raziya, he stopped his car and got out to walk. It was after 2:00 a.m. when he saw an Army truck and several troops mulling about a government roadblock down the road. Farshid returned to his car, drove up to the roadblock, and obediently killed the engine.

"What's going on?" he asked, all innocence.

The sergeant on duty said, "We're not exactly sure. There was some kind of firefight around here. A local native was found dead — all smashed up. The villagers claimed it was a hit-and-run. We found a car, a total wreck, gone over the side about twenty kilometers down the road. We think it may be the result of local rivalry." He pointed. "Down the road toward Tabriz, you'll find a large military presence. Over there, a real war broke out between two Kurd villages. At least seventy people were killed. You may be stuck there for a while."

"Allah save us! How terrible," Farshid murmured, as the sergeant perused his identity papers and vouchers. When he was done, the sergeant looked up.

"You've got some nice recommendations here. Hard to believe a Jew would be thought of so highly by the Mullah of Isfahan."

Farshid spread his hand. "I'm a businessman. Generosity is a trait of all the sons of Abraham, not just Moslems. I don't discriminate in my charitable works between followers of different religions."

"I'm sorry for offending you. Just tell me what business you had near the border, and I will let you pass."

"I'm in the lead reprocessing business," Farshid answered, handing the soldier a business card, "and I heard that the people from this region have thousands of old car batteries piled up. I came to see if it was worth my while to collect them."

"Well, is it?"

"I'm not sure. Some of the villages claim that, given the current instability, they're going to use the batteries to build barrier walls. I'm going to seek a government ban on using them for that purpose. It would cause an environmental nightmare to have millions of batteries shot up, sulphuric acid leaking all over the place." He shrugged. "If I am successful, it will be worth my while to send a truck to collect them."

"Better go in with a convoy of tanks with your truck, or it may never make it out," the sergeant advised. He waved a hand. "You can pass. Good luck."

Jabala Khandor was an absolute mess. Dozens of troop carriers were all over the road. Occasional gunfire could still be heard, and the acrid smell of cordite and burning organic material was thick in the air. A cursory examination of his papers granted Farshid legal passage, but it still took him until 9:00 in the morning to travel the eight kilometers past all the activity. It was 10:00 p.m. when he stepped at last, wearily, through his own front door.

"So how did it go?" Ruchama asked excitedly.

"Oh, just like another day at the office." He plopped down in his bed and slept for twenty hours.

On the morning of March 14, 1979, Sam Kirby met with his boss back in Fort Worth.

"Moss," Sam announced, "Here's a letter addressed to you from Iran. It's postmarked Isfahan. It came yesterday. It contains only a small newspaper clipping in Farsi."

Javeed was called up from the third floor. As he read the article, Farrell and Kirby watched the jubilation form on his countenance. When he had finished, he yelled, "Ya'allah!" which means, "Oh my God!" As he translated, the two Americans also began to smile.

Page five, Revolution News, March 2, 1979, column four:

Early this morning, Hosain Dagat, Chief Magistrate of the Health Ministry, was arrested by Revolutionary Guards and removed to Gasr prison. He was charged with official corruption. An anonymous tip indicated that he had taken a bribe to ensure safe passage out of the country for two American businessmen jailed for corruption. They had walked out of prison when Revolutionaries opened the gates last February 11. Exactly as the tipster had predicted, $16,500 in new U.S. currency was found hidden in his office at the ministry. Although the usual punishment for this felony is a maximum of five years imprisonment, due to the fact that Dagat himself was appointed to prosecute official corruption, the Islamic Revolutionary Council has preliminarily indicated that Dagat will be hanged.

Farrell stared at the Persian news clipping for several minutes. "Why do you think he did it, Sam?"

"You picked the right man, Moss. Crystal told you that Abbas, or whoever he really is, didn't want to keep the money. I guess this is how he got his way, and made sure the money was repaid." He paused. "Moss, I think we owe him a debt that money can't repay."

Farrell was thoughtful. "You're right. What I think he would really like is for us to bury any recollection of his involvement — and especially of his identity. Perhaps someday, after his 'official duties' have been completed, we'll meet again...."

* * *

The next two years were dull but peaceful in the Levihayim household. The city was wired to blow, the synagogue was hardened for shelter, and no more wise guys demanded Levihayim's assistance.

Then, one day, the peace was shattered.

"What's this in the mail?" Farshid asked his wife. "Looks like a government return address." He slit open an envelope. Ruchama watched his expression sour as he read the letter in his hand.

"A draft notice. It must be some kind of mistake. I'm thirty-eight and have two children. Besides, they should know Jews don't believe in the 'Jihad' against Iraq."

That afternoon Levihayim dragged his buddy, the mayor of Isfahan, to the draft board of the Revolutionary Council.

"What's the meaning of this?" Farshid demanded of the captain in charge. A Mullah was quietly sitting next to the captain, arms folded.

"It means what it says, Mr. Levihayim. The just Islamic government of our country knows no discrimination. Everyone is subject to the draft, and everyone must fight to defend our nation from the satanic designs of Saddam Hussein. Perhaps you're of the opinion that Saddam and Iraq represent the side of good?"

"No, no, of course not. But I was under the impression that, from your perspective, a Jew killing Moslems, as bad as they are, is unacceptable. Even in the Shah's time, Jews were not required to fight Moslems."

"The Shah was a bastion of corruption. He didn't care about the faith — he was only greedy for the money the Jews would pay to stay out of the army." The captain paused. "But your point is well taken. When the mayor called to make this special appointment for you, I consulted my superiors. You will not be serving on the front line." Farshid breathed a sigh of relief. The captain continued, "Your skills at organization and perseverance are legendary here in Isfahan. The army thinks you could be of assistance in military planning."

"But what about my business? I supply thirty percent of the small arms ammunition in the country."

Captain Asfami found it impossible to look Farshid Levihayim in the eye as he answered the question. Asfami was an Isfahani, and like most of the citizens, felt Levihayim was an exception to his concept of a Jew; he was one who truly cared for the people regardless of background. He had hoped that someone else, perhaps in the Home Ministry, would deliver the tidings to Levihayim. But it was not to be.

"Mr. Levihayim, since you have been conscripted into the army, our law requires that all of your resources fall under the aegis of the army as well. Your lead factory is now under military domain. But, please," he urged earnestly, "don't feel too bad. After the war, your property will be returned."

"After the war, you say." Farshid was bitter. "How long is this damn war going to take? We've been at it almost two years, and things look almost dead-even."

"I don't make military policy, Mr. Levihayim. Perhaps in your capacity you will meet my superiors. Ask them." He shuffled some papers, then added, with a placating air, "I will give you an extra week to report to basic training."

"Basic training!" shouted the distraught business man. "You said I would not see action."

"You won't, but those are the rules. All inductees go through basic training. Who knows, perhaps we will soon be marching on Jerusalem to remove it from the hands of the infidel Zionists."

"Against my brothers, you would make me fight?"

"They are not your brothers!" exclaimed Asfami. "Zionists are Europeans who one day, a few hundred years ago, picked up a Bible and got it in their heads that they were Jews."

Levihayim saw where the conversation was going. Resigning himself to his fate, he left the draft office. The mayor shrugged his shoulders; Levihayim knew that his Moslem friend meant well, but was powerless to do anything about the situation in which he now found himself.

Two weeks later, Farshid had been in basic training for six days. He rose a half-hour early each morning to don his *Tefilin* and pray, using the mess hall, which was unoccupied at the time. Now came the Sabbath, and he was resolved not to work. He was tossed into the brig with a warning: he'd better follow orders the following week or the punishment wouldn't be so light.

During the whole of his training, Farshid never revealed his hand. He never let on to the fact that, not only did he already know all the fundamentals he was now receiving, he had been a major in the elite Golani brigade before joining the Mossad. He did, however, act as if he was concentrating on the training and excelled in all tests and activities. When the second Sabbath came around, he prayed alone as usual, then made his *Kiddush* on Coca-Cola, wine being strictly forbidden by Moslem law. For his frugal meal he ate bread and other non-meat products, after which he reported to his training sergeant.

"Sergeant Merveed, I am asking permission for the day off." Before the sergeant could react, he went on persuasively, "I didn't mean to be insolent last Saturday, but it was very upsetting to violate my religion. I am aware of how important it is for our soldiers to be well prepared to meet the enemy, but you must admit that I have done well in my training. Just let me have the day off, and no one will be the worse off."

Merveed was a serious soldier and a devout Moslem. He was also very, very big: he stood one hundred eighty-eight centimeters and weighed one hundred five kilos. At thirty-three, he had been a professional soldier during the reign of the Shah, whom he hated but served faithfully until the revolution. He was also the boxing champion of the Fars province. He had recognized from the start that Levihayim was doing very well, but attributed it to his Jewish intellect.

His glance was noncommittal. "At roll call, we'll see what I can do for you."

Levihayim was suspicious of what Merveed had in mind. As it turned out, his fears were not unfounded.

"Soldiers of the Islamic Republic," Merveed called to the one hundred sixty men in his unit standing opposite him two rows deep, "one man among you is a Jew. That is no problem: we don't discriminate. But this Jew would like to observe his day of rest while the rest of you work for our defense."

On cue, the men broke out in a chorus of boos. Those standing near Levihayim began to edge away from him.

"Levihayim..." yelled the Sergeant.

"Mr. Levihayim, if you please," Farshid interrupted. "I am a respected businessman in Isfahan." Some of the men laughed.

"I apologize," the sergeant said with an ironical bow in his direction. Straightening up with a stern look, he bellowed, "Mr. Levihayim, get over here!"

Farshid stepped forward. There was complete silence among the thirteen dozen trainees. "So you feel you don't need the day's regimen. You have excelled to such a degree that your preparedness for the nation at our most somber hour will not be impaired by your dereliction...." Without warning, as if shot from a cannon, he threw a punch directly toward the dead center of Levihayim's face. Levihayim caught it neatly in his right hand, as he slipped laterally out of its aim. Merveed, though thrown off balance from the force of his momentum, managed to keep his footing due to the support of Levihayim's open palm pushing him back.

"I see you know something about fighting," Merveed gasped.

"You're a good teacher," responded the Jew.

"Let's see how good." Merveed let loose with a kick aimed at Levihayim's groin. Levihayim, like a cat, spun to the left. His right arm rocketed up, catching Sergeant Merveed's rising leg so fast that, when Merveed bit the dust, the back of his head hit the ground before his back came flopping down with a violent thud.

The man was in magnificent shape, however, and got up on his feet immediately. Again the injured bear came at Levihayim, who was facing him with an expression of serene confidence. Levihayim grabbed his right arm and threw the man three meters. This time he landed on his rear.

"Had enough, sergeant? I told you, I took my lessons seriously."

The sergeant didn't answer. This time he came at the Jew more cautiously, slowly closing in, waiting for his quarry to make the first move. The pair circled around, in the manner of wrestlers. At this routine, Merveed was more successful. He was able to spring and grab Levihayim in a bear hug. Vaguely, he wondered why, if this man was such a good fighter, he couldn't have prevented this coarse maneuver.

He was soon to find out how greatly he'd misjudged his opponent. Before he could think to carry out his next move — which was within a split second of contact — Merveed let go in monstrous pain. His broken nose was gushing blood, and his hands were full of it, as was Levihayim's forehead. Several of the men on the line yelled, "Grab him!" Levihayim quickly spun around to face them. Now he was standing in the exact spot the sergeant had been three minutes before. "Come on, come on, who's next?"

The men were silent. Meanwhile, the sergeant's anger overcame his pain. He came up from behind Levihayim and made ready to land a jab to the back of his neck. But too many of the men Farshid was facing mirrored on their facial expressions what was about to happen to him from behind. Instantly, he ducked, swiveled around, and sandwiched Merveed's right arm between his own two arms. The dead-silent brigade heard an audible crack as Merveed's ulna snapped at the elbow. Farshid gave the clump of blood and sweat a hard shove, leaving his vanquished pursuer to writhe in pain harmlessly on the ground.

No one said a word. The men didn't know what to say, Farshid didn't have anything to say, and Merveed couldn't say anything. Levihayim walked back to his barracks. Nobody bothered him for the rest of his Sabbath.

In the official inquiry into the incident, Merveed was strongly reprimanded for attempting to strike Levihayim from behind. Levihayim could have received a severe punishment for his insubordinate request, but instead was promoted to hand-to-hand combat instructor. It was a good thing they didn't know about his other skills, Farshid reflected, or they'd have him in charge of the whole army. After five weeks, he was called into the commanding officer's office.

"You certainly learned military skills very quickly," said the colonel with a twinkle in his eye.

"Yeah, I learn quickly. I did in school and in business, too."

"Anywhere else?"

Levihayim looked up intently at the colonel. "No, that's it, school and business.... Well, I've belonged to a Karate club in Isfahan for the past eight or nine years."

"Mr. Levihayim, we're not the Islamic Council; we're Army. We won't probe into your life any more. That's not our business. The point is, we feel you could be a great asset to the war effort. Would you accept a commission?" The colonel slit open an envelope and took out two sets of silver double bars, along with a slip of paper.

"One brass leaf, or I'll stay an enlisted man."

"I didn't realize you lacked humility to such an extent," the colonel said, surprised.

"If I lacked humility, I wouldn't have settled for less than one star."

The colonel broke out laughing. Levihayim kept a straight face.

Chapter 28

Major Farshid Levihayim was allowed to reside at home and run the "government" lead factory. For the five weeks he was away, production had fallen off by twenty percent. He attended military staff meetings three times a week and, at least once a month, was flown to the front to observe the progress of the battle.

"The Iraqis are pounding us with their air power. We shoot down a decent amount of their planes, but they keep coming as if they had an unlimited supply," General Maluf told Levihayim as the two ducked for cover on the outskirts of the embattled city of Khorramshahr.

"I still say that our best chance is a ground attack. Simply put, we have greater human resources and, assuming we go head-to-head with them, they lose. But it must be on terrain where air power is least effective."

"We already have plans to launch a joint maneuver with the Iraqi Kurds along the mountainous north and eastern border of Iraq."

"That sounds good to me. But it would be most effective if you opened another front. Let's see those maps." Levihayim perused the maps of the Euphrates-Tigris confluence. "See here," he pointed to the huge marsh area which makes up most of the area from Basra to the Gulf coast. "This is the area we must take. It shouldn't be too difficult."

"Not too difficult!" the general echoed in a disbelieving shout. "That area is completely impassable. It's a natural defense."

Farshid smiled. "That's exactly what I meant. There aren't too many Iraqi troops defending that area; they don't expect us to be able to muster a significant position in the swamps. It's our best bet. First, there is plenty of cover in the reeds and swamp grasses. But more importantly, fragmentation bombs have little coverage when they hit water or mud."

"In the same spirit, how are we going to move men through it?"

"With boats. Small outboard motor boats."

Shaking his head, the general said, "Major Levihayim, we have considered that. Our problem is that the Revolutionary guards — with the Imam's backing — insist we must cut off the Basra Baghdad road."

"That's suicide!" exclaimed Levihayim.

"You're telling me. We already tried six assaults; we lost over fifty thousand men and could only hold a position twelve kilometers from the road," the general said somberly.

Farshid stood and began to pace the room. "Well, at least the Imam has figured out an easy road to martyrdom for all those people."

"You go to hell, you dirty Jew," the general laughed.

Farshid whirled around to face the general. The sardonic note was replaced by one of complete sincerity as he said, "Look, Iran can't win this war. We have the people and the determination, but they have the superpowers, unlimited credit, and the high-tech edge. We have to scrounge spare parts for our American-made equipment, from Viet Nam and wherever else the Americans left their stuff behind. Why doesn't the government go for the UN-sponsored mediation and cease-fire?"

Slowly, the general answered, "That's a religious question. This is Jihad, you know."

"I think it's also a political question. I think the Imam Khomeini actually thinks Allah is going to send down a chariot of fire from heaven to destroy Saddam Hussein. But Saddam has also declared Jihad and has just as many clerics on his side. He even sponsored Islamic conventions over the past several years."

The general expressed his opinion of this with a forceful wave of one hand. "Bah, that Hussein! I doubt if he believes in anything except himself."

"I won't argue with you on that one. In any case, we're in a serious deadlock over here. The best we could do is gain a little strategic ground as a bargaining chip, because eventually even the Imam is going to wake up and realize that Allah ain't coming down for him. Did you see that last wave of recruits? I'll bet some of them are still in diapers, poor suckers."

"Look, Farshid," the general said morosely, "if it were up to me, I'd never have taken them. But my hands are tied." He grimaced. "You think politicians interfere with military professionals? They're nothing compared with Ayatollahs."

"It's sad. But I guess those suckers are thinking of the bliss of eternal reward as they run into a hail of hot lead raining all over them.... Getting down to business. I saw a documentary on the Everglades. You know where that is?"

"No. It sounds like somewhere in America."

"Exactly. The Everglades is a huge swamp in southern Florida in the U.S. It has been made into a National Park. They invented a special boat for the region. That's all we need, and we'll get around in the marshes like frogs and snakes. This boat is simple to make. It's nothing but a propeller driven flat-bottomed skiff with a rear mounted, air-cooled, small-aircraft engine. Nothing to get stuck and gummed up. It can even move over water no more than five centimeters deep."

"Sounds like just what we need. Do you think the cursed Yanks will get us for patent infringement?" The general snickered.

"We'll send a notice to the CIA to seize the boats...." Farshid quickly sobered. "Seriously, General — I envision a massive presence down in the marshes. It's highly strategic. We'll cut Iraq off from its only access to the Gulf. They'll have to truck everything in from Kuwait."

Major Levihayim and several other high-ranking officers worked on the plan for three days. By putting their heads together, they all came to the same conclusion. The ultimate objective: Fao Peninsula, a huge base of Iraqi military and naval operations just across the Shatt-Al-Arab waterway from the old international boundary. Levihayim insisted that it was attainable. Slowly but surely, the Iranians pushed their way forward, taking more and more territory in the southern marshlands. Always keeping the Iraqis busy in the north and northeast with limited incursions, they maintained an inexorably expanding coverage of the marsh. By 1986, they were ready to strike.

Levihayim wanted to be close when the invasion of Fao took place, but his Moslem superiors wouldn't allow this. First, he was a Jew, and they didn't want him in a position where he might have to kill Moslems, even if they were the dastardly infidels of Saddam Hussein. More importantly, they needed Farshid Levihayim alive and well; his professional advice was always accurate. On more than one occasion, he was cajoled into making contact with Israeli arms dealers. He would always desist, claiming he had no inside track with the Zionists. But somehow, Zionists would come out of the cracks — on occasion in France, or in South America — always ready to deal, usually for TOW and Hawk missiles, purely defensive ordnance. The price was right, too.

Swarming like locusts, the Iranians overran Fao in a frontal attack. Their buildup of the small speedboats that had been so useful in ruling the swamps became impossible for the Iraqis to stop. Within fourteen hours of heavy fighting, the Iranians established a secure beachhead on the Iraqi side of the waterway. They immediately laid down a pontoon bridge to bring the heavy equipment across. The Iraqis, left alive, retreated like chickens without heads. Baghdad was in turmoil. Half the residents of Basra clogged the roads in their urgent desire to get out of town. The conquest of Fao was devastating.

"So, Major, success!"

"Yes, General. I'll bet you would have drunk to that, had our Islamic Republic not banished alcohol," Levihayim grinned.

"Shhh. That kind of talk could get you shot."

"We succeeded for now. But you can never trust Saddam; he's totally unscrupulous. You see how every time we advance and crush his forces, he immediately goes back to bombing our cities and the civilian population."

"At least Ayatollah Khomeini allows us to respond in kind. That has certainly been one of the major reasons Basra has emptied out. With Fao now unable to protect it on the southern flank, Basra is quickly becoming a ghost town." He paused. "What do you think Saddam will do next?"

As Levihayim and General Maluf spoke together in a Quonset hut on Fao, emergency sirens began to wail. The pair ran out in time to see a squadron of Iraqi jets circling at high altitude. Iranian Phantoms appeared a few seconds later to challenge them.

"Hurry — to the bunkers!" At a run, they crossed the one hundred fifty meters to the hardened concrete command bunker built by the Iraqis less than three years before. Altogether, about twenty officers and another fifty staffers were in the bunker when they sealed the door. The regular soldiers remained outside, in trenches and open concrete bomb shelters — except for those manning anti-aircraft guns, Hawk and Stinger missiles. One Iraqi plane came in low and strafed the base's main runway with several cluster bombs. Only one hit the runway, putting it out of commission for about three hours. Another Iraqi MIG dropped what appeared to be a quarter-ton bomb. It missed the base but exploded near the edge of the marshlands.

"General!" yelled Farshid, "Do you smell that?"

"I smell cordite and TNT. What are you referring to?"

"There's a tinge of gas mixed in. I think it may be mustard gas."

The loudspeakers began blaring in Farsi. "All personnel, don your gas masks!" There was a decent filtration system that cleaned the air inside the command bunker, so that not much of the lethal gas was able to affect the officers. But for the personnel outside, it was another matter.

"I'm going outside," Farshid shouted. He put on his gas mask and headed for the portal.

The general grabbed him by the back of his flak jacket. "No, you can't do that. You are not to engage in combat."

"I'm going out to command, not to fight. It's a mess out there, and all the top brass are stuck in here."

Levihayim twisted his shoulder, freeing himself from the general's grip, quickly went through the double doors and emerged topside. As he had predicted, he was confronted with a mess. Men who hadn't donned their equipment fast enough were coughing and choking. Luckily, the first gas bomb had exploded seven hundred meters off-target. Still, it was close enough to cause a lot of suffering.

"What's the matter, man? Get this Stinger in position!" Farshid shouted at the first rocket man he came across. The entire area was engulfed in smoke, with a definite, though minimal, tinge of mustard gas and clamorous noise all around.

The man turned agonized eyes on Farshid and moaned, "I can't, I can't." Uncovering his right hand, which had been wrapped in a portion of his shirt, he showed Farshid that two fingers were missing. Farshid gulped, amazed at how little blood was leaking from the man's hand. Suddenly, the hair-raising sound of a jet approaching rang in their ears. Farshid grabbed the missile launcher, raised the sight to his eye, and fired in the direction of the plane. The Iraqi jet broke to the left, rising directly into the sun. Two seconds later, the pilot veered sharply to the right and down. The little missile, in hot pursuit, couldn't be fooled.

The fleeing Iraqi realized that the AAM following him was of recent vintage; its electronics were tuned to filter out the IR signature of the sun. His next move was to eject a chemically treated flare, whose IR signature closely mimicked that of the jet's engine. Farshid, on the ground, observed this game being played out as if he were at a wrestling match. As the Stinger began to maneuver toward the falling flare, the major resigned himself to the possibility of defeat for his team. Seconds later, a bright orange flame came shooting out of the MIG's rear, indicating to Farshid that the Iraqi had turned on his after burner in an attempt to put distance between himself and the four kilos of deadly explosive intent on blowing him up. Farshid shrugged his shoulders as it looked like the MIG-27 would definitely get away.

Then an amazing thing happened. The Iraqi pilot didn't bother going into a climb. Perhaps he thought increased velocity was more critical to his evasion attempt. Thus, the jet remained within the angle of view of the Stinger's IR sensor. It immediately picked up the stronger and truer IR signature of the jet and maneuvered back in pursuit of the real target. Sixteen seconds had elapsed since Farshid pulled the trigger. At a distance of six kilometers, the dogfight was almost out of Farshid's visual range. Suddenly, a huge fireball flashed in his eyes from that direction. Twenty-five seconds later, Farshid heard and felt a subdued boom and watched as the flaming remains of the craft fell straight down and crashed silently into the marsh.

A minute later, with the all-clear alarm, the general joined Farshid outside.

"Where's the missile that was in that launcher?" the general asked Farshid, who was still a little dazed.

He removed his gas mask and said, "It's gone to Kingdom Come, and taken an enemy MIG-27 with it."

The general grabbed the $30,000 piece of equipment from Levihayim's hands and shoved it back in the arms of the injured rocket man. "A good Moslem died at your hands. But Sergeant Parvan here will have to get the credit." The general directed his attention to the injured soldier. "Right, soldier?" The sergeant nodded.

"General, I don't need the credit," Farshid replied, "but had that basss... good Moslem let out his payload of bug spray here, you would have had one thousand dead, good Moslems all. Shias, at that."

The General gave a shout of laughter. Farshid remained impassive. The pair escorted the soldier to the infirmary. On the way, he tossed the launcher into the base junk pile.

"So now you see, General, what our buddy Saddam has in mind. Mark my words — that bit of mustard he tried to dump here today is only the beginning. The man is pure slime. If he gets desperate, he'll use real gas, VX or Sarin."

"I suppose we'll have to counter with our own gas. The Holy Koran states, 'an eye for an eye'."

"Now, don't you start making religious decisions. That should be left up to the Imam. Don't you think?"

The general replied frankly, "No, I don't. But I think it will be, anyway. If not for this stupid Jihad, we could have accepted UN mediation. All I hear is, 'We can never give in to the infidels'. Damn it! We've suffered 300,000 casualties already. For what? A few square kilometers of worthless hill country." The general's eyes filled with tears as he spoke to his Jewish friend.

"Now General," Farshid said softly, "it's your turn to watch your tongue. You didn't hear anything. Right, soldier?" The rocket man nodded hazily through the pain in his hand. Farshid turned back to his commanding officer. "I'll see you back at command HQ in Tehran, General." He took the next helicopter out of Fao.

In the following months, Saddam Hussein became bolder and bolder in his use of internationally banned, poison gas. His American and Soviet friends didn't care to admonish him. Their only concern seemed to be to stop the fanatics from exporting Islamic revolution. Actually, the Americans and Soviets were overjoyed to keep the Iran-Iraq war at a stalemate. Oil prices were kept low, and weapon sales were doing a land-office business. Farshid Levihayim was also satisfied. Having the two Moslem brothers busy at each other's throats meant that they kept their paws off of his own people. Nonetheless, he was very concerned. Despite Khomeini's charisma and his powerful grip on the country, he couldn't succeed forever at countering the disillusionment felt by the troops when stepping out into a veritable gas chamber. After careful reflection, Farshid asked for, and was granted, an appointment with the Ayatollah himself.

"So we have a Jewish major in the army of Allah's nation. I pray you don't subscribe to the terror of Zionism." These words constituted Farshid Levihayim's introduction to Ayatollah Khomeini.

Respectfully, he replied, "My first allegiance is to the God of Abraham, whom we all recognize as the Creator and King of the Universe. My second allegiance is to my country. I understand that his eminence has seen my military and civilian record, which proves my patriotism."

The Ayatollah inclined his head slightly. "I will take you at your word, Major. Now, why is it that you seek my confidence? I have no doubt that I have heard the same request a thousand times already. You military people all think alike."

"His eminence is very insightful. In no way do I mean to argue or criticize. Only, as a God fearing military man, I feel obligated to do anything and everything to ensure our victory and to stave off defeat. Perhaps as a non-Moslem I can proffer an objective insight into this war."

"I thank you for your deeply-felt sense of duty and your benevolent intentions, but I must inform you that I have already heard a thousand times from non-Moslems what they think of this war. Certainly you realize that our weapons are manufactured and sold by non-Moslem countries. Procuring those weapons involves arduous political and psychological wrangling. I know very well the opinion of the outside world." The Ayatollah's voice hardened. "But Major, I will also tell you this: it makes not a bit of difference. This is Jihad. We fight not for Iran, but for Allah! We must defeat His enemies — and for this goal, in the end He alone will send His messenger to assist us. All other factors, whether world opinion, Saddam Hussein, America, the Soviet Union, or the Zionists, amount to nothing but a conspiracy of Satan. They have no substantial meaning."

Farshid thought a moment. Then, his manner deferential but firm, he asked, "Is the Imam saying that in spite of their weapons and their backdoor willingness to let us procure those weapons, these men represent the totality of evil? I don't mean to defend my Jewish brothers, but look at what the Israelis have done for us. They have re-supplied our defensive needs and enabled a vast network of international credits and black-market spare parts for our war machine. Isn't it incredible that a country at war with Hizbulla and Islamic Jihad forces, which Iran fully supports, should go to such extremes to make sure we are not annihilated?"

"It is true. But you must understand that the Israelis are smart. Indeed, Jews are very smart; you are a perfect example. What they are doing has only one motive, and it is not beneficence toward the Islamic Republic of Iran. They see Saddam Hussein as a more immediate threat than Iran." The Ayatollah leaned back, a slight smile playing across his lips. Watching Farshid's reaction, he said, "Despite the fact that you are a Jew, I will tell you the truth, for I have nothing to hide and have declared it publicly. After we overrun Iraq and remove its devils from power, and after an Islamic republic is established in Baghdad, it will be on to Jerusalem, to wrest away the Holy City from the infidel Zionists who have illegitimately ruled for the past thirty-seven years."

Farshid had known what to expect when he had entered the simple room and sat down on the carpet opposite Khomeini to hold this conversation. He also knew he had an immediate goal and would not get bogged down in polemics. Stony-faced, he said, "So the Imam feels that no gratitude is due those who assist us because of their own ulterior motives?"

"That is correct. We only have Allah to thank for altering their perverse hearts at this moment. You must be aware of the international political mumbo-jumbo that has taken place in this war. Our spiritual foes, the satanic nations of Russia and America, have both given their public blessings to the satanic Saddam Hussein. Yet they are not in any way allied in the effort. On the contrary, it has become more or less a confrontational issue between them.

"On the other hand, it is as you have spoken. Both of those nations and the arch-Satan Zionists, behind all the political rhetoric, have worked beyond our expectations to sell us the arms we need. The interim defeats and victories are all part of a Divine Plan. Allah's Will and our mission are to suffer and persevere."

"I won't argue with his eminence. I am no religious scholar. I am, however, a military officer." Farshid's manner became businesslike. "I have come to request that his eminence allow our forces, as regrettable as it sounds, to counter the diabolical Iraqi use of poison gas against our people. This can be achieved only by reciprocity. We have the ability to deliver gas to Baghdad. Perhaps that is the message of Allah in this conflict. Saddam has acted foolishly. Allah's desire is for our righteous nation to achieve victory quickly by raining down on our enemy a chemical death."

The Ayatollah sat quietly, eyes cast down to the gaudy carpet surrounding him. "No, Major," he said at last. "It is not the Will of Allah for Iran to use gas. We can never sink to the subhuman level of our enemy, Allah's enemy. Allah will secure victory for us by some other means."

"Is his eminence saying that Iran would never use gas at all? What about on America or the Zionists?" Farshid held his breath.

"I won't answer that question, Major. But now we are talking about brother Moslems, most of whom are coerced and brutalized by Saddam to fight against us. Although we must defend ourselves, as individuals most of the Iraqi people are blameless."

Slowly, Farshid said, "I respect your decision. But his eminence must realize that, from a military standpoint, the war cannot be won if we allow Saddam to continue his gas attacks with impunity. His superpower mentors, who ostensibly subscribe to the Geneva Convention banning the use of poison gas, have been silent on this issue — a curse on their heads. But the result has been that we are having an impossible time motivating our soldiers to fight."

"I don't understand. Our people have no fear of death and martyrdom. A battlefield, wherein explosives and metal fragments can cripple or snuff out life, has not been a deterrent to our magnanimous volunteerism for the sake of Allah and our Republic. Why should the specter of gas be any more ominous in their eyes?"

"The Imam asks a very good question. I don't know the precise answer. All I know is that it is a fact. Morale has gone down significantly since Saddam has stepped up his use of gas. In my religion, although we pray for God's deliverance, we do not rely on miracles. We must make a reasonable human effort; then God, in His Mercy, assists us, sometimes in a miraculous manner. Isn't that also the belief of Islam?"

"Yes, of course. If we believed in relying on miracles, we wouldn't have planes or tanks. We wouldn't send thousands of men to their deaths. We would just be filling the mosques with prayers. But that is not the case." The Imam paused. "The great question is, how to define a reasonable effort? From all of my studies, and from my innermost feelings, our use of gas is beyond the Will of Allah and does not fall within the realm of a reasonable effort. Instead, it would demonstrate our lack of faith in Allah, showing that we cannot be victorious for the cause of righteousness without resorting to reprehensible means."

"Your eminence is very wise. But assuming the Imam has expressed the Will of Allah disqualifying the retaliatory use of gas, is the Imam willing to concede that it may also be the Will of Allah that Iran will not prevail in this war?"

Again Khomeini looked down and was lost for a good two minutes in contemplation. "My Jewish friend, I see that you are also very wise. Indeed, the blessings of our forefather Abraham have descended through the generations to the children of Ishmael and Isaac. I will not dismiss your opinion, which as I told you in the beginning has been poured into my ear on numerous previous occasions. But for the time being we will pursue the war as we have for the past six years. If I see little or no progress in the coming year, I will consider it a sign from Allah and reevaluate the manner in which I interpret His Will."

"Does that mean the Imam will consider the use of gas? Our military and industrial complex just needs the word and we can begin to stockpile."

"No, that's not what I said! We will say what will be," answered Khomeini in a stern voice.

Having come this far, Farshid was not about to back down. "Shall we begin to manufacture? That's all I'm asking."

The Imam calmed down and again thought silently for a moment with downcast eyes before responding, "I agree to very limited quantities. Perhaps it will be necessary to use gas on some future occasion against infidel nations that may choose to engage us."

Farshid viewed the conversation as a breakthrough. He could see the pain on Khomeini's face as he authorized a mitigated permission concerning poison gas. Farshid was now confident that in the near future, if the Iraqis went overboard in their use of chemical warfare against Iran, counter-measures would also be approved.

The Ayatollah waved his hand, indicating that the meeting was over. Silently, scribes and tape-recorders had been working away to chronicle the word of Allah on earth as expressed by the Ayatollah. The Imam extended his hand; Farshid grasped it with his own two hands, kissed it, and backed away out the door.

Chapter 29

"So, what was it like speaking to the Ayatollah?" Ruchama asked when Farshid arrived home.

"I must admit, he's a very great man," Farshid said, shrugging out of his jacket.

"Great man?" she echoed indignantly. "He'd have the head of every Jew decorating his fence posts, if he could get away with it."

"Maybe the head of every Zionist living in Jerusalem, but not because of religion. Let me tell you what I think. The man really believes in what he's doing. I've studied Islam in depth — I had to for this project. Its law, in some ways, is very close to our own Biblical and Talmudic law — only it's a slightly mangled adaptation. Have you ever read the Koran, my dear?"

"No, I wouldn't pick up that book."

"A lot of its aphorisms are straight out of Proverbs. On the other hand, it contains some gross errors and transparent alterations. Mohammed was an illiterate peasant, brilliant, but delusional. Even the Koran records that his family initially thought he was nuts. He picked up most of his knowledge from conversations with the Jewish merchants who frequented Mecca and Medina."

"What do you mean by 'transparent alterations'?" Ruchama inquired, her curiosity overcoming her indignation.

"Who was commanded by God to sacrifice his son, but at the last moment was stopped by an angel?"

"Abraham, of course. We read about that every Rosh Hashanah."

"Correct. Now, who was the son about to be slaughtered?"

"Isaac. Why?"

"According to the Koran, it was Ishmael, forefather of the Arabs."

Ruchama burst into laughter. "Now I understand what you mean by transparent. That is so ridiculous! Do the Moslems really believe that?"

"Of course they do. They say that we, the Jews, changed the story."

Ruchama started laughing again. "The Jews changed the story? I suppose the Jews miraculously got hold of every Torah and translation of the Bible that had been written for two thousand years before Mohammed came on the scene and forged Isaac's name in place of Ishmael's."

She was still chuckling when Farshid said, "You think that's funny? When and where did Haman live?"

"Right here in Iran, of course. He tried to kill the Jews in the time of Esther and Mordechai. The tomb of Esther and Mordechai in Hamadan is revered as a holy site by Jew and Moslem alike."

"Yes, but when did they live?"

She frowned, trying to remember. "The way I learned it, it was about twenty-four hundred years ago."

"That's right. Now, when were the Jews enslaved in Egypt?"

"Oh, I'd say about... thirty-three hundred years ago."

"Exactly. But according to the Koran, Haman was Pharaoh's advisor and suggested that he throw the Jews in the Nile River."

This time, Ruchama's laughter was uncontrollable. Trying — with a marked lack of success — to catch her breath, it took four attempts to get out the words, "I s-suppose Mohammed also received the Ten Commandments on Mt. Sinai?" Gasping, she collapsed on the sofa in hysterics.

"No dear," Farshid said calmly. "They got that one right."

When she'd regained her composure, she shook her head. "I thought you said there's wisdom in the Koran. It sounds like pure nonsense to me."

"The Sages of the Talmud might have agreed with you. The Book of Ben Sirah was excluded from the twenty-four books of the Bible because of one sentence that was deemed to be foolish advice. But really, as I told you, much of the Koran contains wise and righteous counsel sprinkled with a corruption of Jewish concepts and laws. Look, even among the rabbis, some are old-fashioned fanatics who are doubtlessly sincere in their beliefs. On the other hand, we have a lot of rabbis who interpret Jewish Law and lore in light of the times."

"You mean like the reformers in America?"

"No, of course not," he answered dismissively. "I'm talking about rabbis like the ones we met when I gave you your divorce decree. There's also the rabbi who was a great influence on Benny Harkesef's life. These men are seriously religious and great scholars. They are the true spiritual leaders of our people."

"Look, darling," Ruchama said, still pondering Khomeiinism, "from the time of our remarriage, I've changed my attitude toward religious observance. But I'm still kind of skeptical about rabbis running a country."

"Oh, Ruchama, how can you think like that? Just open a Bible; it contains so many sins and crimes that prescribe the death penalty, you'd think no one could survive in our faith. Yet, the Jews, with our traditions, have survived through the millennia. You don't see the rabbis demanding wholesale executions like the clerics here do. The problem with Khomeini and all of Islam is they think we're still living in the seventh century. They can't make the transition to the twentieth century. That's because the Koran is not a 'living book.' It stagnated hundreds of years ago.

"Khomeini — and, to a lesser extent, other Arab leaders — are so absorbed in the literal application of Koran that they will never succeed in making a sincere impression on the heart and mind of twentieth-century society. But that doesn't mean that as an individual Khomeini is not a great man. In the West, they don't understand him; they just view him as some kind of antiquated monster."

"Well, he is, isn't he?" Ruchama interjected

"No, he isn't. I really think he acts for the sake of heaven. But since the ideology he espouses is theologically flawed and inherently false, it's not going to continue in the same form in the future. It will change, completely change. The question is: how will that change appear in the next generation? The students and followers of Khomeini may take all of his 'sticks' after he's gone, but will leave the 'carrots' in his grave...." As usual when thinking out loud, Farshid began to pace back and forth across the room. "Perhaps his succeeding clerical heirs will become draconian in their effort to shore up the Islamic Republic. On the other hand, the Iranian people may foment a counterrevolution, demanding reforms that bring Iran closer to the modern society than the Shah envisioned.

"Khomeini is a great man. He's been able to unite this country merely with his charisma and radiant personality. Lacking those characteristics, his successors may have to use external sources of motivation to hold onto their power. One way may be to rally the public in a Holy War against Israel. Even Khomeini has admitted that his goal is to free Jerusalem from the Zionist infidels. The fanatics who follow him may take that cue literally...." He turned to face his wife. "Ruchama, my dear, that is precisely why I was sent here."

Soberly, he added, "Still, I hope our work will never be needed."

Just three years after Iran, having sacrificed 262,000 of its citizens, and Iraq, having lost 105,000, called a halt to their stalemated war effort, Iraq paid back its friends in Washington and Kuwait by invading the kingdom to which it owed billions. After receiving the full fury that Western technology could deliver in the Gulf War, Iraq ostensibly capitulated. But the turn of events in the Middle East by the new Millennium — notably, Palestinian independence and President Bill Clinton's cruise missile attack on Saddam Hussein (a veiled attempt to stave off Clinton's impending impeachment) — finally brought the former foes, Iran and Iraq, as well as ten other Moslem nations, into a cogent alliance.

Fifteen years after Farshid's meeting with the Ayatollah, his worst-case scenario became a reality: his life's work was needed.

Recalling the success Ayatollah Khomeini had in firming up the Islamic revolution through the rally call of Jihad against Saddam Hussein, the now teetering Islamic government of Iran determined that leading a Pan-Moslem Jihad against Israel would be opportune. Little did they know that one moonless night thirty-four years before, four men had been deposited upon their shores....

*   *   *

On that fateful day, July 1, 2002, the prayers in Isfahan's Great Synagogue continued until sundown. At 7:45 p.m., the evening service finished. Farshid Levihayim turned the key of the deadbolt lock, which opened the outer heavy metal doors. To the frustration of the worshipers, who were in a hurry to return home to eat, the doors would not open.

"They've blockaded the doors from the outside!" one woman screamed.

"Just keep pushing," Farshid Levihayim ordered. "We haven't heard anyone out there since the morning. We'll get the doors opened." The four strongest young men got into position, and heaved forward against the door. It budged, opening a crack. All at once, the mass of people waiting near the door backed away as a foul stench from outside effused into the building. It took five more heaves before the door was sufficiently ajar for a man to step through. Shmuel Moinzada was the first one out.

There was an instant of stunned silence. Then he screamed, "There are dead people all around! Hundreds, maybe thousands — and at least fifteen piled against the door." He flung out his arms. "God has saved us and destroyed our enemies. It's a miracle!"

The crowd broke into cries of awed jubilation. "God is the Almighty. God is the Almighty!"

The bodies were moved from the walkway leading from the synagogue's gates to the park across the boulevard. Levihayim led his three hundred people through the surreal landscape of formerly hostile aggressors, peaceably "asleep" all around, toward a line of ten buses that had brought many of those slumbering figures to the rally. Now the young men removed the drivers, slumped over their steering wheels, and filled the buses with the entire Jewish community. They filled the tanks with diesel fuel at a nearby gas station. Farshid Levihayim left 250,000 rials in the cash register for the attendant who, at the moment, was lying serenely on the floor.

Four hours later, the buses arrived at the outskirts of Shiraz, where a full-scale revolution was in progress. Within one day, the municipality was in the hands of a new ad-hoc political party, the Modern Democrats. A similar phenomena took place in Tehran as millions of people — including hundreds of thousands of women who'd divested themselves of their Chadors — marched on the Majlis (parliament). Tehran and Shiraz had not been targeted in Levihayim's operation. Now their populace, which had enjoyed the blandishments of the Shah twenty-three years before, was motivated to expel the fanatic clerics from their dominion and send them back to their mosques.

Four days later, 262,000 fresh graves were the only evidence remaining in Iran of this major conflict. That same day, Farshid Levihayim was in Tehran, meeting with the new Modern Democratic government and assisting it in drafting a letter of apology to the Jewish Nation.

PART THREE:

ROBERT BENSON

"And he will turn back the hearts of fathers with sons, and the hearts of sons with their fathers, lest I come and strike the land with utter destruction."

Malachi 3:24

Chapter 30

Benny Harkesef was born in Milwaukee, Wisconsin. His father, Herman Silverberg, left his wife and eight-year-old son to fight in the war of Israeli independence with Herut in 1948. He arrived on the *Altalena* together with a company of dedicated fighters hailing from all over the world. Luckily, he disembarked from the ship at Kfar Vitkin; nineteen of his buddies were cut down a day later by Ben Gurion and company off the coast of Tel Aviv.

Silverberg himself never saw action. The rifle he was issued, a Carcanna 6.5mm, jammed while he was chambering the first round. All of his efforts to get it repaired were to no avail. He waited anxiously for a post card from the gunsmith, but never saw the weapon again and never saw action in the war. Eight months later, the armistice with the Arabs was signed. Unlike most of the other foreign volunteers, Silverberg decided to settle permanently in Israel. In 1950, he brought his family to the Holy Land.

Benny picked up the language and Israel's secular culture with ease. Within two years, he had caught up with his Israeli-born peers in every way, even though the family continued to speak only English at home. Years later, on February 17, 1968, he made his first trip back in the U.S., walking ashore on the rugged Virginia coast, soaking wet and encrusted with salt, at 3:00 a.m.

It was not long before he was dry and dressed in a business suit that he had removed from a waterproof bag. That bag also contained the rest of his gear, $100,000 in cash, and his papers. The papers included an impeccable copy of an American passport issued in the name of Robert Benson, a Wyoming driver's license, and a Ph.D. from Cambridge in nuclear physics.

The following week, Benson had established himself in a modest house in the extreme northwest corner of Washington D.C. — the heart of the Jewish community. He found jobs as a substitute teacher in the Jewish Day School and a physics instructor at Montgomery County Junior College. The pay was weak, but he didn't need money; he needed only to establish his authentication. After fourteen months of quiet living and moderate participation in the community, Robert Benson married Barbara Weiss of Kemp Mill. Twin boys, Daniel and Harold, were born ten months later. Until 1980, Robert Benson was active, but Benny Harkesef remained dormant. He did, however, maintain his skills — and vastly improve some of them — by keeping current with the quickly developing computer world.

The time was ripe for him to emerge.

"Dr. Benson, why do you want a job with the NSA?" asked the department head of satellite telemetry.

Benson was the picture of earnest self-confidence. "I have a background in nuclear physics. Computers were not very interesting back then, but all that has changed. Over the past few years, I've held jobs writing scientific programs. At the same time, I made sure to understand the electronics of digital signal processing. I can't think of a more challenging and rewarding job than to work for our nation's security in the most high-tech field available."

"You have extremely high scores on all of the aptitude and psychological tests. The agency would like to hire you."

Benson made no attempt to disguise his pleasure. "Thank you, sir."

"Hold the thanks until you hear the rest, Mr. Benson," the department head suggested with a thin smile. "You will have to pass a Top Secret security clearance for the job. That could take up to six months and be quite a nuisance for you, your family, and your neighbors."

"I wouldn't expect anything less for the security of our country."

Sure enough, at the following Sabbath service: "Aryeh son of Hirsch is called to the Torah," shouted the beadle of Ohev Shalom congregation. Robert Benson rose from his seat, walked over to the small stage in the center of the sanctuary, and ascended the steps. Before he could recite his blessing, the beadle whispered to him. "Bob, I got a strange call yesterday. The caller wouldn't identify himself, but he asked all kinds of questions about you."

"Did you tell him what he wanted to know?"

"Well, at first I answered a few things which he could have found out by looking in a phone book. Then he asked a few other questions that seemed innocent enough. Finally, he started asking things that I didn't really know, or have any business knowing. After I hung up, I felt a bit foolish." He peered at Benson. "Are you in trouble or something?"

"I'll talk to you later.... *Borachu*...." Benson continued with the service.

Three months later, the National Security Agency hired Robert Benson. The process of security clearance was indeed grueling and, occasionally, slightly embarrassing. But in the end, Robert Benson was exactly where he wanted to be. It had taken him the full ten years to get there — not because it took that long to become qualified, but because that was how far back the F.B.I. clearance check probed for information.

Within three years, Benson became department manager of satellite communications at NSA. Throughout this time, he worked diligently to build his contacts. Wednesday afternoon golf became quite a habit with him eight months out of the year. He also organized a group — seven of his colleagues at the Agency and six generals from the Pentagon — that would go down to Hilton Head for a three-day golf package every October. Apart from his technical knowledge, his opinion of satellite utilization was highly sought after by the big brass.

"Bob," said General James Woodson in a phone call to Benson's office, "your firmware design of the Global Positioning System has passed all the preliminary tests. We're going to launch the first prototype next week from Goddard."

"I'll be there," Bob Benson promised, smiling with satisfaction.

"Of course, of course. I was just thinking about your insistence that the positioning data be made available to the public. Our main concern, though, is military priority."

"I agree, Jim. I voiced my opinion for political considerations." He geared up for presentation of a carefully thought-out argument. "Let's face it, the system is going to cost a pretty penny: twenty-four high-orbit satellites and all the ground-control logistics. I think the last official estimate was ten billion dollars... for sure that figure will go up." He waited for the general's acknowledgment, then continued, "If we were to encrypt the system, the Ruskies would have to send up their own system."

"Maybe that's not a bad idea. We aren't going to break those Pinkos militarily, but we might break them economically."

"I agree with that too, Jim. But this system is not a weapon *per se*. It also has tremendous possibilities for civilian application. If the government doesn't put the system into the public domain, AT&T or some consortium will build it anyway. Don't you see the advantage of the government retaining control of the system? The private sector will never build a system like this, if ours is available to the public, cost-free. The Russians won't spend money they don't really have, if they can use ours. Comes a crisis, we can shut it down or control it on a selective basis...." Wryly, he added, "You'd be surprised at how fast legacy navigational systems will fall apart once the GPS becomes widely available. You know how it is — kids can't count past their fingers anymore without a calculator."

Thoughtfully, General Woodson said, "I see your point. Sort of a dual system — a functional standard public domain signal, and a precision encrypted military signal."

"Exactly. Your idea of breaking the bank in Russia is a good one, too. Although it's not my department, there's talk in the halls here of another expensive satellite system — one that would not only be able to track ICBMs, but could knock them out with power lasers and other radiating signals. Sort of a Star Wars scenario. If the Russians had to compete with that system, they'd be out-antied."

"That's really interesting." Woodson's tone acquired a decisive firmness. "Bob, I'm going to make my recommendations to the Joint Chiefs to go for your civilian GPS."

Robert Benson nodded to himself, pleased.

Chapter 31

Ira Rabinowitz strolled into Benson's office. The two had begun as respectful colleagues in the intelligence business but had gradually become friends. "Bob, I'd like to ask you something."

Rabinowitz had met Benson through their overlapping work, though the two were in different agencies. Ira was a top analyst for Army Intelligence. But quite often — at least twice a month — they would meet at NSA HQ to discuss progress on the work Benson was doing. Rabinowitz had an almost photographic memory and a keen insight into the value and veracity of satellite data. Benson's input into the signal modalities was important in factoring in the exact locations of gathered information. Their relationship had been purely professional until the day a black-hatted Jew, a mathematician at the agency, stuck his head into Benson's office and invited him to attend a prayer service; the mathematician had to say *Kaddish* for his father. Benson took a yarmulke and prayer book out of his desk drawer and rose from his desk. Since Rabinowitz was also Jewish, he was asked to help make up the quorum of ten. From that day on, Rabinowitz seemed to discard the businesslike facade he had always maintained around Bob Benson. Soon, they were socializing after work, and even their wives became friends.

"OK Ira, shoot. What's the question?"

Rabinowitz hesitated. "You know, I think it's better if we talk somewhere else." Not only was the agency not bugged, but there were also special noise generators present throughout the building to suppress any listening devices. Nonetheless, Rabinowitz didn't feel comfortable revealing his heart and mind to his friend right on the NSA grounds.

That evening, at the Royal Dragon restaurant in Rockville — a dimly-lit place he'd chosen more for its air of discretion than to savor a delectable meal, Ira Rabinowitz confided, "Bob, I know you're a traditional Jew, and I imagine that, like the rest of us, you must have some Zionist tendencies. I have a huge problem with Reagan and his administration. Three years ago, when the Israelis destroyed the nuclear reactor in Iraq, the world — including the U.S. — roundly condemned them. But everyone in my department let out a cheer when the news came through."

"My department, too," Benson concurred.

"Officially, though, America supported Iraq. Of course, that's our policy now; we're more concerned with the specter of Islamic Revolution in Iran than with the madman Saddam Hussein."

Benson shrugged and forked up a bit of meat. "I think the President has it right."

"Oh, I don't disagree. But it bothers me how the administration simply dismisses Israel in order to curry favor with the Arabs. I know they're playing this game for the sake of oil, but I detect — and I know how to detect — a tinge of anti-Semitism behind the scenes."

"That's possible. But as long as it remains behind the scenes, we still have the greatest country on earth," Bob Benson replied. He had a feeling about where the conversation was heading. "Ira, you haven't touched your food. What's the point in going to a restaurant if you don't eat?"

Rabinowitz dismissed the food with an impatient wave. Placing a hand flat on the table, he said urgently, "Bob, there's more to it. Do you remember the presidential order for information exchange with all satellite data on Middle East strategic info?"

Benson sighed. "Of course. What's the problem? We've got Israeli generals coming into the agency all the time. They often come packed with goodies."

"They might. I'm afraid we're not reciprocating in kind."

"What are you talking about? I never heard them complain."

"They probably don't know there's anything to complain about." Ira found his napkin and twisted it nervously in his fingers. With lowered voice, he said, "I could probably be executed for what I'm about to tell you — but if you care about Israel, you won't get angry with me for breach of security. Over the past six months, I've been analyzing some highly technical data on Iraqi military movement. Those guys are preparing to snuff out little David. You can't imagine what's going on in the pictures I've seen. Bob, *that material is not getting to the Israelis!*"

"How do you know that? You're just an analyst. You're not a politician."

"Yeah, but I prepare all the material for submission. The stuff I'm talking about, I was told, doesn't go out." Rabinowitz picked up his water glass and drank deeply. Immediately, their waiter appeared over his shoulder, pitcher in hand, to refill it. It was all Ira could do not to scowl at the efficient fellow.

"Everything all right, sir?" the waiter asked genially.

"Fine," Benson and Rabinowitz chorused. Nodding in a self-satisfied manner, the waiter moved away — to Ira's intense relief. He leaned across the table to whisper, "I know enough to keep my mouth shut. Even so, I tried to probe a bit as to *why* this material wasn't going out. It was indicated that the Israelis only get material on a Need-To-Know basis. This didn't qualify. That's when I kept my mouth shut. Need-To-Know — hell, the stuff being withheld is *vital!*"

Still Benson said nothing. His friend prompted, "Well? What do you say, Bob?"

"Maybe you should consider going over the heads of those making the decision."

"Bob, my friend, I thought of that. But before doing something that would probably get me fired, I planted a trap — to see just how high the decision is coming from." He shook his head, lips compressed in anger. "It's not my superiors and not theirs either. The final say is coming from way up top."

"You mean the President?" Bob asked in quasi-shock, fork suspended in mid-air.

"No, not the President himself. Let's face it Bob — the President is a great guy and he's ninety-nine percent in terms of policy. But that's all. He more or less leads this country in a general political and moral direction, but knows nothing about specifics or technology. His talent is his showmanship. It's his appointees, his direct underlings, that really make all the decisions."

"Are you saying his appointees have him hoodwinked?" Bob Benson himself was hoodwinking his pal Ira Rabinowitz, but it was necessary — for both their sakes.

"I wouldn't characterize it in exactly that manner. I suppose they could give plausible reasons why keeping this data secure is for the overall benefit of Western Society. But I also suppose that it wouldn't pain them overmuch to see Jews taking some major hits, before the U.S. jumps in to save the day.... They know the Israelis have the brains and the will to take care of themselves. The State Department just doesn't feel like augmenting Israeli defensive capabilities. They feel it is wiser to create a circumstance where Israel will be more beholden, more dependent on the U.S."

Bob commented, "Sounds like a pretty smart policy to me. We do the same with every other ally. No?"

Ira glared at him. "Hey, are you a Jew first, or an American? I love this country, too. But if I can stop another Jew somewhere in the world from getting killed, maybe it's my obligation."

Deliberately, Bob set down his fork. He fixed Rabinowitz with a very direct gaze and asked quietly, "So what are you proposing? Do you want to become a spy for Israel and take it upon your shoulders to determine which info they're entitled to see?"

Ira glanced quickly around the darkened ambiance of the restaurant before returning to meet his friend's eye. Miserably, he said, "I don't know Bob. I just don't know. I took an oath of secrecy just as I'm sure you were required to do. I take polygraph tests every five years. Thank God, I've got almost four years before the next scheduled one. The truth is, I have no idea how to begin. I'm not trained in any way; I have no contacts to conduct a viable information path."

Benson thought a moment, while his companion waited tensely and the food grew cold on both their plates.

"Ira, I hear what you're saying. Your 'treasonous' thoughts won't go beyond me...." He shook his head. "It's a tough one. What if you're caught? I'm not worried about Israeli-American relations — they'll survive. I'm worried about me. In other words, all the Jews working for the government. We'll be looked at as a fifth column — if, that is, we can even hold onto our jobs. It would be a disaster of major proportions. As you, yourself, just said, you're not a spy. I think you can expect to get caught."

"I didn't even think of that." Ira put his elbows on both sides of his plate and rested his head in his hands. "Bob, everything you're saying is true. I know it as well as you do. It's just that I can't think about what's going on behind our brothers' backs without getting a giant pit in my stomach." He lifted his eyes with a deep sigh. "But I suppose you're right. Oy, what sacrifices we sometimes have to make!"

Two weeks later:

"Hey, what the hell are you doing?" Ira Rabinowitz yelled at the driver of the car behind him, which had soundly bumped his rear on Colesville Road. The two cars were now pulled over to the shoulder. The rear bumper of Ira's Chevy Chevette was badly dented; the front bumper of the black Lincoln Town Car limousine was not damaged at all. As Rabinowitz got out of his car he noticed the limo's diplomatic tags. Its windows were so darkly tinted that nothing inside was visible. After a moment, the back door opened and a man emerged.

In a thick foreign accent, he apologized to Rabinowitz and invited the hapless American into the back of his car to exchange information.

"I'm really sorry. My name is Horon Barak. I'm a second attaché from the Israeli embassy."

"Well, okay," Rabinowitz said grudgingly. "It almost seemed as if you hit me on purpose! You're lucky I happen to be a Jew; I'll accept your apology."

"Thank you." The other's tone was quietly ironic.

"But, apology or not, there's a good few hundred dollars in damage to my car. Let's see your insurance card."

"Never mind insurance. The embassy will take care of you." Barak took out a thick wad of bills from his breast pocket and held it out to Rabinowitz. "Will $20,000 cover the damage?"

In the limo's dark interior, Rabinowitz tried to look into his counterpart's face. No one offered to turn on the dome lights. Finally, he mustered the courage to ask, "You're giving me $20,000? Hell, my whole car isn't worth three thousand! Who are you, and what do you want?"

"I told you, I'm an Israeli diplomat, Mr. Rabinowitz."

"How did you know my name?" Rabinowitz asked in surprise.

"It's my business to know. Mr. Rabinowitz, our government would like you to have a new car. Please take this money. We damaged your car, and we owe it to you. Don't worry — there's plenty more available."

"More? I don't get it. I told you, my car isn't even worth that much."

In the dimness, the diplomat's voice was low and even. "Well, Mr. Rabinowitz, perhaps you have something *we* could use that is worth that much, and more."

All at once, it was as though something clicked in Ira's brain. He knew exactly what the man was talking about. Incredible! It was almost like a prophecy come true.... "What do you know about me?" he demanded.

"Very good, Mr. Rabinowitz." Barak was pleased. "I assumed you would want to cooperate. You're an analyst for Army Intelligence. You have access to all satellite data on our enemies that we should have been routinely permitted to see.

Unfortunately, we have enemies other than Arabs — even some in the U.S. Department of State. But God has never let our people down for very long. We found you, and we think you may have been looking for us."

Rabinowitz, still incredulous, found himself bereft of speech.

That evening, Benson got an urgent call from his friend Ira. "Bob, you've got to come over here right away!"

"To your house?"

"Yes. And hurry!"

"Ira, what's going on?"

"Never mind that now. You'll hear as soon as you get here. Just —"

"Hurry, I know. I'm on my way."

Curiosity vied with apprehension on the short drive to the Rabinowitz home. His friend met him at the door, eyes glittering feverishly with some hidden excitement. He drew Benson into a small study and closed the door behind them.

"Bob, you won't believe this. I think it might be a small miracle! An Israeli intelligence officer contacted me today. I haven't the foggiest idea how he found me, but he did."

"That's interesting." Slowly, Benson removed his coat and set it down on the loveseat beside him. His mind was whirring as he analyzed the possibilities of the situation. "Did he seem to know anything about your type of work?"

"I thought the man was either a prophet or had our place bugged. This guy is a pro. I didn't answer any of his questions, but he offered me big bucks. For the first time, I had the desire to accept. I now see why the government goes through all the absurd precautions, the oaths and the lie detectors. You give me the biggest patriot, and this guy will have him broken down in twenty minutes. I mean, it was amazing!"

"You must be reading a lot of Tom Clancy novels lately, Ira."

Ira clasped his hands and let them dangle loosely between his knees as he said simply, "Bob, I mean it. I could feel myself being transformed into a different person as he was describing how easily I could have it all."

"Did he tell you how remote the possibility of getting caught was?"

"Of course. All I had to do was follow his instructions to the letter. He even promised that the Israeli government would bail me out in the worst-case scenario."

Benson leaned back and crossed one ankle over the other knee. Almost casually, he asked, "So, did you take the money?"

"He offered me $20,000 up front. I didn't take it. I actually felt bad — I'm no mercenary. I told you a few weeks ago that I thought about this purely to save Jewish lives. I guess you can say I was even a little insulted by being offered money. On the other hand, I realized that this guy was just doing his job. He couldn't have known my innermost feelings." He flashed a quick grin. "But I'll tell you, Bob — millions of dollars for a man with a $40,000 salary can sure help."

Benson looked at him gravely, not a flicker of an answering smile on his face. "Ira, I'll respect any decision you make, but we're going to have to end our friendship. I just can't afford to have any relationship with you at this point."

"You don't mean that?" Ira sat bolt upright.

"I do, Ira."

"You expect me to get caught?"

"I do."

Rabinowitz shook his head, as though to shake off Benson's prediction. "I can't take that into consideration. I don't even care about the money. As for the Jews in the government, the government can't discriminate against all Jews just because of the actions of one. If that were true, with all the black criminals around no African-American would be trusted beyond sweeping the floor."

"Ira, about the racism, you're right. But to victimize all the Jews — well, to be frank, there are many in high positions who would relish the chance. You told me yourself: they're withholding vital info that should have been handed over to Israel."

Ira leaped to his feet. Standing over Benson, he declared, "Bob, I've made up my mind. God has put me in my position to save the State of Israel. You remember when that jack ass Kissinger assured Israel not to be alarmed by the Egyptian military buildup just before the Yom Kippur war?"

"Who could forget that? But Nixon did bail the Israelis out," answered Benson.

"Yeah, just in the nick of time. I don't believe in bailouts. Sometimes, they're too late — too *damn* late. No, my friend. I don't care if I die, I'm going to do whatever I can, even if I have to rent a tractor trailer to move the data out."

Robert Benson stood up, too. He and Rabinowitz stood eye to eye for a long moment. Then, still without a word, Benson reached for his coat and left.

Chapter 32

At 3:00 a.m., about nine months after his last conversation with Rabinowitz, Barbara Benson, Robert's wife, was rudely awakened by a frantic pounding on the door of their home.

"Who's there?" she called in a shaking voice, lips pressed almost to the door. Harold came running out in his pajamas.

"It's Ira Rabinowitz!" came a hoarse whisper. "Please, let me in!"

Hesitantly, Barbara opened the door. As she did, she saw three cars race by toward Arcola Road. "Where's Bob?" Rabinowitz asked urgently. "I must see him right away."

Barbara looked dazed. "Ira, I thought you and Bob had a major dispute. I haven't even called Ethel since my husband told me about your falling out last year."

"Barbara, I can't talk about that now. I'm in trouble and I have to speak to Bob. Please wake him."

Barbara ran into the bedroom and shook her husband awake. Benson put on a robe and walked into the living room. He looked angry.

"I told you never to contact me. You're endangering me and my family. Now please leave," Benson insisted. His wife and fifteen-year-old son exchanged a wondering glance. It must have something to do with security. What else could this be?

"Bob, they're after me. Please give me a hearing. Can we go into your den for a bit of privacy?"

"No. Quickly, tell me what you want right here and now."

Ira Rabinowitz had never expected this kind of treatment from his erstwhile most trusted friend. He looked around at Barbara and Harold, who either did not grasp his unspoken hint that they leave, or else chose to ignore it. Turning back to Bob, he drew a breath and said, "The FBI is after me. You've got to help me."

Barbara covered her mouth and gasped. "What did you do?" she asked.

Rabinowitz glanced up at Benson and received a look in return that indicated that he might as well tell. "I got caught spying for Israel."

"You traitor!" Benson said with controlled fury. "You rat. You're going to ruin it for *every* Jew in a sensitive position."

"But, Dad," Harold broke in excitedly, "Maybe Mr. Rabinowitz did it for our people. Aren't you going to help him?"

"No. Maybe you'd better go back to bed. To his wife, he added, "Barbara, this is very dangerous. You go back to bed, too." It was all he could do not to shout.

"As for you," he addressed Rabinowitz, "you've got to get out of here. I'm sorry, Ira, but you must understand why." He paused, hesitated. "Just tell me — briefly — what you've done."

"I gave away the show — maybe ten thousand documents."

Robert Benson stared.

"But I think they were on to me a long time ago. At first, I was giving away satellite photos."

"How'd you get them out of the building? All our copiers deposit secondary records in a safe."

"Ours, too, of course. I couldn't use the office copiers. My handlers gave me a phenomenal briefcase. At least, it looked like a briefcase, even when opened. It had some kind of reproduction mechanism inside. I never took it apart to see how it works — but work it did. I was able to copy and store fifty documents at a time in it."

"So if you think they were on to you a while back, how come they only closed in now?" asked Benson.

"I think they had some kind of cryptic system, which even we analysts weren't aware of. It creates an electronic log each time a file is opened or documents are taken out for inspection. They must have realized that I was only interested in the satellite photos that should have been given to Israel by treaty. But as I went through the documents, I also came across a series of memos that probably had no business in Israeli hands."

"Did you give those to the Israelis, as well?"

"I told you, I gave away the show. I began to rationalize — I realize it now, under the psychological control of the Israelis — that any and every document may be germane to Israeli security. Anyway, about those memos. I followed the paper trail to dig out the whole story. It proved that certain operatives in the Defense Department secretly supplied the poison gas technology Saddam Hussein is using right now on Iranian troops and his own Kurdish villages." Ira clenched his fists. "Bob, he's not doing it under the noses of his American supporters — he's doing it at their behest!"

"You're insane," blurted Benson in unaffected anger.

"No, listen to me Bob. Maybe the generals involved, who include your buddy Woodson, did it on their own. But what I found was incontrovertible evidence of a cover up. One that goes all the way to the top of DoD. It was only after I dug up that material that I realized there was a system to log all documents that had been reviewed. I think that's why they're after me now. It's as if I hit a hornet's nest."

"Hornet's nest? Godzilla's nest! Ira, I think they may want to kill you. What's in the briefcase?" Benson pointed to the leather satchel in Rabinowitz's hand.

"Those are all the documents I put together proving what I just told you."

"You mean, your copies?"

"No, this time I took the originals. I only left the building an hour ago. It was really late, everyone knows me, security was lax. I exited through an emergency door. I didn't realize how fast they could get to the scene when the alarm went off."

Rabinowitz's breathing grew shallower and more rapid. "Bob, my handler told me in a worst-case scenario, I'd be let into the Israeli Embassy. I want to go there, but there's no question the Feds would recognize my car. There are probably five hundred Feds surrounding the area by now."

"Don't be a fool. Even if you get in, the Israelis will be forced to hand you over. If you have cash, I'd hail a cab and head for Baltimore or Philadelphia." He walked to the door. "I'm sorry, but this is it, my friend. You can't stay here any longer."

Reluctantly, Rabinowitz nodded: he might not like it, but he fully understood. Benson watched him go. While upstairs, from their bedroom windows, his wife and son did the same. The front door closed gently behind him.

Rabinowitz hid behind some bushes adjoining the Benson's home until, after an interminable hour's wait, he finally saw the light on the roof of an approaching cab. Nervously, he asked the driver to take him to Philadelphia.

"That will be two hundred dollars. You have that kind of cash, Mister?" the driver asked in a heavy West Indian accent.

Rabinowitz fumbled to remove a wad of bills from his wallet. The driver's eyes lit up as he saw what amounted to a thick stack of $100 bills. He drove off in the direction of I-95. In the rear of the cab, Ira Rabinowitz leaned back in his seat, eyes closed.

No more than ten minutes had passed before the driver pulled over at a deserted rest area. Rabinowitz's eyes flew open. "What —?"

"Mister, I need more money. Two hundred won't be enough."

Half-asleep, Rabinowitz fumbled with the bills in his pocket to offer another hundred.

"Will this be enough?" he began — then looked up to find the muzzle of a wheel-gun pointing directly into his face. "Oh, no," he gasped. His hands went instinctively over his head. "Okay. Okay. Just don't shoot."

"Gimme all of it!" the driver demanded.

Rabinowitz dropped the entire wad onto the back seat. Gripping his briefcase, he quickly opened the door and jumped out, making for the woods as fast as his portly frame would carry him. A shot rang out, missing him by a good margin. The cab sped off. After catching his breath, he went over to the public phone. It was still dark.

"Ethel, I'm in all kinds of damn trouble."

"Don't tell me about it!" Ethel squealed, obviously terrified. The receiver was wrested away from her. "Mr. Rabinowitz," came a deep male voice over the phone. "Where are you?"

"Who are you? What are you doing in my house?"

"Steve Forman, FBI. I think you know by now, Mr. Rabinowitz. Your wife is under arrest. Tell me where you are, and we'll meet you."

"I'm in New York," Rabinowitz lied.

"Tell me where. I'll have someone from the New York office pick you up in five minutes."

The phone clicked in Forman's ear.

Afraid the call might have been traced, Rabinowitz began walking swiftly down the shoulder of the highway. Minutes later, a Maryland State Trooper pulled up behind him, flashing his utility beam. Rabinowitz resigned himself to the fact that he had been caught.

"Is everything all right, mister?" the trooper asked, politely enough for Rabinowitz to realize there was no all-points bulletin out on him yet.

"No sir. I've just been robbed."

Rabinowitz was invited to get into the trooper's car. Safely inside, he told the sympathetic policeman how the cab driver had robbed and shot at him.

"Look officer, I'm okay — just dead beat. All I want right now is to get home. I'll call tomorrow to file the report. I didn't pay attention to the cabby's name or tag number. He turned off his lights as he tore away.... Please just take me home."

The officer called into the station to report the incident. Rabinowitz heard the response over the radio. "That's the sixth time this month we've had that same MO. Cab drivers in D.C. have become almost as bad as the passengers."

"Hey, you better watch your tongue Matt; that smacks of racism. I'm taking the victim home," the officer said.

"Ten-four."

Rabinowitz thought this propitious. He hadn't believed his old friend, Bob Benson, when Bob had told him that the Israeli Embassy was the worst place he could head for tonight. Besides, he had the most damaging information of the century right in the briefcase in his hand. He gave the address to the trooper, who obliged by heading directly for the place he was told. Within two blocks of the embassy, Rabinowitz noticed all kinds of strange, parked cars. Most had two men in the front seat, eyes carefully scanning the walkways. None paid the least attention to the police car Rabinowitz was riding in. The car stopped right in front of the gate.

"Here's your address, Mister. It looks like an embassy to me."

"Yeah, this is it. Thanks a million. I'll be in touch." The officer got out of the car to open the back door, which had no handle from the inside. At the precise moment that the two FBI men standing ten feet down the sidewalk had turned around for a second, Rabinowitz dashed through the outer gate. The Maryland State Trooper thought that odd, but didn't catch on until, within seconds, a flurry of activity began.

"Catch him. It's Rabinowitz!"

By this time, the first light of dawn prevented Ira Rabinowitz from enjoying the protective concealment of night. But it was also too late for the Feds — or so Rabinowitz thought. The super spy was ushered into the embassy lobby. Asking for the ambassador, he was received by a third attaché who spirited away his briefcase. Also waiting inside were four FBI men.

"Mr. Rabinowitz," said another attaché who came out to meet him, "The FBI has requested that we turn you over. I think you will be accused of spying." The conversation was in view of the American agents, but out of earshot.

"Accused? You know damn well that's true. But you're going to get me to Israel. I don't care anymore about living in America. I'll be put away if I stay here. For what I've done, Israel should make me President."

The attaché shook his head gravely. "Mr. Rabinowitz, this is a very serious matter. I'm afraid the American government is very angry with you. Now as a loyal Zionist, which we recognize you to be, you wouldn't want American-Israeli relations to be damaged. That would spell a greater disaster than if the Arabs started another war."

"What are you saying?"

"I'm afraid we are going to authorize those men over there to escort you out."

Rabinowitz looked at his fellow Zionist, his fellow Jew. "You rotten, filthy piece of scum."

The attaché stared stoically at Rabinowitz, not deigning to answer. As the American G-men clamped handcuffs on him, Rabinowitz turned to the Israeli and said, "May the fires of hell burn you for all eternity." Rabinowitz spat.

Chapter 33

"Dad," Harold Benson asked his father in agitation, "couldn't you have done more for Ira? He's been put away for life. Here, read this."

Benson read the news article describing how the government had partially reneged on a plea-bargain arrangement, clamping a life sentence on Ira Rabinowitz for unauthorized disclosure of classified material.

"This is terrible. I could never have imagined he would be put away for life, just for giving secrets to a friendly nation. He wasn't even charged with espionage." Benson put down the newspaper and fixed his eyes on his son. "I'll tell you Harold, the last sixteen months have been hell for me and for all the Jews at the Agency, and it's all because of Rabinowitz. If I had done anything other than throw him out when he came running to me for refuge, your father would have been sitting along with Ira in a dank cell."

"But Dad, didn't he do it for the Jewish Nation?"

"Yes, Harold. I must admit, that was his motive. There's no doubt about that."

"Dad, what if you were in the same position? If you knew information, or you could do something that would save Jewish lives — or even save Israel from destruction — wouldn't you do it? Even if it meant great personal sacrifice?"

Robert Benson looked long and hard at his son. For seventeen years he had raised his twin boys as traditional Jews, with a mainstream American-Jewish attitude toward Israel and Zionism. Harold had obviously, on his own, developed an emotional attachment toward his coreligionists, which displayed a mature character.

He made up his mind. "Harold, let's go for a ride."

"Where to, Dad?"

"How about the C&O Canal Park?"

The federal park was essentially a thin strip of land that followed the Potomac River for many miles. The mule path that had once been tread by hundreds of mules pulling long, narrow canal boats from Washington to Cumberland, Maryland, was now a foot and bicycle path. Thousands of tourists enjoyed the beautiful and historic park each year. High above the Potomac River, overlooking the Great Falls, father and son had a fateful conversation.

"Harold, I didn't know that you were such a Zionist."

Harold flushed. "Look, Dad, I don't consider myself a true Zionist. I'm not ready to get up and move to Israel, that's for sure. But it's obvious that Ira Rabinowitz was ripped off!"

"I agree, Harold. But there was nothing I could do for him. You must believe me."

"Why do you say that? You could have hid him and made contacts for him to get out of the country. He obviously would have been happy to wind up in Israel." Fretfully, the youth shook his head. "I still can't understand why the Israeli Embassy threw him out like a used rag."

"Harold, sometimes one must make smaller sacrifices in order to ensure and secure more important things."

"Are you saying Ira was just some small-time operator? The government's reaction seems to indicate that he must have been a pretty big fish."

"I'm sure he was. The Israelis may only begin to recognize the importance of his information in years to come. But we still don't jeopardize bigger things just to be nice and to show our appreciation."

Harold stared at his father. "I don't get the analogy. What bigger things are you talking about?"

This was the moment. Benson found himself reluctant and eager to talk, all at the same time. He turned away from the Falls, feeling the spray on his back and hearing the roar of the water in his ears. "Harold, my son, can you keep a secret?"

"Of course!"

"No 'of course.' I mean, could you keep a secret if your life depended upon it?"

"Dad, you're speaking in riddles." Harold was confused.

"I'm sorry. This is what I mean. Rabinowitz was a spy. Right?"

"Yeah, obviously."

"His life depended upon secrecy. Maybe he even told me what he was doing. If I spilled the beans, he would have been caught sooner. If I had been compelled to tell what I knew about him and refused to speak, I could have been imprisoned, or worse. Right?"

"I suppose."

"So you see, I kept his secret."

Harold gripped his father's arm and asked tensely, "Did he really tell you?"

"He did."

The hand dropped suddenly. "Dad, did you have anything to do with his getting caught?"

Benson felt like slapping his son. He caught himself in time. He still hadn't revealed his incredible secret — it was no wonder that Harold couldn't imagine what his father was about to say! He smiled, then began laughing at the quizzical expression on his son's face.

Calming himself, the elder Benson answered, "No, Harold, I didn't. Now swear to me that you will keep what I am about to tell you absolutely confidential. You may reveal it to no one without my permission."

Harold, frightened at his father's seriousness, managed the words, "I swear."

"Rabinowitz was an amateur spy. Do you know what that means?"

"I guess it means he just decided on his own to make contact with the Israelis and give over information that he was in a position to find. He was never trained or recruited."

"Exactly. Well," Robert Benson looked around at the desolate overlook. Though there was no one in sight, he lowered his voice as he said, "I am a professional secret agent for Israel. Major Benyamin Harkesef, Mossad Aleph-Shin 30."

Harold Benson was speechless for a minute.

Robert continued, "I was born Ben Silverberg, which was changed to Harkesef when I was ten — a literal translation into Hebrew. At that time, thirty-seven years ago, my parents moved to Israel. In 1965 I was recruited by the Mossad, and in 1968, Robert Benson was born on the shores of Virginia."

Father and son looked intently into each other's eyes for an endless moment. Then Harold straightened up and asked slowly, "Why are you telling me this?"

"Because I see that you are mature, and it is part of my long-term mission, which I will explain, to enlist a reliable successor. I see in you, my son, whom I truly love, one who understands and is willing to live the covert life necessary to carry on my project, to which Ira Rabinowitz's work pales in comparison."

"You mean, you have also been giving NSA secrets away to the Israelis all along? Maybe you even took the job for that purpose?"

"Oh, I specifically took the job as part of my project. But it doesn't entail transferring secrets, though perhaps it will at some later time. My work is quite independent. It is so secret that no one at the Israeli Embassy even knows of my existence. I did, however, tip them off about Rabinowitz."

Harold's head flew up. Angrily, he said, "You mean you warned them that Rabinowitz was caught and they should be prepared to throw him to the dogs?"

"No, you don't understand. I tipped them off that Rabinowitz had vital information he was willing to give them."

Harold was amazed. "But I thought you tried to discourage Ira when he came to you!" He stopped, frowning as he thought back. "That must have been around the time the Rabinowitzes stopped coming over to our house."

"It was all a show. Ira Rabinowitz has no idea who I am. You are the only person.... I shouldn't say the *only* person; there may be others on the continent who know about this project and my role in it. But you are the only person whom I have told."

"What about mom?"

"She doesn't know. Remember, Harold, you are sworn to secrecy, even from her. Most women — and most men, for that matter — are weak. It's better they not know, especially when there is no purpose in it."

Benson spent the next three evenings explaining the entire project to Harold, and insisted that he change his major from biochemistry to electrical engineering and computer science. During the following two years Harold excelled in computer programming, especially in the area of digital signal processing. Father and son replicated all of the satellite communications FORTRAN programs which Robert wrote at the Agency. In addition, Harold began to design a ground transmitter, which could implement the satellite control programs.

In the meantime, Benson's other son, Danny, had decided, with his father's blessing, to go into nuclear physics. He was accepted at MIT. Danny Benson knew nothing at all about the secret life his father and brother shared.

Early 1991:

"Well, Harold," Robert Benson said, "it looks as though the U.S. military GPS system is about to get its first workout."

The two were sitting in the small den which Harold sometimes jokingly referred to, when they were alone, as Mossad headquarters. He glanced sharply at his father now. "You really think Saddam Hussein won't back down?"

Benson shrugged. "I hear the talk in the halls. I even heard from my buddy, General Woodson, last week."

"He was with you at the Palm Springs Amateur Open?"

"He sure was. He's a great golfer; he had the tournament's only eagle. Anyway, we were in a threesome together on the final round. After sinking a twenty-two-foot putt, he came over to me and said, 'We're going to kick Saddam Hussein's butt. We're going to throw everything we have at him — except for nukes of course.' I caught him in just the right mood. He revealed that the military was just itching to try out all its new toys, including the brand-new Tomahawk cruise missile which is GPS navigated."

"But Dad, I read in the Post that Saddam Hussein would use poison gas. He's got Scuds, too. Don't you think he'd use them if he got hit too hard?"

Benson took a sip of the soft drink at his elbow. He relished these private moments with his son, the one person in his life with whom it was safe to drop the mask. "I really think our electronic gadgetry will work so well, he won't have much of a chance. I asked Woodson, what if Saddam uses gas? Woodson turned serious for a moment and said, 'Bob, everything I've told you is classified. I've known you for ten years and you've got full clearance. If Saddam releases one ounce of gas on our boys, we nuke him. He's been warned about that.'"

"What else did he say?" Harold was fascinated by this insider's view of U.S. military policy.

"I asked him about Israel. Woodson replied, 'They're going to have to sit tight. We've got most of the Arabs behind us, but we have to tread lightly. Israel has been warned to stay out of this one.' But what if they're attacked? I asked him. 'You Jews only think about Israel.' I kept my cool — that's my job, after all — and told him I had relatives over there. He apologized for his remark, and said the American government would spend a lot of resources to cripple Iraq's ability to hit Israel, but they may have to suffer a bit."

"Did you tell him that wouldn't be satisfactory?" Harold demanded.

"Of course not. I agreed with him." Benson studied his son with affectionate detachment. "Your technical training has gone very well, Harold, but you still mix in a bit too much emotion to be an effective secret agent," he mused aloud. Then he smiled. "You'll learn, my boy. In due time, you'll learn."

Chapter 34

By the summer of 1991, however, Harold Benson was not doing very well.

"Harold, dear, is something wrong? You haven't looked well for the past few weeks," Barbara Benson asked her glaze-eyed son.

"I'm okay," Harold said curtly.

"But you've been so pale, and your eyes —"

"I said there's nothing wrong, Mom!" Abruptly, Harold walked past her and disappeared into his room. Mrs. Benson looked at his closed door, worried.

He was about to start his last year at College Park. His grades had been perfect up until the most recent semester. Robert Benson noticed that his son's clandestine work together with him had slacked off of late, but he couldn't mention that to anyone except for Harold himself. His wife, concerned, brought the subject up as they prepared for bed one night.

"Bob, have you noticed any change in Harold lately?"

"For the better, or for worse?" Bob smiled.

Barbara didn't think the question was funny. "I'm very worried about him. Maybe he's coming down with something."

"You could be right. I'll try to convince him to see a doctor."

But seeing a doctor was something that Harold Benson adamantly refused to do.

One afternoon the following week, Barbara Benson, following her husband's instructions, called him at work in the middle of the day. Harold had just informed her of his plans to go out with friends. "He'll be back late, he said." Robert came home immediately.

Over moderate protest, Barbara acceded to her husband's urging to take a shopping trip. He waved her off with an indulgent smile that quickly vanished the moment she was out of sight. Without further delay, he set to work.

The door to Harold's room was locked. It was no problem for a man of Robert Benson's talents to slip a Slim Jim into the door jamb and pry it open. But, knowing his son and his skills with electronics — many of which he learned from his father — Benson removed a piece of electronic equipment from his briefcase. He switched it on and set it to scan the frequency range often used by alarm sensors. Thirty seconds later, he recorded the frequency and then pushed another few buttons until the LCD display read, DISARMED. The Mossad sleuth looked around the room, which he hadn't frequented for several years, and began to search the most likely places first.

He looked under the mattress, though he didn't really expect to find anything in that quintessential hiding place. He pulled out the drawers — not that he expected to find anything significant in them, either; but there was always the chance that something was hidden behind them. Still nothing. As he was putting away one of the dresser drawers, a strange object in it caught his eye. It was a large suction cup attached to a hook; the kind used to hang towels on a tile wall. The old secret agent's mind went into high gear. Why would his son keep such an item in a drawer? Benson took it out and began to play with it. He pressed it against the wall, but it didn't adhere very well to the flat latex paint. Then he moistened it with some spit and pushed it against the floor. To the linoleum tile, it adhered very well. He went around the room trying different tiles, each time having to break the suction by peeling up the edge of the rubber cup. Then he moved the bed slightly and tried the tile that was under the bed frame, adjacent to the wall. With the help of the suction cup, this one lifted easily from its perfect fit beside the three tiles around it.

Benson easily pried up a cutout of plywood from the floor — and found what he was looking for. In the ten-inch space between the downstairs ceiling and the upstairs floor was a small vinyl bag. Inside were four small glass vials of white powder. He put everything back, except for a small sample of the white substance, which he poured into a Ziplock sandwich bag. Then he relocked the door and electronically reset the alarm.

"Bob, it's crack-cocaine," said the lab technician in the basement of NSA headquarters.

The next day, the younger Benson looked more worn and unfocused than ever. "Harold, we've got to talk," Bob said quietly.

"About what?"

"You have a problem, and I think it's getting worse."

Harold whirled on his father. "Look, Dad, you and Mom have been bugging me for the past few weeks. How many times do I have to tell you there's nothing wrong? Maybe you two are just getting old. You know what I mean?"

Robert Benson looked intently into his son's eyes. They were bloodshot and glazed. Benson whispered to his son, "You've got a drug problem. It won't fly."

Harold glanced up in sharp surprise. Then, recovering, he answered arrogantly, "You're crazy." Benson slapped him hard across the face. Harold yelped, and pressed his hand to his stinging cheek. "Sorry, Dad," he muttered. "I didn't mean to say that. I guess I've been staying out too late. I'm just tired."

"No, Harold, you're on crack. Admit it."

Harold became agitated again. "Why are you saying that? You think I'd do a stupid thing like that?"

"This is why." Benson took out a vial from his pocket and dumped a pinch of the white powder on the table in front of his son. "This is yours."

"Where did you get that?" Harold mumbled in disbelief.

"Where, you ask? Just where you hid it — under a floor tile in your room."

Harold's jaw came down. He was speechless as the slow tears welled up in his eyes.

"Harold, your mother and I want to send you for treatment." Robert Benson lowered his voice, adding, "You must go. Our work is too important. You can't function reliably in your condition. It's imperative, you understand?"

"Yes, Dad. I understand."

Harold spent the next two weeks in a rehab clinic in Pittsburgh. Then one day, Barbara Benson got a call.

"Is Harold Benson there?"

"No, who is this?"

"This is Dr. Irving Horowitz of the Sunrise Park Rehabilitation Clinic in Pittsburgh. Harold has taken all of his belongings and left. It must have been last night. His treatment regimen is far from complete. We were hoping that he only suffered a temporary relapse and went home."

Barbara bit her lip. "Oh, I hope so too. But he's not been here...."

With trembling fingers, she dialed her husband's number at NSA.

"What?" Benson exclaimed into the receiver. "Gone?"

"Yes. The doctor said he wasn't ready to go yet, that he still needs treatment. Oh, Bob — "

"Sit tight, dear. I'll be home right away."

Danny, Harold's twin brother, was brought into their confidence. With his assistance, Robert assembled a list of Harold's friends and closest associates. The next four hours were spent contacting them by phone. Finally, Benson found one who would talk straight with him. It was Sheila Bergman, a former girlfriend.

"Yeah, I knew he was snorting crack, that's why I broke up with him. One night about three months ago, he picked me up. I told him he didn't look like he could drive. I was so scared, I wanted to get out of the car. When I tried to open the door at a stoplight, he grabbed my arm and punched me. I screamed, which I guess brought him down to earth for a moment, and he apologized. But when he let me off, I think he sensed that I was through with him."

"Did he give any clue to how he got into this business, or who was selling him the stuff?" asked Benson.

"Not really. But I did notice a slip of paper on the floor of his car. For some reason, I picked it up, and must have had it in my hand when we got into that tussle. It ended up in my pocket. I think I still have it. Wait a minute...." Robert Benson drummed his fingers nervously on the desk in his den as he waited for Sheila to return to the phone. "Yes, I found it," she announced breathlessly at last. "It's just a name and a phone number, though."

"Tell me exactly," he said, picking up a pen.

"It says, Snookie 672-8917."

He breathed deeply. "Thank you, Sheila. I think you've helped us."

"Dr. Benson, until he fell into drugs I really loved Harold. But my feelings for him just vaporized into thin air as soon as I found out about his problem."

She seemed to be seeking absolution. He gave it to her. "I understand."

"Well, I hope you find him. Good luck."

It took Benson twenty seconds to cross-reference the phone number to the address at which it was registered. One more advantage of working for the NSA, he thought. It was a public phone on the corner of Good Hope Road and Minnesota Avenue in Anacostia.

Benson felt the slight trepidation of the lawbreaker as he went down Kenilworth Avenue at Eastern and crossed the line into DC from suburban Maryland. Stuffed into his waist was a Glock-23 loaded with thirteen rounds of Black Talons. His Maryland carry permit made that no different from carrying a toothpick in his home state, but by crossing the imaginary line which abutted the nation's Capitol, he was now subject to five years mandatory imprisonment if caught.

At 8:00 p.m., just as the sun was setting, Benson pulled up to the phone booth. No one was using it. But all around him were small groups of young inner-city men, in their teens and twenties, engaged in dealing as if it were Lexington Market. He got out, grimaced at the stench inside the phone booth, and picked up the receiver as if to make a call. His fingers played at dialing a number, but there was no one at the other end of the line. A few of the natives had stared menacingly, at first, at the white face with the gall to get out of his car. They soon disregarded his presence, however, and went back to their dealing. Benson, the receiver still hanging on his ear, looked around and quickly unscrewed the cap of the mouthpiece. He placed a small electronic device in it, which held fast to the magnetic microphone. Screwing the cap back in place, he hung up the phone and headed back to his car. But as he fit the key into the door, he was startled by a voice hailing him from behind.

"Hey, white man, you want something?"

Benson quickly turned around. Four muscular Africans in baggy pants and tank tops were rapidly bearing down on him. "Yeah, maybe I do. What have you got?"

The group stopped about twelve feet away. One of them moved a little closer. "Whatever you want. Speed, Crack. Want to shoot up? Or maybe just a cool drag. We got it all."

"How much for a reefer?" asked Benson.

"You hear that, Bongo? Whitey came all the way to Anacostia for a lousy reefer." The group broke up with laughter. "You're a cop, ain't you?" the criminal asked brazenly, moving in. Benson didn't answer. The situation, he realized, had turned ominous. They had closed in on him, too near for him to draw the weapon holstered in his waistband.

"I'm no cop. I'm looking for Snookie. One hundred bucks, cash, to the first one to tell me where he is."

The group looked around at each other and went into a huddle. Then, as a cat springs, two of the group were around Benson. The spokesman came at Benson with a scowl and let loose with a punch. With lightning speed, the fifty-year-old man threw a block, simultaneously aimed a front kick in his attacker's groin, caught the falling assailant with a back-knuckle to the jaw, and slammed down hard with a chop on the back of his thick neck. The entire fight lasted less than two seconds; the drug dealer was unconscious on the pavement.

"He's a cop!" yelled one of the others.

Benson took the disarrayed criminals' immediate shock as an opportunity to jump onto the hood of his car, bounding over to the street on the other side. One of the criminals fired his weapon, shattering the driver's door window, just as Benson fell safely behind the cover of his vehicle. A second gang member branched wide, about fifteen yards away, and emerged into the street from behind another parked car. He fired his Davis .32; the bullet grazed Benson's right shoulder. A second later, the thug noticed a small red dot appear on his khaki shirt. A split second later, the dot turned into red liquid, pouring out of his chest. The two other criminals dashed off.

Benson got into his car from the passenger side and burned rubber to get away. Despite his wound, he didn't want to be caught in DC with his gun. He was treated, answered the police inquiry into how he was shot, and was released at 3:00 a.m. from Landover (Maryland) General Hospital. He told the police the shooting had taken place in Oxon Hill, in Maryland. The next day he returned to the same site in Anacostia, this time in a rented panel van.

Parking about a hundred feet from the phone booth, he set up a sophisticated piece of radio equipment, clamped earphones to his face, and waited out of sight in the back of the van.

In the course of six hours, three innocuous calls were made from the fetid phone booth. Then he hit paydirt.

At exactly 9:00 p.m.: "Yeah, this is Snookie. You want your regular order? Okay. Meet me at the regular place tomorrow at 3:00."

Snookie hung up. Immediately, the phone rang again. "What you say? Bongo was wasted by a white cop here yesterday? Anyone get his tag? No? And what's with Hoki? They say the cop hit him real hard. I told those boys to learn Kung Fu. He's got a fractured jaw and a bruised neck bone. Well, at least he ain't dead... I'll talk to you later."

The phone rang for a third time.

"Harry, you Jew boy, where you been? I thought you hopped my competition. Put away by your old man in a rehab hole? Look, meet me at the regular place in an hour. Just for coming back, I got some free hot ones for you. Goodbye."

At exactly 9:25, Snookie left the phone booth. It continued to ring, but no answering machine was set to collect messages for this business. Benson followed Snookie, who was driving a '91 Jaguar XJ12, four blocks to a dead-end street next to Fort Stanton Park. He parked about one hundred yards behind the Jaguar and waited. At least ten "clients" came over to the window of the car for several minutes and then departed. By 10:00 p.m., the flow of "shoppers" slacked off. At 10:15, Harold's car pulled up just behind Snookie's. This time, Snookie got out of his car and extended his hand through Harold's window. It was too dark for Benson to determine if Harold was actually the driver of the car. His headlights still out, Benson slowly turned his car around, stopping the vehicle perpendicular to the street. The area was largely deserted, as the park was officially closed, and the junkie had obviously scheduled Harold's appointment at the end of his business hours.

"Snookie," Harold said, poking his head through the window, "I just couldn't take it any longer. I need a fix. I'm glad you're still in busi...." Harold was looking straight into the dealer's face and was bewildered to see a piece of Snookie's skull, brains and all, apparently explode off the top of his head. It was just like in the cartoons.... An instant later, the crack of a rifle shot rang out, and Snookie's carcass fell limp to the pavement.

Harold quickly grasped the situation. Without sparing so much as a look in the direction from which the shot had proceeded, he gunned the engine, spun the car around with a screech that reflected his own terror, and raced away. He didn't even notice the van that pulled away from the curb as he passed it, missing it by just inches.

Robert Benson followed closely behind his son. A few blocks from the scene, Harold began driving normally again. While stopped at a light, Benson put the Remington Police/Sniper model-700 .300 Winchester magnum rifle, capped with a Leupold Vari-X II 3-9x50 low light scope, back into its case. He followed Harold to a greystone walkup in Georgetown and watched as the door opened and Harold disappeared inside. He then drove back to Silver Spring, put away his rifle, and found his way back to Georgetown in the body shop loaner car.

At 6:00 a.m. the next morning, Harold emerged from the greystone, got into his car, and turned the key. Nothing happened.

"Can I help you?"

"Dad!" Harold looked up in fear at his father, who was standing with his arms folded beside the driver's window. Hesitantly at first, then with an empty bravado, Harold got out of his car to confront his father. "What are you doing here? How did you find me?"

"You forget. I'm a professional. Now, why did you leave the rehab center? Why didn't you at least come straight home?"

Harold offered no answers. The elder Benson waited, then ordered, "Just leave your car and come with me."

While driving up NW 16th Street, Robert asked, "What the hell did you think you were doing? You lied to your mother and me about your drug problem. Then you ran away from rehab. You're endangering my entire project. I've worked on it for twenty-five years and *I'm not going to allow it to fail*. You hear me?" Benson gave his son a hard slap across the face with the back of his hand.

The younger man cringed in pain, but didn't scream. "Dad, I'll be honest with you, I don't give a damn about your project anymore."

Robert Benson winced at those words. "What happened to you, my boy? Only a short time ago you were doing great in school, and we almost finished the parabolic super dish antenna. What's made you go sour so suddenly?"

"Yeah, that's it. I've gone sour."

"You don't care about your parents' feelings?"

"I care, I care. But I've got to live my own life. I'm not a baby anymore. I'm not living at home any more."

"That's obvious. Who lives in that greystone?"

"Christine Matthews."

"A Shiktze?"

"Why not? No hang-ups about anything. Who needs a stupid JAP?"

Benson's fingers tightened on the steering wheel. "Harold, you're a Jew."

"Look Dad, I don't care about religion anymore. It's all the same. All people are the same. You and your nationalism. All that clannishness causes wars and hate among men."

"So you've become a philosopher. I suppose the dope has 'freed your think-ing'?" He paused, then asked, "This Christine, she knows about your drugs?"

"She hooked me up with Snoo... with a junkie."

"Who was that? What were you about to say?"

"Never mind."

"No, tell me. I insist. You're still my son, I know better than to start up with drug dealers. I'd be the last one to call the cops."

Harold began to shudder. "What's the matter Harold?" Robert asked with feigned emotion.

"I...I guess is doesn't make any difference. The guy's name was Snookie."

"Was?"

"Yeah. Somebody blew him away yesterday. Not that I was surprised after I thought about it. It's just that I wasn't two feet from him when his brains went fly-ing."

"What are you saying?"

"He was shot dead, probably by some rival drug dealer, just as he was about to fork over some coke to me."

Robert gave his son a sidelong glance. "Did you call the cops?"

"What the hell for? You think I give a damn about the pusher? There's plenty more out there."

"Didn't seeing the guy killed in front of your face send any message to you? If I had seen a snake about to inject its venom into my veins, then witnessed it mirac-ulously snuffed out in front of me, I wouldn't be looking for another snake to bite me. I'd be thanking God from the bottom of my heart."

For a moment, Harold was silent. As if speaking to himself, he said, "You know, that dawned on me, for about five minutes. When I first tore out of there, I said to myself, if I live through this, I'm going straight to the closest synagogue to pray hard."

"So why didn't you?" Benson tried not to let the intensity creep too obvious-ly into his voice.

"Once I crossed the 11th Street Bridge, I began to think rationally again. It's like I was telling you — drug dealers get blown away every day, like squirrels get run over in the street."

"You call that rational? Harold, what about your love for your people? You became my partner in the project."

"Big deal." Harold shrugged, once again in possession of himself. "People split up all the time. Marriages split up, partners split up. You're no worse off than you were a few years ago when you still had me hoodwinked."

"But, Harold," Benson said slowly, "you swore secrecy."

"Look, Dad. I don't give a damn any more. I told you — religion, Israel, it means nothing to me. Just leave me alone. I have my own life to live! Now tell me what you did to my car."

Robert didn't answer for a long while. When he spoke, it was only to say, very quietly, "Please come see your Mom for a few minutes, then I'll drive you back to Georgetown."

Harold offered no response. When the car stopped at the light at Colesville Road and East-West Highway, he grasped the door handle and, without warning, catapulted himself out of the car.

"Harold! Come back!" Benson shouted. The traffic behind him began to honk wildly. He had no choice but to drive off.

Harold caught the subway and made his way back to his girlfriend's apartment. He opened his hood and found the distributor wire detached. Plugging it back in, he started the car to make sure nothing else had been disconnected, then went inside, well-satisfied with the morning's work.

The next day, Harold and Christine were on their way to Reston, Virginia. Ms. Matthews knew of another good source for crack she had heard about from college friends. The couple had been stoned all night and not quite up to driving, but they started out regardless. Taking the Clara Barton, they got on the entrance to 495, just at the bridge to Virginia.

"What are you doing?" Chrissy screamed frantically, as the car began to accelerate like a dragster.

"Nothing — nothing," he gasped, fighting the car. "The throttle must be a little stuck."

"You're up to seventy. Were going to get caught by cops. Slow down, damn it."

"I can't. I told you. the pedal is stuck. The brakes... the brakes don't work. Damn, damn, daaa...."

The steering wheel — as if a demon had taken control of it — turned sharply to the right. The car hit the guardrail head on, flipped over the forty-inch concrete barrier, soared across the C&O Canal, and crashed into the rocky Potomac River, ninety feet below.

*   *   *

The *Shiva* was very hard on Robert, Barbara, and Danny Benson. Hundreds of friends and co-workers filed in to pay their respects, but the family was inconsolable. The following Monday, Benson went to the synagogue for the first time in seven weeks. He wanted to say *Kaddish* for his son.

"Aryeh son of Hirsch shall rise to bless the Torah," called the beadle of Ohev Shalom congregation. None of the other twenty-five men at the service could have known that Benson, the typical American Jew, would understand *every* word the Torah reader chanted.

"If a man will have a wayward and rebellious son who does not hearken to the voice of his father and the voice of his mother, and they discipline him, but he does not hearken to them; then his father and mother shall grasp him and take him out to the elders of the city and the gate of his place. They shall say to the elders of the city, 'This son of ours is wayward and rebellious; he does not hearken to our voice; he is a glutton and a drunkard.' All the men of his city shall pelt him with stones and he shall die; and you shall remove the evil from your midst; and all of Israel shall hear and fear."

Benson showed no emotion as he walked back to his seat. But inside, where his innermost secrets resided, he felt a great solace in the age-old words he had just heard.

*   *   *

"Mr. Benson," came the voice on the phone, the first evening after Robert returned to work. "I'm Captain Williams of the Virginia Highway Patrol. We're very sorry for the delay on the report. Unfortunately, it took all of three days to determine whether Virginia or Maryland had jurisdiction in your son's case."

"I understand. What did you find?"

"The autopsy report has confirmed that both your son and the woman killed with him had restricted substances in their blood at the time of the accident. Obviously, there will be no prosecution. The wreck is at the Fairfax police pound. You can come and see it or retrieve any belongings." Apologetically, the officer added, "Though, to be honest, there's not much left of it. Certainly nothing of value."

"I'll come anyway. I just have to see it."

The next day, Robert Benson took off from work at noon and headed for Fairfax, Virginia. He was shown his son's car. Its nose was compressed to only one third its normal length, the entire passenger compartment buckled and crushed. Only the trunk hadn't seemed to suffer too much, considering the monumental trauma.

Benson looked at the police sergeant who had escorted him to the car. "Sir, please, leave me alone here for a few minutes." The officer headed back to the main yard house. He was scarcely three steps away when the bereaved father broke down and wept bitter tears.

Presently, rubbing his eyes to clear them, Benson began to walk around the car. He peeked into the engine compartment. It was nothing but a mass of mangled wires and metal. Then he bent down and looked at the undercarriage. He pushed back the boot of the rack and pinion hydraulic piston and removed an eight-inch metal sleeve attached to a pair of wires and a little black box.

He slipped the box and wires into his pocket, threw the metal sleeve into a junk pile a few steps away, and took out a handkerchief to wipe his face. Benson threw the tear-dampened cloth into the broken-out windshield, and drove home.

Chapter 35

In June of 1992, Danny Benson graduated Cum Laude from MIT, with a B.S. in nuclear engineering. He came home for the summer, resting up in preparation for an M.S. Ph.D. program to which he had been accepted in the same institution.

"Hey, what are you doing, Danny?" his father asked on the second morning after he came home.

Danny had strapped onto his head and arm the black leather boxes that Orthodox Jews wear during weekday morning prayers. "Just praying. You know what *Tefilin* are — you bought these for me when I was *Bar Mitzvah*."

The answer was gently ironic. "I know, I know, but that's just what it's for — *Bar-Mitzvah* boys. What's come over you? Are you becoming Orthodox?"

"Is that so bad?" Prayerbook in hand, Danny paused, then continued with real enthusiasm, "Dad, three of my professors last semester were Orthodox Jews. There's no contradiction between Orthodox Judaism and science; those guys are just as brilliant as any of the other profs. One is even a rabbi of a synagogue. He invited me over to his house to eat on Friday night. Would you believe that the man is totally transformed on Shabbos? Turns into a Hasidic Jew, fur hat and everything. At first I thought it was some kind of a joke. But after going there a few times and hearing him speak, I began to realize that not only is he serious, but his knowledge of religious studies is just as brilliant as his lectures on quantum mechanics."

"I have no problem with that," Robert Benson said. "We have always kept kosher in the house. I go to services a few times a month. Just don't go overboard."

"Don't worry, Dad. I know how disappointed you were when Harold went off. I'd do anything to please you and Mom. I really mean it. This has always been a traditional household. I thought you'd be happy to know that I plan to carry on that tradition, and then some."

"You're right." Benson relented. "Actually, I was baiting you. After Harold died, I used to go to *Shul* a few times a week to say *Kaddish* for him. I even bought a new pair of *Tefilin* at that Jewish bookstore on Georgia Avenue." He eyed his son thoughtfully, as though assessing him. Danny glanced at his prayerbook, obviously ready to begin his morning prayers. His father said, "Tell me, Danny. How serious are you about pleasing Mom and I?"

"Completely serious. One thing the professor, I mean the rabbi, said in one of his lectures — and this came as a great surprise to me — was that the hardest of all the Commandments to fulfill, is the one about honoring your mother and father."

"Oh, I understand that," Benson nodded. "It makes perfect sense. Remind me in a few months; there's something you could do for me."

"Tell me now, Dad," Danny urged. "I'd be glad to do it."

"Let's just wait a while."

Danny Benson was deeply interested in electronics and computers. One of the courses he would be taking — and for which he had already spent $120 on a nine hundred page textbook — had a detailed chapter on electromagnetic waveforms. After studying the chapter, Danny spent another six hundred dollars on an EMF (electromagnetic frequency) sensor and an A to D (analog to digital) converter that connected up to his 486 computer. He tested the device on all kinds of signals: radio, TV, microwave. Soon, he began to recognize the different waveforms they generated. The computer program that came with the sensor created a database that allowed him to store the pictures and data of each, so that he could compare them and run analyses of their characteristics.

Generally, he would hold the sensor within a few inches of the EMF source he was attempting to chart, but one evening, while working in his room, he just left the sensor on. On his screen was a weird waveform that he didn't recognize. The signal was very weak. Cosmic rays, he figured, or some other type of radiation with which he was not familiar. Nonetheless, he thought it odd that the waves seemed so orderly. They did not fall into the common, random "noise" patterns.

A week after school resumed, he attempted to find an answer.

"Professor Chernitzski — I mean, Rabbi Chernitzski?"

"I'm wearing my beret at the moment; call me Professor. When I'm in a *Shtreimel*, you can call me rabbi." Danny laughed.

"Over the summer, I was fooling around with an EMF sensor...."

Chernitzski cut him off, "Those things are expensive. I didn't realize you were so rich, Danny. You're going to have to make a bigger donation to my Shul." Danny laughed again, then doggedly pursued his question.

"It might be called a sensor, but it's not very sensitive. It's little more than a toy. I saved some waveforms whose identity I'm not sure of. I thought they might be cosmic rays or some other junk from outer-space, or radiation given off by the sun."

That afternoon, Danny loaded his diskette into the professor's PC. For two minutes, Chernitzski gazed wordlessly at the image on his monitor.

"Those aren't cosmic rays or anything of the sort. I'm not quite sure what they are, but from the uniformity of the waves, it looks like a high frequency IF (intermediate frequency) wave from a transmitter." Chernitzski's finger moved across the screen. "It would indicate some kind of a man-made radio signal generated by a nearby transmitter. Did you ever try your... toy, near a radio station?"

"You know, I never thought of that."

That same evening, Danny borrowed a UPS and carried his computer out to his car. He drove out to the WBZ tower, where he switched on both his computer and the EMF sensor. Just as Chernitzski had guessed, Danny found that there were many similarities to the mysterious waveform. Two days later, on Sabbath, Danny prayed at Chernitzski's synagogue. After services the rabbi came over to him and said, "This is not really what we talk about on Shabbos, but you know that disk you gave me?"

"Sure — the one with the mysterious waveform."

"That's right. I showed it to a good friend of mine who works for Raytheon. An Arab American, and a brilliant fellow. He develops top-secret military communications computers. He took one look at the picture and said, 'That's an IF from a satellite signal.' I asked him if it was perhaps from a telephone company. He said, 'Oh, no, that's pure data flow; it's modulated quite differently.' He looked closely at the data description on your analysis chart and said, 'Looks like a military band. I really shouldn't say any more about it.... But this must have come off a transmitter hooked to a dish antenna very close to whoever picked this up.' Curious, isn't it?"

Danny thought for a minute. "Yes, it is. You know, I just thought of something. Of course — it's obvious. But it doesn't make a bit of sense...."

"What doesn't make sense, Danny?"

"My dad has a top-secret job with the government. He rarely talks about what he does. But I know it has to do with satellite communications and military navigation." He leaned forward, lowering his voice. "Rabbi — I mean, Professor, *Shtreimel* or no *Shtreimel* — could the signals my father works with all day have rubbed off on him? I know he was home when I made these studies."

"No, Danny, not quite. Not unless he was some kind of miracle worker!" The two laughed, then began to make their way out of the synagogue along with the last of the worshipers.

The matter was dropped until Danny went home in early December for the midterm break. With a good clue as to the type of waves that had baffled him in the summer, he was curious to get to the bottom of the mystery. On the third evening that he tried, the signal returned. This time, Danny moved the sensor — attached to a six-foot cable — to various points around the house. He wanted to see if the signal changed depending on its location.

It did. His computer sat on his desk, near an outside wall of the house. As he moved his "magic wand" closer toward the house's interior, the signal gained in strength. The same thing happened when he moved it up toward the ceiling. He set his computer on a chair in the middle of his bedroom and plotted a chart of the signal in three locations throughout the room. He took all the data and fed it into Mathematica to triangulate a three-dimensional survey of the signal's maximum-strength location. He ran the program ten times before he was convinced that a satellite dish sending and receiving military signals was only thirty feet west of, and six feet higher than, the upper northwest corner of his room. He stared at his results, his brain awhirl with confusion. What did these results mean?

Four days later, Robert and Barbara Benson drove off to New York to attend the wedding of their rabbi's youngest daughter. By Danny's calculations, whatever was up there must be directly above a linen closet near the staircase on the second floor. He brought a stool over to investigate.

To his surprise, he discovered that the ceiling in the linen closet could be pushed up, and that it led to an attic that he never knew existed. Propping up a ladder, he made his way up to the secret chamber, flashlight in hand. The young sleuth almost lost his mind — not to mention his balance on the ladder — when he saw the five-foot dish antenna and the sophisticated electronic equipment surrounding it. An ordinary 486 PC was there also, hooked up to the elaborate system. Danny switched it on.

It took him four hours to figure out approximately what was going on. At length, he managed to hack his way into the part of the program which was headed DTC on MGPS. He entered that menu and found a column of numbers, headed by an X, a Y, and a Z. These, he guessed, must be coordinates of some kind.

This was as far as he wanted to go. He switched off the equipment, put everything carefully back in its place, and went back to his own room. The last step was to return his computer to his desk. Then he lay down in his bed and began to cry.

His father was a spy, working right under the noses of the government! He only hoped that — like his father's old friend, Ira Rabinowitz, rotting away in jail these past seven years — his father was not an enemy spy.

Several days later, while Mrs. Benson was in the kitchen, Danny sat with his father in the living room. Nervously, he cleared his throat.

"Dad, do you agree with all the rabbis and movements that are agitating to get Ira Rabinowitz freed?"

Benson looked up from his newspaper. "Danny, I hear about that stuff. But I really don't want to talk about it."

"Why not? He was your friend, wasn't he?"

"He became a traitor to his country."

"That's not true!"

His father set aside the newspaper and said, "So you've bought in to all the balderdash his supporters are spewing about him, about how good he really was. You should only know how much the Jews in sensitive government jobs have suffered because of him."

"No, Dad, I didn't mean it in that sense. He was no traitor to his country — because it is quite obvious to me that America can't be considered his country; Israel is."

"Well, if you look at it that way, I suppose you're right." The elder Benson shook his head. "Look, you know my work is highly classified. I cringe whenever his name is mentioned, and I don't want to think about him."

Danny was nothing if not persistent. Watching his father carefully, he asked, "But Dad, didn't his information really help Israel during the Gulf War? They had the knowledge to keep Syria at bay, and had they felt compelled to counterattack Iraq, Ira's info would have put them right on target." He leaned back. "At least, that's what I've heard. I'm sure you know the inside scoop."

There was a tinge of annoyance in the way Robert Benson picked up his newspaper again. Pointedly, he opened it, saying. "I told you, I really don't want to comment about that. Even at *Shul*, everybody knows that I avoid the subject."

"Dad, do you love Israel and the Jewish nation?"

"Of course! Every Jew does. But we live here in America. Our first allegiance is to this country. You want to be a big Zionist? Go live there, Danny — I'd be proud if you did. A lot of our neighbors' children made *Aliya*."

"Dad, would you consider *Aliya*?"

Benson pondered a minute, not in search of an answer to the question, but of what, exactly, his son was driving at. "No, Danny," he replied at last. "I'm a red-blooded American. I don't think I could leave this country. As a matter of fact, because of my job, I'm not allowed to leave the country."

"So your first allegiance is not to Israel. Then where *is* it to?"

"What the hell are you talking about? I must have told you five times in this conversation, I'm a loyal American!"

Danny stood up and walked over to his father. His fists were clenched tensely at his sides. "Then why do you have your own private military satellite processing center in the attic of this house?"

Robert Benson was stunned. He stared up at his son, absolutely numbed.

"How did you find it?" he whispered. "No one knows, not even your mother."

"Answer me, Dad! Just answer me!"

Shakily, Benson brought a finger to his lips. "Shhh. Of course for Israel. What did you think, for Red China?"

"That's what they're now saying about Rabinowitz."

"Oh, Weinberger that bast.... Hogwash. That's nothing but lies being leaked to the press to justify the horrid treatment meted out to Ira."

"Can you prove it to me?"

Robert Benson began to speak to his son in Ivrit, Israeli Hebrew. Although Danny could only catch a few words, he knew it was Hebrew. Now it was his turn to be stunned.

"What did you say, Dad?"

"I said, how did you find out?"

Danny shrugged. "I guess I'm just one hell of a smart Jew."

"Arrogant."

"Not really. I inherited my brains from you."

"I hope that's the case." Benson stirred, as though shifting a burden that had long rested on his shoulders. "I suppose the time has come to tell you everything, and to trust that you will join my operation. I'll start from the beginning.

"Twenty-eight years ago, after taking a battery of tests, I was called into the office of the project commander...."

Chapter 36

July 1965, MOSSAD HQ:

After reading a dossier on the man sitting across the table, Colonel Rafi Schwartz looked up at him. "You have scored well on all the psychological, physical and intelligence tests. Do you know your IQ, Mr. Harkesef?"

"No, sir. My parents were scrupulous never to tell any of their children the results of those tests."

"Very wise of your parents; we have enough arrogance here in Israel. But as you have volunteered for Mossad duty, a modicum of arrogance is not only commendable, it is imperative. So I beg the forgiveness of your parents in advance.

"Your IQ is one hundred sixty-one, passable for the new project I have in mind. If you volunteer for this project, you will not only be devoting your career, you will be devoting your entire life to it. You will be sworn to secrecy, the violation of which will mean your execution. Believe me, Mr. Harkesef, we have the will and the means to carry out that threat."

Harkesef reflected on what he'd just heard. "You say nothing about the danger factor. Are my chances of survival small or nil?"

"On the contrary," Colonel Schwartz assured him. "You will probably never find yourself in the remotest danger. But as I said, the project calls for a lifetime commitment — literally. You are on the job until you die at a ripe old age."

"Is it some type of mole operation? On foreign soil, perhaps? Will I receive a new identity and pretend to be someone that I am not?"

The Colonel smiled. "I can see the IQ test was pretty accurate. Let me just add that, for all the sacrifices you will be called upon to make, the reward will be great. Great, that is, if you believe in the survival of the State of Israel. As you are well aware, we have many enemies. We probably have some that we don't even recognize today. I am sure there are even some who are our friends today; tomorrow they may sour on us for various and sundry reasons. Your mission, together with sixty-nine others, will prepare our nation to survive a worst-case scenario." He fixed Harkesef with a steely eye. "Make your decision."

Harkesef was startled by the abrupt command. "By — by when?"

"Right now."

"No. You must give me time to think about it."

"Too much thinking is no good. In our business, you must react."

Harkesef shook his head and said quietly, "I'm not in your business yet. If and when I decide to be, *then* I will be trained to react. I know from the past two weeks of tests that you won't find too many men who can qualify. I need three days to think."

"One day."

"Thirty-six hours, that's what you really mean," Harkesef stated categorically. He wasn't used to beating around the bush.

Colonel Schwartz nodded. "Not a minute longer."

"Tomorrow evening," Benny Harkesef said evenly, his face betraying none of the turmoil he was experiencing inside. He looked long and hard into the penetrating black eyes of Rafi Schwartz. For a brief moment, he thought the Mossad Colonel had mesmerized him. Schwartz extended his hand as the two stood. He knew he had his man, which was more than Harkesef knew.

The drive from HQ to his home in Hertzlia became reckless as his mind wandered. At first, his thoughts were dominated by the sheer bravado of such a vital and secretive mission. But by the time he reached the Ramat Gan road, he had begun to think about the realities of the project. That was when the trembling started. He imagined having to cut himself off from his entire past and start out again as an entirely new person.

"Maybe that's why man is born as an infant devoid of intellect and reason — so that he may slowly mature and develop through the care and training of his parents and his society, unlike other beings who must fend for themselves from the earliest age." Benny Harkesef was well-educated. Though he had majored in nuclear physics, he was well-read in most subjects. He thought now about a psychological report he had once read. A study of infants had proven that those babies deprived of human contact until the age of two were irreparably damaged mentally. He thought about his own present situation, and the effects of spontaneously coming into a new existence. How would he react? Would there be irreversible scarring? Part of the training for the mission, he was certain, would doubtlessly deal with these issues. The thought settled his anxiety a bit.

Unfortunately, his absorption in his thoughts caused him to make a left turn at the wrong light. He soon realized his error. Moving on down the block — the sign said 'Rabbi Akiva Street' — he searched for a convenient side street in which to turn around. Then, as he realized what he had stumbled into, he gritted his teeth.

All the men walking along the sidewalk wore long beards, and the women were dressed as eighteenth-century peasants, skirts down to their ankles and sleeves to the wrist in the sweltering heat of summer. He tried to turn up one side street, then noticed that it was one way. He turned up another. Slightly lost, he looked around to survey the best way to get back to the main highway. Distracted by his confused sense of where he was and the lingering thoughts of the day, he had no idea that he was in trouble until he heard a shout, "Look out!" Quickly, he faced forward and slammed on the brakes. The car must have slowed to five km/h when he struck a pole where the road suddenly curved.

At impact, his head flew forward, right into the windshield. The post became slightly canted, though not too terribly. Nor was the dent on the Mazda's bumper very deep. A cut on Benny Harkesef's forehead was the major calamity of the incident. Although he was never unconscious nor in fear of a concussion, the blood spurting from the contusion was liberally staining his paisley shirt.

He got out of the car. A group of children paused in their game to run over, curled sidelocks flying, and ask if he was all right. With his right hand pressed against the cut to suppress as much bleeding as possible, he dismissed them with a disdainful, "Yeah, I'm okay. Just get away." He knew, subconsciously, that he would never have reacted with that tone of voice had the children not been wearing the corner-stringed square garments over their shirts and those ridiculous sidecurls. His reaction would have been different had their heads not been shaved nearly bald — aside from the *peyot* of hair at their ears — and bedecked by large, black yarmulkes. Had they even been wearing knitted *Kippot* with a colorful border, he knew that the words that emanated from his mouth would not have been so bitter.

Benny Harkesef was not a man to ignore the uncomfortable. The more he thought about his reaction to those children, the worse he felt. This was not so much because he had yelled at a bunch of draft-evading little parasites, but because, if he did join the Mossad, he would have to maintain complete control over his emotions. He looked up at the street sign that had put such an effective stop to his progress: Rashbam Street.

A minute later, a bearded, middle-aged man emerged from the closest building. In his hand was a wet towel. Silently, he handed it to the wounded young secular Israeli. Benny stared at the man, who wore the same hairstyle and outer garment as the boys looking on from across the street.

The rabbi spoke. "Please come into my house and rest a minute."

Benny Harkesef, though loath to enter the house, decided that this was a perfect opportunity to school himself in the conscious control of his feelings. The rabbi sat him down at the dining-room table, then went into the adjacent kitchen to bring a pot of tea and a plate of cookies. He handed his guest a yarmulke and said quietly, "Put this on and make a blessing." There was a manifest glow to the man's personality that led Harkesef to do as he was asked. He even found that he remembered the beginning of the blessing from his youth. The older man filled him in when he got stuck on the last three words, which Benny methodically repeated.

The rabbi watched him eat a cookie and take a sip of his tea before he spoke again. "I see in you a strong and intelligent character. But you mustn't daydream while you drive. The Torah prohibits us from placing ourselves in danger."

"You don't understand," his secular guest protested. "I'm not religious. I don't follow the Torah."

"Still, you could have endangered others. Even from your perspective, isn't it imperative to preserve life and not endanger it?"

To preserve life, Harkesef thought. *That's what this project is all about.*

The rabbi went out, brought back a clean bandage and applied it to his guest's wound in a very professional manner. The bleeding had stopped. Meanwhile, the rabbi's wife prepared a hot meal for the unexpected visitor. He protested, but the rabbi urged the young man to stay. Benny found it difficult to take his eyes off the rabbi's face. There was a sincerity and depth of personality that emanated from within in a way that the young secularist had never before encountered. He looked around the dining room, and all he could see were wall-to-wall books. He sensed that his host had read *every* one of them, but decided to inquire anyway. "Are you a rabbi?"

"I am just a person, like you and everyone else. Thank the Almighty, I was raised to believe that one should immerse oneself, his entire being, even his entire life, in the study of the Law of God. That Law is expressed in print. The books you see around us — those are books of the Holy Law."

Benny's eyes turned to the pile of books at one end of the table. There must have been at least fifteen of them, some piled open on top of each other. Then he began to think about his decision and Rafi Schwartz.

"Rabbi, I don't understand much about what you do and what you believe in. But let me ask this. What would you say about a person who dedicates his life to saving other lives? I don't mean just some kind of suicide military mission. I mean a lifelong project whose entire goal is to prepare the way to save lives during some emergency in the future."

The rabbi looked deeply into the young man's eyes. A great fear welled up in Benny's heart. He was frozen to his seat. Eyes closed, the rabbi swayed gently as he pondered the question. It lasted only three or four minutes, but to Benny it felt like an eternity.

The rabbi's eyes suddenly popped open and found Benny's. The only words he spoke were, "Yes. You must do it."

Benny Harkesef was stunned. For the first time in his life, the thought crossed his mind that there must be a God and that he had met His prophet. His newfound practice of forcibly controlling his emotions came into play now, as Benny mustered the courage to respond despite his amazement and bewilderment.

"Rabbi, I don't understand. *What* should I do?"

"You hit the pole because a great and grave question hung heavily upon your mind. You must have been in a state of deep perplexity. You were given the opportunity to volunteer for some kind of security mission — that much you have practically told me outright. I see in you a profound intellect and good character, despite the fact that you weren't raised with Torah observance." He smiled at Benny, adding persuasively, "Nothing happens by chance, young man. God sent you to my door for a reason. Dozens of people seek my advice and opinion every day. If God determined that you must be brought here now, it must be for some vital purpose. I've thought through many options, and have concluded that the answer is 'yes'."

"Rabbi, I don't even know what the mission entails," the younger man said miserably. "All I know is that it might require that I permanently cut myself off from everyone I know and start out as a stranger in a strange place. How can I commit myself?"

The rabbi looked at him with penetrating eyes that held a world of compassion. "No, my son, you're wrong. God — *your* God, whose love makes the love of your parents and friends pale in comparison — will be with you everywhere, every step you take." He paused. "I think I have an idea about this mission, perhaps even more than you realize. A great leader of our people once had a similar mission. He was a judge and a warrior. No man ever possessed the physical strength of this man."

"Samson!" Benny burst out.

The smile came back. "I see you have some knowledge of the Torah."

"We learned in grade school about heroes who meet Zionist criteria."

The rabbi inclined his head in acknowledgment, then continued, "But Samson was subverted and revealed his secret. In his last moments, he prayed to God to restore his strength for just one moment, during which he managed to severely injure the enemy. If only he had kept his secret and retained the power to destroy the enemy, perhaps the Final Redemption would have come about in his days.

"But the opportunity was lost, as it has been lost time after time throughout our history." His tone became commanding. "You must keep the secret and act only to fulfill your mission. Do not be cajoled into making the same mistake as Samson."

Benny frowned. "I don't remember the story very well. It's been a long time, and none of the students took Bible seriously. I do remember that Delilah, his wife, was a Philistine. The teacher taught us that it was only the rabbis in recent times who made a prohibition against marrying gentile women."

"That is not true. Samson married her only to position himself to help save his people. He was the greatest undercover operative in our history. Unfortunately, his success in his mission was not complete, because of his mistake in revealing the secret of his strength." The rabbi's eyes twinkled. "That was not the first secret he revealed. The first was the riddle of *Samson's Lion*. Did Zionist education teach you about that?"

In the face of Benny's silence, the rabbi took a Bible down from the shelf and began to read.

"Samson went down to Timnath, and in Timnath he saw a woman of the daughters of the Philistines. He went up and told his father and mother and said, 'I have seen a woman in Timnath of the daughters of the Philistines. Now take her for me as a wife.' His father and mother said to him, 'Is there no woman among the daughters of your brothers and in all my people, that you go to take a wife from the uncircumcised Philistines?' But Samson said to his father, 'Take her for me, for she is fitting in my eyes.'"

The rabbi looked up for a brief moment and then continued.

"'His father and mother did not know that Samson was acting on a mission from God. He was seeking a pretext against the Philistines, who ruled in Israel at the time. So Samson and his father and mother descended to Timnath. They reached the vineyards of Timnath, and behold a young lion came roaring toward him. The spirit of God came upon him and he tore it apart as one tears apart a kid, though he had nothing in his hand. He did not tell his father and mother what he had done. He went down and spoke with the woman, and she was fitting in Samson's eyes. He returned after some time to marry her, but he turned aside to see the fallen body of the lion, and behold, a swarm of bees was in the lion's carcass, with honey. He scraped it into his hand and went, walking and eating. He went to his father and mother and gave them, and they ate, but he did not tell them that he had scraped it from the body of the lion. His father went down to the woman and Samson made a feast there, for that is what the young men would do. It happened when they saw him that they took thirty companions to be with him. Samson said to them, 'Let me pose you a riddle. If you answer it for me during the seven days of the feast, I will give you thirty sheets and thirty changes of clothing. But if you cannot tell me, then you will give me thirty sheets and thirty changes of clothing.' They said to him 'Pose your riddle and let us hear it.' He said to them, 'From the devourer came sustenance, and from the bold came sweetness.' They could not answer the riddle for three days. It was on the Sabbath day that they said to Samson's wife, 'Entice your husband to tell us the riddle, lest we burn you and your father's house with fire. Did you invite us here to impoverish us?' So Samson's wife wept near him and said, 'You only hate me and do not love me. You posed the riddle to the sons of my people, but you did not tell me'. He said to her, 'Behold, I did not even tell my father and mother, shall I tell you?' She wept near him for the remainder of the seven days they had the feast. It happened on the seventh day that he told her, for she had distressed him. Then she told the riddle to the sons of her people. And the people of the city said to him on the seventh day before the sun had set, 'What is sweeter than honey, what is bolder than a lion?' He replied to them, 'Had you not plowed with my calf, you would not have solved my riddle.' Then the spirit of God came over him and he went down to Ashkelon and struck thirty of their men. He took their clothing and gave the changes of clothing to those who had told the riddle. He became angry and went up to his father's house. Samson's wife was given to his friend, whom he had befriended.'"

The rabbi closed his volume, and for the next half-hour expounded on Samson's intentions in the entire incredible episode. He explained, "The Philistines were in power at the time, and the Jewish Nation was at a loss to throw off the yoke of those immoral and idolatrous people. Samson, understanding the great martial talents with which God had endowed him, realized that he must infiltrate the Philistine ranks and decimate their leadership. By marrying a Philistine woman, he convinced them that he was willing to betray his own people. Then he set up the circumstances so that he could justifiably take revenge against many of their people. He kept his plan so secret that even his parents had no idea what he was doing. Certainly the Jewish Nation had no clue. Samson was even arrested and handed over to the Philistines by his own people; that too was part of his plan to destroy the oppressors. In the end, the pressure Delilah put upon Samson to reveal his secret was unimaginable, and she finally triumphed."

"But Rabbi, if the great Samson gave away his secret, how can it be expected that I won't? I am only a man. Over the course of years and years, I may slip up and be discovered or make a devastating mistake."

The rabbi closed his eyes again, deep in thought for a few seconds. "Your youth belies your wisdom," he said finally. "But remember this: no endeavor goes perfectly smoothly. God gave Samson one last opportunity to redeem himself, and he did so by pulling down the pillars of the building and annihilating the Philistine leadership, which had come to watch him being made sport of. Though he died with them, this represented the greatest success of his lifelong plan." He focused directly on Benny, speaking slowly and with great emphasis. "If you retain your focus and your dedication to the project, it makes sense that you, also, will be given an opportunity to redeem yourself. But it is imperative that you eliminate any obstacle that may threaten your success."

The eerie feeling overcame Benny Harkesef again. Reluctantly, he was beginning to think there might be something to the religion he'd dismissed all his life. He was truly amazed at himself for feeling suddenly that his life was lacking something. He had been missing not only knowledge, but also interest and a positive attitude, for the past twenty-four years. He was intelligent enough to be deliberate, and now he was also determined to control his emotions and immediate desires. He would investigate Judaism further, he decided, as soon as he had the chance.

As for the rabbi's counsel that he should go on the mission, he wasn't about to formulate the decision of his life based on the word of another man, even if that man seemed to be genuinely holy.

After a simple but wholesome meal, Harkesef thanked his host and promised to keep in mind everything that he had learned from this unexpected encounter. As he opened the door to leave, the rabbi said, "I didn't tell you before, when I explained Samson's riddle, but this you should know: the Philistines, after forcing the solution out of Samson's wife with a death threat, didn't really answer the riddle. Oh, they solved it well enough to warrant Samson's revenge, but it was not the explanation Samson had in mind!"

"What was the true answer?" Benny asked eagerly.

"Some day, Mr. Harkesef, some day.... One more thing. Please come close."

Taken aback, Benny hesitated, then took four tentative steps in the rabbi's direction. The rabbi placed his right hand upon Benny's head and pronounced the priestly blessing. The young man bowed his head a bit under the pressure of the rabbi's hand. After the three-sentence blessing was complete, Benny left the house. He got back into his car, and sat a few minutes thinking. Then, accepting the rabbi's admonition — if not as a religious obligation, at least as common sense — he cleared his mind and drove off.

The next evening, Benny Harkesef found himself at GSS headquarters, still undecided in his mind. Colonel Rafi Schwartz greeted him with a firm handshake, and sat him down in a luxurious lounge. "Well, Mr. Harkesef, have you made up your mind? And by the way, what did the rabbi tell you?"

Harkesef was astounded. "You had me followed?"

"You're an expensive piece of meat. I'll be honest — don't get a fat head, now — we really think we need you for this project."

"*You* tell *me* what the rabbi said. You probably had me bugged." As he spoke, Benny Harkesef began to grope his clothes, just as one would for a tick or a burr. He couldn't find anything.

"Honest," said Schwartz in all sincerity, "we didn't go that far. We were surprised when you turned off into the interior of Bnei Braq. We thought maybe you'd had some kind of spiritual inspiration. But when we spotted you crashing into the pole, we figured you must have been lost in thought. It's not the first time one of our candidates went bonkers thinking about his mission.... So what did the rabbi say? He's considered one of today's greatest rabbis by the Orthodox. It's some coincidence that you happened to crash just in front of his building."

"Perhaps it was no coincidence," Benny offered noncommitally.

"Oh, please. Just what kind of hocus-pocus did the rabbi tell you? He tried to make you into a believer?"

Benny grinned. "I'm not going to tell you what he said. But you'd better watch out: he's definitely a great and holy man." The grin disappeared. "Let's get down to business. I have to know more about the project before I can make up my mind. I'd do practically anything for my country, but this seems to be an extreme sacrifice."

"I can't tell you any more until you commit and swear secrecy."

"In that case I'll have to decline," Benny said, completely insincerely. He knew how spooks operated — ninety-nine percent bluff.

The colonel suddenly dropped his charade. "You will receive a new and secure identity, show up somewhere in the world, and start a new life. From that vantage point, you will continue to work at a natural pace to build up our country's defenses."

Benny feigned puzzlement, "Wouldn't it be easier to build up defenses right here?"

"A good offense is the best defense. Now really, that's all I can say until you give me the word. I suppose I can tell you the tentative code name of the project, which will probably be changed later anyway. I made it up myself. You'll be surprised because I took it right out of the Bible: Operation Samson's Lion.... What's the matter, Benny? You all right? Maybe you struck your head harder than you thought. I'll get a doctor."

Rafi Schwartz grabbed the phone and called a GSS staff doctor. He became visibly frightened as he unsuccessfully tried to rouse the ghostly white figure slumped beside him on the couch. The man was lost in a profound stupor.

August 1965, MOSSAD training camp:

"Men," Colonel Rafi Schwartz announced in an authoritative and serious tone, "the mission for which you have all volunteered is not only the most bold and secretive in the history of our country, but it will probably prove to be the most vital in years to come. I am sure you are all sitting on pins and needles to hear about the destiny you have embraced. You all have iron guts and a penetrating intellect; you wouldn't have been chosen otherwise." He paused, then continued in a singsong chant, "'From the devourer came sustenance, and from the bold came sweetness.'" Changing expression, he began to laugh. Sixty-eight of the sixty-nine men sitting at their desks in the classroom were puzzled.

Harkesef raised his hand. "'What is sweeter than honey? What is bolder than a lion?' The riddle of Samson to the Philistines."

"A Bible scholar," said Schwartz facetiously.

"I'm no Bible scholar, but I have the utmost respect for the heroes of our people. I'm surprised at you, Colonel Schwartz. Despite your name, I have no doubt you descend from Oriental Jews. You're just too dark to be an Ashkenazi."

"I won't deny that — but so what?"

"So what, you say? Since I've come to live in our land, I've met all kinds of Jews from the four corners of the earth. Among the non-religious Americans, Russians, Poles, etcetera, some are so alienated from religion that you can't distinguish them from non-Jews. But among the least observant Sephardic Jews, I've never met a single one who, deep down, didn't possess a strong faith in God. I suppose it's an ethnic thing." He shrugged self-consciously, aware of the stares of the other men all around him in the classroom. "I just happen to think your secular facade is a bit affected. That's all."

Schwartz glanced around the room. "All right, Mr. Harkesef, let's say for argument's sake that you're right. Now tell us how you made the connection with Samson's riddle?"

"Recently, I happened to hear an interpretation from a rabbinical perspective on this subject. To my mind, it rings truer than the Zionist take on the subject. Samson wasn't perfect, but his intentions from beginning to end were to destroy the enemies of our people from within their own camp. I volunteered for this job knowing that I would be going under cover, perhaps for the rest of my life, with the same intentions as our Biblical ancestor." The other men looked at Benny Harkesef with a new respect.

Rafi Schwartz nodded. "Very good, Mr. Harkesef. A very perceptive guess. You are close, but not quite there." He turned to address the group at large. "Now, men, you understand a little about why I've named our operation 'Samson's Lion.' But let's set all that aside for now, and continue discussing the mission itself.

"Your training will take two-and-a-half years. You have already been sworn to secrecy, and I trust that secrecy will be scrupulously maintained. To your friends and relatives who pester you about what you are doing, you will tell them that you have joined the navy's submarine corps and are in training; the rest is classified for state security. This answer will not only satisfy them, it actually contains an element of truth.

"The bulk of your time here will be spent learning ordnance, electronics and infrastructure. We are not going to concentrate on TNT, cordite or plastics. That's kid's stuff. You're going to learn the state of the art, and once you're out in the world, it is expected that you will keep up with the state of the art.

"Right now, as the world suspects, Israel has developed thermonuclear weapons. Yes, the H-bomb, as well as various fission devices. As I speak, we have a GSS team of scientists and engineers working on a tactical form of a very special weapon, which may or may not be ready in time for the beginning of the project." Rafi looked soberly at his hand-picked trainees. "This may seem cruel, but that word must be expunged from our lexicon. For when it comes to the very survival of our people, nothing is cruel — and this project concerns survival. The weapon will rain death without major physical damage, similar to nerve gas, but much cleaner and more effective. We cannot yet fit an entire device in a briefcase, though that may change in a few years. But that is of no significance. We are not under any time constraints. The model we need will be ready soon. The American inventor of this device is one of our boys, Sam Katz.

"The second field of expertise you will acquire is civil engineering: suspension bridges, skyscrapers, tunnels and railway systems. However, you will not be concentrating on the art of building them. You will learn how to demolish them. You will learn where and how the support structures are constructed, so that you may topple them with the least amount of energy. You will learn how to plant destructive devices that can be remotely controlled. These devices will be designed to remain in place — dormant for many years, perhaps decades — to be detonated only if and when necessary.

"The systems you will devise are to be updated as technology advances. Once you're out on your own, each of you will decide exactly how, where, and when to plant your bombs. Only by prearranged signal from headquarters will you detonate your devices — your life's work."

Schwartz gave the group a minute to digest what he had revealed. There was an utter silence in the room as the impact of his speech began to sink in. When he judged that a sufficient interval had elapsed, the colonel continued his astonishing presentation.

"We Jews are family-oriented. Many of you must be wondering how family relations will fit in with this... long-term project." He smiled thinly. "Well, in addition to the bad news that you will be permanently cut off from your family and friends here, there is good news. A vital portion of this project calls for each of you to establish a family in the place you will be stationed. You will marry and raise children, in order to accomplish two objectives. One: as cover, to conceal your true activities. And, two — listen carefully, now — this project may extend beyond your useful lifetime. Therefore, when the time comes, you will reveal everything to one son whom you deem fit to continue your work. He will take over in your place, for the sake of the next generation."

Even from this tough bunch, the intake of breath was audible.

Harkesef raised his hand, and was acknowledged. "Colonel, this whole project seems to emanate from some kind of oracle. It reminds me of the Orthodox, who take religion so seriously that it has become a pervasive way of life."

"Very good, Mr. Harkesef," Rafi Schwartz grinned. "I see you have an exact understanding of what our training program hopes to accomplish. With your attitude, I wouldn't be surprised if our training program forges on ahead of schedule." His laughter ended the session.

For the next twelve months, the students became well-versed in the fine art of stealth: how to change their identity, not merely on paper, but in terms of their very personalities. They learned how to seek employment in areas that would enable them to carry out their work, planting the infrastructure of destruction within the infrastructure of a civilized society. Over the following eighteen months, they studied the fundamentals of nuclear, biological and chemical weaponry. They also learned martial arts. Rafi Schwartz seemed to have a fetish about karate. The daily exercise routine consisted of an hour and a half of kata. By the time the course was completed, most of the men were awarded black belts.

On November 3, 1967, the training was complete. Seventy Israeli men were about to go undercover, to disappear from the face of the earth. These men were casehardened, prepared for any fate. Still, three members of the group who were married confronted Rafi Schwartz at the last class, indicating that they had a problem. For their nation's sake they were willing to abandon their families and become reborn somewhere else on the globe. However, their concern was for the three wives who, in the State of Israel, under rabbinical regulation of marriage and divorce, would never be able to remarry.

Rafi was prepared for this eventuality. Fixing his mesmerizing gaze on Benny Harkesef, Schwartz addressed the men's apprehension. "You have nothing to worry about. All of us will officially be declared dead, and the wives will remarry. Believe me, everything has been arranged. The rabbis have the formula."

Benny Harkesef was worried. He was not married; he'd even dumped his girlfriend the day he swore secrecy to the mission. He hadn't seen a woman since. It was wrong to mislead some poor girl with whom he could not, in good conscience, join under the wedding canopy. Intellectually, he knew the decision was right, but emotionally it left him feeling mildly depressed. One day, in a spirit of restless desperation, he remembered his experience in Bnei Braq, and impulsively decided to see the rabbi again. By the time Benny left the rabbi's office, he had agreed to study twice a week with one of rabbi's students. This routine, which continued until his disappearance, provided an intellectual and spiritual stimulation that did much to fill the empty places in his life.

The evening after Rafi Schwartz had reassured his men about their wives' fate, Benny Harkesef made his way to Bnei Braq to attend his regular study session. But before opening his text, Benny felt the inexplicable compulsion to ask his teacher, who by now was a friend, "Shlomo, a question about Jewish Law."

Shlomo's brows lifted in mild surprise. "Go ahead, ask."

"You know that I haven't become observant, although I've gained a high respect for the Orthodox. Nonetheless, when it comes to marriage and the other ceremonies of the life cycle, I appreciate that these areas should remain in the domain of the religious leaders." He paused, waited until Shlomo had nodded to indicate his grasp of Benny's position, then continued intently, "Now, my question. What happens to a married woman if her husband disappears? If, for example, he disappears in battle, or was on board a ship that is lost at sea, is there a period after which he is presumed dead and his wife may remarry?"

Shlomo Klein was a man who was totally immersed in his studies. Whether the question was practical or academic had no bearing on how he listened to it or how he proposed to answer it. "According to *Halacha*, she may not remarry unless there is a witness who saw the husband dead. Presumptions of death are rarely acceptable, especially in cases of loss at sea. It is always possible that a man could have survived a shipwreck, gotten hold of some kind of flotation, and drifted to a distant place. Therefore, the wife is considered still married and may not take another husband."

Benny suspected that Rafi Schwartz might have been bluffing on this issue; after all, his only concern was the success of the project. How much did he really know or care about the religious strictures that might cause three abandoned women to suffer?

But Benny did care. After his study session, he headed over to the great rabbi. Although extremely busy, the rabbi excused himself from his guests and met for a few minutes in a private room with Benny. There was a third man in the room.

"Mr. Harkesef, I'd like you to meet my son, Chaim."

Benny was impatient. "I'm happy to meet you," he nodded politely at the younger, bearded man at the rabbi's side, then turned back to the rabbi, "but I really must speak to you, sir."

With a gentle smile, the rabbi said, "Reb Chaim happens to be a far greater man than I am. He will take my place with you now. Just listen to whatever he tells you, as if I had told it to you." The rabbi returned to his study, leaving a puzzled and annoyed Benny to deal with Rabbi Chaim.

The young rabbi regarded Benny steadily, not speaking. Under that unwavering gaze, Benny worked quickly through his annoyance. He decided to take the father at his word. Abruptly, he asked, "Rabbi Chaim, what can be done for a woman whose husband disappears and never returns? Can she be freed to remarry by some rule of Jewish Law?"

As Benny observed the other man's countenance, a shiver began to crawl up his spine, just as it had a few years before when he had met the man's father. The elder rabbi, too, had submerged himself in deep thought, only to emerge with words that seemed in some eerie way to pinpoint hidden truths....

"You are not married, so you must be asking on behalf of your friends. I realize that you are leaving soon. May the Almighty grant you success in all of your endeavors.

"This is what you must do: you must bring your married friends to Rabbi Nisan Karlin of our local Rabbinical Court. Do not turn to the Chief Rabbinate of the State. Don't tell your friends why; just get them into your car and drive them to the Court. Their wives will be free. *But you must bring them.*"

"What shall I tell the rabbi when I bring them?"

"Nothing at all. He will take care of them. It won't take long at all. But remember — if you are to help those women, you must do this." The rabbi's voice grew no louder, but his tone was imperative.

"Yes, sir, I will," Benny felt compelled to answer. The elder rabbi, he realized, had not been pulling his leg about the greatness of his saintly and scholarly son.

The following evening found a curious Eli Kedem, Shefi Mordechai and Alon Barnash pestering Benny for the duration of the entire thirty-five minute ride. They wanted to know what their mysterious excursion was all about. Benny remained mum. No good, he instinctively felt, would come from crossing the rabbi — and only good could result from this evening's work. As he turned into Rabbi Akiva Street, the men began mocking him. "So you're taking us for a blessing to some hocus-pocus rabbi? I hope you didn't tell him about the project," Barnash warned.

"Of course not. But what we are going for is even greater than a blessing. You'll see." The men continued to mock, laugh and nag until Harkesef pulled up in front of the address the great rabbi had given him — Rabbi Karlin's home.

The three husbands, two of them fathers already, were admitted and seated at the table. Across from them sat three rabbis, Rabbi Karlin in the center. The rabbi wasted no time.

"What is your name?" he asked Eli Kedem. Eli told him. "What is your father's name?" Again, although still puzzled, he answered. "What is your wife's name and her father's name?" As Kedem finished answering, he could not contain himself. "What's this all about?"

"I understand that you want to give your wives *Gittin*." Seeing the men's bewildered reaction, he added helpfully, "To divorce them."

"What?" the trio yelped in unison. Mordechai told the rabbi that there must have been a misunderstanding, and excused himself for a minute. He found Harkesef sitting in the idling car, listening to the radio. Mordechai got in, and slammed the door shut.

"What's going on here? You were sworn to secrecy. That includes everyone, even rabbis." In the close confines of the Mazda, his yells were deafening.

Benny turned off the radio and said, "Look, I told nothing. But after three years, sometimes your friends get an inkling of what's going on. We've all told our loved ones that we are going to enter the submarine corps. That in itself always represents danger. I was surprised that the project accepted married men at all — but I suppose that makes it more credible when we... disappear. I simply took it upon myself to alleviate any undue suffering that would not jeopardize the mission."

Mordechai looked mulish. "Dragging us to a rabbi —"

"That rabbi in there knows what to do. I don't know exactly what he has in mind; *I'm* no rabbi. But have a little mercy on your own wife! Why should she suffer for the rest of her life? Don't you love her?"

A bit more calmly, Mordechai said over the convulsions of the idling Wankel motor, "You heard Rafi. The rabbis will come up with some solution, they always do."

"It's not so simple. Schwartz may be a great undercover man, and his genius at planning is mind-boggling, but he's no religious authority."

"Benny, you just said it. Rafi must have everything planned out. Why are you meddling into his plan? Don't you see it could ruin everything?"

Now it was Benny's turn to glare. "Hey, who do you think Rafi Schwartz is — God's right hand man? He's great at his job, but he's just a man."

"Just a man, you say. I'll let you in on a secret. You know how he's stressed unaided martial arts in this course?"

"I'll say so." Benny grimaced. "He has us going through kata ninety minutes a day, as if we were a bunch of Samurai living in the seventeenth century. I suppose it instills a certain discipline, even if its defensive value will prove useless."

Folding his arms across his chest, Mordechai said, "Just shut up a minute and listen. Last month I was riding with him in the countryside during a break. I asked him if it was true that he had studied karate in China with one of the elder masters and had earned a tenth-Dan black belt. He smiled but didn't answer. Suddenly, he told me to pull over to the side of the road. Beyond a barbed wire fence, a herd of cattle was grazing. He climbed over and motioned for me to follow.

"As he approached, several cows ambled away. With a light-footed step, almost like a dance, he caught up to one and began to stroke it on the head. I thought he was cracking up. Within three minutes the animal seemed lulled and lay down on the ground. Then I saw your 'just a man' perform the most amazing feat I've ever witnessed a person do. It was almost like a magic trick. I swear, *he had nothing in his hand*. I saw some movement of Rafi's right hand, but it was too quick to define exactly what he did. The next instant, he was holding up the cow's bloody heart as if it was an apple dripping in honey. There was a small slit just below the animal's breastbone; a surgeon couldn't have done it any neater. But I knew Rafi had no knife.

"Half a minute after the demonstration, he replaced the heart in the animal's chest. We drove over to the farm house and, without comment, Rafi paid the owner."

"Did it come alive?" asked Benny, shaking and covered with cold sweat.

"No," laughed Shefi, "It wasn't really magic, it was skill. But a skill that transcends what is considered a man's capability. He admitted that he had learned the discipline known as Sun Yen, a martial art that combines knowledge, skill and mental power into Qigong, as he labeled it."

Benny shook his head, as if to clear it. "That *is* amazing. But it doesn't have any bearing on my moral obligation. Listen to me, Shefi — just follow Rabbi Karlin's instructions. It's the least you can do for your wife."

Shefi Mordechai looked into his friend's eyes, which were frankly teary. He reflected for a long moment. Then, without further word, he stepped out of the car and returned to his chair in the rabbi's dining room.

Rabbi Karlin continued with his questioning. "Do you willingly agree to grant a divorce to your wives without compulsion?"

The other two, who hadn't gone out to talk with Harkesef, were still confused. Shefi Mordechai spoke up, "Eli, Alon, say yes and just follow instructions." The two complied, following Mordechai's unhesitating lead.

The rabbi finished his questions, and explained to the three husbands that they must contact him at a later date, after parting from their wives to embark upon their ominous journey. He assured them that he had no idea where they were going, or why. They accepted his words, and promised to call.

Chapter 37

For five hours Danny Benson sat transfixed, listening to his father's tale. By the time Benson finished his monologue, Danny was crying. "Dad, you most certainly are a professional. Now I see that you are a *Tzaddik*, too. With everything that's happened, you have succeeded in remaining completely beyond suspicion. I would be honored to join you in the project, but doubt if I could ever come close to your skills."

"It's all training, Danny. Just follow my lead carefully, and in a few years, not only will you be my successor in the project, you will augment it and exceed even the level of my work."

Danny heaved a deep sigh, wiped his eyes and mustered a smile. "I'll try. That's all I can promise. But it's an awesome responsibility. Until I stumbled upon your operation in the attic, I didn't have the foggiest that you were involved in anything like this." He paused. "I guess you're assuming that your fear of being discovered, and the rabbi's admonition that you would have to redeem yourself, were unfounded."

Robert Benson became white as a ghost. Leaning closer, Danny pleaded, "What? What is it, Dad?"

Benson shook himself out of his thoughts. Smiling at his sole surviving son, he said, "I'll be okay. I'm back on track."

"But what —?"

"Oh, nothing. Let's skip it for now. There are so many important things we need to talk about...."

*   *   *

Back in Boston, Danny Benson began to expand the scope of his education. He signed up for a Hebrew course given at B.U. and surreptitiously sat in on a poly sci course in Middle Eastern affairs at Harvard. After six months, he became fascinated with politics and considered abandoning his Ph.D. program to concentrate on the Israeli political scene. His father convinced him to finish, but to maintain his interest in Israeli politics on the side. Danny was tall, handsome, and strong. He was very popular among his fellow students. At the Boston Hillel, he met Nancy Applebaum, a grad student in poly sci, and they became good friends.

"The right-wing parties in Israel sure made a mistake. I read in the papers how their disunity cost them the election and got Rabin elected PM," Danny told Nancy one morning in the cafeteria.

"A good thing, too." Nancy was petite, with shoulder-length chestnut hair that she had the habit of flipping back with a toss of her head when expressing an opinion. She did this now, adding, "the intifada has been going on for almost a decade. With Rabin in power, at least there's a remote possibility of a comprehensive peace plan."

Danny frowned. "That's exactly what I'm afraid of. You don't understand, Nancy: Rabin is at a point in his life and his career where he would negotiate a terribly dangerous deal. It's always risky to send in a 'mellowed' politician for such a consuming diplomatic coup."

"I didn't realize that you're so right-wing, Danny," Nancy said, staring at him.

"It has nothing to do with right-wing or left-wing. It has to do with the psychology of idealism. A person who remains focused on his idealism and his sense of purpose will be more careful about making drastic changes — especially a change that will affect so many people on a permanent basis." Danny drummed his fingers on the cream-colored Formica tabletop, formulating his argument. "Look at Begin. He was as right-wing as they come. Still, he was able to negotiate with Sadat. After fifteen years, that peace is still holding strong. But remember, Begin had just come to power. You couldn't characterize him as a worn-out politician looking for his place in history and willing to take major risks. Rabin, on the other hand, has nothing to lose. He's a relatively old man, he doesn't believe in God and Torah...."

Nancy cut him off, "And you do?"

"Of course I do. I'm not exactly Orthodox; I don't observe everything in Judaism. But I believe that God gave the Land of Israel to the Jews. It seems to me, if you don't believe that, why should the Jews have any more rights in the Holy Land than the Palestinians?" He spoke slowly now, with the cadence of a man delivering a deep-felt credo. "I believe in the inalienable rights of the Jews to live in Israel. I believe it is justified for the Jewish people to wage war against any Arab who would deny them that right. What justification is there for 'Jews' who don't believe God gave us the land? What source can they claim as giving them title to a land whose ancestors departed from it two thousand years ago?"

"That was very well put, Danny," Nancy smiled. "You said that like a man up on a political soapbox. A man with a message that people will want to hear." At his dismissive gesture, accompanied by a blush at her open admiration, she added, "No, really, you were very good. You know, Danny, I think you have potential in this area. Why don't you take a public speaking course?"

The following week, Danny Benson signed up for a Dale Carnegie course. He gained so much that, immediately upon completion, he signed up for four more of the courses. In June of 1995, Dr. Daniel Benson took his first job with General Dynamics. He was able to live in the Washington area, a necessity in order to work closely with his father. By this time, Robert and Danny Benson had become accustomed to conversing in Hebrew. This had been Danny's idea.

"Dad, my heart is in politics, not in physics anymore. But I am committed to the project."

"That's no contradiction. Quite the opposite, in fact." The elder Benson regarded his son thoughtfully. "I've noticed that you have great personal skills,

Danny. I want you to capitalize on them. In its strictest sense, each local project has a narrow military objective. As a facet of the global plan this represents a powerful tool, given a dire situation, to defend the existence of our Nation. But that in no way excludes your right — and your obligation — to find a broader and more personal context from which to help defend our people from destruction. If you possess the ability to do so, there's no imperative for you to sacrifice that ability merely to remain on the project."

Danny felt an immense lightening of a burden he hadn't even known he was carrying. "Dad, has anyone ever told you that you're brilliantly sensible?"

"Yeah, Rafi Schwartz, thirty years ago," Robert Benson replied, grinning ruefully. "I don't suppose I'd be here today if that were not the case. But we were given some latitude — actually, a great deal of latitude — to enhance the effectiveness of our work. We were not just foot soldiers with marching orders. I think you may be very successful, Danny. You look right for some big position."

"I look right — is that what counts? How about intellect?"

"Of course looks count. We live in very vain times. How do you think Clinton got elected?" The father clapped the son on the shoulder. "Go for it, Danny. I'll help you wherever I can."

In September of 1995, Danny was elected president of the synagogue. He didn't realize what he was getting into. On a microcosmic scale, the job was as big a headache as being a head of state. The petty issues uncannily paralleled the major ones that all governmental leaders must face. The job was a monumental challenge for Danny, and a great experience in leadership.

At the end of October, the synagogue sponsored a trip to Israel. Danny was to lead the trip. None of the congregants knew that he was fluent in Hebrew; that might have raised some questions. An Israeli guide ferried the group around and translated when necessary. Their first Saturday night in Israel had nothing listed on the itinerary. Danny seized the opportunity to make his way to Bnei Braq, looking for the rabbi who had made such a powerful impression upon his father many years before.

He was distressed to learn that the rabbi was no longer alive, but pleased to hear that his son, Rabbi Chaim, had taken over the father's unofficial pulpit.

Danny presented himself to the rabbi. His name brought about an immediate reaction. "Reb Shmuel," the saintly scholar said to his assistant, "I'd like to talk with Dr. Benson alone."

"But I'm sure the American doesn't speak either Yiddish or Hebrew."

"Don't worry. We will communicate, somehow."

Danny pretended not to understand a word they were saying. The British-born assistant left the room, leaving Rabbi Chaim and Danny Benson alone in the book-lined study. Danny glanced around at the heavy, holy tomes, then turned his gaze with open curiosity on the bearded man seated opposite him. In Hebrew, Rabbi Chaim said, "You look just like a man my father befriended over thirty years ago. I am guessing you must be his son. Therefore, I conclude that you are probably fluent in Hebrew."

Danny had visited the rabbi on his own whim, curious to see for himself whether the wondrous stories his father had told him retained any credence. Now, he was stunned to see how accurate his father had been.

Danny opened his mouth and, for the first time in his life, spoke the Hebrew language to a person other than his father.

"Your memory amazes me, Rabbi Chaim. From a few casual meetings with my father years ago in your father's house, you figured out who I am."

The rabbi inclined his head with a warm smile. "I've been expecting you. My father, of blessed memory, told me that some day your father, Benjamin Harkesef, would return. My father is gone for ten years now, but I was confident that, in some form, his foresight would be fulfilled. I knew the moment you stepped into my office who you were."

"But your father said that my father himself would return. That hasn't happened."

"A son is an extension of his father. There must be some valid reason why your father could not come back.... But my guess is that it won't be more than a few years before he, too, will return."

Again Danny was stunned. He began to understand the feelings his father had described, and why he had sometimes compared the rabbis' words to prophecy. Carefully, he asked, "Do you also know about my father's work?"

The answer did not come at once. Endless seconds ticked by while the rabbi composed his answer. At last, he said, "All I can say is this: my father told me that someday your father's project would play an instrumental role in alleviating a terrible situation. He didn't go into detail. Over the years, whenever I thought about this, I prayed that someday I should have a greater insight into the specific way that might come about." He looked at Danny. "Today is that day."

Awestruck, Danny waited at the edge of his chair, certain he was about to hear big things. The rabbi's manner, in contrast, was eminently calm as he continued, "In our circles, we are not Zionists. We actually abhor the concept and ideology of Zionism as defined and developed by the secularists."

"I understood otherwise!" Danny broke in. "Isn't Zionism the aspiration of the Jewish people from time immemorial?"

"No, my friend. It is an artificial replacement for the genuine aspiration of our nation. It is a foreign concept — one which vies with God's true Command. The Jewish Nation is not defined by its common language, territorial borders, racial and ethnic commonality, artistic and cultural styles. Nor is the true Jewish Nation composed of individuals who merely give lip service to the appellation, Jew. There is only one factor that defines us, one ideology: the Torah, acceptance and adherence to God's Law. Anything else, is not only unauthentic, but a danger to our people. We are suffering today under a regime whose founders not only disowned God and repudiated the Torah, but took their ideology directly from our spiritual enemies, and thus have formed an impediment to the Final Redemption."

The argument was not new to Danny Benson, savvy to Israeli politics. It was, however, the first time he'd heard it from a scion of the ultra-Orthodox community.

"Would you say that the failure of the Likud to retain power a few years ago, has resulted in added misery to our people?"

"*You* answer that question," the rabbi challenged. "I don't want to comment about a specific political party — they all include constituents of various ideological stripes. The essential problem is secular Zionism. Please understand, besides its decadence as viewed by the Upper World, it is devoid of logical justification and certainly doomed to the wastebin of political philosophy.

"The founders of the Zionist State, who had discarded the Torah, claimed a right to create a state in the Land of Israel based on two factors. First, and most important, the Jewish Nation had once dwelt here, two thousand years ago. Second, the Holocaust sympathy factor, which the Zionists were able to exploit after World War Two. But with the passage of time, *sympathy...* a transient sentiment, will soon fade away. As for Zionism, four or five generations have already passed from its inception: that is just about the limit of a false political ideology — note the fate of Communism in Russia. The great-grand sons of the old Zionists, who deny that the Almighty promised the Land to the Children of Israel, will come to repudiate the justification of their forebears who founded this state. They won't relate in any way to the remote past, to *ancient history*." The rabbi tilted his head questioningly as his eyes probed Benson's. "Make no mistake, we would accept the concept of land for peace — if indeed there would be peace. I see that you are a logical thinker. Have you ever pondered the psyche of the Israeli framers of the Oslo Accord?"

Once again Danny was subject to the shivers: the sage seemed to read his mind. "What the rabbi is saying is that the left-wing Zionists...."

The rabbi interrupted, "The secular, godless Zionists. Left or right is only incidental."

"The godless Zionists, perhaps subconsciously, have cultivated the *first sprouting* of the disintegration of their own ephemeral substitute for Torah, which they coined 'Zionism'. Perhaps they'll wake up one day and ask, 'How are we any more privileged than the Arabs? What right do we have to kill Arabs in dispute over this land?' A movement based on this conclusion, if left unchecked, will drag down — along with its own foolish proponents — those who do believe that God promised the Holy Land to the Jewish Nation."

"Exactly!" The rabbi beamed. "You have confirmed my opinion of you from the moment you entered my office. Now, listen to me very carefully."

Danny Benson sat up to demonstrate his complete attention. Rabbi Chaim said, "The Satan has prevailed these past three years in order to allow the barb of Oslo to stab into our nation's bosom. It has not penetrated the heart — yet. I am sure, now that this huge blow has befallen our nation, that God in His infinite mercy will grant us some respite and the opportunity to recover. I don't see this regime lasting much longer."

"But, Rabbi," Danny protested, "Rabin is fully entrenched! Master politician that he is, he will stop at nothing to remain in power until he has given back the entire land. You know their tactics — giveaway programs and such."

The rabbi smiled. "You still lack full faith, Dr. Benson. There is no obstacle which can stand in God's way. The question and the test for our people will be this: when given the opportunity, will we do what we must?" His eyes were piercing as twin lasers as they bore into Danny's. "I believe that *you* would."

"What are you saying, Rabbi?" Danny was considerably taken aback. "I'm a nobody. I have no influence, no connections, and not much money."

The rabbi stared intently at the young man. Again, a fear and trembling rippled through Benson's body. "My friend, you will have all three, if you need them. But it will still be up to you to succeed. I wish you all the best, and may God be with you every step of the way."

It was a blessing and an exhortation, which left Danny Benson shocked and perplexed. "B-but Rabbi, I don't understand what you want me to do."

The rabbi called his assistant back into the room, then stood up to shake hands with Benson. Taking his cue, Danny departed. He stepped out into the street and filled his lungs with the warm night air. In some obscure way he realized that, though on his own, he was nevertheless subject to both the prompting and the protection of a Great Guiding Hand....

A week later, as Danny waited at the airport for his return flight to be announced, a frenzy erupted throughout the main hall. Shouts of "What's going on?" flew through the air as people ran about clamoring for answers. After a few minutes, the P.A. system crackled to life, asking for everyone's attention. The hall became still. Into the expectant hush came the announcement, "Prime Minister Yitzchak Rabin has just been assassinated."

A great cry rose up from the throats of travelers and airport personnel. A chill traveled down Danny's spine. He turned toward the wall to conceal a subdued smile. The days of prophecy may be gone, he thought to himself, but my father was right: some of our sages still come pretty close.

Chapter 38

In the year 2001, the government of Israel fell apart again, and new elections were called. Although his looks and finesse didn't hurt, Daniel Benari was elected Israel's Prime Minister primarily for his brains. His colossal human mind became apparent on the day he emerged from obscurity, as a twenty-nine-year-old American immigrant.

Surprisingly, his brilliance had not been widely recognized back in the U.S. He had a Ph.D. in nuclear physics from M.I.T. and worked at various mid-to-high-level jobs — considered smart enough, but only run-of-the-mill for an M.I.T. Ph.D. Danny Benson was no Nobel Laureate. He was just one of many, a man who knew his work, retained a low profile, and whose moonlighting preoccupied much of his time.

All of that changed from the moment he stepped off the plane at Lod airport in early March of 2001. Benson became Benari. Instead of heading to Weitzman (Israel's premier institute of science) or the Technion (Israel's foremost institute of technology), the young physicist made for the headquarters of each of the Israeli government's coalition partners — a government on its last leg, staring at the specter of an ignominious demise. The Palestinian state had been declared and, within ninety minutes, inducted into the United Nations. The Post-Oslo accord still hung on by a thread, as the government buckled under the pressure to return yet another two hundred square-kilometer parcel of West Bank land to the Palestinian Authority.

Out of every office, Daniel Benari emerged successful — uncannily successful. He entered with good looks, a razor-sharp mind, and big, big bucks. When he'd made his intentions known to his father, the money had appeared miraculously in his bank account. Each of the party hacks ended the visit with the awestruck sense of having witnessed a rising star. Danny's demeanor was impeccable, but it was the timing — the prophetic timing — of his appearance that planted the seed of hope in a coalition of desperate and despondent politicians. Indeed, the need for a Messiah created the imagery of that persona.

Daniel Benari was all things to all men. When he met with the Likud hawks, Benari out-hawked them. When he met with Labor moderates, his logical and congenial approach lulled them. When he met the party heads of NRP, Shas, and UTJ, he donned a small black yarmulke which, he promised, was always kept in his pocket. He also made sure that one short length of string from a ritual four-cornered undergarment "accidentally" hung out from his shirt. His talk was inundated with God-fearing expressions, reminiscent of Begin, who had been quite traditional, the first Prime Minister to really win the hearts of the ultra-Orthodox.

He spoke English like the American Jew that he was, yet his Hebrew — except for a slight American accent — was indistinguishable from that of the most erudite Sabra. Within three weeks, he had garnered the support he needed to go out on the stump. At first, he was introduced at political rallies as a new immigrant and brilliant physicist, and given five minutes as the last speaker. But the responses he drew around the country were so enthusiastic, and the media attention so positive, that his position in the queue quickly advanced. Two weeks into the campaign, Benari was not only the primary speaker, he had risen to the top of the slate. A new hope was born in the party, for this man had a way about him that transcended partisan politics and exuded a broad appeal. He took the country by storm.

"My fellow citizens, Israelis, Jews. It is imperative that we come together in unity now. Never before in our history, perhaps, has this been so important. So many divisive issues have converged in the past ten years. We must resolve those divisions or we are indeed doomed. The rightists and the leftists are at each other's throats over what to do with the new Palestinian State. The rhetoric and vile behavior of the secularist camp against the religious citizenry is outrageous.

"Among our youth who have been raised with the secular perspective, there is a profound breakdown which will certainly doom our nation in a generation or two if left unchecked. Poor educational performance, drugs, violence and promiscuity run rampant among our teens. Why, the Zionist ideal is flickering and nearly extinguished in our own young people!

"On the other hand, we view the Orthodox and the ultra-Orthodox with suspicion and even hatred. To be sure, they are pushy and 'holier than thou' in attitude. It is difficult to countenance those whom we view as arrogant. But just remember — that is exactly how most of the gentile nations of the world view us. When we're despised, even if only surreptitiously, we characterize the reaction as 'anti-Semitism.' We must understand that, by hating the Orthodox for those very same reasons, we are practicing anti-Semitism. The Orthodox are raising a generation that is well-educated, not only in religious studies, but in secular studies as well. Their self-contained community is proving far more disciplined and morally stable than secular society.

"The Orthodox parties have unified, while retaining most of their respective, unique characteristics. The NRP still sends all of its boys to the army. The ultra-Orthodox continue to receive deferrals from military service in order to study in divinity academies. This issue, which once divided those parties, has been buried. Yet, at the same time, the ultra-Orthodox have become so devoted to the land that I would characterize them as ultra-Zionists.

"We have viewed with trepidation the encroachment of the ultra-Orthodox. They seem to be overrunning the country. You can't travel five kilometers without seeing another new, and totally Orthodox, neighborhood under construction. They have succeeded in recruiting thousands of children from secular families into their schools. They have attracted thousands of nonobservant people to return to

Jewish religious life. The blasting rock music, once typical on an Egged bus, has now been exchanged for the moralistic preaching of Rabbi Amnon Yitzchak."

Here, Danny's voice would rise with inspirational passion. "This is what I say to you, people of the State of Israel! Wage your spiritual wars only with mutual respect and intellectual arrows, and may the best man win! Let us seek unity with the Orthodox camp in the spirit of brotherhood. If we disagree, so be it — but we must put an end to our feelings of contempt and hatred and stop allowing them to lead to open, violent confrontation and unfair treatment.

"I ask for your vote in this election so that I will be able to draw our nation together as one. That is the sum total of my platform. The Palestinian state poses a huge problem which bodes poorly for a simple solution. But if we draw together, we will endure — through the strength that we will forge by that unity, and with the help of the Almighty. Thank you all, and success."

This was Daniel Benari's message, delivered from Dan to Eilat. The voters responded with a sixty-four percent popular vote for Daniel Benari. His closest competitor garnered only twenty-one-percent of the vote in the first round. It was a landslide. It was a mandate.

After Benari's inaugural speech in June of '01, electricity filled the air of Israel. Orthodox baiting and bashing changed from a respectable pastime to an activity in which only the most debased class of secularist indulged. At the same time, the Orthodox activists, at the behest of the Prime Minister's office, initiated a sensitivity training program aimed at the Orthodox public. The leading rabbis all approved the program and its results were successful beyond belief. By the end of the summer of 2001, hostilities between the political party members and the religious and secularly-affiliated were remarkably diminished. Only the die-hard fanatics, widely disdained by both sides, continued to cling to their feeble reminiscence of past confrontations.

It would be logical to assume that somehow, some way, the new spirit of unity and brotherhood among the Israeli people would spill over with residual effect on the Palestinian Arabs, so that the entire region would flourish in peace and prosperity. After all, when a particular spirit fills the air, it is often, magically, *contagious*.... The reaction, however, was just the opposite. Even in the past, the various Arab groups — Hamas, PLO, Hizbullah, Islamic Jihad — had always coordinated in their effort to kill the Jews. This was so despite the fact that they hated each other's guts. If not for their common desire to see the Israelis disappear from existence, they would have been at each others' throats. Now, the kindred spirit welling up in the House of Israel acted to harden Arab resolve. The Arabs became terrified of the formidable threat that Jewish unity presented.

Contrary to the dreams of the Oslo Accord framers, the intent of the Palestinian State had never been for a peaceful coexistence with the Jewish State. This became publicly manifest when most of the Moslem countries rallied behind the Palestinians to embolden their demands for more concessions. The harmonious activities among the Jews was a panacea for Israel, but infected the other residents of the Middle East with venomous hate.

One month after Benari took office, he received a call from the Secretary of State of the new State of Palestine.

"Mr. Benari, the President wishes you the best of luck… and wishes to remind you of a few issues."

"I thank the President, Mr. Huseni," Benari said politely. "What is it that he would like to remind me about?"

"Now that Oslo and Wye have been fulfilled, the time has come to speak of the next stage in the restoration of our Palestinian rights."

The call was not unexpected by Benari, a keen student of history. It was only a matter of when and how much.

"I don't know what there is to talk about. We can't return to the pre-'67 borders."

"We don't expect you to," Huseni replied wryly. "But just as you have autonomous enclaves of Jewish settlements here in the West Bank, we must begin to speak about the Arab enclaves in Galilee, Haifa and Jaffa. I think a referendum of those residents might demonstrate their desire to be ruled by their Palestinian compatriots. That is only logical, is it not?"

Benari paused for a moment, with only the sound of his breathing to let Huseni know he was still on the line. "Secretary Huseni, are you talking about Israeli Arabs?"

"There is no such thing, Mr. Prime Minister. They are Palestinians, who through the grace of Allah, were never forced from their land."

Benari carefully considered how to maintain his decorum. "I think that this is the time for both nations to settle down and exist within the present situation for a while. Perhaps after demonstrating our ability to peacefully coexist for a few years, we can talk again."

"Mr. Prime Minister, the peace process must not stop now. The present momentum will carry us to a true peace, a peace that will last a thousand years — a peace in which the complete rights of *all* the Palestinian people will be restored and Arab and Jew will be able to live as neighbors."

The PM held back a laugh as he responded, "Mr. Secretary, I will have to talk this over with my cabinet."

Huseni's tone quickly changed. "Listen here, Benari. The world will support us. Even your Americans will not stand behind you if you take the intransigent position of no further negotiations."

Daniel Benari was no coward. Huseni's words rang true in his ears: Israel would indeed have to weather the pressure of the world. But Benari was confident — more than confident. He was prepared to embark on an entirely new road, a road to independence, a road that would lead the Jewish Nation out of dependency on America and the rest of the Western world. For he knew a secret which had first been told thirty-five years earlier. His very existence was an outcome of that secret.

Benari cast off his diplomatic facade. "Huseni, go back to your President and tell him these three words exactly as I say them…. We are ready."

PART FOUR:

THE BEGINNING OF THE END

"And he saw the angel of God standing between earth and heaven, with his sword drawn in his hand, stretched out over Jerusalem"

I Chronicles 21:16

Chapter 39

July 2, 2002, 11:40 a.m. (GMT+2) (4:40 a.m. EDT Washington), The Prime Minister's Office, Jerusalem:

President Abe Lewis gripped the receiver tightly, his knuckles turning white with pent-up frustration. He was speaking to the Prime Minister of Israel, and the conversation was not going at all as he'd hoped. Daniel Benari seemed bent on his course. Israel would continue its outrageous retaliatory attacks against Arab countries, despite America's almost frantic disapproval.

Lewis took a deep breath, then adopted a newer, more conciliatory tone.

"Look here, Danny, even I have only so much power. I have little control, at this point, over the Russians and the Red Chinese. I'm losing control over my own people. The vermin are crawling out of the woodwork. Not since the oil crisis of '73, when we heard 'Burn Jews, not oil,' has there been such an anti-Semitic clamor. Now, of all times, the first Jewish president looks like he'll be the last. The Arabs once trusted me. My platform was, 'Elect Lewis, avoid Middle East war.' I've failed. I have no reason to exist in the eyes of half the people. What can I do?"

"You can go home."

"I *am* home, you fool!" Lewis yelled, his calm going up in smoke.

"No, Abe, you're not." Benari's answer was quiet, but very emphatic. "You're a Jew. Your home is Israel."

The phone clicked hard in Benari's ear, and went dead.

* * *

"Mr. Benari, there's a weird call on your secured line," the secretary notified the Prime Minister, five minutes after the President of the United States had hung up on him. "There's no one on the line, but I hear men talking in the background." The gray-haired woman, normally tough as iron, bit her lip as her eyes met Benari's. "Something about this call scares me."

"I'll take it, Miss Cohen." Benari pushed the flashing line button on his speaker phone and listened silently.

A harsh, unfamiliar voice came to his ears first. "Abe, you can't lead the country. We are recommending that you resign."

"Who the hell are you to tell me to resign, General Sherman? You want to send this country to hell in a hand basket? We can't have the military bossing around the executive." This voice Benari did recognize. He had heard it over this same line just minutes before.

It belonged to the President.

"Abe, take it easy," General Sherman said. "This is for your own good. The Israelis are out of control. We don't have time to fool around. There are people dying like flies. You know very well that we may be forced to take military action shortly." There was a brief pause, then he drew himself up and continued, more formally: "As chairman of the Joint Chiefs, I've been delegated to let you know that we commiserate with your predicament."

"For me it's a predicament, and for you not?" Abe Lewis snapped back.

"Let's say, it's less of a predicament."

"You mean, just because fate would have it that I was born a Jew, I can't properly address a problem brought about by other Jews? You know that's ridiculous."

"Look here, Abe — we're only trying to take you off the spot. Are you telling me you could order a full military strike against Israel?" General Sherman demanded.

Abe Lewis stared up at the ceiling, deep in thought. "I could do anything that is in the best interest of the United States. I took an oath to that effect, and I intend to live up to it."

"In that case, you had better give the order. We're running out of time."

"Damn it, I won't give the order. The only order I'm going to give is for your termination!" The President pushed firmly on his emergency buzzer. But no troop of Secret Service agents entered. Instead, the door opened to admit a troop of fourteen uniformed MPs.

President Lewis swiveled around to glare at General Sherman. "What's the meaning of this, Sherman?"

"Mr. Lewis," Sherman said in a deceptively deferential tone, "I deeply regret to say that I must hereby declare you officially deposed from office."

"What?" yelled Lewis. "You can't do that. We have a Constitution — or have you forgotten that little detail? You want me out, go to Congress. Now you get the hell out!"

Nobody budged.

"Men," the President barked at the line of MPs standing by the door, "As Commander in Chief, I order you to arrest General Sherman and leave my office!"

Nobody moved a muscle.

General Sherman now addressed his men, "Take Mr. Lewis to the quarters we have prepared for him in the Pentagon."

"Yes, Sir," said the staff sergeant with a smart salute. Lewis, looking dazed and furious at the same time, was escorted to the door by two large MPs.

"Oh, one thing, Mr. Lewis," said the General, "I need the nuclear release code."

"Never!" Lewis snapped.

Sherman picked up the President's briefcase, the one that contained the decoder processor needed to arm U.S. ICBMs. Softly, he said, "We'll see about that."

After Lewis was led away, Sherman scouted the office. He soon began opening the desk drawers. In the lower right-hand drawer he found a red telephone whose light indicated that the line was live. Sherman picked up the receiver and asked sharply, "Who's there?" He heard the line click and go dead.

*   *   *

At 4:57 a.m., the doorbell rang at the Benson residence in Silver Spring, Maryland.

"Bob, there's a man at the door for you. He won't give his name. Should I let him in?" Barbara Benson asked her husband.

Benson looked up sleepily. "Who is it at this hour?"

"He has a foreign accent, perhaps Israeli. It might have to do with your work. It must be about the Middle East crisis." Barbara Benson spoke the words without a clue as to what she had just said. Her husband knew better. He got up, tied a robe around himself, and went to the door.

He found a stranger on his doorstep, tall and olive-skinned. In Hebrew, the man said to Benson, "Come with me immediately. There's an urgent message from your son, the Prime Minister."

Without a word, Robert Benson followed his visitor into the limousine idling in front of his house. He picked up the encoded phone that was on line with Israel and heard a dearly familiar voice exclaim, "Dad, there is a God!"

Benson answered in more subdued fashion. "I know that, Danny. What's happened? You know it's not wise for you to contact me like this."

"Well, I couldn't wake you to look at your email." Danny sounded excited as a schoolboy as he crowed, "Dad, this is it. You'd better say a prayer and be prepared to act. President Lewis called me about a half-hour ago, urgently pressuring me to call off the 'action.' I could hear in his voice that he was scared stiff. Well, it wasn't five minutes later that I got another call from him. But this time, he never spoke to me."

"Danny, what are you talking about?"

"He must have hit the redial button on his phone. I suspect he wanted me to overhear a conversation with General Sherman, who had just entered his office. Dad, you won't believe this. Sherman and the Joint Chiefs have kidnaped the President. I'm not joking."

Dazed, Robert Benson found it impossible to respond. His son pressed, "Dad — Dad, did you hear me?"

The elder Benson cleared his throat, which felt as if it had suddenly filled with gravel. "Yes," he said slowly. "I heard you. Sherman is an anti-Semite. He's a great military tactician, but I could never understand why Lewis appointed him chairman." He thought a moment. "I think this crisis is about to explode. You're perfectly right, Danny, we need to pray. I'll do what I can."

"Dad, should I call a halt?"

"You're the PM. You're going to have to make that decision. I don't mean to push you off, I'm just not sure how this whole thing is going to play itself out." He paused, then added candidly, "I must admit that I was kind of surprised when you gave the signal to let loose."

"Dad, I made the decision and did it, and that's all I can say. At the spur of the moment, I said to myself, we've had it with the Arabs and fanatic Moslems. We have the capability; we're going to end this problem now. I called Rabbi Chaim in Bnei Braq, who gave me his blessing. But when the utterly disdainful reaction of the whole world began to pour in, I began to rethink the issue. I still think I made the correct decision, but now this development with President Lewis.... I'm kind of dumbstruck."

"Danny, this business is too complicated for my small brain. I don't see any way that I can do anything about the President. I'll do what I can to protect our people, but — like I said — I haven't the foggiest how this will play out, so how can I advise you?" Benson thought out loud, feeling his way slowly in the dark solitude of the limousine. "Maybe the time has come to relent. Maybe, by doing so, you can save Lewis' skin. On the other hand, we don't know if the Arabs are ready to cave in. It would be a shame — and maybe much worse — if, after beginning the job, you didn't finish it. At least if Lewis were around, he might be able to negotiate something. I just don't know...."

Silence — the silence of shared uncertainty in the face of an unknowable future — settled onto the line. Then, abruptly, Robert Benson blurted, "Yes — I know what you should do. Call Rabbi Chaim back immediately. Ask him!"

His son's astonishment was almost palpable. "Look, Dad, I know he's a great man. But we're talking about the whole game here. This is it — all or nothing. How can a rabbi save a President, fifty-six hundred miles away? Do you expect a rabbi to know about the military and political intrigue?"

"Danny, I don't think you understand me. This matter has gone beyond politics, even beyond war. Trust me — call him."

"Chaim, you have an urgent call. It claims to be from the Prime Minister's office," the rabbi's wife called to her husband, who was poring over his books in the next room. He took the call. His wife looked on as he listened intently, pausing only to say every now and then, "Go on." Finally, he answered with these words: "Mr. Benari, you must be more scrupulous in studying the weekly Torah portion. If you had listened carefully to this past week's reading, you would have heard the answer to your question. All the answers are in the Torah, you know."

"I believe that," Danny Benari said. "But I'm not qualified to interpret them. That's why I called you, sir. At this point, I'm not sure that my decision wasn't a great blunder."

"Blunder? It's explicit! 'Behold, I have given him My Covenant of Peace'....

"And now, Mr. Benari, I am very busy with my studies. I bid you success and a good day." Rabbi Chaim hung up.

Danny replaced the receiver, frowning. The answer posed a greater enigma than the question. It had been an hour since the Prime Minister had stumbled on the earthshattering news about the President of the United States, and he was no closer to knowing how to react than he'd been before....

Suddenly, a wild idea popped into his head. He hesitated, then smiled. As a gambit, it was worth a try.

"Miss Cohen," Benari told his secretary, "Get General Sherman of the U. S. Joint Chiefs of Staff on the line for me."

Half an hour after Marine One, with the President and General Sherman aboard, landed inside the Pentagon grounds, Sherman was summoned to the phone.

"This is Benari," the Israeli Prime Minister said tersely. "I want to cut a deal."

Sherman was taken aback. At once, a frightening possibility arose in his mind. Was it possible that the Prime Minister knew what had transpired in the White House a little while earlier? But — how?

Could he possibly have been on the other end of the phone in the President's office?

"What kind of deal?" Sherman fished. "You should be talking to the President, not me."

"I've already spoken to Lewis. He's all washed up. He can't run your country any more; he should resign. I want to deal with you directly, because I know if any finger is on the trigger, it's yours."

Sherman still wasn't sure if Benari wasn't bluffing. "Why don't you just call off your goons?"

"It might be too late for that. Too late, that is, without some kind of a deal. We've got to come out of this alive. No retribution — you know what I mean."

"No, I'm not sure. But are you saying you would consider ceasing your attacks?"

"Do we have a good line?" Benari snapped. "That's exactly what I just said. I want to meet with you privately. Just the two of us."

Sherman said slowly, "That might be difficult."

"General Sherman, listen very carefully. We've got your mad embassy bomber, Rastafani. Just deal with me, and he's yours."

The general thought for a minute and then said, "All right. How do you propose we accomplish that?"

"I'll fly in on an F-16. We'll meet at some small airport."

"How can a fighter jet fly fifty-six hundred miles? Even with wing tanks it can't cover more than two thousand at most."

"We've got a tanker up in the air off the coast of Spain."

"Still that leaves over three thousand miles."

"What do you want from me, Sherman? You want to know all the secrets of how we extend flight range?" Benari chuckled, a sound without mirth. "Don't worry about me; I'll be there if you will. How about Chestertown on the Eastern Shore of Maryland? It's only an hour from Washington."

Sherman told Benari to wait a minute. Two minutes later he was back on the phone. "The runway is only thirty-seven hundred feet long. You can't land a fighter there."

"Listen here, Sherman, I just told you we Israelis have methods. We can land an F-16, without instruments, in less than nine hundred ninety meters. If we ever get out of this one, just remind me and we'll give you the flap design modification. I can be there...." Benari looked at his watch, "at midnight, your time. Get me clearance."

"I'll be there. You'll be cleared."

"Alone, right?"

"You're coming with a pilot, I'll have just a driver with me. No — perhaps I'll drive myself," Sherman said confidently.

"I'll see you tonight, then."

"Tonight."

Chapter 40

July 2, 2002, Headline, the Evening Washington Times:

The entire press corps has been asked to leave the White House. Unusual military activity has erupted throughout the Presidential complex in expectation of imminent action over the events in the Middle East. A new spokesman for the President has spoken to reporters lined up on Pennsylvania Avenue. He states that the situation is so tenuous that the President has cleared the White House of extraneous personnel for the time being, but that press releases will be issued on any turn of events. Pundits speculate that the Jewish President may be gearing up to attack the Jewish State. It is reported that the U.S. has at least three-hundred ship-based Tomahawk cruise missiles in the Sixth Fleet, now racing from the Persian Gulf to the Red Sea. Another fifty B52-launched cruise missiles are believed to be standing ready at Diego Garcia in the Indian Ocean.

Below this headline was an interview with Mortimer Zenner, chairman of the Conference of Presidents of Jewish Organizations.

WT: Mr. Zenner, does your organization — which, we presume, represents the vast majority of American Jews — agree with the carnage that Israel has wrought upon the Arabs in the past two days?

MZ: We uphold Israel's right to defend herself against foreign aggression. The Moslem Coalition started this and remains a threat until it agrees to cease hostilities.

WT: But don't you feel the response is out of proportion to the initial attack?

MZ: The response has come from unknown forces. I can't condemn Israel for any action until we know for sure that it was Israel that acted.

WT: Are you saying that you don't believe the attacks came from Israel? Who else could have perpetrated them?

MZ: Of course, it is logical to assume that Israel was behind these defensive actions. But it might just as easily have been a group of rogue individuals or an organization that acted beyond the control of the Israeli government.

WT: In your position, haven't you inquired from upper level people in the Israeli government if the counterattacks were from Israel?

MZ: I have. The official response has been that they have no idea who is behind the attacks.

WT: It has now been established that seventeen Arab and Iranian cities have suffered Enhanced Radiation explosions, killing over 350,000 people. The toll from the Aswan Dam collapse has not been reported due to the Egyptian government news blackout, but experts have predicted at least 200,000 dead and up to 4,000,000 homeless. Do you really believe that any individual or organization other than a government could produce weapons of such massive destruction?

MZ: Since the fall of communism in the Soviet Union eleven years ago, there have been all kinds of rumors about nuclear materials that have disappeared, and their ultimate destinations.

WT: If the President ordered an attack on Israel, would you support him?

MZ: We support any action that is in the best interest of the United States, Israel, and the entire family of nations. We don't believe that action will include a military phase targeted at Israel.

WT: We know that you are close with the President. What do you make of his current reticence regarding speaking with the press?

MZ: It's atypical of him. I don't understand it. I tried to call him less than an hour ago and couldn't get through. He seems to have appointed an entirely new staff in the aftermath of this crisis. I just don't understand it.

WT: Thank you, Mr. Zenner.

*   *   *

At 11:38 p.m., a small military jet circled the General Aviation Park at Chestertown, Maryland. The runway lights were switched on as the control tower gave the go-ahead for the craft to land. With flaps full down, the jet was still moving at one hundred sixty knots when it plopped its gear down fifty feet past the beginning of the runway. Screaming reversed jets and burning brakes brought the plane to a dramatic halt in only twenty-six hundred feet. Within five seconds of coming to a full stop, ten HUMVEEs raced out and surrounded the craft. Each bore a 50mm machine gun, which it trained on the plane. One hundred troops waited in the darkness for the passenger to disembark.

But no move was made from the plane. There was no communication. After ten minutes, Major Humphrey Jones, commander of the mechanized regiment sent to "greet" the Prime Minister of Israel, climbed up onto the wing of the F-16.

"I can't see anyone in there. Someone give me a flash light." A few minutes later, shining a flashlight through the cockpit window, the major still couldn't see anyone. He undid the latch and the bubble popped open. Sure enough, the jet was empty. The soldiers gaped at each other, perplexed.

At 10:45 that same evening, a BMW-740 was racing north on Route 213 at close to ninety miles per hour. Rounding the bend two miles past Starkeys Corner, the driver slammed on his breaks as he saw a police car with flashing lights four hundred feet up ahead. A sawhorse bearing a large iridescent sign stating POLICE

ROAD BLOCK had been set up across the road. The BMW came to a full stop, and the officer walked up to the driver's window.

"You were doing some speed coming around that bend; eighty-seven to be exact. Six people have been lost in that spot in the past year. I've got a radar gun set up one thousand feet down. Your license and registration, please."

"Officer, I'm on official government business. I have an appointment that I must make. It's urgent."

"Sir, your license and registration," repeated the policeman, a bit more emphatically. The driver resigned himself to comply; he had almost an hour in any case.

"George Adley Sherman!" the officer exclaimed, as he reviewed the Virginia driver's license. You're not the chairman of the Joint Chiefs of Staff?"

"I am one and the same."

"Well, in that case...." The policeman began to hand back the general's license, while, with his other hand, he drew out a 200,000-volt stun baton and shoved it into the general's neck. A second later, General Sherman was out cold.

Robert Benson immediatly popped the trunk on the BMW. A quick check with an electronic gadget around the vehicle indicated that the only signal-generating tracer on the vehicle was a standard Lo-Jack, which Benson disabled within minutes. The general was stripped down to his underwear and searched. Benson found a Berreta-92 military issue in a belt holster and a Walther PPK backup in an ankle holster. The unconscious figure was thrown in the trunk, arms and legs manacled behind his back. After shutting the trunk, Benson dislodged the suction cups holding the flashing light bridge to the top of his rented white Ford Crown Victoria, and peeled off the police decals from the car's flanks. He then grabbed the roadblock sign and strode five hundred feet into the woods to dump it. The Crown Vic was then driven off the side of the road, where it crashed into a tree.

At 12:30 a.m., the automatic garage door at his unoccupied Silver Spring residence descended, with the BMW safely inside. Benson had seen his wife off to Israel earlier in the afternoon.

"Who are you?" the still-groggy George Sherman, hands and feet still firmly chained, asked his captor. "David, Shlomo or Ehud? You're Israeli, aren't you? It was someone in Israel who overheard my escapade in the White House yesterday. I wouldn't be surprised if it was Benari himself. We've got one hell of a crafty Jew in that Lewis. You can bet he'll never see the light of day again."

"You underestimate our abilities, General. It is you who may never see the light of day."

"Oh, they'll find me all right." Sherman glared. "What the hell kind of man are you anyway? Give me back my clothes."

"I'd gladly give them back to you, but I think you'd have a hard time putting them back on, tangled up the way you are. In any case, if you were thinking about pressing the panic button on your waistband electronic beacon, I might as well let you know that it's lying at the bottom of the Chesapeake Bay."

Sherman looked chagrined. Physically, he wasn't doing too well either. Benson brought a turkey baloney sandwich and fed it to the bound prisoner.

"Now, General, I'd like to ask you a few questions." It was already 1:30 a.m. "Tomorrow is Independence Day. I think Abe Lewis would like to celebrate it as such."

Sherman didn't comment.

"Where is he? The Pentagon is a pretty big place. The largest building in the world, I'm given to understand, in terms of floor space." When there was still no answer, Benson stepped up closer, the courteous veneer gone in flash. "Where is he?" he yelled, slapping Sherman on the face. "I'll go in myself if I have to, to get him out. If I see that's impossible, I'll inform the press. I'll be happy to let the court system of this great country handle you. You traitor, you'll be lethally injected. You hear that?" Benson slapped him up some more. Sherman gritted his teeth but was adamant in his silence.

Benson calmed himself and spoke softly. "Listen, General. How would you like to escape with your life? You help me get Lewis freed and restored to office, and I swear I'll let you go. You'll have twelve hours and $50,000 cash to flee wherever you want. After that, you're on your own. I swear, not a word will cross my lips. If you're eventually caught, it won't be because of me."

Sherman looked up at his captor and laughed. "You still didn't tell me who you are."

"It's not important! Just respond to my offer."

"Tell me something," the general said laconically. "Benari wasn't on the plane, was he?"

"I'll bet you expected there was a good chance he would be. I saw the military force sneaking onto the airport grounds. I realized at that point that you were the same rat that kidnaped the President. Due to my 'police duties' in escorting our chairman of the Joint Chiefs, I wasn't able to be there, but I'm sure your men got the surprise of their lives when they discovered the jet was empty."

"Empty!" shouted Sherman. "Who the hell could have landed it?"

"The pilot of course. Who else?" Benson saw the puzzlement on Sherman's face. "Okay, okay, this one I'll explain to you. Wasn't it you who signed the order for one hundred IAI (Israel Aircraft Industries) Hunter Drones? You should have known that we have the technology. Just a minute." Benson left the room. In the short time he was gone, Sherman scouted around, but his captor had prepared well. There was nothing immediately at hand to help him out of this situation. He heard Benson call out in a strange language which, although Sherman couldn't understand a word, he figured must be Hebrew. A minute later another man in a business suit entered, with Benson following.

"Meet the pilot," Robert Benson said. "We'll call him Alpha Sierra."

Facing the pilot, Benson said, again in English, "Alpha Sierra, meet General George A. Sherman, former chairman of the Joint Chiefs of Staff, U.S. government."

"Former?" Sherman barked.

"Does your memory fail you, General? The President fired you yesterday. Alpha, tell the general how we operate."

The pilot opened a small aluminum case, which contained a modified computer console and screen. "General," he said in a heavy Israeli accent, "On my final approach, I came in low over the Bay and ejected into the water between Bodkin Point and Rock Hall. The plane was on autopilot. Within three minutes, I was sitting in an inflatable dinghy and opened this computer, which is really a remote flight console." Alpha Sierra switched it on and turned it in Sherman's direction. "It was easier to land that jet than if I'd been sitting in the cockpit. When I reached the shore, I changed clothes and hailed a cab." He grinned and snapped his fingers. "Voila, here I am!"

Sherman was despondent — exactly the emotion Benson had been trying to elicit from him. But he wouldn't agree to Benson's terms.

Benson spoke quickly in Hebrew to his man. "Your job is to watch this man. If, somehow, he pulls a Houdini, kill him. I've got important business to take care of." Benson switched on the TV in the room, changed out of his police uniform into a business suit, and departed.

Chapter 41

"General Woodson, General Woodson!" The reporters clamored at a 9:00 a.m. Fourth of July press conference at the Pentagon. The General pointed a finger at Sam Ashley of CSPAN.

"General Woodson," Ashley called, "Is the report in this morning's Washington Times true? Have the Joint Chiefs kidnaped the President?"

"How dare you ask such a question? Of course we haven't kidnaped him."

"Well is it true that he's right here in the Pentagon?"

"Due to security issues, we can't comment on the President's whereabouts. I will, however say this much: due to the immense crisis in the Middle East, the President has sequestered himself to run the country from a more secure venue than the heart of D.C."

"Do you mean to say, that since the U.S. may be preparing to attack Israel, the President is afraid of some kind of Israeli retaliation?" asked Sheila Ling of ABC news.

The General regarded her gravely. "We see their hand. It has always been rumored that the Israelis maintained nuclear capabilities, but they have always denied it. We now see they are a most formidable power, perhaps rivaling that of our country."

Bob Donovan of CBS was next. "General Woodson, could you explain to us why General Sherman, your chairman, is not conducting this press conference?"

Expecting the question, Woodson was primed to answer. "General Sherman is extremely busy planning a possible military solution to the present crisis."

Donovan then dropped the bomb he had waiting in the wings. No one could have known this, but he had it from a perfectly reliable source. "General, rumor has it that General Sherman is nowhere to be found. Do you have any information that might confirm or deny this?"

Hundreds of TV cameras brought home to the country that there was something seriously amiss as the normally ultra-confident Woodson stammered, groping for words. "There's... uh, there's, n-n-no truth to that rumor." Ruthless, the cameras picked up every bead of sweat.

The rest of the press corps remained tensely silent as Donovan continued to probe. "General, are you all right? You seem distressed."

"I — I'm fine." Woodson's hand shook as he lifted it to wipe his brow.

"General," Donovan pressed, "my sources have revealed that General Sherman disappeared after he was to have held a secret meeting with top Israeli officials. Can you confirm this?"

Words eluded Woodson. Several of his aides, in a belated attempt at damage control, started leading him away. The clamor of hundreds of reporters resumed as each tried to get in one last question.

Colonel Edward Pume, spokesman for the Joint Chiefs, quickly replaced the general, and stood up to make the anticipated announcement of a full military alert.

"In accordance with Resolution 771 of the United Nations, passed July 2, 2002, Israel was found in violation of the UN's non-aggression statute. In addition, they have violated seven other clauses, which deal with nuclear provocation and the use of unconventional weapons. The UN has also passed Resolution 772, which condemned the Moslem Coalition for their missile attack upon Israel. That coalition has already responded to UN pressure by accepting and signing a cease and desist order, and by officially declaring their coalition defunct.

"Israel has refused to respond in kind. Due to the immediate threat to world peace, on July 3, 2002 — yesterday — the UN passed Resolution 773, which authorizes the use of force to prevent Israel from carrying out any additional aggressive acts. The United States, in conjunction with France, England, Russia, and China, is preparing to organize a military force for that purpose." He nodded abruptly at the press corps. "There will be no further questions for now."

With that, all the top brass who had been lined up at the conference about-faced, and beat a hasty retreat inside the Pentagon doors.

The scene had been witnessed by millions of concerned Americans whose day off from work afforded them the opportunity to turn on the tube in the middle of the day. Among those watching were the fifty-four members of the Mount Royal Gun Club who had scheduled a meeting on the national holiday. Tim Krale, the club's president, switched off the TV and got up to speak.

"Ladies and gentlemen, our country is in crisis. Who here doesn't think that General Woodson was lying through his teeth?" No hands went up. "This is the greatest conspiracy in the history of the nation! It's a genuine military coup d'etat. I have no doubt that the President has been kidnaped." Murmurs of agreement were heard among the group. Krale held up a hand for their attention.

"Friends, the founding fathers of our country were prophets, true prophets, when they wrote the Second Amendment into the Constitution. I move that we take up arms against the insurgent and treasonous regime of the Joint Chiefs of Staff, as provided for in the Constitution and as our founding fathers explicitly expressed in the Declaration of Independence!"

Dave Shelby, an obstetrician by profession, took the floor. "How the hell are fifty of us going to face tanks? I might be nuts, keeping a collection of two hundred thirteen guns around my house. But I'm not *that* nuts!"

Jane Weaver was acknowledged next. She addressed Shelby directly. "Doc, you've got it all wrong. The founding fathers were in the same situation with the entire British military. We can't worry about that. Tim's right — we've got to act, and act now!"

A cheer rang out from the group — hellbent on preserving the Constitution. The resolution was immediately passed. At 2:00 p.m., fifteen cars, carrying a total of more than fifty people, arrived on the outskirts of the Pentagon. All carried concealed sidearms, but prudently left their long arms in the car trunks. When the group arrived, three of the fourteen news agencies Shelby had called had camera crews waiting.

A CNN microphone was pushed into Shelby's face.

CNN: Dr. Shelby, we understand you represent the Mount Royal Gun Club of Baltimore.
DS: That's right.
CNN: Is it true your club is here at the Pentagon to demand that the Constitution be restored as the Law of the land?
DS: Something like that.
CNN: Is it also true that, should the Joint Chiefs refuse to meet your demand, you intend to use force of arms?
DS: We will uphold the Constitution. You are familiar with the Second Amendment?
CNN: Are you claiming to act as a militia?
DS: I think that is an accurate characterization.
CNN: Does your group disapprove of the impending confrontation over the Middle East crisis?
DS: Foreign affairs are not our concern. What we're concerned with is what's going on right here. We have a duly elected Commander in Chief who is being held illegally incommunicado and being forcibly restrained from executing the charge of his office. We demand that he be reinstated immediately, so that he, and he alone, can make the necessary decisions about the crisis.
CNN: You don't really believe the President has been kidnaped?
DS: If I had the slightest doubt, I wouldn't be here.
CNN: Don't you think your 'militia' suffers a slight disadvantage in firepower against the U.S. Army?

As the interview proceeded, twenty troops were sent out of the building to monitor the situation.

DS: Back in 1990, the Russian people had no arms at their disposal, yet they overcame the Russian Army and restored the rule of law. You remember what became of the generals who fomented the coup d'etat against Gorbachev?
CNN: Doctor, perhaps you could remind us.
DS: They met Hari Kari. And I don't mean the baseball announcer. (Pause) Actually, we have an ally who will ensure that we prevail in this struggle.
CNN: Who is that?
DS: You! I want every loyal American watching this broadcast to take up arms against the insurgent United States Army. I want every American soldier to dis-

obey any order which can only be authorized by the President or which counter-mands the Constitution!

The soldiers used their walkie-talkies to contact the military police, who have jurisdiction on federal grounds. Six MPs came running out. A corporal told Shelby to leave. With the TV cameras whirring, Shelby responded defiantly, "You have no right to tell me to leave. I am a citizen, a taxpayer, and a voter. I declare your supe-riors decommissioned."

The MPs began to snicker. The corporal said, "Sir, you have five minutes to get off the property. If you don't, you will be arrested."

Shelby stood firm, but ten members of his group backed off to the parking lot, seventy-five yards away. The corporal was looking at his watch. There was dead silence. The cameras panned continuously back and forth between the two sides of the standoff.

The five minutes expired. The corporal stepped some fifteen feet away, turned around so that his back was to Shelby and the cameras, and spoke into his walkie-talkie, asking for instructions. Pulling a pair of handcuffs from his belt, he started toward David Shelby, who, with arms folded and a stern look on his face, didn't budge.

"By order of the United States Army, you are under arrest."

Three of the MPs came over and grabbed Shelby as the corporal was about to clasp his right hand. Suddenly, a shot rang out. The corporal fell dead. The other MPs let go of Shelby, hitting the ground. Armed only with sidearms, they began to fire in the direction of the parking lot, from which the fatal shot had come. Within twenty seconds all the MPs were incapacitated, and pandemonium had broken out.

A soldier on the roof, manning a machine gun, opened fire, riddling twenty cars in the lot like Swiss cheese. One shot from Al Powalski, who had placed thir-tieth at the Camp Perry high-power competition, more than countered the two hundred rounds the soldier had expended. The camera crew, seeking cover wher-ever they could find it, did their best to keep their cameras pointed at the action.

July Fourth, the most appropriate day for remembering the Declaration of Independence, was being commemorated in a shockingly unexpected way on the Pentagon lawn. Millions of viewers witnessed the beginning of a war between the Mount Royal Gun Club, upholding the Constitution, and the United States Army, under whose control it was anybody's guess. Nonetheless, as tanks and armored vehicles were being dispatched from Fort Meade, Maryland, the unbelievable began to happen. Forty Bradleys (armored fighting vehicles) succeeded in turning onto the 295 headed for Virginia, but soon became bottled up as hundreds of cars, whose drivers had listened to the news bulletin and the tail end of the confronta-tion live on the radio, stopped their cars in the middle of the road. The soldiers in the Bradleys got out, yelling at them to move. The drivers refused. Spontaneously, they began driving their cars onto the shoulders and down into the median, com-pletely sealing off the road. Cell phones and CBs buzzed, notifying drivers coming up from the north to block the Bradleys' exit from the other end. Forty-five minutes after they'd started for Virginia, two hundred soldiers switched off their engines, climbed out of their vehicles, and sat down in resignation on the grass.

On the Pentagon lawn, the score stood at eleven servicemen dead, and one gun club member slightly wounded. After the initial three minutes of live fire, the confrontation reverted to a tense standoff. The Virginia State Police were on the scene near the Pentagon within twenty minutes. They were hesitant about arresting the members of the gun club, who were still poised, guns in hand, behind a line of parked vehicles. Still, the police presence brought about an easing of the deadly tension in the air.

The grass-roots reaction that had begun to sprout on Route 295 soon made itself felt at the Pentagon. Shortly after the Virginia troopers appeared, cars started rolling in, and the momentum grew apace. The Mount Royal Gun Club was a member club in the conglomeration known as the Union of Baltimore Gun Clubs, which touted over two thousand members and operated a sophisticated target range in suburban Baltimore. More than eighteen hundred gun club members soon arrived at the scene. They pulled their cars up on the Pentagon's lush green lawn, one parking behind the next until a ring of five hundred vehicles had been formed, completely surrounding the building. Camo fatigues of every shade and pattern clothed their bodies, helmets of every war and every nation bedecked their heads. The gaudy and sundry mix seemed to turn the event into a costume party — one hell of a serious party. What made it so serious was the awesome and terrifying assortment of firepower they carried.

There was a significant mix here. The majority were carrying either Colt AR variants, former Eastern Block AK models, or Ruger Mini-14s. But there was a nice representation of oddball weapons, many of them extremely formidable, such as the Barret 50s and magnum-caliber large-game rifles, .375 H&H Magnums, .460 Weatherby Magnums, and .500 Nitro Expresses which, crowned with super-scopes, were deadly accurate as well as deadly powerful.

The renegade military leaders inside the Pentagon could see that their enlisted men were no match in small-arms combat for the seasoned, card-carrying NRA members. By 4:00 p.m., the news began to spread that a squadron of Apache attack helicopters was on its way from Fort Bragg, North Carolina. By now, three rings of cars circumscribed the Pentagon. The crowd had swelled to over ten thousand red-blooded Americans, hundreds of reporters, and dozens of local and state police. Suddenly, like a flock of birds ascending in unison, small helium-filled promotional blimps and balloons rose up from the crowd, their wire cables suspending the airborne flotilla between five hundred, and two thousand feet above the ground. The lead Apache hit a nearly invisible cable, which insinuated itself quickly into the rotor and left the helicopter sucking in the blimp of Al's Chevrolet. As the hapless blimp was being mangled to bits, its strands of plastic and nylon diminished the chopper's lift to such an extent that it had to make an emergency crash landing nearby. The other helicopters were immediately called off.

Up until six o'clock, the majority of the country — though bewildered at the strange events in and around the nation's Capitol — still looked upon the militia men, and the talk show hosts, who were insisting that the President had been kidnaped, as right-wing lunatics and conspiracy freaks. All that changed when the six o'clock news came on. In an emergency press conference that was broadcast nationwide, the flamboyant governor of Minnesota came on the air.

"I've ordered state and local police to blockade and prevent any hostile activity from the military bases in our great state. As commander in chief of the Minnesota Militia, I hereby order all hands to get in their cars and head for Washington. Take all the guns and ammo you can pack!"

Chapter 42

"Jim," said Chief of Naval Operations Earl Stillman, "What do you make of the hubbub out there?" The two were standing near a window in the command room on the fifth floor.

General James Woodson spoke without removing his eyes from the spectacle on the lawn below. "I assume we'll have it under control by tomorrow. In the meantime, we'd better act in the Middle East crisis."

"It's been forty-one hours since George went to meet Benari... or, should I say, an empty jet," Stillman fretted. "I'll be damned if I know how those Israelis pulled that one off. I'm convinced there's been foul play."

"I have no doubt about it, Earl — and I have no doubt the Israelis are the ones behind it. But that's one of the casualties of this game. Unfortunately, we cannot report the truth. At this point, our best bet is to attack Israel in accordance with the UN resolution. That will only help us to gain credibility with the American people."

Stillman turned to the general. "Jim, I know there's no love lost between you and the Jews, but we've been allies all these years. They're still the only half-reliable and sophisticated country in the region. I tell you frankly, I'm hesitant. The Israelis are smart. They have Sherman — and, so far, we have nothing."

"At least we have their F-16..." The phone rang.

"General Woodson."

"Speaking."

*   *   *

The caller was the commander of the group that had been sent to meet the unoccupied Israeli jet. "My men spent the day checking out that Israeli jet, and I have to tell you — that thing is a wonder. There's a scanning CCD built into the windshield. The control computer leads to a transmitter, and the hatch was designed to automatically close after an ejection. No doubt you've got one hell of a smart Israeli pilot, probably a Mossad man, walking the streets of America this minute."

"I wish there was only one. Go on...."

"Not ten minutes ago, a recorder in the jet blared out the message, *'This craft will self-destruct in five minutes. Clear the area.'* My men raced out of there like rabbits from a fox. By golly, that thing went up in a spectacular fireball! No one was hurt, but there is literally nothing left but a hole in the ground."

*   *   *

Woodson hung up the phone without comment. His jaw was set and a deep line was etched between his eyes. Stillman studied him. "What's the matter, Jim? You don't look so good."

The answer came like an angry expulsion of air. "You were right, Earl. So far, we have nothing.... I think you're right about treading carefully with the Israelis. Maybe if we punish them a little, show some muscle, they'll back down."

"As long as you have in mind minimal loss of life," said the Chief of Naval Operations, "we're on."

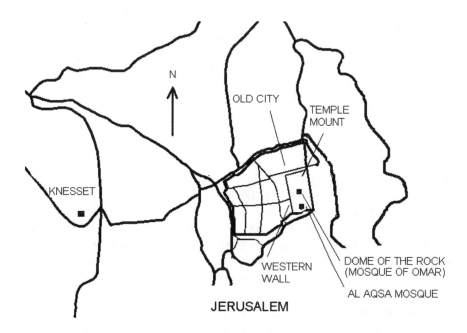

July 4, 2002, 3:42 a.m. (GMT+2), Zahal Surveillance Command HQ, Tel Aviv, Israel:

"Hey, Reuvy, one of our surveillance satellites picked up the signature of a B-52 heading toward us from Diego Garcia. It's now about eight hundred kilometers away, over Saudi Arabia."

"There's not much we can do about it until we see it has hostile intentions."

The pair of radar men huddled over the scope and the computer screen, watching intently. Suddenly, they jumped up in fright and sounded the alarm. Six cruise missiles, AGM-86A ALCMs, had been launched against Israel. They quickly fell though the sky and, within two minutes, were cruising along the contour of the country, out of radar view. All over Israel, air raid sirens sounded. The best men in the business fired six Arrows at the slowly approaching killers, but had little hope of destroying them. The Arrow was a tool that just wasn't made for the job. They couldn't even find the low flying beasts.

"Benari, this is General Richard Boyle of the U.S. Air Force."

"I know who you are, General. You must remember, I'm an American."

"Well, that's debatable.... In any case, we have six cruise missiles flying toward your country as we speak; they should arrive in ten minutes."

"Destroy them immediately, or General Sherman will be returned to you," demanded the PM.

"It would suit us very well if you returned the General," Boyle said, startled. "I see you've confirmed our suspicions about his disappearance."

"General, there's no time for games. We will return Sherman in twelve pieces. *That* is what I meant!"

There was a small silence. Then, "Listen carefully, Benari. We don't intend to hurt anyone. I called you to inform you that the missiles will strike the Knesset and level it. This is a symbolic strike. We want the campaign of carnage against your neighbors to stop."

"Is that why you've disobeyed the most fundamental principles that your nation was founded upon, and kidnaped your own President? You're a criminal! You deserve to be strung-up. I'm certain that will be your fate. How many are there now, camped out around your fortress? You'd better believe we get CNN over here. How many General — a hundred thousand? Two hundred?"

"I'm not going to engage in a debate with you," intoned Boyle. "I'm merely warning you to get everyone away from the building. At this hour, I don't suppose there are too many. Good bye."

The missiles came in over Jordan, crossed the Dead Sea at an altitude of fifty feet, and snaked their way up a mountain ravine twenty-eight hundred feet above sea level, toward the Holy City.

July 4, 2002, 8:56 p.m. (EDT), Military Command Center, the Pentagon:

A huge, computer-generated map of a two thousand square mile area surrounding Jerusalem appeared on the wall.

"A beautiful sight, isn't it General Woodson?" said the control officer to the commander of the Army, as every person in the packed room watched the six small red LEDs moving across the field toward the Israeli Knesset. In front of the each light was a white line which connected the moving red lights, representing the missiles, with their target. The white lines grew shorter and shorter as the five hundred fifty mph flying bombs approached their quarry.

"T-minus fifteen seconds," came the voice across the P.A. system. Suddenly all the white lines shifted thirty degrees to the right. Four second later, as everyone in the room stood in bewilderment, the first red light flashed and went out, followed a quarter-second later by the second, then the third, fourth, fifth and sixth. Each red light flashed and was extinguished. The cruise missiles had detonated but, quite obviously, not on the intended target.

"What the hell...? Major!" Boyle barked at the control officer. "What was that? Did we hit the target?"

The major was at a loss. He shook his head. "I don't understand it, General. I just don't understand it. Those birds were flying perfectly. They should have hit their targets within thirty-five feet of dead center. I just don't understand it."

"Well, where the hell *did* they hit? There are hundreds of thousands of people living in Jerusalem — including lots of Americans."

The major had regained his composure. Brazenly, he said, "Look, General, I didn't order or plan this operation. I just follow orders. Anything — you hear me, *anything,* whether man or machine — can be flawed. Nothing is perfect, except God in Heaven!"

The general's initial reaction was to have the major arrested for his insolence. Then he had second thoughts. He pictured the hordes of citizens still flooding in, chanting and yelling outside his window. He thought about the thousands of guns and millions of rounds of ammo those people possessed. And he began to take very seriously the possibility that he and his fellow Joint Chiefs had made a mistake of catastrophic proportions....

He was jerked out of his thoughts by a phone call. Woodson and Stillman looked on as Boyle listened to the caller. Beads of sweat sprang out on his forehead. He hung up and collapsed wordlessly into his chair.

"That bad?" asked Stillman.

Without looking up, Boyle said, "My God, worse than imaginable."

"How many casualties?"

"Two, possibly three," Boyle answered despondently.

"Two or three!" Woodson shouted. "That's less than we anticipated. What's the matter with you, Dick?"

Still without looking up, Boyle said dully, "Gentlemen, there is a God, and He is a Jew. The God of the Jews is the true God. I now realize that Jesus and Mohammed must take a back seat."

"What are you talking about? You've buckled under the pressure! General Woodson, look, he's cracked up! It's just too much for him!" Stillman was beside himself.

Now Boyle did look up. He began to laugh. "Gentlemen, I think we may wash our hands of this devastating mishap. Indeed we built the missile, aimed it, and pulled the trigger. But, weee... did not alter its course. That, apparently, was the proverbial, and seemingly literal, 'Act of God.' Our missiles have laid bare the entire Temple Mount."

Everyone in the room gasped. Boyle nodded. "Yes, Gentlemen. The Dome of the Rock, aka the Mosque of Omar, and the Al Aqsa Mosque, among the holiest sites in the Moslem religion, no longer exist. What remains is a rubble-strewn plateau, upon which many Jews believe their Third Temple is destined to be built." He gave a hollow chuckle. "It now appears that there is great potential for that eventuality."

The shocked silence was so thick it was almost palpable. The control commander walked slowly over to the general, flipping through a fanfold computer printout. Into the silence, he said, "General, I apologize for my harsh words before."

The general, head down once more, waved him away, mumbling "Never mind."

But the major didn't go. "I want you to have a look at this," he urged. "Incredible!"

Boyle glanced at the printout, then back into his lap. "Just tell me what it means," he ordered dully.

The major turned to address all of the top brass present. Pointing to a plot that ran a few pages, he began, "We have here a printout of the error codes that are updated one hundred times per second on the military GPS. Our cruise missiles use this system exclusively for guidance. Take a look at this sudden dip in the graph. Here, on this other sheet, is the digital interpretation on that four-second dip. This is simply amazing! It shows that the digital signal, which the GPS computer on board the missile interprets to guide it toward the preprogrammed target coordinates, was altered.

"Specifically, it was tweaked to return a course plot that reinterpreted the target latitude by .0246 seconds and the longitude by 10.178 seconds, thereby causing the missiles to strike the Al Aqsa Mosque and the Dome of the Rock, respectively. It is almost impossible to believe that these were the result of a random glitch. Both targets were hit dead center, turning these thirteen hundred year old historic shrines into landfill rubble."

General Boyle stood up and said, "That's exactly what I just said. The major is correct — it is impossible to believe this was an accident. That was the gist of the call I just took. The entire Arab world does not believe it was an accident. They believe the United States has purposely destroyed their holy site."

The tense silence that fell now made the earlier one seem like a pleasant interlude. Boyle continued speaking, his voice strained and doom-filled.

"Jihad, gentlemen," he said. "It's all out Jihad. Whether we like it or not, we have fallen into the same bed as our erstwhile 'friends,' the Israelis."

Chapter 43

"Great work, Dad," Prime Minister Danny Benari told his father, Robert Benson, over a digitally-encrypted Internet voice line.

"Yes, Danny. I must admit, those four seconds were extremely rewarding, considering the thirty-four years of work I put into them."

While still on line, the secretary buzzed the PM.

"What is it?" he asked. "I'm on an important call."

"Two men are here to see you. They said they have an appointment."

"Oh, yes. Admit them immediately." Into the phone, he said, "Dad, do you remember Alon Barnash?"

"Do I remember Alon? Alon is there? Put him on."

As the two old friends were speaking, Danny sat Moshe Mitzri down to talk. He had already heard the headlines about this man, who was his own age, and his exploits. He hadn't realized that this son of Samson's Lion was Orthodox, and was utterly amazed that, being raised Moslem, he could wind up that way.

"Moshe, I'm traditional myself; I believe in everything, but I don't observe everything. I began to worry the day before yesterday that perhaps my decision to start this mess might have been hasty. My father, the former Benny Harkesef, told me to call Rabbi Chaim. Do you know him?"

Moshe's eyes lit up. "Rabbi Chaim is the greatest man alive. Tell me what he said."

"All he said was, 'Behold, I have given him My Covenant of Peace.'"

"It's obvious what he meant. We just read that last Shabbat."

"Obvious to you," Danny said with mock indignation.

"Okay, okay, you never learned in a *yeshiva*. Listen here. Pinchas the grandson of Aaron the priest, publicly murdered a Jewish prince who was performing an immoral act with a Midianite princess. Most of the people condemned his act of violence more than the immoral act, and were ready to lynch him. But it was his very act of zealotry that saved the nation from destruction. I think Rabbi Chaim was telling you not to give in to any pressure, that your action was proper, and that your deeds will bring about an ultimate and true peace."

Daniel Benari was satisfied with that explanation.

The older Benson wound up his conversation. "Alon, it's been great talking with you. I hope to see you in a few days, when the situation is under control. But I must be getting off the line; I'm expecting guests very shortly." Benson hung up.

July 4, 2002, 9:21 p.m. (EDT), Military Command Center, the Pentagon:

Woodson clapped his hands together. The other chiefs turned to see what he'd come up with.

"General Boyle, I think you were a bit hasty in your deduction. I'm not exactly going to reinstate Jesus, certainly not Mohammed — but maybe Darwin. Maybe God is not quite as Jewish as you have surmised."

"What are you talking about?" Stillman demanded.

"This 'accident' came about as the result of a highly evolved human brain. I think we might have a mole in our security... and I think I might know where he is."

"A mole?" Boyle retorted. "In control of the whole damn military navigation system?"

"Yes. Exactly. My old pal Bob Benson. It makes perfect sense."

"I've heard that name. Isn't he Benari's old man?"

"Exactly," Woodson said again. "As far as I know, he's still with the NSA. Pretty high up. Until about fifteen years ago I worked with him extensively." His eyes swept the room with an air of triumph. "Gentlemen, Bob Benson is the 'father' of the GPS system."

"Come on, Jim," Boyle protested. "Just because he sat at a desk with a computer screen, theorizing and designing, how could he have altered the system so precisely? All the control signals are encoded and encrypted, rock-solid. What you're saying is simply impossible."

"Impossible, you say? We'll see about that. I'm going to order another missile attack on little David. Let's see how impossible! Stillman, you have an aircraft carrier in the Mediterranean. How far off the coast of Israel?"

"Less than three hundred miles."

"Good. I want four Tomahawks fired at downtown Tel Aviv."

"Hey, what are you saying?" Stillman protested. "We're playing with fire. I don't want to start World War III. You see what the Israelis have already done to much of the Arab world. They might have us wired up, too."

"We'll destroy the missiles over the sea, before they hit. Major Simmons," yelled General Woodson, "have you got any radio locator equipment in the Washington area? Somewhere not surrounded by the hordes?"

"I think we have a warehouse near White Oak, with a few trucks."

"Are they marked 'military'?"

"We're not that stupid."

"Excellent. I want three of them aiming their antennas directly at 3116 Pleasant Road, Kemp Mill, Maryland — Robert Benson's house." Woodson rubbed his hands together in a show of grim determination. "We'll catch him."

"But, Jim," CNO Stillman said excitedly, "if your hypothesis is correct, isn't it possible that Benson has Sherman?"

"Not just possible Earl. I'm certain he does."

July 5, 2002, 8:00 a.m. (EDT), UN Headquarters New York:

"The vote is one hundred forty-one to two. Resolution 777 is passed in the General Assembly condemning the United States of America for, intentionally or through gross negligence, destroying The Al Aqsa Mosque and the Dome of the Rock in Jerusalem."

July 5, 2002, 4:02 p.m. (GMT+2), Office of the PM of the State of Israel, Jerusalem:

"Mr. Benari, you have a call which, according to the computer, originates in Baghdad," his secretary announced.

"This is Aziz. We forgive you for the deaths in Basra and assume that you are prepared to strike Baghdad. We want to make a deal. You set the terms." Before an amazed Benari could reply, Aziz added in explanation, "The coalition is defunct. We just don't want to be hit again."

Benari drew a deep breath. "Very well," he said. "Here's what you must do...."

Air raid signals went off just as Benari was about to "negotiate" with the Iraqi foreign minister. "I've got an emergency, Aziz. Call me back later. Don't worry, you won't be hit until we can talk again."

"Mr. Benari!" The secretary was beside herself. "Four Cruise missiles have been fired from the American carrier Rickover! They're aimed to strike Tel Aviv in fourteen minutes."

July 5, 2002, 2:10 p.m. (GMT), U.S.S. Rickover off the coast of Egypt:

"Captain!" cried the commander of fire control. "Captain, the missiles have gone haywire! They're veering off course."

"How many of them?" the captain asked frantically.

"All of them. They turned in pattern just like a quartet of Blue Angels."

"How far are they from the target?"

"Seventy-five miles."

"Detonate them all." The captain began to walk away from the command bridge.

"Captain, they won't detonate. Nothing happens at all. We've totally lost control."

Slowly, the captain turned. "Where are they heading?"

The other man shook his head, dread in his face and voice. "I can't believe this. It's like a demon has taken control. They're heading straight back toward us! We'll be sunk!"

The code red alarm was sounded throughout the entire craft. All hands were ordered to their battle stations. Ten F-15 fighters scrambled to intercept their own cruise missiles. By the time the jets met up with them, there were only nine minutes separating the six thousand crew members of the carrier from certain destruction. Thirty-five AA missiles were fired before three of the Tomahawks exploded, the pieces falling harmlessly into the sea. But one seemed to elude destruction and continued on its course at five hundred fifty mph, thirty feet above the waves. A wail of despair rose up from the men and women on board the huge craft.

News of the American cruise missile demolition of the Temple Mount had reached the Rickover's crew. Once the right-wingers and the fundamentalist sailors on board began openly decrying the Rickover's missile launch on Tel Aviv, it was curtains for military discipline. Thousands were jumping into the warm Mediterranean waters as the flying bomb came into view over the horizon. Now even the interceptors couldn't fire their remaining few missiles, since they, too, were liable to strike the ship instead.

"Why aren't the Phalanxes working?" the Captain shouted frantically to his warrant officer.

"There's nobody left in charge of CIC. I saw Ensign Wright jump overboard along with most of the crew."

"What about — oh, what's her name? Yes, Ensign Jameson, Peggy Jameson?"

"Captain Gilcrest, I hate to tell you this, but she's still in sick bay. Her abortion yesterday went bad. She suffered a hemorrhage."

The captain stayed with his ship, standing and watching as bedlam reigned over his crew. His mind was struggling to comprehend the broad picture of the past five days' events. He, too, realized now that his CNO had become a pirate, and that he should have refused the order to fire the missiles. Then a deeper thought dawned upon him: had even the Commander in Chief himself ordered him to violate the Law of the Ultimate Commander, he should have defied that order.

He was at peace with himself. For his error in judgement, in about ten seconds he would be paying the ultimate price.

July 5, 2002, 9:11 a.m. (EDT), outside of 3116 Pleasant Rd, Kemp Mill, Maryland:

General Woodson disembarked from a helicopter, which landed in a schoolyard on University Boulevard. He was met by one of the locator trucks.

A young radio technician hurried up to report. "General, look, we have a lock on a signal. It's a satellite frequency all right. Digital encrypted code, and it's coming right from that house, 3116. You're amazing!"

"Don't be so amazed, young man. It was an experienced guess."

Woodson had also ordered a platoon of soldiers flown in from Fort Meade. The citizen mobs that had taken the law into their own hands did not yet have the capability to block a helicopter. The platoon surrounded the house as Woodson called on his cell phone.

"Hello, Bob, is that you? It's Jim Woodson."

"Jim! It must be about ten, twelve years. You've done real well for yourself, General of the Army and all."

"You haven't done that bad either. A son the Prime Minister of a country. I'm happy for you."

"Hey, Jim, how's your driver working for you these days? I can never forget those monster shots that last time we were down at Hilton Head."

"Oh, it's still moving, but I guess age is catching up with me a little. How's your lob wedge treating you? You had a killer short game."

"It only gets better. Anyway, what can I do for you?" Benson asked casually.

"You can come outside with your hands held high, high up. You have five minutes, or my gun ships will level your house."

"With Sherman in it?"

"Oh, so that's where he's been. We've missed him these past two days. What are you guys doing there, having a poker party?"

Benson's voice hardened. "Woodson, you know you're finished. I want you to know, from the bottom of my heart, that I believe that when you first kidnaped the President you really believed he couldn't manage the crisis. But it was downhill from there. You've turned into a Hitler. As we speak, the cruise missiles you shot at Tel Aviv ten minutes ago have been turned around and will sink their mother ship who sent them. Everyone under your command, from Pentagon control to the operators on board the Rickover, are soiling their pants, because they have no control over those missiles.

"Woodson, you swear to God to release the President safe and sound, and those missiles will be stopped. You gave me five minutes, I give you ten. Generous, aren't I?"

"Benson, the men and women on board that carrier are innocent. I know you wouldn't do it."

"They may be innocent, General — but then again, in every game of war there are sacrifices. You fired those missiles at the heart of my people, civilians even more innocent than the military personnel on your carrier."

"Benson, I swear, it was only a ploy to flush you out. We had every intention of pre-detonating those birds fifty miles offshore. I swear to God. Hell, if I knew that you could jam their controls...."

Benson realized that, for the first time, Woodson was telling the truth. "Listen, Jim, it's Sherman for the President. Take it or leave it."

Benson put Sherman on the line. "Jim, give up. We're doomed and there's no purpose in this anymore. The whole thing was a miserable failure — a complete backfire. Let Lewis go."

Benson took the phone back. "Sherman is right, and I'll prove it to you. Turn on WTOP."

Without replying, Woodson told the driver to turn on the radio. He listened carefully to the silence on 1500 AM. To Benson on his handset, he demanded, "What the hell are you talking...." He broke off. From his car radio, in his own voice, came the echo, "What the hell are you talking...."

"Jim...."
"Jim...."
"The whole country is listening...."
"The whole country is...."

Woodson banged his fist down on the dash, switched off the radio, and began to sob.

July 5, 2002, 9:21 a.m. (EDT), Military Command Center, the Pentagon:

Everyone stood watching silently as the missiles turned back toward the carrier. "Admiral Stillman, there's nothing I can do," a technician said. "General Woodson was right — this Benson guy has completely re-encrypted the psuedo-random control codes of the entire GPS system. For him, it's ultimate power — for us, those twelve billion dollar satellites are now space junk."

They watched on the huge screen as three of the missiles disappeared before they came within thirty miles of the carrier. The last one, however, seemed to have slipped through the hail of fire from the admiral's war planes. Stillman stared at the screen. When the missile was forty seconds away from blowing his prized craft out of the water, Stillman pulled out a Colt Mustang .380 from his pocket.

The silent apprehension of one hundred twenty-five men and women, eyes glued to the screen, was deafeningly shattered when he stuffed the barrel into his ear and pulled the trigger.

July 5, 2002, 2:22 p.m. (GMT), U.S.S. Rickover off the coast of Egypt:

By now, a line of over five thousand men and women were floating in the sea trailing behind the carrier, which was steaming along at twenty-six knots. Ten fighter jets were circling wide overhead, their pilots just beginning to grasp that within a few seconds, they would have nowhere to land.

Then, as the captain stood alone on the deck, watching and waiting for the end to meet him — the end never came. At the last second, with the missile just one thousand yards from its target, it nosed up and flew past the captain, sailing one hundred feet over his head. He was knocked to the deck by the whoosh of the air.

Stumbling back to his feet, he looked around just in time to witness the Tomahawk take a dive and crash harmlessly into the sea, three miles away.

With less than five hundred crew members left on board, including only two helicopter pilots, the captain ordered the jets not to attempt a landing. "I'm going back to pick up my people. The rescue may take half a day and you won't have enough fuel to stay in the sky for that long. I suggest that you eject, and we'll pick you up, too," squawked the captain over the radio to his fighter pilots.

"Captain, Captain!" yelled the lone signal officer left on board. "I just got an urgent email addressed to you."

The captain walked over to the ship's computer and clicked OPEN.

FROM: Daniel Benari
EMAIL: pm@netvision.co.il
SUBJECT: U.S. fighter crew
TO: Captain William Gilcrest, U.S.S. Rickover
EMAIL: wgilcrest@rickover.navy.mil
7-5-02, 16:36 local time (GMT+2)

Dear Captain Gilcrest,

Your planes are welcome to land in Israel. They will not be detained. They may refuel and return to the carrier as soon as convenience allows. Our escort jets are on the scene and will lead them back to our base. You can also expect the first of our twelve rescue choppers to land on your deck with your sailors aboard, by 18:30.

Daniel Benari, Prime Minister of Israel

Woodson's revelation that the cruise missile attack was only feigned had been enough to make Benson divert the lone cruise missile, making it nose up and fly over the carrier instead of destroying it. In the same vein, Woodson could no longer seriously threaten to blow up Benson's house with his boss, General George A. Sherman, inside. Woodson raced back the half mile to his waiting helicopter and took off.

Chapter 44

July 5, 2002, 9:32 a.m. (EDT), The crowd camped out around the Pentagon in northern Virginia:

"Folks, most of you just heard the live broadcast where two Generals, including the chairman of the Joint Chiefs, confessed to kidnaping the President. Until now, many of the press and the diehard liberals still believed that everything having to do with our government was fine. I now call on the featured speaker of the day to lead us into battle. The G-man himself, G. Horton Richie!"

An ear splitting cheer rose up from the crowd of more than 600,000.

Richie brought his lips to the microphone of the two thousand watt P.A. system the NRA had set up earlier that morning. He spread his arms as a signal for full attention, and waited. After a minute, silence prevailed.

Into the hush, Richie said simply, "The record speaks for itself." He pulled the mike from its stand, half-turned to face the enormous complex behind him, raised a clenched fist and said, "Admiral Stillman, General Boyle, General Harman, and you, General Woodson, if you're listening, thirty-five years ago you were my buddies. We became men together. I've paid my debt for my crimes like a man. Now it's your turn to do the same."

A huge roar went up from the crowd. It took the G-man three minutes to restore silence. "Let President Lewis go!" he shouted. Then, deliberately, he began to chant, "Let Lewis go! Let Lewis go! Let Lewis go!" The crowd joined in, the chant rattled the windows of the building. Five long minutes later, Richie raised a hand for quiet.

"We're waiting," Richie said, once again directing his words at the Pentagon building.

Silence.

"Okay." The slow intake of Richie's breath was audible to the crowd. He turned back to fully face his people. "Good citizens of America, as you must be aware, I am a convicted felon and may not hold public office." Richie pulled out of his pocket and unfolded a sheet of paper. Waving it high, he continued, "Here in my hand is a power of attorney signed by Mrs. Richie granting me authority to represent her interests at this rally." Richie paused for a moment to allow the import of his words to sink in. "Do you accept Mrs. Richie as commander of the American Militia, with all the legal implications as expressed in the Constitution of the United States?"

"Yes!" thundered the crowd.

"All opposed, raise your hand."

Out of the sea of humanity, not one hand was held high.

"Good. On behalf of and representing the commander of the American Militia, as I've now dubbed it, I declare it our solemn duty to defeat and depose the military leaders, and their lackeys, who have perpetrated this diabolical insurrection against the Constitution and the citizens of the United States. Therefore, you are ordered to raise your weapons — high-powered rifles only, please, no handguns or .22s, we don't want any accidents — toward..." Once again, Richie turned and pointed at the Pentagon, "this building!"

The soldiers on the roof, numbering about fifteen hundred, quickly disappeared, scampering back inside the massive fortress.

"Now, listen carefully. When I give the signal, you are to fire one round, and one round only, into the window that lies in a direct beeline from your position." He quickly assessed the throng. "Behind the cover of about twenty-five rings of vehicles, we are perhaps four hundred men thick. I want all of you behind the innermost five rings of cars to aim for the first floor windows. The next five rings go for the second floor windows, and so on. I'll give you about four minutes to reckon your relative position so as to choose your target."

The minutes passed in a rustle of movement from the crowd. A sea of rifles aimed upward, stainless barrels flashing in the sun. Richie gauged their readiness, then intoned, "Ready... aim..." Unexpectedly, he shouted at the Pentagon, "Hey, you there, inside — my old buddies! You ready to give up?" Silence. Then, gradually, the beat of a chopper became audible in the distance.

Richie asked a nearby militiaman for the pair of binoculars slung around his neck.

Everyone was still poised, waiting for the G-man's signal, when he barked into the microphone, "That's the lousy traitor, General Woodson, returning in his helicopter. I countermand the previous order! Everyone is to direct his aim toward the chopper."

In a twinkling, the sea of rifles rippled and reversed direction. Richie shouted, "Do not fire until I give the order. When I do, let loose with everything you have. If you have the angle, aim for the rotor — the closer to the drive shaft, the better."

*   *   *

"Woodson, Woodson!" Boyle yelled over the radio, "Get away, get away. You'll be shot down!"

"Dick, what the hell? It's all over. Stillman is dead; Sherman is out of it, and I am too. I'm coming in," lamented the dejected Army Chief.

*   *   *

Five hundred thousand gunsights followed the slowly moving Jet Ranger. It was not more than fifteen hundred feet above the ground now, carefully avoiding the menacing conglomeration of lighter-than-air craft littering the sky in its path. By the time it had meandered beyond the armada of sky-borne debris, it was in a dead hover over the Pentagon, almost as if to say, 'Shoot me.' The G-man shot his right hand high and cried, "FIRE!"

The gunfire was deafening, even for the hundreds of thousands who came prepared with ear protection. Almost instantly, pieces of the rotor went flying in every direction. The chopper fell out of the sky like a rock, crashing into the atrium of the Pentagon. None of the crowd was able to view the actual crash. But a plume of thick black smoke rose from behind the building, filling the sky above.

Every eye watched that coiling dark smoke, mesmerized. Richie, too, stared upward at the result of his handiwork. No one spoke. There was scarcely a muscle that twitched. It was as if the whole crowd — the whole world — was holding its breath, wondering what was coming next.

The sound, when it came, jerked them all out of the trance with a startling abruptness.

It was music. The Pentagon's P.A. system blared a recorded version of *Hail to the Chief.*

Swiftly, Richie commanded the crowd: "Gentlemen, and ladies, AT EASE!" The rattle of dropping magazines clicking loose, actions locking open, and guns being set down was audible through the music.

"ATTENTION!" Richie bellowed.

The Pentagon doors opened. President Abraham Lewis emerged from the building, followed by a retinue of military and civilian personnel. Six hundred thousand men and women stood at attention, their open right hands touching their foreheads in a salute as Lewis took the podium. His message was succinct.

"Ladies and gentlemen, citizens of the United States — I thank God this disgraceful nightmare is over."

A prolonged cheer erupted from the crowd.

"As for the Middle East crisis... we're out of it."

The crowd cheered even louder.

A helicopter bearing the markings of the Maryland State Police hovered low over a clear area five hundred yards away. Robert Benson, accompanied by George Sherman — now in police handcuffs and escorted by two Maryland troopers — made his way through the parting crowd toward the podium.

The President extended his hand to Benson, who met him with a bear hug. For a long moment, the two shed quiet tears on one another's shoulders. Benson slipped a piece of paper in Lewis' pocket.

"What's that?"

"That's the prime number key code to unlock the new signal encryption on the entire military GPS system. I didn't want to entrust it to anybody else... Abe, you must do something for me," Benson whispered to the President.

"Anything."

"Pardon Rabinowitz."

Sherman was pushed up to the microphone. He was sobbing much more bitterly than either the President or Benson, whose tears were those of joy. The general wiped his nose with both hands, which were closely manacled together, and composed himself enough to speak two simple, shuddering words: "I'm sorry."

FINALÉ:

ARMAGEDDON

"And saviors will ascend Mount Zion to judge the Mountain of Esau"

Obadiah 1:21

Chapter 45

July 5, 2002, 6:00 p.m. (EDT), UN Headquarters, New York:

NEWS RELEASE:

Due to the information which has emerged over the past twenty-four hours, the general assembly has voted to amend Resolution 777, condemning the United States for the destruction of the Moslem holy sites in Jerusalem. It is now apparent that Israel was an accomplice in the missile attack, directing the incoming missiles to strike the Dome of the Rock and the Al Aqsa Mosque. Therefore, the family of nations, by a vote of one-thirty-seven to five, adds Israel to the U.S. in its condemnation, and has ordered all member nations to form a military task force to invade and dissolve the present government of the State of Israel. The dissenting votes are Israel, the United States, Iraq, Jordan and Iran. These States have also informed the secretary general of their refusal to participate in such action, even at threat of sanctions, and of their refusal to allow the use of their territory or airspace to any nation participating in the implementation of any such military option.

July 6, 2002, 10:05 a.m. (MDT), The office of Gem Tours, Nampa, Idaho:

"I'm sorry, Mr. Horrace. All flights to Tel Aviv are booked for the next three months," the travel agent in suburban Boise said crisply.

*   *   *

All his life, Gaylord Barnett Horrace had been a schlemiel. Late for everything he ever did, his friends were used to applying to him the maxim, "Nice guys finish last." Horrace recognized his limitations and didn't complain; no one would listen to him anyway. In 1994, he was sent by the New Israelite Church of the Messiah — of which he was a most devout follower — as a missionary to Rwanda. Under his tutelage, a classroom full of poor teenagers began to display their first interest in learning to read. And, for the first time in his life, the twenty-two-year-old Horrace felt the satisfaction of personal accomplishment.

The teenagers had idolized the blond, blue-eyed American who, in his broken French, showed them that someone cared.

Then one day, only three kids showed up to class.

"Where is everybody?" he'd asked a sixteen-year-old by the name of Kolawi.

"They're dead."

"Dead?" shrieked Horrace. "What happened?"

The youngster shrugged. "Some men from my Tusi tribe came through our village handing out machetes, and told us to go kill Hutus. So I kill. The only ones I knew well were the others in the class. Master Gaylord, you know Timbala? He had a birthday party last week. He invited everyone in the class, so I knew where he lived. When I got to his house last night, five other Hutu kids from the class were also there, so I kill them all. Now Master, can we continue with yesterday's lesson? You were teaching us about the Good Samaritan. Please finish that story."

Horrace stepped outside and puked. He never entered the class again. Instead, he hired a cab to Kigali and caught the first flight back to the U.S.

*   *   *

He eyed the ticket agent anxiously. "What about by ship, then?"

She clicked the keyboard and scanned her monitor for five minutes, then said, "There are no passenger lines that sail directly to Israel anymore. But let's see. Here's one from Naples.... Booked. Ah, here's one from Piraeus; no — that, too, is booked." She looked up. "Look, Mr. Horrace, in the past three days our agency has sold 3,652 plane tickets to Israel. The week before, seventeen. I guess everybody has the same idea."

"I suppose you're right," he said unhappily. "But I'm convinced this is *it*. The Second Coming is imminent.... What about getting me to a destination near Israel, where I could travel the rest of the way by some sort of overland route?"

"You're not going to get there from Egypt, Lebanon, or Syria. Let's see about Jordan." Three more minutes of computer work turned up the same results: "Booked solid."

"What about Saudi Arabia?"

"Isn't that one of the hostile Arab nations? I think the papers wrote that over 50,000 were killed there during this crisis."

"I think I'll go anyway. At least I'll be close. Hopefully, I'll figure out something after I get there."

"I don't think it's safe, even though the President apologized for the bombing of the Temple Mount and had the renegades arrested. But, as you wish."

The travel agent scouted the flights and was surprised to find that all flights from Europe to Riyadh were completely booked. This jammed up the few flights originating from the U.S.

"All I can find for the next ten days is a flight to Jidda on Ethiopian Airlines, via Addis Ababa. From Jidda, Saudi Arabia, there is a bus to Aqaba in Jordan. The ride takes twelve hours. Under normal conditions, there is a tour of Eilat from Aqaba. If all goes perfectly, you might get to Israel that way."

Horrace snapped at the offer. "I'll take it!"

At 10:00 p.m. that evening, the flight took off from Kennedy. Horrace, the only blue-eyed blond, felt uncomfortable among all the swarthy passengers on board. At 4:14 p.m. the following day, the plane landed in Ethiopia. Horrace remained in his seat. After a tedious, two-hour wait, a cleaning crew came on board.

"Does anyone speak English?" asked the worried passenger.

The workers indicated that they didn't understand. Finally, Horrace disembarked and ambled over to the front desk. "My ticket says this flight is continuing on to Jidda. It's an hour and a half after scheduled departure. What's going on?"

A uniformed airline employee gave him a cheerful smile, and said, "That leg of the flight was canceled."

"Why?" asked Horrace, highly incensed.

"Not enough passengers."

"So how am I going to get there? Why wasn't I told? I've been sitting on the plane for two hours, waiting."

The agent shrugged his shoulders.

Horrace forced himself to breathe deeply. When some measure of calm had returned, he said, "Okay, when is the next flight?"

"I don't have any idea. Come back next week."

"Next week?" Horrace yelled, "What kind of airline do you run? Look, I've got to get to Jidda. Any other options?"

"There's a ferry from Assab to Mocha, in Yemen. From there you catch a bus to Hodeida or Taiz and transfer to the Mecca Haj bus. That's the Hejira route everyone around here takes."

By the time Horrace crossed the Straits just north of Bab Al Mandeb, he understood what self-sacrifice meant. The ferry was designed to carry a maximum of ninety people. On this trip, it was loaded up with close to four hundred. The captain announced in Amharic, Arabic and French that, after being seated (on the floor; all the benches had been removed), no one was to get up or move about the ship. Squashed in like a sardine, Horrace felt it was hardly necessary to make such an announcement. But when the rickety ship came within two hundred meters of the pier on the Yemeni side, everyone started shoving toward the port side in an attempt to position themselves closer to the gangplank. There was pandemonium as the ship suddenly shifted in the water, listing dangerously. The pilot made a quick maneuver, turning the wheel sharply to starboard, which righted the vessel. Ushers on board began beating the people with leather-covered clubs, like riot police, forcing them back — pressed together even more tightly than during the one-hour trip — to the center of the hull. Horrace made it alive to dry land. He considered it a miracle.

Three hours later, sore from a bumpy ride on a vehicle that resembled a junk-yard school bus, he alit in Taiz. Appearing an absolute oddball among the dark-skinned, rag-clad populace surrounding him, he reflected on the scene before him. He was standing in the Souk, a central market, in the twenty-first century, but easily counted at least fifty donkeys and ten camels for every car that wedged its way through the dung-strewn streets. After fifteen minutes, he found the "high class" hotel and checked in. The room he was given was actually just a bed, for although he took the best the hotel had to offer, he still had to share the room with another guest.

Horrace got the surprise of his life when his roommate came in that evening and switched on the light. He glanced up from his bed — and there was another character out of a storybook. But it was not a South Arabian storybook; it was a Brooklyn, New York or, more accurately, a Carpathian Mountain storybook. The man who had unwittingly woken him from his exhausted sleep wore a long black coat and round, wide brimmed black hat, a long black beard, and two long, curled locks of hair hanging down in front of his ears. He was a Hasidic Jew of the ultra-Orthodox Satmar sect.

"Oh, I'm terribly sorry!" the Hasid gasped. "I didn't realize someone was put in the room with me." He studied Horrace more closely. "You speak English, I hope."

Horrace sat up on the bed, rubbed his eyes to make sure he wasn't dreaming, and answered, "I'm an American. Gaylord Barnett Horrace. Nice to meet you." Horrace extended his hand.

"Yossel Berger from Williamsburg, New York. Where are you from?"

"Nampa, Idaho."

"What on earth are you doing here?" Yossel asked his blond compatriot.

"I could ask you the same question. But I'll bet our purpose has more in common than we might think. You represent some church group, right? I myself did a tour of duty back in the middle nineties in Africa."

The Hasid chuckled. "Mister Horrace, I think you may not quite understand. Have you ever seen someone like me before?"

"Not exactly."

"Never been to New York or Montreal?"

"Nope, can't say that I have."

"Well, can you keep a secret?"

"Sure, sure."

"I'm a Jew," Berger said proudly. "But I don't advertise it around here."

Dazed, Horrace pinched himself to make sure he wasn't suffering some kind of medical condition brought on by his arduous travels.

"Look, Mister...."

"You can call me Gaylord."

"Okay, Gaylord. You said you thought we're here for the same thing. What did you have in mind? You don't look like you had such an easy time getting here."

"You can say that again. I'm still not sure I'm not dreaming. Actually, I never wanted to come here. Let's say, my plans got diverted. Well, I'll start from the beginning. I don't know how long you've been here...."

"Two weeks," the Brooklyn native riposted quickly.

"Do you know what's going on in the world?"

"I've been listening to the BBC. Sounds like the time of *Moshiach*?"

"What was that? Did you say Messiah?"

"Yeah, that's exactly what I said."

Horrace pursed his lips and exhaled. "That's a relief! I seem to remember hearing that the Jews didn't believe in the Second Coming of Christ. I guess it isn't true."

"Hey, wait just a minute. I said *Moshiach*. I didn't say anything about Yoshke."

Yossel removed his broad hat, to reveal a close-shaven head and a large, black skullcap underneath. He placed the hat on the dresser, asking over his shoulder, "You some kind of Christian fundamentalist? You believe the Jews are the devil and all?"

"No, in our Church, we don't hate anybody. We love all mankind."

"Is that why you burned my forefathers? Out of love?" The Hasid carefully removed his long, black coat and hung it in the closet, his back to Horrace.

"No, no, Mr. Berger. You've got the wrong religion. I'm a New Israelite. You know, the New Israelite Church of the Messiah Jesus Christ. We love our fellow man. We are God's Chosen People."

"Hey, just a minute!" Berger spun around. "It's the Jews — you know, the Children of Israel — who are God's Chosen People. Don't you read the Bible?"

"Yes, of course. And that's just what I said. We are the Children of Israel."

"What's going on? The Jews are the Children of Israel." Yossel Berger sat on his bed, staring at his roommate.

Horrace pondered a moment, still slightly groggy. "Yes, but we are the new Children of Israel," he explained.

Yossel shook his head vigorously, earlocks swaying with the motion. "Mister, the Jews are the Children of Israel — new, old, whatever you want."

"Look," pleaded the bewildered and worn out Christian, "can't we save this argument for another time? I'm beat. I want to get some sleep. Tomorrow, it's on to Jerusalem."

"Jerusalem!" Berger yelped. "How are you going to get there?"

"I don't know. We'll see tomorrow...." Horrace yawned mightily. "Now, if you please, the light. I'm zonked."

"Sure, sure." Berger tugged the frayed string dangling from the ceiling, switching off the light, but the light in his mind remained lit up with 50,000-candle power.

Chapter 46

Berger was just folding his prayer shawl when Horrace woke up. The curtain was partially drawn, and a sliver of bright Middle Eastern sun was in his eyes.

"Good morning," he said to his fellow American, as Berger inserted the prayer shawl into an embroidered velvet bag.

"And the same to you," the Hasid replied affably.

"You know something? You never told me what you're doing here. With what the Jews have done to the Arabs lately, I doubt if the Yemeni government would appreciate your presence here very much."

"*Some* Jews, Gaylord; some Jews. The group I belong to is anti-Zionist. The government here knows that, and lets us come to visit with the local Jews. Most of them are in a pitiful situation."

"Jews — living here in Yemen?" Horrace was incredulous. "This is the middle of nowhere. It hardly seems to have changed at all from Biblical times."

"You're right. But that's not always a drawback. They have no TV here, no movies, and no scantily clad women." Berger grinned, adding, "But I guess for you that might be a drawback."

"You don't seem to know much about the New Israelite Church of the Messiah."

"You're right. I never heard of it until last night."

"Well, we still believe in the old fashioned moral standards too. All those things you mentioned are strictly taboo in our religion. And, believe me, it's enforced, too."

"Don't you have young people who, er, fool around, take drugs and other things?"

"We have a few like that, but they're immediately expelled from the church if they don't shape up after a stern warning. No, we don't tolerate all the nonsense going on in American society. We are about as conservative as they come. But we don't hate anyone."

"Sounds good to me." Yossel Berger assessed Horrace thoughtfully, then seemed to make up his mind. "Gaylord, before you leave for Jerusalem, I want you to meet a man who lives here."

"I don't know if I have time. I've got to find out when the bus leaves for Mecca."

Berger broke out in a fit of laughter. "Mecca? Is your church a branch of Islam?"

"Of course not!" Horrace answered indignantly. "We are the true Christians, followers of Jesus Christ the Messiah."

"Gaylord," Berger said, serious now, "I like you, and I want you to know — we don't have much to do with gentiles."

"Neither do we."

"What are you talking about?" Berger asked in confusion, "You're a gentile yourself!"

"Not according to our definition. I think I told you, the New Israelites *are* the incarnation of the Children of Israel."

The Hasid lifted both hands. "Okay, okay, let's not get into that argument. Just come with me this morning. You won't be sorry."

The pair walked for about three-quarters of an hour from the hotel. Horrace was aware of the odd picture they made: he in his conservative American summer-wear, the bearded Hasid, as always, dressed in a long black coat and dignified black hat. As they went, Horrace marveled at the simplicity of the small, square houses baking in the relentless sun. Heat and dust were everywhere. Still, Yemen, he decided, had a stark charm that appealed to him. The sky was bluer than he ever remembered it being in Idaho.

"Here we are," Yossel Berger gestured at a hovel, no different from the dozens of others they had passed this morning. "This is the home of Mori Menachem Shabazi. A very wise man." Reverently, he went up to the door and knocked.

"Menachem is not home. He went to the market," they were informed by the sage's wife.

Apologizing for disturbing her, Yossel told her they would wait outside. Twenty minutes later, a donkey came around the corner, bearing Menachem and his bundles of greens and clusters of fruit.

"Yosef, my friend! Why are you waiting outside in the sun? Please, come in, come in. You've made my day! Now I have guests to share my fresh fruits with."

He slid down off the donkey and came to stand before them. Horrace saw a man of less than medium height, olive-skinned, with warm but very penetrating dark eyes. He wore a thin white beard and long side-locks, similar to those of Yossel Berger. Taking Yossel's arm with his right hand and Gaylord's with his left, he practically dragged them inside. With no time lost, they were soon seated around a low table situated in the middle of the carpet.

Horrace studied his host. The Yemenite Jew's face reflected a youth and animation that belied his true age. As he extended his hand upon Berger's bilingual introduction, Gaylord Horrace, devout Messianic Christian, was taken aback. He had never before met anyone that had made such a powerful impression on him, by appearance alone. The man greeting him was the personification of humility and love, wisdom and kindness. What Gaylord Horrace didn't realize was that he was struck by this perception only because he had spent a lifetime of religious devotion, longing for the image of just such a persona.

Berger turned to Horrace, smiling. "Mori Menachem says he's happy to meet you. He said you are a precious soul."

Horrace still sat transfixed as Menachem got up and left the room. Finally, the American pulled himself together, and took a sip of the mint tea that Mrs. Shabazi had brought. She had deposited it before them, silent as a wraith, smiled slightly in response to his thanks, and disappeared again into the back regions of the tiny house, where her husband now joined her.

"Yossel, although I don't understand a word, it sounds like Menachem and his wife are arguing in the kitchen. She, at least, seems to be talking a mile a minute."

"You're very perceptive. They're speaking Yemenite, a Jewish dialect of Arabic, which I don't understand either. But I've been through this before, they're arguing over who will have the privilege of serving us the traditional fruit platter brought to guests."

Sure enough, Menachem came in bearing the tray laden with dates, figs and grapes. He set it down on the low table around which the three men were sitting. Reciting a blessing over a grape, Menachem put it into his mouth. Yossel answered "Amen" and motioned to Gaylord, who did likewise. Menachem looked intently at Gaylord for a few seconds, then spoke in Hebrew to Yossel.

"This man is not a Jew, but he is a very righteous man."

"What did he say?" Gaylord prodded anxiously. Berger told him.

There was a short silence as the trio ate fruit. It was broken by Horrace, who asked Berger to find out whether Mori Menachem thought that, in light of the recent events in the Middle East, the coming of the Messiah was at hand.

Menachem listened to the question, closed his eyes tightly and said, "I can't be completely sure. But since it is very likely, we must depart for Jerusalem immediately." He sat up, the decision apparently making itself. "Yes, we must leave right away — for Gog from the Land of Magog is on his way even as we speak."

Yossel Berger was floored. Having spent the past week and a half with Menachem, he had discovered that the simple Jew knew the entire Bible, Talmud, the Code of Maimonides and the mystical Zohar by heart. In his discussions, which sometimes lasted eight or ten hours, Yossel had learned that this man with the penetrating smile not only knew these works and understood them, but that he thoroughly lived and breathed them, too. It was almost as if the books were his home and his country. When discussing the Zohar, Yossel noticed how frequently Menachem seemed to drift off into another world, then quickly return. Yet, amazingly, Menachem Shabazi was the most self-effacing man Berger had ever met. Gaylord Horrace received the same impression, just by looking at the man. Yossel Berger spoke for another ten minutes to Menachem in Hebrew, then turned to Gaylord. "I'm going with Menachem. He wants to leave tomorrow morning, a half-hour after dawn. He asked if you would come along with us."

Horrace's excitement was so great that his head swam. He felt perilously close to fainting. It was Menachem Shabazi's penetrating eyes on him that jarred him back into a state of alertness. "Of — of course I'll come! I'll do anything the mori says."

Menachem smiled quietly, pleased. Berger nodded, as if he'd known that no other answer was possible.

*   *   *

Back at the hotel, Berger was packing his belongings when the dam burst in Gaylord Barnett Horrace tear ducts and he felt like he was about to be carried off to heaven.

"Yossel, I can't hold it back any longer. That man, Mori Menachem — do you know who he is? Do you understand whom we've met, and are about to accompany to Jerusalem?"

Berger turned slowly, and said, "I think I do understand, maybe even a little better than you might. After all, we speak the same language and serve the same God."

"No, Yossel, I don't think you understand. You've never studied the New Testament. I'm convinced — and I'm positive that Menachem Shabazi is keeping it a secret... but he is none other than Jesus Christ incarnate! Yossel, we're on our way to Jerusalem with the Redeemer himself." Rapture nearly overwhelmed Gaylord as he spoke.

Berger was unimpressed. "Hey, calm down, just take it easy. There's no doubt the man is great and, for sure, what we call a hidden saint, but I think you're carrying your dreams a little too far. I assure you, he'd be pretty angry if you told him that you thought he is Jesus. Let me tell you a little about his background. Some of it I heard from him, but mostly from speaking with the few local Jews...."

Shabazi was born in a village on the outskirts of Taiz on the Ninth of Av, 1937 or '38 — no one knew for sure, not even Shabazi himself. He was a quiet child but, like all Yemenite Jewish boys, studied conscientiously. He knew all the prayers and much of the scriptures by heart. Typically, he could fluently read texts upside down and sideways. In those days, books being an expensive and rare commodity, six to eight boys had to learn together from one book — some of them, consequently, viewed the printed page from unusual angles. The first hint that Menachem was an extraordinary youngster came when he was about twelve.

"Nechama," Yehuda Shabazi called excitedly, as he came in from work one day shortly after Passover of 1949. "Pack up, this is it. We're on our way to the Promised Land. Our ancestors have dwelt in this land for twenty-five hundred years — but next week we will fly in a great iron bird, back to the Land of Israel!"

Nechama was the practical one. "Not so fast, Yehuda. Don't you think we should check out living conditions, jobs, schools for the children? There are rumors that the new government in Israel is made up of apostate Jews."

"You believe that nonsense?" Yehuda waved a dismissive hand. "What's there to worry about? So not every Jew in the Holy Land observes as he should. In time, God will change his heart. We're going! All our friends and neighbors are going, too. The emissary from Israel, Rabbi Eliyahu Levi, has told our congregation that almost 50,000 Jews from Yemen have signed up...."

The entire Shabazi family spent the next week packing their belongings, especially their valuables, the silver and gold ornaments that Yehudah Shabazi made in his craft shop. They were inserted into heavy cardboard tubes, around which valuable Persian carpets were wrapped. When they got to the airfield after an arduous, six-day trek to Aden, they found the huge Constellation perched majestically out on the field. There was no terminal building, no customs house — just a big iron bird in the center of a crudely graded dirt runway.

Rabbi Levi from the Jewish Agency was there to meet those who were on his list. He himself was of Yemenite origin, but had been born in Jerusalem. He sported a beard and thin side locks of hair, just as his clients did. He also wore the same long gown and head covering. But although he spoke the Yemenite-Jewish dialect of Arabic, he did so with a heavy Israeli accent. Most of the Jews had never seen a large airliner before, let alone ever flown in one. As Rabbi Levi instructed the passengers to hand their belongings to the airplane staff to carry up a ladder into the luggage hold, many argued with him, insisting they didn't want to allow their precious articles out of their sight. They lost the argument.

"Hey, lady," called Rabbi Levi, catching sight of a middle-aged woman carrying a bundle of sticks up toward the passenger compartment, "Where are you going with that wood?"

"You said it would take over six hours for this 'eagle' to carry us to the Promised Land. We have to eat on the way, you know."

"You eat sticks?"

"No, sir," she answered with dignity. "But we are not animals. We must cook our food first."

The rabbi chuckled to himself. He'd known these people were naive, but he never thought they would consider building a fire on an airplane in flight. "Don't worry, madam, plenty of good food will be served on the journey. The Jewish Agency has taken care of everything."

Everyone was on board, the door was sealed, and the engines started. Yehuda Shabazi and his eight children sat together in their corner; all the seats had been removed to squeeze in more people. Besides, the Yemenites were used to sitting on the floor of their own homes. Little Menachem stood up and began to walk toward the Israeli emissary.

"Where are you going, little boy?" Levi asked. "You must be seated as the bird takes off, or you could fall and get hurt."

"I'm not going!" the boy declared. "Open the door, I want to get off."

"Come now, everybody wants to be in the Holy Land. Everything is so wonderful there. Not like here — so old-fashioned, dirty, and miserable with all the hateful Arabs."

The boy kept making for the door. Levi grabbed him and began to carry him back to the area where his family was sitting. Menachem kicked him in the shin. Wincing in pain, Levi let go for a second. The boy grabbed the Rabbi's side locks and tugged as hard as he could. But instead of screaming in pain, the emissary gaped as two wads of "hair" came off in little Menachem's hands. Attached to each, was a piece of adhesive tape, which had been hidden under Levi's hat.

Menachem turned toward the people on the plane, threw down the theatrical props, and cried, "You see? This man is a phony. He is the wicked and rebellious son we read about on Passover. He is leading us to doom, maybe even to kill us and steal our belongings in the belly of this bird."

For a moment, everyone was in shock. Menachem took the opportunity to run over to the door, pull the handle and jump down two meters to the ground. He did so after the plane had actually started rolling toward takeoff. Finding a lone donkey that had been left behind, he made his way to the grave of his ancestor, the Poet and Holy Saint, Mori Shalem Shabazi, and prayed with all his heart. From there, he rode the ten kilometers back to Taiz, where he went straight to his great-grandfather's house. The elder sage, at his advanced age, had declined to leave the homeland that his people had lived in for twenty-five centuries. From that day, Menachem was recognized in the village as a brilliant and diligent student. Three months later, he received his first letter from his mother.

My Dear Son,

God must have alerted you to something. Everything you said was true. In Yemen, the Jewish Agency workers impressed us as religious and sincere. Once we arrived in Israel, their men all went around bareheaded. The women who worked with us wore short pants and sleeveless blouses. It was painful and embarrassing for our people, who, in Yemen, had been used to modest dress and reverent behavior. We knew something was wrong, but what could we do? We were taken to a temporary transit camp, Rosh Ayin. At first, we could not understand why it was surrounded by barbed wire, but we found out soon enough. As for our belongings, our gold and silver, we never saw them again. Our complaints were met with such hollow excuses — it's as if we weren't considered human beings.

The worst thing that happened to us has me in tears ten times a day. I just can't get over it. I pinch myself. Why didn't we get off the 'eagle's wings' with you? Your little brother Yitzchak is no longer. One week after we first arrived, the Jewish Agency woman said that all children must go for a physical examination in the city. That evening, when two-year-old Yitzchak was not returned, I asked where he was. They told me, they found he was sick, and that he would be in the hospital for two or three days. I didn't think he was sick, but I believed that maybe with more modern medicine, they knew better. After three days, I started to complain. They said they would find out. That took another three days. And then, God save us, they told me Yitzchak had died. I was beside myself with grief. Your father begged them to take us to our baby, but they said he was buried already.

They didn't even let us go to the funeral, they didn't let us see his body; they never gave us any paper-work. There is a lot of paper-work in this country. I never learned to read and write, but they make your father sign twenty papers a day. Our baby dies, and nothing — he's gone, just as if a locust had died. These people are so evil I can't believe God doesn't strike them down without mercy....

The barbed wire was put up after the first wave of Yemenites arrived. These so-called Jews from the Jewish Agency, who are worse than the worst Moslems I ever experienced back in Yemen, put up barbed wire to keep out the good Ashkenazi Jews who tried to come into the camp to teach Torah to the children and tell us about the religious schools and organizations. I saw with my own eyes, which I couldn't believe, one of the Yeshiva boys sneak into the camp. He made a hole in the barbed wire. He brought books with him and was teaching Torah at night. A counselor from the Jewish Agency caught him, called his cohorts, and they beat the boy so badly that even those evil ones had to call an ambulance.

This is the worst nightmare of my life. At least you, my son, despite your tender age, had the sense to stay in our homeland. You are my joy. God be with you.

With much love,
Your Mother

Menachem cried and cried as he read the letter that had been dictated by his mother to his father to write. His father included his own note, saying that everything his mother had written was true.

Yosef Saba, Menachem's great-grandfather, told the youth he must mourn for at least one day after hearing about the death of his brother. But Menachem refused.

"Sabi, my brother is not dead. Why would these evil people bring all the Yemenites to their new country just to kill them? The adults they need to fight in their army against the Arabs and to clean the floors. But why would they kill babies in their mother's arms?" He gazed at his great-grandfather with dark eyes that were already filled with penetrating wisdom. "It's so simple, Sabi. They have kidnaped these children to sell to other evil Jews who cannot have children of their own."

The old man shook his head. "So now you've changed your mind? You told me that you warned the people they might be killed. Now you are saying it doesn't make sense that they would kill the babies! Oh, Menachem, why do you deride the new leaders, who have merited God's miracle of returning our people to their homeland after two thousand years of exile? You speak slander and bear tales on your fellow Jews. That is a great sin, you know."

But the boy would not be swayed. "Sabi dear, you have too much faith in men. These people don't observe or believe in our Holy Torah. No good can come from their deeds. You hear me, Sabi — *no good can come*. They are the disciples of the devil. They don't bring redemption; they prevent it. I said our people were in danger of being killed?" Slowly, Menachem clenched his fists, finishing in pain and grief: "I meant that those godless Israelis would kill the spirit which was vibrant in the hearts of our people."

"Enough, Menachem. Enough! Even if there is some truth in your words, you must not open your mouth with such condemnation. It will only bring about Heavenly Accusers against our people."

"No, Sabi. I must respectfully disagree. The forces of evil must be publicly exposed, so that the faithful will be awakened to rise up and defend the Will of God."

Sabi was sorrowful. "Menachem, my son, you are too young and too delicate to be involved in these matters. I pray they won't distract you from your studies."

For nine years, Menachem dwelled in the tents of the last few remaining sages of Yemen. Late in 1958, Mori Siman Tov Sharabi, the last of the great *Kabbalists* in Sana, passed on. With his master and teacher gone, Menachem Shabazi bid his seventy-nine-year-old great-grandfather, his friends, and few remaining relatives farewell, and departed.

Ten years later, he returned. Varied rumors floated around: he had traveled to America, to Israel, to Tibet, China or to Japan. Menachem himself never talked about where he had been. All he said was that he had gone off on a personal exile, to gain insights and knowledge that were not possible to acquire in Yemen. The few remaining Jews in Taiz and the cities near the central coast speedily came to recognize the special character of the man who immersed himself in Torah study and purity day and night. But although he was happy to speak to people, to answer their questions, and offer advice, Menachem Shabazi steadfastly refused to accept any title or official position. He continued to live the simple and humble lifestyle that had been customary of Yemenites for close to one hundred generations.

Yossel concluded his story, "Well, that's what I know about Menachem Shabazi. You can believe whatever you want — but, please, keep your Christian ideas about him to yourself."

Gaylord Horrace didn't keep it to himself. After finding his way to the Taiz central post office and waiting two hours, he got in a call to his Uncle Luke, who also happened to be an elder in the New Israelite Church of the Messiah Jesus Christ.

"Uncle, this is Gaylord."

"Where are you? Your mother called yesterday to say you were heading for Jerusalem. My flight leaves tomorrow."

"I couldn't get a flight anywhere close to Jerusalem. But the Almighty has been kind to me. More than kind."

"Just get to the point. Where are you?"

"I'm in Yemen."

"Yemen?! What on earth are you doing there?" hollered Luke Horrace.

"It's a long story, and I can't talk much now. Just listen carefully. Change your ticket, and come straight here now."

"Have you gone crazy? I've got a group going on one of the last available flights for months, and you want me to cancel it and go to some God-forsaken desert to meet you!"

"Listen to me, Uncle. I am headed up to Jerusalem too... but I have been deemed worthy by God to escort the Lord Jesus Christ himself."

A hollow groan met his ear. "Oh, Gaylord. I always knew you were a little strange."

Horrace said quietly, "It's true, Uncle. I've met him."

"What are you talking about?"

"I swear, I have met the Lord himself. He's been hiding right here in Yemen, like a thief in the night, and he's on his way to Jerusalem tomorrow morning for the Second Coming. He's in the form of a saintly humble Jew. But I'll tell you Uncle, when he looked at me for the first time, I knew — I had met Christ. He is an exact picture of the man we've been learning about in the Church. Please believe me. Have I ever been dishonest with you?"

Horrace could almost hear the wheels turning in his uncle's head, Slowly, Luke Horrace said, "But... but... Jews don't accept that Jesus came the first time. How could you possibly believe that Jesus would come back as a Jew for the Second Coming?"

"Uncle, I'm afraid that teaching of our Church may need a little reinterpretation. The future will testify to its true meaning. But this man *is* the Lord; there is no doubt about it."

"Well, you sound pretty convinced," his uncle said cautiously. "But I don't think we could make it there before you leave."

"There's only one road north, and we're lucky there's that. I think you'll be able to catch up with us. Or better yet, meet us north of here. You might find a flight to Jidda, Saudi Arabia."

There was a short silence. Then, "I must be nuts, but I'll see what I can do. I just hope you're not going to make a fool out of me."

As Horrace was leaving the post office, an old man brought in a load of newspapers on his head. They were plopped down on the floor with a thud. Horrace noticed four copies of the International Herald Tribune among the others. He quickly purchased one of them.

July 7, 2002, Headline:

The World in Turmoil

UN Organizes the Largest Multi-National Force in History:

Over three million men from across Europe and Asia, from South America to Africa, have been hastily dispatched to the Middle East to invade Israel. Since the breakdown of reliable air navigation systems a few days ago, the UN high command, now headed by Russia's Field Marshal Vassali Urmenkoff, has decided that the most direct method of replacing the government in Israel is by ground assault.

Although the UN military command would not answer questions, we have reliable information that the attack will come from the northern front first. The area is mountainous and contains ample vegetation for ground cover, as opposed to the Southern aspect, a barren desert which the fully navigational Israeli Air Force could easily and effectively defend.

The United States, under President Lewis – who was restored to power after a failed military coup five days ago – has warned that the United Nations Organization could be expelled from its headquarters in New York if the proposed attack on Israel is implemented.

American General Commits Suicide:

General Richard Boyle, head of the United States Air Force, who participated in the aborted coup which had President Abe Lewis held incommunicado for three days, hanged himself using bed-sheets in his solitary confinement cell in the Lewisburg Federal Penitentiary in Pennsylvania.

General George Sherman, former head of the Joint Chiefs of Staff, is also interred at Lewisburg, awaiting trial. It is expected that he will be convicted and sentenced to death for treason, unless President Lewis commutes his sentence. That possibility is thought to be remote.

American Jewish/Israeli Spy Pardoned by the President:

At a ceremony in the rose garden of the White House, Robert Benson — who happens to be the father of Israeli Prime Minister Daniel Benari — received the Congressional Medal of Honor for his covert role in uncovering and foiling the conspiracy against the President. Another recipient was the Mount Royal Gun Club of Baltimore, which ignited the massive protest rally at the Pentagon. Most noteworthy of all was the clemency decree handed down by President Lewis to the notorious spy Ira Rabinowitz, who had been languishing in jail for seventeen years.

Until now, all presidents, from Reagan to Clinton, have steadfastly refused to grant clemency to the man who spied for Israel, a close ally of the United States. In the past, even President Lewis had informed the Jewish groups lobbying for Rabinowitz's release that he would never do so. On this occasion, there was no public or private protest from the Justice Department or the intelligence community.

Rabinowitz, in tears, thanked the President and told reporters he would be leaving for Israel this evening on a special flight.

Chapter 47

"Gaylord, my friend, come quickly with me." Yossel led his roommate, upon his return from the post office, back downstairs and out of the hotel. Two streets away, he introduced the blond American to a local Arab in traditional garb. "Gaylord, meet Abu Hamza Ibn Fayet. He deals in used cars. We need a car to get to Jerusalem."

"A car?" asked the perplexed Christian. "I thought we were taking the bus to Mecca."

"Please. Is that the way you treat the Messiah? You told me, yourself, that Menachem is the Messiah. Shouldn't he go in style?"

"I suppose you're right. What's that got to do with me?"

"You're going to drive."

"Me? Don't you drive?"

"Only an automatic. You told me you're from out west. You drive a stick, don't you? "

"Sure, I drive a stick."

"Good. Ibn Fayet has a great 1983 Vauxhall. He wants just sixteen hundred dollars for it. It even has air."

"What's a Vauxhall?" asked Horrace.

"Some English car. Don't worry, it's good enough."

"So," asked Gaylord, "You're going to buy it?"

"Me?" The Brooklyn accent was suddenly more pronounced. "I'm a *Schnorrer*; I collect charity for a living. *You're* going to buy it!"

"What makes you think I've got that kind of money?"

"You have a VISA card, no?"

"A MasterCard."

"Same difference. Go to the bank." Yossel looked at his watch, "It closes in fifteen minutes. Cash out to your limit. We're going to need gas and oil, too."

Horrace shrugged his shoulders and followed Yossel and Ibn Fayet to the bank. This was not the time to think about petty things like credit card bills. He had met the Savior, face to face!

In the end, Gaylord Horrace dished out more than eighteen hundred dollars, including taxes and tag transfer, to become the new owner of a twenty-year-old car.

"Say, Yossel," Horrace asked, "don't you think 75,000 miles is pretty low for a car this old?"

"No, that number makes sense. All the cars around here get haircuts before they're sold."

At 6:35 a.m., Yossel and Gaylord drove over the dirt paths to Menachem's house. They found him waiting outside with only two small bundles of belongings. One he slung over his shoulder, the other he cherished against his bosom. Menachem got into the car without saying a word, and they were off.

Gaylord proved to be a very good driver. The road, although paved, was a miserable patchwork of blacktop, asphalt, concrete and crush-n-run. He never drove the car over forty-five, in order to conserve gas and not to tax an engine whose quality he couldn't be sure. At 9:15 a.m., they reached the frontier with Saudi Arabia.

Yossel planned to handle the border police himself. The policeman who peered in thought it an odd mix: a dark suited American, a blond American, and a Yemenite.

In broken English, the officer asked, "Where are you going?"

Yossel got out of the car and said, "To Mecca. We're going on the Haj."

The bewildered policeman asked, "Americans?"

"Why not? Aren't there Moslems throughout the world?"

"But you Americans destroyed the Temple Mosque. You should all be killed."

Yossel shook his head vigorously. "Hey, man, that was the Zionists. Don't you read the papers?"

"The Zionists *and* their American lackeys. Now get back in the car and hand over your passport. Who's the man in the back shading his head with his cloak?"

Before Yossel could answer, the policeman knocked on the back passenger window. With hand motions, Gaylord showed Menachem how to roll it down. The policeman bent down to look through the window. With some trepidation, the two in front watched as Menachem moved the *Talit* that covered his head and half his face for the policeman to see. Immediately, the officer's knees began to shake; he slowly backed off and almost inaudibly uttered, "You may go through."

Gaylord started the car. For ten minutes nobody said a word. Then Gaylord whispered to Yossel, "I told you we're taking the Lord in the back of this car. You didn't believe me."

"Gaylord, my friend, you might be on to something."

It was late afternoon by the time the car drove into the town of Qunfida. Menachem told Yossel that they would stay overnight there.

"But, Mori, the car has lights, and it is cooler at night. We can make it to Jidda in about five more hours."

"We stay," said Menachem, in a firm but polite tone. Stay they did. Finding another small, unassuming hotel — this one made the Taiz Inn look like the Sheraton — they booked a room, which constituted the entire sleeping quarters of the hotel. The place had ten beds, with two others being occupied at the time. At 4:00 a.m. Gaylord was awakened by the traffic out in the street. He looked out the opened window, and saw lines upon lines of buses. They were all old and painted a drab green, of the school-bus variety. It looked like an army convoy. Then he saw a man lean out of one of the lead bus's windows. He couldn't believe his eyes.

"Uncle!" he shouted, waving frantically. "Over here!"

The bus stopped, as did all the buses behind. New Israelites, hundreds of them, got off and made their way toward the hotel. The vast majority were forced to wait outside. Gaylord dressed hastily and went downstairs. He was breathless with excitement. "Uncle, I didn't think you believed me to *this* extent! How many people do you have with you?"

"Nine hundred. Most of the original tour. I had to convince another two thousand not to come until I confirmed your claim. These people wouldn't wait."

"I think it would be rude to wake Menachem now. They'd better wait for morning." As Gaylord and Luke Horrace were talking in the minuscule lobby, they heard a roar coming from outside. They ran out. People were bowing, and each one in his own way was shouting, "Praise the Lord," "The Lord has come." Luke Horrace looked up. There, at the window, was Yossel looking out, trying to quiet the crowd.

"Is that the Lord Jesus, of whom you spoke? He looks a little like him from the popular pictures."

Gaylord began to laugh. "Uncle, just tell the people to wait for morning. They shouldn't be making such a commotion at this hour."

At 6:30 a.m., after Menachem and Yossel had said their morning prayers in the room, black boxes affixed to their foreheads and left arms and prayer shawls draped from their shoulders, they joined Gaylord and emerged into the street. Suddenly a sea of humanity descended from the buses and surrounded the trio. Yossel said, "Please, please, go back to your buses. What on earth do you want?" He was stunned when one of the men said, with a slight Western drawl, "We've come to greet the Lord. Are you the Lord our Savior?"

Yossel turned to Gaylord and demanded, "What's going on? You know any of these people?"

"I know them all. They're from my church in Nampa."

"You have something to do with their coming here?"

"Everything to do with it. Well, actually, I only called my Uncle Luke. He told the others. Do you think we could arrange for them to greet the Lord? Just to say hello?"

Without waiting for an answer, Gaylord turned to the crowd with upraised arms, asking for their attention. "Friends, friends, quiet down. That's no way to greet the Lord! Now let me introduce you all." Gaylord turned to Menachem, who didn't understand a word of English. Assuming that Yossel would translate, he said, "The folks would like to greet your honor. Maybe even escort you on the journey."

After Yossel, in a highly skeptical tone, had translated the first request, Menachem protested gently, "I don't understand what's going on. These seem to be nice people — gentiles, that I can see. But very decent people. Why would they want to meet a simple Jew like me?"

The people formed a line and each one shook his hand. He greeted them all simply, warmly and without the slightest pretension. Very few of the people were impressed. He seemed to be a nice, gentle fellow who dressed as if he came out of biblical times. But that was all.

Luke Horrace pulled Gaylord to the side. "Gaylord, that old man is the Lord? What a fool I've been, bringing all these people here like this!"

"What do mean, uncle? Didn't you look into his eyes? The eyes tell everything."

"So he has nice black eyes. They match his swarthy skin. What is he, some old Arab? He can't even speak a word of English, and you expect me to believe he is the Lord and Savior?"

"Uncle, where does it say the Lord will speak English? Can you show me in the Bible where it states that Jesus was a fair-complexioned, blue-eyed blond? The Bible states that the Lord was born a Jew. I told you before you came, this man Menachem is a Jew."

"And I told you the Jews lost grace two thousand years ago. You know they'll only be saved when they accept Jesus Christ as Lord and Messiah. We are the legacy now of the Children of Israel."

"Uncle, that's what you say. No one knows exactly how to interpret these things. Maybe the Jews just use different words, but have the same general idea about the Messiah. I tell you that man is holy — more than holy." He shrugged. "You want to go back to Idaho and take all these people along? Go ahead; I'm staying with Menachem and my new friend, Yossel Berger, who is also a Jew, but from New York."

As they were arguing, they noticed that the crowd, which had gathered around Menachem and Yossel, had suddenly become dead still. Luke and Gaylord looked around to see what was going on. Matthew Jonas had approached Menachem with his twelve-year-old son, Bartholomew, who had been born with Down's Syndrome.

In English, the tears streaming down his face, Jonas cried, "My son, my only son, Bart was born retarded. But he's the nicest boy you'd ever want to meet. His mom and I love him dearly. We cry every day, because he can't even talk. We know he understands a lot, and returns our love in many ways. Please Lord, is there anything you can do for him?"

As he was talking, Matt Jonas was looking straight into Menachem Shabazi's eyes. By the end of the plea, he began to see what Gaylord had described to his uncle over the phone. It was something that Luke Horrace still didn't perceive. Jonas fell to his knees even before he had finished speaking. Menachem gestured that he was not pleased to see the man on his knees before him. Seeing he wasn't communicating, Menachem, too, fell in a squat opposite Jonas and helped the sobbing man to rise. He was still grasping the man's arms when the retarded boy walked toward Menachem, staring at him. Yossel was about to explain everything, but the sage waved him off. "I understand the language of the heart."

Menachem Shabazi extended his hands beckoning the boy to come closer. The boy came forward and put his left hand on the sage's face. Menachem stooped slightly to kiss the boy on the forehead. Then he whispered something into his ear. A smile spread over Bart's mongoloid features. Still beaming, he turned to his father and said, imperfectly but discernibly, "Fada, Menahem my friend."

Matt Jonas fell to the ground. He grabbed at the bottom edge of Menachem's long robe and showered kisses on it, pausing only long enough to yell, "The Lord has come, the Lord has come!" Everyone standing around fell to their knees and began repeating in unison, "Praised be the Lord!"

Menachem became frightened. In a whisper, he looked to Yossel for an explanation. He'd had no idea that the boy had never uttered a word in his life.

"Yosef, my friend, why are these people falling to the ground? I just told the boy that I am his friend and all of a sudden these people go crazy.... Come, we must continue our journey, and let these people continue on to wherever they were going."

Yossel didn't bother explaining. Menachem, he felt, would figure it out soon enough. But as the car got back on the main road heading North, nineteen buses were now following behind. Matt Jonas and Luke Horrace, along with thirty-five other men, lined up at the post office to place calls back to the States.

"It's true, it's true!" Elder Horrace shouted into the phone to his superior in the church hierarchy. "We have met the Lord. He's not a Christian; he's a little black-eyed Jew. But there's no doubt — he is Jesus Christ incarnate!"

As the Vauxhall traveled down the dry, hot road along the Red Sea, Menachem asked Yossel to act as interpreter as he spoke to Gaylord.

"Gaylord, my friend, why were all those people so thankful that I spoke to the boy? He has a most precious soul."

"Lord Master, the boy had never uttered a word in his life until you healed him."

"I healed him? Perhaps it was not his purpose on this earth to speak. According to our great sages, this strange-looking child has a special, pure and sanctified soul, which must merely return to breathe the air of this world. Don't any of your wise men understand that?"

Gaylord hesitated, then said sorrowfully, "Lord Master, the wise men in my land have devised a test that can detect if a baby in its mother's womb suffers from Down's Syndrome — so that the embryo can be aborted before it is born."

Menachem looked at Gaylord aghast, then broke down and cried.

Chapter 48

The convoy arrived in Jidda at four in the afternoon. Word got out quickly, and the twenty-two-year-old mayor, Prince Feisel Bin Farheem, nephew of King Khalid, came out with his police entourage to meet the group. After speaking with a few of the Americans, he expressed a desire to meet their Lord. He shook hands with the old Yemenite and spoke with him in Arabic in front of everyone present. "So you are the Lord?" he said mockingly. "Do you come in the name of Moses, Jesus or Mohammed?"

The smile which was almost a fixture of Menachem Shabazi's face turned grim. "Sir, I don't know what you're talking about. I'm no Lord. I'm a simple man who prays to the Almighty three times a day."

"Then why are all these people following you?"

"Who said they're following me?"

"They did!"

"What? I thought they are just headed in the same direction, perhaps with the same destination."

"And where might that be?" asked the insolent prince.

"I'd rather not say." The smile was back. "It's been nice to meet you. I must be on my way. I'm just one of three in my party, I think I might be holding them up."

The prince raised his open hand and began to direct a forceful slap at Menachem's face. But contact was never made. Menachem, who had half-turned toward the car, made a barely perceptible defensive motion with his hand, and continued walking toward the waiting vehicle. The prince was very embarrassed. Not only had his hand stopped short of slapping the old Jew who had refused to tell him where he was heading, but Bin Farheem found that he couldn't move his hand at all. It was paralyzed at the spot where it had been stopped.

He thought at first that it had just gone numb, then discovered that he couldn't move it even by tugging at it with his left hand. Suddenly, he became terror-stricken. The hundreds gathered around had already begun to smirk, thinking he was putting on an act of buffoonery. His chief of staff ran up to him. "Master, what happened? Why are you making these ridiculous gestures?"

"The Jew, that man these Americans call Lord, he has cast a spell on my hand!"

The officer pulled his gun from his holster and aimed it at Menachem, who was about to open the car door, thirty-five meters away. "Stop!" shrieked the prince. "Put that away, and go over to tell him I am sorry. I want to apologize."

"But Master, he's a filthy Jew. Only one week ago, his Zionist brothers murdered 12,000 pilgrims at Mecca — and you wish to beg his forgiveness?"

"Shut up, you fool! Just do as I say, and make sure you ask him humbly. You hear me?"

Cowed, the chief of staff mumbled, "Yes, sir."

Menachem got out of the car before the aide de camp came close. He didn't say anything, but ambled back to the prince. The prince now looked at him directly and began to tremble. Menachem began rubbing his hand and sensation slowly returned to it. The prince flung himself onto the ground, prostrating himself at Menachem's feet. Menachem bent and said to him, "May the Almighty grant you health and long life." Slowly, the prince stood up. Seeing Menachem's smile, he began smiling in response.

"If it please my Master, would he stay in my house as a guest for the evening?" offered the prince. Menachem told him he must discuss it with the others of his party. A conference then ensued between Shabazi, Berger and Horrace. They returned to Prince Feisel and accepted his offer.

The house was palatial. Yossel Berger explained to the prince's house crew that Menachem would eat only meat that he himself had slaughtered. That afternoon a sheep was brought to the courtyard and Menachem Shabazi slaughtered it with the knife that was among his meager possessions. He then carefully cut out the sciatic nerves from the hind legs, and the layer of fat surrounding the abdominal cavity. Yossel remained with the lamb throughout the entire process, his eyes never leaving the meat until the prince's kitchen help had completely cut it up. Throughout the trip, Berger had eaten no meat. Back in New York, he was strict about abstaining from any foods not made under Satmar kosher supervision. Now he was seated at the table with the King's nephew, side by side with the holiest man he had ever met, aside from the Grand Rabbi of Satmar who had passed on twenty-three years before.

When Yossel first came to Yemen and told Menachem that he was a devotee of the Grand Rabbi of Satmar, Menachem was elated. Heaping praises upon the Grand Rabbi, Menachem began quoting passages from his writings by heart. When Menachem cut off a juicy piece of meat from the broiled rack of lamb, Yossel passed it on to Gaylord, on his other side. Menachem handed him the next plastic plate of meat. Yossel was in a quandary. Could he step down from his standards and eat of a non-Satmar slaughtering? Menachem was smiling, his heart yearning for the others to enjoy the fruit of his labors. The decision was a very hard one for Yossel. His plastic fork moved slowly, with obvious reluctance. The prince and Gaylord were watching the strange scene with wonderment.

Finally, Menachem said something to Yossel in his Yemenite-accented Hebrew. Yossel, who had lost nine of his one hundred ten kilos since arriving in Yemen, brightened at once, then dug in with gusto.

A few minutes later, Gaylord leaned over to speak in a low voice to Yossel. "I saw that you were hesitant to eat the meat. I'll bet you weren't so sure about the sanitary conditions." When Yossel didn't answer at once, Gaylord pressed, "What

were you worried about? If it's good enough for the Lord, it's good enough for us."
He paused, but Yossel still said nothing. At last, exasperated, Gaylord asked, "Well,
what did he tell you to make you change your mind?"

Yossel made a dismissive motion with his fork. "Ah, you wouldn't understand.
And even if you did, you wouldn't believe me."

"Try me," said Gaylord.

"Mori Menachem told me that my Rabbi, Rabbi Joel of Satmar, who had died
over twenty years ago, once came to him in a dream and told him that he would
eat from the meat Menachem had prepared."

Gaylord's eyes widened. Though he did not catch the entire significance, he
grasped a little of the import of what he had just heard. Fervently, he murmured,
"I believe, I believe...."

After the meal, Menachem recited the entire grace after meals out loud. Those
present answered amen, except for Yossel, who also quietly said the entire prayer.
Then Menachem turned to the prince and said, "I thank you for your hospitality.
You are truly a son of Abraham our forefather. I will now answer the question you
asked this afternoon. We are headed to Jerusalem."

"I knew it, Master. I knew it then. But then I was an infidel; now I am a believer. Until the Master reproved me this afternoon, I was vexed by the measure of retribution the Israelis dealt my Moslem brethren. Still, it can't be denied that we started this round. But why did they have to hit us as we were begging for mercy on
the ground? Why destroy our shrines in Al-Quds (The Holy City)?"

"Honorable Prince," answered the sage with his mesmerizing gaze, "don't take
it so hard. It was the Will of the Almighty. For thirteen hundred years, the shrines
of Ishmael, servant of the One God, have maintained and protected the holiest
spot on the face of the earth from desolation and defilement by pagans. The demolition of those temporary edifices has now cleared the way for the Eternal House
of God. May it be the Will of the Almighty, soon in our day, that we merit the
rebuilding of the Temple in Jerusalem, a House built with fire, to which all mankind
will turn to offer their prayers and thanksgiving."

Bin Farheem digested Shabazi's simple but profound observation, smiled and
replied, "Master, you have allayed my anger."

The next day, the Vauxhall was traded in. At the prince's insistence, the trio
now rode in his own stretch Lincoln Town Car. Four passengers and a driver were
now on the way to Jerusalem — the Prince had joined the trio. When word leaked
out from the palace about Menachem Shabazi, the wondrous Jew, the original
nineteen busloads of New Israelites were joined by fifty more buses of Moslems. In
addition, by morning, fourteen charter planes from Boise arrived in Jidda, bringing another four thousand Messianic Christians to the scene. By the time the caravan of pilgrims stopped over in Umm Lajj for the night, the story was front-page
news in papers around the world.

It shared that privileged space with the other big news story of the day: the
impending UN attack on the brazen and cold-blooded government of Israel.

Chapter 49

July 10, 2002, 9:00 p.m. (GMT+2), The Prime Minister's Office, Jerusalem, live on Kol Israel TV:

"I make this announcement to you, the people of Israel, with trepidation in my heart. I would gladly tender my resignation if that would pacify the UN, but I am told that this is not the case. The course of events, with or without myself at the helm, seems unstoppable. Still, I am confident that — with the help of God — we will prevail.

"The unfortunate news I must report is that the UN has successfully mobilized a huge force in the north. It is believed to approach two hundred divisions from nations around the world. Our satellites have indicated that there are practically wall-to-wall mechanized fighting forces along the entire north bank of the Litani River, from the coast eastward to Marbudun. The northern line continues all the way to Mesmiya to the east and then forms an eastern line south to Dera'a near the Jordanian border. That represents one hundred kilometers of solid soldiery — perhaps 4,000,000 men in all. They are preparing to launch a greater invasion than D-day, almost sixty years ago. They also have hundreds of troop transports within one hundred sixty kilometers of our coastline.

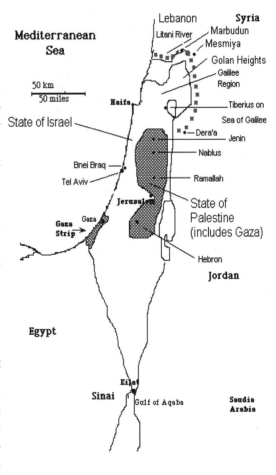

"Our military high command has assured me their seaborne attack force is under control. Due to the fact that their air navigational capacity has been severely impaired, their ships are relatively unprotected and vulnerable to our air force. I have given warning, through the good offices of President Lewis of the United States, that any hostile military ship that crosses a line within one hundred kilometers of any part of the State of Israel will be sunk. So far, they have kept back. We are still hoping the ground forces to the north will peacefully disengage.

"Now for some positive news. Our friends, King Abdullah in Jordan and...." the Prime Minister audibly swallowed hard, "Saddam Hussein in Iraq, along with the new democratic government of Iran, have troops lined at their borders to prevent any of the UN forces from entering their territory.

"And now for some better news. The Saudis, not trusting the west, yet bent on avenging us for the mysterious deaths last week that plagued their nation, had mobilized 200,000 men and much of their armor to the south of Aqaba. But just an hour ago, I received a satellite report that they were ninety-percent disengaged. An unconfirmed report has it that the governor of the Hijaz district, under orders from Prince Bin Farheem, mayor of Jidda, has called for total disengagement of the northwest corridor along the Red Sea.

"Now — the most amazing news! It has been confirmed that an international force, growing every minute, is on its way north along the Red Sea highway heading toward Eilat. As of a half-hour ago, the road was clogged with buses, cars, tenders, donkeys and camels carrying some 250,000 people. The line extends forty miles.... Just a minute, I've been handed a note. It's a fax from World Lubavitch headquarters, 770 Eastern Parkway in Brooklyn New York..

Have just chartered four-hundred planes. Request special permission to land at Eilat/Aqaba shared airfield.

Rabbi Y. Shementov

"If you're listening in New York, this is the Prime Minister. Permission granted, but please, no more.

"Now what is this hubbub in Saudi Arabia all about? I'm sure you've read the news reports and listened to the talk shows with all the talk of Messiah. This is still completely unconfirmed. The center of attention in this caravan of, I suppose, the faithful, is Rabbi Menachem Shabazi of Taiz, Yemen, who started out three days ago from his native land. I have asked Rabbi Chaim, our Chief Rabbi, about him. Rabbi Chaim only said, in these words, 'Rabbi Menachem is certainly a holy Jew.' There are also unconfirmed reports that Rabbi Menachem is performing miracles for the following. Rabbi Chaim has admonished all those who would jump to conclusions at this time. He said, 'Miracles by themselves mean nothing. The only true test of the Redeemer of Israel is if he stands up to Amalek and the sons of Esau and defeats them.' I hope it won't come to that with the hostile forces to the north. But no one can say for sure how this will play itself out.

"People of Israel, listen carefully. Here are my instructions. I want the entire Galilee evacuated except for our military forces. This mass exodus must begin as soon as I finish this message to the nation. With so many of the enemy poised to invade, a huge area to the north will most certainly become a battleground. We can always rebuild the structures. There's no need for civilians to be in the middle of this. No doubt, the enemy will attempt to break through our northern lines to enter the State of Palestine, which will welcome him with open arms. Thus, we must expect our enemy to make it to the outskirts of Jerusalem. As I speak, our troops are mobilizing around the city from the north, the south and the east. I ask all Jerusalemites to open their hearts and their houses to their brethren of the Galilee as this saga unfolds. With God's help, all will be able to return home safely."

July 10, 2002, UN Middle East High Command, Sidon, Lebanon:

"Paging Marshal Vassali Urmenkoff, please take line ten."

"Urmenkoff speaking."

"Vassali, this is Roland Duncan of Her Majesty's Royal Tank Division."

"Yes, General Duncan."

"I'm having problems with some of my men."

"What kind of problems?"

"They're scared."

"All war is frightful. How could it be otherwise?"

"No, General. This is different. They claim to be afraid of God. Of attacking His people."

"That is rubbish, Duncan. Offer a quick firing squad to anyone with those kinds of thoughts. They have one obligation — to follow orders from the UN High Command. When this is over, the entire world will be ready for a One-World government. Every person alive will realize that this is the only possible just and equitable political system."

Slowly, General Duncan said, "Your words may prove true, Marshal Urmenkoff. But the seat of that government may not be in Geneva. It may very well be in Jerusalem!"

"Look here Duncan," Urmenkoff rejoined sharply. "If you also speak rubbish, I'll send you back to London. Now go take care of your troops."

Duncan changed the subject. "What about the convoy heading up from Arabia?"

"Lunatics. Lunatics all, there is no lack of those in the world. They mean nothing."

"What about their leader, the Yemenite?"

"Six grams of lead from my Tokerev will take care of him. He's a nothing. A cult leader, like the American, Jim Jones, twenty-five years ago. It does amaze me how many suckers are taken in by these kinds of superstitions. In one way, it was the greatest tragedy when communism fell twelve years ago in my homeland. At least we were well on the way to eliminating the vagaries of religion and superstition. Now we've regressed a hundred years, practically back to the Dark Ages." The musing tone was replaced by a curt and absolute order. "Take care of your men, General. That's an order!"

"Yes sir!" Under his breath, Duncan amended that to, "I'll try my best, anyway...."

Chapter 50

July 11, 2002, 10:00 a.m. (GMT+2), The Prime Minister's Office, Jerusalem, live on Kol Israel TV:

"I am begging the entire nation not to go to Eilat. The entire highway for two hundred kilometers is completely jammed. All hotels and private homes are bursting at the seams. As of last night, we have twelve merchant ships in the Red Sea following the travelers, to supply food. The logistics of sustaining a group of this size are already overwhelming; it will be impossible for the stores and restaurants to service the 1.4 million people expected to be in Eilat by tonight.

"I have some more good news to report. Saudi Arabia has officially withdrawn its support of UN Resolution 777 and will not allow UN forces on its soil or airspace. The southern front can be considered safe from hostile forces. On behalf of the State of Israel, I thank Prince Feisel Bin Fahreem for influencing his government to change their stand. The Saudis have also begun to shuttle food and supplies, via helicopter, to the mass of pilgrims heading our way.

"Of course, we have been carefully studying the movement of the UN forces in the north. We must thank God that, according to reliable reports, many of the soldiers are not anxious to engage in this battle. Our nation, though smaller in number, has the iron will to survive. The enemy, greater in number, is weak of heart. With the help of God, we will prevail.

"I expect an attack very shortly. The enemy knows that, beyond a brief and limited time, their window of opportunity will evaporate.

"Just a minute. Stay tuned.... I have just received an E-mail from the President of the United States.

"It reads, 'I thought it prudent to inform you of a demand that has been forwarded by the United States to the Secretary General of the United Nations. We reiterate: be informed that if your multinational force attacks Israel, the United States will immediately banish the United Nations Headquarters from United States sovereign territory. No other warnings or negotiations will be considered.'"

July 11, 2002, UN Middle East High Command, Sidon, Lebanon:

"Marshal Urmenkoff," Roland Duncan said, smiling, "I've just received official notice from 10 Downing Street. All British forces are to return to their bases."

Urmenkoff's face, always on the crimson side, turned nearly purple with rage. "You cowards. You damnable cowards! Good riddance to you. We don't need any weak-hearted mice in this battle. We need men who are prepared to destroy this menace once and for all."

"We'll see which menace will be destroyed." Duncan said softly.

"Go to hell, Duncan!"

"I wouldn't have imagined that a person like you believed in hell." With that, Duncan turned on his heel and departed.

July 12, 2002, 3:00 p.m. (GMT+2), Eilat, Israel, live on Arutz (channel) 7:

"Friends," the reporter shouted into the microphone, trying desperately to make himself heard above the din. "In just two minutes, we will be granted an interview with the man who is the focus of all the attention. I might say, the focus of world attention. I must thank Rabbi Shabazi's traveling secretary, Rabbi Yosef Berger of New York, for making the arrangements for this interview. We understand the rabbi will be spending Shabbat right here in Eilat, before journeying on toward Jerusalem on Sunday." The crowd, already at the boiling point, rose to a fever pitch. Excitedly, the reporter screamed into his remote microphone, "Here comes the secretary! This is incredible — absolutely incredible!"

Yossel Berger fought his way to the reporter's side. Like Berger himself, the reporter was bearded and wore ritual fringes hanging below his shirt.

"Are you Haggai Segan?"

"Yes, I am. Can we begin?"

Segan was led into the lobby of the Sheraton hotel, past the police barricades. He was instructed to sit on the plush carpeted floor, where some fifty or sixty people were already seated in a circle. Menachem Shabazi was there too, his head draped in a *Talit*. Clutched to his bosom was the small Torah scroll he had written himself and brought along from Yemen. He turned toward the Orthodox reporter and smiled.

Segan shrank back. The radiance from Shabazi's face and eyes took a minute to get used to. Shabazi extended his hand and spoke in his Yemenite-accented Hebrew, which posed no problem at all for the Israeli reporter.

HS: Rabbi Shabazi, first I would like to thank you on behalf of the station and all the listeners for granting this interview. I understand from my station engineer that, with all the taps and hookups, the number of listeners to this live conversation may number close to one billion.

MS: Haggai, friend, first let me say that I am flattered by all the attention. But I am not a rabbi. If people want to call me rabbi, I don't have the strength to argue. I am just a simple Jew. Unusual events are taking place in the world. In the few years the Almighty has granted me to study His Torah, I have seen signs that indicate there is a great possibility that those events offer us, God's Nation, and even righteous gentiles who wish to join us, the opportunity to publicly sanctify God's Name. Have you met my friend, Gaylord Horrace? Gaylord, come closer!

Yossel Berger called out in English. Gaylord couldn't believe that he was being summoned to appear with Menachem Shabazi on worldwide television and radio. Menachem spoke to Gaylord, with Berger translating.

MS: Gaylord my friend, Haggai Segan has been so kind to ask to talk to me. Perhaps you have something you would like to say?

The TV cameras zoomed in on the tall American, whose tongue was practically paralyzed. He managed a wave, then quickly receded.

MS (with patent and genuine humility): I hope someone will explain to me what has happened here. For sixty-four or sixty-five years, I have lived a simple life, as my ancestors before me had done for twenty-five hundred years. Now hundreds of people seem to be following my journey to Jerusalem. Haggai, my friend, do you know the explanation?
HS: I think so, Honorable Rabbi.
MS: Please, please, just call me Menachem.
HS: The people recognize you as the Messiah. They would like to hear your confirmation.
MS: I am honored. But I am sure there are rabbis in the Holy Land who are more worthy than I to lead our people to redemption.
HS: Then you don't deny that you are the Messiah?
MS: What is the Messiah? He is a man like other men. He is imbued with the spirit of the Torah, and infused with the selfless dedication to lead his flock by the Word of God, like King David, his forebear. Anyone could be the Messiah. If the people say Rabbi So-and-So should be the Messiah and the people are totally sincere in heeding the rabbi's decisions, then he is the Messiah. There is no magic, nothing mystical about the matter.
Rabbi Akiva thought that Bar Kochba was the Messiah. Bar Kochba was a great Torah Scholar, a strong man and a mighty military leader. Accept his authority, and you have a Messiah! Let me tell you the opinion of a simple Jew. The coming of the Messiah is not dependent so much on some mystical character emerging and performing miracles. That's for grandmother tales and small children. In the time of Samuel the Prophet, the people clamored for a king. Samuel, through prophetic vision, found that Saul, son of Kish, possessed all the qualities needed in a king, and anointed him the Messiah. Even King David referred to Saul as Messiah. The people really have to want a king, to give him respect and authority, and to be dedicated to observing the entire Torah, down to the most minute detail. When the people will learn to love God and their fellow man, the divine aura that will flow forth from them will imbue the individual of their choosing. Then his energy of spirit will be magnified and we will have the Messiah; we will create the Messiah. It's a very simple formula.
HS: If the people want Your Honor to be that king, will he accept?
MS: I told you before, I am sure there are great rabbis and deans of Yeshivoth who are much more qualified than myself. Let the people decide.
HS: Which people should decide, Master?
MS: Menachem, just plain Menachem. I am no master. It's just my opinion, but the decision must begin with the true masters of the Torah, the recognized great

rabbis, deans of the Yeshivoth, and private Torah scholars. They must convene and choose the most worthy candidate to be king. After they agree, then the devout communal leaders must meet and accept the candidate. After that is done, then the masses of pious heads of households must agree. Then the candidate who is selected must accept, be anointed — and we will have our Messiah.

Unfortunately, in our history from time to time there have arisen false Messiahs. Many of them were indeed great scholars and devout individuals. But they did not follow the pattern that I described. They hastily accepted the role after acceptance by the most ignorant people first. Or they declared their position without proper authorization. Since the people themselves were spiritually unprepared to empower a true Messiah, it was inevitable that their chosen one would be an impostor. Much suffering, for many generations, came from those false messiahs. If we stand at the gateway to the era of the Messiah, this time it must be done right.

HS: Menachem, sir, are you saying that the rabbis should convene now?

MS: No, it is too close to Shabbat. Better they should convene on Sunday.

The world was amazed. The saint who in only a few days had attracted millions of followers, who until this moment hadn't spoken or given any instructions, was now advocating a convocation of rabbis to select a Messiah.

HS: Are you saying that the rabbis should form some kind of court?

MS: If they want. Who am I to tell them what to do? But I think God is waiting. We have enough men imbued with the knowledge and spirit of Torah that I think they can find seventy-one colleagues to meet together.

HS: Seventy-one…. Is His Honor suggesting that the Sanhedrin be restored?

MS: Why not? Did God decree it should never be restored? Now is a good time, I hope.

Listeners worldwide, but especially in Israel, were stunned. The Sanhedrin, the ancient equivalent of the modern Supreme Court, was the august rabbinical body that had made authoritative decisions regarding Jewish Law until shortly after the destruction of the Holy Temple in Jerusalem.

HS: What does His Honor say about the UN force about to attack our nation?

Menachem suddenly stood up on his feet. The anger that gathered on his face caused those around him to melt in fright. He raised his fist.

MS: You wicked ones — come! Menachem has no fear of you. I fear only the Lord of Hosts. Don't you touch my anointed ones! Come and stand up to me.

The simul-translation went out on stations throughout the world, even to the UN troops camped on the Litani River. Within minutes of Menachem Shabazi raising his fist, Field Marshal Urmenkoff received a call from the commanders of three of the four German divisions; they were packing up. The phone rang again as soon as it was hung up, two French divisions were going home.

Menachem's entourage, now numbering close to two million in encampments surrounding Eilat and Aqaba, and another two million packing the road toward Eilat, went into a frenzy at hearing his fiery words. When Channel-7 News Central interrupted five minutes later with a bulletin announcing the German and French disengagement, the roar of the crowd was all that could be heard over the airwaves. It was an elemental sound, filled with awesome grandeur and unimaginable power, like a primal bellow torn out of the earth's belly, or ripped from the fabric of time itself. For ten minutes it continued unabated. Then, with some minimal semblance of order restored, the interview resumed.

HS: The Sabbath will soon be upon us. Do you have any message to send to all the listeners?

MS: To all my fellow Jews. We are all guilty of sin; no man is perfect. Let us all observe this Shabbat and the next, and hopefully, by our own actions, we will merit God's Divine Protection from the massive evil which seeks our imminent destruction.

HS: But what if the enemy attacks?

MS: Defending our people and our nation is not a desecration of the Shabbat. In fact, it is the greatest mitzvah.

HS: Thank you Menachem — and Shabbat Shalom.

Chapter 51

The State of Israel was in a tizzy. On the one hand, preparations for war continued unabated. On the other hand, hundreds of thousands of secular Israelis, entire families, were banging on the doors of their religious neighbors, begging for instructions on how to observe the Sabbath.

A civil war spontaneously broke out in the State of Palestine. Most of the cells of Islamic Jihad, Hizbulla, and Hamas took up arms, declaring that they would not allow UN forces to cross their territory. The official Palestinian government, now also in turmoil, was still preparing to welcome the UN troops. All funds from Iran, Iraq, Saudi Arabia, and Omar Rastafani in Afghanistan were cut off to the terrorists. But those terrorists themselves, being for the most part devout Moslems, were fearful of crossing swords with a man who quite possibly was the Redeemer. The automatic weapons, which the Palestinian Authority had distributed so capriciously in violation of Oslo, now came back to haunt them. In addition to the fundamentalist terrorist groups, thousands of non-affiliated Palestinians, disgusted by the massive corruption in their government, joined the battle against it. Skirmishes and battles raged on every side, turning the Palestinian political scene into a giant demolition derby. All sides had factions pro and con; all control, rhyme, or reason seemed to have disappeared from Samaria and Gaza. In three days, at the height of the conflict's intensity, more than 100,000 Palestinians were killed by their own brothers and neighbors.

On the fourth day, the gunfire began to wane, as the billion rounds of automatic rifle ammunition — stowed away for years to dispatch the Zionists — began to run out. No nation, nor even the UN, dared intervene. Like a huge forest fire, the consensus seemed to be that, sooner or later, the flames would burn themselves out. In Hebron, the fighting was so vicious that most of the Arabs evacuated their families. The Jewish enclave remained safely ensconced behind its walled section. Government troops and some Hamas fighters tried to enter the Jewish neighborhood, but were brought down by gunfire from both directions.

The most important outcome of the chaos in Palestine, as far as Israel was concerned, was that it forced the UN force to postpone its attack. With each passing day, the force dwindled further. As of Tuesday, July 16, 2002, only one million men of the original four million remained ready to invade. By this time, Menachem, who seemed to have gained the three million that the UN lost, stood at the outskirts of Jerusalem. Still riding in Prince Bin Farheem's white limousine, he was met by Prime Minister Daniel Benari, who greeted him warmly.

"Rabbi Menachem, our nation is at the brink of a great war. As Prime Minister, I must lead them into battle. I ask for your blessing."

Shabazi did not allow him to continue. His demeanor, utterly gracious during the introductions and greetings, suddenly switched to anger. The simple Yemenite told the prime minister, point-blank, "You want a blessing? If you trust my opinion, here is what I will tell you. Yesterday, seventy-one rabbis — with the approval of a vast majority of rabbis and devout citizens in our land — were selected as our nation's high court. They will carry out justice. The sins of this State's past leaders must be atoned for. Let the seventy-one rabbis judge them. Regardless of the outcome, the judgment alone will atone." Gravely, Menachem inclined his head. "Then, Mr. Benari, you will have your blessing."

The Prime Minister was puzzled. "I don't understand. On many of the radio talk shows over the past few days, the main topic was the renewal of the Sanhedrin. Many scholars objected and said it couldn't be done, because the Temple has not been rebuilt."

Shabazi looked at Benari and smiled. "Did I ever say the rabbis formed the Sanhedrin? They are just a court of our greatest rabbis, that's all."

"Then why did you declare last week there should be seventy-one?" Benari persisted.

"If the Torah numbered the leading sages at seventy, there must be a reason. Besides, hopefully the Temple will soon be rebuilt, and then this court may truly become a Sanhedrin."

"So you mean, right now they have no power. It's only in preparation for the future?"

"No, Mr. Prime Minister. I believe they have power right now. We need them to judge the guilty among our people, so that we will merit the rebuilding of the Temple. How can we wait for the Synod to convene, if we lack the merit? Isn't that simple?"

"I suppose so." The Prime Minister, like so many others, was struggling to assimilate so much change in so short a time. Respectfully, he said, "Now please Master, tell me which cases should be brought before them. I will see what I can do about it."

"'One who steals a man and sells him, and he is found in his hand, shall surely be put to death. A soul for a soul,'" Menachem quoted.

"Your Honor — we don't have a death penalty, except for war criminals. But we do punish kidnappers and murderers to the fullest extent of the law."

"No, Mr. Benari. You do not understand. *You* are the kidnappers!" Menachem hastened to qualify that bald statement, which had the Prime Minister gaping in shock. "I don't mean you, personally. I mean the demons who ruled the Jewish Agency when my Yemenite people were brought to this land fifty-three years ago. My own brother was one of those victims." To Benari's horror, Menachem began to weep. His shoulders shook and the tears flowed, as though his grief was as fresh as it had been half a century earlier.

"Rabbi Menachem, that was so long ago," the Prime Minster said in a tone calculated to soothe. "Those babies are probably grandparents by now. It's not as if they were murdered. Sure, the plan was misguided. But the Yemenites were so poor when they came; many of those children found themselves in a better situation. They had the opportunity to start new lives in a new country, without the burden of poverty and being one among families of eight or ten children."

Shabazi's face grew red with rage. When he glared directly into Daniel Benari's face, the Prime Minister became more ashamed than he had ever been in his life. He felt like crawling into a hole. "Perhaps they wouldn't have been so poor, had your degenerates from the Jewish Agency not stolen all their money!" the sage shouted through his tears.

Then, just as suddenly as Menachem had become enraged, he calmed down. "Mr. Benari, I just quoted you from the Torah: 'He shall surely be put to death.' Let the prosecutor do his job; the defender shall do his. The Synod of rabbis will decide the Law. Regardless of their decision, the act of justice alone will help atone for the crimes.

"Rabbi Meshulam has a list of most of the perpetrators who are still alive. Your government has sinned greatly by persecuting Rabbi Meshulam and falsely imprisoning him. You realize, of course, that he was jailed only in order to intimidate him and stop his cry for justice. Your job is to demand the arrest of those elderly criminals and to let the court decide their fate. This will be as great an atonement for the kidnappers as it will be for our nation."

All Benari could say was that he would get to it immediately.

Shabazi was not finished yet. "Innocent blood has been spilled — blood that must be avenged. We must invoke human justice to merit the favor of Divine Justice."

Benari, taken aback, said, "Is Your Honor referring to the murder of Yitzchak Rabin? We have jailed the assassin, but our laws don't allow us to execute him."

"Mr. Benari, do you have one of those little telephones I see most of the people carrying here?"

"Yes, of course." Startled by the curious request, the Prime Minister took a tiny Nokia from his breast pocket.

"Call the prison which houses my distant relative, Yigal Amir, and tell the warden to free him immediately."

Benari started to protest, then shrank back at the stern look he received from the little Yemenite sitting beside him. He tried to speak, but found himself literally at a loss for words.

"Go ahead, Mr. Benari, or I will have to ask you to leave me alone."

Amir was pardoned immediately and without reason. After his brief phone conversation with a dumbfounded prison warden, Benari replaced the Nokia in his pocket. He was sweating like a mule.

Menachem Shabazi visibly relaxed once this transaction was complete. "Mr. Benari," he said, "it is clear that this bothers you. But this was your first act in atoning for the injustices that have tainted our holy soil. Rabin, with his own hands, spilled some of that blood. It was crying out from the earth for forty-seven years. Now, at last, comes atonement."

Benari managed to regain enough of his gumption to carry on the semblance of a normal conversation. "It's well known that Rabin, along with Ben Gurion, participated in the murder of thirteen innocent Jews who were fleeing the burning *Altalena*. Yesterday, I met my grandfather for the first time, and he confirmed the story; he actually eye witnessed six of his friends from the ship being cut down by Ben Gurion at Kfar Vitkin. But — but Rabin's assassination had nothing to do with the *Altalena* incident. It had everything to do with Rabin's land-for-peace accord with the Palestinians."

"That," Menachem said serenely, "might have been *Amir's* reasoning. I am speaking about Divine Justice."

"Still," Benari persisted, "wasn't it wrong for Amir, as an individual, to take the law into his own hands — to serve as judge, jury, and executioner for an act which *he* perceived to be criminal?"

"Of course it was wrong. But let us be honest: from his perspective, there weren't any channels of justice available to adjudicate the criminals who maintained political dominion over the nation! At the time, there was only a very selective and corrupt 'justice'.... Besides," Menachem added, "Amir was used by others in fulfillment of their own political machinations. Those others are still walking the streets as free men. Seven years is long enough. He has served his time. But, as I mentioned, Mr. Benari, the reality of the assassination was the fulfillment of Divine Justice."

"Do you mean to say that Amir was merely a puppet and, therefore, not blameworthy?"

"I told you — blameworthy to an extent. Seven years worth."

Thoughts began to fill Benari's head; thoughts of the entire scenario that was now being acted out on the stage of the world. What was really going on? Who really is in control?

"Your Honor," he said sheepishly, "according to what you're saying, is it possible that the entire Arab campaign against Israel for the past fifty-four years is Divine punishment for the sins of the founders of this State, who abandoned God and observance of His Law?"

Shabazi broke into a smile, which answered the question more powerfully than words could. A sudden panic overtook Benari, his forehead breaking out in a fresh sweat.

"Our retaliation for the missile attack? *We* were to blame — *our* crimes brought the misery upon ourselves, and then *we* punished the puppet who was sent to give us the message?"

Menachem continued to smile. "You are beginning to understand Mr. Benari. I praise God for appointing you Prime Minister!"

"I was elected by the people, and by a good margin," Benari blurted.

"That's what you think. I thought you were beginning to understand. Perhaps I was a bit hasty in that judgment? In any case, let me explain one more thing to you, and we'll leave it at that. God does not always pick messengers to deliver punishment who are themselves completely free of blame. Just as Amir was blameworthy to an extent, the Arabs also needed a measure of 'rehabilitation' for the degeneracy of their culture. Who was it, if not the Arabs, who introduced the world to the tactic of urban terrorism? For fifty years they have waged their war of... *liberation,* in the bus stations, market places and schools, blowing up women and children and riddling them with lead. Who ever heard of brave warriors who dump a wheelchair-bound old man overboard from a ship at sea? What other people hail the act of detonating a bomb in a civilian airliner 10,000 meters above the ground as heroic? Hopefully, the dose of medicine they received two weeks ago will not only permanently dissuade them from acting as God's executioner, but also will help to heal the sickness manifest in their national soul.

"But as you see, my friend here, Prince Feisel Bin Farheem, as well as several other former Arab enemies, have come around since the attack. Perhaps our brother Ishmael is already on the way to recovery. We must now focus our attention on our other brother, Esau — and specifically his grandson, Amalek, whom medicine cannot cure."

Benari bowed his head in submission. As the silence stretched, he lifted it again, and curiously met the Yemenite's eye.

Menachem continued, "As I was saying, so much innocent blood has been spilled in this land that only with the intervention of the Almighty Himself can we ever expect a full atonement."

"I don't understand, Your Honor. Apart from a few politically-motivated killings, murder is not that common among our Jewish population."

"I'm not talking about the Jewish population as a whole. I'm talking about the leaders of this government who rejected the moral compass that has guided our people for over three thousand years. Leaders who, in their arrogance, committed *spiritual genocide* against the pure and innocent Yemenite and Oriental Jewish children. It was inevitable that this crime would bear bitter fruit: creating a generation of monsters who turned to apostasy, immorality, and even murder. Yes, we must pray for God's Mercy — but we must also do our part to ensure that earthly justice is carried out."

"Again, sir, I will do my best." Benari hesitated, then asked with ill-concealed eagerness, "If we can accomplish the justice you've spoken of, will we win an easy victory over our enemy?"

Menachem smiled, lifting his palms. "Mr. Benari, the Almighty has not yet seen fit to restore prophesy. I can't answer that question. Again, we must resolve to keep God's commandments and not worry about matters that are out of our hands." He paused thoughtfully. "However, if you wish, I might suggest a strategy for fighting the enemy. Thank God, in their efforts to sort out where they stand on this matter, our Palestinian friends have won us a few days reprieve. But that will not last forever."

Benari leaned forward. "Of course. I will take to heart whatever the Master says."

"There is no need for loss of life in this battle. That is," Menachem amended, "no need for our people to die."

"Is the Master serious? No Jew will die fighting the UN force?"

"Perhaps a few whose merits do not outweigh their sins…. But I anticipate, from the reports of the last few days, that most of our people have found, or are trying to find, their way back to God's Commandments."

"That is most certainly true," the Prime Minister said proudly. "And I, among them."

Twinkling, Menachem murmured, "I suspect you were not so bad even before this week. I can see that the woolen fringe sticking out from your garment is slightly yellowed with age."

Not for the first time since they had begun to talk, Benari was struck by the power of the Yemenite's perceptions. It was difficult, if not impossible to get anything past this man.

For the next hour, Menachem Shabazi lectured the amazed Prime Minister on the strategy to be used by the Israeli army to engage the enemy. The white limousine then drove him to the first neighborhood in the newer section of Jerusalem, where Menachem was welcomed by a host of rabbis and Torah scholars. There was an emotional reunion with his four sons and two daughters, who had departed Yemen many years before. They were all married. One son lived in the Har Nof neighborhood, where Menachem Shabazi stayed the night.

Chapter 52

Late the following afternoon, Daniel Benari came in his helicopter to pick up Menachem Shabazi and take him up to the Temple Mount for the service connected to the fast of the Ninth of Av. The chopper circled the barren Mount. All the rubble from the mosques had been cleared away, leaving a nearly-flat plateau covering some one hundred forty dunam. The police had cordoned off the area and it was completely clear. Below, throngs of people were making their way to the Western Wall plaza. The plaza filled quickly, and there were still hundreds of thousands trying to approach.

"Can you land over there?" Menachem asked the pilot, pointing. The pilot complied, carefully bringing down the helicopter in a clearing beside the Spring of Shiloah.

"Come, Daniel. Come, Yossel, quickly. We must immerse."

"But Master," Yossel protested, "it is now the week leading up to the Ninth of Av. How are we allowed to bathe?"

Menachem hesitated, then sighed. "Must I explain everything? If you must know, your Rabbi Joel of Satmar and Rabbi Israel Abuhatzera of Tifallal appeared to me in a dream and instructed me to immerse here, and you also; it is a mitzvah. We shall mark the Ninth of Av this one last time on the Temple Mount." He seemed distinctly uncomfortable about the need to openly describe these dreams, and the Heavenly favor they implied.

Without question, Yossel followed his master into the spring, as did the Prime Minister. The cool, pure waters were a great relief to Menachem and Yossel, who, had not bathed since the previous Friday, in Eilat.

The helicopter lifted off from the spring and returned to the Temple Mount, landing in the precise spot that Menachem indicated. After making the required rent in his cloak — a symbol of every Jew's grief over the destruction of the Temple — Menachem borrowed a roll of yellow police tape and walked out with it about three hundred meters. There he stopped, calling to Yossel to hold the roll while he himself unraveled the tape and set the end down at the stone wall, which faced the Mount of Olives.

"This is as far as we are permitted to go. Beyond this yellow line, we must wait until the Almighty grants us a higher state of purity." Seventy meters beyond the yellow tape, the smooth surface that characterized the rest of the area was interrupted by a huge, flat rock that jutted two meters above ground. A trickle of water, emerging from the rock, slowly wore a path toward the hillside east of the Temple Mount.

Benari asked sheepishly, "Did the Master know where to draw this line through spiritual emanations from the holier ground beyond?"

Menachem turned his warm smile on the Prime Minister. "Mr. Benari, I am just a man, like you. But I have been diligent in my studies. The Talmud, in the tractate Middoth, gives all the measurements of the Temple site; anyone can look it up. With the Arabs controlling the area for thirteen hundred years, it wasn't possible for a Jew to come up here and walk off the measurements. Now it has become a simple matter."

It was the Prime Minister's turn to smile. At Menachem's behest, he put in a call to the Minister of Religions. The Minister was to announce publicly that the Temple Mount plaza would be opened to all those who immersed themselves, and that Rabbi Shabazi had decreed it permissible to immerse for that purpose even on the eve of the Ninth of Av. By dusk, four hundred thousand people filled the Temple Mount up to the yellow line. No one dared cross that line. A three thousand watt speaker system was set up, with huge speakers extending sound not only within the limits of the Western Wall plaza and the Temple Mount plaza, but throughout the streets of the Old City.

One million candles lit the area, as that number of people and more sat on the ground to lament the destruction of the Temple beneath the very ground upon which many of them sat. Rabbi Menachem took out a scroll, written by his own hand, which contained the complete five chapters of Lamentations authored by the Prophet Jeremiah. He chanted the sadly melodious words in the traditional Yemenite tune, amplified electronically for all to hear. Thirty-five minutes later, a million people in tears continued to recite the traditional elegies for the tragedies that had befallen the Jewish Nation over the past two thousand years. Suddenly, Menachem Shabazi stood up and spoke into the microphone.

"My friends, I know that most of you are not in my view. But thousands here will testify as to what I am about to do."

From his bundle, Shabazi took a small, cubical, white stone. He held it up for all to see. Several TV cameras turned their powerful beams on the old sage. He did not protest.

"Here in my hand is a stone, about eight fingers long, four fingers wide, and four fingers high. It is perfectly formed, just like a brick. But I assure you this is no brick. It is a stone, and it has been in my family for nearly twenty-five hundred years, handed down from father to son. It was perfectly shaped, without a metal tool, from a remnant of King Solomon's Temple wall." He looked around at the sea of humanity. "If the people will allow me, I would like to find my way to the corner of this great, barren plaza."

The human sea split before Menachem as he walked toward a spot in the northeast side of the dirt plateau. A camera crew was allowed to follow him. He stopped near the edge of the slope facing the Absalom memorial. There he bent down and pushed the stone into the earth about three centimeters.

"I hereby dedicate this — the cornerstone of the Third Temple!" A deafening cheer welled up in the plaza above, the plaza below, and the city beyond. It was a full fifteen minutes before silence was restored.

"I declare this day a Holiday. But the day is not over. Until sunset tomorrow, let us remember all of our people who perished in the tragedies of our history. Let us remember those who were spiritually destroyed by many of the men and women who founded this State in the misguided belief that the God of Israel was no longer concerned with the holy mission of His sons.

"Let God, on this, the last Fast of the Ninth of Av in the history of the Jewish Nation, hear our plea: 'Return us, O Lord, to you, that we may repent. Renew our days, like those of yore.'"

Chapter 53

Friday, July 19, 2002, saw much activity throughout the Land of Israel. Some of it was military in nature, but the vast majority involved the observance of the second Sabbath since Menachem's arrival. In addition to purchasing and preparing provisions for the day of rest for the country's four million Jewish citizens, the needs of an additional three million Jews and two million non-Jews, who had arrived within the past ten days, had to be met. Hundreds of thousands of gentiles graciously accepted the task of standing guard over the roads and streets. They were prepared to remind any Jew who might forget, who might attempt to enter his car or take a smoke outside, that it was prohibited to do so on the Sabbath.

During the first Shabbat, the previous week, the hostility and animosity between neighbors, secular and religious, began to earnestly melt away. At Benari's election it had achieved a state of dormancy, but now it was actually disappearing. This Shabbat, the feeling of solidarity, of being a single united people, was manifest everywhere. Impossible under ordinary circumstances — there will always be those diehard extremists, who even at the gates of hell, refuse to budge from their positions — but then, these circumstances were anything but ordinary. Transportation is a two-way process. The planes that shuttled back and forth to bring millions of people to the Holy Land, also carried away close to one million. Four hundred thousand of these were non-Jews: one hundred thousand foreign workers, fearful of the impending invasion, and 300,000 Russians, most of whom had feigned a Jewish identity in order to escape the economic morass of Russia during the nineties. A full half-million Jews, resentful of the *religious coercion* of the lunatic nouveau-religious, which now comprised seventy-five percent of the population, decided to "switch rather than fight" and fled the country as well.

At 1:15 a.m., the silence of the night was crudely broken, when machine-gun fire and thousands of artillery rounds suddenly let loose from south central Lebanon in the direction of the Israeli border. For three hours there was no letup, as the UN forces worked to 'soften' Israeli positions before commencing the invasion.

Not a single round of return fire landed north of the Litani River. As the fire lit up the sky like day, two thousand pontoon bridges were hastily erected, spanning the river, and untold thousands of tanks and armored pieces began their journey south toward Jerusalem. By 5:00 a.m., more than five thousand tanks and armored vehicles stopped at the frontier, twenty-five kilometers south of the river. No resistance was met along the way.

"Gentlemen," said Field Marshal Urmenkoff to the generals of his staff, "The Israelis seem to be playing a very smart game with us. They have withdrawn under our noses. I understand the mentality of the Jew; he will not die for someone else's territory. But for his own, he will pull out all the stops to defend. Thus, I expect that the next twenty-five kilometers will not be as easy as these first."

Urmenkoff was wrong. The UN, dug in at the border, set off another monumental barrage of cannon fire, showering a line fifty kilometers wide and fifteen deep with deadly ordnance. But not one man was killed. For, as Marshal Urmenkoff found out by noon on Sunday the 21st of July, no one was to be found in the entire region. The UN troops, more thinly spread along the eastern Syrian side, had completely recaptured the Golan Heights and were now overlooking the Sea of Galilee.

"General Chang," said a Ukrainian lieutenant gazing upon the city of Tiberius, fifteen kilometers across the lake, "I can't see any sign of activity in the Israeli city yonder. It seems to be completely deserted. The communal farms surrounding the lake likewise show no sign of life."

Chang grabbed the binoculars from the scout, and looked for himself. "I don't understand it. Get word back to Urmenkoff. That's an order!"

"Yes, sir." The lieutenant scurried away to do as he was bid.

July 20, 2002, 11:00 a.m. (EDT) WINS NEWS RADIO 1010 AM, New York City:

Ten thousand city police, augmented by one thousand FBI agents, entered the UN Headquarters building on 1st Ave and 42nd Street at 10:45 this morning. Over intense protest by the Secretary General and several Security Council members, the President gave the corps of international diplomats three hours to remove their documents and equipment. Britain and France had already moved out on Thursday, when the general assembly voted to give final approval for the attack, which began last evening at 7:15 local time. The mayor has implored the citizens of New York not to stage protests in front of the UN. This would only impede the ability of the police to take control of the premises and to seal it off. The President has given all the UN missions, scattered over a wide area from Suffolk County in Long Island to Morristown, New Jersey, forty-eight hours to evacuate their premises. Local, state and federal police will seize the missions after that deadline. According to 1010 WINS news reporters on the scene, this is a very aggressive and serious police action taking place on the East Side.

July 21, 2002, 8:30 a.m. (GMT+2), Jerusalem, Israel:

"Dror Tzioni, you stand accused of kidnaping Yekutiel Tanami, son of Salim and Naomi Tanami, and selling him to Mr. and Mrs. Bernard Weismann," intoned Rabbi Shlomo Dekelbaum, bailiff for the Synod of seventy-one rabbis meeting for the first rabbinical court hearing.

The elderly defendant shook his head. "I don't remember too well. You have arrested me for events of long, long ago — over fifty years. I was young and idealistic in my Zionism then. I was only following orders." Tzioni was very nervous and began to tremble. "Why are you doing this to me? You're not a legitimate court of law. Let the High Court of the State of Israel try me!"

"Mr. Tzioni," snapped the bailiff, "We won't stand for any contemptuous remarks in this court. You will receive a fair trial in accordance with the Torah."

"I'm not interested in the Torah. If I hadn't been stopped at the airport, I would have been out of this crazy country," Tzioni sputtered indignantly.

"Mr. Tzioni, if you are found guilty, as accused, your crime is very severe. In numerous countries of the world, such as the United States, you would face the death penalty for kidnaping. The fact that you might have gotten away with your crime for fifty-three years is immaterial. Do you feel that an eighty-seven-year-old Nazi war criminal should automatically be reprieved, just because he wasn't caught until now?"

Tzioni looked around nervously, unable to articulate the obvious answer to the question.

"I call on Salim Tanami to testify," said the bailiff.

Over the next hour, three more witnesses corroborated Tanami's testimony. Dror Tzioni, then twenty-three years of age, had taken the seventeen-month toddler from Naomi Tanami against her will, claiming the child needed inoculations and a checkup. The mother pleaded for permission to accompany the child, but Tzioni insisted that the rules did not allow her to come along. The next witness was Tamir Weismann, a son adopted by Bernard and Hilda Weismann in 1953, and stepbrother to Yosef Weismann, who was born Yekutiel Tanami.

"I have here a file of paperwork which I found after my mother's death in 1993. It contains the adoption and related documents, which she kept concerning me and my brother Yosef, who died in the Yom Kippur war."

Mr. Weismann presented the file to the judges. One particular paper was most interesting. It was a handwritten note, signed, *Dror Tzioni*.

Memo To: Bernard Weismann, 12-9-49

The child I spoke of came here to Israel with Operation Magic Carpet. According to other immigrants who arrived at Lydda, this child's parents died during the arduous overland trek from Sana to Aden. I incurred numerous expenses in procuring the child and taking care of the necessary paperwork. If you want the boy, I will need threethousand Israeli pounds. There are other takers, so please get back to me within forty-eight hours if you are serious about this matter.

Dror Tzioni

At first, Tzioni denied writing the memo, but his signature was matched against twelve other samples from government files. It was clear he had indeed authored the memo. Tzioni, now fearful for his life, recanted and admitted his involvement in the affair. The next witnesses were Yehuda Basson and Tzvi Hammer, two former yeshiva students who had volunteered to work with the new immigrants. Examined separately by the court, both offered identical testimony.

"Yehuda and I were secretly notified by Mr. Tanami that his young son had been taken from his mother's arms by Tzioni. We knew Dror T. quite well: he'd had us arrested and expelled from the transit camp after we came there to teach the Yemenite youth Bible and Mishna. The P'eylim organization had sent us, and had told us that we had express permission from Youth Aliya Central to give the classes. But about two hours after we arrived and were permitted by the camp guard to enter, Tzioni, the chief youth director, rudely barged in on our class and told us to leave. After a short argument, we continued the class, only to be arrested for trespassing twenty minutes later. Yes, we knew Tzioni.... After receiving word that the child had been taken away, we immediately went to the Tel Hashomer Hospital, looking for the child. One of the nurses, who happened to be religious, told us that Tzioni had brought the child in for evaluation. She showed us the log, which already stated that the parents were "unknown," the child was a foundling. Later, we went back to the camp and confronted Tzioni over this matter. He became completely enraged when we warned him that he had better return the child and that we were onto his game. By the time we returned to Tel Hashomer the next day, the record of the child's admittance had been removed from the files."

Tamir Weismann was returned to the stand and testified that his brother had sported an unusual birthmark on his back, which exactly matched the one described by Salim Tanami. Fifteen more witnesses came and testified that Tzioni had committed the same crime with at least twelve other Yemenite babies. After three hours of deliberation —

"Dror Tzioni, you are found guilty of kidnaping and selling your victims for profit. The Torah prescribes the death penalty. The rabbinical court must decide whether it will be carried out, or a substitute punishment meted out."

No punishment was ever meted out. Seventy-six year old Dror Tzioni was found dead, hanging in his cell the following morning.

Chapter 54

By Tuesday, July 23, 2002, the entire Galilee, from Acre on the Mediterranean coast to Bet Shaan near the Jordanian border, was in UN hands. Not a single Jew had been killed or captured, for not a single one remained in the region. Although the UN force advanced cautiously, expecting a surprise from its Israeli foe at any time, none ever came. The Russians, Chinese, Cubans, Africans and a smattering of other various nationalities that made up the force, occupied the territory without resistance.

"Marshal Urmenkoff, what do you make of this tactic? Why have the Israelis retreated? Taken all of the their civilians, as well as their military, clean out of the region?"

The Marshal, frowning, shook his head in bafflement. "I've never experienced this tactic before. In Russia during the Napoleonic War and even in the Great Patriotic War (WWII), we Russians used a tactic that always proved victorious in the end. We would allow the enemy to besiege our cities as long as we could reasonably hold out."

"How long was that, Marshal?" interjected Chang.

"Until about half the population was still alive. Now, listen carefully. We would then evacuate the remaining population and the majority of the fighting force to the interior of the country and burn the cities to the ground. It was highly discouraging to our enemies to see that the long, hard-fought siege earned them no booty in the end. All of this was well-timed. Our enemies always started their offensives in late May, expecting an easy conquest before winter set in. We would hold them off until October; at that point they were sunk.

"But that tactic couldn't possibly apply in this theater. First, the Israelis have left their cities completely intact. Second, there is no environmental factor that would serve their interests in such a retreat. Third, in Russia, retreating to the interior meant, for all practical purposes, a virtually unlimited expanse. I would guess that all the Jews of the Galilee stand at this moment no more than one hundred fifty kilometers from their homes. They have nowhere else to go."

Chang asked, "So what do you think? They're not stupid. I would say, perhaps they intend to use Tactical Enhanced Radiation Weapons against us. That is why they left their structures intact and only removed their population. We see from the past few weeks how experienced they are in the use of those weapons."

"I've considered that, Chang. I don't think so. We also have ERWs at our disposal, but we are prohibited from using them unless attacked first. The Moslem coalition had no nuclear capability, only poison gas, which — given enough time to prepare — is easily defended against. No, Chang, the Israelis know they must defeat us quickly, almost instantaneously. We are too spread out for them to attack us with neutrons and their population, especially now, is too concentrated to survive a neutron bombardment in retaliation. They won't risk it." Once again, the Russian shook his ponderous head. "Now you see why I am baffled."

"You've seen what's going on in Jerusalem. Perhaps they expect their God to rain down fire to consume us."

"Not you too, Chang!" the Marshal snapped in exasperation. "You're supposed to be a loyal Communist."

"I was only joking."

"Chang, this is no time for jokes. Listen here, I want you to send one division on an exploratory invasion of Samaria. That's all we should need. You are not to engage the Palestinians, unless fired upon. We were granted permission by the government to cross the border and traverse their territory on our way toward Jerusalem, but we all know it may not be that simple. There are still many factions warring within Palestine, and the government may not be in control of all areas."

Indeed, heavy fighting had re-erupted in Nablus and Jenin, where Hizbulla and the Islamic Jihad were bountifully supplied with TOW missiles by some unknown source. By now, the random and unbridled shooting in every direction had largely ceased. Hamas officially aligned itself with the Palestinian government. It took until August 15, with two additional divisions of troops, for the UN and the Palestinians to gain a foothold in Samaria. The mountainous terrain provided perfect cover for the guerrillas, who popped off UN tanks like a turkey hunt. Before they made it to Nablus, each side had suffered over 50,000 casualties, the UN losing three hundred fifty tanks. In the meantime, the UN organization was nonfunctional for the three weeks it took to establish hasty new quarters in Geneva, Switzerland. The government of Switzerland didn't want them, nor did any other nation to which the Secretary General had appealed. Invitations came in from Zimbabwe and the Uzbek Republic, and were politely declined. Finally, after a week of wrangling, President Lewis convinced Switzerland to let the beleaguered UN in temporarily, until they could find a permanent home.

All UN resolutions and pleas calling upon Israel to negotiate were ignored by Prime Minister Benari, just as Menachem had instructed him. The Israeli ambassador to Bulgaria did, however, arrange a secret meeting with the Secretary General.

"Danny, this is Nimrod Eitan. Through the good offices of President Norcescu of Romania, I met privately with the Secretary General. He's ready to deal. One hundred ten nations have withdrawn or refused to send a contingent to fight us. He sees the UN falling apart at the seams. My advice is, let's do it. I can understand why you've held out this long. It has been to our great benefit — I'd never have believed it would turn out this way. But enough is enough; we'd better deal now."

Benari said thoughtfully, "Nimrod, I understand your position.... But I'm not sure if we can't get some more mileage out of this tactic. I'll get back to you. Just sit tight and don't make any more contacts on your own. You wait for instructions, you hear?"

"Yes, sir."

Six hours later, Eitan's secretary buzzed him. "A Mr. Gelbworth is here to see you."

"Ask him what he wants."

"Your Excellency," the secretary said, "I think you had better see him." Without waiting for confirmation, she led Gelbworth into the ambassador's plush office.

Standing in front of Nimrod Eitan was a man who wore a large, round, black hat, a long black coat, a long beard and dangling sidelocks. "What do you want?" Eitan barked, when he had conquered his first astonished reaction. The stranger handed him a letter. The scowl still on his face, Eitan ripped open the letter and read:

19-8-2002

Dear Mr. Eitan,

The man presenting this letter to you is Rabbi Zisha Gelbworth. He is your replacement as Israel's ambassador to Bulgaria. As you read this note, you are hereby terminated. I have stayed your diplomatic status for forty-eight hours, enough time for you to put your affairs in order and return to Israel (if you wish). Please brief Rabbi Gelbworth on any pending matters you were pursuing with the government of Bulgaria. Thank You.

Sincerely,
Daniel Benari, Prime Minister of Israel

Eitan lifted his eyes from the letter, and gaped at the black-clad figure before him. "Mr. Gelbworth, what's this all about? Why are you replacing me so suddenly?"

"I don't really have any idea," Gelbworth shrugged. "I thought your term must be up, or perhaps you wanted to pursue other matters."

"You mean, Benari didn't tell you what happened here this morning?"

"No, he just told me that I was to replace the present ambassador. I've never been in the diplomatic corps before, but Rabbi Menachem Shabazi told me that I must go."

"Weren't you a member of Parliament — from the Agudat Israel party?"

"Yes, that is true."

Eitan slumped back in his chair and motioned for Gelbworth to take the seat facing him on the other side of the desk. "I'm going to tell you exactly what happened. Perhaps you could explain to me why this draconian measure was taken. I called the PM this morning and I told him that I had, on my own initiative, made contact with the Secretary General of the UN, and that we can now negotiate...."

Gelbworth broke in, "Mr. Eitan, please. You need say no more. I have the complete picture now." He studied the man he was to replace. "Perhaps you are not fully aware of what has been happening in Israel over the past six weeks."

"Of course I know. You fanatics have gained control of the government."

"Fanatics, Mr. Eitan?" Gelbworth echoed softly.

"Yes, fanatics — and the Prime Minister has gone along with all the nonsense! Just as the Islamic Republic of Iran collapsed, the central office of fanaticism has taken up residence in Jerusalem. I suppose these wholesale executions have ushered in the messianic era?" Irritably, he clenched his fists. "This past month has been one long deja vu experience. I remember when Khomeini returned from exile and turned Iran upside down. Now the crazies — not just Jews, but even Christians and Moslems — are declaring this Shabazi the Messiah. I see him as the reincarnation of Khomeini."

"How many executions have there been? Mr. Eitan, let's be honest."

"According to the news, three. But I'm sure there are more to come."

"Mr. Eitan, you should really get up and offer me the chair you're sitting on."

Angrily, Nimrod Eitan got up. But Zisha Gelbworth smiled and waved him to sit down. "Please, I don't care about the chair, I'll have plenty of time to sit in it. You are laboring under a fundamental misunderstanding. Just calm down and let me explain. Do you admit that it was wrong to kidnap the Yemenite children?"

"Yes, I must admit, that was a sad chapter in our history. But the perpetrators were just a few rotten apples."

"No, Mr. Eitan, not just a few bad apples. You look to be about forty-five; you were not yet born at the time. I was a student in the Ponevez Rabbinical Academy in Bnei Braq. I visited those camps." Gelbworth leaned forward and looked sternly at Nimrod Eitan. "The secularists looked upon the materially primitive Yemenites as subhuman."

Eitan got up and roared, "That's a load of hogwash!"

"No, Mr. Eitan, it's perfectly true. However, they felt that the Orientals could be transformed into *menchen* — that is, Israeli humans — with the proper indoctrination. Prior to that *transformation*, they were fair game to be treated as subhuman. Well, Mr. Eitan, the secularists were wrong. They were wrong how they treated the Oriental Jews, whose religiosity they ravaged, and they were wrong in their own abandonment and disdain for our tradition. A tradition, which has carried us thirty-three hundred years, down the ages, as a nation. Since the Supreme Rabbinical Court has been established, they have tried over nine thousand cases. As you mentioned, three people were executed. One was a police captain who beat a seventy-year old Hasid to death during a raid on a synagogue on the Holy Sabbath."

"I remember that case. Wasn't that over twenty years ago?"

"It was in 1986," replied Gelbworth, "the Maariv newspaper reported that the police had raided the place after youths who were stoning cars had taken refuge inside. That's a media distortion. The truth, Mr. Eitan, was that a convoy of provocateurs had just driven through Meah Shearim. The police were on hand, hiding in the wings, when seventeen cars driven by radical, anti-religeous Meretz people came through, honking their horns on Shabbos to bait the Chareidim. The group of four stone-throwing, fifteen-year-old boys was too fleet-footed for the police, even though they were set up. Our rabbis had warned the entire community that stone throwing must stop. But, as you've just pointed out, there will always be a few bad apples, wild youths who don't listen. In any case, the police lost the boys and didn't know exactly where they were. Frustrated that their quarry had gotten away, they entered a local *Shul*, enraged and filled with vengeance. Old Shmuel Biderman stood up in the middle of the evening service and told them that no youths had run into the premises. Captain Jimmy Naboni — himself of Yemenite origin, a spiritual victim of the Jewish Agency — mercilessly clubbed the old man twelve times on the head. The poor man died later the next day, on the holy Shabbos, in Misgav Ladach Hospital." He paused. "What do you say now, Mr. Eitan?"

Eitan bowed his head and acknowledged, "That was shameful. But police are trained to be aggressive. They wouldn't be effective if they always acted like pussy-cats. Sometimes it can get out of control."

"Don't fool yourself, Mr. Eitan." Gelbworth's voice hardened. "I can picture the hate in Naboni's eyes, and the sadistic thrill he felt with every whack of his billy club. Here, read this." Gelbworth took out a recent news article from *Hatzofeh*.

Major Jimmy Naboni of the Israel Police, was executed this morning for the 1986 murder of Rabbi Shmuel Biderman. As Naboni was led to the gas chamber, he was granted his last request: to see Rabbi Menachem Shabazi. Rabbi Shabazi came willingly, and helped Naboni with his last rites in accordance with Jewish Law. The press was well represented witnessing this unusual event. The exchange between the two follows.

JN: Please Mori, I wish to repent my sins.
MS: You have done terrible deeds. But much of the blame can be laid at the door of the former government, which nurtured you to rebel against God and His Torah. You must accept your punishment. Your soul will be purified if you truly repent at this moment and accept your atonement.

Naboni fell at the rabbi's feet, crying bitterly.

JN: I'm sorry, so sorry. I apologize to Rabbi Biderman and his family. After fifty-five years of darkness, God has given me clear vision. I killed a saintly man on Shabbat, in the synagogue. Oh my God. Oh my God. What have I done? What have I become? I beat thousands of my fellow Jews as they protested the evils of the government. I was just following orders, but I did so with zeal. I was a mon-ster, I was a Nazi. I beg... I beg forgiveness from all those I violated. God has given me back my eyes. I cannot live. I cannot live. Please Mori, beg God to for-give me. I am so weak....
MS: Get up. Get up and listen to me. Do you remember the Shema?
JN: Yes, Mori, yes.

Naboni bellowed the Shema prayer, so loud that the cameramen had to attenuate their mikes. His death, he said, should serve as atonement for his sins. Shabazi whispered something into his ear.

JN: And atonement for the sins of my people!

Amazingly, after weeping so long and so bitterly as he pleaded with the rabbi for forgiveness, Naboni straightened up as a serene expression settled on his face. He turned to Rabbi Shabazi.

JN: Thank you. I am ready to die. I go with joy, for it is the Will of God. All my life, I rebelled against His Will. Now, in His Infinite Mercy, I was given this final chance to fulfill God's Will with joy.

Again, Rabbi Shabazi whispered in Naboni's ear. Immediately, Naboni seized the sage in a warm embrace and began a renewed and even more profuse bout of sobbing. A few moments later, he stepped away from the rabbi and walked, unescorted, through the door into the gas chamber. He wouldn't even let the warden close the door; he did so himself. The warden, of course, sealed it from without. Naboni went over to the cot and laid down. Two pellets of cyanide were released inside the chamber. Naboni had been looking out through the window. Slowly he closed his eyes. Everyone was surprised to see a smile cross his lips as the bleep from the overhead heart monitor faded away and ceased.

Tears rolled down Rabbi Shabazi's face as he chanted the Hashkava memorial prayer.

MS: He who has Mercy on all of his creations, He should have pity, clemency and mercy on the soul, spirit and essence of Yitzchak son of Yehuda. May the Spirit of the Lord give him rest in the Garden of Eden.

Several police officers noted afterward to the press that they had been under the impression that, although always called Jimmy, Naboni's given name was Gamliel, not Yitzchak. Rabbi Shabazi declined comment.

By the time Nimrod Eitan finished the article, he was in tears.
"Rabbi Gelbworth."
"Yes."
"I'm sorry about what I said." Eitan got up, but Gelbworth again waved at him to remain seated.
"Mr. Eitan, ignoring the UN it is not merely a tactic. This war must be fought to its conclusion, not just pushed off for a later time. Now do you understand?"
"Yes, rabbi." Slowly, Eitan got up, walked around the desk, and took the chair next to Gelbworth's. "Please rabbi. Go sit down over there. The desk is yours now."

Chapter 55

The city of Nablus was almost as deserted as the Galilee. It had suffered, however, a great many more casualties until its population, using its better sense, left town. On August 22, 2002, the UN, together with Palestinian government forces, finally began to prevail against the Shiite Iranian-backed forces whose backers had diametrically changed their positions vis-a-vis Israel. The rift between these groups had always existed, though in the past the various factions had united to face their common Israeli enemy. In the present chaotic climate, the equation had completely changed, confounding all previous alliances.

No one knew exactly where the mass of Palestinians had fled. Some had made their way to Jordan, others to Syria and Lebanon. Large numbers headed back to the Gulf States where they had once worked. Since the attack on Israel the previous month, the Palestinian economy had come to a grinding halt. The border with Israel had been sealed, and most Arab workers were now unemployed. Leaving town became the obvious option.

The huge UN force occupying the Galilee began to thin out. Several additional divisions were sent into Samaria, to reinforce those heading south toward Jerusalem. With time on their hands — time to think more clearly — at least fifty more divisions were called home by their respective governments. Of the original 4,000,000 men and women ordered to conquer the Jewish State, only 400,000 remained, more than half of them holding the easily gained north, the remainder on the warpath headed toward Jerusalem.

"Marshal Urmenkoff," said the Chinese military representative, "believe me, it's not that I have any fear of the God of the Jews striking me down. But things are going very poorly. Hardly any troops remain from the West. Our troops have met bitter resistance from Arab factions, who are using the opportunity to wage war with the Palestinian government. Our progress to Jerusalem has been terribly impeded — and not one Jew has fired a shot. I'm afraid we may be no match for them at this point, even in a ground war."

"Chang, we don't set policy. We only implement it. The last vote in the UN was ninety to sixty-three to continue this campaign."

"Yes — but besides our two countries, the ninety votes included all those nations whose combined economies don't add up to the gross sales of the McDonald's in Tiananmen Square."

"That's not the point, General Chang."

"What really is the point, Marshal Urmenkoff?"

"The point is, what direction is the world going to take: toward progress, science and true egalitarianism, or superstitious fundamentalism? The world has evolved beyond the need for a mythical archetype that the ancients called God. In those ages of darkness, when there were few scientific solutions to matters that plagued mankind, all one could do was to call out for help from an imaginary supernatural power. Today, man's destiny is completely within his own grasp. Most devastating diseases have been cured. And for those that we are still working on, we know we have the technology to eventually conquer them.

"Science and technology are the true answers to the prayers of the ages. But those fools in Jerusalem, who in the past two months have increased their following to include tens of millions around the world, are unwittingly plunging the world back into the darkness that it took mankind four thousand years of history to emerge from. That, Chang, is why we must fight on."

General Chang was not convinced. "Now, really, Marshal Urmenkoff. I see that you attribute the entire frenzy in the Jewish State to the sudden advent of Menachem Shabazi. If not for his influence, you are probably thinking, the Israelis would have negotiated some kind of settlement after cooling off for a few weeks from their brutal attacks. But Marshal Urmenkoff, even before Shabazi's emergence, the idiotic failed coup in the United States, which took that country out of the fray, must also be characterized as a disastrous blow to the UN's cause. Isn't it unfathomable that the coalition holding the Arabs together to annihilate their old enemy should so quickly and miserably crumble? Isn't it inexplicable that, after fifty-four years of fighting conventional wars and haphazardly battling internal terrorism, Israel should have all at once pulled out the stops in the region, killing hundreds of thousands of innocent civilians? Isn't it strange that all these factors should come together to encumber the just and peace-seeking efforts of the United Nations?"

"Chang, are you inferring that all these occurrences are anything other than a bloody coincidence?"

"No, of course not, Marshal. But who is to say that we won't encounter some other "coincidental" setbacks?"

Urmenkoff said disgustedly, "Chang, Chang, you are a great military man. But you...."

The Marshal's cell phone began ringing in his pocket before he could finish his thought. He whipped it out and listened a moment.

"What! That can't be. Move all unaffected troops toward the front. I mean now!"

Urmenkoff looked dejected as he disconnected. Chang wondered what new setback had befallen them now.

July 1, 2002, 12:00 p.m. GMT+4.5), Professor Hilwani's Office, Herat Afghanistan:

"I apologize for not having been perfectly honest with you when you first sought my advice. But I will be now — perfectly. The actual species of black fly that bit you is classified as *Simulium hilwanei*. Do you understand? I developed it from the venustum subspecies. How does it vary from its progenitor? It was developed to become the host of the *Trypanosome alwazei*. That title should also be revealing. This protozoan is a variant of the *Trypanosome gambiense*, of African Sleeping Sickness fame. It was genetically isolated from its prototype and is five hundred times more resistant to the body's autoimmune system. Thus, it reproduces and infects the body, as you are experiencing, by taxing the inflammatory cells within a few hours instead of months.

"Now you know what I know. Who am I? I am entitled to ask you the same question. But I won't, because I already know. You are Omar Rastafani, a great philanthropist. Why, it was through your own magnanimity that the parasite which now afflicts your own blood was developed.

"You are also a man of God. You pray with fervent devotion, five times each day, for Allah to destroy Israel. As you must know, your Moslem colleagues recently made a futile attempt to accomplish just that."

Hilwani leaned back against his desk, the H&K pistol trained relentlessly on his captives.

"But most notably," he finished, "you are a murderer. Very soon to be retired."

"Hilwani," said the wealthy terrorist leader, Omar Rastafani, in a barely audible voice weakened by fever. "Save me, and a hundred million dollars will be yours."

"Make it two hundred million and it's a deal," answered the professor, whose deadly flies had just ravaged the terrorist camp.

Rastafani gave Hilwani a ten-digit number and a password. After switching on his computer and logging onto the Internet, Hilwani found:

www.zuricharabian.bank

He entered the account number and the password. The available balance was 53,210,000 Euros. With a few clicks of the mouse, the entire sum was transferred to another numbered account at the Bern Federal Bank.

"Please, Hilwani. You've done nothing for me. It's been ten minutes. I'm going to die and you've cheated me."

"Now, now, Omar. You still owe me over a hundred million. But don't worry. You will see that I am a man of my word. I just want to check, to make sure the funds were actually transferred."

Hilwani logged into his Swiss account; sure enough, the money was there. He took out a vial marked DFMO and injected ten CCs into the terrorist leader.

"This will spare you from death, but it won't cure you. You will have to stay with me several weeks for an hourly treatment if you want to live. No funny business or you die. I assure you Mr. Rastafani, you'd be lucky to get hold of this drug on your own in less than forty-eight hours. You understand?"

Limp with relief, Rastafani nodded.

"Good. We're leaving the country. I'm sorry you'll have no time to pack, but I'll be happy to buy you some new clothes. If you're lucky, I might find a nice Calvin Klein striped suit for you." Hilwani laughed.

Hilwani dragged the body of Major Kalami and the half-dead Captain Jebli into a closet and called Rastafani's pilot on his cell phone. A few minutes later, Jamiel Falkami carried the weakened terrorist to the waiting helicopter. Hilwani ran back to the lab, stuffed two large jars into a rucksack, and got into the chopper.

"Are you also our leader's plane pilot? We must get him decent medical attention! The flies were infected," Hilwani said at the outset of the fifteen-minute flight to Herat International Airport.

Jamiel Falkami had learned to fly a helicopter at an Israeli base in the Negev during the Afghan rebel war with the Soviet Union. He really wanted to fly a jet, but the Mossad only reluctantly trained a few to fly helicopters. Israel had no intention of letting the rebels fly jets. Jamiel, however, was a bold and assertive character. These characteristics had helped him get the job of flying for Rastafani. Indeed, Falkami had over a hundred hours of Lear Jet flight experience. Not that he ever flew the bird, or took lessons. But he had sat next to Habal Shatil, and scrupulously watched his every move in flying the craft.

"As a matter of fact," he said now, "I am his backup pilot. But the master is very ill. It might take too long for Habal, master's first pilot, to get to the airport. I will fly the master. Where are we going, Professor?"

"I've made contact with a colleague of mine in Vienna. He has made all the arrangements."

"Vienna! I've never filed a flight plan to Europe. Besides, we must stop to refuel."

A flight plan was filed to include a stop in Istanbul. From there, Falkami said, it would be easier to file for the next leg of the trip. It took Falkami four passes over the runway before he had the guts to cut the engines and land.

"What's the matter?" yelled Hilwani. "I thought you said you know how to fly this thing!"

"I do, I do. It's just that I came in a bit too high. With the master in his condition, I wanted to make sure the landing was extra smooth."

Finally, when the plane did land, it touched down so hard they were lucky the landing gear didn't snap. As it was, the plane came to a full stop on the dirt, one hundred meters past the end of the runway. Hilwani didn't have much of a choice; he had to continue the perilous journey.

The next leg of the trip did not go as planned. Ten minutes out of Istanbul, Hilwani said to the pilot. "I see the beautiful Mediterranean below us. Take a bearing of one hundred eighty degrees, Mr. Falkami."

"But that won't take us to Vienna. The master, he needs quick treatment."

"Who said we're going to Vienna?"

"You did, Professor."

"I think you misunderstood. I said I made all the arrangements with a colleague of mine from Vienna. I never said we were heading there."

"Then where are we headed?"

"We are heading to where Master Rastafani can get the very best treatment. Egypt."

"Egypt? Since when do they have good medicine?"

"Master is wanted in most other nations. He'll be turned over to the United States. Egypt has the best medicine of any nation that will take him in and let him go."

Falkami turned the plane south. "Look here, Professor, we don't have a flight plan. We're flying into dangerous territory."

"Just hug the coast and we'll be all right."

"The coast. Are you crazy? In a half hour we'll be close to Israel."

"I meant out over international airspace."

Forty minutes later, two F-16s pulled alongside. The Lear Jet pilot grimaced as he recognized the six pointed light blue stars decorating the wings of the F-16s.

"Professor, I told you flying so close would mean trouble."

"What trouble, Falkami? We're in international territory. Looks like we're at least twenty kilometers from the coast. All right, change course. Take a bearing of one hundred ten degrees."

"You're crazy! On that heading, we'll be in Israeli territory in two minutes." Falkami turned around — to see the barrel of the Professor's H&K pointing straight at him. He shuddered, then reached for the controls. The chase planes signaled for the Lear Jet to follow.

"Who are you, Professor?" asked the frightened pilot.

"Who am I? I'm just a real nice guy. When you told me how great your training was in Israel, I felt it would be a shame to come so close and not give you the chance to enjoy a reunion with your old Mossad buddies."

Falkami began descending as instructed. As Israeli Air Force jets do not have civilian band radio, the pilot just made an internationally understood hand signal for the Lear Jet to follow. Suddenly at 11,500 meters, Falkami pushed the flight yoke all the way forward. The jet started to dive.

"What are you doing? Level this thing off or I'll kill you."

"Save your bullet Professor. In another minute, we're all going to die. You're Mossad, aren't you?"

Hilwani jumped into the copilot's seat, grabbed the yoke, and tried to pull it back to level off the craft. It was a struggle between him and Falkami, who was pushing forward with all his might. Hilwani's efforts managed to moderate the rate of descent, but after thirty seconds the plane was still heading for the sea at a rate of five hundred eighty-five knots. At three thousand meters, Hilwani let go of the yoke with his right hand and fired one shot at point-blank range into Falkami's temple. The bullet passed through his head and smashed the windshield quarter panel. The pressure dropped slightly, but at two thousand meters, it wasn't significant. The plane leveled off. Still, Hilwani's heart was pumping hard. He didn't know how to fly a plane.

Grabbing the mike, he yelled, "Mayday, Mayday. Tel Aviv do you hear me?"

"This is Tel Aviv. What's the matter with your plane?"

"The pilot is dead. Call the air force and tell them not to shoot at me. I have a VIP on board."

"Who are you? We've got you on radar with the two chase planes."

"I'm Mossad Aleph-Shin 47. I don't know how to fly this Lear Jet. I think I can keep it steady in the air, but I don't know how to land it."

"Just hang in there. We'll contact air force and try to figure out what to do."

Two minutes later: "Major Mordechai — Shefi Mordechai?"

"Yes, I am he," answered the voice from the plane. "I haven't been called that for thirty-four years."

"Major, this is Captain Yoram Chai of the air force. Do you see a button near the center of the instrument panel which is marked AP? That's the autopilot. Switch it on."

Mordechai did so. Immediately, the craft's progress seemed to smooth. He let go of the flight yoke and saw that it was making slight adjustments by itself, locked onto the heading to which it had been set when switched on.

"Now Major, we want to get you and your passenger in alive. I'm afraid that, with no experience, even with coaching your chances of landing the thing in one piece are quite low. Still, we've got some pretty nasty daredevils around here. If you cooperate, we might be able to help you. I'm going to try to get you a pilot."

"If I could land this thing myself to pick up a pilot, I wouldn't need you guys!" Mordechai shouted frantically.

"Major. Just listen carefully and we may be able to deliver him to you. It's worth a try. I've got a Harrier STOVL twin trainer taking off right now from a base in Ashkelon. He will be on you in four minutes. Turn the yoke to the right until your level indicator shows a two mile turn, and then press the autopilot button again. That will get you into a wide circling pattern."

On the radar screen, Captain Chai saw that the maneuver was executed. "Very good. Now, you're going to have to reduce your speed. We have you at four hundred seventy-five knots. Pull back on the throttle and reduce to two hundred. The auto pilot should keep your altitude steady at twenty-five hundred meters."

Three minutes later, the plane had slowed to the desired speed. "Now, Major, we want to get your speed down even further. Flip the switch on your left marked, Flaps."

Mordechai did so, and listened as the flap motors fully rolled back the wing flaps and then came to a stop. The nose of the plane moved up slightly until the autopilot compensated by adjusting the tail elevators.

"Major, your air speed should be down to ninety-five knots. Are you losing altitude?"

Mordechai looked at the altimeter, it was slowly rotating counter-clockwise. The plane was down to eighteen hundred meters. Without instruction, the novice pilot pushed forward on the throttle until the jets were roaring and the descent ceased. He looked up. There in front of him, about three hundred meters ahead and fifty meters higher in altitude, was the TAV-8B trainer flying unimaginably slowly. Then he witnessed something he had only read about in a magazine article about the barnstorming era of the 1930s. Dangling from a tether was a helmeted man, a parachute on his back. He hung about thirty meters below his craft and was slowly approaching. The two chase planes stayed on the scene. Mordechai figured they were radioing in exact positioning movements to the pilot of the trainer, who couldn't see his man hanging below. The dangling man waved to Mordechai as he passed three meters to his left and behind. A minute later, Mordechai heard the creaking of the door mechanism and then the wind rushing by as the door opened.

At 7:20 a.m. July 2, 2002, setting foot on the ground in Ashkelon, Shefi Mordechai cried as he bent down to kiss the tarmac.

As a black Mercedes pulled up to the plane, Shefi Mordechai took off his left shoe and sock. His identity was positively confirmed.

There was no time to be wasted. At Mossad headquarters, the screen enclosures and water circulating equipment were set up in a lab, exactly as Mordechai had instructed. Taking his jar of flies from his rucksack, he released them into the artificial environment that was now their new home. They set to work immediately — breeding. Rastafani was taken to a comfortable cell, given a full regimen of treatment, and was perfectly well in two days. But the Mossad, at the behest of Prime Minister Benari, decided to keep his capture a secret for the time being.

"How long will it take you to get a useful population of these bugs, Major Mordechai?" asked the Mossad chief.

"We can acquire one generation in about ten days. But I'd prefer to wait until we can get the second generation. We'll need about twenty rabbits by next week."

"What for, Major? You've developed a germ that makes rabbits kill the enemy?"

"No, sir. The flies have to eat. They only eat blood. Now if you want to volunteer, we can save the money on rabbits. Don't worry, these flies aren't vectored."

"We'll get you your rabbits."

By that day in late August of 2002, as Vassali Urmenkoff was slumped over in a state of depression, Major Shefi Mordechai had developed four generations from the initial one thousand flies he'd brought back from Herat University. Flying around in the multi-partitioned chamber were close to 20,000,000 black flies: *Simulium hilwanei*.

After asking for the third time what was troubling the Field Marshal, Chang finally got his answer.

"General Chang, those bloody Jews have pulled a fast one on us. Do you remember the report from the Afghan terrorist camp that the Israelis hit at the beginning of this affair?"

"No, Marshal!" Chang's eyes widened. "You don't mean...."

"I do mean. The entire Galilee is infested with what seems to be the same black flies. Over 150,000 men have been bitten and are scrambling in panic away from the front. There's no more control or military discipline. Many have abandoned their guns and posts and have fled for hospitals in Haifa, Beirut, Damascus, anywhere they can go. Others have officially been given leave by their national commanders and are headed home. Not one division remains intact. I understand the Israeli army has landed paratroopers and will seize back control of the Galilee within a few hours."

"Are our men putting up any resistance?"

Urmenkoff grimaced. "None at all. Those who couldn't go anywhere are surrendering by the thousands, begging for treatment. Those crafty Israelis certainly know their entomology. This strain of fly is completely insensitive to DEET, the standard UN-issue insect repellant."

"But aren't the Israelis afraid their men will also be afflicted?"

"I don't understand it, Chang. I just don't understand it. I suppose they developed another repellant which the fly is not immune to."

Slowly, General Chang asked, "Are you saying, Marshal, that the time has come to throw in the towel?"

Urmenkoff stood up. "Never!" he said defiantly. "Not even if I must fight this battle myself. We still have 180,000 men and good equipment. We are only fifty kilometers from Jerusalem. Hopefully, the UN high command will send reinforcements if we can make some more progress."

"They'll have to drop them in, Marshal. We are almost trapped now, with Israel back in control of their northern border."

"So they'll drop them in."

"Marshal, you don't give up," mused General Chang.

"Not as long as there remains any chance to eliminate these vermin."

Chapter 56

August 24, 2002, Nablus, Palestine, UN Command:

"Marshal Urmenkoff," said his Chinese subordinate, "I have good news. Perhaps the best news since this disastrous campaign began."

"What's that, Chang?"

"Tests now show that the flies Israel set upon our men in the Galilee were not vectored. No one has become ill; none of our men will die."

Urmenkoff slumped down in his chair, nervously wiping his face with his hands.

"Marshal, what's the matter? You don't look well."

The Field Marshal jumped up and angrily barked at Chang and the other generals in the room, "Why *should* I feel well? I don't give a damn about the men! We have no army left in the Galilee!"

No one commented. Urmenkoff was still the commander.

The battle for Ramallah took two weeks. The terrain was very difficult. The warring Islamic factions fought to the death, always well supplied with the most sophisticated weaponry. UN tanks were constantly being knocked out of commission. But at the same time, the former anti-Israeli terrorists were slowly being eradicated, as were the Palestinian regulars who fought side-by-side with the UN forces. Many of them also defected, questioning what they were actually fighting for; ninety-five percent of the civilian population had disappeared, including the Palestinian government which fled to Switzerland. The Palestinian State, effectively, no longer existed.

"Prime Minister Benari, this is General Uri Matar. I would like permission to give air support to the Hizbulla forces north of the Ramallah hills. They are taking very heavy shelling. I'm afraid that even the mountain caves won't protect them for very long. The fire is so heavy, the mountains are slowly being leveled."

"I'm sorry, General, I empathize with you. But I have instructions not to directly involve any of our military forces in this fight. Hizbulla, Islamic Jihad, Fatah offshoots and the Mujahedin are fighting for Palestine, not for Israel."

"But Mr. Prime Minister, we're already supplying them with weapons. The longer they hold out, the more the UN troops will be thinned out. Perhaps they won't even make it to Jerusalem as a viable force."

"General, I understand what you're saying, but I just can't authorize it."

"Why not? Is this an order from Shabazi? What's come over you?"

Benari's voice softened dangerously. "Yes, it was a suggestion from Rabbi Shabazi. Uri, you still don't understand who this man is. Haven't *you* started keeping the Shabbat since he came?"

"Of course I have. I'm not personally convinced, but with everyone doing it, I wouldn't buck the flow. Look here, Danny, I admit that Shabazi is the most charismatic man of the century, and that his military strategy has been uncanny until now. But what can it hurt to give those former terrorists a little air cover? Believe me, I'm not doing it just for the sake of their lives. It might mean we can delay the UN another few weeks or few months. Samaria has practically emptied out its Arab population. If the UN were to pack up tomorrow, I would grant complete clemency to the former terrorists. There might remain only 50,000 Arabs on the entire West Bank. The Palestinian State is gone already. Have a little pity."

"I'll see what I can do. Don't make a move until you hear from me."

Matar did make a move. A squadron of six F-15s came in fast and low over the north side of Ramallah City. Five never made it past the city limits to the east, but were blown out of the sky by UN Hawk anti-aircraft missiles. The sixth was badly damaged but managed to circle around back into Israeli territory, where the pilot ejected.

"Matar, Uri Matar. This is Benari. *What have you done?* According to Menachem you have jeopardized the possibility of victory. You're fired!"

Silence.

"Uri? Uri, say something...."

Over the line, Benari only heard the sharp report of a single gunshot.

By September 7, 2002, Urmenkoff and his remaining 120,000 troops had overtaken Atarot Airport south of Ramallah. They were now poised against the northern reaches of Jerusalem City. The warring Arab groups had lost over 150,000 men since the beginning of the battle one month before. What remained were 10,000 well-armed soldiers who occupied the abandoned housing complexes on the north rim of twenty-first century Jerusalem.

Even before Menachem Shabazi's march to Jerusalem began, masses and masses of people had flooded into Israel: Christians, Jews, Americans and Europeans. But by the time the UN troops crossed the frontier into the Galilee, the tide began to turn. Not only were fewer and fewer people coming, many of the those who had come began leaving, fearing a major conflagration. Now, as the Jews in Israel and around the world ushered in Rosh Hashanah, the Jewish New Year, hundreds and hundreds of extra flights were scheduled to fly out the thousands of panic-stricken people scrambling to escape the country.

"Master Menachem. What should we do? The country is emptying out. These past two months, Israel had seen wild economic growth from all the tourism. Should we try to mollify the people to stay?"

"No, Mr. Benari. I am certain that the vast majority of those fleeing the country lack true faith. We need a strong willed populace at this time. Even the newcomers who remain, like my friends, Gaylord and Prince Bin Farheem, augment our spiritual fortitude. Those who flee, do not. Just let them go. Arrange more flights, if necessary."

Rosh Hashanah in the Old City was spectacular. The foundation of a new stone wall now surrounded the entire Temple Mount. This outer wall was vastly expanded beyond King Solomon's original boundary, set in place more than two thousand years earlier. Bulldozers had worked feverishly for six weeks to fill in earth and expand the plateau of the Temple Mount to the east. The eastern wall, built by Sulieman the Magnificent four hundred fifty years before, was torn down to enable the expansion. The terrace now covered over one hundred eighty dunam (forty-five acres). This new design, approved by Menachem Shabazi and the Synod of seventy-one rabbis, could easily accommodate 1,000,000 pilgrims, even without a miracle. Hundreds of separate prayer quorums were set up on the court within the foundation of the new walls, each holding services with a distinct ethnic format. Prayers were still conducted at the Western Wall, whose plaza was not as full as the huge terrace to the southeast.

On Sunday night, the eighth of September, after the prayers concluded, Menachem spoke into the PA system which reached into every corner of the Old City.

"People of Israel! I know that you have been repenting for the past seven weeks. The enemy stands only ten kilometers north of us but, thank the Almighty, the enemy within our hearts has been all but expunged. Our Synod of rabbis has heard almost 20,000 cases since the movement for *national atonement* has begun. The innocents have been exonerated and the guilty have been punished. A week from tomorrow we shall all return here, to this Holy ground, in fast and prayer. But it shall be a joyous occasion. Yom Kippur of the year 5763 will be the final Atonement for all the sins of our people. Thereafter, a great joy will overcome our nation as we anticipate God's Countenance to soon shine down upon us.

"There is still work to be done. We have one more week left — seven days for each man among us to engender true love and unity with his neighbor. Let everyone dig deep into his memory to remember even the slightest offence that might have been done to him. Let each one forgive with a full heart. If there is a matter of financial claim, form a rabbinical court. Any three Talmud scholars may be convened for this purpose. But, heed my words: by Monday a week, let there be no issue outstanding between one man and his fellow. Ensure this, and God will release His bountiful blessings upon us before we face our enemy."

A great cheer rose up from the million-plus men and women in the city.

The following week was busy indeed. In every synagogue, groups of three men, sitting at numerous tables, were hearing petty cases. Millions and millions of shekels were changing hands, both parties overjoyed to have the burden of responsibility lifted from their shoulders. In more than half the cases, debts were simply forgiven. The electricity of brotherhood and love in the air energized the entire population. Even the few die-hard antagonists who had obstinately chosen to remain in the country found themselves infected with this spirit. The everyday greeting, even of complete strangers, became, "I forgive you with a full heart."

Prior to Sabbath, the 14th of September, 2002, posters were plastered all over the country.

> **Please, all good people! Make sure to eat three meals this Sabbath. No one — man, woman, or child — must be delinquent in his or her duty to eat the third meal this Sabbath. No Sabbath of Repentance sermons should be so long that they prevent the congregation from having ample time to eat the third meal. Eat in joy. It will bring down a great blessing.**
>
> **Menachem Shabazi the Yemenite**

Chapter 57

From the time the UN forces reached Ramallah, one thousand Israeli tanks and one thousand artillery pieces formed a wide, north-to-southeast arc. The ten-kilometer defensive line started north of the Ramot neighborhoods around Ammunition Hill, continued along Sheik Jarah, Wadi Joz, Jericho Road, traversed the new east ridge of the Temple Mount, south to the UN House, and tapered off in the south at Talpiyot East.

On Yom Kippur, the remaining Arab forces fighting the UN troops retreated from the vacant Jewish neighborhood of Neve Yakov. Their effort, with unlimited TOW missiles, had done its job on the invaders. Of the five thousand tanks and armored vehicles with which Joint Commander Urmenkoff had started out, less than two hundred remained. Still, the resolute Field Marshal plowed on. His ground troops now numbered only 75,000. Arab forces, for and against the UN, were almost completely gone. All of the Palestinian regulars had either thrown away their arms, dog tags, and uniforms and run away to find their families, or joined the groups fighting against the UN. Belatedly, they realized that the UN invasion had destroyed their country. Not more than one thousand former terrorists remained alive. But, almost robotically, they continued to pound the slow-moving UN lines with heavy fire.

At 7:00 p.m. on September 16, 2002, two thousand 1000-watt halogen lamps spontaneously came alive, activated by preset timers. As the sun was setting on "The Closing of the Gates," Yom Kippur 5763, the artificial light now enabled 900,000 Jewish men, all dressed in white prayer gowns, to follow the remaining prayers in their books. For *Na'ilah*, the concluding service, all the small, disparate congregations joined together, led in the Yemenite rite by Menachem Shabazi. Most could not hear the cantor, but followed in refrain as a wave rolls over the surf. At 8:05, silence pervaded the entire city of Jerusalem as Shabazi put the 1.5-meter-long spiraled ram's horn to his lips and blew a blast that wafted across the hills for thirty seconds. After this, Shabazi finished the *Kaddish* Prayer, and the throngs of the Children of Israel broke out in jubilant song and dance.

*   *   *

Earlier that afternoon, five kilometers to the north, a brigade of UN troops had broken through the decimated Arab lines and captured the first block of houses in Sho'afat. A total of 99.9% of the Jewish population along the northern city limit had heeded the Prime Minister's warning to evacuate the area the previous week. But four families, who belonged to the recently defunct Human Culture Society, refused to leave their homes. Throughout the entire two months, they would meet several times a week to decry the religious oppression and fanaticism that had gripped the nation. Although they were prevented by the masses in the streets from driving their cars on Shabbat, in the privacy of their own homes they continued to violate the Sabbath and to consume non-kosher foods. The neighbors, who by now had evacuated, used to invite them to Sabbath meals and to participate in discussions. But the Congregation of Four remained strident and derisive toward anyone who attempted to convince them that they were making a big mistake.

Thus, as the UN troops swarmed around their building, the group — which had huddled together throughout the fighting — came out of their bomb shelter waving UN flags and welcoming the soldiers. Four men, three women, and seven children emerged from their lair to greet the saviors who would rescue them from the forces of darkness crazily dismembering civilized society in the modern Zionist State. Leora Nimrodi, whose husband and eight-year-old daughter had gone ahead with the others, remained in the shelter to change the diaper of two-year-old Hofshi, when she suddenly heard a volley of automatic-weapon fire. She left the baby for a moment to peer through the small window in the upper level of the cellar. Horrified, she was glued to the spectacle of twenty black, white and Asian soldiers ripping the clothing from her daughter and the other women. She wanted to cry out, but the sight of her husband's bloodied corpse among those of his friends and most of their children, left her paralyzed. Before her eyes, three of her best friends and her own daughter were savagely violated. All twenty of the platoon, laughing and frolicking, took turns demonstrating their domination over these female representatives of the vile Jewish enemy. After twenty minutes, the sadistic orgy came to an abrupt end as the lifeless bodies of its victims were dumped a few meters away from the bullet-riddled men. Leora finally tore her eyes away from the limp bodies of her former comrades and her own young daughter.

The sound of a vehicle reached her ears. Turning, she saw a car pull up near the group of soldiers. A huge man, his chest strewn with military decorations, got out.

"What's going on here?" asked Marshal Urmenkoff.

Captain Mombosho, an African and the highest ranking soldier present, saluted and answered. "We found Israelis. They tried to appease us with UN flags and warm greetings, but we knew better than to buy that ruse."

"What's with these female corpses?" The Marshal came closer and viewed the copious blood staining the remnants of their tattered clothing. The scenario was all too evident. He waved off Captain Mombosho as the latter was about to answer. "Do me a favor Captain," he said curtly. "Just burn these bodies in one of the bombed out buildings. Do it at night."

Leora Nimrodi ran back into the shelter and locked the door from the inside. Unfortunately, she could not lock her ears. She listened fearfully as soldiers rummaged around in the untouched apartments upstairs.

*   *   *

On the Temple Mount at 8:30 that night, no one had broken his fast, nor did the slight hunger bother the masses waiting expectantly to hear from Menachem Shabazi again over the PA system.

"Dear people of the Israelite Nation. Go forth in joy to eat your bread, for the Almighty has heard your prayers. Go tonight after you have tasted a morsel, and begin to build your *Succah*. Even if you nail in only one board tonight, that will be sufficient. Tomorrow will be a great day of joy for our nation.

"Our enemy is now preparing its last stand. Hurry, return to your homes in every corner of the country to prepare for the Holiday, for the joy that will emanate tomorrow will be as great as the elation when our forefathers left Egypt. Just be careful to continue to love and respect your neighbor as you have done so wonderfully all this past week. To the gentiles who remain among us, show utmost respect. Invite them to join you in the festive meal this coming Shabbat of Succoth."

* * *

At 2:00 a.m., Leora Nimrodi gathered her courage, unlocked the heavy steel shelter door, and carried her slumbering baby outside. One lone guard was slumped over, snoring, in front of her building. As stealthily as she could, she opened her car door, and put the baby on the passenger-side floor. For one moment the thought crossed her mind that there must be a God; the possibility had been banished from her mind from the time she had turned eleven. But now, here she was, alive. Her baby, Hofshi, was alive. And miraculously, the car was parked facing down a steep hill. She had hated when her husband did that.

Slowly and quietly, she closed the car door, not letting it catch all the way. She turned the key halfway, releasing the steering wheel and putting the car into neutral. It immediately started rolling downhill. At a distance of one hundred fifty meters, the speedometer showed twenty-five km/h. The slope of the hill now leveled off, and she threw the shift-stick into third gear. The car bucked and surged forward as she pressed the pedal to the floor. Twenty seconds later, a hail of bullets shattered the rear window. Leora took one in her left shoulder. For the first time in her thirty-four years, she cried out, "Oh God, save me! Please save me and my baby." The road curved, and she was out of the sights of the soldiers behind her.

Seven minutes later, Leora Nimrodi finally passed out from loss of blood, just as her engine coughed and failed by slowing down in second gear — directly in front of an Israeli M1 Abrams tank guarding National Police Headquarters.

* * *

At twelve noon on the following morning, the nation was amazed and exhilarated. Three hundred meters off the coast of Haifa's deepwater port, a T-Class conventional submarine surfaced. Twelve naval vessels quickly surrounded it. Crowds standing on the shore and peering from tall city buildings were roused by radio and television reports to direct their attention toward the blue waters of the Mediterranean Sea. By 1:00 p.m., some two hundred thousand people were lining the streets of Haifa. By 2:30 p.m., it seemed that all those who just the day before made the pilgrimage to the Temple Mount, now overflowed the streets and squares of Haifa, many with binoculars viewing the black metal fish that bobbed gently in the waves. Over four hundred thousand Jews from all corners of the land heard the news and spontaneously made their way to the coast beneath Mount Carmel.

At 2:45 p.m., men dressed in neatly-pressed Navy uniforms, emerged from the hatch and lined up along the smooth deck. Exactly 12,651 days late, the men of the *Davar* cruised up to the Naval pier in Haifa port. The INS Dolphin, sister submarine of the *Davar,* had been repaired and repainted for this ceremony after twenty-five years of inactivity, and now bore the name *Davar* II. Fifty-nine of the original seventy men stood at attention as the long, narrow boat nestled up and was lashed to the dock.

Daniel Benari stood on the pier along with the twenty members of his cabinet, the one hundred twenty men and women of the Knesset, and the seventy-one rabbis of the Synod. Masses of people were in tears as the men of the *Davar* walked down the gangplank and shook hands with the Prime Minister as they filed past. A cheer welled up from the crowd as Daniel Benari and his father shook hands and fell into a sobbing embrace. After a minute, Benny Harkesef straightened up and continued walking with his wife, Barbara, to the cheers of the crowd. Alon Barnash, after greeting the PM, continued on, arm in arm with Fatima — now Ahuva — to his right, with his son Moshe to his left. At Moshe's left walked Admiral Ariel Mizrachi, ritual fringes prominently hanging over his belt, forming four corners. Eli Kedem plucked Ruchama from the crowd on his march up the pier.

Shefi Mordechai was escorted by his eighty-six-year-old mother. Each brave soul who had sacrificed and dedicated his life, each one with his own story, a book unto itself, filed by to the cheers and tears of the nation. For although the Mossad never lifted its rule of secrecy, by now everyone had figured out the secret of thirty-four years past.

Eleven men were not present to return in glory to their nation. Among them were Rahamim Heguy, Yona Lieberman, Gutzi Karmel, and Rafi Schwartz. Indeed, Colonel Rafael Schwartz, the brains and impetus behind Operation Samson's Lion, was most missed. He had posited Samson's riddle, but was not present for its resolution. None of the crew had been briefed, nor did they know exactly where their fellow agents had been stationed, except in the case of Alon Barnash. And even though the remaining men on the sub knew where their colleagues had been deposited, many of those traveled far and wide to settle in their assigned destinations. Only Rafi knew everything. It was he who had designated the place and the objective of each brave soul. The fates of the missing crew members were unknown; the eleven might have died of natural causes... or otherwise.

*   *   *

At 3:30 p.m. in Shaarei Tzedek Hospital in Jerusalem, three high-ranking military officers and the assistant chief of Israel Police were busy debriefing the recovering Leora Nimrodi when they were rudely interrupted by a familiar face.

"What's going on here? Why are all you he-men crying like babies? Mrs. Nimrodi, I am Yossel the *Mohel*. You have a beautiful baby down in the nursery, but as the nurses were changing his diaper, they were shocked to find that the two-year-old was uncircumcised. What's your maiden name? You *are* Jewish, aren't you?"

Leora Nimrodi, moved the IV tube to one side and sat up in her bed. "Yes, of course I'm Jewish. I was born Leora Mordechai, December 21, 1967. In the Human Culture Society, we considered circumcision superstitious and barbaric."

Yossel mumbled to himself, "Mordechai, Mordechai, I just heard that name." In a flash, he grabbed the remote on the night table and switched on the TV. All present turned their attention to the picture of thousands of people in Haifa welcoming back the brave men of the *Davar*.

Suddenly, Leora screamed out, "My father, my father! He went down with the *Davar*. I never knew him."

"Sir," Haggai Segan the Channel-7 reporter on the scene said to one of the returning sailors, thrusting a microphone into his face. "Sir, the nation is in a state of disbelief. What do you say upon returning home after thirty-four years?"

"I am happy to have served my country and my people. The way things are turning out with Rabbi Shabazi here, the heart of the nation as one, the UN army crumbling at the hands of Arab terrorists, and the Palestinian State in shambles, is simply miraculous. This saga reads like the prophecies of old. It is absolutely beyond my wildest dreams. I just feel deeply saddened that my friend and commander, Rafi Schwartz, is not among those of us who have returned."

"What are you going to do now? Do you have any plans?" asked Segan.

"Yes, of course. I actually returned just after the initial attack, two months ago. Most of the others on board also returned shortly after their missions were complete. Due to the classified nature of our work, we were required to remain silent until today. I am planning to see my wife — actually my ex-wife, she has probably remarried — and my daughter, Leora, who was two weeks old the last time I saw her. I would assume that I am a grandfather by now."

Leora Nimrodi was bawling. Yossel and the high brass sitting in front of the TV were similarly drenched with tears. But this time, they were tears of joy that replaced the tears of tragedy that had fallen from their eyes upon hearing of the brutalities that befell the Congregation of Four in Sho'afat.

After a minute, Yossel the *Mohel* pulled himself together, switched off the TV, and turned to Leora. "So Mrs. Nimrodi, will there be a *Bris* today?"

Leora nodded, too choked up to talk. "Don't worry, ma'am. Yossel will make sure that your father will be the *sandek*, to hold his grandson during the celebration. General..." Yossel looked down at the name tag, "General Leventhal, I give you the assignment of contacting Major Mordechai and bringing him up here. Now that's an order!"

* * *

After all the brave sailors/agents had filed by, they joined the throngs of people. Once again, the entire nation stood at attention as twenty-one guns were fired in unison eleven times, to honor those who did not return. No speeches were delivered. No speeches were necessary.

The feeling of joy was overwhelming. The atmosphere of unity was inexorable. Finally at 4:00 p.m., the crowd broke up to head home and continue their festival preparations.

In Jerusalem, the din of gunfire and distant, exploding ordnance sounded insignificant as crickets in the ears of the four hundred thousand men in old shirts and worn pants busy hammering together their Succoth huts on balconies, roof tops and yards throughout the Holy City. The women were lined up at special shelters to invite guests, complete strangers who had been displaced from their housing in the northern reaches of Jerusalem. So many invitations came in that numerous families were committed to eat each meal of the seven-day holiday at different homes. The people were almost completely oblivious to the fact that the remnant of the greatest fighting force in the history of the world was slowly progressing toward them. They had complete faith that God would fight for them and would vanquish the enemy, just as He had until then.

The evening of September 20, 2002, was beautiful. The sky was clear, the stars shone bright. The Hebrew Nation throughout the Holy Land, and especially in Jerusalem, was alive in song and joy as the people sanctified the Holiday from within their makeshift dwellings. Every individual felt the almost tangible Divine Presence hovering above his head, offering protection from the destructive elements that loomed ominously nearby. Displaced Jews felt more at home than they had in the past, sitting in their own living rooms. Not one guest was left in his or her hotel room to eat the commercial food available there. They, too, were invited to take part in the holiday spirit.

The Temple Mount was now dominated by military equipment. Due to the fact that Jews do not take up the palm branch, citron, willow and myrtle branches on the Sabbath, not as many people came out to pray at the Holy site as in the previous week — only two hundred thousand. The day was very hot, and up on the Mount there wasn't much shelter from the sun. One hundred thousand non-Jews, one-fifth of whom were local Arabs, remained in Jerusalem as the festival of Succoth was invoked. At high noon, in the heat of the day, many walked to the homes of their hosts to enjoy the festive meal, as they had the night before. This time, however, the hotels were surprised to see a good number of their guests returning to eat in the air-conditioned dining rooms. Even the Arab guests, who were used to the heat, grumbled about their discomfort as they excused themselves to seek a cooler ambiance under their own solid roofs. Turmoil broke out as the hotel restaurants quickly ran out of food, unable to accommodate those whom they had anticipated would be eating out. As the situation became known in the city, tens of thousands of women brought food to the hotels — food that had been abundantly prepared in anticipation of the gentile friends who, as it turned out, could not take the heat outside in the thinly-shaded Succoth huts.

By late Saturday afternoon, as the sun was going down, the gentiles who had retired prematurely due to the heat of the day were back out on the streets, greeting the Jews and spreading the good tidings they had heard on the international news broadcasts. The UN had recalled its troops. The war was over. Most of the Jews were overjoyed, and spontaneous dancing broke out in the streets. The gentiles happily joined in.

But the rabbis, sages and Torah scholars avoided these ad hoc celebrations. They knew that the news was preliminary and the celebrations premature.

Chapter 58

"So, Marshal, it's over," chided General Chang.

"No, Chang, it can't be. We've come so far. We are so close. We cannot stop now. We will not stop now!"

The Chinese general stared at the Russian Marshal across the expanse of Urmenkoff's desk. "What are you talking about? I'm packing up my 20,000 men and returning to China. Ten Jumbo jets are on their way to Atarot right now. Hopefully, the runway will be fully patched by the time they arrive at 8:00 tomorrow morning."

"Chang, stay with me," Urmenkoff urged. "I have 15,000 Russian troops. It's my hope that most of the Africans will stay. I am certain the German, French, New Zealand, Austrian, Polish, Lithuanian, Latvian, and other assorted soldiers who remained with us after their governments recalled their contingents, will remain to the end."

"Urmenkoff, you're insane! We can't possibly win. I'm absolutely astonished the Israelis haven't finished us off the way a man squashes a beetle."

"You give them too much credit. Look how we devastated the aircraft they set on us three weeks ago. They haven't dared to send any more."

The normally unflappable Chang grew visibly agitated. He snapped, "Either you're fooling yourself, or you're fooling me. Just tell me this, Urmenkoff: why would you want to pursue this? Do you have a personal vendetta? Or perhaps I should be asking if you have a suicide complex!"

"Chang, how many times do I have to tell you — this struggle is the most justified in the history of mankind." Urmenkoff shot out of his chair and began to pace his office with his long, confident stride. "Look at the American president, Bush. He was so close to wiping out Saddam Hussein in the Gulf War. At the last minute, perhaps twenty hours from total victory, he withdrew. Schwartzkopf also played the fool. He should have defied orders. Had he done so, surely he would be sitting in the White House instead of that wretched Jew, Lewis. I will not be that fool. Now do you understand?" He whirled around to face the general. "Listen to me, Chang, I'll guarantee ten thousand Euros for each courageous soul who stays on."

Chang was still doubtful. But consciousness of Field Marshal Urmenkoff's impeccable military reputation, coupled with his generous offer, made him reply slowly, "I will allow my troops to join you on a voluntary basis."

From the night of September 21, 2002 until just before dawn on the morning of September 22, 12,500 "dedicated men" — mercenaries, now — finally succeeded in destroying the last remnant of Palestinian resistance. The stateless army swept south and established a battle line with their one hundred twenty remaining tanks and cannons on the mountain ridge that extends from Mount Scopus to the Mount of Olives. As the sun rose, Marshal Urmenkoff, standing on the roof of his command post, the old Hebrew University building, was struck by the beautiful view of the entire walled Old City of Jerusalem.

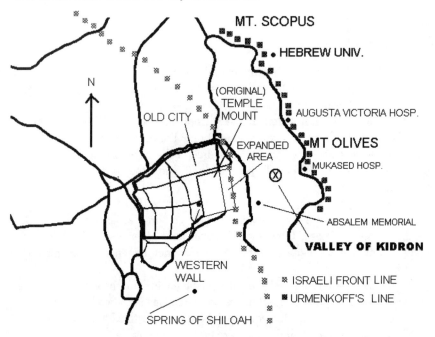

"How much more beautiful this would have been," he thought, "had the great gold Dome of the Rock remained standing." The Marshal marveled at how, in two short months, the Jews had moved mountains — including part of the very one he was standing on — to expand the plateau of the Temple Mount an additional thirty percent over its original size. The bulldozers were silent now. In their place and surrounding the occupied half of the city were Israeli tanks and cannons, as far as the eye could see.

The Marshal knew he was outnumbered. He knew he faced a more formidable fighting force than the one he'd cobbled together, even had the numbers been nearly equal. He knew he faced a more determined force — a unified nation of people defending their land, against a hodgepodge of soldiers of fortune.

But a conviction had welled up from the depths of the Russian's soul: there was no turning back now. He did not allow himself the luxury of thinking about his decision too logically or philosophically. At this point, it had simply become something he was determined to do.

The remaining 12,000 soldiers — five hundred had died or deserted during the night — from dozens of nations around the world, faced off with 100,000 Jewish soldiers on the hills across the valley. They stood just eight hundred meters apart. At 8:00 a.m. Urmenkoff was about to order his army to commence shelling, when a loudspeaker from across the valley boomed out in English.

"Field Marshal Urmenkoff, this is Daniel Benari, Prime Minister of the State of Israel. Our guns are aimed at you. In thirty seconds, we are can turn you and all of your men into ash. Listen carefully, Urmenkoff: our sage and mentor, Menachem Shabazi of Yemen, will meet you alone in battle. He has proposed that if you win, Jerusalem is yours. Of course, if he wins, it won't matter to you what happens. The deal is, both our armies hold their fire.

"Look for the red flag near the southeastern corner of the Temple Mount. The man with the white beard, wearing a flowing white robe, and holding a tall palm branch and a huge lemon-like fruit, is Menachem Shabazi. He is a Holy Man — a direct descendant, exactly one hundred generations removed, of King David. He carries no sling and no sword." Despite himself, for the first time a hint of uncertainty crept into the Prime Minister's voice. Over the loudspeaker, the uncertainty was magnified a thousandfold. "I myself don't understand what will take place... but he has instructed me to make you this offer. Menachem Shabazi asks that you meet him in the center of this great valley. Bring ten of your most loyal and devoted men. Menachem Shabazi will bring only three. All must be unarmed."

Urmenkoff took up his most powerful megaphone, and blared across the valley, "Shabazi, I take your offer! But even though you are old enough to be my father, you must know that I will have no mercy on you. I will tear out your beard at its roots. I will stuff the silly sidelocks, which grow in front of your ears, down your throat. I will strangle you with the strings that hang from the corners of your white cape. Your remains will be placed in a glass jar of formaldehyde and put on display in a museum, captioned: *Ancient, superstitious man, now extinct.*"

Urmenkoff observed, through his powerful binoculars, that Shabazi was waving his palm branch up, down, right, left, forward and backward; that he was deep in prayer, and oblivious to his threats. After ten minutes, he handed his palm branch and citron to an aide, then descended from the Temple Mount with three men in tow. They were a strange assortment: Yossel Berger, the Satmar Jew, Gaylord Horrace, the American Christian, and Feisel Bin Farheem, the Arab prince. As they passed the Absalom Memorial, Benari's amplified voice called out across the valley, "Marshal Urmenkoff, are you coming? I thought you agreed."

Through his powerful field glasses, Benari could see Urmenkoff beginning to sweat, wiping his forehead profusely. He got into a car. A troop tender followed and rode south along Mount Scopus road, past the vacant Augusta Victoria and Mukased Hospitals, down to the Valley of Kidron below. Within five minutes, Urmenkoff and ten other men, from ten different nations — all high-ranking and all large-framed — got out of their vehicles and stood in a line behind Urmenkoff, facing the Old City. It took Shabazi and his three friends twelve minutes, walking, to approach the enemy on the bolder-strewn dirt lot, midway between the battle lines.

At precisely 8:47 a.m., the two sides finally stood facing each other, twenty meters apart. Shabazi's head was still covered by his *Talit*. He spoke to Yossel in Hebrew, asking him to translate what he had to say to the Russian Field Marshal.

"Vassali Urmenkoff of Hassan Gog in Armenia. We go back a long way."

"I've never seen you before in my life," the Russian answered callously.

"I said, a long way. I mean generations. Do you even know your own line-age?" asked Shabazi.

"And you, through your magical powers, have figured out my lineage?" the Field Marshal sneered.

"Not magic, Urmenkoff," Menachem answered calmly. "Do you see my American friend here, Gaylord Horrace? He's an expert at tracing family trees. According to his research, you are a fourteenth-generation direct descendant of Bogdan Chmielnicki."

"That is amazing!" Momentarily, Urmenkoff dropped his guard. "There *is* such a tradition in my family."

"But it goes further back than that. Chmielnicki was an seventieth-generation direct descendant of Haman, son of Hamdatha, who was an sixteenth-generation descendant from Amalek. Exactly one hundred generations, Urmenkoff. You are familiar with your forebear, Amalek?"

"You mean the character from the Bible, 'The Book of Superstitions'?" The Russian made a dismissive gesture with one broad hand. "I don't believe that any such character ever existed. But from the little I know, this mythological Amalek people whom you claim I am descended from — they had the right idea about the Jews. For even back in those days, they stood up against those who would foist upon the world the myth of an All-Powerful God."

As Berger translated these words, a fire welled up in Menachem Shabazi's eyes. The ten officers standing behind Urmenkoff shrank back from the piercing look, but Urmenkoff himself was unmoved. Suddenly, Shabazi shouted something in his native Yemenite Arabic. Without being asked, Prince Bin Farheem translat-ed.

"The Book of God that you deny also states, quoting Balaam the evil prophet: 'Amalek is the first among the nations, but his end will be eternal destruction.' Indeed, 'first among the nations.' The decendants of Amalek headed up the effort and *led* the other sons of Esau in battle, to destroy the Children of Israel. You ten cowards who stand behind your king — each one of you is a descendant of the bitter foe, vizier of the Persian Empire, Haman, who tried to obliterate the Jewish Nation twenty-four hundred years ago. Your 12,000 up on the mountain descend from the Amalekite sheep whom King Saul's army pitied and failed to destroy."

The Prince translated faithfully but looked quizzically at Menachem, who explained further. "Twelve thousand Amalekites donned a disguise of sheep skins in an attempt to save themselves from the Israelites. Those who stand behind you on the mountain, Urmenkoff, have followed you like sheep, even after all the nations, the sons of Esau, withdrew their support for this evil campaign.

"I have been commanded by God not to pity you, or your ten, or your 12,000. My strength shall not ebb, as did the might of my ancestor, Samson. I will not repeat the error of my progenitor, King Saul, who failed in his mission to destroy Agag the Amalekite king and his 12,000 sheep. Of Haman's thirty sons, ten were hung, ten were killed by Jewish defenders and ten escaped by living as paupers. Today, twenty-four hundred years later, justice will catch up with you.

"My forefather, King David, was not allowed to build the Lord's House; too much blood sullied his hands. But your blood, and that of your cohorts, will not contaminate.... For the hands that will spill *your* guilt-ridden blood will bring only purity to the world."

Urmenkoff let out a laugh, then straightened up, anger burning in his eyes. "Come on Shabazi, you little runt. Your strength is that of a fly; you won't have a chance to repeat any error. Come on and meet my fist. The only blood you will be sullied with will be your own!"

Bin Farheem translated into Arabic. Menachem remained expressionless. The scene was being viewed live by the entire world. Although Benari had ordered police barricades to keep people away from the front, five hundred TV cameras, equipped with super unidirectional microphones, picked up the action better than a live, unaided view from four hundred meters away.

The silence was deafening as the whole world observed Menachem Shabazi prepare himself to face off with the remnant of Amalek. Urmenkoff, arms folded across his chest, and his men also watched as Shabazi took off his *Talit*, folded it neatly, and handed it to Yossel Berger. He then grasped the hem of his long white cloth gown and lifted it up, folding it back two or three times. The loose white pants he wore were exposed up to his waist. Shabazi turned to Yossel and nodded. Yossel removed a narrow black sash, dyed with crimson stripes, from a satchel he had brought along. Shabazi took the sash and tied it around his waist, securing his folded gown to his loins. Last, he slipped off his leather sandals so that his feet were bare upon the ground.

Millions everywhere, friend and foe, looked on in awe. The collective heart of the entire world was pounding madly, waiting to see how the drama would unfold. Only Urmenkoff seemed to keep his cool, snickering openly at Shabazi's meticulous preparations, and clearly impatient for the action to begin.

Shabazi, now ready, stepped forward and cried out in Hebrew. Yossel translated.

"You!" He pointed at the two-star general standing at the extreme left of the line. "Your name?"

The general stepped forward and said, "I am Jose Alverez of Argentina."

"No!" shouted Menachem Shabazi. "That's a lie! Who is your real father? Tell the world if you know."

For a brief second, an expression of abject fear crossed Alverez' face. Then he brazenly picked up his head. "My father was Dr. Joseph Mengele."

Shabazi pointed to the next man in line who, without further prompting, stepped forward and said, "I am General Dimitri Valeskaya. My great-grandfather was Joseph Stalin."

The next, the lone American, stepped forward unasked, and defiantly declared, "General Elmer Wagner. Great-great-grandson of the German composer Richard Wagner."

Next came the Palestinian. He directed his attention at Prince Feisel Bin Farheem and spoke in Arabic. "I am the proud grandson of the Grand Mufti Haj Amin El Husseini. I am here to avenge the destruction of our holy site."

The Prince replied in Arabic, "May the dung of a thousand camels pile high on your grandfather's grave."

Looking El Husseini directly in the eye, he spat in his direction. El Husseini took an angry step forward, but was held back by Urmenkoff's arm.

Next in line was the Frenchman, Edward Drumont IV, who said, "Dreyfus the traitor got off the hook. But you will not!"

Each one in succession proudly gave his name and his relationship to some "prominent", Jew-hating ancestor. When all had finished, at Urmenkoff's behest they stepped back behind him. He commented, "So now you see, Shabazi, my assemblage of men of character, some of the finest thinkers and leaders the twenty-first century world has produced. They represent, along with the troops who have stayed the course, the heroes of humanity, willing to contest the defeatism of the feeble-hearted politicians who originally sent them on this just mission."

"Send them first, Urmenkoff. Let us begin." Bin Farheem translated for Shabazi.

"How many?" Urmenkoff mocked. "Two, perhaps? Any one of them could tear your limbs from their sockets."

Shabazi, calm as ever said, "Send them all. None merits a longer life than the others!"

Urmenkoff laughed again and said, "Shabazi, all the news reports talk about your humility. But I see that the king of the Jews is actually highly conceited."

Shabazi repeated, "Let's begin."

Without warning, the meek-looking, one hundred seventy centimeter, bearded Yemenite exploded into the air, his torso straight as an arrow, his legs kicking high above his face, one after the other in rapid succession. He landed 2.5 meters away and immediately leaped up again, this time extending his arms in an imaginary forward-punching motion, one after the other. Next he landed and wheeled around, powerfully flicking his elbows out and up, out and down. His gymnastic performance was like a dance — a most spectacular dance. It took him full circle around his opponents. They turned around, following his motion, keeping their eyes glued warily on him. Of them all, only Urmenkoff refused to turn. He stood defiantly facing the Temple Mount, ignoring Menachem Shabazi's mesmerizing gyrations.

Shabazi let out a blood curdling yell and like a springing cheetah, leaped toward General Jose Alverez. In a lightning motion, which could only be observed in the slow-motion instant replay of a TV camera, jabbed his opened hand forward under the Argentine's rib cage, withdrew it, and jumped back. The TV cameras were pointed at Alverez as he looked around in bewilderment. Two seconds later, still on his feet, his eyes rolled up in their sockets. A torrent of blood spewed from his mouth as, grabbing his stomach with both arms, he dropped to the ground.

Four of the other generals rushed over to him. Shabazi was upon them in a flash. Raising their arms in defense, they quickly surrounded the old Jew before he struck. No human *eye* could catch the series of movements which sent the four men reeling like four sides of a banana instantaneously peeling back. Each one landed with a crash on his back at least two meters from Shabazi, who was now standing alone in the center. Four large, strong soldiers were writhing in pain and screaming on the ground, one bleeding from the nose, one holding his groin, one gripping his fractured knee cap, the fourth clutching his neck.

Shabazi jumped out of the circle to run after the Frenchman, Colonel Drumont, who in abject cowardice was fleeing the scene. As Menachem caught up with him thirty paces away, the hoary sage flew at the anti-Semite with a drop kick that struck the back of his neck. Shattered cervical vertebrae sent bone shards spinning. His spinal cord severed, Drumont was dead before he hit the ground.

Valeskaya was right behind Menachem. Yossel Berger opening his mouth for the first time since the spectacle began. "Menachem, look out!" he shouted. "He has a knife!"

The Russian had decided to break the rules, but it made little difference. He was hovering over Menachem before the agile maestro had risen from the flying drop kick. The Yemenite stayed on his back, circling around, following his attacker's movements. After a full minute, during which Valeskaya attempted to gain a positional advantage, the Russian lunged at his quarry with the twenty-three centimeter dagger he had kept hidden under his belt. For the brief moment that the Russian was on top, Shabazi was almost totally concealed. Then the one hundred twenty kilo Stalinist rolled over on his back, and Shabazi stood up over him. The hilt of the dagger was all that was visible, sticking out of Valeskaya's left eye socket.

The man whom Urmenkoff had termed conceited walked over to rejoin the four who had attacked him in unison. Three of them had regained their feet and were standing next to each other as he approached. Passively, almost in a death wish, they stood there as Menachem seemed to sweep his hand through the air in a wide arc. Each was struck in succession in the neck and fell to the ground, never to rise. The fourth, in a seated position, took what seemed to be a tap to the back of the neck. He, too, keeled over and slumped on the ground, motionless.

The three remaining soldiers, frightened beyond death, took up baseball-sized rocks from the ground and hurled them at Menachem, who was only ten meters away. Two of them he caught in his two hands, while the third whizzed over his head just as he ducked.

Urmenkoff yelled at them, "Don't you dare run away! He's worn out; you can prevail!"

The three, by this time totally bereft of their capacity for independent thought, rushed forward together to attack with their hands. Shabazi jumped quickly to the left, so that when the men turned toward him, they were positioned in a line; only the leftmost opponent now faced Shabazi. Before the two in back could come around, Shabazi had gouged out the eyes of Elmer Wagner. Two globs of vitreous humor ejaculated back, splattering against the sage's white gown.

As the others came straight at him, Menachem jumped out of the way. The lightning sidestep caught them by surprise, making them appear almost drunk in their unbalanced stumble forward. Menachem instantaneously whirled around, grabbed the one to the right by his hair, and jerked his neck back. The long-range microphones picked up a poignant crack. Shabazi shoved the cadaver forward, and it crashed into Kathim El Husseini — knocking him to the ground like a bowling pin.

The Arab lay on his back, begging for mercy. For the first time since the fight began, the mikes picked up, under his breath, a comment from Shabazi. The TV commentators translated from the Arabic: "You used your tongue to express a lifetime of bitter hate against God's Nation. Out of one side of your mouth, you misled my people with peace babble. From the other side, you fanned the flames of terrorism, murder and mayhem among the Arab masses."

With that, Shabazi's right hand bolted forward, this time in what the viewers perceived as slow motion. Blood spurted and tooth fragments went flying as the sage pushed his hand straight through El Husseini's lips and teeth. The hand emerged ten seconds later, gripping a slimy human tongue dripping with blood. He held it up and flung it at Urmenkoff. "Here, you king of Magog, you heir to Agag, you son of the Devil. This is what remains of your great thinkers and twenty-first century leaders. Put this in your museum!"

Urmenkoff caught the tongue in his hand, the tip flying up to slap his face. Meanwhile, Shabazi redirected his attention to the wailing General Wagner, aimlessly staggering in circles. A quick, powerful heel-palm to the tip of his nose, sending bone and cartilage into his brain, took Wagner out of his visionless agony.

Without warning, a volley of gunfire fulminated from Mount Scopus. Everyone was caught off guard. Yossel Berger and Prince Bin Farheem were struck and fell to the dusty earth. Gaylord Horrace hit the ground and scampered behind a large rock. Urmenkoff angrily turned around and raised a fist at his own troops. Menachem Shabazi turned toward the Temple Mount and raised his two hands high. Then he fell down in a crouch behind a nearby boulder. The initial gunshots had not been directed at Shabazi, for Urmenkoff was in the line of fire. The next moment, the entire city of Jerusalem shook as if hit by an earthquake.

*   *   *

"Alon," Prime Minister Daniel Benari shouted at Colonel Barnash, standing five meters away. "*Now!*"

The returning men of the *Davar* had been invited by the Prime Minister to watch the spectacle from the Temple Mount, together with the rabbis of the Synod and the members of Knesset. Benari gave Barnash the privilege of pushing the four-button sequence on a remote controller which his son Moshe had constructed only a few days before.

The entire Mount Scopus to the edge of the Mount of Olives exploded in flame. The shock wave that was generated rocked the ground for six kilometers around. Like a volcano, thousands of tons of rock and dirt erupted from the ground. All of it soared up into the sky angled slightly toward the east. No lethal debris fell to the earth west of the mountain ridge. It was ninety seconds before the fire storm, which had flared half a kilometer into the sky, finally died down. Everything underneath the huge wall of fire was incinerated by its massive release of thermal energy. Only the scrub brush and the wooden beams of the former Hebrew University campus and the vacant hospitals continued to burn, surrounded by the charred and twisted remains of everything else present, animate and inanimate.

Benari turned to his father. "Dad, how did Menachem know the Amalekites would cheat?"

"You should ask a better question," Benny Harkesef — formerly known as Robert Benson — said. "How does he seem to know everything?" Incredulous, he shook his head. "I still can't believe my eyes. I just can't believe it. It may be true that he is a great Kabbalist and mystic, and that by invoking Divine incantations he has power over men. But this man is super-rational too; he knows how to plan and execute. Although it's almost unimaginable, I think it's possible that this battle is not being waged purely through supernatural means. It seems to be a perfected form of martial arts. The incredible thing is that an old rabbi who's spent his entire life poring over books could have developed such mastery."

"An amazing man," the Prime Minister murmured, then grinned wryly at the understatement.

"He is that," his father agreed. "Since his arrival here a few days after I came, he's been the mastermind behind this entire campaign — demanding unnerving restraint while our enemies did away with one another. When he insisted that the Temple Mount be expanded, I understood very well that more room is needed. But, Danny, you did very well in listening to his every instruction. Yes, everything the old Yemenite Rabbi requested has been vindicated in grand style. At first you couldn't understand why he insisted that the tunnel bypass road under Mount Scopus, leading to Maaleh Adumim be diverted to pass under the Mount of Olives. You had a hard time approving the budget for the super-hardened tunnel walls that Menachem insisted be formed in a parabolic curve pitched fifteen degrees toward the east. I could feel your frustration when you bewailed the fact that you were just able to push the project through to a cabinet of skeptics by explaining that the excavated earth would become the source of landfill for the expanded Temple Mount. But the day before yesterday, when Menachem insisted that the tunnel be sealed off with one hundred seventy full LP gas tanker trucks parked inside and wired to blow, every specification of his design became perfectly clear. This man's planning ability is astounding; I just can't get over it. If I were a bit less rational than I know myself to be, I would swear that Menachem has been steering and manipulating our enemy to its destruction from day one." He pointed. "Look at that ridge up on the Mount of Olives, Danny! It's practically split in two!"

*   *   *

The ten-minute diversion, which further eroded Urmenkoff's renegade force to a total of one, didn't seem to faze the sole survivor of Amalek's legacy. Nor did he seem to be disconcerted that his chances of winning in hand-to-hand combat against this sagacious master — despite his size and his own considerable boxing skills — were about the same as his chances of obtaining reinforcements from UN High Command. It was do or die, or perhaps do *and* die. But Vassali Urmenkoff was prepared to *do*.

Menachem Shabazi turned his attention back to his last opponent — the most critical opponent he would ever face — just in time to see this corporeal analogue of the Satan pull a Makarov from an ankle holster. At a distance of twenty meters, Shabazi began to move. He resumed the super-human cavort that marked the commencement of battle. The first three shots missed by a wide margin. Shabazi suddenly stopped, staring down his opponent in a war of nerves. But Shabazi guessed right again, for just as the Marshal's sights were lined up to his satisfaction, pointing directly at his head, Shabazi leaped away and continued his dance at a dizzying pace. The fourth and fifth shots missed by a meter or two.

Gaylord Horrace decided it was time to step in. With Urmenkoff's back to him — the determined gunman was closely following Menachem's unpredictable movements — Horrace picked up a rock and hurled it with all his might. The rock struck the marshal squarely in the back. The Russian bear winced in pain and spun around, firing two more shots in quick succession at the American. One bullet grazed Horrace's arm. Menachem Shabazi let out another ghastly scream as he raced toward Urmenkoff.

The magazine in the Makarov 9x18mm, auto-pistol held eight rounds. Seven had already been expended. Urmenkoff realized, to his chagrin, that he had wasted two rounds on the insignificant American. Frustrated and aware that he had only one last chance to accomplish his goal, he resorted to the highest-percentage option. This time, he did not try for the instant-kill head shot, but fired point-blank at Shabazi's chest from a distance of just three meters.

Shabazi stumbled back and fell to the ground, deadly still. The unified moan of three hundred thousand men echoed throughout the valley. Urmenkoff tossed away his empty gun and threw up his clenched fists in a show of ecstasy.

*　　*　　*

Shefi Mordechai, in the stands along with the crew of his mission, suddenly turned to his friends. He was in a frenzy. "Alon, Eli, Shimon, Benny. All of you, come quickly. Come over here! Incredible!"

Close to sixty men gathered near Mordechai, who had his two hundred power Celeston telescope aimed at the scene. Benny Harkesef was the first to take a look. After five seconds, he stepped away from the eyepiece in a state of total bewilderment.

"Dad, what's the matter?" the Prime Minister demanded. "What happened? Tell me what you saw!"

But Harkesef couldn't reply. He didn't seem to be able to think. He merely mumbled to himself, "He had nothing in his hand. He tore the lion apart, though he had nothing in his hand." He wandered back to the bench and sat down, utterly dazed.

*　　*　　*

Vassali Urmenkoff walked over to the perfectly still body of Menachem Shabazi. The last heir to the nefarious dynasty of Amalek got down on his knees in front of Shabazi's face. He pulled up his victim's eyelid, expecting to see a fully dilated pupil. Instead, a very real and very powerful human hand exploded in fury at the Russian's forty-five centimeter neck. With the first blow, Urmenkoff, barely alive, was gasping for breath; his windpipe and gullet hung out through a gaping fissure in his throat.

The victor ran over to Gaylord Horrace, tore off his shirt, and bandaged his disciple's arm with it. Meanwhile, Berger and Bin Farheem had risen shakily to their feet. Berger, soaked in sweat, struggled out of his black jacket, pulled his four cornered fringed garment over his head, and undid the velcro straps that held his Kevlar vest in place. Shabazi returned to his impotent nemesis, who was wheezing in agony. The Yemenite sage bent over nearly double with his back toward the Temple Mount, so that the cameras had no view of what he was doing. There was a blur of movement. Then Menachem stood up, turned around, and raised in his right hand for all to see. It held the head of the final male of Amalek.

He cast the head down beside the lifeless torso.

Within half a minute, an ambulance was on the scene to take Gaylord Horrace away, but he refused the help. Menachem Shabazi untied his black and red sash, pulled off his bloodied gown, and released the body-armor that clung to his sweat-drenched chest. From his satchel Yossel pulled out a clean change of clothing, which the sage donned. The faithful servant removed a container of water from the satchel and poured it over Menachem's outstretched hands. Word by word, with fervor and intensity, Menachem pronounced a blessing, which the microphones picked up and faithfully transmitted to the watching throng. Thousands answered Amen in unison as he wrapped his *Talit* around his head.

Arm in arm with Yossel Berger, on his right, Gaylord Horrace on his left, and Prince Feisel Bin Farheem on Horrace's other side, Menachem Shabazi began the walk back toward the Gates of Jerusalem. Meanwhile, soldiers abandoned their tanks, rabbis and politicians their benches. Spontaneously, a veritable sea of humanity began running down the hills to greet and escort the victorious sage into the Holy City.

The first reporter on the scene managed to push a mike into Berger, the spokesman's, face. "I suppose this is it; Menachem Shabazi by unanimous acclaim is declared King of Israel. What does Rabbi Shabazi say?"

The Hasid turned and, in an undertone, asked his mentor if he would comment. Menachem stopped, as did everyone following. Into the reporter's outstretched microphone, he cried in a mighty voice, "The Lord shall be King forever — your God, O Zion — for generations eternal, Hallelujah."

The concurrent recitation of the people thundered throughout the valley, almost as loud as the explosion that had rocked it twenty minutes before.

The Prime Minister of Israel could not fathom what shocking revelation could have caused his father to be oblivious to the nation's jubilation. "Dad, Dad, what's the matter? Wake up! Menachem has killed Urmenkoff, the Amalekite. It's over. It's all over, Dad. Come, we must greet Menachem."

By now, most of the men from the *Davar* mission had raced down the hill together with the rest of the crowd to hail their newly crowned leader, but five of them had remained behind with Benny Harkesef. Harkesef looked straight into his son's eyes and confessed, "Danny, my son, thirty-seven years of my life and that of my fellows" — gesturing with his hand at the five that surrounded him, and pointing to those on their way downhill — "have come together in the last forty-five minutes. 'What is sweeter than honey? What is bolder than a lion?'"

"Dad —"

Harkesef raised a hand. "Let me finish. You'll understand in a minute.... Major Mordechai's telescope happened to be directed at Menachem Shabazi's left foot, as he lay still waiting for his enemy to approach. Between his big toe and the next was a marking. In tiny lettering, it said *Aleph-Shin 01*."

The Prime Minister was staring at his father now, his face wearing the same mask of incredulity. Nodding slowly, his father continued, "We once thought of Rafi Schwartz as the mastermind who crafted and commanded the boldest under-cover military operation in the history of the world. But now it is clear that Rabbi Menachem Shabazi, the humble and saintly hero of Israel, was the true master-mind who created and portrayed the character of Colonel Rafael Schwartz!"

Daniel Benari swallowed, tried to speak, then gave up the attempt.

"My son," Harkesef said softly, "it is mind-boggling — and yet, in hindsight, so obvious! From the very beginning, thirty-seven years ago or perhaps even before that, his sole plan and objective was to restore the throne to the King of Kings. As a warrior he waged a ferocious battle, but as the victor, he is the Prince of Peace. The riddle of Samson's Lion has been solved. 'From the devourer came sustenance, and from the bold came sweetness.'

"Even the Philistines, who solved the riddle, had no clue to the secret under-lying the words. What was their true meaning? In true fact, they had a double meaning. In his time, Samson was referring to *himself*; a lone individual, who devoured his enemies and sustained his people. A bold and powerful man, with bare hands he tore apart his people's oppressors; yet at the same time, in sweet-ness, humility and self-sacrifice he sequestered himself for the sake of God's Nation.

"But as a prophecy, Samson's visionary words were fulfilled on this very day: *Menachem* is the man whose spirit is bolder than the lion, yet whose love for his people — and for all mankind — is sweeter than honey."

People, as far as the eye could see, Jews, Arabs, Americans, Europeans, Africans and Asians marching joyously together, were accompanying the King's new emissary triumphantly toward the Holy City. Benny Harkesef smiled radiant-ly at his son, put an arm around his shoulders, and turned him toward the valley.

"Come, Danny. Let's go!"

INDEX OF CHARACTERS NAMES

Abulafia, Nissim: Caretaker at the Western Wall.

Agag: King of the Amalek Nation whom King Saul pitied and failed to kill as he was commanded. Samuel the prophet killed him later. *

Alwazi: Afghan professor of epidemiology who develops a micro-organism biological weapon.

Amalek: Grandson of Esau who was the forebear of a nation bent on destroying the Hebrew Nation. The original anti-Semite. *

Balaam: Biblical gentile prophet who sought to curse the Jews, but blessed them instead. *

Barnash, Alon: Alias Abdallah Ibn Gash. Mossad agent in Operation Samson's Lion who destroys the Aswan Dam.

Barnash, Ahuva: Alon Barnash's first wife; mother of Ariel Mizrachi.

Barzadeh, Raymond: Mathematician, who helps H. Moss Farrell find Israeli agent in Iran.

Benari, Daniel: Daniel Benson.

Benson, Barbara (nee Weiss): Wife of Robert Benson.

Benson, Daniel: Later changes his last name to Benari. Son of Robert Benson and Prime Minister of Israel.

Benson, Harold: Son of Robert Benson. Brother of Daniel.

Benson, Robert: Alias of Benny Harkesef.

Benun, Ozer: Admiral in Israeli Navy in charge of purchasing submarines.

Berger, Yossel (Yosef): Orthodox Jew, Satmar Hasid, follower and servant of Menachem Shabazi.

Biderman, Shmuel: Elderly Orthodox Jew murdered during synagogue services by police officer Jimmy Naboni.

Bin Farheem, Prince Feisel: Nephew of King Khalid of Saudi Arabia. Mayor of Jidda, follower and servant of Menachem Shabazi.

Bolgazi, Abbas: Alias for Farshid Levihayim (Eli Kedem), used when assisting H. Moss Farrell to get his employees out of Iran.

Boyle, General Richard: General of the American Air Force.

Chaim, Rabbi: Most respected rabbinical personality in Israel.

Chang: Chinese general during UN invasion of Israel.

Chemeilnitzki, Bogdan: General of the Cossack army who massacred the Jews in the Ukraine and other parts of Poland in 1648.*

Daryoush: Employee in Farshid Levihayim's lead company.

Duncan, Roland: British general during UN invasion.

Eitan, Nimrod: Israeli ambassador to Bulgaria who is summarily fired.

Esau: Son of Isaac and archrival brother of Jacob (Israel). The Romans (aka Edom) were descendants of Esau.*

Falkami, Jamiel: Omar Rastafani's pilot.

Farrell, H. Moss: Texas computer magnate who works to free his kidnaped employees during the Iranian Revolution.

Fashwari, Nabi: Kurdish tribal leader of the village Jabala Tarmuk; cousin and arch rival of Khalil Fashwari.

Fashwari, Khalil: Kurdish tribal leader of the village Jabala Khandor; cousin and arch rival of Nabi Fashwari.

Gelbworth, Zisha: Orthodox Jew, replacement ambassador to Bulgaria.

Gilcrest, Captain William: Captain of U.S. aircraft carrier in the Mediterranean.

Haman son of Hamdatha: Vizier to King Acheshverosh in fifth century B.C.E Persia. He was a descendant of Agag and Amalek and plotted to kill all of the Jews in the Empire.*

Harkesef, Benny: Alias Robert Benson. Born, Ben Silverberg. Mossad agent in Operation Samson's Lion who infiltrates the NSA and gains control of the GPS system.

Hilwani, Ibrahim: Afghan alias for Shefi Mordechai.

Horrace, Gaylord: An American and a member of the New Israelite Church of the Messiah, who became a follower and servant of Menachem Shabazi.

Ibn Gash, Abdallah: Arabic alias for Alon Barnash.

Ibn Gash, Fatima (nee Baktari): Wife of Alon Barnash in Egypt. Her Hebrew name is Ahuva, the same as Barnash's first wife in Israel.

Ibn Gash, Mustafa: Son of Abdallah Ibn Gash who finds out he is Jewish. Later changes his name to Moshe Mitzri.

Ilsamik, Faruk: Aswan Dam employee.

Ishmael: Son of Abraham and Hagar, half-brother of Isaac. The Arabs descend from Ishmael (and other sons of Abraham and Hagar).*

Javeed: Iranian employee of H. Moss Farrell who assists in the employee escape from Iran.

Jebli, Captain Mahmud: Captain in Omar Rastafani's Afghanistani terrorist army.

Kalami, Major Sirhan: Major in Omar Rastafani's Afghan terrorist army.

Karlin, Rabbi: Arranges divorces in Bnei Braq for agents of Operation Samson's Lion.

Karmel, Gutzi (Amos): Mossad agent in Operation Samson's Lion. The smallest member of the group.

Kedem, Eli: Alias Farshid Levihayim and Abbas Bolgazi. Mossad agent in Operation Samson's Lion who plants ERWs in Isfahan, Iran.

Kedem, Ruchama: Wife of Eli Kedem, later remarries him in Iran.

Kooreesh: Employee in Farshid Levihayim's lead company.

Levi, Rabbi Eliyahu: Charlatan rabbi sent by the Jewish Agency to bring Yemenites to Israel in 1949.

Levihayim, Farshid: Alias for Eli Kedem.

Lewis, Abe: Jewish President of the U.S.A.

Maluf: General in the Iranian Army; commanding officer of Farshid Levihayim.

Matar, General Uri: Israeli Air Force general who countermands orders.

Merveed: Iranian drill sergeant who starts up with Farshid Levihayim.

Mizrachi, Ariel: Naval doctor. Son born to Alon Barnash before departing on mission.

Mordechai, Shefi: Alias Professor Ibrahim Hilwani. Mossad agent in Operation Samson's Lion in Afghanistan who develops Black Flies to vector deadly biological agent which decimates Afghanistani terrorist camp.

Muhamma, Dr.: PhD in Education who leads Egyptian students on trip to Israel.

Naboni, Jimmy: Israeli policeman who brutally murders an Orthodox Jew.

Nimrodi, Leora: Atheistic daughter of Shefi Mordechai.

Pinhasi, Avraham: Relative of Ruchama (Kedem) Levihayim, from Shiraz, Iran.

Rabinowitz, Ira: American intelligence analyst who becomes a spy for Israel.

Rastafani, Omar: Billionaire Afghan terrorist leader.

Richie, G. Horton: Militia leader and defender of the Constitution.

Saadatmand, Joseph: President of the Isfahan Jewish community and friend of Farshid Levihayim.

Schuman, Meir: Rabbi in Jerusalem who helps lost Jewish souls return to Judaism.

Schwartz, Colonel Rafael (Rafi): Commander of Mossad Operation Samson's Lion.

Segan, Haggai: Reporter for Israeli Channel 7.

Shabazi, Menachem: Yemenite rabbi and hero of Israel.

Shelby, Dr. Dave: Medical doctor who represents the Mount Royal Gun Club for the press.

Sherman, General George Adley: General and Chairman of the Joint Chiefs of Staff of the American military.

Snookie: Inner-city drug dealer in Washington DC.

Stillman, Admiral Earl: Chief of Naval Operations.

Tzioni, Dror: Jewish Agency counselor who kidnaps and sells Yemenite children.

Urmenkoff, General Vassali: Russian Field Marshal, commander of UN invasion of Israel, archetypical anti-Semite and descendant of Amalek.

Weatherby, Captain Hillman: British naval captain, chief engineer of submarine division.

Woodson, General James: General and Commander of the American Army.

Yoshke: Jesus. (Yiddish) *

(* indicates non-fictional character)

GLOSSARY OF UNCOMMON TERMS REFERRED TO IN THE BOOK

Abeed: Black Africans (Arabic), literally: slaves.

Aguda: Ultra-Orthodox political party in Israel, which represents Hasidic sects.

Agunot: Plural of Agunah. A woman who may not remarry, either because her husband has disappeared or because he refuses to grant her a Jewish divorce.

Aliya: Immigration to Israel, (Hebrew).

Arrow III: Anti-missile missile, developed jointly by Israel and the United States, and manufactured in Israel.

Ashkenazi: A Jew whose customs follow the Central and Eastern European rite.

Baal Tshuvah: A Jew who has returned to Orthodox faith and observance.

Bar Mitzvah: A Jewish male who is obligated to observe Jewish Law after the age of maturity, at thirteen years.

Bnei Braq: Orthodox Jewish city in Israel, just north of Tel Aviv.

Borachu: Blessing recited just before reading the Torah.

Bris: Circumcision procedure required of all Jewish males at eight days of age.

Chador: Highly concealing head covering required of women in some Moslem countries. (Persian)

Charedi: Devout (Hebrew), an ultra-Orthodox Jew.

CIC: Command Information Center. Electronic weapon systems control department on board a naval vessel.

EBCDIC: Eight bit alpha-numeric-symbol system used on IBM mainframe computers.

Eretz Yisrael: The Land of Israel. (Hebrew)

Felafel: Fried chickpea balls eaten in Pita bread. (Hebrew and Arabic)

Get (singular), Gittin (plural): Jewish divorce. (Hebrew)

Goy: Gentile. (Hebrew)

GPS: Global Positioning System. A system of satellites that that transmits a digital signal that is used to locate a position on earth, and to navigate ships, aircraft and missiles.

GSS: General Security Services: parent body of the Mossad.

Halacha: Jewish Law. (Hebrew)

Halitza: Jewish religious ceremony to release a widow, whose husband died childless, from the obligation to marry his brother. She must remove his shoe. (Hebrew)

Hamdalla: Thank G-d. (Arabic)

Hasidic Jew, Hasid: A Jew who follows the teachings of Rabbi Israel Baal Shem and his disciples.

Hatzofeh: Orthodox Zionist Newspaper. The organ of the Mizrachi/NRP political party in Israel.

Hebron: Palestinian Arab city, which has a small Jewish neighborhood, twenty miles south of Jerusalem. The tomb of the forefathers, Abraham, Isaac and Jacob, is located there.

Hejira: Pilgrimage to Mecca. (Arabic)

Herut: Right wing Revisionist Zionist political party in Israel.

HUMVEE: Hummer all-terrain, 4WD, wide track, military vehicle.

IAI: Israel Aircraft Industries.

JAP: Jewish American Princess. (Pejorative)

Jenin: Palestinian Arab city, sixty miles north of Jerusalem

Kabbalistic: Of the Kabbalah, Jewish mysticism.
Kaddish: Prayer sanctifying God's Name, recited by mourners. (Aramaic)
Kippa: Skullcap. (Hebrew)
Knesset: The Israeli Parliament. (Hebrew)
Kollel: Advanced program that grants fellowships to married Jewish men to continue Torah studies. (Hebrew)
Leben: Yogurt. (Hebrew and Arabic)
Maariv: (1) Jewish evening prayer service. (2) Secular evening Israeli newspaper. (Hebrew)
Mamzerim: Plural of "mamzer." An illegitimate Jewish child who may not marry a proper Jew. (Hebrew)
Menchen: Plural of "mench", a proper man. (Yiddish)
Meretz: Left-wing, antireligious, socialist political party in Israel.
Mikva: Ritual bath; immersion in it removes specific types of spiritual impurities. (Hebrew)
Minyan: Quorum of ten adult Jewish males required for public worship. (Hebrew)
Mishigat: Craziness or idiosyncrasy. (Hebrew)
Mishna: Part of the Talmud, which cites cases of Jewish Law. (Hebrew)
Mitzvah: Commandment or good deed. (Hebrew)
Mohel: Professional ritual circumsisor. (Hebrew)
Mori: My Master, the Yemenite term for a rabbi. (Hebrew)
Mossad: The Israeli secret service.
Moshiach: Messiah or anointed one. (Hebrew)
Mujahedin: Moslem fighters for freedom and holy war. (Arabic)
Majnun: Insane. (Arabic)
Nablus: Palestinian Arab city, thirty miles north of Jerusalem. (Shechem in Hebrew)
Nachal: Program in Israel, which combines Jewish learning or Kibbutz work with army service.
Negev: Southern desert in Israel.
Ninth of Av: Fast day, commemorating the destruction of the Temple in 69 C.E. Jewish boys born around this time of year, have traditionally been named, Menachem.
NRP: National Religious Party, Mizrachi, Religious Zionist political party in Israel.
P'eylim: Orthodox organization in Israel, which promotes Jewish education to nonobservant Jews.
Peyot: Sidelocks of hair worn by many Orthodox Jewish boys and men. (Hebrew)
Phalanx: Six-barreled, radar guided, 20mm machine gun that fires four thousand rounds per minute (CIWS).
Ramallah: Palestinian Arab city, twelve miles north of Jerusalem.
Ramle: City in central Israel.
Reb: Honorable title, like Mister. (Yiddish)
Rosh Hashanah: Jewish New Year, A Day of Awe on which the ram's horn is blown.
Sabra: Native-born Israeli. Literally: a cactus pear, prickly on the outside, sweet on the inside. (Hebrew)
Sanandaj: Kurdish city in western Iran.
Sandek: Godfather. The man who is honored by holding the baby during the circumcision. (Yiddish)

Sanhedrin: Seventy-one-man Supreme Court of Jewish Law which ceased to exist shortly after the destruction of the Temple. (Hebrew)

Schlemiel: Unlucky person. (Yiddish)

Schnorrer: Charity collector. (Yiddish)

Sephardic: A Jew whose customs follow the Spanish-Portuguese rite. Oriental (mostly from the Arab countries) Jews follow a similar rite.

Shabbat Shalom: Sabbath greeting, meaning "Have a peaceful Sabbath."

Shabbat: Sabbath. (Hebrew)

Shahab: Iranian version of the Russian Scud ground-to-ground missile.

Sharia: Moslem law. (Arabic)

Shas: Orthodox political party of Sephardic and Oriental Jews in Israel.

Shema Yisrael: Supreme declaration of faith in Judaism. "Hear O Israel, the Lord our God, the Lord is One." (Hebrew)

Shiktze: Non-Jewish girl. (Yiddish)

Shiva: Seven day mourning period for close relatives prescribed in Jewish Law. (Hebrew)

Shofar: Ram's horn, blown on Rosh Hashanah and other solemn occasions. (Hebrew)

Shtreimel: Fur hat worn by Hasidic Jews on Sabbath and festivals. (Yiddish)

Shul: A synagogue. (Yiddish)

Succoth: Jewish autumn holiday of tabernacles, booths. Jewish men eat and sleep outside in branch-covered huts for seven days and wave a palm branch, citron, willow and myrtle branches on each day of the holiday.

Talit: Prayer shawl (Hebrew). It has fringes on the four corners.

Talmud: Multi-volume encyclopedia of Jewish Law and lore compiled fifteen hundred years ago. (Hebrew)

Tevet: Tenth month of the Jewish calendar.

Tefilin: Leather boxes that contain parchment prayer scrolls, worn on the head and arm of Jewish men during weekday morning prayers. (Hebrew)

Torah: General term for all Jewish Law, ethical and moral teachings. Literally: the Five Books of Moses.

Tzadik: Saint. (Hebrew)

Tzitzit: Ritual fringes on the corners of a four-cornered garment. (Hebrew)

Ulpan: Intensive course in the Hebrew language.

UTJ: United Torah Judaism, a political coalition in Israel of ultra-Orthodox Jews (Aguda and Degel Hatorah).

Yarmulke: Skullcap. (Yiddish.)

Yeshiva Bachur: Young unmarried man who learns in a Yeshiva.

Yeshiva: Academy where only Torah subjects are studied. (Hebrew)

Yored: Israeli Jew who moved away from Israel. (Hebrew)

Youth Aliya: Branch of the Jewish Agency, a Zionist organization whose purpose was to indoctrinate immigrant youths in Zionism. During the early days of the State, most chapters endeavored to dissuade new immigrants from religious tradition and observance.

Zahal: The Israel Defense Force, acronym for the Israeli army.

Zohar: Second century book of Jewish mysticism and hidden ideas of the Torah, attributed to Rabbi Shimon Bar Yochai.